Beyond Thuria Trilogy - Book 3

ASCENSION

JAMES TODD LEWIS
AUTHOR OF *THE THURIAN SAGA*

Ascension

Front Cover Credits:

Artistic Credit: Cover Characters, Chapter Flourish, & Breaks:

Kat Miller
(www.furaffinity.net/user/foxenawolf)

Cover Background: Genesis Eve Whitmore (little-tales.com)

Editing and Review Assistance: James W. Lewis, Jr., Deborah
Williford, & Nathan M. Edwards

"Honor to all. Honor from all. Honor … above all."

Revision 1.1.2

Contact e-mail: author @ jamestoddlewis.com

ISBN 978-1-940929-20-0

To every one of you who leave ratings.

To every one of you who let me know where there are mistakes.

To those who question and probe and think about what I have put into words.

You are the best!

With thanks eternal to my God,
my family,
and my friends.

Books
by James Todd Lewis

THE THURIAN SAGA:

The Rescue: The First Visitation of Thuria

The Aftermath: Secrets of Thuria

The Ascent: Conflict on Thuria

The Summit: Rise of the Anati

Purebred: Soul of the Mixed Blood

The Fallen: Search for the Path

Trials of the Teldear

Beyond: Incarnation (Book 1)

Beyond: Resurrection (Book 2)

Beyond: Ascension (Book 3)

Table of Contents

Author's Note vii

Introduction ix

Chapter 1: The Lost Land 1

Chapter 2: The Renewed 22

Chapter 3: The Empty Answer 43

Chapter 4: The Faint Promise 60

Chapter 5: The Uncertain Suitor 82

Chapter 6: First Dates 99

Chapter 7: The Attoria Inception 120

Chapter 8: The Beginnings of Refuge 140

Chapter 9: The Simpler Life 158

Chapter 10: The Course Corrects 179

Chapter 11: Walking as One 200

Chapter 12: A Truer Voice 223

Chapter 13: The Scandal Lever 239

Chapter 14: The Refugees of Privation 262

Chapter 15: Rediscovered Countries 284

Chapter 16: Agonized Veracity 310

Chapter 17: Revisions of Nurture 332

Chapter 18: The Turnings of Trust 352

Chapter 19: Preset Agendas 376

Chapter 20: Familial Relations 398

Chapter 21: Pinnacle Rhymes 428

Chapter 22: When Shadows Fall 454

Chapter 23: The Teldear's Method 478

Chapter 24: Of Light and Shadow 500

Chapter 25: Shift at Mid Sol 522

Chapter 26: The Workings of a Matriarch 545

Chapter 27: The Plan for Knowing 569

Chapter 28: Shadows in the Dark 597

Chapter 29: The Renovation of the Guides 616

Chapter 30: The Last Chapter 636

Epilogue 654

Abbreviated Thurian Reference 674

Preview of *The Legacy of Aris* 678

About the Author 683

Author's Note

Thank you for reading this book, and as always, I hope you enjoy it!

This story is about a world far away from our own. If a human were to visit there, they would find things both foreign and familiar. While our way of marking out time – days, weeks, years – would not be, a system for tracking the moments certainly would exist, and does. On Thuria, there are mountains, rivers, beaches, and forests, but the continents would not be recognizable to us, and the mountain ranges and courses of rivers would be unfamiliar. Governments, families, and businesses still exist and serve much the same functions for Thurians as they do for humans, but not exactly as our own. This world is a different world.

This book contains some material not intended for children. Parents and other responsible adults are asked to do their part in ensuring that any story with mature subjects and themes does not end up in front of eyes too young and for which it was not intended. There are some episodes of violence, occurrences of suggestive material, and moments of coarse language; however, these are not prevalent.

To my normal introduction, I need to add a special thank you to my Lord and Savior, Jesus Christ, who has gifted me with the resources, the time, and the help to publish ten books in this, *The Thurian Saga*. In 2007, I started writing again after a more than fifteen-year hiatus, and apart from a piece of hand-written fan fiction, *The Rescue: The First Visitation of Thuria* was my first book. It started as an experiment, something potentially throw-away, but in the end, there are now nine new books that are a part of that story that takes characters from near infancy to where, in this book, you'll find them. I was even able, after some massive renovation, to take the book I wrote in college and publish it as a part of this series. This has been amazing journey of sharing and friendship, and it's brought kind words to me I will always treasure.

With this book, the main arc of the characters from *The Rescue* comes to its conclusion, but I hope to keep writing, and I hope to bring these characters into the other works. I write for my own enjoyment, yes, but as I say above, I truly hope you enjoy these stories, as well.

Again, my sincere thanks. See you in the future.

James Todd Lewis

Introduction

To my diary, although it makes me wonder if anyone has ever really been named "Diary." I'm writing this because a very nice Vulpi psychologist, a Doctor Emmeniama de Kestrick, suggested I should do it. If I'm talking to this Diary individual, I suppose it would be rude to not introduce myself. Hello, my name is Akashar. Yep, that's it. Just Akashar. I don't have a last name, not even a fake one. I thought about making one up, but every time I tried to after the accident, it just didn't seem right. Since you are just named Diary, then I'm thinking this may be okay with you. At least, we're not alone. I know of a few others in Shanandrae who are the same way.

You see, Diary, I'm hoping you can understand me because I really have a hard time understanding myself. You see, I don't have all of my memories. In fact, I don't even know how old I am. All I know is that about sixteen seasons ago, I was found outside of the hospital grounds of Shanandrae Commons hospital. I wasn't in very good shape. I had a really high fever and stomach problems, well not true, they were intestine problems ... ones bad enough to kill me. They nearly did. Doctors told me that they had to work really hard to save me. I'm grateful, Diary, but there's a part of me that almost wishes they would have let me die all the way. No, you see, I look at that sol as the one where a part of me did die. That's the part of me that remembers who I really am, remembers my name and my past and everything else about me. That's what died, and I, sadly, am all that's left.

I don't suppose everything about that old life died. I could read and write, some, but not really well ... or good? I can never remember. Yeah, and it's true, I can never remember. The skills are there like the talking and the reading and the writing and walking and all sorts of other stuff, but I can't for the life of me get back the memory of when I learned those things. Some Thurians who lose their memories have flashes of their past. I don't have a thing, not even in dreams. I might have been rich. I might have been important. Now, I'm poor and a nobody. I'm so poor, I tell others, that I don't even have memories. Well, I'm not like really destitute or anything. I have a job and earn enough to feed myself, although I am still paying on my medical bills. Everything anyone sees or knows of me, as far as I can tell, began about sixteen seasons ago.

This, Diary, is the point where most Thurians start to get *that* look in their eyes. When I get to this part of the story, they doubt I'm telling them the truth. They think I'm hiding something, something horrible I did. Whenever I talk to someone with a connection to enforcement, I generally see them scribbling down notes. They've tried to find out who I am for seasons and seasons. See, what will happen is that I will tell them those things I said just now, and they'll go off and check. Several sols later, I'll get a visit from them, and then they have the second look in their eyes – pity. I don't know which look is worse, honestly. If they haven't gone off the cliff thinking I am actually part of some giant government conspiracy, they will finally believe me, and the dreadful part of my existence is there for all of them to see.

No, it's not just not knowing who I am. It's not knowing what I've done that really scares me. When I was found, no one came looking for me. Why? Had I done something horrible and that's why I wasn't worth someone's time? Maybe, I was just this hopeless charity case – the Thurian you can't get off of your sofa. What if my memories are gone because I saw something horrible or did something horrible that is just too bad to remember? What if I am hiding something and even I don't know it? Worse, was there someone out there who needed me, and I wasn't there. I'm not there. Damn. I'm almost convinced I'd be happier to have lost my own tail rather than to not have any memories because now I don't know if there is someone out there I murdered or rapemated or abandoned or hurt in countless other ways. It's really hard for me to not know that, and it drags me down.

And it's not just me who doesn't understand how my past can be a mystery. Everyone from birth, except me, is genetically recorded in the master naming index. Those indexes are backed up and copied and all sorts of other stuff to make sure nothing gets lost. I'm not in there. I'm not. I've heard theories from others for seasons about what that means, and I'm not happy with them. I could have been taken from my mother at birth, raised and then forced to be someone's possession or pet. That genetic thing would have the ability to track down close relatives. Yeah, they aren't in there, either. So, was like my whole family taken at birth and raised by themselves? Doesn't seem likely. There are stories of Thurians who get their records erased from the genetic indexes, but that usually only happens with the help of someone very rich and very powerful. Again, why bother? I'm not worth anything to anyone.

Now, I'm sorry, Diary, for complaining so much and making it sound worse than it really is. See, I was rescued, nursed back to health, and then found the Creator's Path and a bunch of really helpful Thurians who took care of me and helped me get a new start. Trade school was paid for as I worked as a janitor at the chapel, and now I'm a mechanical technician over at FridgeTech; we do geo-cooling for lairs and offices. Hey, I say that a lot, it seems. Well, it is true. It's a good job, and I get to help out. Our chapel is small, and I still help them clean up, and I make enough at FridgeTech to take care of myself. It's not a bad life; I just wish it had more history to it.

Well, I don't want to bore you, Diary, with the tales of my confused and messed up life, but I appreciate you listening. You're very nonjudgmental, and I like that about you. Speaking of like, I'll say just one more thing. Over the past moon, I've noticed a brown and gold Faelnar kind of keeping an eye on me. I think she works in the hospital, too, where Doctor Emma is, and when I've asked about her, she seems pretty popular with the nurses and doctors. I'm not totally sure what she does, but she gets called in when things get really bad with a patient, or so I hear. Lots of bad in these sols – Sahnassites and Vanarrans going after each other, mostly, but a lot of folks like me just plain lost. I'm lost in not knowing who I really am, but I believe the Creator knows, and I believe and have faith.

She spoke to me, this Faelnar. She said I reminded her of someone she lost long ago. It was someone close to her, I think. She said his name was Ash. Funny name, but I suppose I can't talk. I picked Akashar as a name because I heard on a VidStar program someone talking about ancient Nephti settlements. If nomads came across land that had an abandoned village or farm or something like that – temple maybe, they'd call it *akashar*. The word was meant to describe a lost land, one that was used for some purpose but now no one knows for what. Ash, though. At least Ash might have the ashes of his past. I don't even have that.

I figured that she'd just kind of ignore me after that, seeing as I'm not who she thinks I am, but she hasn't done that. I seem to run into her from time to time, and she's very nice to me. I won't lie to you, Diary, she's attractive. I'm not sorry to see her as far as her looks go. As far as what's on the inside, she's a little guarded. She has a close friend, a sister maybe, who works with her at the hospital, and she's also very kind to me. I don't see her as much, only when I go to visit Doctor Emma. I get the sense that this Faelnar – her name is Vanalla, by the way – wants to know more about me, but I try to keep it light, on the surface. After all, there isn't much below the surface, at least that I can tell. Thurians deserve more in a mate than a half of someone. As old as I am with as many memories as I have missing, I'm not even that.

Oh, wow. I just read all of this, and I'm writing in circles. Doctor Emma is right. I need to do something to figure this out, come to peace with it at least. She prodded me, last time, to read Vanarra de Gonari's biography from the last chapter to the first, and so I think I'm going to try doing that. I might try to set up visits through work, but again, I'm not sure I want to. No! I'm doing it again and in the same paragraph! Okay, I'm going to try. I'm going to try to get real help.

Thank you, Diary, for listening. It means a lot to me. I think it helped. Maybe when I sort myself out, I can help you. It would only be fair. I'll talk to you later. Thank you again.

"Kylie," Vanarra asked softly from the bridge of the Haven, "are you *sure* we can't do it?"

"Positive, Van," the Vulpi-Izar said, standing in her physical form on the bridge of the ship. "There is a pawful of individuals whose history is locked out. The Allarrae call them *focus points*, but what it really means is that we are prohibited from doing a back-scan on them, even near them. That's not something that you or I can authorize, and I very much doubt Me Sha would do so, either."

Vanarra leaned back and looked at the image of Akashar working in a new lair, setting up its geo-cooling system. "He's so close to what I remember but having just aged a bit."

"Your nose tell you anything?"

"I've been close enough to smell him, but I ... don't know," the mixed blood sighed. "It's been too long, lifetimes and lifetimes. Same color eyes and the voice is so close whenever I can get him really talking to me. Given that he's one of these focus points, I should just take it that he is the one, the other surprise that Theo said he'd spring on me to help me grow closer to what I needed to be."

"Focus points can occur outside of the Allarrae's influence. As I said, he's not the only one."

"Show me the others, Ky," Van bade. What appeared on the screen was a sampling of about twenty-six individuals, none of whom bore any resemblance to the Perratti Lupar who was her first love so long ago. "I don't remember focus points ever being mentioned in either my experience or Sahni's."

"Hmm, not true, Van," her inner Sahnassa warned. "See, I don't or didn't mess around much with histories and time, but I've heard the term before. It wasn't during my time on Thuria, but as I understand the concept, it's serious. It's not something we can play around with."

Kylie, who had been listening in on Vanarra's inner deliberations, continued the thought. "Time travel is ... a ticklish thing, even for the Allarrae – a power they don't use for more than observation if they have any alternative. They have fought and defeated enemies in wars that were scattered across time; they got very good at it. All of those battles caused them to put down some serious laws, and these focus points are one of those laws. According to the description, a focus point can occur naturally when the causality nexus is-"

"Save it, save it, save it," Van told her, frustrated, putting up her paw. "I couldn't ever get temporal mechanics or the definitions they used. The short answer in all of that technical gibberish is ... no. No, I can't backscan him to determine if he is *my* Ash. If he is the Ash I knew, yanked away at the moment of death, like Mom, I now have no way of knowing – not even by talking to him. He won't open up to me. He's polite. He's kind. He's ... distant."

"My observations," Kylie softly inserted, "are he's that way with pretty much everyone. He's opened up to Doctor Emma a little bit, but even then, I can tell he's holding back. What I've been able to glean from my scans, medical records, and other historical files are that he's completely unaware of his life prior to sixteen seasons ago. We're pretty close to the anniversary, too – just a few sols ago. I've watched him making diary entries and the like. He's afraid that his past might be horrible."

Vanarra was now in a full force rant. "It was! He was a pathetic orphan cast out Anati mongrel bastard who wasn't able to steal enough food to keep those living with him from nearly starving to death! He was thrown out and wandered into the forest by the Pinnacle Academy or the Pinnacle Center back then! He was ... scared out of his mind, terrified of his own shadow. He almost wet himself when he first saw me, but then the way he looked at me as I talked – like I was some kind of amazing miracle – made me want to help him. I spent time combing nits out of his fur, cutting them out, sometimes, teaching him, making love to him, helping him to know how to live, and now look in the viewer, kits. There he is or ... may be. Dammit, I wish Theo would just tell me it's him!"

"I'm sorry, Van," Sahni breathed. "I know – I really do – how deeply you cared for Ash. We still don't know for sure if that's him or not."

"It couldn't be anyone else, kit," Vanarra offered up, closing her eyes and laying her head back. "Vanassa's not complete yet, and I know that Ash's loss is something that still hurts me. Besides, Theo told me there would be multiple surprises, and my Mom is only one – so there's more. This cub is just a little too close to my memory for me not to feel the old hurt. It's strange, though. It's more like a ... representative hurt, or at least I thought it was. My soul bled from my body onto the sidewalk the night I lost him. Parts of it never ever came back. I've had lifetimes of joy, but this still aches. It couldn't be anyone else. It just couldn't…"

Chapter 1: The Lost Land

Vanalla stepped into the hallway at just the right moment to catch Akashar or "Shar" as he left Doctor Emma's. Quietly, stealthily, she slipped up beside him, just behind, and tried to catch a whiff of his scent. "Hello, Vanalla Ashallo," he said kindly, and she stopped in surprise.

"How did you know I was there?"

"You've been there three times out of three that I've visited here. This was number four," he offered, turning his deep green eyes back towards her with an air of humor. "You were quiet and even stealthy, but it's always between here and the entrance to the cafeteria where you greet me and ask me to have lunch with you."

Vanalla sighed and shook her head, taking a step back from him. "I guess this is the point where you complain to the hospital administration or get a restraining order or something of the like."

"No, I don't think so," he offered quietly. "You don't follow me around outside of here, and you seem genuinely happy to see me. That's a good thing."

"I don't want to get in the way of what you're doing with Doctor Emma, though," Vanalla replied, sensing his patience in dealing with her.

An impression struck him, however, that although he was supposed to be going to the chapel to help with one of their projects on his sol off, there was clearly something missing in her life that she thought he could fulfill. What his eyes showed him, no matter how professionally dressed she was, was also an enticement to linger a bit – she was beautiful. "If you showed up when I was on the way in and kept me from going or interrupted us, that would be different. You make a point of not doing that. You seem to make a point of being here, instead. Being here … to see me." Vanalla bit her lip and nodded. "Why? I'm not the one you lost a long time ago, at least as far as I know. You said he died, right?"

Vanalla nodded. "Yes, and I'm sorry. I don't mean to try to stuff you into his paw shoes, but…" She looked away, and he could tell that she was trying to control her emotions. Seeing it, he stepped closer in concern, and she turned her head back to him and smiled. "That's it. You … are a good soul. I don't know if you know how I can tell it, but I can. Just now, I wasn't sure what to say, and I feel a lot of difficult things when I talk to you. I'm … nervous when I talk to you, and if you only knew me, that's a pretty surprising event. Now, some would just back away or keep their distance. You worried for me, Shar, not about me – for me. I'd like to know someone like that, and I hope I could be that to you."

"But," he softly pressed her, "isn't there still the chance that you're just putting all of your memories on top of my fur, draping me in them?"

She looked up at him and slowly shook her head. "Until I get to know you, how will I ever tell? Maybe that cub not out of his teens I lost so long ago isn't you – not in any way. After all, like you said, he died. However," she offered stepping a little closer to him, "maybe he was kind to me and let me be kind to him, and maybe that isn't so foreign to either of us. It doesn't require you to be him, it just asks if you are someone *kind* of like him – namely, kind, like him."

He smiled and, embarrassed, bowed his head. "I like to think I am. I pray that I am."

Vanalla's ears perked up a bit. "You … are a believer? You have a faith?"

"I do. I follow the Creator's Path."

"Something we share, then," she told him. "Something we can talk about that doesn't have much to do with the one I knew before."

"He wasn't a believer?"

"No," she said gravely. "No, he wasn't. It's not a happy thought."

Akashar began to see the depth of her hurt and loss over this individual from her past, and that reflected off of his own loss – his own missing past. "No. Losing someone like that is … difficult, and it truly challenges your faith. You know, you've asked me three times to share lunch with you, and all three times I've said no. You haven't asked, now, but this sol, I have a little time I can spend if you'd like."

"To introduce ourselves to one another?" Van agreed hopefully. "So maybe I don't see you as this individual I lost so long ago, and you don't see me as this somewhat stalkerish obsessive crazy Faelnar."

"I may be very different than what you're expecting. After all, I'm visiting Doctor Emma … for a reason." She nodded, her eyes closed. "So long as you understand that and … respect my choices, then yes, I'd be happy to have lunch with you."

"Thank you, Akashar. I agree with what you've said. You have a very special kind of wisdom, I think. This way?"

"This way," he agreed and started to walk beside her down the hall. "It's an unusual compliment," he added after a moment.

"What?" she asked, smiling as they entered the cafeteria and got into line.

"That I have wisdom."

"A special kind," she told him. "One that is braver than most, and one that requires I treat you as a Thurian, not an image of one. That's self-respect. I like that."

"And you are … interesting," he told her, faltering slightly, as he went through the line picking a few things. "I'm not all that polished, I guess. Was he?"

"He was just barely more than a baby cub, and I'm not going to compare him to you. However, you could guess the answer."

"I suppose. Wherever I got my education, it was … serviceable, but not very refined. I've tried to improve it, over time."

"Really?" Van asked as she walked over to the register to pay for her meal. Waiting for him, she offered, "My treat? Only fair since I asked."

"I … suppose so," he replied, a little guarded.

"You're really thinking this through carefully, aren't you?" she observed, making his blush fur rise a little. "It doesn't obligate you, in any way. If anything, I owe you for the bothering I've put you through. Please?"

"Alright," he agreed, and in a moment, they were both seated at a table. "Thank you."

"Thank you for saying yes," she told him, not looking at him as she stirred some things together on her plate. "Would you like to say thanks over the food?"

"I'll defer to you," he stated, his eyes still nervous.

She smiled and nodded and then closed her eyes, bowing her head. "Thanks to the Creator from whom all blessings come, and thanks for the ways made for us and the paths for us to tread. May this food be to our nourishment while we nourish the souls of others."

"Well said," he noted earnestly, looking up into her eyes with a bit of a searching expression. "You're not new to that prayer."

"No, not new at all," she chuckled, realizing that she had just confirmed for him that she also had a faith and such wasn't just talk, and that led to a new realization. "Wow, this … must be really difficult for you."

"Difficult?" he asked as he started to eat, his eyes never leaving her.

"Yes. Trust. Everything I say, you doubt. You're very polite about it, but still."

"When you don't have memories from a huge part of your life," he quietly admitted, "you'd be surprised how many go out of their way to pretend to be a part of what you can't remember or try to jolt you in some way to try and fix you."

Van chewed for a bit and then nodded. "So, that's it. A big part of your life is missing?"

"Yes. Minus sixteen seasons, I'm … pretty well a blank slate. Woke up not knowing anything about who I was – not even my name. I've spent a lot of fruitless time trying to find out who I was, and now I'm hoping I can just put that blank spot in my memories behind me."

"And be happy with who you are, now," Vanalla offered, not looking at him, but nodding acknowledgement. "You found your way to the path, and that is probably the most profound good you could do for yourself. You have a job, and I have to admit that I was curious about geo-cooling. It's a little expensive, but it pays for itself in under five seasons. That's better than most corporate investments."

"I agree," he offered, a slight smile on his face. "Nothing is right about a place if you are too hot or too cold, or everything has a musty or damp smell. I've been in fine hotels where, when we entered, I felt like I could barely breathe. Afterwards, when we fixed things, it was so much better."

"Clears the air," Van acknowledged. "I, if you would permit me, would like to do that, as well, since you've been kind enough to tell me what's going on with you. You're not the only individual I know missing a big part of their past. My ... adopted sister, I guess you would call her, was someone I discovered here in critical care. She was found, injured, at a construction site with her memories in a jumble. We've become close."

"And she's all better now?" he asked, but there was an edge to it of distrust.

"Physically, her wounds are healed, and she has started a new life. She has forsaken that which she can't return to."

"Does she remember any of it?" he pressed, but then shook his head. "No! It's ... not the gold-on-gold Faelnar, is it?"

"The very same! It appears I've not been the only one being watchful, Akashar," Van teased a little, biting her lip. "She's taken, unfortunately – well, great for her, but not so great for anyone else who might want to hunt her."

"I saw the bracelet," he admitted. "She ... is very nice, true. Was she a blank slate, too, even with the authorities?"

"No genetic records, no. We're still trying to figure that out. Physically, though, she's alright. Spiritually, she's also found the Creator's path."

"And a mate?" he asked, and she nodded. "How does he know – well, maybe that's a rude question."

"Might still be important; go ahead," she told him as she took another bite.

"How does he know who he has *actually* joined with? She could be someone – if you'll forgive this – with a horrible past, maybe even one that could have been dangerous."

"It's almost certainly the case, based on what we know. She was horribly abused and thin when she was found. Someone treated her abominably, shamefully. Still, think on this. We've had some friends in enforcement scour every known criminal database looking for any sign of her. She's gone in and been modeled in three dimensions and searched every database the world over as far back as it makes sense to search. They can't find anything she did wrong. Now, she could have done wrong in secret, but there's nothing that proves it. I've gotten to know her, care about her. I think that she's proven I can trust her, and I don't think her mate is wrong about that, either."

He looked at her, and she could tell by his expression what he was thinking, even without Tana's help. "Hold on there. I mention her only so you can talk to her, but go through Emma, first."

"Why wouldn't the doctor tell me to if it would do good for me? She knows about your … sister, right?"

"She's not allowed. Patient doctor confidentiality prohibits it."

"Confidentiality that you just broke?" he asked.

She looked down at her plate and chuckled. "Damned, you're good. You might do indoor cooling and so forth, but the mind sitting behind those eyeballs is pretty freaking incredible. Your honor, the counsel for the defense would just say that, by way of confession, she is a dear friend, and I've spoken with her about you, and my … interest in getting to know you a little better."

"How is that going?" he asked having just swallowed another bite.

"Rocky, but pretty amazing, actually. Shenaria gave me permission to tell anyone her story if I thought it could help. Strange as it seems, once I learned you had lost your memories, she came to mind. Now, if you'd fallen off a wall over a cliff and found yourself dangling a hundred tracks in the air and had nightmares about it, afterwards, I'd recommend a different friend. Running into an ancient pair of historical figures in a nightmare and waking up to find your tail shaved, yeah – different friend altogether for that one, too."

He looked at her, his guarded expression softening, and he chuckled. "Okay, okay. It's really hard for me to trust anyone. Frankly, I give you decent marks finding out that I'm missing my memories. Lots of Thurians presume I'm lying and trying to hide something bad or shameful."

"Ever thought of trying the enforcement angle? Looking yourself up, or are you satisfied that everyone else who hasn't believed you already covered those hunting grounds?"

"Yeah, there were one or two who were really thorough about it, laid everything out in front of me on paper – must have spent a bunch of money doing it. They didn't find anything, and yes, I believed them." After eating another bite and looking at her for a moment, he asked, "What kind of bad life experience would have referred me … to you? You don't have to-"

"I do," she told him, smiling softly but in a way he could clearly see her pain. "Coming back to the grave where your mate was buried and finding that the grave had been violated. Finding his bones … gone, sent who knows where. Not your specific problem, I'd guess?"

"No," he offered, surprised. "I'm … sorry. Do you know why he was targeted?"

"Perhaps, I blame myself," she told him, spearing a soft tuber root. "Maybe, it was something in the way I lived my life that caused it. It wasn't on purpose and not the kind of thing you can guess is coming. I've thought a lot about what I said about him and who might have heard it, taken it, passed it on, ending up in … well, with his grave desecrated. I know that by the teachings of the Creator's path, where his body is really doesn't matter, but … there's a part of me that will always be hurt because that happened."

"That's two, then, you've lost," Akashar noted.

"Both died of unfortunate, but natural, causes and not by violence of any kind; you can imagine how I feel when someone tries to pin that on me."

"Fair point," he offered. Looking down, he saw his food was already gone. "I'm done," he breathed, seeming a little sad.

"It was good," she told him. "Thank you."

"Bringing up such heartache isn't good."

"It isn't *fun*, but I believe it's good – in terms of it being meaningful. Please, ask Doctor Emma what she thinks, and if you want to talk with Shenaria, I can arrange an introduction, or you can just go to her, yourself. I'll tell her, with your permission, that we spoke."

"I'd have to really think about what to say," he admitted to her.

"You did just fine in speaking with me. She's a sweet kit – not difficult to talk to. Why are you worried?" she queried, but then saw the guilty look in his eyes. "You thought a lot about what you would say to … me if you did say yes, didn't you?"

"If you actually invited me after all of the times I turned you down. I … tend to consider my choices very carefully," he explained, standing and nodding to her. "Some poor choices just after I was found caused me to be more cautious. I'll admit I was prepared … for a very different encounter."

"I hope it wasn't a disappointment," Van told him earnestly as she also stood.

"No. No, you're not. Give me a little time, Vanalla, and … maybe we can have lunch, again?"

"I'd like that, Akashar. I'd like that very much."

"Give … give me a moon, please. I'm just starting to make progress with Doctor Emma, and … there's a lot I'm not ready for, yet."

"Just be kind to me when you see me, Akashar, please. That's all I ask." He looked at her, curious about that request but then smiled. He nodded to her and then stepped away, leaving her at the table. Before she could count to three, a Nephti nurse was standing beside her. "Well?"

"Cute. Really cute," Selena observed, her tray in her paws. "You two would make a nice couple, I think."

"I guess," Van breathed but couldn't help but wonder if that she and Ashalam standing next to each other would be considered a cute couple in this time. "What's up with you? Everything quiet? No primal stars being divas or secret refugees hanging about?"

"Not right now," she stated. "Mind if we sit?"

"No, that's fine. I have a few." She sat as the nurse sat down in the chair just vacated by Akashar. "How have you been?"

"In the ward, we've been fine," the Nephti told her as she put her napkin cloth in her lap and started to cut up her grazerloaf. "We manage all of the more normal cases, but the one where it's getting pretty difficult is the ward they set aside for the Vanarran poisoning cases."

"The purebred curse," Van breathed angrily. "There are so many. Oh, sorry." Closing her eyes for a moment as the Nephti said a quiet prayer of thanks for her meal acted as a break in conversation.

"It's alright. I appreciate it. Yes, there are so many, as you were saying, and all ages. This has been going on for a long time."

"Notice you haven't been seeing many Vanarrans out and about, either. They are pretty well hunkered down in their compounds and temples – worldwide if what I'm hearing from our dear Doctor's new love is true."

Selena smiled naughtily as she finished chewing a bite. "Like a whole different Thurian, that Vulpi is! She's actually listening for a change and a bit more open minded. Guess we just needed someone to plow her field, so to speak."

Vanalla laughed quietly, closing her eyes and shaking her head. "Now, you! I will say that it has … relaxed her a little."

"Oh, don't play it down. It's been all Triani and I could do to keep from pulling on her tail about it, but we so much like being on her good side, we're afraid to take the risk. She nipped at you a bit, if I remember. She doing better on that score?"

"Well," Vanalla hedged, "since Shenaria, she's not really been reaching out to me for any of her cases."

"And here you go getting all friendly with one that's not so different from her. How's she doing, anyway? I see her in the gift shop, and she looks so happy!"

"Oh, my," the Faelnar chuckled. "Couldn't be any happier! After she and Trax were joined, they are positively the model couple – so much so that it's a little difficult to be around them. What?"

"Yeah, I heard about that," Selena confessed guiltily, but not without a great deal of sympathy. "You gave up … everything for her. That's a debt she'll never be able to repay, and what's more, I've seen the way she acts when you are around. She knows it. I'm so sorry, Vanalla. I pray that you find someone wonderful. What about this cub you were talking to? Something possible there?"

"I don't know," came the sad musing, but then an eyebrow fur raised over her right eye. "What I *do* know is that you strike me as someone quite worthy of your namesake – Grand Matriarch Selena de Orturu. You're pretty good about talking to Thurians, understanding their problems, being assertive in defense of them. Those are qualities that would serve you well in a family house."

"Me, a Grand Matriarch?!" Selena clearly rejected the idea. "You don't know what you're saying, Vanalla."

The gold and brown Faelnar let her head rest in the hammock of her joined paw fingers and smiled a knowing smile. "Well, you'd be surprised, and of course not as a Grand Matriarch, but as a matron – someone who, in the old times, used to reach out to and help guide families. Hey, I'll tell you a secret. Have you done much study on the Grand Matriarch Selena of old?"

"Just a bit. I kind of ran from the subject in school because my parents were overly fond of the historical connection. Every time a report came up about it, I kind of chose a different topic."

"Well, then you may have missed one essential part of her background. She started in school learning how to be … a nurse." The nearly unpleasant scowl from the Nephti who was chewing her food and couldn't respond caused Van to raise her paws, placating Selena. "No, no! Check your history and see. That was what her undergraduate and graduate studies were in, and she served a number of seasons before dropping out to raise a family and then, just as she was about to get back into the workforce, her house snapped her up. She did very well."

"I'll check your story, I suppose," Selena offered, the edge off her annoyance. "And no, I never heard any of that. The truth is that

… well, I was kind of asked, recently, what I thought about matrons and what their roles should be. I think our house is trying to follow de Dothnar's lead in steering their matrons back towards what some are calling the more *traditional* role. I … I can't say I'm opposed, but," and she looked sternly at Vanalla. "I'm *not* ready to sign up!"

"Not yet," Vanalla chuckled and was about to get up to go, but then saw two more friends heading in their direction. "Oh, good thing I didn't have any pressing engagements."

Selena whirled around and looked, smiling. "Mishiph, you old prowler you! You stalking younger prey?"

Triani, her fellow Nephti nurse, wasn't taking that joke unchallenged. "Oh, well, if you've got what it takes to attract a fine male like this…" Swishing her tail and flexing her hip to the right in a rhythmic motion caused one of the nearby Nephti males to growl. "Oh, do shut up, Kirbal; you have six kits and cubs already. You don't want me; you want a therapist." He laughed heartily, nodding, and went back to his meal. "May we join you?"

"If you don't cause a riot," Van chuckled but used her paws to pull back both of their seats. "How are things?"

"Pretty challenging," Mishiph admitted as he sat down and settled himself, looking depressed as his eyes came to rest upon his meal. "Grazerloaf. Why … why this?"

"It's not bad," Selena told him. "At least not when you put the sauce on it."

He looked at her with all of the pity he could muster. "I'm so sorry for you, child. To think that your sense of smell and taste have deserted you at such a young and tender age."

Selena growled at him, darkly, and it looked like she was ready to truly go after him, except Vanalla intervened. "Now, now! I had it, also, and I actually survived. I may have to find me a fully aged and seasoned grazer steak after work to make up for the abomination, but it will keep me on my hind paws, at least."

"I'll need that," he told them. "We're struggling to find ways to cover the demand for pediatricians and pediatric nurses for the child recovery wing – the one where we're curing the Purebred curse. I'm afraid our dear director is finding himself pressed into reaching out into … interesting labor pools to draw out more paws to do the work."

"Really?" Van asked.

"Do tell," Triani pressed him.

"I'm afraid I better not," he warned. "I have only caught scent of it, and I'm not sure it's true. Even if what I've heard is true, I can't say I disagree with his logic. What has me heartbroken was looking at the backlog list. As usual, the other hospitals are doing far less than their share; so many of the families are coming to us. It appears, by the age of the cubs and kits we're seeing, that the Vanarrans were very active in the last twenty seasons."

Van closed her eyes and shook her head slowly, angrily, her ears down, back fur up, and tail lashing. "Jail ... is far too gentle for those who did this."

"Oh, there will be some of that," Mishiph told her after chewing through his first bite. "Report says enforcement took ten into custody on Thuratan and at least six times that if you add up all of the other continents, and they're nowhere close to the end of the second wave of the investigation. However, that wasn't as fascinating as what I heard. Six of the Vanarrans who were awaiting trial were attacked by the other inmates and had to be moved into solitary. They're having to do that the world over."

"Seems even prisoners get pissed when you mess with children," Selena seethed. "It's deserved. That said, I don't think the Sahnassites..."

Van put her paw on the nurse's sleeve. "Hold ... that thought. Look towards the door, but do it slowly. Don't attract attention."

Mishiph's Faelnar grace allowed him the ability to make the glance quick and hardly noticeable, but the rise of his back fur was unmistakable. "Well, it is true then. That's director Kinness with someone who looks like..."

"Yeah," Van supplied, keeping her eyes off the doorway and trying very hard not to attract attention. "Loyal Elite of the Sahnassites, robes and everything. Frills on it, too. Might be the local pack leader, you think?"

Triani looked back at her food, her expression sour. "I haven't seen that much of them, but from what I have seen ... yeah, you could be right."

"And they're coming over," Vanalla groaned quietly. "So, not my most fortunate sol."

There wasn't anyone in the cafeteria who wasn't watching the director enter with someone of the Sahnassites, and Van couldn't help but look up, as well, when they got in relatively close range. The director stopped at their table and nodded to them before speaking. "Good sol. I hope you're having a pleasant lunch?"

"Already had mine," Van told him, standing, trying to add a slight rasp in her voice that wasn't there normally. "I was just going."

"Oh, very good," Kinness responded. "This is Loyal Elite Kallain de Mistral of the Sahnassites. He has generously offered to help supply additional medical staff for the curing of the Vanarran poisonings. It seems they have quite a number of board certified doctors and nurses who could be of assistance. We are … discussing the possibility of including them to help increase capacity. I was wondering, Vanalla, if you would be so kind as to show him around the hospital while I meet with the board of directors? If our deliberations go well, then we'd need him brought back to the boardroom in about half an interval to an interval or so."

Van took a quick breath and then plunged in, using her normal voice. "As always, I'm happy to assist however I can. Should I take him to that ward, as well?"

"Please," Kinness directed. "Loyal Elite, this is Vanalla Ashallo, one of our most dedicated and effective *volunteers*, especially when it comes to helping with some of our most difficult cases. She's been a light to many who have truly needed it."

Kallain held her in his steady gaze as he bowed. "My honor, and I must compliment you on such a *noble* endeavor. To offer such service without a *shade* of a possibility for payment is truly exceptional, one might even say it … transcends the normal."

Van decided to let just an edge of warning slip into her voice. "Your *compliment* … is most appreciated. I think we should begin immediately, with the second level?"

"I will happily accept your most enlightened guidance," he stated graciously, bowing low before her. Throwing Kinness a deeply resigned look, Vanalla led the Loyal Elite out of the cafeteria and down the hallway.

"Kinness," Mishiph grumbled looking up at him. "That was not a nice thing you just did to that kit."

"I had to. The board is having the exact same reaction you are, but we are falling behind badly on trying to help these kits and cubs, and we need all of the help we can get. I need the time to talk them into just listening and treating his proposal seriously!"

"But, sir!" Triani protested. "The Sahnassites?!"

"Nurse, if Dame Geistana de Oterbythe, herself, were here and willing to put on a nurse's apron to help those poor children, I would sign her up and gladly so, right now! The board has utterly tied my paws and blunted my claws in terms of trying to use overtime as a way to manage this tide, and our community has never had a greater or more impactful need! We're trying to pull new graduates from the medical academies early and begging those who retired up to twenty seasons ago to come back and help, but it ... is ... not ... enough. We have to do something!"

"I don't disagree, Kinness. I just wish it wasn't Vanalla you had to task with that."

Kinness patted him on the back, gently. "She's got the easy job, Mishiph. It's me who has to go deal with the rabid prowlers in the boardroom. Wish me luck."

"You'll most certainly need it," the elder Faelnar told the mixed blood as he retreated.

In the hallway, Vanalla pressed the elevator call button and waited in silence alongside the other Faelnar. When it opened, they both stepped in, and Van raised a paw to warn off a couple of orderlies who wanted in. When the door closed, she looked at Kallain with a pained expression as she switched off the elevator's controls, effectively holding them in place. "Of all of your disguises," he told her, evenly, "I believe I am perplexed by this one most of all, my Noble Shade. So, is this where you live your ... normal life amongst other Thurians? I have wondered about that, if you even fully existed on the material plane."

"And just on the voice, too!" Vanarra groaned, sidestepping his question. "*What* are you doing here, Kallain?"

He ignored her obvious annoyance and commented, "Your voice was simply the first aspect which collected my attention, as I heard you speaking from some distance away, and it is a voice I have marked in my mind. However, despite your attempt to mask yourself, I studied your eyes and the lines of your face. As you kept those similar to the Vanarra de Gonari seen in history books, the answer was not difficult to divine." His answer from the Faelnar was a resigned shaking of her head and a grunt, which he interpreted – rightly – as reluctant acceptance and an appreciation of his faculties. "To answer your question, however, I must tell you that this course of action was not one that I originated. Nevertheless, it appears sound on multiple levels."

"Oh, how so?" Vanarra asked, curious.

"First, from the Sahnassite point of view, our funds are highly constrained, our influence and reach have been reduced, and our numbers are dropping moon after moon, as you are well aware. Second, we have a number of skilled professionals in the medical field and other vocations who can apply their skills whilst using their earnings to support our order. This is seen as one of the few remaining sources of income and will likely be adopted across the planet. Now, as your loyal vassal, I must point out that some efforts must be made, however problematic, to re-introduce members of our order back into society. When the Sahnassites are no more or their faith has been lost, they must still be able to provide for themselves. In that way, I attempt to facilitate a peaceful path to unwind and disperse the Sahnassite influence. Finally, in respect to both of my loyalties, if we reverse the injuries done to others, then I can scarcely call it a poor choice."

She leaned against the side of the elevator and looked at him. When he glanced at the door, she shook her head. "We're okay. I'm tucking this little moment between others so they won't be noticed. We have the time. Oh, Kallain! My operatives knew you were in the hospital and knew that you were talking to the director, but they didn't know he'd suddenly get an itch to seek me out for your tour. I was hiding out in the cafeteria for a while trying to stay out of sight."

"Such are the intricacies of fate," he offered, "and the abilities of an aware and alert mind."

Pacing a bit in the elevator, she nodded. "True. Now, what you suggest has merit, and as usual, it is very well thought out. I presume you're being very selective about who participates in this program and who does not?"

Kallain nodded. "No one who is or has been key in the rites of Mavia would be included, nor those I consulted for the downfall of the matriarch. I am concerned about too much temptation there, and our order does not need any more ill will directed at it. The provision of our resources for this purpose should be a plausible recommendation, even to the board of the Commons. There are legitimate medical needs in our community, as you might guess, and unlike our Vanarran counterparts, our doctors studied in academy alongside those not of our faith. Their qualifications are still valid. So, yes, those choices will be careful, but they must be made in order to prevent those amongst our number becoming frustrated to the point of violence or inciting violence in others."

"Thank you," Vanarra told him, giving him a nod, which he returned, before looking at the door.

"One of many appreciable differences in serving you and serving the former matriarch of de Dothnar is that even when you are angry and surprised, you are still reasoned. Your frustration is as much self-directed as it is outward, and you still manage to compliment my abilities and provide gratitude for my contributions. I will keep my interactions with you here sparse and only as we are directed into one another's presence by those in leadership. Would that be satisfactory?"

"I would appreciate it," she nearly whispered, grateful he had looked away, and she did the same. "When I first came back, Kallain, I was very much on my own, just getting the lay, if you will. I found a place to belong during that time – this place. I've made friends and helped and kind of become part of it. Now, I could sit enveloped in shielding and mystery and everything – remove myself, but I feel a desire to speak to regular Thurians, help them. Maybe, I even need it," she confessed.

"And, you share your heart," he added, softly, looking at the floor. "To that end … I must ask, if you do not mind, about the fate of Shalana. We have heard … different things – that she no longer lives, for example."

She leaned against the wall of the elevator and looked at him, and she could see he was clearly struggling with this conversation, something the Allarraen amulet around her own neck confirmed. "She's alive and well, but Shalana was involved in some of the attacks on the Vanarrans inside of the prison, and it earned her three more felony counts – long ones. Some kits just don't know when to stop. You're ... missing her, it seems."

He nodded and put his paw on the grab bar. "I am finding myself often lost in thought about the disgraced Matriarch of de Dothnar, although I know it is just biology that is betraying me. She was someone who, had she been mentored properly at an early age, could have done enormous good or at least lived a far less avaricious life. Her fierceness of spirit could have been a true benefit to her, the community, and to ... a mate. Is there any sign that she has repentance in her heart?"

"Nothing yet, but I think her lawyers are still trying to lie to her a little longer to pull every bit of funds they can out of her before they throw her off the cliff. Give it time, Kallain, and you might find occupation elsewhere, for your attentions. She may well not be worth your wait."

"Seeking someone with all that is transpiring around us would be difficult, and I confess my attraction to the Nephti now strangely eclipses my desires for those females of my own breed – with apologies. I know that is about the most heretical thing a Sahnassite can utter."

"None needed," Vanarra chuckled. "I'm certainly not a Sahnassite, my best friend is a gorgeous Nephti, and I'm only about half Faelnar, anyway."

"Well said," he replied, smiling. "And so, my Noble Shade indeed does lead a life among other mortals. Does she also seek a home for her heart?"

"She tries," she told him, shaking her head. "And it didn't work out, although I think how it did fall through was to the greater good. I'm kind of trying to talk to someone new, but it's so very tentative. There's a great deal of growth that has to occur between us for even the beginnings of an intimate relationship. I'm kind of hoping for a brighter sol down the trail on that subject, I suppose."

"Distractions are difficult problems for both of us, truly, but it is ... difficult not to want this to be over and for us to find ourselves in what some would call a normal life," he admitted. "So, my Most Noble Shade, do I have your permission to proceed with my plan?"

"Yes, you do. I think it's a very good idea, honestly. Just be very careful around here and protect my identity. Make sure those you send are well behaved, too, as you said. There are a lot of good Thurians I care about here."

"It will be done," he promised. "How fare our Vanarran adversaries?"

"Eating their own, more or less," Van explained. "Spending down their bank accounts, selling off land and possessions just as the Sahnassites are compelled to do. Unlike your group, however, they are finding it downright dangerous to venture into public without good security. We have also been tripping up several of their more dangerous methods of gathering cash, such as selling off their projectile weapons."

"That has been the subject of discussion in our chambers, as well. It is something I refuse to permit on the grounds that we must still be able to defend ourselves. However, anything commercially purchased through legitimate means sold to a reputable dealer does help remove excess weapons from our midst, so the number of stunners and stun prods has dropped. I take it this meets with your approval?"

"It does, and I was aware, actually," she told him, smiling a little predatorily. "And … as for your hopes for a normal life or a life with a little … Nephti companionship, I appreciate what you're doing for me and the loyalty you're showing not only to me but to the lives of those in your charge. So, to that end, I want to help you, maybe even reward you? Tell me what you think about … Melissiana?"

"My aide?" he asked, a little confused. "She could represent the riskiest and ill-considered-"

"She desperately desires your attention and approval, and someone of your intelligence could help her to grow and grow well in the way Shalana never had the chance to. I've looked into her background in the same way I looked into yours, and so I know her very well. Did you know that her genetics are very close to that of Shalana? They are distantly related, but related. Also, she keeps your secrets, even when pressed by those of your order who are against you, and she is being pressed right now. Chuffar still has his representatives around you, and they are trying to undermine you. It's something we've been frustrating, subtly, but in her case, we've had no need to intervene. Regardless of your decision about pursuing her, I would advise you to keep her close and happy."

"I ... truly don't know about this," he admitted to her, and Kallain looked as uncertain as she had ever seen him.

"I," she told him, walking in front of him and crossing her arms, "care about you, and I care about her. There is a difference in ages but not beyond that which is normal. She is very careful about how she reacts in front of you, as she knows your abilities and has training of her own to hide how she feels. When she's alone, however, the walls fall away, and her desires for you are ... evident, let's just put it that way. I am not demanding or requiring that you do anything, but I wanted you to know, and I wanted you to know that if you pursue something with her, we will also look after both of you, protect both of you. I already know you'll be careful, for her sake and yours. How this develops is up to you, but when it is over and I fulfill my promise to you for your safety and survival, I pledge to ensure hers, as well." She saw his doubt, and through Tana – the stone at her neck – she felt how torn he was. "Shalana is just not going to be an option, Kallain. She has too much blood on her paws, and you know that. You know that she cannot be trusted, and thanks to the crimes she has committed, she will be in prison until well after the age of childbearing. There was some small chance for her redemption, but she's given it up. Her life is ruined, and Melissiana's is just starting. She ... you can help, and she will adore you for it, even more than she already does."

"Is it not Melissiana's free will and choice that you compromise by this pledge?" he challenged, but she could see he was interested.

"No. I'm promising to help you both and protect you both, not go inside of her head and condition her to love and obey you beyond her will. Kallain, her will to do that is already there, and I'm just removing the veil between you so you know of her affection for you. Do you find her at all attractive?"

He was silent for a moment but then nodded. "I have very little knowledge of her … form, I guess you would say, for she is always in loose robes around me."

"She is fit, attractively provisioned, and healthy in every respect. Much of the work of keeping herself so she has done in your name."

"But you have invaded her mind and soul to learn this?"

"No, Kallain," Vanarra countered. "We've listened to her utterings when she thought no one could hear. Someone always could, and I've heard her prayers to the goddess. Treat her kindly and openly, and she will be yours. Very seldom have I seen this possibility, Kallain. These things are usually poorly formed and badly balanced, but here, I'm telling you that the way is clear between you, if you wish it."

"I will … consider what you have said, earnestly. I was nearly unaware of the biological facts of rut for myself, but now, my … exposure has made its presence evident again. I suppose I could let it die, but…"

"Being lonely is difficult, and surrendering that part of who you are is not required. Also, I make you this promise – when the time requires it, I will confess the truth of who I am even to her."

He bowed to her, very deeply. "Your consideration of me and my wellbeing is beyond anything I have ever known, Noble Shade, and at every exchange, you again earn that title, which is why it remains my favorite name for you."

"I appreciate the Noble part, at least how it's intended, but the Shade?"

"You are always like a mist that appears and disappears at will, and like a ghost, you see what cannot be seen by other mortal eyes."

"Well, as soon as I cease our little temporal stalling action here, that door will open, and we'll have loads of mortal eyes on us. I was looking … nervous and slightly on edge? Right?"

"I do believe that is true, and I was trying to radiate … polite peacefulness."

"Oh, well said," Van agreed, taking her place. "Ready?"

"She is … well-constructed, you said?" he asked, seeking a clarification at the last.

"*Very* well *proportioned.* If your preferences were at all affected by the Nephti you appreciated prior, you'll find more than one reason to forget the previous ever existed, dear Kallain. Also, her rut peaks in two sols, just in case that information would be helpful to you."

He breathed deeply and sighed, filing the information away without reacting to her implicit taunt. "Polite peacefulness. I am ready."

Just before the door finally did open, Van suppressed a smirk.

Chapter 2: The Renewed

It is a pleasure to meet you. The facilities you offer here will provide some welcome relief to those of my order who have such challenging tasks ahead of them," Kallain told a somewhat stunned Shenaria as he greeted her in the gift shop. Thanks to her various trips to the Haven, the gold-on-gold Faelnar – Vanarra's mother – knew exactly who this was, but meeting him face to face was not something she had expected.

"It's my hope they'll be happy … with the service they receive," Shenaria stumbled, returning the Loyal Elite's bow. "Also, I know of no more important work right now."

"Your knowledge is exceptional," the Loyal Elite offered and then turned and left the shop. Van's chuckle and eye roll after shaking her head made her mother shrug her shoulders in confusion.

"Just tell her everything is okay, Ky," Van told the Vulpi-Izar mentally as she followed the Elite.

"Will do. Yeah, he totally made her, too. Nice. Glad we trust him," Kylie breathed out, nervously.

"As you are keeping tabs on him continually, not much to worry about there, and speaking of which, I think we'll need to increase the approach warning radius for him and anyone else we deal with."

"Like duh," Kylie replied sourly in Van's mind. "Damned if he didn't alert until he actually stepped into the hospital. I set the parameters on him too low."

She was alongside the Faelnar now as they walked back towards the boardroom. "So, she was one of yours, I see," he offered quietly. "Not ... well trained."

"No. Very new. She's a bit of a rescue. She's also been following the news well enough to know who you are," Van whispered back, "with the addition that I put her and several others wise to our agreement."

"Agreement?" he queried.

"Survival. If something happens and you seek them out, they are supposed to watch for you and give you aid – hide you – in the stock closet if required. However, there may have just been that little part I added onto the end of that requirement."

"Which was?"

"You won't see him unless something is seriously messed up."

"Unfortunate that you should have to amend that sage observation," Kallain nearly teased her, "but I hope to be here more frequently ensuring that those of my order perform to the required standard, and no more."

"Got it," Van told him, and then quieted as they turned the corner and approached Kinness, standing in front of the board room door. He looked nervous and just a little upset, and what concerned Vanarra more was that his uncertain gaze rested on her. Kallain noted it, also, and stopped an appropriate distance back to allow the two of them to speak in privacy.

"I'm sorry, Vanalla, but I've had a very difficult time convincing them to see him. However, when I explained that I placed the Loyal Elite Prime into your company, their attitudes shifted. Now, they want to know *your* opinion."

"My ... opinion?!" Van nearly screamed, but she kept it at a whisper. "I'm just a volunteer!"

"Who has had an essential and critical role in averting three major possible media nightmares and rendering key mental health assistance to patients our own doctors had issues with. They also might have gotten wind that you assisted the hospital in getting payment for Shenaria's treatment. That's why they want to see *you*."

Vanalla took a deep breath and nodded. "Okay, okay. Let me talk to the Elite for a moment."

Kinness watched her carefully as she went to the side of the robed Faelnar and had a brief conversation. When she walked back, she told Kinness, "I should ask to be on the payroll for this."

"I think it's because you're not that they trust you."

"Fine. Who is in there?"

"The board … and Emma."

"Oh, damn," Van groaned. "Okay, fine. Let's see what kind of a mess I can make this sol!" Van walked forward and opened the door, leaving a somewhat nervous and uncomfortable Kinness in the company of the Loyal Elite Prime of the Sahnassites.

"Vanalla," Doctor Emma called to her. "Please, can you sit? The board would like to ask you some questions."

"However I can help, Doctor," she told the psychologist as she took her seat dead center in an almost-circle of august and wealthy Thurians in business suits.

"Forgive us for this imposition, Vanalla," the distinguished Pantera directly in front of her offered. "However, you have provided aide to this hospital and exceptional service – not to mention insight. We have your help with Fireclaw Destiny, Laxar, and Shenaria, not to mention your generous provisions to reimburse the operating capital of this hospital above and beyond for her care. You have, also, by reports of our head of volunteers, been responsible for providing very timely reminders for us to review our disaster policies and provided our security team warning when private investigators were unlawfully intruding onto our premises. Beyond all of this, our … well, our security guards like you. A lot."

Vanalla was curious, but then followed the cut of his eyes over the side where Shashee Dupree – now officially the mother of three – stood, back to her pre-pregnancy weight and looking very attractive. "Okay, when you put it that way," she offered, sending a rueful smile in Shashee's direction, "I guess I might be able to offer you some insight. What are your concerns?"

"We're grappling between two major issues here," a Lupar off to her left side confessed, and she could tell that he was very earnest about what he was saying. "We are responsible for the safety and welfare of all of the patients in this hospital, but we are facing a crisis where two groups of patients' needs are in potential conflict, and we're concerned that danger and violence may be part of the mixture. We do not doubt that, if allowed to enter this boardroom, Loyal Elite Prime Kallain de Mistral will be able to provide every reason for us to accept his order's services."

A Faelnar just beside him shook his graying gold head and almost grunted, "We've checked into the certifications of the doctors presently working with the Sahnassites. They're all current. They're all legitimate doctors with standing credentials."

Vanalla eyed him, carefully. "So, you want them to help, but you're afraid of having them help because you think having them here will cause conflict. With whom?"

"The Vanarrans, for one," the Lupar replied. "Maybe, some of our other staff when they are being proselytized."

"Okay," Vanalla told them, trying to ignore Sahni's remark that this group might even be smart enough to listen to her. "Let's take them one by one. First, the Vanarrans. Are your upgraded security measures in place from when the Vanarrans wanted to nab Laxar?" and she looked at Shashee as she asked it. The mixed blood nodded nervously as they all turned around to look at her. "Same policy for limited entry?" Again, Shashee nodded. "Have you added special security to the ward where these particular therapies are happening? If the Vanarrans shouldn't be let in anywhere, it's in there or anywhere near there."

"Not ... specifically," Shashee explained. "My supervisor may be doing something about it, but I'm not sure."

"Yes, well," the Pantera stated darkly, "we can *make* sure, and I see where you're going with that, Vanalla. It's reasonable to put heightened security on the entire ward because we might not be able to know who is Vanarran or a Vanarran sympathizer."

"A high security ward would be suggested," Van put forth and added, "hopefully not with too much additional in the way of staffing or cost."

"Guard, make sure-" the Pantera started, but Vanalla corrected him.

"Shashee," Van inserted.

The Pantera was a little fussed by her insistence on the use of the mixed blood's name, but he did so, nevertheless. "Guard ...

Shashee, please take the matter up with your supervisor and have a proposal to the director no later than by close of business this sol. So, we may be able to deal with the one problem, but what about the impact of the Sahnassites on the rest of our staff?" he asked his fellow board members.

"Potentially," Vanalla offered, again drawing the attention of everyone in the room, "you might find the Loyal Elite open to the possibility of certain restrictions on the members he provides. I think it would be completely reasonable to require doctors, regardless of their religious affiliation, to follow your code for professional dress and comportment. I take it that no other doctors or nurses are allowed to openly try to persuade patients or their families to join any group not affiliated with the hospital?"

"Yes, you're right," the Faelnar told her. "They are allowed to offer prayers and encouragement, but not try to sell anyone anything – a policy that I feel has both a good and a bad side."

"Without doubt," Van agreed before reminding them, "but the fact this policy is already in force means that the staff offered by the Loyal Elite will have to abide by it."

"So," the Pantera summed up, "no robes or arm bands or whatever, dress the same as any other doctor and behave as any other doctor. Do you think they're even capable of that?"

"Looked at the news recently?" she challenged him, gently. "They lost all funding from de Dothnar, and they have been selling off land and assets like crazy over the last six moons – even The Guides statue is back in the paws of de Gonari, de Dothnar, and a little consortium of others. They … need you, and so they will have to do what you say to get paid. You do need them to help these poisoned kits and cubs."

"What about the press?" the Lupar asked. "The newsarotzi! There will be a media blood hunt on this *when* it leaks out!" Emma cringed a bit at that.

"Then don't let it leak," Vanalla told them. "You have contacts in those same services who are friendly towards you. Reach out to them and control the story by getting your version out there, first. This program wouldn't be open to just those of the Sahnassites, correct? Would you offer it to, say, Creator's Path doctors now serving elsewhere?"

"Of course," the Pantera agreed, and he was trying very hard not to smile. "It would be a general invitation, and while no one currently involved in a case would be allowed to assist, the invitation would be open to members of the general public regardless of their religious affiliation. That, I do believe, is a story we could live with. Who would be a good first reach out, media wise?" he asked, again to the board.

"I believe that Doctor Emma may have a contact – Alanar de Kestrick – who has worked with her on stories in the past. I believe he did a fair and thorough job with those interviews, did he not?"

Emma was trying to hide her blush fur, and it was clear she was uncomfortable with the question. Nevertheless, she said, "He has been very aggressive in reporting the faults of the Vanarrans and Sahnassites alike, and so if we want to gauge our policy, he would be a good first test for us."

"Might as well ask a harsh critic, because we're going to get those, anyway. Doctor, just start by telling him we're *considering* it," the Pantera offered, "and give him the parameters we've described. If he's favorable on it, I'd like to know by the time we get done tonight with the Loyal Elite. Is that something you can manage?" he asked. "Next interval or so?"

A little stunned, the Vulpi stood and nodded. "I think he is off this evening, and I might be able to reach him. I can try."

"Please. I want this wrapped up with a nice bow on it by the time we leave here. If we even have half a chance of getting our staff up to some reasonable level to deal with this influx, then we've got to act. If we don't, the insurers might start getting nervous. They're funding this as reluctantly as they do everything else, but they are *with us* at the moment. I don't want to lose that."

"I'll be right back." With an uncertain glance at Vanalla, the doctor was away.

The Pantera then looked over Vanalla's shoulder and shook his head. "Dammit, Mishiph, if you weren't dead on. We had parts of it, but nothing so damned clear cut."

Vanalla turned and saw the elder Faelnar approaching her. "This board has many reasons to be grateful to Vanalla Ashallo, regardless," he told them. "I've also worked closely with her."

"And, you carry yourself well in such an environment," the Pantera offered, standing and walking over to her. "Name's Holosar de Katscha," she was told as she stood and took his large paw in a clasp. "Would you mind if we imposed upon you for occasional insight regarding this process as it goes forward?"

"Not at all," she told him seriously, "if I can be of help. The focus here is twofold. Make sure we heal the patients and make sure the hospital gets paid so it stays open to heal who needs it next."

"That's about the size of it," Mishiph chuckled. "Oh, and if you're wondering what I'm doing up here, I'm retired from the board. They let me sit in if they need someone who doesn't pull their claws."

"I've seen you mad, and it doesn't thrill me." That sent up a chuckle if not a good laugh from several in the room. It was clear that Mishiph was very well appreciated by almost everyone, and he had intentionally done her the favor of including her. As the stone around her neck searched his thoughts on the subject, Van got the impression that he liked her and recognized talent when he saw it.

"If he only knew," Sahnassa inside of Van breathed out in a chuckle. "If he only knew."

"I'm so sorry that this is taking an extended period of time," Kinness offered the Loyal Elite.

"No apology is needed, for a long deliberation would be a thorough one, and that is what is best required in this instance. I see the concerns of both sides, and while there is the potential for a common trail, there are also many issues and concerns to ponder."

At that moment, the door opened, Vanalla and Mishiph stepping out. "They've taken a short recess," Mishiph told them.

Kinness looked at the elder Faelnar crossly. "*You* suggested this – pulling Vanalla into that den of … well, into the boardroom."

"I was a bit surprised, but I think we might be in a good place. Would either of you mind or object if I took the Loyal Elite aside for a moment and helped frame up where we are? It may remove ... obstacles." As the question had been asked right in front of the Loyal Elite, there was not much of an option to refuse, and so Kinness nodded. "Loyal Elite Prime, with your agreement," she offered, directing him to an open office down the hall.

In a few moments, they were seated in the office leaving the door open. "I have to admit that your influence in these precincts is ... surprising if you were trying to maintain a low profile," he told her quietly.

"Ever actually *read* my history?" she shot back, and she had the satisfaction of seeing him smile. "I've tried, and the head of the volunteers just happens to be an ex-board member still in good standing. The work I've done has earned me their ears, and I just filled them up pretty good. They're open to the idea, but with conditions – no surprise. No robes, no religious identification, and no preaching on property or trying to win converts. If you're here to work and here to help, then those are the rules not only for you but for everyone else, myself included. They're going to screen Vanarrans out of the ward where your group will be working, but not being able to pick out Sahnassites from regular doctors or volunteers from other groups will be a plus. They're also going to preempt the media by seeking coverage, not hiding this, using newsarotzi contacts they already know."

"My dear Noble Shade," Kallain offered, his tone nearly lecturing, "if you wish to avoid yet another religion offered in your newest name, you had better exercise care. I sense that these actions are your wisdom and not fully theirs."

She grimaced at him. "You wouldn't be totally wrong. I know. However, I'm still a hospital volunteer."

"And advisory counsel to the board of directors of a major institution. In this instance, I am very grateful."

Standing with him, she agreed, "Yeah, but in other instances, it could get tricky. They'll likely want me to monitor the arrangement, at least to some degree, but that's my problem. Your problem is can you sell this with the other members of your order? They going to live with these restrictions?"

"It is an even hunting ground with no favoritism. This, they should be grateful for. With funds coming in, our outreach can occur in other quarters. I will also make transportation arrangements that will not draw undue attention."

"Yeah, no big limohovers coming right from the Sahnassite complex if you please."

"Such is the heart of what I have to offer them – service, with discretion."

"Then," Vanalla told him, smiling as they left the office, "the bargain might well be struck. May it go well for you, in there." Kallain and Mishiph already had the boardroom doors open as he approached, and he followed them inside.

Two intervals later, Vanalla was again "escorting" the Loyal Elite Prime back to his awaiting conveyance in the parking garage, Shashee following at a discreet distance.

"You were right," he whispered to her. "The bargain is struck and very well done, indeed. If I might enlist your services in dealing with those of my order, then all of my other meetings would conclude with such ease and efficiency."

"Hardly easy," she told him, "but they at least decided. Hey, about that. You know that … advice I gave you earlier?"

By her tone, he could hardly misunderstand what she meant. "Melissiana," he breathed. "I am still … unsure."

"Well, you need back-up, and you are alone. We weren't at all sure they'd put you in Chuffar's place, but they did, and you've done well. However, your aide could cover for you and be an enormous help to you. Moreover," she told him, shaking her head, "and most importantly, she's smitten with you, Kallain. She's so far into you that she may never be able to be with anyone else. That's one incredible offering and a serious responsibility. You need her, too, cub. You are just about as intelligent and logical as anyone I have ever met, but you can't do this alone. You need help, and you could have her love. I can't order you to do anything, but as someone you've come to trust, I'd ask you to strongly consider confiding in her and opening yourself to her."

"It is uncertain ground for me, but you assure me that the ground is not at all unsure," he told her, his brow furrowed in concentration. "And yet while I try to think about how unfair this must be to her, fairness would hurt both of us?"

"Yeah. Quick, let's save her from her crush on you so she doesn't spend the rest of her life with someone she fell in love with from her ears to her tail-tip. See, that way she can spend the rest of her life looking for the second best, which is what we all want out of life."

"Sarcasm becomes you, Noble Shade," he told her, smiling slightly. "If it were not for our guard, I would thank you more ... traditionally for the service you have done me."

"That's good enough, right there," she told him, pleased. "Also, I am screening what she can see and hear. She thinks we've been silent this whole time, not even looking at one another as we walked."

"You're distorting both sound and image?" he asked.

"It's a wonderful way of making sure that we can protect you and Melissiana from discovery, and we'll do that. Now, we're at your vehicle, so everything you say from the moment I stop talking, Shashee will hear."

He nodded and then bowed to her. "Thank you for your assistance, tonight. You have been very kind in your aid to us, and we will remember it."

"Good night, Loyal Elite Prime. May you be safe," Vanalla told him, bowing. In a few moments, the Loyal Elite had departed.

Shashee walked up behind her and told her, "You ... are freaking amazing, you know that? I was scared out of my mind in there! You interrupted and corrected him like ... three times!"

Vanalla shrugged. "I'm a volunteer! What are they going to do, fire me?!" At that point, they both laughed as they started making their way back towards the hospital.

When Vanalla finally did arrive home, conventionally, it was well after sunset. However, as she opened the door to her lair, she found her mother sitting on her sofa looking anxious. "Mom? Hi, what's up?"

"Loyal Elite Kallain is what's up!" Shenaria told her, concerned. "He knows who I am, now, doesn't he?"

"He's a very keen observer of behavior," Van told her as the door closed, the same instant she reverted back into her authentic form. "And, as it happens, voice."

"Why couldn't you just change it?"

"Everyone else around me would have noticed," she explained as she put her things down. "Honestly, I didn't make the best decisions when I first came back to Thuria. I sort of kept a little too much of myself, and this sol, it finally bit me in the hindquarters, but it's not so bad. Don't worry, though. We're watching Kallain, and I believe he's going to be even more aligned to us."

"You said he'd been acting a little erratically, recently."

"Yeah, about that. He … has a problem, and it's been difficult for him to come to terms with it," Vanalla offered, sitting down beside her mother and hugging her warmly. "I love you, Mom."

"I love you, my daughter," she told Van, returning the gesture. "I am always proud of you." They were just quiet for a moment, this greeting the one that gave them back that deep and wonderful connection that had been taken from them when Shenaria was assaulted and supposedly killed in the de Gonari Mercy Garden more than fifteen hundred seasons prior. The temporal slight-of-paw done by her benefactor, Theo, to bring her mother forward in time had a major impact on Van, filling so many of her hurts and regrets. Her mother, Shenaria, seemed interested in the subject and wanted to return to it. "What problem does he have?"

"Because of his … exposure, his *intimate* exposure to former matriarch Shalana, he had actually bonded with her, and his Faelnar lineage nor his Sahnassite training prepared him for that."

"That horrible female!?" Shenaria nearly bleated. "She's repulsive! How … how could he?"

"It's biochemical, Mother, hormones and pheromones and enzymes – things he couldn't control. He's been suffering with actually feeling his rut, and when his rut was on him, what did he want to hunt?"

"Shalana?"

"Well," Van hedged, "more generally, just Nephti. His erratic behavior was partly from that, partly from stress, especially understandable given the intensive pressure he's under as leader of the Sahnassites. Still, he's making good decisions, and it's one you're going to be able to help me keep an eye on."

"Really? What's that?"

"Some of the Sahnassite doctors and nurses will be joining the hospital staff to help cure the ones the Vanarrans poisoned. Plain clothes, no robes and no trying to make new converts for the goddess. After all, what they want most of all right now, from their point of view, is pay – funds to keep the Sahnassites going. Kallain also thinks this may be a good way to help shed members of his order peacefully, and it wasn't his idea, but he felt he needed to support something to keep them from collapsing."

"Isn't that what we want?" Shenaria queried.

"Controlled crash or maybe even less harsh than that, a smooth settling over time. If it happens too fast, the Sahnassites might decide that taking a more violent approach to preserve their status might be preferable. If it slowly drains away over time, there's not as much chance they'll turn violent. However, I did something for Kallain this sol that he really needed," Van chuckled and smiled smugly as she snuggled into her mother.

"What?"

"I told him his aide had a huge, barely manageable crush on him, and … it just so happens, she's a Nephti."

"Oh! Well, that should make him happy, I guess," Shenaria said doubtfully.

"It actually will give him a confidant, and we've checked her out. She's more in love with him than the Sahnassites and worthy of being in our little circle. Kallain's faith emphasized worshiping what amounted to a Nephti goddess, at least in Sahni, and so he already had a pre-disposition to the breed. Besides, you have a little experience on the Nephti side, right? And as a Faelnar, too!"

"What do you – I guess you're right, at least half way right that is, you mess!" the gold-on-gold Faelnar shot back as she tickled the ribs of the mixed blood laying into her, making Van squirm and cackle. "So, yes, your mother is a Faelnar who also loves her some Nephti, with a side of Perratti, granted, but still."

"Believe it or not," Van, still chuckling, pulled away and looked at her mother as she spoke. "Trax, by genetics and blood, is far more Nephti than Perratti.   Your darling mate is more like Sahnassa than he is Bushor, for example, if you remember that history you've been reading."

"Yeah, no wispy muzzle fur," her mother agreed.   "Does … that make you feel good that I fell in love with someone who is mostly Nephti?"

"He's a good soul, Mom, and that's what makes me happy. Speaking of which, where is he?"

"My lair mate is helping his friends tonight, and I can't begrudge him that.   The whole lot of them are studying for final exams.   They're over at our place, next door, so that they can study in peace away from the academy, and … they're staying the night."

"Wait, that means you're bunking who – Lallie, Dexer, Racea, Ariasta – all of them?"

"Yeah, and it's going to be an all-nighter.   I was wondering…"

"My bed, sleeping next to me," Van stated firmly.

"Thank you, my daughter.   I love you so much."

"Well, you should," a disembodied voice filtered into the room. "She's very kind and very clever."

"Rahnahi!"   Van called out, and the once poet matriarch materialized on the sofa in front of them.   "So good to see you!   So, what earns me those kind accolades this sol?"

"Well," Amyra offered, appearing next to her, "your match between Kallain and Melissiana is going exceptionally well.   We've been watching after them, as you suggested, and it's done.   They're solidly together."

"So fast?" Shenaria queried.

"They've worked closely together for six moons and been in each other's general vicinity before.   There's a little biology that's playing a role, as well; I'm sure your daughter told you."

"She did, and … although I had to steal her hunt to do it, I do have some experience with this."

"Oh, Mom," Van chuckled, reaching out and hugging her, "I couldn't be happier for you two."

"Yes, very kind of you, my dear, and you have my eternal thanks, but ... what about you?" Shenaria asked her daughter. "This ... Akashar. Ky sort of let on that you might have talked with him this sol?"

"Yeah, right before I got Kallain dropped into my lap. He's ... very cautious, oh so very cautious and skittish about his own past. I feel for him, and I want to help him just like I did you. I can't figure out why Theo did that to him – dropped him here on Thuria sixteen seasons ago and let him live all alone. If ... if he is Ash-"

"What does your heart tell you, Vanarra?" Amyra asked.

"That he is Ash, but older. His experiences are lost to him, it seems, but there's some thread of that cub still in him. I don't know; I just wish I knew for sure – I wish I could back-scan him. This *focus points* stuff just seems like the crap lazy authors in novels come up with when they want an excuse to complicate the plot," Vanarra grumped.

"Well, sadly enough," Rahnahi explained, trying to placate her, "this is something we know about. See, when someone is going to ascend, there are contributing individuals, events, and time streams that all have to flow together. Some of these don't matter, but as you have already experienced through reuniting with your mother, some truly do." Vanarra reached out her paw and held her mother's. "Very much so. However, as you move closer to ascension, the events around you become more and more critical. Sometimes, they can be distractions. Lyssia, Tanatta, and Bushor isolated themselves in the woods to reduce the distractions, but it also limited the interactions with those who could distract them. Now, what's more, you were *their* primary focus point, their final one."

"I ... I was what?!" Van asked, confused.

"You *named* them! When you named them, not even Merialla could hold them back for long. It was done," Amyra told her. "Now, I know what you're thinking, and not because I'm reading you, but because I know you too darn well." That made them all laugh a little, but Amyra soon continued, "You are not the type who even would be able to isolate yourself, and that's not required for everyone.

However, my guess is that if this individual *is* Ashalam, he's been put into time and in the condition he's in for the express purpose of contributing to your ascension, just as Shenaria was. However, when you were reunited with your mother, you jumped significantly closer to that event that will cause Vanassa to come into being. Now, help has to be subtler, and Theo must use even his powers very carefully."

Vanarra considered that for a moment and thought out loud, "I get my mother back, and the event comes closer – a lot closer and more likely. Sahni and I are even doing those sessions every so often where we bring Vanassa into being for short periods of time. However, now that I am closer, what is it like an … exclusion zone? It may have actually, what, harmed me for Ash to come back with all of his memories intact?"

"Well, if he came back now exactly as he was," Shenaria asked Van, "wouldn't he be a little young?"

"He would be, at that," Van realized. "Not that Theo couldn't solve that problem if he wanted to, but then … that's more interference. So, this version of Ash, the one who is older and doesn't have his memories, has to appear sixteen seasons ago and live through to this time – my time."

"Maybe, Vanarra," Amyra warned. "The truth is, we don't know. Theo might know, but he will keep such things to himself if past history is any indicator of the present. He would tell you that it helps to ensure the impact of what he's doing."

"I hope that Vanassa is truly worth all of this," Van mused, a little sadly. "I mean, it's a lot for poor Ash to go through if that is him. He's … hurt and lonely and confused."

"And *alive*, child!" Rahnahi reminded her. "That has to count for something! He's also found the Creator's Path, gotten schooled, got a job, and built a life! I'll also confess that I've been … snooping around him a little."

Amyra groaned and shook her head. "Oh, of course!"

"Just checking for *her*. Tana, your amulet, probably picked up on this for you, as well, but I'll say it out loud. He's barely capable of maintaining a friendship, and he and Doctor Emma have a lot of work to do. This isn't going to be a relationship that goes anywhere fast. This is going to be the work of seasons, at the least."

Vanarra closed her eyes and shook her head. "How can I not wait? If it is truly him, my dear Ash, then he's lived sixteen seasons without me, already. If it's not Ash, then here is a very sad and lonely soul who needs someone."

"And if he eventually falls in love with someone else?" Shenaria asked, worried.

"Then he'll be okay, and I'll be happy. Knowing that he, like you, is in a brand-new life is wonderful, as Rahnahi said. Vanassa is not going to come about by me sulking. Besides, I ... learned something in my last little join up with Sahni that's going to help with that. She's ... sorta pregnant!"

"What!?" Shenaria bleated. "That ... that didn't take long!"

"Well, a few moons," Van contested. "However, it's looking good. A little Faelnar Nephti on the way for them, now."

"Cub or kit?" Rahnahi asked.

"You don't know?" Shenaria asked, but then apologized, "I'm sorry. I'm just surprised by that."

"Contrary to popular belief, it appears, we don't know everything – although we do know a lot. Cub," Amyra posited, earning an angry look from her peer. "I like to stay in touch with Alahari and Lyshantor, that's all. We've been comparing notes, and some of what we're learning about the cults here is informing their actions on Thuriana."

"Something Sahni will have to get involved in?" Van queried.

"Don't think so. They're thinking they can kind of keep her out of it for now, and if not, they have someone else tapped for the Teldear position, only if needed, you understand. If Sahnassa does have to interact, it will likely be in the form of a mentor, like Dynaea was to her, actually."

"Anyone we know?" Van asked.

"Someone you knew did. Corelliana de Caterra's Vulpi servant who died in the assault on the home estate – Vialla. She's been living on Thuriana for about thirty seasons, now. She's grown a lot, and Lyshantor says she has immense promise. Even if she's not needed to keep Thuriana moving in the right direction, I think he wants to cultivate her as a protégé."

"Sounds pretty good," Rahnahi agreed. "So many of them were lost during that time period; it's good to know that some are getting that second chance."

"Thuriana's problems aren't anywhere near is complex as what we see here on Thuria. Most of what they're trying to do is just stop problems from happening in the first place, as we..."

Van completed Amyra's sentence, "Will spend quite a few seasons doing the clean-up here for problems that were allowed to fester for a long time. You know, I've wondered about that – why wait until things got as bad as they did before intervening? Why not send us in, earlier?"

"Minus the existence of the cults, themselves, and the weakness of the houses," Amyra offered, "Thuria wasn't doing so poorly. Alahari showed the both of us worlds in far worse shape than this one. While this is a situation that needs to be addressed, it's not as bad as it would have been had we waited another ten or twenty seasons to jump in. Can you just imagine?!"

"I'd prefer not to. Wow, that could have been awful," Vanarra groaned putting her head in her paws. "Sahnassites attack Vanarrans, blame the Creator's Path, and then the Vanarrans strike back. Both of them pulling hard on their contacts in government and house leadership. Creator's Path under assault for violently attacking another faith..."

"Shalana would have killed the soul of my house," Rahnahi opined, "plain and simple, or worse, would have just merged with the Sahnassites to create a power that would be difficult to stop. As it is, they're ... doing okay."

"Yep, heard the catch in the voice," Van noted. "Not great, I take it."

"They're having some new internal struggles we're keeping an eye on – nothing serious. There's just a lot of clean-up and recriminations from all of the blackmail material Shalana had. While it was never made public, all of the senior dames know most of it, and there's some desire to elbow out those who were particularly impacted by bad judgment or temptation."

Amyra supplied the rest. "In a few seasons, they should have their act well enough organized to start trying to win back some of the houses' rights. Right now, they're not cohesive enough in their senior leadership to even attempt such a thing. We've sort of been helping them realize that. On the positive side, they're helping their own, again."

"I'll take it – we knew this was going to be a long game, anyway. The Vanarrans have pretty much been on my plate," Van told them. "Ky and I have been tag-teaming that one, and it's really starting to fray pretty badly. I'm keeping my eyes on the kids, and so far, they've been pretty insulated from what's going on – the budget cuts, the trials, the indictments – enforcement prowling everywhere. However, it's not going to stay that way. With the loss of the lab, however, and the discovery of the *alleged* crematorium, child safety enforcement has been making regular stops to count heads. Although the Vanarrans have halted any sort of breeding program, we'll need to seriously start working on Lasrihal at some point, soon."

Shenaria, always awed by the august company, had been hesitant to speak, but now quietly ventured, "Wasn't Fireclaw going to help with that? I mean, she's done such an amazing job raising funds to cure the kits and cubs poisoned by the Vanarrans."

"She is, but she's also trying to finish out her last few seasons strong so she'll bank a lot of winnings and good will that can be used for that," Van explained. "I just talked to her about it, and she's always asking about the Vanarran cubs and kits. They really touched her. She's been sneaking away and spending time with Javoth de Bosnar and Laxar when I'll let her get away with it."

"Any chance they'll pair up? Javoth and Fireclaw?" Shenaria asked, trying not to smile.

"No, believe it or not! They do work well together and like each other, though – more like me and Flint than me and Bucky. They've been mapping a few things out, and they've started to draw up a strategy to make it work – land purchases, fund raising, other groups that could contribute or be served. They're putting a lot of thought into it. Of course," Van explained, "when it starts up again, it won't actually be in Lasrihal. That's a major Vulpi city now – well, Vulpi and mixed blood."

"I always wondered about the kinds of things that went on there," Rahnahi noted. "I wondered what the long-term implications would be."

Kylie then appeared in their midst. "Sorry about that," she said, patting Shenaria on the shoulder as she had jumped, startled.

"It's okay, it's okay! At least, I don't swear like Fireclaw when you surprise me," the gold-on-gold Faelnar commented, panting a bit, and the others laughed.

"I've been kind of tracking some of Fireclaw's ideas and tweaking on them, well, through Vosh-"

"Yeah, I've practically lost my hover half of the time," Van sighed, leaning back and closing her eyes.

"It's worth it," Kylie admonished her. "Fireclaw would make a worthy choice as Teldear, I think. She's really growing, and your daughter is helping her. This new Lasrihal plan is as much Vosh's as it is coming from Javoth and Fireclaw. Anyway, as far as the original Lasrihal, present sol, I've got a good sense of what's going on there, and in many ways, it's not better or worse than other cities other than it has a strong core of Creator's Path followers, and they've frustrated the efforts of both the Vanarrans and the Sahnassites. It's been so bad that both sects had plans to go in and undermine Lasrihal, specifically, but the truth is, it's one of our best strongholds for anti-sect sentiment."

"And our lovely little sects are now far back in their burrows just trying to weather this storm," Van breathed, smiling, "and they won't on our watch. Now, we just have to start laying the foundation for the houses' to get their rights back, get their place in Thurian society back."

"Is that going okay?" Shenaria asked.

"Well, I'd say," Amyra offered. "Mind you, right now, we're just trying to make sure that the Vanarrans and Sahnassites lose their influence in the legislative circles. We've kept Alanar very busy."

The gold-on-gold Faelnar tilted her head as she tried to puzzle it out. "Oh! You ... you have been helping all of those politicians get found out for the bribes and things like that?"

Rahnahi leaned back and put her hind paws on Van's low table, sighing, "You'd be surprised how easy it is to get someone to look where someone doesn't want them looking. A recording accidently running or a Thurian trapped in an alley who happens to be recording the audio of a very interesting conversation. We have to be careful, though. We can't rip the hide off of all of them as quick as we'd like – it has to look like enforcement is just more attuned to it. In some ways, it becomes a self-fulfilling prophecy; we help them catch someone, and now they want to catch more and go after them on their own."

"But it's only foundation," Van noted. "We don't have the first law repealed or the first new law approved. Legally, it's all status quo, but we've got to change the representation before the laws can be changed, and even then, we might have to pry some corrupt judges out so they don't throw away our new laws once we get them passed."

"I just have to say," Shenaria told them all, looking around, "you just don't know what it's like to sit in a room like this and hear such amazing things! We're sitting in a living room discussing the future of this entire world, and unlike everyone else, all of you can actually change it! I ... I would never have imagined such things were even possible a season ago – well, a season for me, that is."

Amyra stood and went to Shenaria's side, sitting opposite of Vanarra. "While that may be true, we are only influencing, tipping small events here and there. If Thurians had the hard-headed determination to go all Vanarran or all Sahnassite, nothing we are doing would stop them. There are millions and millions of Thurians on this world, and we're not forcing them to think or believe anything. We're simply ensuring that those who would take that right away from them are prevented. We can't force Thurians to make the houses great again; we can only remove the obstacles so the ideas have a fighting chance."

"Still, thank you all for letting me see this and know about this. It's a treasure to me. One I will share with Trax and, maybe, with a kit or cub of our own," she put in, shyly, "soon."

"What?!" Vanarra blurted. "No one told me about this!"

"It's her private business," Kylie admonished her, but that didn't stop Van's stare from boring into her mother's eyes.

"Well, I've been talking to Ky, you know, about the best way and what the options are and ... stuff, so ... maybe?" Shenaria was clearly worried about her daughter's opinion but hoped the presence of her elders would help moderate Van's reaction.

"It's not going to be easy," Van warned her.

"It wasn't easy the first time," Shenaria gently returned.

Vanarra sighed and snuggled into her mother's side, relenting. "True. True. Bless you for that; bless you forever for that. No, if anything, Mom, I'll help make up for what you went through before; you deserve that. Just … let me be there for you, okay?"

"Of course. If you're not too busy."

"I will never be too busy for you," Van promised.

Chapter 3: The Empty Answer

Vanalla sat in the cafeteria of the hospital, just finishing up her meal when someone walked up to her table. "Oh, Akashar," she told him, appearing a little surprised. "I'm glad to see you. Would you like to sit? What's wrong?" She could tell that he wasn't happy and that he was nervous. Still, he nodded and sat.

"Well, Vanalla, it's … it's about you and … me spending time with you, even here. I've been advised by my doctor that I truly don't need to form any … special kinds of attachments right now, given where my therapy is, and as much as I appreciate your attention and kindness, I just can't accept it. I can tell that you like me, and I can tell that if we spend time together, you will want to draw closer to me. I'm not a whole and complete Thurian, and it won't work, and I don't want to hurt you. I won't allow myself to do that. I also don't know what this therapy is going to bring out. I can't ask you to walk this horrible trail with me. I have to ask you not to try to spend time with me; even lunch here is something I shouldn't do."

Vanarra, Sahni, and the presence of Tana enshrouded within the golden crystal stone hanging invisible from Van's neck, knew this was coming. Kylie had warned that Akashar had been open with Doctor Emma about his curiosity concerning this lovely brown and gold Faelnar, but the Vulpi's admonishments had convinced him to sever not only his forming ties with Van but those with a female customer who had taken a heavy interest in him.

Van's head bowed, and she breathed, "I understand. You have to take care of yourself and your own healing, and I would never stand in the way of that. I can't imagine what you're going through, and I certainly would never want to make anything more difficult for you."

"I'm glad … glad you understand," Akashar told her, embarrassed, and it was clear his resolve was starting to waver given the kind thoughtfulness of her response, and moreover, how his gentle rejection was clearly paining the Faelnar. "I am … so very sorry."

Vanalla stood and told him softly, "Don't be. Other than friendly greetings, these can be the last words we ever say on the subject, but I will tell you this, Akashar, and I ask that you truly hear me. You needn't be an abandoned and forsaken land, forever, and that which was deserted can be loved and flourish, again. For as long as I am alive, I will be there for you if you need me, even if it is only as a friend and only many seasons from now. *I'll take care of you,* and that is a promise that I *will never* … break. Be well, Akashar."

The stunned mixed blood male just sat, stunned and impacted by her words in ways he could barely fathom, watching her leave.

Just beyond the entrance, Vanalla issued a sigh as she looked at the floor, "Well, wasn't that fun," she thought, but then looked up into the eyes of Doctor Emmeniama de Kestrick. The Vulpi's countenance stopped her for a moment – an odd mix of concern and hesitation she'd not seen frequently, especially when the concern was directed at her.

"I'm sorry, Vanalla. I think, for him, it's the best," she stated softly.

Walking over to close the distance to something more social and private, Van agreed, "I know. I know; I can see it, too."

"Can we talk and walk? Would you be willing to?" the Vulpi asked, but there was a bit of insecurity there that again made Van wonder.

"Sure. Why don't we go up on the observation deck? Not many up there right now, if any, and it will be private."

"I understand," the Vulpi stated and led the way. While they were in the elevator and after a few silent ticks, Emma asked, "Can I ask, please, what you saw in him that caused you to agree with me?"

As the door opened, Van led her out onto the deck high above the city before answering. "His fear and anxiety are … overwhelming him. It's different than with Shenaria. He's … adjusted to it, and this has become his norm. He doesn't seem to have any tie to a past life, but he clings to this mystery of what it is or might have been, and it's never good – only bad. I can see it in his eyes. What's worse is that his separation from others seems to be driven by a need to protect them. Protect them from who? Him. He … he thinks he's that bad, that his past is suddenly, after so long, going to rise up and claw strike anyone he's close to. I might be wrong, Emma, and I've only talked with him a little bit."

"I don't know that you're wrong," the Vulpi psychologist told her. "I don't know that you're right, either. However, his caution is not without some merit. Shenaria's case was the … oddest, most frustrating, most downright incomprehensible one I've ever worked. I still don't understand how she is down there, in the guest shop, joined, and living a perfectly healthy and normal life – other than the fact that she *still* thinks she's Shenaria Anasto, well – Shenaria Lasser, now. She's happy as can be, loves you like a sister, and is just the nicest kit!"

"Still trying to figure her out?" Van asked, smirking a bit.

"No. I've officially stopped trying, but I will be there for her if she needs help, so please let me know if anything crops up."

"I will," Van promised.

"Yes, but Akashar," Emma hedged looking over the balcony. "I've … kind of seen more than a pawful of Akashars in my time."

"Really?" Van asked, turning around.

"Yes. If you weren't in this area twenty seasons ago, you might not know this, but for a good, long while, we had kits and cubs like Akashar turning up somewhat frequently, two or three per moon. They would have no knowledge of their pasts but would be full of fear and foreboding about it. We ended up running it down to an illegal recreational drug called Wipe Out, and for some Thurians, it created a type of brain damage that *wiped out* their ability to recall memories at will. Now, the memories are still there as a part of composite, holistic brain function – that's why they can walk and talk and still look after themselves. Sometimes, the ability to recall is only compromised attempting to reach certain key memories."

"Like before he was found," Van conjectured, and the Vulpi nodded.

"He was brought into the emergency center in really rough shape, but we don't have a toxicology report on him we could trust because the drug would also read as what was commonly used for emergency anesthesia. According to his medical history, they dragged him straight into the operating room and got to work on him. He may have been a Wipe Out victim, but saving his life took precedence over finding that out. He's symptomatic, though, in the way I've seen others. It's a difficult treatment, and it's a long treatment, and there have been cases where some or a part of their ability to recall memories comes back. Their ... whole character can change in an instant. He's not ready for a long-term relationship or even a short term one. He needs treatment, counseling, and observation."

"Hence sending him to me with the message to not try to pursue anything with him."

"I offered to do it," Emma confessed, "but, he wanted to. He sort of ... insisted. I hope you were understanding. I glanced in at the last, he seemed pretty stricken. Can I ask what you said?"

"I told him that I would be there for him if he needed help, no matter what, no matter for how long. I told him he didn't need to live thinking he was abandoned and unused, forgotten."

Emma put her paw on Van's. "I've heard much worse; that was very kind and pretty impressive, honestly. It's a huge commitment to make to someone who might not wake up the same Thurian as when they went to sleep. Can I ask why you feel you have to offer him that?"

"I'm not that different from you, in a way," Vanalla told her. "I see hurting, and I want to help. I won't lie to you, Emma. He touched me in a special way, and I felt a connection to him, probably an echo of something I lost or thought I had long ago. Can I ask you a question?" The Vulpi nodded. "What happened when one of those cases you tended never got their memories back?"

"We'll generally know within the first two seasons of treatment if that is going to be the case. Akashar is a little bit like Shenaria in that there isn't a record on him which means we're unable to use any aspects of his previous identity to jump start his memory recall. Still, the time period is about the same. I'm just happy that he's committed to treatment; some never do."

"Do you know anything about him?"

"His schooling when he was found was very basic, although serviceable. There have been cases where mixed blood children like him were from some rural village that didn't have genetic records. There was a very intense effort about ten seasons ago to make sure everyone on the planet had a genetic record, which is why Shenaria is a bit more of a mystery. Other than that, he's done well on his own, I guess, at least from an enforcement and employment point of view. As you know, however, he's keeping himself alone except for his work."

"That, in itself, isn't healthy," Vanalla told her.

"Nor is plunging into a relationship while trying to work through what he has facing him," Emma contested. "Nor ... is it healthy for you. You've been such an immense help to me, here, Van, and you've been my friend. I hope you still are. You helped me get into a relationship with Alanar, something I've never had, and your importance to this hospital has also increased. I saw it, myself, in the boardroom. How you took on the chair – impressive. I care about you, and I am worried. I've seen one exactly like Akashar go full charge back into a life of illegal drugs and crime to support it once his memories came back. Before, he was ... nice and kind. It's like, without his memories, all of his addictions didn't exist. Once they returned..."

"Sounds bad."

"Yeah," Emma acknowledged. "One of my first cases after getting hired, and he's probably still in jail. As much as I hate to say it, what Akashar needs for the next two seasons, at least, is a relationship with himself and with me, as his therapist."

"I'll abide by what you say, and what he's asked, but I meant what I said, Emma."

"I know," the Vulpi told her. "I know, and I'm not sure that you wouldn't make the same statement to any hurt child or suffering mother or ailing grandama, here. You're that good, and that's why we need you, and why ... why we love having you here."

Van could feel that the Vulpi's words were sincere, and gently, she drew Emma into an embrace and thanked her. "For some answers, I guess we have no choice but to be patient."

Dear Diary,

Wow, okay, this is really hard to write. It's been three seasons since I started therapy with Doctor Emma, and this sol she told me that there was now almost no chance of me ever recovering my memories. I wanted to be angry at her as if this is somehow her fault, but it appears that I'm in the three percent who might have been affected by a drug or an event who will never get their memories back. It's not her fault, and I've shared so much with her that she's listened to and helped me work through that I can only feel grateful. I've been as honest with her as I know how, but only not with one thing. What I won't tell her is that about a season ago, I've posted pictures of myself under a false account on the TransNet registry saying this was a missing Thurian. The only response I've gotten in the last season was from the old Faelnar in our central office who spends all of his time looking at TransNet. After that, I took it down.

Looking back, I think she's been preparing me for this, and we've talked this alternative several times over the many sessions. Dear Creator, who am I!? Well, when I broke down in her office this sol asking that question, she told me – Doctor Emma did. She said that I am a kind, considerate, strong, and very patient Thurian who now has his answer. When I asked her exactly what answer she thought I had, she told me that I could be sure that the Thurian I was now was who I would be, and that if I wanted to engage in relationships again, I could do so. She said I had the confidence that, in nearly twenty seasons including a full course of therapy and no other identity or report of who I might have been, Akashar is who I am and who I will be. Her last advice ... shocked me, though, I have to say.

She told me that, while I was being treated, she was allowing another form of mental illness to exist in me, and now, that is what she wants to treat. She said I'd been isolated, emotionally, for so long that it isn't healthy. When I looked at her, she smiled and told me that she was already joined. Yeah, I blushed. Muzzle still hurts; I blushed so freaking hard! However, she said that although the emotional connection between her and I had to stay as doctor and patient, I should – no, she said must – seek out opportunities to start building loving, compassionate, and emotionally deep relationships with others. I must have again reacted, because she added, "in the cafeteria, perhaps."

I know who she meant – Vanalla. I've not forgotten that sol when I told her it would be best if we didn't talk because of my therapy. She … told me she would be there for me, for … I'm sorry, Diary. I had to stop. I had to wipe the viewer's surface, after. I thought she would just move on, you know? I thought she'd leave or find someone else, and it wouldn't matter, right? It was just an empty promise – that's what I thought. Then, I saw her hugging a mixed blood Nephti-Perratti, but it wasn't anything more than just being family. I saw her walk with that mixed blood into the gift shop, and then he kissed the gold-on-gold Faelnar who works there. Now, that … that was a kiss. I happened by later to buy something, and I asked her why she was so happy, and she told me that she and her mate were going to have a child.

I walked out of there with so many questions. What if that mixed blood was me? What if the one having the child was her … no, I can't go there. Not yet. Sorry, again. Have to quit now. I don't know what I'll do.

Vanarra's heart almost stopped as she stared at the Haven's main viewer. "What's he doing!?" Akashar was seated with his legs dangling over a very precipitous drop on top of one of the two hundred track tall buildings in the middle of Shanandrae. He was seated up there, looking at the sunset, crying. "Kylie, what the mange is he freaking doing, and you had better be dreaming up a really creative way to catch him if he does something stupid!"

"That's why I called you. I need for you to get a read on what he's feeling. He got his news this sol, news that he won't be getting his memories back."

"Trigate me behind him, Ky, on a surface that won't buckle or make noise. I'll go clear so he can't see me. Just be careful."

"Yep, got it," Ky told her. "It would totally stink to startle him. Okay, Trigate in three, two, one, zero."

Vanarra appeared behind Akashar, a few tracks away, standing on top of some flat stone roofing material, and as she went invisible, Tana confirmed for her that he hadn't noticed. Crouching down, she watched him and waited for Tana to gently sift through his emotions.

"He's praying, Van," Sahni told her, concern and grief in her mental voice. "He's asking forgiveness over and over, again, for something, but we're having a hard time piecing together exactly what." Van was very grateful in this moment, that the Sahni living in her thoughts had bound herself so closely to Tana, the presence of her former aide inside of the golden jewel hung around her neck. Sahnassa had given voice and perspective to Tana's perceptions, and Tana's insight had benefited them more and more, especially in circumstances where they had to influence someone. "Oh, it's … it's Emma. He's grown close to her during the therapy, and now, he's trying to … wait, no. It's not just that. It's us, too. It's you, Van. He's afraid of reaching out to you. He doesn't know how or what to say, and he thinks he hurt you back when he told you he needed to not have relationships during therapy. Oh, Van. I … I feel for him. He's suffering."

"Needlessly," Vanarra sighed. "We've got to get him off this ledge, cuddle kits, and that's all there is to it. Maybe get word to Emma or give him some advice?"

"Well, if you appeared up there," Kylie inserted, "it would do nothing short of freak him out – probably send him over the edge right there."

"Mother?" Vosh's voice sounded in her thoughts. "I am hovering just below him in a contingency position should he slip or intentionally jump, although I do note a wide balcony just below him. I am masking his presence from any observers below."

"Good kit, you are," Van breathed out, mentally.

"I will note your affection for me, Mother, on my service record," Vosh told her in something akin to a joke. "However, the presence of another form is indicated – one defined as more lighthearted and casual than you would normally portray."

"Normally?" Van asked, curious and a little put off.

"She's right," Kylie put in. "You normally go for the dark brooding dangerous types. The only time I've actually seen you lighthearted in disguise, recently, was when you were setting up Kallain for his run-in with Melissiana. One of your best matches of all time, granted, but you did that with a bit of a light touch."

"Yeah, they have worked out well together," Vanarra noted, smiling to herself. "Okay, so a lighter touch. What else is up here that someone would care about?"

"TransCom equipment, emergency StarSat transceiver relays – there's a whole host of things available for someone with a fluorescent vest and a hard hat to fix. I'll find something that can be broken and needs your tinkering if I'm guessing where you're going with this."

"I hope. Just be ready to catch him in case I screw this up, please," Van told her as she willed herself inside of the access shaft a floor down.

Akashar had been lost in self-reflection and self-doubt ever since trying to finish his diary entry, and that had caused him to return to the one place where he knew he felt at peace. Walking to the transport stop, riding it, walking into the TranStar building felt like he was buried, nearly entombed in the city, suffocated by his troubles as much as its high buildings and crowds of Thurians. Thanks to a favor he was owed by one of his customers, he had acquired the access to come up to the roof hatch and walk about above most of the city. It was where his spirit felt lightest, the freest. This was where he felt he could think – sort out his thoughts, and he had so many thoughts to sort out, this sol.

Although there was a balcony two levels below him, it felt like he was sitting on the edge of the world, and thankfully, he felt like he had more than adequate paw holds if a breeze wanted to kick up and push him forward. It was only a mild breeze tonight, and it helped soothe him as he cried and wept before the Creator. He kept replaying the conversation he had with Vanalla – telling her that he didn't even want to have a conversation with her until his therapy was done. The entire reason for his therapy – to discover his identity – had now been proved useless, and he had, therefore, hurt the Faelnar's feelings and pushed her away for no good reason. While he understood that he didn't know back then and had valid reasons for what he did, it still pained him deeply to have done needless harm to someone else for what amounted to selfish reasons.

"What do I tell her, now? Do I tell her – What's that?" he asked, his eyebrow fur raising as he wiped his eyes with the back of his paw, all the while keeping his right paw firmly gripped to the grounding rail. Sure enough, the door opened, and he sighed. His solitude had been broken when he least wanted it to, when he was just about to try to puzzle out what to do concerning the beautiful brown and gold Faelnar.

"Oh, dang!" he heard someone swear. "I ... I ... mange, I just can't do this!" Leaning over and looking back, still with careful attention on his grip, he saw a short male Perratti in an electrician's uniform trying very hard to stay right up against the central roof access. This individual hadn't seen him, as yet, so it gave Akashar a little time to right himself from his miserable introspection and take in his new and very reluctant companion atop the TranStar building. "I'm gonna quit. Just take another job – that would be easier."

"Friend?" he called, and the brown Perratti with terrified silver eyes startled, yelped, and looked in his direction.

"Oh, gods!" the male bleated. "You've got to be kidding me! No, please! You're going to try and jump, and I'm going to try and stop you – because it's the right thing to do, but then I'm going to fall and die, and…"

"Peace, please," Akashar breathed as he rolled backwards, putting as much distance between himself and the edge of the building as he could in one movement. "I *didn't* come up here to jump."

"Wha … you think just the walking off version or rolling forward's better?" the Perratti tried to joke, but then the breeze blew around him, and he yelped again and held onto the building as if it might blow away without warning. "Freaking cruel joke sending me up here – the boss knows I hate heights! It's like I can feel the whole building move every time it does that! Did he tell you to come up here, too? Just to scare me half to death?!"

"No, no," the mixed blood placated walking closer. "I just come up here to think, sometimes. It's actually a lot safer than you might think, if you'd like to see for yourself."

"No ... way! I get close; I lose my balance, and then I'm a splotch of brown Perratti goo on the ground!"

"This building has balconies for the executives a few levels from the top. It would probably be really uncomfortable to hit them, accidentally, but you'd just slide into their plants or patio furniture."

"Yeah, I'm still not going over there," the Perratti told him as he approached. "They can't pay me enough for this."

"Pay you for what, friend? What were you sent up here to do?"

"I have to change the relay ... there, over there, on that thing!" he said, looking around for a moment and then pointing to an electrical box on a raised platform, nearby – about half way between the edge and where they were standing, now. "But I'm not going to! It's probably a straight drop to the bottom just on the other side!"

"Actually, there's a good twenty tracks of building left. You'll be fine. I work as a tech over at a lair cooling and heating business."

"Any openings there?" the Perratti asked, again trying to make light. "I'm totally quitting this bad joke before I become the punch line!"

"I think you'll still have this job, friend, and I have some time. Can I help you?"

"You ... know your way around up here, so ... so sure. Okay."

"Here, take my paw, and we'll walk over. The ladder is on the other side, you have to walk past it and around. What's in that metal box, anyway?"

"Regulation required emergency communications relay. Gets tested every moon, and this time ... oh my gosh, I'm going to get blown right off of this!" he nearly shrieked, holding onto the mixed blood tightly.

"No, you'll be fine. Now, we don't have to go any closer to the edge. We just have to go up the ladder, alright?" The terrified electrician nodded and then made his way up the ladder with Akashar having a paw on his back. While the mixed blood followed him, he was fumbling for keys and finally found the one he was looking for, keying open the panel.

"Oh, yeah, yeah, it's totally … totally burnt out – fried. Can you find the wire snips?"

"Sure. Here they are. Oh, yeah – it's totally dark. Might have been struck by lightning, and oh, mange, that's something else I have to check."

"If this is connected to the lightning rail?" The Perratti nodded, nervously, as he sorted through his toolbox looking for the items he needed. "Well, that's a … that's a lot closer to the edge, but I can help you there, too."

"Oh, friend, I … I don't know your name-"

"Akashar, and you?"

"Beran de Oterbythe. Pleased to meet you, but really wish it was at a lower altitude. I was about to say that I don't think I could do this without you. You said you were up here thinking?"

"Yeah, I've had kind of a rough sol, maybe more than that. I have a job and all, doing okay there – business is brisk, and the customers are actually pretty easy to work with most of the time, but I'm kind of having to face up to undoing something I did."

"Oh really? Mind spilling it to me so I can take my worries off of how high up I am?"

Akashar chuckled. "You know, it will be okay, I think. Just don't pass it along."

"Secret's safe with me so long as word doesn't get back to my manager that I peed my pants up here."

"You did?"

"Not yet, but it's likely. So, this thing you did?" Beran prompted.

"I had to go get some … time where I didn't have any relationships to work some things out, and just before I started this three seasons ago, there was this Faelnar who was interested in me. She was pretty amazing, but I told her I didn't want to talk to her, anymore. I thought that I might find out some bad stuff, and I didn't want to drag her down with me, you know?"

"Yeah. I know. Hate to involve other people when I'm in a mess, but ... it helps sometimes."

"Well, I had a doctor tell me not to, and so I kind of took her advice. Thing is, three seasons later, nothing. My doctor has released me from treatment and says I need to get on with my life. This ... Faelnar told me, that last time we talked, that she would be there for me, no matter what. My doctor even hinted I should seek her out, but it can't be true, right? I'm just a stranger to her."

"Oh, I don't know about that, pal," Beran contested as he vigorously cleaned the contacts of the relay. "I knew this one kit whose steady hunt got framed for drugs and was sent away for six seasons – six whole seasons! Before he went away, he tried to break it off to save her pain, but that little kit wouldn't hear of it. I mean, they hadn't even been going together but a little while, but she must have just known she loved him. Well, he gets released, and she's standing right there to pick him up. They don't go home; they go to the local government office with him still in the clothes he was arrested in six seasons earlier. They get joined. Still together, now, happy and with kids!"

"Wow," Akashar breathed. "I ... have never heard of such a thing."

"You wouldn't – it's good news, right? The only thing that ever gets published with the newsarotzi is the bad stuff. There have been a few others in my time, as well – like this academy cub who met a kit just one moon from graduating and going into the military. He gets stationed overseas, and they can't talk for moons on end, but when he gets home two seasons later, she practically jumps his tail and, well, it's a good thing they got joined so their kids could be born under the covering of honor, if you know what I mean."

Akashar leaned back against the right side of the electrical box where the Perratti was working and just shook his head. "Beautiful, precious kits who barely know you and then just pledge to stand around for seasons waiting for you? Why? I mean, why would they do it? Why wait all that time when they could have their pick of males?"

"My uncle Philleasar told me that he thought some kits instinctively knew who was the best match for them – it's maybe by scent or body shape or gesture or some other things, but some just do.

Other kits were just as dumb as six bags of turf-burrower poop and couldn't even start to decide on the male for them, even at their own joining. If a female has her eyes on you like that, though, it's a treasure. Don't pass it up; it may not work out, but you're off to a better than average start. I sure wish I had someone with their eye on my tail that way. Okay, that's got it. Now, where's ... where's this lightning ground rail?" Shar raised his paw and pointed to the area about one track from the edge of the building. "I'm ... going to die of fright or have a spasm and fall off, or-"

"Hey, I'll help you. You have the new grounding cable?" The Perratti pulled out a thick coil of wire from his satchel. "So, what were you supposed to do?"

"Look at the cable and the connectors, and if anything needs to be replaced, replace it. I'm pretty much feeling like I need to replace my job right now."

Shar chuckled lightly and walked towards the edge where the connector was supposed to link into the rail. Beran started to hyperventilate even when he got close. Kneeling down, he looked at it. "Yeah, it's ... loose and corroded. Probably why your relay blew in the first place. Do you think you can make it over here?"

"Would you ... be embarrassed if I crawled?"

"Not if it worked for you. Honestly, I'd say you're very brave. Phobias are hard to overcome."

Beran slipped down the ladder and crouched on the ground, dragging his tools behind him. "What about you, oh, he who hangs his legs over the abyss – what scares you?"

"Well, honestly, heights do – a little bit. See there's a reason why I feel okay being up this high with this specific building. I ... kind of had to jump off it once." Beran just looked at him, stupefied. "No, seriously – we were doing some air work for one of my former jobs, got stuck up here when the door locked on us. A storm blew in, and this was sort of the highest thing. After almost getting struck by lightning twice, one of ours remembered the balconies a few levels down. I was about to pee myself, to be honest, but yeah, we made it. Never been too scared of heights after that."

"I don't want to try your ... method," the Perratti told him, trembling. "So, head here is totally ... totally weathered away, metal is all gone, and ... and what wasn't gone is fried. Not enough to take the full force of a strike."

"And this building gets them, for sure," Shar agreed. "Got the replacement parts?"

"Sure, sure," he said, turning over on his side and pulling his tool box close so he could reach inside without getting up or getting any closer to the edge. "So, this kit of yours. She pretty?"

"Well, she's not mine, well, not yet, I guess. However, if what you're telling me is right, maybe she already is. I don't know."

"Bud, I didn't ask about her ownership history; I asked if she was pretty?"

Akashar chuckled as he watched the Perratti get the new wire clamp and high tensile fasteners and start to prepare them. "Yes, she's pretty."

"Gorgeous?" Beran pressed. "I mean, like pretty face, nice slender body, maybe a great rack up front?"

Shar bit his lip a little and said, "Well, yeah. She's got that Faelnar sleekness and that amazing tail, but up front she's ... nicely proportioned."

"Damned! All that and she's freaking keen, too! Buddy, other than helping me out, what the mange are you doing on top of this building?" Beran fussed. "You ain't got thinking to do; you got *talking* to do!"

"What if she has moved on, and this was all in my head?" Shar asked, his real fear coming out.

"Then go to a bar, buy a pretty kit a drink, and tell her the story of how you jumped off this building. That makes *me* almost want to hunt you," he chuckled. "Hey, any keen females when you did it? Any unattached?"

"I'm afraid it was an all cubs adventure," Shar told him, smiling. "I suppose you're right. She'll either talk to me or she won't, right?"

"Well, she sure ain't talking to you right now, is she? Only one way to improve that situation," he told the mixed blood as he screwed in the last of the clamps around the wire, the bracket now firmly attached to the grounding rail. "If she is one of those who has her eyes locked on you, then you'll get the opportunity to get your eyes locked on her and more, if you catch my meaning. Pretty damned soon, you could have a very warm bed and a big smug grin across your muzzle. Ah, all done here. Good, I get to crawl back now as I tie it off."

Without asking, the Perratti started shuffling along back towards the control box, stopping to clamp the wire every few tracks or so. That left Akashar with time to think, and there wasn't anything incorrect about what Beran had told him. Although it was a little crassly stated to his tastes, rejection didn't seem that bad against the possibility of spending time with that lovely Faelnar. Although the thought of intimacy with her was certainly appealing for its promise of physical pleasure, as well, Akashar had the sense that if she did love him enough to wait for him, she would have been saving up and holding a gift for him that no one ever had. It was a gift he wouldn't have accepted from anyone else until now, but in this present time, with Doctor Emma's permission, he really could say yes.

"Beran?" he called out to the Perratti as he stood up.

"Yeah, what – I miss something?"

"Thank you."

"Don't mention it, and as I think my pants are still dry, don't mention that I ... I had a problem up here, okay?"

"Our secret," Akashar told him.

"Yeah, well, thanks to you," the Perratti said, finally standing up and walking around the utility box to the roof access entrance. "I still keep my job, if not my sanity. Would you believe, Akashar, was it?" The mixed blood nodded, joining him inside. "They gave me two more jobs after this. I better go, but..."

"But what?"

"Are you going to be okay, buddy?"

"Yeah, and ... I think I'm going to take what you've said to heart. Tomorrow."

"Tonight," the Perratti sternly insisted.

"I don't even know where she lives, what her number is, and all the offices where I might ask are closed," he told him.

"Okay then, but tomorrow! If you're brave enough to jump off this damned crazy building to save your tail, then you should be more than brave enough to go chat her up all nice and proper."

"You got a steady, Beran?"

"Had," the Perratti bemoaned, shaking his head as he stepped into the lift. "She met one of my friends, and now *they're* together. Introductions and counseling service – that's me. I should be on percentage! This one's free – you helped me out, after all."

After a few passes, they had both made it to the bottom of the building, clasped paws, and said goodbye. Akashar found himself wondering, still, what he would say when he next came to the table of the pretty Faelnar, but he knew this at least – he *would* say something.

Chapter 4: The Faint Promise

"Okay, kits, how did I do?" Vanalla asked, walking around the bridge as the pudgy little Perratti male.

"Well, as usual, oh honored Teldear," Kylie quipped, "*you* are going to be the best one to determine if you were successful or not. Do you think he would have actually jumped?"

The Perratti faded back into Vanarra at that moment. "I don't … think so, and Sahni and Tana don't, either. His feelings are really mixed up, though. He did become very dependent on Doctor Emma over the last three seasons, and his heart's a little torn. He knows she's joined and doesn't want to mess with that, but it's difficult for him to pull away. However, I owe her. If she'd pointed him at a Vulpi friend of hers, Akashar could have very easily gone in that direction."

"He'd be really stupid if he did," Trax said as he entered the bridge.

"Heya, big cub," Van greeted him, happily. Walking over and hugging him around the neck as he did the same to her around her waist. "Good to see you! What are you doing down here?"

"You, too, Van," he chuckled, still overcome by the fact that his childhood fantasy was actually walking around and also his dear friend, not to mention his adopted daughter. "You, too. I was spending time with Ria as she sketched the statues back in the bay. Hey, is that who I think it is?" he asked, breaking the hug and looking at the main viewer.

"Yep, and it looks like he got his news, namely that he's not getting his memories back."

"Oh, how did that go?"

"I found him sitting on the edge of one of the downtown high-rises," Kylie told him flatly as she walked over for her hug, as well.

"Holy crap!" he groaned as he briefly held her. "That's not good!"

"Well, kind of a mix, actually, come to find out," Van told him as he let go and walked to her side. "He was in therapy with Emma for a really long time, and he sort of developed an attachment to her – which is bothering him."

"Yeah, kinda should as she's joined," he noted. "Emma happy with Alanar?"

"Very," Kylie stated. "Emma's gotten better at her job, too, well ... except in this case from poor Akashar's point of view. She told him he's likely never going to get his memories back, and it was a really tough hit for him."

"I can see as it would be, but that means he's not going to suddenly turn into someone else, right? He knows that?"

"I think with all of the time that's gone by, nearly twenty seasons, he sorta gets that," Van told him, slipping into the command chair. "However, he's worried he offended me and that the last three seasons of him trying to avoid me preclude any chance I'd ever be interested in him or care about him."

"So, you kind of had a chat with the poor cub or have one planned? A dream maybe?" he teased.

"You! Hey, I used what I had available at the time to figure you out – still not sure I got it right," Vanarra grumped. "I kind of went up in disguise as a chubby little Perratti tech scared to death of heights. He was good, and he helped me. He even opened up a little. I pushed him some, too, in all fairness."

Just then, the main viewer played back Van's "encouragement" for him to seek out the Faelnar and talk to her. "Ky!"

"No, no," Trax told her. "It'll work, I think. I think it will – it was good. Sometimes, when males get lost in grief and self-doubt like that, it doesn't hurt to club them over the head a little."

"So, did you just stop by to check in on my love life and so that Kylie could show you that I do a really awful Perratti impression?"

"No, but it's a bonus," he chuckled. "Actually, Ria reminded me that I need to talk to you ... probably because she wanted to be alone while she painted. Racea reached out and said that her matrons are sort of not answering her on when the houses might be getting some of their rights back. I was kind of getting curious about that, myself."

"Yeah," Van breathed, "it's not going well. They are being stonewalled, as you say, by several in the assembly who mysteriously don't even want to entertain the subject. The problem is that de Dothnar's funds are in a pretty good place, and they want to go for a court challenge. However, Ky's been doing a little knocking around along with Amyra and Rahnahi. This ... resistance isn't all on the up and up – it's not all honest disagreement."

"Government corruption? Bribery?" he asked.

"Yes," Van told him plainly, a little surprised. "Good guess."

"Yeah, *Thurian politics*," he told her, shrugging. "Seen it for a while."

"And you're not a *complete* idiot," Kylie threw in by way of a tease.

"Gee thanks – high praise from the Vulpi with a brain the size of a small moon," he jabbed back, and she put her paws on her hips, clearly perturbed.

"Alright, you two," Van intervened. "Since you are so smart, as Kylie – moon brain – says, speculate who is standing in the way of bringing the repeals to the floor of the assembly. Let's see how you do."

He took a few steps away as Kylie threw a bunch of images of well-known Thurians from the political branch on the screen. "Well, it won't be any of these, not directly," he shot back, and the screen went dark as the Vulpi mumbled something about him not being an easy target anymore and no fun. He paced a bit and sat, thinking it over. "Politicians ... don't generally vote their ideals, if they even have any. They vote what their constituents want them to. In particular, they vote their deep convictions based upon the deep bank accounts of their wealthiest contributors. So, the question is who can keep this from coming to the floor as an invisible third party."

"That's presupposing," Van warned him, "that it's just contributor motivation that's pressing them. Remember, de Dothnar has a big war chest thanks to their defunding of the Sahnassites, and it's growing all the time. You did say bribery, didn't you?"

"Wow, I was right on that one, too. Okay. This means one of them, or even several of them, have been compromised, and no amount of money is ever going to turn them," Trax posited, and Van nodded. "Okay, so it still works back to who is pulling someone's scruff where they want them to go. It ... could be the Sahnassites, but that doesn't work well because Kallain has such a presence, especially after his elevation to Loyal Elite Superior. I mean, someone under him might be doing an end-run around him, but you'd know that and help him stop it."

"Okay, that's good," Kylie commented. "That's just plain good."

He nodded and smiled. "I have been paying attention at dinner. So, if it's not the Sahnassites, maybe it's the Vanarrans. You know, all told, they are having a surprising case of *not being dead, yet*. Shouldn't they be standing on their last wobbly paw, more or less?"

"Ah, Trax, sweet Trax," Vanarra breathed. "Very, very close. It is the Vanarrans, and you are right, they have secured a secondary source of funding that is under the view of the newsarotzi. Alanar and his crew don't even suspect. Watch this." Van nodded to Kylie, and a diagram appeared on the main viewer. "This is the result of Ky's careful searching and listening and tracking over the last six moons."

"Six ... moons?" Trax asked, just staring at Kylie, confused. "That's a little slow unless ... someone's been taking Foundationalist lessons?"

"Not bad, Trax," the Vulpi told him, "exactly, and that has all kinds of implications. First, here's the pitch. They've been trying and failing in several little ventures with my help, but this time, they've got several key assembly delegates under their sway, and they have them by the scruff of the neck and by the base of the tail, too. However, corrupt politicians are one thing – after all, if they've done something worthy of blackmail, we usually don't have any issues with letting them suffer for it and simply be replaced with someone who doesn't have a blackmail problem."

"Tough love, for sure, but why can't you just pull the plug on these delegates?"

"Two reasons. First, if we can free them of their blackmail concerns, then they have proven sympathetic to voting for the houses' restoration. They might even do so as a revenge vote. Second, however, is that the Vanarrans still have a cadre of potential stealth candidates waiting behind these guys to take over and take an even harder line against the houses' rights."

"So, we either find someone to release these idiots from their blackmail shackles," Van commented, "or wait for a full elections process where we shouldn't actually interfere even though we know that the Vanarrans have been cultivating house-hostile candidates for some time."

"Wow," Trax breathed. "They … they were setting this up for a while, weren't they?"

"There was a reason why the Sahnassites struck first, trying to throw a wedge between the Creator's Path and the Vanarrans in front of the newsarotzi. The Vanarrans, especially, have significantly improved their influence with the government in the past few seasons. It's not that they've used it, you see, but they obtained it – decades ago in some cases – just to have it for a time when they needed it, like now. Kallain told me that that information was accidently slipped to his side regarding about just how many of the assembly delegates, not to mention the potential replacements, the Vanarrans had a lock on. The Sahnassites hoped to destroy that investment by creating an angry constituency that would demand action against the Vanarrans."

"Wow, deeper and deeper all the time," Trax commented, shaking his head. "So, where do the Foundationalists lessons come in?"

"Well, our dear Kallain isn't the only one with a fondness for history, and although he was much further along than most," Kylie told him, "he's not alone. The Vanarrans have been studying patterns in society for season upon season, looking for the pressure points where they could act according to their advantage. One of the things they learned from history was that the Foundationalist attack on

Thuria was one of the most well-planned, well-coordinated attacks in history and was completely invisible to all of the electronic surveillance mechanisms in place by the government. The houses, also."

"It's a shame that Shaelen de Dothnar isn't around. After the Foundationalists attacked, he completely changed the way they acquired intelligence, and he looked for ways to locate these verbal and paper message networks," Van breathed out, sighing.

"Well, that's where I took my inspiration from," Kylie noted, pointing at the viewer, "although I have a couple steps up on what he had access to. When these five key assembly members inexplicably voted to block legislation to repeal some of the most harmful oversights of the houses, I back-scanned them and started looking at all of the individuals who spoke to them. Van's been helping me and using Tana and Sahni to sniff out when they became particularly fearful. Someone ... has been very, very clever. Face-to-face meetings, only – threats never communicated any other way."

"Yeah," Van noted, "and now we have to be twice as clever and undo their work. All this without a major hero appearing in history. Now, if we can take care of our poor blackmailed politicians, then we can get the legislation approved. Afterwards, we can spend the next few seasons culling out the Vanarrans' paw-selected replacements, at our leisure. However, we have to start somewhere, and we need to start now. Carinthia isn't the patient sort, and she might start her own investigation – or heck, her own blackmail campaign – if we don't get hold of this."

"Yeah, not stellar leadership there," Trax commented. "At least from what I hear from Racea and Ariasta, she's no Rahnahi."

"Well, she hardly could be," a disembodied voice entered the room.

"Uh, sorry about that, Honored One," Trax said quietly to Rahnahi as she formed in front of him, paws on her hips. "You're just the standard everyone looks to."

"You need a more careful understanding of my history, baby cub. Without Dania, I wouldn't have been half of the matriarch you thought I was. Carinthia needs work, carries too much pain and scars from all those seasons under Shalana, but she *can* bring up some who are better than that. Besides, I'm helping to see to it."

Trax suddenly cocked his head and asked her, "Oh, was … that where you were during the whole Akashar on a rooftop thing?"

"It was well managed by Vanarra, and yes, Amyra is doing the same with her house. A lot of apathy and resignation to fight there. However, Van," the ascended poet offered turning towards the mixed blood who had walked up beside Trax, "I think we're about there. We need cubs and kits on the inside now, ones we can *direct* and not just influence. I'm working on some of those as side projects right now. However, I'm starting with green twigs – I can't pull someone like Fireclaw, too noticeable. However, give me a generation or so, and you'll have solid candidates ready to move the house forward."

"Hey, about Fireclaw," he asked, "did I hear something in the TransNet about her retiring from primals?"

"Yep, this is her last season. Vosh has been helping her train and stay in good shape, so she's still competitive and fairly dominant, but we three have been talking about the next phase for her. The *Lasrihal* project phase. It's something that in the next few seasons we kind of have to see to. I think-"

"Van, hate to pause you on that," Kylie warned, "but we have an interesting event at the capital. Looks like Temple Master Dartha is being let in to see Assembly Delegate Rasalan de Oterbythe."

Vanarra looked up as she reached out with her mind. "Vosh, you listening to this, too?"

"I continually monitor your communications, Mother," the Terspear replied evenly. "I am at a point in the training sol where I can disengage with Fireclaw and attend to this mission, if you would be so inclined to authorize me for it."

"Authorize her for what?"

"Basically going to the assembly building and following the Select on the poor beleaguered politician's schedule. He's one of the ones we want to pry free," Vanarra explained.

"Oh," Trax replied. "What was he supposed to have done?"

"Had intimate relations with a minor when on the campaign trail just before being elected. One problem, though – she *wasn't* underage. She's just one of those kits like Letta who always looked young because of her size. She was over the legal limit at the time of their ... relations."

"How much over?"

"Two seasons," Van explained. "Voshy, get in the vicinity in stealth, and tell Fireclaw that she can't come with you – not this time."

"Mother, I'm now being asked to relay a message."

"Oh, gosh," Van groaned putting her paw over her eyes. "Just ... just put her through on audio. It just doesn't sound right having you repeat the things she says sometimes."

"Yeah, and I totally heard that," Fireclaw's voice complained. "Come on! You've stuck me on the sidelines for ages, coach! Put me in, please! You know I can carry it off! It will look better if she has an assistant. I can't be washed up in both of my possible lines of occupation!"

"Alright, as you've *trained* with her, I'm willing to allow it, but I will be watching and giving directions – you had better follow what I say, kit. No initiative permitted on this mission whatsoever."

"Done. We'll be ready in a few passes."

"Vosh," Van called quietly, "make sure she gets it, please."

"Yes, Mother, but I believe she will be capable in this endeavor. She and I have discussed it, frequently."

"So be it, my dear, but I'm relying on your judgment."

"She has excellent judgment," Trax noted, paternally.

"Your support has been noted, Grandfa," Vosh replied, not just a little smugly. "We will accomplish the mission, Teldear. You have my promise."

"Very well, daughter. Love you. We'll listen in," Van told her.

"She will," Kylie reassured Vosh. "We both will. Okay, here's the start of act one – enter Temple Master Dartha," the Vulpi noted as she pointed at the viewer.

"Well," the male middle-aged Perratti offered uneasily. "It's been ... a long time since I've had a Vanarran Temple Master grace my office. Welcome, would you like to have a seat?"

"Thank you," Temple Master Dartha stated evenly and took her seat in the fine prowler-hide chair. "We have had a recent change in our leadership structure, and I have been elevated to the post of Grand Temple Master for this region."

"Oh, really?" he replied, pretending to be surprised, but in truth, he had heard this from his staff earlier in the moon. "Well, congratulations are in order, then."

"Delegate Rasalan, there is not much for us to celebrate, actually. Our interests continue to be under assault on every front, and now, even from this very office."

"I'm ... sorry," he replied, swallowing a little as he sat down at his fine old harlock wood desk. "I don't understand."

"Word has been circulated to us that you are starting to entertain several pieces of legislation which would undermine the very foundation of our society, restoring a harshly restrictive and oppressive culture that refused to let our order, when in its infancy, grow and flourish."

"I'm sure I don't understand. We ... we haven't brought anything to the floor regarding any restoration of the houses' power."

Her brown eyes held him critically. "You deny that individuals at the very highest levels of de Dothnar's leadership have not been to see you?"

"No," he replied, a little nervous. He had been visited, once, by this one's predecessor before his unfortunate turn of bad health, and he wondered if his period of freedom from his prior mistake was now at an end. "As a public official, I am obliged to listen to all of my constituents' needs and ideas."

"Yes, but three visits from them in the last moon, along with a visit to their estate, you see, might tend to ... wear one's resolve down, make one consider directions that would not be in the greater best interest."

"There are many," he gently challenged, "who believe that the harsh restrictions on house autonomy have not served our best interests, as a collective society. For example, if they were to disband

and reassemble under the guise of a ... religious order, they would not be so impeded."

"And yet, then, they would be unable to function as the holding of public ownership in companies and speculative interests would be considered illegal." That made delegate Rasalan stew, somewhat, because he knew, without fail, that the Vanarrans had only held onto as much power and wealth as they had by orchestrating secretive agreements with various corporate packs and firms. "It is ... a nice office," she noted, looking around. "It would be a pity if a series of bad decisions were to pry you from it."

"What are you saying?" he pressed.

"I'm saying that we have evidence that your judgment has not always been sound or even ... legal. There is a considerable number of your supporters who are convinced you are completely upstanding and faithful to your mate in your joining. If they were to become ... disabused of that notion, it may not be enough to remove you from this place. However, knowing that you hunted but a female baby kit would certainly be more than adequate to turn this lovely plush office into a jail cell."

"So," the representative said, stewing. "You ... haven't forgotten, then."

"No, and neither will you. You, who took a precious mixed blood kit, someone's baby daughter who was just a little confused by her very first rut, and what did you do? Well, we have ... all the proof we need to review fully for the newsarotzi what you did. You need our guidance, it appears, as your inbred nature overruled your better judgment. If you believe that the houses should have their ancient power back, then you are showing poor judgment and influence yet again. There were too many of our order who suffered and died because of house power, and we are not willing to stand by and let someone like you give it back to them. So, even as other faiths remain silent on the matter of trying to curry favor with these once murderous houses, we won't stand for it."

"Then, your business here is concluded?" the tan and black Perratti pressed, impatiently, his blue eyes snapping with anger and barely controlled rage.

"Not … quite," she smiled smugly, sitting very comfortably. "There is an investigation which is utterly pointless and invasive against us in the area of securities purchasing. You are aware of it?"

"I am," he replied.

"We would consider it a very … useful … favor if it could be de-prioritized against other work. The investigation is regarding an item so long ago that it hardly seems relevant as so many of the key defendants amongst our order were killed by the Sahnassites. We would be unable to make any sort of reasonable defense, and it does seem as if someone in your district prosecutor's office has a special dislike of both us and our order. Would you mind looking into it? If you were able to, we might be able to leave you to your own devices for say, a few moons – provided that no other lapses in judgment were evident, regarding the houses."

"Fine. I'll … I'll look into it," he told her, nearly growling.

"A fine sol to you, then," she said, standing. "This office … suits you. You should do everything you can to stay in it."

"It seems … a very difficult position being a Vanarran right now," he nearly growled. "Especially in leadership. Can be quite risky from time to time, it seems."

She stopped at the door and turned back to him. "Hardly a deep concern for our interests as every one of us knows exactly what you did, and so long as there is one of us left, someone will be around who can tell everyone. Farewell on that thought, Delegate Rasalan.

He didn't say a word to her as she left, and when the door closed, he turned his chair away from the door and started angrily swearing. The old Temple Master, Lashure, had visited him only once three seasons ago, and his warnings were actually far more delicately delivered than those of this enrobed Vanarran arrogance. He had nearly committed to the Matriarch, Carinthia, that he would look into the process for repealing the restrictions against the houses. "Now, what do I tell her? The Vanarrans said no, and so I can't?" He leaned over and put his head in his paws, feeling sick and angry and just a little ashamed.

After about five passes of that, his intercom buzzed. He hadn't actually calmed down, yet, fully, but he did manage to press the button. "Yes, Annalisa?"

"You have two ... females here to visit you, and it appears they are interested in making a sizable donation to your campaign. They have been passed by security."

He wanted to tell them to go away, but his campaign war chest was running a little thin the longer he delayed bringing legislation to the floor to repeal the house restrictions. It would stay thin, also, if the dames of house de Dothnar were denied. Sighing, he felt as if he was just looking for one horrible weight to counterbalance against all of the others, and the more that were added, the more the chance of a calamitous collapse. "And the Vanarrans hold a rope around the keystone that can bring it all down." Still, he realized, that if he were to have any chance at reelection, he would need some funds, and so he told his administrative assistant, "Please, show them in."

Trying to regain his composure, he straightened his desk and stood at the ready. What entered his office made him work to keep his welcoming smile in place. The two females Annalisa had told him about were curious, to say the least. The one who was clearly the leader was a large, black Pantera with silvery grey eyes and a noticeably muscular build. Accompanying her was her assistant, or so it seemed, a bookish looking Vulpi female in glasses and modest, if nice, clothing. What the Pantera was wearing was utterly striking, especially since he understood how much those kinds of dress clothes cost. She might as well have entered his office wearing money.

"Good afternoon," he greeted them warmly. "I'm glad you were able to drop by this sol! I'm sorry, your names are?"

The black Pantera's voice nearly rumbled like a distant thunderstorm. "Vossia de Katscha, private investments broker. My assistant, Tessie de Khaetria."

He offered his open paw to them, directing them to sit, and then he too, retook his seat. "My pleasure to meet you. I am Assembly Delegate Rasalan de Oterbythe. What can I do for you?"

He watched the dark-furred female pause and wait until his own assistant closed the door after leaving the room. When it was just the three of them, she nodded to her own assistant who began speaking. "We're here, this sol, Delegate, because of certain concerns we have over the rights of young females. We are concerned that, on certain tertiary school campuses during select events, there are a number of rapematings and event statutory rapematings that are occurring on a regular basis."

Rasalan swallowed hard. He hadn't taken either of these for Vanarrans, and he couldn't help but wonder if Temple Master Dartha wasn't making a point. "I … see. Yes, it's something to be … concerned about, surely." The location where he had been seduced by a female that was far too young was actually at a large tertiary school during an evening fundraiser. After he had delivered his speech, he had found himself alone walking through the hallways back towards his hover. That's when his fantasy and his nightmare both began, and what was worse, he could look into the silver eyes of the large and imposing female in front of him, and he knew she could just see him squirming.

"Especially of concern to us, however," the assistant offered, "is when these females are conscripted to play the role of victim in order to achieve certain outcomes from those who are unfortunate enough to have been marked as targets."

His astonishment was also not missed by the Pantera. "Why," he asked, "do I have the feeling that the points you are raising are … directed at me?"

"Delegate, you were just visited by Temple Master Dartha of the Vanarrans," the assistant offered. "It should not be hard to guess that we followed her visit, intentionally."

Just then, Vossia, the Pantera female, slipped out an image from a portfolio she carried and placed it on his desk. Looking at it, horrified, he realized that it was a posed and barely clothed nubile mixed blood – one that was seared into his memory. "Six seasons ago, Delegate," the assistant stated calmly. "She found in you the hallways of Starsand Tertiary in your home district when you were alone. She approached you in a very … alluring way, gathered your attentions during what had to be the peak of your rut, and then proceeded to make prey of herself, so to speak. You were later told by certain parties that she had become pregnant by you which was unfortunate as the kit, despite her appearance, was actually below the age of consent."

"So … you know, and what-"

"They lied to you," the Pantera rumbled, a soft smile on her muzzle. "She was of age. Here is her birth certificate retrieved from the secret archives of the Vanarrans." Another document was placed on the desk in front of him, and this he reached for and read eagerly.

"How did you get this?"

"I *invested* some funds to acquire access to the encrypted information found on a search of the Vanarran temple shortly after it was destroyed. We have evidence that the Vanarrans bred this specific female, trained her for the purpose of seducing and compromising key leaders in the assembly, such as yourself."

"Are you with ... enforcement?" he asked, his paws shaking.

"No, we're with a private organization, and its name is equally private," the assistant offered, gently. "However, we acquired this information on yourself and several others, and we had to decide what to do with it."

"We could just do what the Vanarrans are doing; blackmailing you to keep you doing what they want, but their interests don't exactly match ours," the Pantera stated evenly. "So, we had the interesting idea of cutting their leash on you to see if you'll turn around and bite them."

"Where is Sephie? Is that really her name?"

The Vulpi shook her head. "I'm afraid that she was one of the ones who perished in the destruction of the Vanarran Temple. As you might have noticed, she was very highly mixed, and later was part of their staff tending to certain key Vanarran children on the grounds. The children made it out, as you know, but ... Druana Anasto ... did not. The various Temple Masters have probably hinted or indicated that she was willing and ready to turn evidence against you should they require it of her. I can assure you there was no child, and what she did to you, she was ordered to do. Here is a record of their entire blackmail procedure and records, including the records on you. You will find several of your fellow delegates are also on this list." The Perratti delegate took the offered data wafer, paws shaking.

"We hope," the Pantera stated, "that you can provide your colleagues the same kind of ... relief that we are providing you, and that collectively, you might compare stories to see exactly what legislation the Vanarrans are trying to hold back. This information, properly redacted and provided to enforcement, should be enough for them to search their own archives and determine the chain of custody is accurate – more than enough to stand up in a court of law."

"And what do you gain out of this?" he asked them, carefully.

"Start putting forth what they don't want you to, and we'll get what we want," Vossia told him. "Besides, in the future, perhaps, maybe a small favor done out of the gratitude you have for both this assistance and the generous draft left with your office. After all, none of your colleagues are getting a bonus to their campaigns by having their leashes cut, and … it's not like we could blackmail you. We just utterly destroyed the method by which it was being done."

"Bringing this up will cause me some damage … especially with my mate," he groaned.

"Why should it, Delegate?" the Vulpi, Tessie, queried, a bit of a wicked twinkle in her eye. "There is no one to testify against you, and there was no other proof in their possession – we actually doubt that even they know the full details of what they're trying to accuse you of. They don't have back-ups of the drives like we do."

"Although it is truly regrettable such a lovely kit has died," Vossia offered gently, "she was both a pawn of the Vanarrans and a criminal, not to mention well above the age of consent when your interaction occurred. I think turning this evidence into an issue directed against the Vanarrans could be a good direction for you. I suggest you advise your fellow delegates to take the same trail."

The delegate leaned back in his chair and nodded. "Fair enough. Damn! You have made this a pretty good sol for me. Thank you."

Both females stood, and he did, as well. "Then we'll be on our way, Delegate. We would appreciate being able to see you with … limited notice in the future," the Vulpi told him, nodding a bow.

"Absolutely and unconditionally," he promised. "Again, I … I truly owe you for this."

"Favors," the dark Pantera said wryly as she reached for the door. "It's what our government runs on."

Akashar walked into the hospital cafeteria feeling a little uneasy to say the least. In three seasons, it hadn't changed that much, but the changes that were present he noticed because he had not crossed the threshold from the hallway in all of that time. It was silly, he knew, as he scanned around, looking for her. Not seeing her present, he found the line and entered it, choosing his food all the while wondering if every staff member knew that he was the one who had pushed Vanalla away. She, to judge from conversations in the hallways, was just as important as before and maybe even more now that a steady flow of cured Vanarran victims was leaving this hospital. It had become the primary facility on all Thuratan for the kind of treatment required to help those afflicted by the "purebred curse."

What was also interesting was that she had been seen escorting and chatting quite companionably with Fireclaw Destiny, the renowned primal star who was in her farewell season. Some of the hallway chatter offered by a couple of the nurses had been accidentally in his hearing, and he had learned that the primal star had been treated here several seasons ago, helped by Vanalla, and the two seemed to become friends. It didn't hurt that he had followed Fireclaw avidly since her turnaround from scoundrel to benevolent philanthropist. He knew she wasn't exactly his type, but ever since being able to finally read through the story of Vanarra de Gonari, albeit backwards, it was interesting to see someone who looked a lot like her performing at the top of her league. She had a flair for the dramatic in a world where his own drama had been long, slow in unfolding, and in the end, wholly unsatisfying in most respects.

As he finished his meal, he realized that this, also, was going to be one of those respects. She wasn't coming, and he chided himself putting his tray away that he had just expected her to be here eating at the same time she had been three seasons prior. As he departed and wandered towards the main entrance, Shar realized that having a lonely meal when he hadn't intended to was likely exactly what the poor Faelnar had endured at least for a period of time after he pushed her away. "And for no good reason," he groaned, glancing into the gift shop.

There, the gold-on-gold Faelnar was just finishing up with a customer, but it was clear that as her eye caught his, recognition flashed between them. Uncertain, he wavered, but she smiled and motioned him over. A little embarrassed, he nodded and went to greet her. "Good afternoon," he offered unsure of what more to say.

"To you, too!" she warmly offered stepping out from behind the counter, a noticeable bump adorning her stomach.

"I ... remember, now," he explained, smiling. "You just had the news not long ago, right?"

"Well, it's been a few moons, and so all of my clothes are starting not to fit," she grumped. "I'll be wearing bags before long, but my little one is doing quite well, so I'm told, and unlike last time, I don't feel sick every morning."

"That has to be a help," he acknowledged. "Congratulations."

"Thank you! Were you looking for something specific?"

"Well, perhaps more ... someone, and I don't know if she'll actually want to talk to me, but I think I saw you and your mate with her – a brown and gold Faelnar, Vanalla. Do you know her?"

The golden Faelnar chuckled, "We're sisters, actually – adopted, but still! I recognized you, true, but I thought you were still working on something and couldn't see anyone."

"Well, the work is done now," he told her, sadness unintentionally seeping into his tone.

"It ... didn't go well?" she carefully asked, clearly concerned.

"It ended with a result, just not the one I had hoped for. However, I'm being ... encouraged to seek out someone to spend time with and, perhaps, explore what that means for me."

"Well, I have time for a break, and you look like you need a friend to talk to. I'm available," she told him firmly.

It was a turn of events he didn't expect in the least, and he just stood bemused and a little shocked as she put out the sign indicating she was going to be away for a quarter interval. "You ... don't have to."

"Yes, I do," she told him, fixing him with a nearly stern expression. "She told me a long time ago that you might come and talk to me about my experience; you never did. So, you've come here now, and you're going to hear it, and I'm going to listen to you. Come on, the break room is this way." Bemused and feeling slightly out of control of the situation, he simply followed the Faelnar back through the rear of the store and into the private hallways of the hospital. The moment they entered the break room, a mixed blood security guard started to approach them. "He's with me, Shashee. Special case," the Faelnar explained. "I'll make sure he doesn't get into any trouble. We just need a moment to talk."

The mixed blood still looked uneasy at the idea, but then it was like she, also, recognized him and said, "Oh! Okay. Just make sure you stay with him back here. You on break?"

"Yes, I am."

"Okay, I'll ... keep an eye on you for a bit, but if one of the others comes back here, you'll probably have to take him out, Ria."

"I understand. We'll be discreet," she promised, and to that end, she offered Shar a seat in a booth facing away from the entrance that was obscured by the beverage machines. With a nod, the security guard departed leaving them the only two currently in the room. "We should have at least the time of my break, since everyone else's breaks are scheduled, and I can take mine at off-cycle times. We're too close after lunch for any of them to be coming back here."

"Thank you," he told her nervously. "Uh, did Vanalla tell you why I might have come to you?"

"Why don't you tell me, and tell me your name, please. I'm Shenaria or Ria, if you're nice."

"Mine is Shar, short for Akashar," he offered, "and that's as good a place to start as any. It means forgotten place. Nearly twenty seasons ago, I ... was found very sick and with no memory of who I was. Now, Doctor Emma has done therapy with me these last three seasons and told me that my memories prior to that time are probably ... gone forever. She's helped me get past a lot of the guilt and fear of what I might discover, and to be truthful, I've also done some things on my own to see if anyone would recognize me as a missing Thurian."

"Nothing came from it?" she gently queried.

"Oh sure. After three moons, the guy in our office who never gets any work done spotted me and wondered if there was a reward on offer. I had to discontinue the TransNet account I used because he was messaging me so much. Other than that, no. She's ... she's probably told you that she once had an interest in me-"

"Has," the Faelnar calmly asserted to him. That stopped him, and into his stare, she slowly nodded. "You heard me. *Has.* Now, why, knowing all of that, would she send you to me?"

"She said you had been through something … similar."

"I was found about four seasons ago just outside of a construction site. My issue was that I was badly injured, and it took surgery to put me to rights again, but I'm okay now – one on the way, even. My memories before I was found are a little … interesting."

"How so? But you have them, at least?"

"My memories are of being the *original* Shenaria Anasto, mother of Vanarra de Gonari. Not someone *named* after her – the real thing." Into his silence, she nodded, smiling knowingly. "Yep, that's what they all say. So, you woke up with no memory of who you were, and I woke up with memories that were utterly impossible."

"I … I don't know what to say," he confessed.

"No one ever does," she told him. "Emma certainly didn't. I about drove her crazy with her trying to figure me out. Thankfully, she was forced to give up and just let me be after about a moon or so."

"Only a moon, why?" he asked, a little taken aback. "I've been working with her for three seasons!"

"No money," Shenaria explained, shrugging. "I had no records and no income, so no way to pay the hospital back for the surgery, the emergency care, the room, the food, any of it! Once I was physically well, they had to let me go, and Doctor Emma had to step out of the way and just let me get on with my new life. Shar?" she asked because he closed his eyes and lowered his head, his brow tightening. "What's wrong?"

"I'm … feeling a little angry right now," he growled out, "like I've wasted the last three seasons only to find out my memories will never come back, ever." Her soft, warm paw reached out for and held his arm, gently, causing him to look up into her earnest expression.

"Don't. Doctor Emma is a good soul, and I've worked here long enough to realize that. What you have to understand is that if she's been helping you for three seasons just to make sure that you aren't going to be surprised by memories that come back and bite you in the tail, then you should be grateful. Very grateful!"

"But after all this time, I still really don't know who I am!" he told her desperately.

"You think I feel any different than you?" Shenaria pressed him. "Even if I'm not the Shenaria of old, I'm way away from where I started, and everything is so different for me – sometimes scary. I've come to understand, Shar, that my existence is no longer governed by who I was, but by who I am, who I choose to be. I have chosen to simply accept that I don't have any other identity than what I told you, and I have chosen to accept that I own my choices now in spite of that. I've ... not chosen horribly, by most accounts, and I've had help – Vanalla's help. She taught me that who I was doesn't matter."

"How can it not?!" he challenged her. "There could be lives ripped apart in your wake, by either the harm you did or the good you failed to do. Does that not haunt you?"

She rose up and stared at him, critically. "By the laws of Thuratan, both you and I are beyond the window for the statute of limitations on any crime as designated by our mutual psychological diagnoses. So if you or I did something really horrible in a previous life we can't remember, the government doesn't hold us responsible for it because *Doctor Emma* has said we shouldn't be held responsible. Do you know what? She's right. I've worked really hard to build a new life here; I've studied and gone back to school in computer engineering where I'm hoping to graduate *before* my little cub is born. I'm also working on being a mother and a mate – working very hard at those tasks, actually. I found the Creator's Path and ways to serve others for their good and not for mine. What about you? What have you done?"

Her intense delivery put him back in his seat a bit, and he was forced to swallow before answering. "I found the Creator's Path, also; I ... got training, and I'm paying off my medical bills. My insurance, where I work, paid for the therapy with Doctor Emma, and they seemed to be happy that someone in the office was taking advantage of the program. A surprise to me, yeah, and you're right. For the last three seasons, I've been finding out that what I lost won't come back, and..."

"You are still, in the end, who you chose to be?"

"I am who I chose to be," he stated, eyes glazed, looking down at the table. "I choose to follow the Creator's Path, work ... hard, and live a pretty empty life, otherwise. Kind of lonely."

"Doesn't have to be," she offered, putting a paw alongside his muzzle as a tear dropped to the table. "Vanalla is special, Shar, truly special. She chose me, and I am so much the better for it. She chose you, and she sticks by that choice. You don't have to accept that, but I wish you would, for your sake and maybe for hers, consider it."

She nodded, and he glanced up at her, smiling as she took her paw away. "You're ... good at this. Doctor Emma could take lessons from you."

"I'm not a doctor, and you did get good care from her. There are over a hundred cubs and kits who are now starting to build a life again thanks to her. We ... were just the odd cases, and I still say she helped you."

He leaned up and nodded. "I suppose so. I wish I had spoken with you sooner-"

"No," Shenaria demanded of him. "No regrets. Those only weigh you down, and what they really are is doubts that the Creator actually does have a path for you. Sometimes, because we are distracted and confused, we can think we're off the path when we're really not. You're still taking care of others and still doing good for the Creator's glory and not for your own; you're there. Don't lose your way on this."

"How do I ... reach out to her?" he asked. "I went to the café, and she wasn't there."

"She's not going to be there every sol. She's attending Ceelie's graduation from secondary along with a friend. The kit was one of the ones who was helped, and she's making amazing progress. She'll be back tomorrow, and ... I think white sahnassas are her favorite flowers. Just one with a little water vase clipped onto the stem. I sell those, actually."

He couldn't help but chuckle at her bright and smiling delivery. "Shenaria ... Ria, thank you. Everything you've said has been an immense kindness to me and a help. If I need to, can I see you, again?"

"You can," she offered slyly, "but only for unofficial professional counseling and public social occasions. As you can see, I'm already emotionally engaged with someone else."

As she stood, he smirked a little as he, also, stood. "Evidently," he offered, pointing at her stomach. "Nevertheless, thank you."

"You are most welcome. Now, break's almost over, and I'll walk you back out to the public areas. I have to do what most pregnant kits have to do in this condition, frequently so. Thankfully, there's a bathroom on the way."

"Oh, we'd better go then!" he chuckled and extended his paw indicating she should go first.

Chapter 5: The Uncertain Suitor

Akashar was nervous; he had been nervous all sol. Shenaria's parting shot before she disappeared into the facilities was that she was nearly sure that Van would be on the observation deck of the hospital tomorrow at mid sol. It hadn't been easy for him to arrange a second half-sol off from work, but he had worked late into the evening on an emergency job, and so his employer didn't have much cause for dissatisfaction. As he paced, holding a single white Sahnassa that had been purchased from the gift shop not fifteen passes prior, that thought struck him. His employer valued him enough to allow for all of the therapy over the past few seasons and his request this sol. He was among the most senior technicians in the office, true, but as he always helped to train those who were hired on, he could miss a little bit of time, and undoubtedly, this was worth it.

"Has," he said to himself, feeling a little faint just as he had when Shenaria told him. "She *has* an interest in me." Part of that repulsed him out of habit, but the part of him that had just started to grasp the freedom he would have in a solid identity was overjoyed and excited by it. "What can she really know about me?"

He looked down over the city of Shanandrae wondering that, but then a few odd recollections started to click into place. Vanalla was something of an informal leader in this hospital, and hence, it withstood examination that she would have kept some kind of tacit track on his progress and may have even delved into his background and records a bit. "Perhaps, she does know a little about me, after all."

Akashar glanced at his PawLink to get the time and realized that it was about five passes after noon. "I ... wonder if she's coming," he whispered.

"I did," she breathed from not far away. His startled look at her drew out a chuckle. "I've been here for nearly five passes, but you were so involved, I decided it would be best to wait for a bit. Besides, it was kind of fun sneaking up on you."

"Vanalla, I'm sorry," he offered, shaking his head. "I ... owe you an apology."

"No, I owe you an apology. I startled you, after all," she told him, turning around and letting her elbow hang over the railing a bit as she looked at him. He could tell that whilst she was dressed for work, she was dressed very nicely.

"No, that's ... not what I mean," he stated as he approached her, the flower offered before him.

"Thank you," she replied, taking the flower and smiling. "Did my sister tell on me, or were you just a good guesser as to my favorite flower?"

"I must confess, your sister has been most helpful to me, in many ways. I have regretted the way I told you that I needed time for my therapy, and I hurt you, I think."

"You were honest as to your needs, and I respect that," she told him, sniffing the flower. "Emma ... stopped me in the hallway, and although she wouldn't tell me anything else, she told me that you were free, now, to pursue associations outside of therapy. I take it that means that therapy is going well?"

"Did Shenaria not tell you? My therapy ... failed, at least as far as what I was hoping for," he explained. "In a regard, though, I suppose it was successful. I can now, at least, stand before you and believe myself to be an honest representation of the individual I truly am. I can, at least, say that this individual won't wake up some sol being someone completely different – someone you wouldn't know, a stranger. I'm nearly that to you now, but..."

"Not quite, cub. Not quite," she told him. "The last three seasons have been very busy for me, although not in a relationship sense. The choice to take the period you needed to find yourself a firm grounding for your paws was well-timed. I can appreciate the frustration you have, Akashar, in not finding a different answer. I think the assertions you make about being who you truly are go beyond those that I can make in promise to you. The soul you talk to is mine, and the heart of who I am is who I am. In time, however, you might find that my outside appearance … changes."

Her admission was delivered apologetically, and Shar thought he knew the reason. "I will always remember you how you are right now, but as I learn more about the soul who speaks from within, I think that the outside won't matter as much for either of us. In three seasons, my image of you has not dimmed at all, save for the thought I believed you wouldn't have any use for me after so long. I was afraid to reach out to you, and at the same time, regretting the lost chance we had for building even a friendship." He looked over the railing down at the ground far below. "Made me pretty sad, honestly. I felt as if things were nearly hopeless."

"But still, you came looking for me. Why?"

He looked towards the horizon, apparently steeling himself before he spoke. "Because any hope that I might still have a place in your life, however small, was worth any chance of being rejected. I've … talked to a friend who helped convince me that by not reaching out to you, I was doing nothing more than guaranteeing that there would be no hope."

His eyes cut to the side in a worried glance, and she stepped over beside him and put her paw on his. "There's a lot of trails ahead, and neither of us knows how much we should truly hope. We have to get to know one another, first. I'm willing to risk myself for you, Akashar. My soul requires nothing less of me."

"That is very kind, Vanalla," he told her, "but I am uncertain, though, of how to even get to know you better. The couples I've seen, when they talk, bring up experiences – their histories of growing up, and I don't have that. You do."

"To be a true relationship, there has to be equality, yes," she acknowledged, looking towards the horizon. "What you do not have is a past, and if I were to simply lay mine before you over and over again, that would drive a wedge between us."

"But I would want to know it," he told her. "I'm interested in you. I think you're important enough for there to be that inequality."

"In time, yes," she agreed, "but in the short term, it would serve us poorly as a foundation. In an office where I once worked, the boss there had a policy – she never asked about the history of anyone who worked for her. She only judged those in front of her based on what they did, how they performed. Besides, it may be far more ... interesting for us to try and sort one another without relying on life histories. So, until sometime later," she deferred, "I won't speak of anything about my past before I came to Shanandrae, less than five seasons ago. That past will simply not exist; it will be as if I can't remember it."

He smiled a bit, struck by the import of her statement. "That would mean that I actually *know* more of my past than you do. Oh, that ... that would be a rare gift. Are you always so kind?"

"While I have only the last five seasons as a reference," Vanalla told him in a teasing tone of voice, "I think most would say yes to that, with very rare exceptions."

He chuckled, shaking his head. "Indeed," he offered, smiling. "Hopefully those who have known me during the seasons I have *as a reference* would say the same. Can I ask you some questions, then, about who you are now?"

"Of course," she stated slyly as she turned to him, an impish grin on her muzzle. "*That* I can recall." Her expression changed, then, and she looked worried. "Look, I am playing a bit of a game here with you, trying to be fair, but I don't want you to think for a moment I'm ridiculing what you've been through. You have my admiration and respect for going through three seasons of therapy and many more of simply living to get where you are on this sol. Please, Shar, know that, okay? If you tire of this or it wears thin…"

"I don't think that's possible," he told her, his gaze into her golden eyes turning warmer. "Your kindness shows itself more and more, pass by pass. I am enjoying this game, Vanalla, and it puts me at ease in a way that I don't know if you can fully understand. It's perfectly okay."

His paw on hers made her smile, and she breathed out, "Then ask."

"You are a … volunteer with this hospital?" She nodded in answer. "There are other volunteers I have noticed, but you seem to be different than they. What is your role here?"

Again, she nodded and answered, "Fair observation. Some volunteers that come here are either the very young or the elderly, and their primary skills are not those that are the most useful for a place like this. It's wonderful that they want to help, but if someone is a trained architect – now retired – they are only going to be so useful in a hospital setting. My knowledge and skills are different, more attuned to the line of work. I have some medical skills, some mentoring skills, some psychological skills, amongst others, but what that means is that when doctors or nurses or hospital administrators talk to me, we are talking the same language. We can collaborate. Now, I wouldn't make a diagnosis, officially, for a patient-"

"But you might point a nurse or physician in a direction they might not have considered?" he asked, and again, she nodded. "Fascinating. How did you – wait, and there it is, again. I … I see the point in this game of yours, Vanalla. It does make us equal. Thank you."

"You're welcome. Have other questions?"

"I do, but I'm a bit embarrassed to ask. Are you … friends with Fireclaw Destiny?"

At his nearly hopeful expression, her smile broadened. "Yes, and do I detect the ardor of a true fan?" His blush furs riding higher, he nodded. "Should I set up a little meet and greet?"

"I … I wouldn't wish to impose, and my attentions are actually focused somewhere else right now," he humbly told her with a nod in her direction, his paw still on hers. "I would just ask you to say this to her – thank you for what you are doing to help these poor kits and cubs. I would root for you on the field just for that, alone."

"She has been good about that, hasn't she?" Shar nodded appreciatively. "I will deliver your message, and for that reason, she'll want to meet you. I'll tell you a secret, Shar, if you promise not to tell." At his nod, she continued, "The hospital thinks that we're about sixty percent through helping all of the kits and cubs poisoned by the Vanarrans. Once all have been helped, she wants to turn her attention in a direction that may surprise and even anger some. She wants to begin raising funds for ... the Vanarrans."

He stood bolt upright at that moment and looked at her, incredulous, breaking their contact. "You can't be serious."

"I am. The Vanarrans she wants to help are those who were innocent of their crimes. The guilty will be in prison for sure – most already are, but what of the others? Conditions in the Vanarran compounds are starting to deteriorate, and they are approaching a point where they will have no more land or possessions to sell off. What then? How will those of their number who did nothing wrong live in our society?"

"But they are wrong, aren't they?" Shar questioned her. "Vanarrans shouldn't exist. They were force-bred, frequently against their will, while they used kidnapped doctors and scientists to help them."

"Doesn't matter – they're here, now. They're living and thinking and self-aware. Do we just snuff them out because they weren't meant to be?"

Shar looked hard at the horizon for a moment, but then he shook his head. "No, that can't be the answer. It *was* the answer for mixed bloods like me in our history. From what I've read, the de Caterra tried to snuff us out, the Foundationalists tried to snuff us out, and for seasons before the houses – by their discrimination – were trying to do the same. Well now, I've disappointed myself. Shouldn't I appreciate what it feels like to be lost and think that everyone's paw is against me? That will be them, won't it?"

"It will," she told him, nodding. "And they need a future that becomes separated from the religious cult that's come to be known as the Vanarrans. Fireclaw and I have been talking and think that a name like *Alkinda* might be the new species name they need to be tagged with. In the end, what we think is just a suggestion, but that might be what they land on. Have you ever heard of the Lasrihal project?"

"Yes. For the Vulpi recovering from rut trance, as I recall. Well, Vulpi and some Perratti and mixes of those, as well. I went to a cooling and heating conference there – something my office paid for. It's a lovely city, but their museum is a bit ... disturbing."

"Full-sized life mock-ups of the rut trance process, indoctrination scripts, example uses they were put to," Van agreed, turning to face the horizon, as well. "Yeah, not good."

"And what was done to them on a regular basis as a part of their recovery – it seems almost as much abuse as what they were subjected to when controlled."

"Only it wasn't, Shar," Van told him, coming back close beside him and putting her paw on his. "What they went through created needs in them that would never be fully understood by someone who hadn't been through that experience or wasn't completely familiar with it. It's repulsive to us because we think they should have been freed and allowed to carry out their life. We think that, maybe, seasons of counseling, alone, might have cured them."

He looked at her, anger and recognition fixing his expression. "Again, Vanalla, I disappoint myself! What if, like me, it *wasn't* enough?! What if *no one* understood them – how would they ever be helped?!"

"And hence, Lasrihal," she told him. "And hence, a new Lasrihal for the Alkinda. Its borders might even have to be protected from those seeking revenge for their kits and cubs. It wouldn't matter that only the innocent but misguided would be permitted within it."

"And with no way to build a life," he nearly growled, his own sufferings coming to focus. "No one to help them, be kind to them – they will die! I would have died had it not been for the charity of other Thurians."

"And now you see the dilemma, my dear Shar. Now you see what drives Fireclaw ... and drives me to help them."

He was quiet for a few moments before turning to look at her. "It is, perhaps, the single most noble thing I have ever heard of anyone attempting. I don't know how I could help, but I want to. I feel, strangely, like I share some aspect of their pain. The Vanarrans don't have the issue of having amnesia, but the memories they do have would be ... useless, wouldn't they?"

Vanalla nodded, sadly. "Everything they were taught is pointless. They worship the Great Mother and the Perfected One, with Vanarra de Gonari supposedly their Great Mother and this new species supposedly their perfected ones."

"Van, do you think that the Grand Matriarch Vanarra de Gonari ever intended any of this? As a mixed blood, they've tried to talk to me, get me to join them. They say that she did."

Van chuckled ironically. "No, Shar. Nothing could be further from the truth. Both the Sahnassites and the Vanarrans failed completely to understand what their namesakes believed and wanted out of life. Both of them loved their families, their houses, and their Creator. They followed the Creator's Path, and those who took their names and twisted them abandoning everything they stood for did so just for the purpose of having power. Did you hear about the governmental black-mail case with the Vanarrans?"

"I was listening to that on the way over – Newsarotzi Nine, I think."

"Yep, the story just broke. The Vanarrans and the Sahnassites are nothing more than modern sol Foundationalists. One group wants to create their own breed to the exclusion of all else, and one wants the existing purebred species to be all that exists."

"All those lives caught in the middle, disposable to them," he whispered. "Now, as things have fallen apart for them, the Sahnassites can just kind of fade back into society, but that's not happening for the Vanarrans. I … I thank you for explaining this to me, Vanalla, and I appreciate your insight. I want to spend more time with you, also, if that would be okay. Dinner, perhaps?"

"Two sols from now, I'm free, and … I would be honored, Shar. So, shall we do the dance of the PawLinks?" she asked, mischievously, holding up her own.

"The auto contact transfer," he chuckled. "Are you sure that our PawLinks are ready for such a … significant step in their relationship?"

Holding hers up, she nodded, smiling, and he placed his alongside hers. After a moment, they both keyed the "permit" button as the devices swapped their contact information. Taking back the devices and checking them, they both saw that each had the other's numbers. "Vanalla Ashallo is a very pretty name."

"Thank you, and Shar suits you, but in time, maybe Akashar won't suit you so much. You are a place and an individual that I want to learn more about and not see abandoned any longer."

"Thank you, Vanalla," he offered, tentatively leaning close and giving her a gentle lick on the side of the muzzle. Her eyes went wide, which worried him for a moment until he saw the smile melting her face. She returned the gesture, holding onto his paw, and it was the most connected he had felt to anyone since his memories began.

"So," Kylie asked carefully as Vanarra entered the bridge. "What do you think?"

"You were watching, of course," the mixed blood sniped.

Kylie took an officious tone and held herself straight upright. "I have a mission responsibility, as assigned, to monitor any threats to the Teldear." Then the Vulpi-Izar's manner reverted to normal. "But, yeah, I was completely dying to know what was going on! It looked like it went well."

"I can sense, even through Tana's cloak, and … I still can taste him, his kiss! Oh, it's so hard to know for sure, but his scent and taste seem a lot like what remember. Oh, it's the curse of being so old, having lived so many seasons! My memories of him are buried beneath an entire lifetime on Thuria and many others beyond that! I remember this little dragonet I became entangled with on Cirrus Nine."

"Uh, Van," Kylie gawked. "Cirrus Nine is an Allarraen world, and by dragonet, you don't mean…"

"See where my life can get a little confusing, from a history point of view? He was still young, about nine-hundred seasons or so, but … he went in and kind of played around in my memories a bit, and well, he might have given me a kind of taste of-"

"He gave you Ash back, the way you remembered him, didn't he? Intimately?"

Van sighed and sat in the command chair. "Yes, before I really knew what was happening. I was … upset with him, after. That kind of broke it off. I couldn't go there, as I just knew that however perfectly he mimicked Ash, the soul inside … wasn't him. Now, it just might be," Van breathed wistfully, "and even if it isn't, I'm feeling very happy right now. Did you see how he reacted when I talked about Lasrihal and the Vanarrans?"

"I did," Kylie admitted, but seemed a little distracted. "I was with Cal from the time I left Thuria until now, and I'm still with him. I had no idea what it might have been like to, well, go on the hunt with an Allarraen."

"Junior tree-screecher Allarraen, second class," Van corrected. "I've had a few others I was close to, besides Dad, but they were basically just good friends, deep friends, but still. Come to think of it, we need to give some direction to a few of our deep friends regarding where the new Lasrihal might pop up. Any ideas?"

"Well, one decent one close by, but it's bound to be a bit controversial."

"Really? Can you show me?" The Vulpi nodded, and a map of the surrounding area appeared on the main viewer. It homed in on an area of land that made the mixed blood swallow a little. "Attoria? Uh, Kylie, you don't mean the same one that is known for the-"

"Massacre of Attoria," the Vulpi apologized. "I know, I know, but save a little marker in the middle of the otherwise overgrown town, there's nothing! There are trails leading in and leading out, but they just stop. One of the reasons Attoria was chosen by de Caterra and later by the Foundationalists was that it is defensible. There are only limited ways in and out." Kylie changed the view to an image of the forest which had overtaken and completely replaced where the town had once been. After fifteen hundred seasons, almost nothing recognizable remained.

"Needs a bit of gardening, right? With like major construction equipment?" Van challenged.

"True, true, but the fundamentals of the location are still solid, and ... have gotten kind of better in time. The river has meandered and widened thanks to the Shanandrae dam; it's rich with fish and wildlife, and the soil – which was fertile enough before the massacre – has gotten far more so. As a bonus, it's also one of the areas that the Sahnassites own and are looking to part with. It's one of their lesser holdings, and so it was presumed, and rightly so, that it would not bring much in the way of funds. Current estimates are that the land value, if it wasn't Attoria, would be forty million or more. However, at this point, I think the Sahnassites would be happy to walk away from it for three. That's nearly eighty courses square."

Van grumbled, "Well, damn, it is a good choice, at least in those respects. Any ideas what kind of resistance we'll face?"

"Ahem," Rahnahi cleared her throat as she materialized on the bridge. "Sort of an informal bit of poking around I've been doing on this-"

"Oh, of course!" Amyra's voice quipped although the ascended Faelnar was not visible.

"I just take an active interest in my Teldear's projects."

"Well, it's not like I don't," Amyra contested, appearing beside her, paws on hips. "However, I thought we said that we weren't going to try and sway Vanarra on this."

"Sway away, kits," Vanarra told them. "Right now, I'm having a very instinctual reaction, and it's not all that pleasant. Even after all these seasons, I can still remember that VidStar."

"Well, that's the thing, dear," Rahnahi told her. "It's not as important to those Thurians living in these sols as it was or is to us who lived when the massacre occurred. Believe me, I have a severe distaste for recalling those events, but it's very fair to say that if you were to ask most Thurians about reoccupying Attoria, they would kind of give you a blank look. Had it been only a hundred seasons, no. Had it been even five hundred seasons later, the answer would have still been no, but the edge would be off of it. Now, so long as there is some memorial to those who died, I don't think many are going to contest allowing that land to be reused. Now, what it's going to be used for is a different matter, and I think she who says she doesn't poke around much actually has been poking around on this."

Amyra shook her head. "Yes, yes, guilty as indicted. I don't think the thought of what's going to happen to the Vanarran innocents has exactly been completely divorced from the Thurians who have been tracking the stories these past few seasons. Even the Newsarotzi and Alanar, to his credit, have been asking the question about what happens to the Vanarrans should they utterly and totally collapse. It's one of those great big problems that no one wants to really talk about or do anything about, but it's looming out there in other Thurians thoughts, and it's a world-wide problem."

"Would Attoria be big enough for the Vanarran population?" Van asked.

"It might serve very well, especially given the number of Vanarrans in prison with no hope of parole. Those who harmed children will certainly never be granted their freedom. Do you remember Select Vassia?"

"Yes, she … she was released, wasn't she?" Van queried.

"Stripped of her title and relegated to lower level duties. She's only remaining in their ranks because she doesn't know of any other alternative. What you told her touched her," Rahnahi suggested. "Maybe it's time that the Attoria plan begins, and maybe it begins with Javoth, with Laxar, with Vassia, and … with Fireclaw."

"The Great Mother lives, again? Fireclaw is sure to hate that," Kylie observed.

Vanarra disagreed. "No, I think this is where the demystification needs to happen. See, Fireclaw is someone who can give them inspiration and leadership, but she can help direct them onto a better path. Fireclaw would never appear in her Great Mother get-up. She would simply be a retired mixed blood primal star who wants to help them. We know her well enough now to know that she's not going to try to co-opt them and make a new cult. If anything, she'll die trying not to. It's just too important to her, now, that she is someone who is worthy of trust and is following the Creator's Path."

"What a change," Sahnassa breathed into her thoughts. "So deeply touched by you, my dearest friend. Tana agrees. Perhaps, when she has the world's attention, when she has her last performance, this can be what she asks of her fans."

There was a stillness on the bridge as Kylie and the two former matriarchs had heard the inner Nephti's assessment. "Yeah," Van finally spoke. "I think that could be her moment. I'll talk to Voshy, and we'll approach her and Javoth to get the idea rolling. Ky, I take it that you've been looking at infrastructure?"

"Yes. It will be a self-sufficient model for a pretty fair amount of time, but eventually, it can grow."

"Got it. Okay kits, sounds like we have a plan. Let me try to help get it started!"

Vosh, in Vulpi form, gently massaged the right hind paw of Fireclaw as she sat in her dressing room. "You performed admirably through the pain, my friend," the Terspear Vulpi told her. "I found Mist Runner's open-mouthed astonishment and subsequent soft use of creative language gratifying."

"Oh, immensely gratifying – the young kitling." Fireclaw looked down at Vosh who had that curious expression that occurred whenever the primal star said or did something that was unusual. "Oh, by saying she is a *kitling*, I am showing disrespect and frustration … with her youth and arrogance – especially in how she underestimated me."

"She did underestimate you, significantly, and tonight's score shows it," Vosh agreed, the slightest of smiles turning up the corners of her mouth. "Your language lacks some specificity and phraseology to deliver an insult appropriate to her distorted self-conception. The Tentalian word *Ringeistar* seems to be the most appropriate word in my memory to describe her, especially if she misbehaves or acts sourly during the awards ceremony. The word suggests that an individual, through their behavior, has regressed into an earlier, less educated and less emotionally mature time of life. However, if one emphasizes the middle syllable and places a hard sound at the end, that version of the word is more severe, indicating that the individual seems to have merited an evolutionary demotion into a lower life form."

Amused, Fireclaw chuckled, "Really? Have a lot of words about insults, do these? Tentalian you said?"

"Yes. The location is Tentalia, a planet in another dimension of reality. They are an ancient species, but one that has progressed very little due to the enormous amount of conflict within their ranks. They have nearly eradicated themselves on multiple occasions over the question of insult. There are very few peace-makers in their – ahem."

Fireclaw's eyebrows lifted over closed eyes, and she breathed out in a relaxed and airy tone of voice, "Welcome, Vanarra de Gonari, Most Honored of All Matriarchs, Allarraen Teldear of Planet Thuria. How may we help you, this sol, Honored One?"

"You … aren't so easy to surprise anymore," Van commented with a little disappointment as she had just tri-gated in right behind the reclining mixed blood. "It's taken the fun of trying to sneak in behind you."

Fireclaw winked at the Terspear Vulpi as she stood. "I guess I was just … relaxed by the kind ministrations of your daughter."

"She tipped you off I was coming, didn't she?" Van groused.

"I'm afraid," Fireclaw offered in a mimic of Vosh, "that my security responsibilities prevent me from providing a clear and definite answer to that question." Feeling the other mixed blood glowering at her, Fireclaw opened her eyes and looked up. "Come on, you know it's not fair for you to make me go all tree screecher, especially when I have to stand up in front of everyone in the Apharium and receive another darned first place prize. All the while enjoying rubbing bright little, tight little *Miss Runner-up's* muzzle in it for the moves she tried to put on me in the wrestling event."

"Yeah," Van smirked, "was keeping an eye on that, but Tana still thinks you bruised your ligaments again with that landing."

"Not the kit I used to be," Fireclaw sighed, sitting up straighter. "On some sols, that's a good thing, but on some sols, out there – phew, not so much."

"Still planning to call it this season and be done with it?"

"As planned, especially because I think we were planning to move forward on something else, right?" the primal star asked.

"The arrest of Temple Master Dartha is starting to move up our timetable," Van offered, sitting beside her daughter and giving her a quick hug. "That story, sad to say, is largely going to bury everything else on the Newsarotzi platter for a while."

"Heh, maybe Temple Master Dartha and Select Vassia can enjoy the same cell," Fireclaw groaned, leaning back, Vosh starting to work on the other hind paw. "Van, your daughter is just darned amazing. Never anyone so giving…"

"She enjoys being with you, don't you, kit?" Van asked.

"I do find it a constructive use of my time, and Fireclaw is kind to me in explaining emotions I do not understand."

"Which ain't much, to tell you the truth," the primal star uttered, tilting her head up as Vosh hit some of her pressure points just perfectly.

"As we've discussed, though, there's a difference between understanding and mirroring. There are a lot of emotions I don't feel very powerfully – thankfully greed and pride are hopefully at least a little less absent from my psyche."

"Well, Vassia's actually out after a season and a half. She was taken back into the Vanarrans, a little unwillingly, but it's the only home she's ever had. She's not a Select now, either. She's Acolyte Vassia. Lowest rank. Her life is pretty miserable, honestly, and for the Vanarran kits and cubs, it will get bad very soon. The child support enforcement officers have started to notice that the children are getting uniformly thin, as are the adults. You have two moons before your farewell speech. Anything you might have thought about saying?"

"Well, goodbye, but I suspect you have an idea. Vosh, where do we stand on the poisoned kits and cubs? Do we have enough to cover their remaining treatments?"

"According to my assessment," Vosh replied, "there are more than sufficient funds in the charitable account to cover the remaining treatment. Funds continue to come in, however, thanks to your highlighting the charity during media interviews."

"How much is there left to do?"

"Honestly, the governmental education has done a very decent job adjusting to the needs of these kits and cubs; a track for them to get them back into the mainstream is now just a part of the national curriculums," Van commented. "All told, it's gone very well. Now…"

"Thin little Vanarran kits and cubs," Fireclaw commented, looking up at Van as Vosh released her hind paw. "It's Lasrihal, then. But … but how do we even get started on it?"

"Well, we need to create anticipation for your announcement during your farewell; something you could tease a little of, tonight? Tell Thurians to save up for?"

"Yeah, totally *can do* on that one," Fireclaw agreed. "Can I bunk over tonight? After Flame and I finish up with dinner, I was just going to go back home, and Voshy tells me that you can go onto an area of your ship and see distant worlds like they are completely real."

"I believe, Mother," Vosh explained, "that Fireclaw is requesting permission for a sleep-over at my lair."

"Heh," Van chuckled. "I'll approve it, but do this for me. I want you to start sounding out the other primal stars on the subject of what happens to the Vanarran children when the Vanarrans can't support them anymore. What happens to those Vanarrans who were innocent of any crimes but won't be able to find work or a safe place to live, when their coffers go bankrupt?"

"Like Vassia?" Fireclaw queried, and Van nodded. "See ... see if they'd be willing to support trying to raise funds like Flame has for the treatments?"

"Yeah. If you trust him not to dump it into the TransNet or in front of the Newsarotzi. Mist Runner is probably not a great choice."

"Like duh," Fireclaw sighed. "Flame's only a little before bailing out, as well. He's looking for something to throw into, and, honestly, both he and his lair mate were asking me the other night. Flame would be good on this, I think. Any idea where we would buy the land?"

"Ever hear of Attoria, near here?"

"The Vulpi monument?"

"Used to be a town, nearly a city," Van replied, "before they were all forced to allow themselves to be murdered. Sahnassites own the land, and it's going to be cheap. We think it's clearable, defensible, and sufficient for how many Vanarrans will need it. We can also use the hover trails near there as a shipping location."

"What would they ship?"

"Lumber, at first – plenty of old trees in that area. Grazers would do well there once the land was cleared, crops, too. It's really fertile land, but ever since the Sahnassites grabbed it over a hundred seasons ago, nothing has been done with it. They had all sorts of plans, but they can't afford them now. Kallain will sell to us if the price is even half reasonable."

"It would be like living in the wilds, again, like the Primalists of old tried to do," Fireclaw commented, feeling a little wistful. "This would be that place we've talked about for them to find their new identity?"

"It would. In Attoria, they could cease being Vanarrans and start being the Alkinda or whatever name they choose. There, they can protect themselves without causing undue fear, and there, with Javoth's help, they could transition away from worshiping the Great Mother to, perhaps, a faith in the Creator's Path. It's not as simple as I'm making it sound, of course, and there will be major issues to work through. However, I can sort of … cheat a little, here and there," Van offered, smirking.

"And how. Okay, my Teldear, I'll get started on that now, because," Fireclaw offered smiling as she looked at the viewer. "They just totaled the points! Hah! Nailed it! Missed again, little Runner!"

"Well, this season, but…" Van mentioned.

"Yeah," Fireclaw agreed, standing up. "No dummy there, really. She's learning and got a good trainer and looks like she's going to sign a choreographer to replace the one who makes her dance like a nervous prowler on hot sands. If I didn't bail now, I'd … I'd have that cute little tushy sitting on my muzzle before too long instead of the other way around. Good enough time to get out in the real world and … do some real good. Thank you for that, Van. I owe you."

"I'll help you, and you're welcome," Van offered, putting her paw on the mixed blood's shoulder.

"And you will have my assistance if the Teldear permits. Mother, I was thinking that I might be a good choice to play the role of Raska among the Vanarrans, especially during the early phases."

"I'll have to think about that, but you may not be wrong. I'll give it serious thought. Alright, Champ, get out there, claim another one for the mantle."

Fireclaw started to walk towards the door, but then turned and looked at her. "And then, claim one for an entirely new species. You're so right, Van – only small stuff happens in that arena."

"Not when you're in it, kit."

Chapter 6: First Dates

Akashar waited nervously at the curb just beyond the hover stop in the upscale district where Van had invited him to dinner. He had only stepped off the transport a few moments ago having ridden for a distance of merely a quarter course. His hover was parked in a safe place, a fair distance off the trail and out of sight – its patchwork of pieces cobbled together from other hovers wasn't something he was proud of. That, however, he could hide unlike what he was wearing. The suit he wore was clearly out of style and a bit worn, something he had acquired from a charitable organization. Normally, his clothes consisted of his work uniform or shorts and a t-shirt. He had been in his work uniform when he had gone to the hospital, and it was nice enough that he didn't feel dreadfully out of place – save for the fact that over its chest pocket was a sewn-in nametag that said "Shar." As he stood, self-consciously waiting for Vanalla to show, he realized that he had been a bit of an idiot about getting ready for a date. While he had bathed and brushed and made sure he looked alright, his wardrobe had never required anything for a casual evening with a female, and it didn't dawn on him until it was far too late.

So, humiliated, he rocked back and forth on his hind paws, his over-tight paw shoes also promising to make his first interactions with the beautiful Faelnar an utter joke. He watched, however, trying to see when she was approaching, the darkening sky making it difficult to see into most of the hovers as they zoomed through the parking lot in front of the shopping center. A very nice green sports hover slipped up to the curb and, seeing it, he sort of stepped behind it, hoping to give Van's hover a place to stop while whoever this was got out or waited to pick up someone. To his surprise, however, the hover slipped backwards slowly, its rider-side wing door open, which gathered his curiosity. As it sat down just in front of him, he couldn't help peeking in. When his eyes met hers, his blush fur jumped immediately to attention.

"Oh, uh ... hi, Vanalla; I'm sorry! Wow, is ... is this yours?!" he asked, amazed.

"I tend to look at her as my baby kit, actually," she joked. "Come on, get inside. She doesn't bite." As he edged forward, she warned, "I might, but she hasn't – well, so far." He slipped inside and grunted in surprise as the seat's bottom was a bit lower than he was expecting. As he tried to lean forward to adjust, there was a ripping sound, and Shar suddenly felt air where there shouldn't be – dead in the center of his back. He looked at her, utterly humiliated, but she just said, "Uh oh. Lean forward, cub. Let me see." Mortified, he did, but then there was the curiously nice sensation of her paw fingers slipping into the hole at the seam and gently lighting on his back. "Yeah, ripped it pretty bad, cub. I'm guessing you had a little difficulty trying to find something to wear?"

"I'm ... I'm so sorry, Vanalla," he pled. "I only have my uniforms and the stuff I hang around in. I hadn't worn this suit since I applied for my current job, and it's clear that I've, well..."

"Grown a little. Pants still fit you relatively okay, but you know, you've done something really nice for me by agreeing to come on a date," she told him. "Now, I want to do something for you. See that clothing store over there? It's going to be our first stop."

"Oh, no, Vanalla, please," he begged, looking like he might actually back out of the vehicle, but the wing door on his side was closing. "You don't have to."

"No, Shar, I don't, but let me ask you something. If our situations were reversed and you were able to help me, would you?" The wash of emotions across his features and look into her eyes told her everything. "Yeah. Thought so. You're going to let me help you so we can both enjoy tonight, and later, we can enjoy other times together, and you won't feel uncertain. Right?"

He closed his eyes and nodded. "You're very kind, but-"

"No buts," she warned him as the hover lifted off. "I can't be very kind and *not* do this for you – the two concepts don't actually work together. So, since you've said I am kind, I'm going to trust your assessment and be kind. You're going to be kind, also, and let me show you just how keen I think you are. Put you at ease so we can both enjoy this night in one another's company?"

The last was a question which was nearly delivered with the timidity of a child, a plea for trust and a promise of sincere concern with no mockery of him intended in any way. "I ... cannot refuse the kindness you offer me, Vanalla. I am so sorry about this; I thought so much about preparing myself that I didn't realize I was ... without anything appropriate – I didn't realize until I actually stepped up to my closet how bad things were. It doesn't cast me in the best light, I'm afraid, and it's a poor first impression."

"We've already had our first impression, Shar, and you are fine. It means more to me that you trust me enough to accept this. Now, if I get you some clothes, and you show up for a date in that suit again – then we *are* going to have a talk!" Vanalla sternly warned, which made him chuckle.

"Upon my honor and by my pledge, most noble lady," he promised as the hover slipped towards the clothing store.

"Hey! You're using the formal statement of promise," Van realized, impressed. "Where did you pick that up?"

"I like to read," he told her, happy that she recognized his phrasing. "And I find some of the histories and biographies pretty good. That is the title of one of Rahnahi de Dothnar's works, as well. Very ... grounded sort, for a matriarch."

"Her friend, Amyra, too."

"I agree – a very effective pair, although I have stopped reading a few of the biographies that were more critical of them."

"Well, I guess everyone is entitled to their opinion," she told him as she finished setting down the hover and opened the wing door. As she got out, she added, "Why did you stop reading them? What threw you off?"

As he removed his jacket outside of the hover, he thought about it. Tossing the ripped coat into the back, he answered, "I guess they didn't seem very ... intellectually honest, I guess is the term. I mean, I know that no one is perfect, but it didn't make sense how they could be both brilliantly scheming and completely incompetent all at the same time."

"No, it doesn't," Vanalla agreed as they approached the front of the store. "And you are to be respected for knowing the difference – not everyone in these sols can. Now, before we go in, I'm paying. Also, I'm not just going to buy you enough for tonight. You're leaving here with enough to give you some options. I just got a bonus, and I want to do some good with it. Helping you would be wonderful good for me to do."

"Bonus, but … you're a *volunteer* at the hospital."

"Exactly!" Van beamed, and before he could ask another question, he was pulled into the store.

Almost an interval later, an extremely grateful Akashar walked out, opening the door for both Vanalla and the sales associate as he carried the generous additions to Shar's poor wardrobe to Vanalla's hover. As she pushed the remote, opening the wing door, the store clerk stepped ahead to quickly deposit the items into the waiting hover. When he was out of earshot, Van asked him, "So, how does it feel?"

"It's wonderful, Vanalla; I just don't know what to say. I never thought I had a chance of carrying off anything like what you've put me in – I have to admit that I feel a bit ridiculous. These seem like clothes meant for someone much keener than I am."

"Ah, but not as I see it. They just help bring out how keen you already are, cub, and the fact that you can't see that, even looking as stylish as you now do means that you are a very humble sort. That's a good quality when you have to get along with someone, being willing to let them go in front of you or even … let them do something for you," she told him. "Thank you for letting me do this for you."

"Oh, no, Vanalla," he said, slipping up close to her and gently kissing her on the cheek, "all of the thanks are mine, and you have made me feel so much better. I catch myself feeling … at ease when I'm around you, and I'm uncertain if that's something I should be feeling."

"I'm nervous, too, Shar," she told him, smiling. "However, I am having glimpses of what it's like just to be with you as a friend, and I like it. I know it's early for us, truly, and let's be honest – thank you." She interrupted herself to nod thanks to the sales clerk as he walked away. As they slipped back into their seats and the doors closed, she continued, "Like I said, I know it's early for us, and we've been very … careful around one another for different reasons. You have your reasons, and I have mine. However, for us to get to know one another, we have to risk sharing with each other. Sometimes, it's going to be like what I just did for you, and sometimes it's going to be talking or helping or many different things. If we don't take that risk, together, then we won't have anything."

His chin sank to his chest, and he shook his head. "You're … just incredibly wise. You are right; I've become an expert at being careful around others. Partly, it's because I work with the public – you know what that's like." She nodded. "Be nice, be tactful, be tolerant. However, even with those who sought to help me when I had nothing, I hid things from them. There were all of those kits and cubs who tried to fix me over the seasons – I cried myself to sleep some nights because of the things they said. I learned to hide my worries and feelings, and I was scared, honestly, to talk with Shenaria. But, she did more for me in a just a few passes than Emma did for me in three seasons. Well, maybe that's not fair, but what she said was powerful."

"She's a good soul."

"You helped her, Vanalla," he told her. "You helped her like you're helping me. That's … meaningful. I look at her life, now, as something I never thought I could have. Now…"

"Now," Vanalla said, smiling, "we'll just have to see, won't we?" He nodded. "Hungry for a little Taprician, or does something else suit you?"

"Taprician food is wonderful, yes. I might need your help when ordering; you might have a bit more experience than I do."

"New experiences mean that you might find something new to like."

"I think the sound of that is very appealing, and again, thank you, dear Vanalla, for all of these wonderful things. What you've done already has made this an evening I will never forget."

"Sounds good to me, and you are most welcome, Shar. Most welcome."

Several intervals later, the two were walking down a path in the woods far outside of the town, Van carrying a basket and an UltraBright. "The meal was incredible, Van," he told her, "and I am so glad I am not wearing what I came in. This walk would have been impossible, and I would have been uncomfortable the entire time. Now, tell me again how you knew about this place?"

"Well, as I told you, some of it … I can't recall," she chuckled, continuing a running joke that had been going on through the evening. When he accidentally asked her a question about her past, she would defer pleasantly in several different ways, and instead of frustrating him, he actually had apologized and thanked her after every one. However, minus about four attempts, he largely didn't have to be reminded. "However, when I returned to Shanandrae I looked around for a patch of land that I needed for a special project, I found this place. I developed a bit of a relationship with the owner – an old Perratti cub, and any night it wasn't in use by his other clients, I had only to ask. Well, as tonight is a very clear, not so cool night, I figured this wouldn't be a bad way to spend the rest of the evening together."

"Passing the time under the stars? Van, you're quite the romantic."

"I try," she told him. "Not something I do frequently, and I wanted to find something low key for us, allow us to truly just talk about things."

"Things," he marveled, "that are. Not things that were." He said it, again. "Things that *are*, and not things that were."

Things that, thankfully, might yet be,

between you and me, but nothing of the past,

ages prior put to rest in place of continuity,

the endless stream of possibility,

trail between you and me,

between you and me.

He looked at her, in wonder, and she explained, "It's a little-known piece from Rahnahi de Dothnar from her book, *Lost Sayings*."

"You really love her work. That's the third or fourth time you've quoted her."

"She's important to me," Van stated after a few moments. "She was a mother to me, in a way."

"You ... are an orphan?" he asked as they reached a clearing.

"Not anymore," she told him. "However, that's well beyond what I can remember."

"When your memories ever clear, it's a story I'd like to listen to," he told her, but then he looked up. "Wow! Amazing how many stars you can see."

For a moment, he just stood there, transfixed as she seemed to be shuffling quietly around him. He had never been out this far from the city and stared into the night sky. As his eyes had adjusted, he was even more struck by what he saw moving at the edge of his vision. Turning, he looked and just followed it, moving so swiftly and so high it just boggled his mind to think about it. "It's the Vega Nine space station," Van explained. "It's abandoned, now. They are assembling Cosmos Lair One, its replacement."

"I'm ... I'm seeing a space station?"

"Small and limited, yes," she told him, placing her muzzle on his shoulder from behind, gently reaching around him. "In time, there will be something much, much better. Little steps on a trail."

"Trail to where, I wonder," he asked, but then a flicker caught his eye, and he looked down. "Vanalla," he breathed in amazement. "Look at that – I had no idea you had all of that in there! Candles on a ... little stand and the blanket and food, too?"

"Like it, Shar?" she asked, sweetly, still staying close to him.

"Yes," he said, looking back at her, "in every way."

"Come, relax with me," she bade gently, taking his paw. "Come along and sit here, and you can slip your paw shoes off."

"I want to be careful with these," he told her as he moved to sit alongside her. "They were just given to me by someone truly special." Laying back carefully alongside Vanalla, he felt unsure – unsure if he wanted to or was able to go further, but a part of him thought this might be an interesting test for them, and for her. What she did next, pleased him. She simply looked up into the sky and reached for and held his paw. "You are very sweet, and this ... this is very romantic."

"I know, Shar, and I don't want to miss your expectations, but..."

"Vanalla, I've never done this before, to my knowledge, so no – I have no experience and expectations, other than I do happen to know what's criminal and illegal." She looked at him, curious. "It was part of my tertiary equivalent's degree. Interesting that they include that, true, but for some of the males I met during the program ... appropriately necessary." She looked back up to the stars and made a little sound acknowledging what he'd said. "I just never considered it would be in my realm of possibility."

"There are those who will take advantage of another, against their will," she told him, "but that isn't the only mistake one can make. In the ... past, just after I came to Shanandrae, I moved a little too fast for a cub, kind of trying to impress him or – it just wasn't the right thing. It can take a long time for someone to realize that, although the attraction is there and it's wonderful, pushing too fast destroys trust, or it sends the wrong message."

"I can see that, and I've heard others talk, for sure," he said. "This, though. Van, being here with you looking up into a sky that's so utterly amazing is just – it gives me peace and a happiness I've never known. That we saw before, it was a space station? How could we still see it?"

"Its orbit is high enough that, for a period of its flight across our sky, it is in light while we are in dark. The same thing can happen in the morning, too, but look there. See those smaller things moving?"

"Wait a moment, I ... no – yes. Yes! That one, and another!"

"Satellites. You can see the larger ones if the weather is perfect."

"And so, tonight it appears to be."

"It does," she agreed, squeezing his paw.

After a few moments of silence, he whispered, "I find myself looking up and wondering..."

"Wondering what?"

"Wondering if anyone is looking back at me. I doubt they could see me from so far, far away. Could there be anyone else?"

Vanalla smiled deeply and answered him. "Maybe. There might be worlds where the sky is fire fruit red, and the trees are crystalline blue and alive. Worlds where the sky unfolds over an ocean of blue and purple clouds tower like mountains above you. Worlds where there is no air or tree or grass and nothing but sand, but beneath that sand, there is the most amazing and marvelous life. Worlds where courses and courses of gas surround a hard center with pressures that would crush us flat – still, life floats in the clouds even as lightning bolts the size of whole continents course from one side to the other. In all you're seeing, Shar, couldn't there just be one place like that?"

"What you describe amazes me," he confessed, just shaking his head. "I never thought of it. Never thought it was possible. I looked up from the city and just saw a few points of light. The night was mostly … empty."

"Well, there is a lot of empty up there. That's just a science thing," she confessed.

"And … life, floating through the clouds – that's a new thought to me. Everything I've seen on VidStar, the creatures look … sorta like us."

"Well, that's a little silly, isn't it? We may have a unique look as far as the cosmos goes. What if there are … jeweled rocks that think and talk or black sludge that builds buildings or long insect-like animals that live underground but with intelligence that would put both of us to shame? What about flyers who can think, who live for honor and pride and territory? What if there was light that could sing to the center of your soul, Shar? It wouldn't look like us, no. It could be different and…"

"Scary?" he asked, looking at her.

"Doesn't have to be," she answered back, looking into his eyes, deeply. "There are horrors even on this world in plenty, some in Thurian fur to say nothing of some of the larger prowlers and even a few of the grazer types you wouldn't want to happen on. I'd … hope there would be a mix, and that although the bad would be there, so would the good. And, maybe you'd find the bad and help it to become good. Just because a thing is unknown doesn't mean it's bad. It's just different, maybe lost and scared."

"It's amazing," he breathed at her, his eyes wide and his expression bemused. "Talking to you is like … watching a thunderstorm far away. You can see the edges of it, the clouds at its borders. Then, there are flashes, and just for a bit, you can see the most amazing detail. I … I was stuck up on the roof of a high building in a storm like that. We actually had to jump onto a balcony for safety, but … but as we sheltered there, I saw the storm in a new light. I had been terrified, and then, I wasn't. I was grateful. I was grateful about surviving, of course," he offered as she snuggled a little closer to him. "Still, as I watched the storm move off and we waited for someone to let us back inside, I saw things in that storm I never expected to see. Like … like you."

"Haven't much seen my stormy side, yet, fortunate for you," Van teased quietly.

"What I saw wasn't frightening. The flashes I saw took something amazing and made it even more amazing. I've never forgotten that experience. Whenever I feel … uncertain, I go back to the building and sit up there, on top, and I just think. I remember what it was like to be so afraid and then find such beauty in what I had feared. I'm not making much sense."

Vanalla put her paw alongside his muzzle and responded, "Sense enough, Shar. Sense enough. Being here with you, talking with you like this, is … an echo of a preciousness that I thought had been lost forever. Like the strains of a song played with only the melody until you hear a full and accomplished orchestra play a new piece, and then you realize that you may have fallen in love with just a tune, but there was so much more than that for your ears to hear. What was kept and loved is still kept, but there is new and more and greater with depths that were invisible. The mind reels, the soul wonders, and the heart glows brightly with new promise."

"And there you are again, a flash of lightning across the clouds," he told her. "Treasure of a lifetime."

She leaned towards him and angled his head so that their foreheads touched. "Thank you for this night, Shar. Thank you for sharing with me."

"And you with me," he told her, nuzzling her gently. They just stayed that way for several passes, enjoying one another's company.

Finally, she pulled back and looked at him. "You have to work tomorrow, I know. We should get going." Her smile told him she wished that they could stay like they were forever, but that she respected him too much to let herself get carried away. His nod and a gentle lick on the side of her muzzle set them to their tasks.

In a few moments, they had wordlessly packed all she had brought and started their walk back. They were content to just hold one another's paws, and so they stayed until they arrived back where Vanalla had picked him up. "Is this where your hover is?"

"Actually, I ... I parked it down the way because I am a little embarrassed by it. Kind of a mix-up, like me; well, the truth is far more than I am. I kind of assembled it together from parts. It gets past the registration inspection, albeit barely. As opposed to this lovely ride, it's more about necessity, I suppose."

She looked at him seriously. "Shar, cub, I want you safe. Tell me where to drive, and I will take you there. After all," she offered, smirking a little, "I've already seen the suit."

"Ugh," he groaned in disgust. "You ... turned this into such a marvelous evening, Van. Thank you. Head back out to the main trail. It's tucked just behind Shining Way Hover Repair Center. I have a friend who let me park it there. He helped me put it together, after all. A good soul."

"You'd know one if you saw him, for sure, Shar. Very well." In a few passes, they were standing in front of the building. "I can drop you off here."

"Thank you." They both got out and stepped in front of the landed hover. When they came face to face, he held his new clothes in one paw, so it was just a little awkward, and Van could tell he didn't know what to do.

"Thank you, dear Shar, and I pray we'll be able to spend time like this together soon, if you like."

"I like, and I promise to come dressed for the occasion," he offered, lofting the clothes a little higher in his paw. She leaned in, holding his cheeks gently in her paws and kissed him with just a hint of the intensity hiding in her soul, leaving him nearly breathless.

"Good night, Shar. Sleep well, and sweetest dreams."

"You, too," he breathed, smiling. "You, too."

She who had once been Select Vassia – now elevated well beyond that role – tended to her sacred holy duties, the ones she had been given ever since being released from the prison of the unbelievers. The rod of her authority worked its sacred duty by her paws' wielding as she traversed her mystic pathways from the blessed early dawn well into the sanctified night. She put fatigue behind her and even the need for food as the work she did served the Great Mother and the Perfected one in unparalleled measure.

At least, that was one interpretation. As Vassia slumped in the corner of the bathroom, her mop in her paws, her body aching and hungry, a tear squeezed out of her eye. It wasn't the truth. She was, as all Vanarrans of thorough mix, left with no place to go other than back into the paws of her own kind, and although none of the failures of the past could be laid at her hind paws, the weight of them was simply too great for her to escape. She had been the one tending the sacred twins, Tabuck and Arlani, when the world of the Vanarrans was ripped apart. She was dragged in by the authorities along with several others and expected to be martyred. However, although the rest were put in confinement for the rest of their lives or put to death, she had been released merely a season and a half later.

There had never been any collusion – yet she was suspected. "I … sold out my fellow Vanarrans to save myself. Yes, that's what I did," she breathed out the lie as her soul ached at an intensity to equal her body's hunger. "I was responsible for causing the destruction of the nursery. I have no share in the successful breeding within our kind that those two poor kits brought about. All the success is someone else's, and I am … nothing."

She was shaking, trembling. Her rations had been cut again because of the ongoing struggles of her faith, their financial trials now added to by the imprisonment of their Temple Master for blackmail. The elderly Grossir now held sway as Temple Master, and he spared no courtesy or kindness to the one who had taken his position and humiliated him before the council. She knew that she would be fortunate, indeed, to survive under his tenure. Exhausted and hungry and wearied to the bone, Vassia finally dropped into her cot well after high night, a sol of mundanity all that waited beyond the closing of her eyes.

Vassia woke, appearing to have somehow ended up in the closed terminal of the transport station of Shanandrae. She just stared around her, at her surroundings, the loneliness, the quiet, the strange ways that things meant to be in illumination looked when they were cast in darkness and shadow. A part of her wanted to call out, ask if anyone was there. In truth, however, she was nearly too terrified to move. Ones of her kind venturing alone had been found and abused, injured, and some had even died at the paws of purebreds. The "purebred curse" had now been refocused. What was a curse to purebreds became the purebreds acting as an almost universal curse to anyone who looked as she did.

There were paw steps approaching her, and terror struck Vassia. Wildly searching this way and that, she tried to figure out where the paw steps were coming from, and more importantly, where she could hide. Darting around, panting because of her weakness, she could only find a dark corner to fold herself into, hoping that her brown fur and dirty robes would not give her away.

Being crammed into this tight little space gave her almost no ability to see but a thin slice of the darkened lobby area just beyond, and heart pounding, body quivering, she waited. Golden paw prints, to her utter amazement, appeared and disappeared on the floor in time with the sounds of their movement. She tracked their progress with an ever-increasing sense of dread as the arc of those imprints drew them closer and closer and closer to her hiding place. Whatever this was that was stalking her knew precisely where she was; it hadn't been fooled by her pathetic attempt to hide.

"Hello, kit," a voice called out for her, and that voice was warm and understanding. It took Vassia a moment to place it, but it was the same voice that had yelled at her when she was in prison when her faith in the Vanarrans and their cause still held strong. It echoed through her mind and body in a way which made her crumple to the floor.

"Please, no!" she called out in her thoughts, but her voice echoed her plea throughout the whole space.

"Peace, yes," Vanarra called to her, coming into being, appearing as a physical presence directly above where the golden paw prints had stopped. "Peace to you, Vassia. You've paid your debts. You've learned the truth, haven't you?"

"I'm ... nothing, anymore, and that's my only truth," she wept, her mental voice of anguish carrying as if swept by the wind out of her very soul, its imprint ricocheting off this wall and that.

"No. Not true, Vassia."

"No longer a Select. No longer bringing our order glory. No longer have ... an order with any glory."

Vanarra's form solidified all the way and looked around the space. "When you sleep, you come here? Why? It's not the first time you've dreamed of it, right?" Van looked at the empty darkness of the place. "Trapped here, aren't you? I ... did that to you. I suppose I did, in a way."

"I'm nothing more than trapped, and I have no future. I want nothing other than to simply not be anymore." The whisper echoed throughout the space as if it had been chanted by hundreds in time with her, a chorus of the darkness of her soul. "I am nothing to anyone."

"What they have you doing, yes," Van mused, waving a paw across an open space on the floor. A tall wingback chair appeared, and she took her place on it. A stool appeared in front of her, drawing Vassia's eye. "You are cleaning their filth from morning until night for no thanks and ever dwindling amounts of food. On a positive, they're skimping on what they give you to keep the children fed – that's good at least, but you need to know something, Vassia. You ... are *someone* to me. My name is Vanarra de Gonari; I am over seventeen hundred seasons old, and you are someone important to me, kit. You can have a wonderful, free, and fulfilling life ahead of you, and I want to give you that."

Vassia turned her eyes away, closing them against a false hope, asking, "How? You're just a vision in my head."

"No, I'm not *only* a vision in your head. Come out here, kit. Let me help you; at some level, you have to believe that I could help you if I wanted to."

"Why do I have to believe that?"

"Because if I could take everything away from you, don't you think I could give some part of it back?"

"Pointless," Vassia's mind echoed in the cavernous space. "The order is finished, dying, and our kind will die with it."

"Your order needs to die because it was a lie and sought to destroy the truth. Did you read the Creator's Path while you were in prison?"

"I ... had a cell mate who did, and she would read me things. I don't believe anything, anymore. I don't want to believe in anything, anymore. It all failed me."

"You were failed by a lie, Vassia. You will not be failed by the truth. Open your eyes and see that."

Vassia did as she was bidden, reluctantly, and found herself bemused by what she saw. Instead of the transport station, she was in a beautiful forest at night, felt a breeze lofting the smell of fragrant blossoms weaving their scents into her nose, and the clean air brushing by her fur. The chair where Vanarra sat still remained – not a throne, but mildly suggestive of one, and as Vassia wandered out of her dark corner, she saw the stool was still there, too. However, between the two of them were large plates of food, and a shift of the wind brought those aromas to her – the need to eat pulling her forward as if she had been collared and leashed. "Sit now and eat."

"Just a dream, right?" Vassia asked although she did comply. "It ... won't really help me."

"When you wake in the morning, you tell me if you feel hungry or not. When you fall back asleep tomorrow night, I will feed you, again. Give you strength for what is to come. This is a beautiful place, Vassia. It, like you, has a dark history, but like you, it can be redeemed. Sit, enjoy the peace and the food, and then lay in the grass and rest. If you do as I ask, you'll awake in the morning in far better shape than when you laid your head down."

Before Vassia could say anything, her mouth already watering at the food, both Vanarra and the chair disappeared, leaving her alone.

Unable to keep herself from partaking, she began to eat, the food and the place she was in seemingly restoring her very soul. She was seeing a beauty in this shaded grove at night she had never thought possible, and the more she ate and the better she felt, the more joy seemed to surge inside of her. Finally, she had her fill and felt drowsy and pleasantly full. "Lay in the grass?" she wondered, looking around. Not far away, the shaded boughs of the grove opened into a small clearing, and Vassia was drawn there.

The grass was low, clean cut, and dense. In the center lay a soft blanket, and bemused and more comfortably full than she'd been in a very long time, Vassia sat down. Her eyelids started to droop of their own accord as sleep demanded she pay heed and succumb. Lowering herself, still feeling uncertain, she was struck with how many stars held their place in the skies above her. Laying fully back to get the best view possible, she had the strangest sensation that she wasn't lying on the ground so much as lying against it, held to a vertical surface by gravity with the night sky's majesty standing full in front of her. "What ... have I missed?" she asked herself in her thoughts. "What have I never seen? Why?"

The food had been different than their normal, bland, non-distracting meals. It had been wonderful, and its flavors and aromas drove her to eat ravenously. Now, everything else commended itself to her just as potently. "Why? Why were we like we were? Is that why we failed? Did we miss the beauty of everything that was ... created?" Her mind thought that a blasphemy even as she articulated it in her thoughts, but like a rude child being stared at angrily by a parent, this distaste of blasphemy cowered under her harsher assessment. "It kept us controlled. It kept me controlled. They keep me ... controlled. I've seen too much, now. I've felt and tasted too much," she whispered. "I would be happy embracing my death, here. For at least here, there is peace and joy and beauty." Closing her eyes, she felt herself slip back into a restful sleep, more completely therapeutic than any treatment she'd ever had.

What seemed like an eternity later, she blinked awake. Sitting up, she once again realized that she was lying on her cot in a musty room. However, unlike all of the other times she had woken up in the last three moons, she was comfortable, well rested, and not at all hungry. "How did ... how did she do it?" Vassia wondered, confused.

Getting up and starting her sol began the process of trying fruitlessly to find an answer to that question.

Late that night when rest was finally afforded her, Vassia felt tired, yes, but it wasn't the bone-crushing weariness that had assailed her every prior sol. Her hunger had started to gnaw at her a little, as they had actually forgotten to give her any ration for one meal, and she had to go without. Closing her eyes on the cot made her hope once again that the dream she had would repeat itself, and if it did, she would have more questions about the future Vanarra had spoken of.

Again, her eyes blinked open, but they opened to a view of the sky streaked with the fading light of the sol and scattered with stars all growing into brilliance. "Oh, thank you," she said softly as she stretched out.

"Hi there, kit," Vanarra's voice greeted her. "Hungry?"

"I ... well, I am. Thank you for the meal last night. I don't know how you're doing this, but you were right. I wasn't hungry most of the sol, and I was rested. I ... felt like I was actually alive for a change, but..." She sat up and looked into the golden eyes of the mixed blood.

"But?"

"Everything and everyone around me is still dead or dying. The ... the order is dying; their spirits and their resolve are dying. You said that was right, but you don't want us to die. How can we *not* die?"

"You need a place outside of the order to survive, to build a life and grow. You are right, Vassia, the Vanarrans are dying as are the Sahnassites, but unlike the Sahnassites, the Vanarrans can't just deny their beliefs and fade back into the rest of society. The world now knows how you were created, and they know what this order did to make that happen. While some will treat you fairly, the numbers will be small. You need a shelter, a safe and secure lair."

"You can offer that to us? To me?"

"Only to those who will leave the path of violence and seek a way to live in peace. I brought your order down, I and those I serve. Now, I want to save your lives and give you a chance to choose differently – follow a new path."

"The … the Creator's Path? It will be awhile before I can put my trust in anything like that again."

"But it's not impossible?" Vanarra asked, and after considering a moment, Vassia shrugged and nodded. Van's smile helped the once Select stand as much as her offered paw. "Come then, I have food for you and … a proposal. It's also something to look forward to. It's possible to live this in real life, you know? Not live it solely as a dream, and also find new dreams to add joy and happiness to your soul. Want to try?"

"I … I will hear, and I will listen," Vassia breathed. "I thank you for the meal, Great Moth- what should I call you?"

"Vanarra or Van. I don't want to be anyone's great mother, Vassia, but I would be honored to be your friend and help you, if you'll only let me."

Vassia took her fellow mixed blood's paw and walked in the direction of the well-set table. "Why would you help me? My … carelessness caused your two children, Tabuck and Arlani, to die in a horrible fire."

"They didn't die," Van told her. "I took them away just before the carrier hit. For the record, also, they weren't my children. They were someone else's."

"You have them?!" Vassia shouted as she stood looking down at Vanarra who had seated herself at the table.

"Yes, and I'm keeping them safe. However, I'm doing it in a unique way, so they'll live, but you'll never know them as Tabuck and Arlani – that's too much of a burden for any child. Now, sit and eat. It will get cold." A little numbly, Vassia did as she was told.

"It's … very good. Thank you."

"I hear the question in your tone of voice, though. It isn't what you asked before; it's actually this question…"

In Vassia's voice, the question, "Why me?" sailed above them, echoing into the night.

The struck expression made Van smiled knowingly. "I can sense your thoughts, your feelings, and you have to understand that this is a big part of why I'm reaching out to you. Here's the thing, what I told you three seasons ago was true. You would have killed the scientists or the children if you had been ordered to. That was who you were, then. It was only a trick of coincidence – some would say – that prevented you from getting those assignments. At least, that's what I thought before I went back and looked at your past a little more closely. You did have a part in the decisions that prevented you from killing others. Make no mistake, you misused them. You did take part in some of the forced breeding sessions as a consultant."

"I … I did," came the shamed response.

"And that's what I'm interested in. Not the fact that you participated in those things, but now that you're ashamed of it. So, if I gave you all the tools you needed to restore the Vanarrans to their greatness, lie and cheat and steal and poison as before, would you?" Vassia stopped in mid-chew and just stared at Vanarra. "Yeah, not so much that, either, kit; I can tell. However, here's the second question that's burning in your soul…"

"Now, what do I do?" the voice of Vassia asked, mournfully, and instantly, the once Select's head bowed to her chest, and she wept, her paws folded under her chin in as much of a fetal position as one could imagine while still sitting. Vanarra reached out for and gently took her paws, holding them, cradling them. "Don't … don't have anything," she sobbed, "anyone – alone."

"No, and that's just it, Vassia. I don't want you to be alone. I want you to have a purpose, a good and noble purpose, and I want you to have those who can share in your purpose. I want you … to be a Great Mother." The questing eyes looked up in shock, still running with tears. "Not a goddess, not someone to be worshiped, but someone who is needed, someone who is loved. The children and youth of your order are numerous, and every one of them is in danger. There are few among the Vanarrans, very few, who could teach them, nurture them, help them grow up into productive Thurians. There are fewer still who have what I see in you to help grow them into a kind that will not be hated by the rest of Thuria, but respected and honored. Your life's goal will be to see that those children you raised raising children of their own, and those children walking alongside other Thurians as equals. You are one of the cores of this new community, and in this, Vassia, your life will be beset with challenges and frustrations and weariness, but all of that will fall away when small, warm bodies snuggle up to you in the most genuine and all-encompassing of loves – the love they share with their mother."

Vassia just looked at Vanarra, struck by that and unable to speak. Van let go of her paws and looked off into the distance. "The way you were raised, what I've just said is very foreign to you, but it still claw-strikes you down deep – it's instinct. We are females, you and me, and it's a part of who we are to want to bring children into the world and nurture and protect those already here. Their admiration and love put something back into our souls we can't get any other way. The Vanarrans turned children into projects – the successful ones and the unsuccessful ones. The children I've seen in the walls of the Vanarran estates are all precious, and that includes those with a tail slightly more Faelnar or a muzzle just too Perratti or too something else. Some of the ones who aren't to the Vanarran standard, I can already tell, will become artists that would shame Saiphar de Kestrick, authors who could write circles around even Rahnahi de Dothnar, and some who could govern a family or a corporate pack far better than I ever dared. Vassia, the mop and pail will never love you, and neither will those left in the order. You have to know that."

"I do. The ... current leaders have made that very plain to me."

Van looked at her, and she put her paw on Vassia's. "I will. I will love you like a sister and a dear friend, and those you work with will love you, as well. The children, if you are kind to them and care for them and truly give yourself to them, they will love you, too. They will, Vassia; don't doubt it."

She took Van's paw in hers, holding it and looking down at their paws. "I'm ... horrible with kids. I'm not going to be any good at this."

"You won't be alone," Van promised, looking back at her. "I have two others who can truly help you, and you'll find that in time, there will be many, many others. Also, when I looked into your past, children were only what you were measuring them for, and at some level, they knew that. Now, you're not measuring, you're caring for them, developing true mercy and concern for them. Little ones have a good instinct of knowing who truly cares. When I cared for the orphans in Shanandrae, it was one of the happiest times of my life. By the Creator's good graces, kit, I could wish no greater gift for you than what I felt, and if you know the truth of my history, you'd know I wasn't in a good place to care for children, either, at the start. In time, you won't be *the* Great Mother, but I think, Vassia, that you will be *a great mother*."

"I ... couldn't hope for anything better for my life, I don't think. I feel so lost, but this thought, this path you're putting in front of me is the first real hope I've had in a long time. So, if we are successful, if we can safely raise the Vanarran children into adults, then what will they do?"

"They will apply themselves first in the place where they live, building a better and stronger community. The location we have selected has good natural resources, both those which can be farmed, harvested, or mined. In time, they will trade these goods with others for what they need. There will be many technological creature comforts beyond them for a long period of time, but they will become skilled artisans, crafters, and builders. They will be sought for their skills. In time, the Purebred curse which has become the Vanarran curse will fade from memory, and those of a new name will leave that legacy behind."

"You said that name to me before, I think," Vassia offered. "Alkin?"

"That's right; for now, I suppose until someone else can choose better."

Vassia closed her eyes and concentrated. "It's ... close, but it feels off somehow. The word is a bit harsh to my ear, I think."

"I started with *all kinds*. Alkin seemed to flow out of that."

"All kinds," Vassia mused, opening her eyes. "Alkinda or even ... Aelkinda. I feel more comfortable with that."

"Who knows?" Van replied, smiling. "In time, that may be what it comes to be. I have to make some arrangements now that I know you agree, and so you'll be here a few more sols, but then, I'll get you out. For now, eat, and let's talk more about how this will all come to be."

"Vanarra?" Vassia asked, and Van nodded. "Thank you. You may not be our Great Mother, but you are very good. Very good and ... kind." In happiness, Van wrapped her arms about the female who had once insulted her in a transfer stop and let her feel what it meant to be truly loved.

Chapter 7: The Attoria Inception

A triumphant Fireclaw took her place at the top of the Apharium winner's platform, her final performance meriting her a first-place finish – hard won, but she was victorious, nonetheless. Below her, she saw several of her rivals looking up at her with frustrated admiration. "Yeah, they totally wanted to bust me down a few levels so I left with my tail between my legs, but that wouldn't help much for what I have to do next."

Lafira, the lovely little Perratti announcer, walked up the stage after the music and cheering slipping up beside Fireclaw. Looking down at the smiling yet uncertain female, Fireclaw reached around her and offered her an embrace. "You've been a big part of my success here, kit. Thank you for everything." The softly spoken praise caused the Perratti to bury her head underneath Fireclaw's neck, and she could tell that the announcer had been utterly stunned that she mattered to any of the competitors. "Hey, you and I need to talk later, too. I might need your help with something."

"Sure, Fireclaw. Thank you! Thank you!"

They parted as the upsurge of applause which had marked their embrace started to wane, Lafira composing herself as best she could. Fireclaw's gentle motion to the crowd helped them settle, and as the Perratti's voice was a little shaky, that was needed. "Fireclaw … Fireclaw Destiny, thank you so much for all of the wonderful … wonderful memories you've given us here. On behalf of literally thousands of children for whom you've fundraised for their treatment, we are so grateful for your contribution not only to this sport but to all of the Thurian families touched by your kindness. Your performance as a competitor is truly legendary, and you leave this sport standing at the pinnacle in every way, including in our appreciation and honor!"

The roar of applause was deafening, and the adulation did not cease for nearly three passes. At this, she briefly hugged Lafira again and took the offered microphone. "Thank you! Thank you, all! Bless you and thank you! All of you made all of the good we've done possible!" Fireclaw tucked the microphone under her arm and applauded the crowd, mingling their continuing applause and cheers with hers. When she took out the microphone, she motioned for them to settle once again, and respectfully, the applause slowly ended. Looking at the Perratti, she asked, "If it's okay, I'd like to make one final request of these amazing and generous Thurians."

"This is your moment," Lafira told her. "It is all yours." The Perratti stepped off the platform, but also ushered the other competitors down, leaving Fireclaw Destiny alone.

"Thank you, thank you, everyone. I began my career, I'll admit it, using the looks of the Grand Matriarch Vanarra de Gonari that I had been graced with by my two loving parents. They were never, once, ashamed of me for who I was – a mixed blood. We live, this sol, standing upon the shoulders of the real Vanarra de Gonari and everyone in her time who fought to give ones like us the opportunity to live and achieve and succeed the same as anyone else. May we have a round of applause offered in thanks to Vanarra de Gonari and all of those who have struggled in the cause of equality and liberty?" The crowd, to her surprise, did far more than politely clap. They stood in great ovation as Fireclaw clapped along with them. When she stopped, however, they took the hint and also sat back down.

"It wasn't always that way, and if someone hadn't stood up and asked more out of us as Thurians, mixed bloods would still be oppressed to this very sol, that I'm sure of." Her more serious tone quieted the crowd to utter silence, and in turn, Fireclaw could drop her voice to its warmest and most caring. "You have stood beside me when I asked you to help undo the damage done to our children by some very horrible adults. I will always thank you for that. I will always be grateful for that, but tonight, as I say farewell to being a primal athlete, I feel that this is my one last moment to take another stand and ask for your help once again. Those who cursed our children and poisoned them are now in jail, and rightfully so, but as some once looked upon mixed bloods with bigotry and hatred and disgust, the challenge for our generation is now rising, and we must decide what to do. We must decide if we will be better than those who came before us."

She took a step down off of the winner's platform and surveyed the crowd before resuming. "Those who are known as Vanarrans are still Thurian, and their children are like those of anyone else – innocent and helpless. They are victims, too, and they are not responsible for the horrible crimes of their elders. They are now, though, a kind unto themselves. They are. If you were to stand in the paw shoes of one of those children and look out upon the world, what do you think you would see? It's no secret that their order is failing, and those children who are not guilty of any crime are falling into hunger and neglect and sickness. Will we allow this to happen? Will we take Thurian souls in different bodies and cast them aside? I pray, in the name of the Creator, that we won't. I pray, desperately, that we've learned to be better."

She took another step down before addressing them, again. "When I leave you, tonight, I will begin the next great chapter of my life, taking care of the innocent infants, children, teens and adults of those we now call Vanarrans, but those who I hope that in time, will have a different name. I want to build them a home, a place apart from the rest of society where we can begin to undo the harm that was done to them, the misleading and abuse that was done to them. I want to build them a place where, under wise guidance, they can learn to contribute to our society and not to harm it. It's my dream that my greatest legacy will not be found in the record books or in awards or trophies. It's my dream that I, one sol, look into the eyes of an adult who grew up protected because I helped. That, dear friends, will be payment enough for my very life."

Stepping to the ground, Fireclaw offered her challenge. "At one time in my past, I treated every Thurian other than me as disposable. I regret nothing more than that. Within the moon, I and a group of those who are willing to join with me will set up a foundation to help relocate the children and teens of the Vanarrans to a safe haven where they can be taught that there is no superior Thurian species, just Thurians who need our love and respect. I am forever grateful that you've given both of those to me over the seasons, especially when I truly didn't deserve it. Thank you, and if you'd be willing to help us, I'd be forever grateful. Thank you, my friends, and may blessings always attend your way."

The applause in that moment was nearly a pressure wave that shook the performance field where she and the other competitors were standing. Instantly, Flame Spike came over and threw his arms around her, his wife and children coming and doing the same. "We're with you on this, okay?" he told her firmly. "You got that?" She nodded, and then competitor after competitor, including her bitterest foes also came up and told her the same. Even Flame Blossom came up to her and promised to join her foundation.

"You showed me kindness once when I didn't deserve it. Please, let me help."

"You're in, kit. You're in for sure. Thank you!"

The applause continued as did the outpouring of support well after Fireclaw had been escorted off the field.

Assembly Delegate Rasalan de Oterbythe smiled and greeted supporters and fellow delegates, alike, as he stepped through the marvelous central ballroom of the Grand Hallows resort. It was the kind of gathering he had been somewhat afraid to hold in the past, with such being inevitably intruded upon by Vanarrans or their sympathizers, always putting a damper on the festivities. This sol, thanks to the incarceration of Temple Master Dartha and the revelations of the mysterious Vossia de Katscha, he had been freed of their oppressive presence and the cold shadow of blackmail. It was a freedom that he and his many likewise liberated cohorts were now enjoying, and this meeting which gave donors to his campaign the opportunity to meet with him in a private conference was actually something he found that he could enjoy.

"No more starving my campaign to suit their needs," he growled, still angry for how they had treated him, Dartha and Lashure and Tigrest, like he was their pet. "Now, I make my own way." As he greeted another wealthy donor, a Faelnar business pack leader, he found his attention wandering a bit. At some level, he knew his freedom was thanks to Vossia de Katscha, a Pantera that was somewhat intriguing to him; her larger size in comparison to him tickled some odd fascinations in his psyche. As he excused himself, he walked over to the resort concierge who had been trying to get his attention. "Yes, Harlo. What is it?"

The younger Perratti replied, "I have just been given this envelope by a Pantera standing outside. She said it was important."

"Important, is it?" he asked, but slipped open the envelope with a claw tip. Inside, he found two items. First, there was a secured draft for two hundred and fifty thousand made out to the name of his campaign, and that made him swallow. It was the biggest donation of the night by an order of magnitude. "Bless my soul," he breathed. The draft was enough to pay off the debts from the last strangulated run for his seat and to add a pleasant padding onto the next one. Inside was a simple note.

"Might I come and join you? Vossia de Katscha."

"The young miss who was outside," he asked the concierge, "was she a black Pantera?"

He nodded. "Dressed very appropriately for the evening's event – very attractively. I was surprised she wasn't on the guest list."

"Did she try to pretend she was?" he asked, fingering the draft.

"No. She simply provided me the envelope, but I did ask her name and look her up."

"Have security search her for weapons, of course, but then please let her in … with my compliments."

"Yes, Delegate," the concierge replied, and then was gone.

Stepping around to the far side of the room, he motioned to a couple of other delegates and then brought them together for a quick conference. "We have an unexpected guest. Vossia de Katscha is here. She just made an impressive donation to our mutual campaigns, but her timing isn't accidental."

"Yes," one of the Lupar offered, "we were only a few passes from taking our key donors into the conference room for them to share their issues and concerns. How does her donation place her in terms of standing?"

"She's first, by a very long trail. You will all be leaving with twenty thousand a piece, if that helps give you an idea."

"Sounds like she's helping you clear your markers, Rasalan."

"I don't discount that, but there will still be enough left over to leave you decently in the black. The point is she's funding our whole caucus. If she can be kept happy, she may fund us even more," he warned them.

"I'll hear her out, Rasalan. Nothing more. I-" It was at that moment that the black Pantera in her black, shimmering, evening dress stepped into the hall, and her entrance gathered the attention of nearly everyone. "Okay, Ras, you didn't say she looked *that* good," the Lupar whispered. "I might be willing to do more than listen, actually."

"By the moons, I've never seen a Pantera look like that."

"She's sharp and *very* professional," Rasalan warned. "She's a player for someone, well connected. Maybe now, we get to see who."

"Sahnassites?"

"No idea," he told them. "However, she's … more of a Pantera than I've ever seen before. If that whole affair with the Vanarrans hadn't scared me straight I might see if she'd entertain a short hunt."

The Lupar looked down on him and shook his head, "With you, Ras, it's only going to be a short hunt. Invite her to dinner, please."

He nodded before making his way over to greet her, again admiring her poise and grace as she made her way into the main banquet room. "I can certainly say you know how to get attention, Vossia de Katscha," he complimented, extending his paw. "You look marvelous, and … you've certainly made our night much more successful."

"Assembly Delegate Rasalan de Oterbythe," Vossia stated as she bowed deeply, providing him a split instant view he knew would haunt him for moons. "I'm gratified my gift was well received." She leaned up and stated, "I take it you've had no more problems with those we discussed in your office."

"The guilty party has been thoroughly and completely dealt with, and ... you've given me a windfall of support by releasing the rest of their chains through me, so it seemed to them."

"My honor," Vossia told him, nodding seriously. "I was given to understand through certain contacts that the subject of Fireclaw Destiny's pet project for the Vanarrans might be coming up for discussion at a later time."

"Yes, yes, at dinner with our highest-level backers," he whispered to her quietly, "and I take it such is a discussion you would like to ... participate in?"

"The dinner also sounds very nice," she replied demurely, her voice just loud enough to overcome the short distance between them. "If I would not inconvenience you, I feel the time is right to make an investment in the future. Would it be ... inappropriate for me to ask you your viewpoint on the Attoria purchase?"

"You have cultivated excellent credibility for this discussion, and I feel it may be sorely needed," he confessed. "There are wildly divergent viewpoints, and I find myself struggling with them. Some believe this is just an elaborate conspiracy to provide the Vanarrans a base to resurrect themselves."

"Deeply implausible, based on the evidence," she countered softly.

"Some are worried that the Vanarrans have found their next Great Mother in Fireclaw Destiny, and that she could rally them."

"Strange, I thought Fireclaw had subscribed publicly to the Creator's Path."

Rasalan considered her for a moment. "So, you support the initiative?"

"Its points are complex, but the logic of its charity is sound. It would be a very interesting discussion, I think; certainly worth my time."

"Well, then I sincerely hope you will be able to join us for dinner; it's braised swimmer fish and select raw vegetables in a seasoned wild berry fermentum sauce."

"It would be my honor. Would you do me the likewise honor of introducing me to some of your peers? I would especially like to meet the ones our efforts freed from the chains of the Vanarrans."

Rasalan nodded. "They owe you a deep debt. Is … this where you intend to collect?"

"This is where I intend to invest more in them than they could ever fathom, yourself included, Delegate. I believe in a strong and vibrant government, and may I say that your work on reversing the family house restrictions has been very encouraging. It is an effort I would happily support."

"Oh, yes? Very good to hear. I … honestly think that we have been missing something in our culture; the houses, like my own, used to add so much to Thurian life which is now absent. I think that we may actually have legislation that will gain the signature of the Grand Chancellor."

As they were approaching a gathering of other Assembly Delegates, she made her comment quick and to the side, "Our resources say otherwise, and that the concern over families abusing their power is still a concern. We can talk later."

He nodded and then greeted the gaggle of very interested males who ended their conversations quickly for the opportunity of speaking with such a lovely and unusual Pantera.

Aboard the Haven, Vanarra, Fireclaw, and Kylie all watched as Vosh worked her way from delegate to delegate as the mysterious and lovely Vossia. "Way to work the room, kit," Van told her Terspear daughter softly. "They all think you are just amazing and mysterious."

"Thank you, Mother. As I am somewhat exceptional against the normal specifications of a Pantera, it is significantly easier to cultivate the mystique we've discussed."

"That," Kylie noted appreciatively, "and you are watching every bodily response they have and tailoring your approach to match, even to when you break conversation with them. It's a trick very few others could do outside of Kallain and his group."

"Amyra," Van asked, "any of them pinning her as a Sahnassite?"

The Faelnar appeared to step into reality just next to her and answered, "Some have thought that, but so far she's disabusing them of that notion well enough. The real prize will be if she can steer this debate onto a more fruitful track."

"Yeah," Fireclaw grunted, "to get our land purchase out of the freaking mud."

"I understand you're upset," Van told her, "but we expected resistance. There is a segment of the Thurian populace which wouldn't mind exterminating all of the former Vanarran children, not to mention their elders. Those who were stuck under the Vanarrans' thumb in terms of blackmail aren't interested in the same situation occurring in the future."

"A myth I will attempt to dispel," Vosh stated.

"Keep at it, love," Van encouraged her. "You're doing very well."

Delegate Rasalan watched the attractively dressed Pantera working the room with practiced ease. "Already stalking her prey," he noted. "I wonder what side she'll take – surely not the Vanarrans' point of view."

"Already sizing her up," the Lupar delegate, Bashir, noted. "She is an attractive and tempting rarity amongst the other Pantera females I've seen in my time. Their normal coarse features have a very refined aspect in her, especially given that lovely frame."

"She's not a hunt, Bash," Rasalan warned. "You may not be aware, but a few of us were being claw-poked by the Vanarrans on the whole subject of house autonomy using sexual scandal as the sharpened claw tip."

"You bravely soldiered on, nonetheless," Bashir answered, his hazel eyes merry as ever.

"No, she gave us *relief* from them. I'm thinking that tonight she plays the role of opponent to the Attoria project. She just might be here to remind us that we were once only so much tail base and neck scruff in Vanarran claws."

"It's not an uncommon position, Ras," the Lupar warned. "Many of my more generous constituents see the Attoria project as an opportunity for the Vanarrans to regroup in a protected area, perhaps with that hot looking former primal star playing the part of Great Mother."

"Possible, yes, but it's mostly just children and volunteers."

"They won't stay children, and they can't do it alone. Some of the less guilty Vanarrans are starting to appear out in society again, and they are being set upon and attacked without actual provocation. Moving them away from the rest of the population who rightly hates them tail tip to ear tops for what was done to their kits and cubs – I mean, it's an obvious step."

The Lupar shook his head as he answered, "What's to stop that bunch festering in Attoria for a few seasons and them coming back all the stronger?"

"Money, my dear representatives," Vossia stated quietly from behind them. To both of their surprise, they had both lost track of the Pantera in the crowd, and she had worked close in behind them. "I would have thought that to be obvious, but I suppose we *could* discuss it at dinner, if such would be permitted."

"Your position on this is ... curious to me," Rasalan admitted, still a little jarred by her appearance. "Especially given our interactions in the past, I am challenged to understand how you could do anything but utterly resist the creation of this Vanarran paradise." His tone intermixed question with the phrase that had been bandied about by various detractors.

"I don't believe a *Vanarran paradise* is possible on Thuria under any circumstances, now. Their aspirations must necessarily be set to lowlier, more practical goals. However, this is an opportunity for them and our general populace, worldwide."

"Delegate Bashir de Narsi," the Lupar introduced himself.

"Truly ... charmed. Vossia de Katscha." Her extended paw for clasping kept her paw fingers more tightly together than normal, keeping the action polite, and her tone and choice of words bespoke that she knew the Lupar to be one who frequently charmed others to get what he wanted. Her response, despite the substance of it, betrayed that he would be unable to charm her, even if he pulled out every trick and technique at his disposal.

"I sense this will be a fascinating discussion," he told her, bowing. "If you'll excuse me?"

She nodded politely, but after he left, she softly uttered to Rasalan. "Watch him. He's firmly in the pocket of the remaining Vanarran leadership, and they line his pockets nicely, despite the woes to their bottom line. They find the idea of Attoria utterly abhorrent."

"Which is why you ... support it?" he cautiously asked.

"Within certain limits, but I did not support the Vanarrans before when I freed you from them, and I do not support them, now. However, the aspirations held by the fanatical religion of the Great Mother is a trail far from the simple need for survival. Those who are volunteering to lead and guide those in Attoria's precincts are not of that stripe of belief. Their spiritual strength will likely flow from another source, one held by the great majority on Thuria."

"How can you be sure that Vanarran beliefs won't make their way into Attoria's water?"

"How does your family make sure that the malfeasance of Dame Geistana de Oterbythe doesn't resurface?"

He swallowed grimly, knowing his history well. "It is taught. It is very much taught by the house and by parents, alike."

"Nothing more complex than this, because they will be living in the protected exile that is punishment for the crimes of their elders."

"How can that be right, either?" Rasalan puzzled.

"I like you, Delegate," Vossia offered with a smile. "You do seem to worry about the right things from time to time. The answer is that it isn't, but it will be within their power to change that through hard work, strong faith, and industry. The Attoria valley has its opportunities, and in time, those can be made marketable. I actually envy them, in a way, if this is allowed to go forward."

"Why? Why would you?"

"They will be reborn in simplicity and come to the simple truths that hard work teaches – the reward of your own paws is food to eat, a lair to sleep in, and protection by the claws of those you keep."

"Are you suggesting a family for … former Vanarrans?" he asked.

"I'm suggesting families for all, Delegate. Families and faith for all, and so, yes. In time and with much proving, the descendants of the Vanarrans – a breed some have already started calling Aelkinda, will need that security. They will always be fewer than us, the breeds Thuria started with, but I remember a long-forgotten writing of the poet matriarch, Rahnahi de Dothnar. She told that one of the greatest losses in the Foundationalists attacks was being able to look towards a future where she might clasp the paw of the one common ancestor that started all of our kinds. In time, although they began in ignoble and misguided circumstances, that dream may again become a treasured part of Thuria."

"You are an uncommon one," Rasalan replied, humbly. "You see them and their welfare as not a curse but as a ... legacy?"

"I see that potential, but moreover our opportunity to set our own legacy into stone. Will we revive the beliefs of the Foundationalists or the de Caterra in our souls, or will we choose a different path? I have my hopes."

"I can see that," he replied, and he felt the sincerity in the tenor of her speech. "So, here is where you are ... investing?"

"I am, in them, and in Thuria. I'm hoping we are better than we have been."

"You tempt me, Vossia, to be like I was before, and you are tempting others by your beauty, still, but ... I have worked too hard over the last moon to make up with the one who shares my bed. I ... there was some level of confession required."

She looked at him sympathetically. "Then allow me to meet her, as well, and I will be friends to both of you as well as supporters of your lives together."

"If not my campaign manager," he stated firmly, looking at the select subset of guests starting to make their way up the stairs to the private dining room.

"We will see, Delegate. I serve another not in the government, but she may be willing to allow me to split my service for the greater good – so long as she thinks you are worthy of it. Her resources are ... impressive, as well."

"Then," he offered, opening his paw in the direction of the dining room, "let us see if I can start working on that worthiness you speak of."

About a quarter interval later, Vossia found herself in the middle of a long table of about twenty other Thurians. "And so, this is dinner, huh?" Fireclaw questioned, her voice a little cross as she examined those settling in and greeting those around them. "Not exactly different than how my sponsor gigs used to be, a lot of the same players, actually."

"True," Van commented from the bridge chair. "All prime movers though; no hangers on. Sorry, Fireclaw. Alright, Voshy, it's all yours. You've practiced, and I think you're ready. Just let us know if you need help."

"I have a full background on all of the individuals here, and I am confident in your training, Mother," the once Terspear fighter told her as a gentle rapping at one end of the table signaled for the guests to turn their attention to the delegates hosting them.

"It is with great gratitude that we welcome you here tonight," Rasalan told them. "For those of us charged with the responsibility for forming the laws and statutes we all rely upon in an ever-changing world, difficult subjects come upon us from time to time, and that's why you have been asked here, tonight. Seldom has such a proposal engendered such charity and controversy as that of the Attoria refuge. To start our discussion, I believe Delegate Bashir de Narsi would like to say a word."

The Lupar nodded and stood up. Taking in the group with a grand gesturing of his arms, he stated, "Tonight, we find ourselves needing not only your generous monetary support to further the objectives we all care about, but also your counsel and insight on the viciously controversial and divisive issue of the Attoria land purchase and resettlement plan. As well intentioned as it is, surely, there are so many potential legal entanglements and ethical issues that I don't expect that we'll be able to sort through them in one night-"

"Well, that son of a-" Aboard the Haven, Fireclaw started to shout at the viewer, but Vanarra put her paw up.

"It's just the first volley, and we already know he's trying to muddy the water. This is why Voshy was chosen for this mission. She's great at two things among others, but these two of note," Van warned. "First, she doesn't get angry. Second, she has a unique way of speaking truth that cuts through most everyone else's obfuscations. Even yours."

"True," Fireclaw sighed as she listened to the Lupar extolling and magnifying all of the complications in such an enterprise. "Better her than me, for sure."

They all listened and watched Rasalan as he squirmed through some of what his fellow delegate was saying. His eyes were primarily on Vossia as she sipped her tea and nibbled her appetizer barely seeming to pay attention to the conversation. There were, of course, strident objections to many of the points Delegate Bashir made by several of the more well-placed and moneyed lobbyists gathered there. Regardless, it was clear that support for Attoria was crumbling around the table, but Vossia still held back until almost the last moment.

A suggestion for the government to form a special commission to review the Attoria request that had been made, largely, out of frustration. Delegate Bashir's taunting riposte to the assertion that Attoria was a caring and controlled way to transition the Vanarrans from a life of violence and misdirection into something better was what had effectively ended the debate, or so it seemed.

The oppressive silence hung over the table until nearly everyone was looking at Vossia's unconcerned detachment as she swallowed a little morsel of food and sipped her fermentum. Her silence and poise through the entirety of the discussion was something that more and more around the table had come to notice, and although raised back fur and slashing tails were now the norm, the black Pantera sat with complete composure as if she was enjoying fine music as an accompaniment to her meal instead of a debate which bordered on a shouting match.

As she put the glass down, she questioned softly, "So please, Delegate Bashir, would you be so kind as to tell me how you will conduct the hunts?"

"I'm ... sorry? The hunts?"

"Yes, Delegate, the hunts. They must be very well planned to ensure a minimum of collateral damage to the ... rest of the population while making certain all of the destitute Vanarrans are apprehended and then processed, to the society's best convenience, of course."

"I'm sorry. I don't believe I understand what you're saying. No one has planned any hunts for Vanarrans. As I stated, the Vanarrans will be easily able to care for their own well into the foreseeable future."

"Truly?" she asked, her golden eyes looking into his with just the right measure of threat and disdain, all the while her voice carrying nothing but politeness. "They are hemorrhaging over five million every single moon, and they are fast reaching the end of the capital property they can sell off, legally, to make up the difference. I imagine they don't have much more than two seasons left, if they are cautious with their funds and can shed a few of their members, that is."

"How can you make these ... assertions? They are just supposition."

She shrugged and placed her paw on a folder that was on the table, one no one had seen her place there. She looked away from him, shaking her head a little and closing her eyes in amusement. "Sadly enough, one of the key pieces of capital technology that was recently sold was one of their back-up TransNet servers. This server, also, had the sum total of their finances current as of ten sols ago. We maintained a perfect chain of custody with enforcement's assistance just to make sure we weren't in the possession of anything illegal. It appears this was just an accidental disclosure, after all. Assertions? Supposition? Perhaps. However, I'm exceedingly good at both math and finance, and my source is the Vanarrans, themselves. So, five million every moon; two seasons running as at present ... maybe three to five if they starve themselves. After that ... I guess the hunts begin, Delegate Bashir?"

Rasalan's admiration of the Pantera female again grew as he saw his cohort starting to wilt. "Vossia, I can't thank you enough for bringing the key facts before us. They certainly color the urgency of this situation in a *very* different light."

"Exactly ... how detailed are these records?" Delegate Bashir asked, almost succeeding to keep the quavering out of his voice, but not quite.

Vossia speared a piece of meat on her plate and held it before her eyes for inspection, everyone at the table just staring, intently, and several were trying very hard to hide their smiles, suspecting what was to come. "You'd be amazed, I'd wager. For example, all of their charitable contributions are listed in exacting detail, including the return on those investments they expected."

"Return? But, you said they were ... charitable donations," one of the females at the table posited.

"Did I?" Vossia questioned, and then she popped the piece of meat into her maw without offering any further answer.

"If I might ask, then," Rasalan quietly put forth, waiting until the Lupar beside him had sunken deeply into his seat. "If the information you acquired is available for review?"

"Available," the Pantera stated, patting the folder, "and fully organized and highlighted for your consumption, and that of the mass media, if desired. I've always been a proponent of clear and transparent communication."

Van smirked as she stated, "And that, my dears, is how you sink your fangs into the neck of an opponent. You're going to owe Rasalan for that one, Voshy. He laid that in front of you very nicely."

"I'll see what I can do about repaying the debt," Vosh's voice came back over the speakers.

Rasalan had waited just the right amount of time before issuing his next statement. "Certainly interesting, and I'd like to see them later, if you don't mind." Vossia's pleasant nod made the Lupar swallow. "Now, if I may entreat you, how do *you* think we should proceed?"

Vossia looked up at the ceiling revealing her very lovely neck and daring anyone to try to take advantage of her. Given how she had just figuratively ripped off the male-hood of Delegate Bashir in front of everyone, no one wanted to do anything other than listen and agree. "You have overwhelming public support, an exceedingly generous and sustainable financial endowment, a serious child endangerment issue, and a dedicated group of volunteers willing to give, perhaps, for the rest of their lives. All of this aimed at the purpose of taking a group most Thurians find abhorrent and integrating them successfully back into your population as contributing and well-adjusted citizens. While there will be challenges, I'm sure, they are … *the right* challenges." She lowered her head, and the twist on her words at the end mentally sealed the issue for everyone there, including Delegate Bashir. It was beyond contest that Vossia's words spoke undeniable truth.

"I agree," Rasalan stated, "and the rest of you believe … similarly?" The group nodded most eagerly. "Then I believe we will have no issue whatsoever, now, pushing this through – don't you think, Delegate, despite the possible difficulties?"

"I ... yes, Rasalan, certainly," the Lupar replied meekly seeming to actually be shorter than the Perratti as he sat.

"Thank you for your contributions, tonight, Vossia. Most enlightening," Rasalan offered, and the group convivially agreed. She closed her eyes and nodded, humbly.

Kylie, aboard the Haven, groaned. "I told you Terspear negotiations tend to be one-sided."

"Woo hoo, kit!" Fireclaw shouted as she bounced. "You nailed it! You clawed him right where the sun don't shine!"

"I do have a question, Fireclaw," Vosh asked as dessert was set before the attendees, Bashir notably excusing himself. "How much of a ... show of appreciation should I offer Delegate Rasalan."

"And so now you're going to *Fireclaw* for moral advice?" Van asked, incredulous.

"We already know he's not well controlled," Fireclaw told her, "and giving him a little bit of flirt and touch – maybe even a light kiss on the side of the muzzle in complete secrecy, you understand, might help us keep him very dedicated and very much in our camp."

"You should do it as if his mate is standing right there, kit," Van added, but then supplemented. "However, historically, his kit has been pretty open, herself, about other relationships. No dating or mating, my daughter, but you can flirt him up a bit. I'll *reluctantly* agree to that."

"I understand the operational boundaries you have set for me, and I will adhere to them out of love for you, my mother," Vosh promised.

A few intervals later, Vossia climbed the stairwell to the private overlook balcony having cast an over-the-shoulder glance at Delegate Rasalan. Had she been a normal Thurian, she would still have been easily able to read his admiration and interest. She could also tell that he was going to wait an appropriate amount of time before following her, but that he would, doubtless, follow her. She made sure that doors were closed and locked on the stairwell so that he wouldn't have any real options as he came after her. As she reached the balcony, she scanned looking for anything that might give away her presence or what she did here, and only one security camera was in evidence. With a quick projection, she made the camera vanish from view, cloaking it in a way so it would continue to send its current balcony scene.

As she waited, she considered the possibilities that this meeting would entail. "He ... likes me," she thought. It wasn't a computation, as it had been in the past; it was something where Fireclaw's training and friendship had influenced Vosh. Fireclaw had taught her to *feel*, a loose association of perceptions and biases synthesized into an average summation – an unsubstantiated abstraction of another individual's likes and dislikes and appreciations, especially about her. She understood, also, that based on her mission requirements, her exterior form was considered markedly beautiful. She had witnessed the Thurians' reactions to her body, and she was surprised that both the males and the females were drawn to her. She could see their eyes dilate, their lips get microshades darker, and their ears and tails change in movement at her masterful maneuvering of Delegate Bashir. Her act of dominance had been noted, and it was impressive enough that both males and females now wanted to follow her, or even wanted ... her. It was a curious aspect of her relatively new self-awareness that was intriguing and puzzling, all at the same time.

"My dear," Rasalan breathed. "That ... that is a truly long climb."

"Making Attoria successful will be, as well, Delegate Rasalan, but you have helped the effort considerably this night." It was said with a finality that brooked no contest, but still, he tried.

As he came closer, the Perratti told her, "I believe such as that over-praises me by many courses against what you were able to do. I have to ask, though, do you actually *have* the records you spoke about?"

"Of course, and to anticipate your next question, they do implicate Delegate Bashir as one of the Vanarrans' last remaining voices of representation in the assembly. He's done well in terms of what they've paid him, two million so far."

"And you just stole away all of that hubris and strut, ripping him exactly where it counts," he noted, reaching the balcony wall and looking up at her, admiringly. "Well done, Vossia. Well done."

"My gratitude for you, though, is genuine, as you played the able partner for me in this contest. Were you intrigued by my tactic of simply ignoring the conversation until all of the most obvious points had already been made?"

"That intrigued everyone, and you, dear Vossia, are now someone who is being asked after. Someone commented to me that it was ... difficult to locate you in the de Katscha family index."

She smiled down at him, reaching for and straightening his collar for a moment, gently, an action which he allowed with raised blush fur. "Intentional. I use a pet name of sorts for myself when I must interact in these circles; it enhances the mystery, you see. My real name is no more or less interesting than the one I used tonight, and I confess I gave you a very generic occupation, as well. While not at all incorrect, it would be folly to believe it is only financial investments I'm interested in. You, for example, are starting to become one of my better investments."

"How so?" he whispered quietly, and she leaned in close over his shoulder and whispered into his ear.

"By becoming an ally to me," she said in a husky voice that mingled seductiveness and danger equally. Leaning up, she looked at him sadly, "This I have done by freeing you from the traps of others, and so, I must not fall to the sweet temptation I feel and place you in yet another. After all, you have a very attractive and talented mate, but I get the sense that you have lost interest in one another. Here, my favored Delegate, is a little investment I make in the both of you. It's something you two can try if you haven't, and I believe it will draw you back together. It's only to be used on her, and it is something which doesn't work on me. Share this with her, as my gift to you both."

He took the envelope and opened it, looking at the contents. His blush furs raised, and he shook his head. "I'd heard ... stories about this, but I've never-"

"Then you *should*. You, dear Ras, are a good cub in very tempting surroundings. I could see how all of them were looking at me, tonight, and yes, you also. There was wanting in the eyes I saw. Some of the wanting was ... well, they wanted me as a female, but some of the wanting *was that* of a wise female *leader*. They want someone clever and strong to help protect them, and after Delegate Bashir's near abuse-"

"They were quite grateful for it. He had cowed them all, and then you-"

She put her paw alongside his muzzle and told him earnestly, "Showed them what it could mean to be kept by and keeper of, once again. I'm not the only one, Ras. I know I'm not. Your mate ... she has it in her, too. You should look to her for that, value her for that. You should love her enough to suggest it – encourage it."

He put his paw on hers and closed his eyes, pressing her paw into his muzzle. "I've been a fool. I was guilty of bedding that school kit, and ... she didn't care. She just accepted it, and she shouldn't have. I ... I can imagine that my own mate has also been untrue to me. Do you know that?"

"If I did, I wouldn't tell you. The two of you need to regain trust in one another, and *you* ... should start."

He let go of her and stepped back, his eyes full of emotions from want to gratitude to acceptance. "The Creator will bless the male who takes you as his own, if he hasn't already."

"I'm not spoken for, but I do sincerely appreciate the sentiment. Do not look for me or hope to hunt when you have already claimed, but simply heed my words and favor me with *that* affection, and I will be most pleased, indeed." She leaned down and kissed him gently on the top of the head. Then, she quietly walked away, leaving the Perratti standing alone on the balcony too stunned to even move. After about half a pass, he finally managed to utter in astonishment a single word. "Wow!"

Chapter 8: The Beginnings of Refuge

Akashar nervously and sadly paced back and forth in the small lobby of the restaurant he had invited Vanalla to, the one where he intended to tell her that they couldn't be a couple any longer. He was feeling close to her but watching everything transpire regarding the founding of the Attoria refuge touched him in ways he barely understood. Even his daily duties at FridgeTech no longer appealed to him as the calls from Fireclaw Destiny to come and be a part of a first in Thurian history drew him. "To be a part of time where we, as Thurians, decide not to repay evil with evil, choose not to shun difference and push it away or think it to be less than us, to … invest in a whole new species. A whole generation."

This was the calling of his heart, and he knew it. As he watched Vanalla enter the restaurant, beautiful as ever, Shar knew that now he had to face the consequences of choosing to follow the path he felt was meant for him. "Uh, hi," he breathed, taking her paw and gently holding it. "So good to see you."

"You, too, cub," she said, slipping closer and nuzzling him a little bit. That nearly made him whimper and give up. "You seem like something is on your mind, tonight."

"Yeah, I have a difficult decision to make, and I wanted to ask you about it," he said, realizing that wasn't true, but hoping it would be a better way to break it to her.

"I'm happy to help you, Shar," she told him earnestly. "Shall we go eat and then you can talk to me about it?"

"Sure, Van. Thank you. They have our table ready," he offered, directing her by way of an open paw in the direction of the only available table in the family style Taprician restaurant. After the few moments required for them to be seated and for the waitress to get their drink orders, he began, "I … am nervous about talking to you about this, because I don't want you to think I'm not doing this – or that I'm doing this to, well-"

"Shar," she offered, putting her paw on his. "It's tough for you, but I understand. Just tell me, and trust me that you can tell me, okay?"

He sighed and lowered his head, but he turned his paw around and clasped hers, gently. "Van, I'm … I'm feeling very strongly led to … to join the Attoria project. That would mean leaving Shanandrae, and it would mean leaving you."

"It will be difficult, Shar. It will be very difficult," she warned him.

He looked up, and he leaned towards her and whispered, "But I am perfect for what they need! I'm a trades worker, a good one – I have … lots of certifications, and I can help these orphans and homeless get theirs!"

"I don't doubt you could," she agreed, "but there are many Thurians who can do that. There has to be something special that's drawing you to this, and I think that before you make the decision you need to understand what it is."

"Van, I … I actually have decided," he admitted. "It barely took one night of thinking about it to know that this is the path I was made for. These kits and cubs, even the adults, will be coming to this place with no idea who they are, who they can be! I can help them with that! I know what that's like. I have almost three seasons of exercises and trials that I went through that I could pour into these – can you imagine what it would be like to be them, Vanalla? Just for an instant? Everything you've ever known is *lost* to you, and everyone is trying to fix you – turn you into something else. I know how not to do that and just be there for them. I was called to this, Vanalla. I'm sorry."

She reached out and opened her paw to him. "I think you've forgotten something about me, Shar."

"What's that?" he asked, confused.

"You expect for me to want to possess you, keep you here and not let you do what you were meant for. No, cub, that's not who I am.

For as long as I am alive, I will be there for you if you need me. *I'll take care of you*, and that is a promise that I *will never* break. You've already applied to the Attoria Foundation?"

"I want to. I want to do that, but I had to talk to you, first. It wasn't fair to do that until I had talked to you."

"You don't need to apply, Shar. I will talk to Fireclaw and the other leaders and get you set up for the first wave. There will be classes once you're there, and we've also managed to get one of the former Vanarran Selects there. You'll meet her. Her name is Vassia."

Akashar just looked at her. "You ... said once you were friends with Fireclaw. I ... I-"

"Didn't believe me?" she asked, smiling a little wickedly. "Then you are giving me a wonderful opportunity for you to believe in me, and that I want the best for you. Shar, I am so touched by your desires, here. You're right. You are perfect for them, and they can benefit so much from who you are and what you can mean to them."

"You're ... you're already part of this? The Attoria project?"

"I am involved," she told him, biting her lip for a moment before adding, "and that's all I'll say, for now. Shar, I don't want to pressure you into a relationship you wouldn't care for, but I enjoy being with you, and now I so deeply respect you not only for your struggle to make your own way, but for this, too! I want to help you and be there for you, even as you do this wonderful and giving thing."

He pulled away from her and bowed his head, his clasped paws at his forehead. He wept softly as his mouth moved in silent utterances she couldn't understand. Slipping beside him, she put her arm about his shoulder. "Shar, cub, are you okay?"

"Yes," he gasped softly, trying to recover his composure. "Yes."

"What ... what were you doing?"

"Thanking the Creator for you, for all you are to me. I thought that tonight I'd have to say goodbye to you and that I would leave one love for another. Are you so kind to me, Vanalla Ashallo, to grant me both? To not hate me for choosing this path?"

She leaned into him, circling her arms around his shoulder. "I will be there for you, my cub. I do not hate you for doing a noble and giving thing. I honor you for it."

He leaned into her, weeping. "Thank you. Thank you, Vanalla. So … so kind of you." Whispering into her ear, he breathed, "Please be with me tonight." He didn't even fully understand what he was asking or why other than he felt the intense need to hold onto her, drink her in completely in all the ways that were possible.

She nuzzled his ear and whispered, "Yes, my love. First, though, we eat, and you can tell me of your hopes and dreams for Attoria, and I will listen."

He nodded, and she sat back down. "Now, my cub, I have to confess that for a time, I must continue to live in Shanandrae to help those here who need me. I will be with you, though, frequently, where you are."

"Some time alone would help me get … my hind paws on the ground and figure things out," he told her. "I didn't want to lose you. Vanalla, I've … never felt closer to anyone than I do to you right now. You give me so much."

She could tell he was tearing up, and so she rubbed the side of his muzzle as she spoke, her voice ironic. "Yes, but … I left my stupid bracelet in the hover so … any chance you could take care of me, tonight?"

He looked up and nodded, whispering, "I will take care of you tonight, Vanalla. I will take care of you and show you what your patience means to me, what your support means, what your … love means to me. That you would give up so much for me."

"Oh, Shar," Van replied, her own eyes welling. "What you give to me, cub, will last in my heart, forever."

They spent the next interval talking about all of the problems and opportunities Attoria would have, and their conversation drew in several others who were interested since he was volunteering for the project. It allowed him to tell his story and even witness to others about the Creator's path. During all of this, Vanarra felt so warm and happy. "I feel him inside of there, Sahni, I do. Seeing him like this, I'm seeing my Ash as he would have been had he been allowed to grow up. What a beautiful heart he has."

"So unselfish," her inner Nephti remarked. "He looked upon his relationship with you as a luxury, something he had to weigh against the necessity of helping kits and cubs who are likely going to start out hating him, thinking nothing good about him at all. He loves you, Van. Tana and I feel it so clearly, but he is noble. In Alahari's time, he would have become a chief."

"His future living conditions may be close to that level of primitive simplicity, but I get the sense that it suits my dear cub. This … this is a relationship where I have to think differently, Sahni, so different than I'm used to. With Trax, I was dating him, pulling him in until what Shenaria did to claim him might not have been different than what I would have done. Trax, though, would have been secondary to the work I was doing, but Shar is going to be right in the middle of a big part of it."

"What will you do tonight, Van?" Sahni asked. "How far will you go? How far … should you go?"

"I'm … not in charge of that, kits," she told her inner companions. "I will accept being his and letting him set the pace of the hunt. Being loyal to him and what he wanted touched him so deeply. It's what I will do."

"Because you love him," Sahni asserted.

"Because I am love to him," Vanarra offered. "I am love offered without demands, and by my soul, I can be that for him. I am his mate, already, from when we lived and loved together in the archive all those seasons ago. We were and are joined in every important way."

"It's better than we did with Trax, teasing him so – testing him. Van, you … you are a better you, I think, when you're with him," Sahnassa offered gently.

"I'm praying that, after tonight, he'll still want to be with me, and then what of that sol when the mask falls away, and the Faelnar he's fallen in love with is not who he thinks she is."

Tana's voice, a true rarity in Van's thoughts, sailed through her mind as the mixed blood's consciousness was pulled in and drawn up. "Love him now, and that love will argue for you when we must tell him."

"Vanalla?" Shar asked quietly, putting a paw on her shoulder. "Are … are you okay? You seemed to just … I don't know, zone out for a moment. I was getting worried." She realized that the couple he had been talking to had walked away to pay, and it was just the two of them.

"And," Van replied, putting her paw on his shoulder, "I was having a very powerful epiphany, perhaps something I've missed my whole life. Shar, I will offer you my lair for tonight, as you asked. I want to be close to you, but how close, my cub, is your choice. Don't do anything tonight to impress me or try to please me, make me happy. I just want to be with you, regardless of whatever we would do. I will not set boundaries, nor will I offer expectations or demands, either."

"Van?" he questioned her, putting his paw alongside her muzzle.

"I'm yours, Shar," she told him softly. "I'm here … for you. For whatever you need."

He rubbed her cheek gently as he brought her closer to his head. "I was a fool to think I had to give you up in order to serve in Attoria. You told me you would be there for me. I don't deserve you, but what … what you're giving me, I am so grateful for. I would love to see your lair, Van. I would love to spend time with you."

She leaned in and nuzzled against him. "Can I drive us, please?" she asked. "I would bring you back to your hover."

Her entreaty struck him in a peculiar way, as if a part of her spirit she'd never shown him was in control. Normally, he'd want to make sure it would be okay, but he realized that she was promising, implicitly, to take care of it for him and what's more, take care of him. "Yes. I'll go pay."

"I'll be along in just a moment," she told him. Trusting, he nodded and stepped away. "Excuse me," she asked the manager who happened to walk by at that moment.

"Yes, lovely one," he questioned in a thick Taprician accent, "what can I do for you, now?"

"The … little patchwork hover in the corner of your lot. Can you please make sure it's okay parking here overnight?" She reached out and put several large notes into his paw.

Smiling, the elder Vulpi turned her paw over and folded her paw fingers around the money. "Keep it. I saw your kindness to him, and I will make sure all will be well when you return. Go, and let the Creator's grace go with you."

"And with you. Honor to you," she replied, touched.

"And to you," he said. She stood then, went to Shar's side and took his paw and then followed him as he led the way to her hover.

When they entered her lair, he looked around. "It's very nice, Vanalla. Very lovely. A reflection of the owner?"

"A little," she confessed. "The previous owner, a friend of mine, did the decorating. However, her tastes and mine are similar." She then felt his paw at her back, gently guiding her. Her first instinct was to question what he was doing, but Van had decided that this night, she would not. She, as she had stated, was fully his, and that was something she deeply wanted him to know. He guided her to the couch and sat her down. Instead of sitting beside her, he knelt in front of her, loosed her hind paws from their shoes, and set them aside. Then, he simply stared up at her for a few moments.

"You are amazing, Vanalla. I only truly see it, now, and I sense this letting go inside of you. Why? Why are you so kind?" She knew the question was rhetorical, and she simply smiled back at him. Nodding back, he then looked around. "If I may … rearrange things a little?" he asked, and she nodded. In a few passes, he had moved the low table between the sofas out of the way and laid a comforter on the floor, throw pillows pulled down laid in front of her. Looking at the window, he then went over and turned off the lights. Curious, but accepting, Van just waited for him. In the relative darkness, she was still able to see him remove his belt and paw shoes and empty out his pockets. Then, he walked over to her and gently took her paws. "I … honestly have no idea why I'm doing this," he breathed, "but, would you come down here with me, please?"

With no complaint or question, no resistance at all, she allowed herself to be led to the center of the floor and guided into a sitting position. "I don't understand this," he confessed. "This just feels right, and your face in this light is just amazing – otherworldly." He reached out and stroked her muzzle and cheek. "It's like you're not even the same individual, maybe not even Faelnar." She watched, with interest, as his eyes roamed her face and then the room around them. "Odd feeling – like even the walls are different. What's happening, Vanalla?"

"I don't know, Shar," Van whispered, "but I know I'm here with you, and that has its own kind of magic."

"Like echoes of a life I never had," he breathed. Then, he just stared at her, uncertain. She reached out and unbuttoned his shirt and started rubbing her paw across his chest.

"If it would please you, you could rest your head in my lap," she told him softly. Biting his lip, he shuffled down to do as she suggested, and soon, they had settled into this new position, and Shar was amazed at how wonderful it felt. Her scent was all around him, and her paws stroked his ears and head along with his chest. It emptied him of worries, of thoughts, and of any appreciation of time. "Are you okay?" she asked softly.

"In a way, I've never been okay until this moment," he admitted, and tears were rolling down his cheek fur. "Sweet, sweet kit. You take care of me in ways I barely understand. Who are you that you could do this?"

She answered, and the words that came from her muzzle she couldn't stop. "I am yours, and it's like I have been for hundreds of seasons. You were the very first to capture my heart, and like two Thurians from ancient times reborn, we are together, and the connection between us has appeared again as if we had never lost it. It takes us and pulls us inside, and all that time we lost fades away because I am again yours, and you are mine, and that is the way of it."

"You are so amazing, Vanalla. I can see things in this way, and it's unlike anything I've ever seen. The room is different, even you."

Still lost in the moment, she asked, "How am I different?"

"I still see you as you are, a beautiful Faelnar, but there is more. There is some other aspect to you that was hidden until now. There is light around you I can't fathom, and it's like an echo of your own soul."

"Can you tell me what it's like? I can't see it," Van asked softly, but her interest was starting to pique in a way that was different than a simple romantic encounter. Inside of her, both Tana and Sahni seemed to lean forward, listening to the answer.

His eyes were half lidded, and he shrugged, his words betraying the comfort and drowsiness he was starting to feel. "Like all around you is being lit with a soft light, but it's coming through you, as well. I don't understand. It feels like I'm seeing it, but not seeing it." He raised his arm and cradled her cheek with his paw. "I'm ... doing it a little, too, but it's like a trick of the eyes. I'm not sure it's even there. I'm not making any sense."

"Just rest in me, then, and I'll take care of you," she offered, her voice soft and sweet. Her gentle rubbing of his chest and head continued to grant him a comfort and contentment he had never felt before, and it touched him. Just as he was about to nod off, he heard Vanalla whisper, "You're the best thing I've ever found."

"You," he ventured at a whisper, "are the best thing ever to find me." At her crooning approval, he finally relaxed and let go – a full sol's worth of worry having burnt his mental energies, and the relief from it too entrancing to resist.

Sometime later, Shar's eyes opened up, and he didn't remember where he was. He felt the legs behind his head and soft paws touching him and couldn't remember who this was. "Don't worry, Shar. It's just me."

"Van ... Vanalla, what are you doing?"

"Letting you rest, and hopefully in a way that's not too disturbing for you."

"It's really amazing, being here with you," he intoned, wonderstruck. "This is new, between us, but ... it feels like an echo of something long ago, maybe before I can even remember. I hope I don't sound too mixed up."

"Maybe, cub, but I like you and care for you so much."

Looking up at her, he just shook his head gently, "Van, you're gorgeous. So ... beautiful."

"And you are wonderfully keen in the most important way."

"What's that?" he asked.

"You have a beautiful soul, Akashar, the most beautiful I've ever met." He sat up then and faced her, his eyes searching her expression. She leaned over and licked him on the side of the muzzle. Then, she looked up at him, her eyes holding his with a question. He looked at her and tenderly returned her affection, his whole body seeming to flood with joy and warmth as he did so.

Wanting even more with her, he slid closer, gently pinning her body between the couch and his own chest. Reaching forward, he gently held her cheek, drawing her in. He stopped, concern coloring his expression, "Do we have enough time for such a … distraction?"

"I am yours, and we have all the time in the world, just for us," she breathed, and he drew her into a long and loving kiss.

Dear Diary,

I've been flipping back through our conversations over the last three seasons, and it's only now that I realize how stagnant my life has been. If it weren't for your enduring patience, I'm not sure I would be able to keep this relationship going. My world has changed so much in just the last three moons. I said goodbye to FridgeTech and enjoyed a much warmer send off than I ever thought I would see. They loved me, cared about me, and I didn't understand that thoroughly until I was saying farewell. I left Shanandrae, the only home I can remember – the place where my memories begin. I thought I was going to leave everything and everyone, but I'm grateful to tell you, Diary, that it's not the case.

You see, I finally let someone else into my life, and it's made all of the difference. Vanalla waited on me through all of the therapy, and she has added a magic to my life that I can't explain. I don't deserve this. I know it, but still, she gives it to me. What's more is that, when we're together, she will wait for me to make a decision, to set the direction – for her, that's amazing. I have seen her, just a little, in her role at the hospital. She's assertive. She's direct. She can even be confrontational if she has to, but when she's with me, I become the center of her universe. I become the one she defers to in all of her choices. It's an amazing feeling to be loved like this, and like I said, I don't deserve it, but it is as if she is telling me that everyone else, including her own self, has less value in her eyes than I do.

We had just started dating after all of that time she waited when I felt called to come here, to Attoria, and serve. I thought she would think I was abandoning her, doing her the gravest injustice – she praised me, Diary, and has supported me. She helped me pack and purchase the things I'd need, and she helped me get chosen to serve here. Every few sols, she comes and visits me. We spend time together, and it's magical. No, it really is! The first night we spent together, I was so nervous, I didn't know what to do, so I just laid out a blanket on the floor. Something started happening then that has happened almost every time we've been together.

According to Doctor Emma, my memories are gone forever, physically not accessible. When I'm with Van, though, I see things. That first night, I saw the inside of this place almost overlaying my vision, somewhere rough and barely constructed with cinder blocks and bricks and power-pack lighting. All of this while Van was touching me, and when we talked, it was like an echo of a conversation I could almost remember. It's happened a few other times, too. When I was walking her down one of the new nature trails Laxar and I helped build, she stepped ahead on the path, and I followed her. I could almost see another form, another female, walking in her place, and the outside of her form seemed to glow in a half light I couldn't explain. I didn't tell her about that time.

She is the light of my life, but even more, she seems to be a light into my past. I thought about reaching out to Doctor Emma, but I don't want to. Part of me feels very strongly that this is my path, what I must walk down. It's also just that, a path. I feel like there is a destination I can actually reach, and I feel that Vanalla Ashallo points the way for me. She follows me and what I say when she's around, but what she doesn't realize is that I am following her, and every time I feel it even more.

This place makes me feel it, too. I was afraid to interact with the kits and cubs who were brought here, the former Vanarrans now called Aelkinda. She, that magnificent Faelnar kit, can play and love on kids like I don't even know. I, who don't remember my own childhood, get to see what one is like through watching her. When she was away, I decided to try to join Fireclaw and some of the older cubs and kits in a game of whisk. Being in that game, playing with kids, I caught flashes of other children, mixed bloods like me. Fireclaw saw me looking around at one point and asked me if I was okay. I swear to you that, for a moment, I saw a real thin cub that wasn't there before, but I knew him. Then, he was gone.

So, who was I? The answers I have now are very little, but I was maybe someone who played with other kids, but maybe we were very poor and didn't get to eat much. I was also a male in love with a magnificent female, and we were certainly poor, but we were happy. She was special, glowing, and I don't know why we parted, but somehow, I see her only in Vanalla. I never see her in Vassia or Fireclaw or any of the other female volunteers. She must be gone now, I guess, and maybe her spirit is somehow living in Vanalla. I think about questioning her about these visions I have, but I don't want to. I don't want to scare her. I want to love her. So, that's, Diary, my life right now – living in Attoria, serving in Attoria, and loving Vanalla, the most amazing female I've ever known.

Akashar woke in his cabin and slipped up onto his hind paws. He splashed a little water on his face before pulling a bottle out and drinking his fill of the same. Looking around, he smiled. It felt good to him to wake with the sun, and it was the rising of the light in the room through its single window which had brought him gently out of sleep. "This is how Thurians should live," he sighed. It was a comfortable time of the season, and perhaps cooler weather would convince him that his romanticism wasn't as well founded, but so far, he enjoyed being a resident of the Attoria refuge. The thoughts of walking underneath the boughs of ancient harlock and aster trees, the light-dappled forest floor, through the small meadows and clearings, were more than enough to get him started. After using the small facilities present in the cabin, he cleaned himself up a little and slipped outside into the cool morning air to find his breakfast.

Walking towards the dining hall, he looked around at the small collection of simple buildings that had been put together or taken pre-fab from generous donors at the start of the project. It was a project that had a plan that would carry Attoria from this very humble beginning forward until, perhaps, with a generation or two's work, a small village would exist. Then, as time passed by, that village might well become a town. That town had the possibility of becoming a major metropolis, just as Lasrihal had. "And here stand I," he breathed out as he looked at the small lake with its dock, one he had helped put together.

"Hey, cub," a female voice called to him from nearby. Looking over, he saw Fireclaw and smiled. He was just starting to get over his star-struck feelings every time he saw her, and it was something she really appreciated, being treated like a normal Thurian.

"Morning, Fireclaw," he greeted as she approached him with a steaming mug of tea. "Oh, thank you."

"Fireclaw," the mixed blood mused. "Yeah, that's what I am, isn't it? Fireclaw Destiny, the great primal star. Well, officially now a primal star *has been*, but still."

He sipped and looked back at the lake before he answered. "You don't want to be those things, anymore or … you don't feel you are?"

"You think my original name was actually Fireclaw Destiny?" she asked, scoffing. "Yeah, right! Tashara de Gonari, that was me. My parents were still members of that family when they had me, but at some point, it just wasn't worth it, and so I became Tashara Sahari. The neighborhood kits and cubs cut that down to Tash, well, until I hit puberty, and then I became, 'Little Van' or 'Vannie' or 'Van-wanna-be.'"

"Children can sometimes be pretty cruel," he offered by way of comfort. "They just don't understand how hurtful they're being."

Fireclaw took a sip of her tea and replied, "Doesn't stop it from smarting, though. That's kind of where I started getting the idea of looking like Vanarra de Gonari. Dance and athletics courses went well for me, and so my parents put me in the tryouts. Next thing I know, I'm in the primals juniors competitions."

"So, the rest was history?" he queried.

"Yeah, kind of sorry history, if I'm honest about it. I worked hard just so I could beat the others and get bragging rights, and the more I bragged, the better I had to get. It's this whole mess, and so one sol, there I am in a hospital room, my career about to go in the dump when your dear Vanalla shows up. Incredible kit, that one. More than you can know."

"It surprised me when she said you were a friend of hers," he told her.

"It still surprises me, sometimes, that she'd have me. I was a real piece of work. Oh, hey there, Vosh! You sleep alright?"

The dark and serious-looking Vulpi nodded as she approached. "All is well this morning with you?"

"Yep, I was just telling him about my old name, Tashara Sahari." The Vulpi's searching stare at both of them, her head cocking slightly to the side, made the mixed blood chuckle. "Dammit, Shar, you can totally see when she's really thinking of something that's going to totally kick your hind paws out from beneath you."

Shar smiled and chuckled a little, for he had been the target of Vosh's somewhat direct observations from time to time. It wasn't anything he could ever deny, but her insights were sometimes just a little too direct for his taste. "Alright, Vosh," he breathed out in a sigh. "Fire away. Otherwise, you'll just be polite and not say anything-"

"And then we'll totally wonder all sol what it was you were going to say," Fireclaw continued, "until it drives us crazy and we come to ask you, anyway."

"It is a logical tactic," the Vulpi said with just a hint of tease in her voice. "No, it's just that both of your names might be something you want to revisit. Might I ask who came up with the name Fireclaw Destiny?"

"I did," she replied without affectation. "It was one of my coaches, though, who suggested I needed a fierce performance name. I was digging around in some dusty old histories and ran across the name Tanatta Fireclaw from Vanarra's time, and I just got a bit creative."

"You could reclaim your prior name here, and it would make you more approachable to the children. It would also demonstrate that you can make choices about who you are and how you wish to be known. For these once-Vanarran youths, that is an important lesson."

"Such a small group we have, though," Fireclaw sighed. "Heartbreaking when we know there are hundreds of others out there, from what Vassia has said, anyway. I agree, Vosh, maybe. So that's me, what about Akashar – only if you want to know, cub."

"I'll listen. Vosh's words seldom if ever don't have value."

"It is just a question," she asked him. "Do you feel lost and abandoned in your life, now? Without purpose?"

Fireclaw smiled and put her paw on his shoulder, gripping it gently. "I guess not," he confessed. "It's taken a long time to get here, but no. I have friends and someone who loves me. I have a home and place where I feel I matter."

"I should say, given how much of this place you've helped build," Fireclaw assured him, dropping her paw. "And, knowing you, there'll be another cubs' cabin built by late this evening, right?"

"It … was what I was hoping for," he confessed. "Those two new cubs are coming, the pre-teens?"

"We're getting them once the hospital states they are in good enough condition for discharge," Fireclaw told them. "They were too malnourished for us to take care of. They needed medical help first, and we'll still have to keep an eye on them once they get here. The legal part is done; the Vanarrans lose them – end of story."

Vosh nodded. "And so here you are, Akashar, not lost and not abandoned with a true and noble purpose, held in honor and respect by your friends for the loyal contributions you make to the helpless. That, and you are deeply loved by Vanalla."

"True," he replied, his head lowering a bit as he blushed. Looking up, he asked, "Okay, so what would you suggest?"

"The name Ashalam means *promised one* but it can also mean *promised place*, a potent counterpoint to your current choice. In tribal times, the term was often used to describe the dowry given in a marriage or a piece of land awarded to a favored son or heroic warrior. I think it suits you."

He looked at her, askance. "You know that's pretty similar to the name of Vanalla's cub, the one she said I reminded her of when we first met."

"Yes, it was his name, and he is the one she lost, who died when she was very young."

Shar shook his head and disagreed. "I don't know that I can fill the paw shoes of another Thurian, Vosh, especially in this way."

The Vulpi stepped forward a little and spoke softly. "You would not be asked to. Remember, he was taken from her when both she and he were comparative children, and you are certainly not that. You are more. However, I have noted that when a couple loves one another, part of what they see in each other is real and part is fantasy, at the start. Successful couples are the ones who accept each other's fantasies and try, in some degree, to make them real. It can be specifics about intimate desires or support of a lifelong dream or a treasured career, but in this case, it would be a memoriam, an honorarium."

"I don't know if she'd like it. It might bother her. I'm none too sure it wouldn't bother me."

"Just think about it, please, Shar," the Vulpi bade. "You are *not* a lost land, and your presence in Vanalla's life returns to her a love she thought she'd never repeat, one she was willing to wait a long time to find once again."

"This … cub she loved, has she ever talked about him to either of you?" he queried.

"She has," Fireclaw mentioned. "I didn't know his name was Ash, but she said he was someone who – I guess the way she put it – she couldn't hide her emotions from, and in his presence, she was always vulnerable, but always safe. I think she feels that way with you, cub. She acts differently around you than she does anyone else."

"How so?" he questioned, downing the last of the tea, but now truly curious.

Fireclaw spoke up after chuckling. "She is assertive, aggressive even, and exceptionally confident. It's not pride, mind you – she really is that damn good. Oh, the tricks she played on me to set me straight, and no, I'm not going into those because I am embarrassed by them, not Van. She is … she is…"

"She is more than what everyone sees," Laxar mentioned quietly. As Fireclaw and Shar turned around, he bowed to them. "Good morning, and I apologize for interrupting, but she was also the one who helped rescue me and found me a home with Javoth. She strongly defends and ably guides. Her heart is true and burns brightly for those she cares for, and it never fails to love."

"Sounds like you are the one in love with her, Laxar," Shar teased, biting his lip a little.

"She is my guide and defender, perhaps a replacement for a mother I never knew, but she is your *love*, Shar. Never doubt that is the truth."

"Did you hear what we were talking about, though?" Shar asked him. "Changing our names, and … me changing mine to match someone she lost growing up?"

"When you awoke, you told me you had no memory of what your name was, and it was from your sadness and loneliness you chose Akashar," the young mixed blood contested. "I say this out of caring for you, my friend. You are lost no longer, in any respect."

Shar looked at the ground and sighed. "You and Vosh sure both share that talent for stating the truth, I suppose. I won't argue with you. I'll ... I'll think about it, okay? I might talk to Javoth, first."

"I would agree," Laxar offered, putting his paw on Shar's shoulder. "Father is very wise about such things, and I would defer to his guidance over my own."

"What you state is sound, young Laxar," Vosh told him, nodding. "There still remains the subject of Fireclaw's name."

"I'm sorry? That ... was up for a change, too?" the youth asked, but his smile drew wide at Fireclaw's embarrassment.

"Tashara Sahari," Fireclaw huffed, "my name *before* I became a primal star. I mean, I had it officially changed and everything. My legal name is now *Fireclaw Destiny*."

"Mine is registered just as properly," Shar chuckled. "Doesn't look like it's going to save me, either."

At that moment, all of their ears turned in the direction of the children's cabins. "The kits are awake and ... arguing, again," Fireclaw groaned.

"I shall attend to it," Vosh told them. "I will resolve their conflict and bring them to the breakfast table in good order. Laxar, would you again tend to the males?"

"I will, although it may take me a little ... longer to get them to the table. Really sleepy bunch, and yes, I did check in on them to make sure they weren't staying up late."

"Alright, Shar, let's get the rest of it going, okay, cub?" Fireclaw asked, and he nodded and walked away with her back towards the dining structure. After they were a few steps away, she asked, "You going to give any of that a serious thought?"

"What about you?" he asked, and she shrugged. "It's ... a lot to take in. Our names define who we are, but maybe mine doesn't fit me so well anymore. We'll see."

"Fair enough," she responded as they stepped down the gravel path.

Chapter 9: The Simpler Life

"Hello there! Good morning!" Vanalla called up to Shar as he was putting the finishing touches on the roof of the new cabin. "It looks about done!"

"Pretty close!" he replied, calling down to her. "It always takes just a little longer than I think it will. However, Attoria is really starting to shape up!" As he finished laying down the last layer of insul-shield, he asked her, "How are things going with Attoria from where you are?"

"Well, I can't complain about the view," Vanalla told him, her voice just loud enough to carry to where he was. He looked down at her and smiled, but then went back to work. "Shanandrae and Attoria are doing ... reasonably well."

"Sounds like you're soft-pawing it, a bit."

"Well, there's a lot to figure out, and not all of it is pleasant."

"There! All done," he called and slipped over to the ladder that was laying across one slanted angle of the roof. As he moved to the ground, Shar told her, "A few more residents will be able to call this their home, now."

"It does look good Shar, and ... so do you," she told him, greeting him with an embrace and a quick lick on the side of the muzzle.

"Sorry," he apologized. "I must smell."

"I like your scent, cub," Van told him, embracing him again, closer and more intimately this time. "I'm looking forward to spending a little time with you, if that is your wish." He pulled back and just looked at her for a moment, and she asked, "Have I ... done something wrong?"

"You, dear Van, are about the most perfect female a male ever had the privilege of hunting, but I'm getting to know you a bit more through the friends you have, here. How you act around me, and how they seem to think you act around them – the two don't match up. Laxar, last evening, was telling me how cunning you were – Javoth, too! Fireclaw started to tell on herself a little bit, at least as far as the hospital stay. The thing is, Van, I'm ... I'm wondering if you're not letting yourself be as free and independent when I'm around."

She looked away from him and stepped a bit away, putting some distance between them. "Don't get me wrong, love," he added consolingly. "You are simply amazing to me, but ... are you caging yourself? Are you putting yourself in a muzzle or on a lead?"

"Sometimes," she said quietly, "I have to be the one who drives things ahead, and I have more than my fair share of experience barking out instructions and directing everyone else. Fireclaw and Laxar ... aren't wrong; I'm good at figuring out how to get things done, even if it's just protecting someone. What if ... what if I don't want to be like that all the time? What if I've discovered, over the seasons, that I ... that I want to be led. I want to know someone I can trust with that, and I want to be able to give control, not just take it. Do you not like that about me?"

He walked forward and put his paw on her shoulder. "I never saw the difference. I never knew about this different you, because you've kept her hidden. I, honestly, love how you defer to me – it makes me feel something I don't know that I've felt before." She looked into his eyes, and he told her, "Respected, maybe even worthy of that respect. I don't mind being with you, and I treasure and even feel a little guilty, sometimes, when you step back and let me choose. It makes me wonder if I'm ... loving you the way you want to be loved. The way you ... desire to be."

His brush of her muzzle with the back of his paw spoke of the gentle and superficial intimacies they had shared. She closed her eyes and held his paw against the side of her cheek. "In my last ... relationship, I charged ahead on that path too quickly, and I hurt the one I was with – confused him and upset him. I know you are a male, Shar, and I know you have desires. I do, too, but again, why should I lead you? Why should I make demands when even watching how you approach me, how you love me, tells me all the more about you? You're not doing it to tease me; you're going slow because you truly want to go no faster. I am here for you, and I will take care of you. I wish to show you my love by serving you, stepping behind you on the path."

"Will I ever get to see the strong and powerful huntress they all talk about?" he asked, biting his lip a little. "Will I ever get to see her stand up to Doctor Emma and give her what for?"

She stepped back and smiled at him. "I am not what I seem, Shar, and neither are you. Part of that, I think, is because we are being graceful to one another as we learn one another. Part of that, I think, is because we want to protect the other. Seeing me in a real rage, trying to blood and kill my target, is ... a bit much. In my first joining, it took a real hard sit down, one sol, where my mate told me I wasn't being tender enough. I was the aggressive one, and ... that was hard to take sol in and sol out. This time, I've resolved to do things differently, if it's alright with you."

He reached down and took her paw. "It heartens me to know you have strength, even if you refrain from using it on me. I do want to know that part of you, though. Could you just tell me about it, like what you're doing to help this place come out alright?"

She looked at him and then buried her head in his neck. "I can try. I'll walk with you if you want?"

"By the moons, Van," he almost groaned out as he held her. "What a treasure you are. Do you ... know about this place? About its history? Any ... secrets about it?"

"I know some, and what I know is yours." She slipped out from under him and then just held his paw. "If we could go in the direction of the dining hall and then beyond it." He nodded, and they began to walk. "A lot of what this place is known for is, of course, the massacre that occurred here, but the massacre wasn't the only crime. This was a village of only Vulpi, and it had been made that way very carefully over time. When others tried to settle here, applications were denied; permits were lost, and even court cases challenging the exclusivity of the place were overturned. After a while, its all-Vulpi heritage was taken as a matter of fact, and the other houses which might have wanted to lay claim to this region were discouraged from doing so."

"Several of them wanted it? Why?"

"The Attoria valley is very rich in natural resources, and those resources are largely still untapped to this sol. It's how we hope to turn what is basically a refugee camp of banished individuals into a thriving village, city, and maybe even metropolis, at some point."

"It's strange to look at all this and imagine that it will turn into something as big as say, Shanandrae or even Windston. I hate to say it this way, Vanalla, but at this point … it's just kind of improbable – on the face of it."

"On the face, it is. The money is only going to last so long as Thurians feel charitable about this place. The Vanarrans are a hostile if thoroughly-beaten group of would-be colonists. Some of them hate each other as much as they hate purebred and pure mixes. They know next to nothing about farming, mining, construction, or anything else someone would need to know living in a rural setting." As they walked past the dining hall and towards a small path in the forest beyond, she continued, "There are a million different mistakes we can make, also – everything from picking the wrong crops, not enough of them, too much of them, to not making sure we keep a viable breeding age population. If you don't pay attention, two hundred seasons from now this could be a ghost town with only one or two elderly individuals still hanging on. Everything we've built could fall apart."

"Sounds … very intimidating," he confessed. "How do we manage all of that?"

"Well, first we have some very good Thurians helping us out," she stated, looking up at him with a degree of admiration that he found utterly captivating. Smiling, she looked back towards the path and continued. "We also have some experts in many different fields committing to come here and be a part of this for the long term. Initially, both they and we will direct what goes on here. Javoth's job is very important, as he and Laxar can help persuade the Vanarrans that they would be better off thinking of themselves as Aelkinda, and not mindless devotees of some Great Mother. Then, they can decide on their own which path to take. It will build, sol by sol, moon by moon, and season upon season. For example, the forest we're walking through right now used to be a very fertile field for uva plants. This ground raises very good creele, and it has a good herd of wild grazers that roam through it – feral ones we can domesticate."

"Uh, prowlers?"

"Prowlers, too, and something to be wary of, but nothing big. Most of them will see you and just run away," Van told him, but then something caught her attention. "There … look up. You see those branches intertwined, woven together? That's original, Shar. That dates back to the time of the massacre. Amazing that those harlocks have held on for so long."

Shar walked around them, looking up. "It's … it's curious. It's like there were two of them, originally, but then these others grew up and were sort of pulled up almost as supports around them. That, and they are in the middle of the forest – lots of cover from bad winds and storms. Thanks to that hilltop over there, they aren't the biggest things in the world, either. Tall enough to … survive brush fires, I'd bet."

"I would say you're right," she told him. "Now, history says that these were treasured by the Attorian Vulpi, but the reason is a little … ominous. You see, this is the path they were led down to be controlled, put into rut trance."

"Do we … go ahead?"

"If you'd like," she responded, smiling at him. He realized, then, that she was asking for his trust, and smiling back at her, he nodded. As they continued, she explained, "Vulpi who had entered puberty were brought here during their second rut or a rut soon after. When their younger friends saw them returning as adults in the eyes of the village, every kit or cub wanted a turn at the secret ritual. The poor victims of this control were trained to advertise it, tease it to the others so that there would always be a willingness and curiosity to see it through. We're passing, right now, what used to be the first of three altars where those accompanying the initiates on their *journey* would encourage them, even as some stayed behind."

"Strange sort of metaphor," Shar reasoned. "I wonder why."

"It increased the peer pressure to actually get them under these arches and on the path, and once on the path, there were only so many options in a dark forest."

"So, what was at the end of this trail?"

"A cave temple to the Faelnar who were the god and goddess of the village. The right sorts of drugs would be administered in *ceremonial* drinks and injected, and the result was a Vulpi pushed well beyond the threshold for rut trance."

"Okay, that was there, then. What's there, now?" he queried.

"When Laxar and Javoth agreed to come here, Laxar was already a budding artist. Over the seasons, actually, he's gotten very good at it, and moving here meant leaving his studio. So, with a little of my own resources, I might have just ... fixed things up for him a bit. It's his studio, now, and he's given his permission for us to visit it."

"Now, this I have to see!" Shar stated, clearly excited to look at the art of one of his new friends. In a few passes, they were standing before a locked door fixed into the mouth of a cave, set back slightly and sealed perfectly. "Okay, this ... is very interesting." He walked up and examined it closely. "Very professionally done – stabilized the rock and everything."

"Wait until you see inside," she chuckled and then opened the door for him. What greeted his eyes was nothing short of a cave of wonders, with colored hanging glass and a carved pathway and lights tucked into special alcoves in the walls.

"Oh, this ... this is beyond anything I could have imagined. Wow! And ... and are these his paintings?!" She nodded, smiling at him. He just shook his head as he looked around. Then, he took a sniff. "Hey, it's ... conditioned air?"

"It is. A small power unit hidden behind the hill provides the light and ventilation. It helps keep his things in good condition. This place can also serve as a refuge, if we need it."

"Yeah, I've thought about that, especially after more of the Vanarran adults come in. Just ... just amazing," he breathed as he walked around and then looked at a beautiful painting of Vanalla. "I told you that kid has a thing for you," he teased.

"He has reason to, as I helped him at the hospital. However, he knows that I am Akashar's, not Laxar's, when it comes to the hunt." Although it was said in good humor, something about it made Shar frown a bit. "What's wrong?"

"Well, a little – can we sit for a bit?" he asked. She sat on a nearby stool and just waited for him, studying him. After he sat down, he took a deep breath. "Last morning, there was a little conversation about ... well, names. Fireclaw, yeah, since she's no longer a primal star and only adopted that name legally for performance purposes. She's considering giving it up, or at least legally changing her name back to what it was – Tashara Sahari or even maybe Tashara de Gonari. The subject also came up about ... my name."

"Your name is lovely. I've grown quite attached to it, not to mention the Thurian who bears it."

He smiled at her compliment, but then shook his head. "I'm grateful, but it doesn't really describe me, anymore. Am I ... abandoned land, anymore? Am I forgotten with no purpose? Am I alone? No. Thanks to you and others like Doctor Emma, I'm kind of found, now. Especially since I've found the Creator's Path, I mean – I should have dropped the name right there. Would it bother you if I did?"

She closed her eyes and took a breath. "It would take some getting used to, but I would. I love the Thurian who bears the name Akashar, not the name of Akashar. What would you choose? Have you given it any thought?"

He stood up, nervously, and started pacing a bit. "Well, that's the tough part of the discussion right there, then, isn't it? I don't have my memories from before I met you, Vanalla, but I remember very well ... everything that happened after. One of those moments, the first instant I really saw you, you said a name to me."

"No, Shar," Van nearly whispered as her paws lighted over her heart. "You don't have to do that. If one of the others..."

"Someone reminded me, and not of the name, but of the fact that mine wasn't right for me – not now. They also let me know its meaning, which you never told me. In fact, you've been so good about not mentioning this cub that I know you truly do not love him in my place. I can see that you haven't tried to put me in his place; if you had, this would have never worked between us. You could have told me to dress a certain way, talk a certain way, like certain things – all of those would have just been masks on top of the real me. You have gotten to know the real me. I can see that. You give everything to me. You let me choose whatever I wish when we're together. You've listened and given and been there for me. I owe you a huge debt for that."

"That's because I love you, Shar," Vanalla whispered. "You don't have to change anything for me."

"It's not for you, alone, love," he told her, drawing closer. "I'm very sorry to say that … it's also for me. Your kindness and patience have changed my life – given me a new life, and I want to be a living memorial to your love and stand in the stead of the one you lost. I want to love you because he can't love you, hold you because he can't hold you, and spend forever with you making up for what fate stole from you. I want to destroy, forever, the regret you feel when you say and think that name, and I want you to know that I care for you that much. I want to be like him in one way and one way, only – I want to stand in your love, Van. I don't … I don't have a bracelet for you, but my name – this name I give back to you. Will you let me do this?"

Vanalla whimpered and put her head in her paws, crying, and he held her, wrapping her with his arms. As she wept, the cave around them seemed to change, and a ghost image covered his vision once again. "Please, call me that name and let me know that I've done at least that much good in your life."

"I'm … sorry … Ash," she wept, snuggling into his body.

"Who have you even been able to talk to about him, Van, since he died?"

"No … one, really. It hurt so much to lose him. It ripped me apart!"

"I'm so sorry. Just cry, Van. Just cry until you can't. You're due that. You're due."

She pulled up and looked at him, dumbfounded. "Echoes of what he told me so long ago … what you just said."

"I feel something, Van, when we're close like this. My memories before, I don't have, but … I see that place, again – cinder blocks and dust and the hum of machines and air, like we're sitting behind some air pushers. It's so strange, Van, but maybe I just see a bit of who he was, through your eyes." Taking his blank stare from the wall, he just looked at her. "You're my anchor, now. You're the one I hold onto and the one I love. Let me be your promised one, please?"

"With all my heart," she cried, reaching around and hugging him. "With all my heart!"

The next sol, aboard the Haven, a merging was taking place that had happened at least twice every season since Trax had wed Shenaria, save for the period that Sahnassa was pregnant with her son, Dashar, named after his father, Dasahar. The magnificent power, Vanassa, was coming into being once again – the perfect melding of the two friends into one being who would, one sol, be the incarnation of their single, mutual future. Sometimes, the merging brought her into being on Thuriana, the Thurian colony created by the Allarrae. However, this time, it was aboard the Haven that she was being formed, leaving an unconscious and helpless Sahnassa on the other end of the connection.

As Vanassa blinked her eyes open, she looked up into the monitor and turned her head to the side. "I don't get used to seeing that, and I don't like it," she complained.

Amyra and Rahnahi, beings already ascended long ago after their lives on Thuria, looked at her curiously. "Dear, why not?"

Vanassa slipped off the table and stood on her own hind paws, and she looked troubled. "Rahnahi, it's like looking at a picture of yourself as a baby, but like when you were very ill and not looking like you'd … survive. Really kind of creepy in a way knowing that she's really back there comatose on Thuriana, and I'm here, but not permanent."

"Well, it will come some sol; you know that. You feel stronger each time, right?"

"I do, or at least I have been," she confessed, but then templed her paw fingers and closed her eyes. "Give me just a moment to … ah, that's it. Wow, I've been doing some complex living in the past few moons, haven't I?"

"They have," Amyra asked her, a gentle smile on her lips. "So, what's got you fussed about it?"

"I think … this comes from dealing with … Ash," Vanassa explained as if she had slipped her paws across a smooth surface and found the distortion that was causing her distress. "And stop smiling so smugly, Myra, I can see it from here even with my eyes closed." That caused Rahnahi to laugh. "So, are you going to tell me what she's keeping a secret?"

"Well, I suppose, although she'll call me kill joy again," Rahnahi complained. "The truth is that Van is … distorting who she is around this individual, and it's really starting to become imbedded in her, leaking into other areas of her life. I know that you are, in some ways, an average between the two of them, but in some ways, you're a multiplication of them. You probably feel distortions far more easily than we do."

"I feel a lot of the supports from my other aspects are stronger now than she," Vanassa noted. "I must be … losing myself in this relationship with him; I'm out of balance. What was a hole or a crevice on who I am is now a lump, of course – the growth of something that isn't meant to be. How's this for introspection – your incarnated future self says you have to…"

"Have to what, dear?" Rahnahi asked.

"Well," Vanassa noted, opening her eyes and looking at them, "that's the thing, isn't it? How does this get put right? I think I know the answer, and … I'm sure I'm not going to like it. I have to tell him. I have to show him, and I have to be who I am. I think I'm doing anything I can to make sure I can stay with him, but this isn't working, either. I can't be this docile around him, this pliant. It just isn't me!"

"But you are a wellspring of patience," Amyra told her, and Vanassa shot her a sternly reproachful expression. "Save your scowls for someone who will actually wilt under them; the praise is deserved, my former matron. However, one of the great difficulties in living as long as ascended do is the danger of becoming less of who we are. Rahnahi, therefore, still writes. I, therefore, still bother her about it."

"Welcome to my on-going torment," Rahnahi grumped.

"While at the same time," Amyra offered, "admiring it deeply and leaning on it as a cornerstone of my world. For a long time, Ash has been a cornerstone of yours, Vanassa. Your mother, of course, was one, but now she is happy and well in front of you. You want the same for Ash, but the relationship between mother and daughter is exactly that – clearly defined, if not always smooth."

"For someone you love, however, as a mate," the Nephti chuckled, "it's not as clear cut."

"These visions that he's having when I'm around him," Vanassa posited, "where do these come from? When they happen, I feel like we're reliving some of that time when we were together in the Pinnacle Center archive's basement. The conversations are like echoes of that, and he's a part of it with me. Am I doing that to him, unconsciously?"

"That's cause for some deep soul searching, but I think the answer is far simpler than that. I've peeked at this cub's mind," Amyra explained. "He can't access the memories he has through the normal process of recall, but there are memories in his mind that go back close to birth as there are in all Thurians. Interval upon interval talking about things with a psychologist was pointless, yes, but that doesn't mean what she said was right."

"That he'll never get his memories back," Vanassa answered. "Okay, so showing and telling him…"

"And loving him, dear," Rahnahi put in. "I get the sense that as he grows closer to you, the pathways to his memories are opening, but it's only through that love he has for you that he can see them."

"And I," the beautiful mixed blood softly uttered, "have to somehow break this to him without scaring him off, chasing him away. I didn't do very well learning about this universe, and … I can't know if he will, either. Still, I must try."

"You, Vanassa, are a smart kit, even when you're two of them," Rahnahi told her. "You know we'll be there for you should you need it. Any issues with the Dasahar side of your life?"

Vanassa smiled and shook her head. "Other than scrambling after little bit, trying to keep him out of trouble. Dasahar loves that kid, and … he loves me. You know, it's strange that I don't need to tell him all about this."

"Well, there's not much to tell, from his point of view. He went through the arrival complex upon reawakening, and I can tell you that, from his transcript, he asked a lot of questions. He was there for a few sols, actually. When you think about your relationship with him, is there any of this false-pliancy that you have to work on?"

"Heck no," Vanassa laughed. "We argue all the time – love each other, but still argue. If anything, when we're done here, I could try to rebalance things a bit. That actually might help me in both situations."

"Sound reasoning, my house's daughter," Amyra told her.

"And I can feel that I've spent all the time here I should. Do me a favor though, if you wouldn't mind. While it helps to see myself when I pull together, I don't need to see myself when I pull apart. Can you, like, blank the viewer this time?"

Rahnahi closed her eyes and then shook her head. "Uh, no. Alahari says you have to face this."

"She says that about everything!" Vanassa groaned. "Fine, fine; I'll face it, but I don't have to like it, and I'm going to *squint*!"

A few passes later, a dazed and disoriented Vanarra was trying to pull herself free of the joining that was becoming far easier to create than it was to reverse. Looking up into the viewer allowed her to see her dear friend Sahni trying to do the same thing, which was unusual as the Nephti generally had an easier time coming out of the union that was Vanassa than she did. "Oooo... Not a good ride that time," Sahni groaned. "I'm feeling a little weak."

It was then that it occurred to Van that she normally woke from these things in her quarters aboard the Haven, not where she had started. "Maybe, she ... she rebalanced the fun, kit – sorry about that."

"I guess it's only fair," Sahnassa started, but then just looked at Vanarra. "Something's wrong, Van. Something is wrong with you and ... Ash!"

Van put her paws in front of her face and shook her head. "Yeah, it's me. Oh, mange. I've been letting myself get so lost in him that it's messing with us."

"In some ways, I suppose it's inevitable," Sahni comforted her. "You did know him before you knew me."

"You predated him, hun," Van reminded her.

"Standing on the other side of an air vent does not constitute a friendship, and ... that's what you've done, isn't it?"

"How do you mean?"

"You've walled a part of yourself off!" Sahnassa accused her and very directly. "You've closed that off, and you're trying to hide it! But you're not just hiding it, Van – you're diminishing yourself!"

"Yeah, yeah," Van groaned, turning away from the viewer and blinking out tears. "I'm getting that pretty loudly, also."

"Well," Rahnahi offered, helping Van sit up, "she felt that something was wrong almost immediately. You have to treat this as serious, dear – it's important." Van could only nod, but she couldn't do much else.

"Van," Sahnassa's voice said softly into the room from the other side of the viewer. "I ... I am responsible for this. What you're doing is something that's more in my nature than it has been in yours. It's my instinct to follow and to want to. That's something that's new to you. You were always the leader."

"But it felt nice to step back and just see where he went, to defer to him. It's ... seductive in its own way. I've never, ever allowed that to happen. I've never just followed someone to see where they would want to go. I've pounced on them – even Trax, even Buck, even ... my lost Ash. All of those little hunts in between. I was the one who decided to go after *them*!" Van was now angry and resentful, and her tone showed it. "I'm tired of being the one who always sets the pace! I'm always the one leading the way!"

"You, my friend, are right, and that's in many ways why it's not you. I know from our sharing," Sahni told her with a voice that dragged the mixed blood's eyes back to the monitor, "that you were very kind to Trax, and that his desires were for you. Intimacy is about mutual agreement because that *allows us* the trust in each other to be intimate. It's why rapemating is the crime it is. What you're doing, Van, is not mutual. You have let him go as far as he wanted to, and it's not enough for you. You know that. I know that. Vanassa knows it, too. You need more from him, and he doesn't know to give it to you. You're killing off a part of yourself, Van, and for reasons we both know, nothing breaks my heart more."

Van went silent and just stared down at a corner of the room since she knew exactly what the Nephti was talking about – namely when Sahnassa had to intervene to change the instincts of a Vanarra set on murdering Tana in a blinded rage for becoming intimate with her mate, Buck. It didn't matter that it was a result Van wanted; her instincts took over. It was one of the events that, when she found out, ripped apart her trust in Sahnassa. "I … I need some time to think, kit. I really do," Van finally whispered.

"Yeah, and you're not the only one," Sahni sighed.

Van looked back into the viewer and asked, "What?"

"Me and Dasahar. I'm … letting myself go in the other direction. As you and I become closer and closer, it's like we want to try out these new parts of our individuality that is a part of the other. I … stink at it. I'm kind of sensing Vanassa's rather plain appraisal of how I am acting as a mate. I owe more than a pawful of apologies to my Faelnar cub. I'll be thinking a lot on the ride home, too, Van. You won't be the only one."

"Alright then, kit. I love you, and I still want this. It's the right thing, but it's just … hard."

"And by that way," Alahari said from the other side of the connection, "you know it is the true path."

The consternated look the two friends shot each other through the viewer at that moment made everyone else, Alahari included, burst into laughter.

A somewhat bemused mixed blood watched hover loads of construction workers and surveyors piling out of their vehicles and starting to lay out marks on the ground with little flags and survey equipment. A gentle paw on his shoulder gathered his attention. "Oh, Laxar, good morning to you!"

"Quite the surprise to wake up this morning and see all of this, but I suppose it's alright. It's part of the plan for Attoria. I asked Father, and that's what he said."

"Javoth okay with you calling him that, yet?"

"About as comfortable as you are with others calling you by the name Ashalam."

"Yeah, but it's only half weird for me. Part of it feels pretty natural – a bit like this," he commented, pointing at the survey crews. "Hey buddy, question?"

"Sure thing," one of the big, burly Pantera responded coming over, putting out his paw. "Name's Jaran."

"Ash," he offered, clasping paws. "This is Laxar." The clasp was repeated as Ashalam asked, "So what's all of this about?"

"The approvals finally got posted for major infrastructure. These cabins are going to start to get some very big neighbors – the first anchor buildings and trails for the new Attoria."

"Really?" Laxar asked, eyes wide. "What ... buildings will there be?"

"Let me call the site alpha over. He'll show you."

As the Pantera went to fetch his boss, Laxar looked in the direction of the cabins. "Ash, sir, I believe that the children are frightened." Watching one of the big earth movers hauled in on a flatbed transport even unsettled Laxar a bit.

"Can you go bring them here, Lax? I think it will be good for them to see this."

Just as Laxar made it to the cluster of frightened Aelkinda huddled together in front of one of the cabins, Jaran walked up with his supervisor, an even burlier Pantera. "Chief, this is Ash."

"Bashar," the site alpha replied, nodding. "You one of the volunteers?"

"I am. I worked at FridgeTech in Shanandrae, lead tech for a number of seasons. You have some plans?"

"I do. What's ... wrong?" he asked, looking at the terrified group of children looking back at him.

"I think they are a little intimidated. Laxar, can you please bring them over here?"

The mixed blood didn't look sure, himself, but he still encouraged them towards Ash and the two Pantera, and soon fifteen kits and cubs followed a cowed-looking Laxar to a few tracks away from them. "Children," Ash told them, "there's no need to be afraid. Everything's alright."

"But … all this equipment," one of the eldest said, "the noise."

"Are they here to destroy our town?"

"Destroy it?!" Bashar rumbled in a voice that made them all tense. "No! We're here to *build it!* Come and look here!" he told them, unrolling the plans on a nearby work table. Curious, the group crowded around the big male as he stood on the other side of the table, Ash and Jaran holding the plans open. "Every good settlement needs a core, a strong center that its citizens can rely on! Lairs to live in, places to store food, places to prepare it, a doctor's office, and all sorts of other key needs for living. See, look here – there will be a park and school and – what?"

The children had started to kneel and close their eyes, bowing towards the big Pantera. "It's their way of thanking you, the way they were taught to," Ash explained as he had been the target of their worship more than once.

The big Pantera rubbed his head for a moment and then stepped around to their side of the table. He knelt down and bowed his head in their direction. "Build master," one of them asked, "why … do you do this? You are providing for us?"

"You are providing for me in a different way," he told them. "I've never been able to build the central core of a place like this. Most every place I've ever been has been built already, and I'm honored to do this for you and everyone who will follow you."

"We, good builder," the former Select, Vassia, said as she took her place kneeling beside the children, "are not worthy of this gift, but what you are offering to create for us, we will treasure."

"Good things were done for me when I was growing up without a mom or dad, and no one would be my friend because of how big I was. I know what life is like … outside of everyone else," he told them. "That is another reason why I am honored to build this for you."

"It's important, also," Ash added, putting a paw on Laxar's shoulder, "that we teach you how to take care of these marvelous gifts. That is another way we can honor the work they do here, by taking care of it."

Laxar spoke next. "We have many fathers and mothers in this place, many brothers and sisters. We would be honored to consider you and everyone in your crew among them." The big Pantera nodded, and the children then filed up to him and touched their head to his. By this time, the entire construction crew had stopped and were watching this happen. When it was over, Bashar stood, wiping tears from his face, the others clapping and jeering him a little.

"Thank you, again," Ash offered. "We'll make sure they stay out of your crew's way, won't we Laxar?" The mixed blood nodded.

"I can attend them for a few passes," Vassia noted, looking across a clearing at Vanalla approaching. "It appears you have a visitor."

Ash parted with the group and met Vanalla about halfway between where she parked and where the construction crew was. He didn't speak to her until he was close to her, and then he took her gently by the shoulders and kissed her on the side of the muzzle. "It's so good to see you. Is everything alright?" He could feel the tenseness in her as he held her.

"So very sensitive, *Ash*?" she asked, obviously questioning the use of that name for him, and he nodded.

"Seems a little odd still, but I find it a bit more pleasant to think about being something found as opposed to something lost. Would you like to walk down to the lake?" he asked.

"Let's take the forest path, instead, if you don't mind," she stated, and it struck him as a little assertive for her, but he agreed. As they started to make progress, the silence lasted only a few ticks before Vanalla started to explain. "I've had a very, very earnest conversation with an extremely close friend, and … they say I owe you an apology."

"An apology, for what? You've been so very giving and kind to me."

"Well, in truth, they pointed out that I've been more than that. Too much more."

"I don't think I understand."

"You might, at least a little," she chided him gently. "I've been deferring to you a lot lately, and really almost getting a bit too caught up in doing that, and my friend pointed out that I'm not being the real me around you, and ... that's not fair to you. I know who I am, but I'm not showing *you* that. I'm not offering my true self to you, my inner self. I'm giving you a tamed down version of me. I'm doing this, and I'm – between the two of us – the one who's probably had more experience in relationships. It's the wrong thing."

"But why, Van?" he asked her, reaching out for and grasping her paw gently, giving her the opportunity to pull away if she wanted. "You're right, and we've talked about it."

"I know, and there lays my little speech about not wanting to always take the lead, but never taking the lead would be something I've never done before in my entire life," she explained. "The why ... has given me a lot of heartburn and a lot of ... fear."

"I don't want you to feel that, Van; I really don't," he told her, "especially about us. Please, just tell me."

She was quiet for a bit longer before finally confessing. "From the moment I saw you in the hospital, I just locked in on you that you looked like my cub from so long ago. You look like what he would have looked like all grown up, and I wanted him back. I admit it. I really do. If I'm honest with myself, I've never been right about losing him, and it has always haunted me, and I was willing to do anything – sacrifice any part of myself just for the chance to walk alongside him again. So, I resolved that I wasn't going to be happy with anyone else. You were who I thought I needed, and to make sure it happened, that we got together, I was going to play a Thurian other than myself. I was going to be okay with it."

"But you couldn't have kept it up forever, right? I ... have to admit that I kind of thought that was what was going on, and that in time, you'd finally be more of that other Thurian I've heard about."

"Oh, really?" Vanalla asked. "Which Thurian is that?"

"The one who is Fireclaw's friend, and the one who was forceful enough with her to sit her down hard about the choices she was making in her life. The one who helped Laxar stand up in front of a room full of scary adults and tell about the horrible things that were done to him. The one who befriended a gold-on-gold Faelnar and loved her like a sister, giving up everything for her. However, I've spoken to Shenaria a few times, and she's mentioned that you do a good job pushing her out of her comfort zone, too. I knew there was more to you, but..."

"But what?" she asked.

"Well, you waited for me for three seasons," he told her, shrugging. "I was willing to wait and spend time with you to get to know the real you, and to hear you speak now, it's like I'm really starting to. Are you afraid, Van, that if you are more assertive in our relationship, I won't care for you?"

"It is a ... concern," she confessed. "My ways of doing things in previous relationships could be seen as rather aggressive, forward."

"I've been a mess for three solid seasons straight, and not much better before that. I know that I don't know anything about being in a relationship with someone like you. Doctor Emma told me that this relationship, between you and me, would likely fail. I don't believe it has to be like that, but I do believe that your friend was right. We're never going to get anywhere if we aren't honest with one another. Were you being honest with me when you told me that you don't want to take the lead when you're around me?"

"I wasn't being honest, not entirely. I like following you, Ash. I'm not going to lie about that. The cub I knew and lost was the only one I could trust to lead me in the right direction. He led me to the first healing I'd ever felt about losing my mother, about some of the other horrible things that happened to me as I grew up. So, yes, I want to and am willing to follow your lead, but if I'm honest, doing it the way I was doing it wasn't something that even he'd put up with. Why ... did you?"

He clasped her paw tighter and just told her, "I was so curious about what this sol would be like when you finally let me see some of the real you, but I was willing to wait. I can't be the only who's hurting, Van. My lost memories aren't the only problem in the world, and just from what you've told me right now, you've had some really harsh things to deal with."

"It's true. Damn, I should have known better," Vanalla groaned. "Well, that's par for it, I guess. With the cub before, I went way too darn aggressive, and with you, I played the pathetically meek and tame pet prowler."

"But to hear your friends talk," Ash told her, "you do know who you really are. You don't need to pretend."

"I'm sorry, Ash, but I still must to some degree. The truth is that my life is exceptionally ... complicated. I have a much bigger paw in things here than you think I do, and not only here, in other places, as well. There are some confessions I can't make, and some details I can't give you."

"Like why I see strange visions whenever you and I are close? Almost like they were memories of another time – another life?" he asked, carefully. "Is this something you're doing?"

"On the love of my mother, I tell you that is not me who is doing that to you. By honor and by my pledge, I am not the one who is making you have those images."

"But," he told her, "you're still holding back. I can tell it." By then, they had gone full circle and were looking at the construction workers laying out the markers for the central core of Attoria.

"The foundation of our relationship, cub, has to be trust. It has to be that I will honestly be who I am and share that with you, even though I can't share every detail about my life. There are oaths I have sworn and commitments to others I have made that I must keep in confidence. I wish and long for the sol when I can share my every secret, but until then, cub, please know this. If even the fur I wear was just a mask, I promise that I will honestly be my own soul around you, not a cheap and meek imitation."

"We do need a good foundation, that's clear," he told her, agreeing. "You've given me a lot to think about, for sure. That part about your fur being a mask, for example. It has been, but I don't think it is so much that anymore. You ... are trying so hard for me, and you want to get this right." He took her by the shoulder and held her beside him. "We share that. I want to get this right, as well."

She buried her head in his shoulder and just rested there. "Mange, cub. I'm sorry. I'm so sorry. Please, forgive me."

"There's nothing to forgive. You realized something was wrong, and you wanted to fix it; you wanted to be authentic to me, and I can't thank you enough for that." She hummed happily and snuggled into him a little more. "So, tell me this, Van. How much did you have to do with everything we're seeing happen right now?"

"I made the plans he was showing, well, me and a few friends," she chuckled. "We had to take into account a lot of things. This place is important, Ash, and it will be a very difficult and tricky path to walk for us to be successful."

"What does success mean to you, Van?"

"It means that the Aelkinda can live here with others living beside them who aren't like them, and everyone can live safe and happy."

"Would you live here, Van?" She nodded. "I will be here, too, then. I promised myself to you, and regardless of what we talked about just now, I still hold to my word."

"And I will hold to mine," she said, wrapping him in her arms and getting as close as she could to him.

Chapter 10: The Course Corrects

Ash held Vanalla in his arms as they slept together in his cabin, their night far more passionate than any they had spent together in the past. Stirring, he felt the naked fur of her chest pressed against him as she nestled alongside. He had been amazed by the fires that burned inside of her, amazed, but not afraid as she feared he would be. There hadn't been a complete consummation of their union, but the explorations and intimacies were just amazing to him. There had been sexual desire, but there were also the incredible moments of just staring into her eyes, and she staring into his. At times, when they were doing this in the darkness of his cabin, his gentle strokes along her body seemed to give her such pleasure. He felt truly connected to her in his spirit. It was a feeling he had never known, before – to know she was his, and he was hers, and eternal trust flowed between them.

Emotions poured from her, too. There would be moments when she would take his paw and guide him, bringing his touch upon her in a way he had never yet dared to do, but in a way that sated some deep part of her soul. She would hug him, after, and nestle into his neck. Sometimes, he caught her weeping, but felt it wrong to do anything more than hold her, his paw upon her back. There were deep wounds in her that he could sense he was helping to heal. "She really did love that cub, and now, she loves me," he breathed out mentally.

He knew her love was a supreme responsibility; somehow, he just knew. She was integral to what was happening in Attoria and potentially many more places, and he felt as if he was just starting to realize how truly amazing she was. Still, in the nighttime quiet of the cabin, Vanalla needed him. There were moments when he was caressing her as she had asked him to, that her eyes closed, her head reared back arching away from him exposing her lovely neck, and her mouth gaped open. It was then, and only then, that he caught glimpses of new visions – a lovely reddish-brown female with golden highlights running through her fur, an unusual fur pattern for a Faelnar, and seemingly more tail than he remembered there being. The face was still his Vanalla, but in all other aspects – color, scent, and breed – this ghost image of Van was different.

"Do I see the female inside of the female, her true spirit?" he wondered, holding onto her. This more assertive, more sensual side of his hunt was intriguing. He could tell that she was still restraining herself, perhaps because of his hesitancy or because of the failures she had mentioned in prior relationships. Still, he had refused her nothing, and he was overwhelmed to see her change through the evening and into the night. At this moment, she rested like someone who had never been able to fully sleep and was now finally granted that privilege. "Oh, Creator, let me be her Ash, please," he begged in prayer. "Let me see her more sols where she is fulfilled like this, then my life would have some meaning and some purpose."

He was stroking her head, still, as the sun started to rise, and light started slowly rousing his love. "Ash?" she asked, not opening her eyes.

"Yes, Van," he answered. "Did you sleep well?"

"No," she answered him. "I didn't just sleep so much as I was able to utterly and completely rest in your arms. Oh, cub, what a treasure you are, more than words can tell!"

"I feel the same way, love, and I'm starting to see so many other dimensions of you."

"Like what?" she asked, looking up into his eyes.

"You are so … beautiful and sensual. I half wonder if the expressions you make when I put my paws on you are real. Could I truly be causing you to experience that much joy … just by my touch?" he asked her, and smiling, she nodded. "You need this, and I could tell, you desire even more. Why did you stop?"

"Because sometimes, I don't know when to," she confessed, embarrassed. "I am not the only one here, and I want you to understand that I know that. You are so different than any other cub I have loved. You love me. You find me attractive and keen to your eyes – I can tell. You are so patient, and it almost makes me wonder if you don't feel urges like when you're in rut?"

"I ... do, but I just haven't known any kind of direction or outlet for them. I think being in rut in your arms would be a lovely place to be, though."

She turned around and backed into him, and when he lifted his arm above her and let it fall to the bed, she gathered his paw and held it against her own breast. "Most cubs, if I were to do this, would start pawing and teasing and stroking, revving me up for more. You simply stay where I ask, give me what I need, but your own needs and wants – where are they, cub? Are you hiding part of yourself, too?"

It was nearly an accusation, but he was able to respond gracefully. "Part of me is hidden, Vanalla, but it's also hidden from me – it is the part I can't get back to. I have looked at other males and seen them as they emerge from puberty. So many of their fascinations and wonderment with the opposite gender are wrapped up into those early seasons. I can't remember those seasons, and my life for some time has been ... hard. Difficult. What purpose does a rut serve if you are only just trying to get by, survive? Even now, I am just a poor mixed blood."

"Not poor, cub. You have me."

"You are right. It *was* true for me. I know it's not," he agreed. "Nevertheless, I am only now catching glimpses of that past, I think, and only when we are together."

"What are you seeing, love?" she asked, a little concern in her voice. She could feel him shift in hesitation, and so she pressed him. "Please, cub. I won't be offended. I just want to know. I care about you."

He sighed and buried his head in the back of her neck. "The image of you ... overlaid with another. Your face, your eyes, yes, but you aren't as I see you. The image moves in time with you, feels what you are feeling. It is still your face, my love. I wonder if it's because you're starting to share yourself with me more fully, and this mysterious presence in you is being revealed."

"You see me as ... someone else?" she asked softly.

"Please, don't be upset. Even in what I'm seeing, it is you – I know it is."

"I'm not upset, and Ash, maybe you are seeing the real me in a way. Sometimes, I am a mystery to myself, but please know that I love you, cub. Never doubt that, even if I became that form you are seeing in your visions, okay?"

"It is you, Van, I'm seeing. I know this. I just don't know why I'm seeing these things or how. I don't know what power makes them come to be. Is it me; is it you; is it the Creator? I don't know." He turned her around and looked into her eyes. "Altogether, though, that means you are the most intriguing and mysterious female I've ever met, and you are deeply in love with me?"

Her smile and brightening eyes were all the reassurance he needed. "I can live with that, and I'm not entirely sure I wouldn't give up everything for it. Every moment we spend together helps convince me."

"Then, I suppose," she said, wrapping herself around him, "that I should spend as many moments with you as I can." They kissed then, at her lead, but he as passionately returned her devotion.

"Myra," Van asked her as they walked through the halls of the Haven later that sol, "do you think I'm doing this the right way?"

"I'm not aware that you are doing anything other than loving him, my sweet kit," Amyra reassured her once matron. "Are you?"

"No, and I'm keeping a close check on Tana and my Sahni within, and we're all being really careful. I've even asked Kylie to keep a close eye on us to make sure I'm not unduly influencing him, accidently."

"You sound a little frightened, Vanarra. That is a strange land for you, I'm sure. I'm also sure that what I have to tell you next won't make it any easier for you to move forward with him, but then again, it may."

Van stopped and watched as Amyra walked into one of the entertainment rooms that Van kept modeled as her library when she was a dame. Taking a deep breath, Van followed her in. "Okay, now what?"

"You have been intentionally ignoring something about Ash when you've been with him, turning a blind eye to it," Amyra confessed, sitting down on the central sofa. "Do you know what that is?"

"Oh, mange," Vanarra groaned walking back and forth, her paw on her head trying to remember. "That … I am the way back into his memories? He's really seeing memories of me? I don't know!"

"Dear, dear. This is really going to surprise you, then. Have a seat." Reluctantly, Van agreed and just waited. "Tell me what he saw when he was with you, last."

"He said that, as we were together, he saw another me, one with my face, but one that was different than I was."

"Not so much who you were, my friend. Who … you … are."

"No! That can't be! Tana swears to me that she was keeping me fully cloaked the entire time! Kylie would have told me!"

"Kylie's vision is limited to what she, as an Izar, can see through the sensors of this ship and its drones. She can't look at Ash like I can, like Rahnahi can, like … you can," the Faelnar told her, softly.

"Myra," Van nearly chuckled, shaking her head. "It can't be that he's seeing through the cloak! That would mean he's…" The look in Amyra's eyes told her everything. "Ascending?! Are you kidding me?! No! No! It can't be! He's just a baby cub!"

"Not true. He's over seventeen hundred seasons old, I'd wager."

"He's not been alive for it! He's not lived through it, I mean!" Vanarra nearly shouted, exasperated and confused.

"Even so, he's nearly forty-eight in biological terms, and that's older than Merialla was when she started to manifest," Amyra contested. "I mean, I've not been trying to spy on you, but he's starting to create some very noticeable disturbances that both Rahnahi and I can sense."

Vanarra was dumbstruck. "It can't be…"

"It is. We weren't sure until the last time you two were together, but his cabin was practically glowing in the dark."

"I'm going to be sick," Van groaned, putting her paw over the front of her muzzle. "I think all of me – we're all going to be sick."

"Any reason why the perpetuation of the one you love beyond his normal lifespan should do that to you?" the Faelnar pressed her gently, putting a paw on her back, trying to reason with her. Van's roiling emotions, the complete inner turmoil of all of her inner presences, prevented any kind of response.

Rahnahi then appeared beside her, as well. "Dear, calm yourself as best you can," she coaxed, but it was clear that Vanarra was having an extremely difficult time with the news, and both Amyra and Rahnahi were becoming concerned.

"We are not only the sum of our experiences," a new voice in the room stated kindly, "we are the sum of *what we thought* about them. What we have believed them to be..." The voice was just enough to catch Vanarra's attention and hold it. Looking up, she saw the delicate features and felt the glowing presence of another Teldear in the room, one she knew.

"Dy … Dynaea!" Van gasped, nearly out of control and hysterical as with consummate patience and grace, the elder Teldear walked towards her and put her hand along the muzzle of the nearly incoherent mixed blood.

"From Me Sha. I come when you need me, and it is by his will that this is done. Peace, Vanarra. Peace, Sahnassa. Peace, Tana. Peace, she who walks in light." The powerful Teldear, ascended multiple times already beyond Amyra and Rahnahi, was able to still and corral the scrambling thoughts of the mixed blood. "His peace I bring to you."

"Teldear Dynaea, thank you," Amyra offered, her own concern finally starting to ebb. "I fear I broke this to her poorly."

"By your actions, you did not fail," Dynaea told her, "but our dearest here is not going to merely ascend when her sol comes; there will be far more to that event. Treasured of Me Sha, tell me the trouble in your spirit at the news of Ash's ascendance."

"That … that if he hadn't died, he would have … he *will* leave me! I can never be with him!?" Vanarra wept.

"That is not true. You are with him, now. You were with him then, and you will be with him still. Amyra's question is worthy, and although I know the answer, you should not feel afraid that Ashalam has caught the spark of ascension from the love in your own heart."

Van looked at her, confused. "I ... I did this?"

"Yes!" Dynaea replied, smiling happily. "You are his catalyst! Without you, he would have never known anything beyond this life other than what awaits in the paws of the Creator. Now, because of you – giver of healing and life – *you* have helped give him a longer life than he would have ever known."

"I ... I caused him to get hurt – I caused him to die – I..."

"Erased all of that," Dynaea contested, "with your father's help."

Vanarra almost became catatonic at that point, her muscular rigidity signaling a collapse in the foundation of who she had always been as the regret and pain shook loose and fell away from her soul. Her past was unchanged, but the one she loved had been spared the ultimate price for her mistake. The guilt that had pulled on her every waking thought after he had been taken from her was suddenly just gone. Gratitude and love for her father flooded into place, her adoptive father who had given her more than she ever thought possible. "Why? Why?" she called out in her mind. "Why ... for me?"

"Because he loves you, dearly, as do we all," Dynaea's voice slipped into her thoughts, and Vanarra wept with joy, curled in a ball on the floor, the touch of three ascended beings insulating her from the world in this moment, allowing that incredible healing to occur.

Shenaria sat rubbing her belly as she relaxed on the sofa of her and Trax's lair. "Forgot all about this part," she groaned as she rested, trying to soothe the painful cramps in her side and back. They weren't indicative of labor, but rather that she had *labored* too freely with lair chores as if she wasn't with a child. "Big cub, too," she huffed. She didn't know if it was due to Kylie's expert care or just her natural genetics mixed with Trax's, but their offspring was stretching the frontiers of her womb, fast. Looking up at the ceiling, she blinked back a tear, but it was a happy one. "Oh, to have these problems – what a joy..."

"Mom?" Vanarra called out to her, and instantly Shenaria knew something was going on with her daughter. Its tone in that one-word question, supposedly for her own comfort and happiness, conveyed what Rahnahi had taught her was the "undercurrent of dissonant resonance."

"I am fine," she chuckled back to her daughter, opening her arm as an invitation for Van to join her. "Nothing's wrong – I was just having one of those really grateful moments." As her mixed blood daughter slipped carefully alongside her, she explained, "I was sitting and aching because I've been an idiot and worked all sol in the lair, and just as I am about to think of complaining, I remember how grateful I am to even have these problems, to have a life! Thanks to you, and thanks to this Theo I still have *yet to meet*!"

Van smirked a little as she heard the complaint in her mother's voice. "Yeah, leader of an expansive multi-dimensional empire of trillions of individual entities – for lack of a better way of putting it – doesn't always have the time to come over and say hi to my mom."

"Oh, you!" Shenaria reached over and swatted her daughter on the shoulder. "That makes me sound so horrible! I just want to say thank you!"

"I know, I know!" Van recoiled dramatically. "He's just busy, that's all."

"Well, even you are so busy that I hardly see you much, anymore," Shenaria softly complained, but some sense told her this was part of the cause of her daughter's anxiety. It was confirmed when her daughter leaned back into the sofa cushions and sighed heavily. "Tell me, Van. I know you have something bothering you. Something that's happened?"

"You're *so* still my Mom," Van sighed, again, smiling. "I've been put on … vacation for a while."

"Oh, why? Who can do that? I thought you were in charge?"

"Well, Theo, indirectly. One of his other Teldear, Dynaea of the Asteravans, has been brought in to help. Mom, I … I took a really big hit this sol. It was a big hit to who I am, who I've always thought myself to be."

Her mother's paws circled around and grasped her right paw tenderly. "Can you tell me about it?"

Van's free paw went in front of her own muzzle as she sobbed. "I … I watched Ash dying, and then his unconscious body was taken away, and he died and was just thrown away, and it's like over a thousand seasons ago. I can see it, in my mind, when I close my eyes as if it's happening right now! It's always been there! That loss has been part of who I was for so long, and this sol, I learned for sure that it … did … not … happen!"

Shenaria thought for a while before she answered. "Like it was with me. Were you this upset when you knew I had been saved?"

Van buried her head in her mother's neck. "Yes," she rasped. "I almost collapsed. My inner Sahni had to talk to me for sols *outside* of my body before I could even half way function again!"

"This is more, though. Either that, or it's harder," Shenaria reasoned softly. "They didn't call in anyone before, did they?" Van shook her head, and her mother felt that. "When you knew about me, what was the thing that made you the most afraid?"

"That I would lose you again," the mixed blood whimpered. "That you wouldn't be able to cope with being in this time. That you would wish to be dead rather than being here…"

"And yet, I am so much happier *in this time* than I was in the one I was born to," Shenaria offered. "Now, my love, I have a tougher question for you. When you knew about Ash, this sol, what was the thing that made you the most afraid?"

Vanarra was dead still, barely seeming to breathe, as she tried to sift through her stormy emotions and doubts. "That … when he learns that I was the cause for him living in this time with no memories, and I didn't tell him, that he won't be able to love me! Worse, that … that he'd do something horrible to himself!"

Shenaria lifted the head of her sobbing daughter and looked into her eyes. "You, my daughter, are exceedingly clever. You, my daughter, are exceedingly kind. You took care to reveal yourself to me in slow, special ways. You appeared to me in the night, cuddled with me, talked to me, encouraged me. You wove dreams into my sleeping mind that made accepting this so much easier. You haven't done these things for him, yet, have you?"

"No."

"Why?" she asked, and her daughter's stunned silence was answer enough. "You've held back because you, as his lover, don't want to force him to love you. That's already happened, both in the past and in the present. Ash loves you, doesn't he?" Vanarra nodded, slowly. "He loved you then, and he loves you now. What does he think of Vanarra Anasto? Has he read any histories?"

"No, I ... I think he's avoided them," Van whispered. "I think the stories disturb him – the abuse I lived through."

"I understand. It disturbs me, too, but you were strong and rose above it – found paw holds and other strong paws to pull you up. I think it's time then, my dear, that with your gentle touch, your guiding paw, he realizes that truth about you, and he should realize that he can do the same, don't you think?" Her daughter nodded, tears still dropping down her cheek.

"I'm ... I'm going to check everything with you, though, first – okay? You've been through this, and ... and what I did with Trax, I-"

"Yes," Shenaria chuckled. "He told me, in detail! Poor little cub! Maybe a bit more like what you did later for him and not the full-on Tana, Sahni, Van challenge, right?" Vanarra, despite herself, laughed at the way her mother had put that. "Oh, yeah, and no more nightmare Vannie-Sahni terror mixes, either. Kylie told me about that little escapade with Ariasta!"

"Well, I ... I felt I needed to jar her, shake her up," Van offered defensively.

"Yeah, she's still a pretty messed up kit inside. I've been helping her. So, I agree. I know I'm not much of anything in the grand scheme-"

"*You're my mother!*" Van said fiercely. "You are so very important to me, and I value what you say."

"Okay, love, then with my assistance, together, we'll work on helping Ash come to love all the beings you are, past – present – future.

Ash slept soundly thanks to a gentle rain striking the top of his cabin and the hectic pace of work in the quickly forming village center earlier that sol. The cabins that he had helped put together were just a little too close for comfort to the rumbling ground shaping equipment that was required to ensure that the foundations and substructures of the new buildings would be constructed to standard. So, he and Vassia, with Laxar's agreement, had taken the cubs and kits on a nice long hike in the afternoon.

It was surprising to him how utterly insulated the children of the Vanarrans had been, and as Aelkinda, they were learning a joy in exploring the forest they'd never known before. He received so many questions from not only the children but Vassia that it was all he and Laxar could do to answer them. Laxar was exceptionally strong on natural facts as he had spent so much time in the last few seasons living amongst the trees in Javoth's private retreat. Questions that were more philosophical had come to him, and although the mixed blood youth had many good answers, Ash tackled some of the more difficult criticisms of the Creator's religion, such as pain in the world and justice.

Vassia's own tentative questions had then started slipping in, harder ones for sure, but ones that he had sat through many a long night and thought about, especially about someone's identity, their past, and what they were responsible for in terms of guilt. The group had stopped in a beautiful mountaintop meadow that overlooked Attoria below them, and a growing overcast had provided shade and a mild breeze for them as they sat upon large sheets that had been brought.

To his immense and warm satisfaction, several of the children and Vassia prayed the prayer of commitment to the Creator and pledged to follow the Creator's path for their life on that very spot. When the group finally returned about the time the construction workers were leaving, a stunned Javoth happily accepted the news and ate with them, answering even harder and deeper questions from Vassia and the rest of the Aelkinda children. It was a sol that Ash knew he would always remember and treasure, not to mention one that he had confessed to Javoth made him hope deeply for others of its like in the future.

Now, as he rested, his mind lost in the warm recesses of sleep, a dream started to form around him, and it was one that he wasn't even fully aware he was in for what seemed like a few passes. He was outside on a cool and comfortable night, laying on a hard surface but propped against a warm and fragrantly inviting presence. It was the scent of a female he smelled and a very enticing one – a bit like Vanalla's, but his mind wasn't operating at a level where he could actually draw together that sort of conclusion. He just knew that it was very nice.

"Ash," a soft and exceedingly feminine voice called to him. "Come on, cub, it's time for us to go. It's nice right now, but I think it's going to start raining soon."

He blinked open his eyes and was mildly surprised by what he saw. He was facing away from whomever this was, but his eyes were focused on a building that he had both seen and not seen before. It was the Pinnacle Center Academy main building, but everything around it was just forest and grassy fields, steeped in the light of a beautiful sunset, one that promised rain later with a great degree of assurance. "I think you're right," he offered and sat up. "Beautiful sky, though."

"Yes. I really like it," she responded, nuzzling into him a bit. She was warm and familiar, but he still couldn't place her in his sleep addled mind. Trying to hide his ignorance, a bit, he decided to pose her a question.

"When you look at that, who does it tell you that you are?" he asked.

"Interesting question," came the response, and there was a moment of consideration before the answer finally came. "It tells me that the world is a lot bigger than I am, and although I love how beautiful it is, it won't show me much mercy. It's either beautiful or ugly without me, and it doesn't change the facts of who I am, who we are. I'm still Vannie; my mother was killed right in front of me, Ash. That hurt me in a way that I can look at the beautiful sunset or our beautiful stolen lair, the Pinnacle Center, and I don't feel much kindness towards it. What about you, Ash?"

"Vannie Anasto?" he thought to himself. "I should know that from somewhere." He sat up and then offered aloud, "I look at it, and I see a reminder that not everything or everyone in the world is bad. It makes me think there's a bigger paw that shaped things other than chance or someone else like us. It … *chastens* me, in a way."

"That's an *expensive* word for you," Vannie chuckled. "What do you mean?"

"It's like someone who knows better than me telling me that I don't have to choose to feel hurt. I could look at that sunset and be resentful of the storm that is going to follow it. I could look at that building and be angry that so much wealth was poured into making it when it could have gone into feeding those without lairs, giving them shelter. I can let those feelings always darken my view, and if I do, it's like I'll never be able to see beauty again. I don't want that for me, and I don't want it for you, either."

Her warm paw encircled his. "You're … chastenafying me now, but I think you're right. I'm sorry I'm this way, Ash. I've needed someone like you for so long. I was lonely for so very long. Thank you for being there for me."

"I think I heard the word *chastening* in what I was listening to, and you're welcome, Vannie."

"Ahem," she grumped. "That's my little kit name."

"Sorry," he said, finally turning towards her. The face that looked back at him in amused disapproval was, at that moment, utterly familiar to him. The lines of her muzzle and gold of her eyes were unmistakable even in the strange mask of reddish brown fur, gold highlights twinkling in it, reflecting the sunset. The connection between them was there, unmistakable and deep, loving and sharing and intimate.

"What?!" she questioned him, her tone soft but still sharp. "You're looking at me like I'm some kind of … freak!"

His expression softened at seeing the fire burning inside of her, a fire he had started to love as he learned more of it. "Because you, in this light, are beautiful and mystical and just amazing. I'm sorry if I made you feel uncomfortable."

"You're forgiven," she replied back into his apologetic expression. "You love me, and that's really all I care about, Ash. I need you so much, and I never knew how deep and lasting love could truly be until I met you. You touch me far deeper than you could ever know."

Her voice had taken a more normal speaking volume, and to his surprise and delight, it was his Vanalla once again – her lovely voice. "I'm seeing more sides of you and more shades of your being all the time, it seems," he commented, smiling at her. "I love you, too, and as I see these new things about you, I love you all the more."

Like a flame that sparked into a blaze, her passion reached for him and loved him. Her scent grew in his nostrils, and it demanded his closeness, his soul-melding intimacy with her. He closed his eyes and kissed and nuzzled her for several moments. When they parted, he opened his eyes and found that they were now within the confines of a small room made of builder's block, and the soft light of a power-pack camping lantern lit the features of this now denuded mixed blood. Her eyes were hungry for him, and her scent penetrated his senses with desire. His eyes roamed her body and found her form exotic and utterly appealing, everything he could want in a female. The tail, far bushier than that of a Faelnar, spoke to a mixed heritage, like his own. "Please, Ash, I … I need you. I love you." As he fell towards her, taking her softness and warmth into his arms, he pushed her back, her soft form yielding underneath him.

His eyes opened, and he blinked, facing in the wrong direction of his cabin's bed, his head nearly hung over the edge. Getting up, he didn't find his beautiful female – only a couple of his pillows. He slowly sat up, the realization that he had experienced a dream finally coming into focus. Reaching over, he grabbed his diary and began writing down every aspect of the dream to the best of his recollection. He thought a lot about the Vulpi part of his love in the dream, and he felt a little ashamed by it. "I know that Vulpi are supposed to be very passionate and great with mating, but really, Akashar!" he chided himself, still using his old name for himself when he felt he was in the wrong. He knew there was nothing, really, he could do about his subconscious turning his dear love into a mixed blood, although he had to confess there was a strange longing there.

"Part of the old ways from thousands of seasons ago? Creatures of dishonor can only find love in each other, not in those pure of breed? She loves me for who I am; I should do the same. Or … maybe I just have the dream all wrong," he pondered as he closed his diary. In a way, it was deeply troubling to think that prejudices from so long ago could still be a part of him, but there were things that Thurians held onto – even terms like TransNet, LineCom, and UltraBright were still used much as they were in the time of Rahnahi.

Many of their technical aspects had improved, but such was a comfort to Thurians to call at thing by the name it was known by in generations past. Further, he knew that some Thurians still wished for the return of the great houses to their full power, and he had to admit that some of his reading of Rahnahi de Dothnar also tugged at him, too. If finances had not been so tight, even he might have joined her old house. He also knew from his own experience that, although there was no longer a second-class status for those of mixed breed, there were still negative reactions from those of pureblood, sometimes. Such explained why even after the once implicit fertility problems had been all but eliminated that those once called Anati were still in the stark minority against the numbers of Vulpi, Faelnar, Pantera, and the like. "And yet this lovely purebred loves me, desires me," he sighed. All of these thoughts made him just want to see his love all the more.

He was thankful that, later that sol, she came to visit him. However, this time something was different. Vanalla always looked as if she had a purpose about her, a mission she was engaged in, and the time she spent with him was an interruption to those plans – one he knew she enjoyed, but an interruption, nonetheless. As she stepped from her hover, there was an air of uncertainty around her. She seemed a bit lost, disconcerted. He was still relatively clean, having showered for quite a long time after that morning's dream, and the duties he had been needed for on this sol were actually more along the lines of acting as an aid for Javoth's much increased Path study group. Thankfully, the rain had made it difficult for the ground shaping equipment to make much progress, at least in the morning, and so the camp had been quiet.

As he approached her, he smiled and greeted, "Good sol to you, my love." As he drew closer, he pulled her into an embrace and kissed her, deeply. It was an action that she seemed to welcome, to want, and at some level, to need even more than in the past. It was this need that made him curious. "I sense you're a little out of sorts this sol? Something going on?"

"Well, yes there is. I've kind of been put on a leave of absence from my responsibilities for a while. Part of it, I have to admit, wasn't completely my choice."

"Who'd you get in trouble, now?" he gently teased, trying to break her serious façade. She smiled and nuzzled into him. "I know your adopted sister has to be getting close to her due time, right?"

"That's certainly true, and she'll need my help, and honestly, I'm looking forward to meeting the little cub or kit that comes to be part of all our lives."

"She doesn't know?" he asked, again looking at her.

"Well, I'm afraid there might be more to this pregnancy than she's suspecting," Vanalla chuckled, taking his paw and walking them in the direction of the cabins and the construction. "Lots of changes here, I see."

"A little much for the kits and cubs. We took a long hike, last sol. I don't know that we won't need to do the same, again, but the results of that hike were very ... encouraging."

"I heard. Javoth called me last night; he's very impressed by you, you know? He says your faith is very simple, very direct, and fully complete."

"If he's said that about me, I'm completely overwhelmed," Ash breathed, shaking his head.

"Regardless, you were an amazing guide to those kits and cubs, and ... that's part of why I'm here, Ash. I ... need a guide, too, right now. I'm having a bit of an identity issue, and somehow, just being close to you – I know it would help. It's not something I can talk about, fully, and if you would rather I didn't impose on you-"

"No, don't say that," he told her, earnestly. "Don't even think it, okay? I will build you a cabin with my own paws, if that's what you want."

"I was wondering if ... this might be a bit ... closer, arrangement. You and I have committed to each other, at this point – do you feel that's true?"

"I do, and as I see more and more of you, the surer I am of that, Vanalla. Can I ask why you were put on a leave of absence, though? What reason they used?"

She was quiet for a moment, obviously struggling with what to say. "Being close to someone, after what I've been through, is something that others have observed me needing. While it's true that I've been distracted from my work by being with you, growing close to you, those I work for don't want my work to be the sole reason for my existence. They say I need this time with you, and they were hoping that you would be willing for us to work, together, on Attoria. That, and work on … us."

"You're starting to show up in my dreams, Vanalla, and in the most amazing of ways," he told her, as they walked towards his cabin. "I'm seeing whole different sides of you, even right now. I don't think I've ever seen you look like your hind paws have nearly been kicked out from underneath you."

"It was a … hard hit, yeah," Vanalla offered softly, "when my friend, someone I work with, clarified what I was going through. I might have, well, curled up into a ball and cried on the floor." His arm grew tighter around her shoulder. "I lost my little Ash, long, long ago, and then I had a lot of bad experiences, found a good cub, but he's gone now, and there were things that happened after with his grave that I just can't talk about. Then, I sort of found someone else, only to have him click better with my sister, and they're now joined and about to have children. I've been … strong for way, way too long. I've borne up, she said, and held onto my guilt and loss. Tried pretending my way through a real relationship with you and…" Vanalla stopped and nearly shoved her head onto his chest, and what he hadn't noticed was how her eyes were filling with tears, warm drops that now soaked into his shirt and the fur beneath.

"Oh, dear Creator," he prayed, wrapping her in his arms, "this one *has* borne up, been the one everyone looks to while everything she needed was left empty. Creator, please help me to help her. Please help Vanalla to know that her caring for me and love for me has touched me, deeply. Help us to find a path together that you would approve of, and please forgive us when we stray. In the Creator's name…"

"In the Creator's name… Ash, please help me. I need to find a way to love you that's truer than what I've been doing, that's closer to you than what I've been doing. I've been trying to coordinate massive plans and solve all kinds of issues, and all the while, I've left us out. I've not given everything I am to you. When I have been with you, I wasn't honestly me, and you could see it, and you still loved me, but…"

"Your commitment to me is something I don't question, Vanalla, and I am more grateful for it than you can know," he reassured her. "You've been hinting, too, that there is an even more real version of yourself hiding beneath, one that loves me, yes, but one I haven't fully seen yet."

She looked up at him with a bit of shock and curiosity. "You ... pick up fast, don't you?" He shrugged and nodded as he invited her inside of his cabin. When they were inside, she sat on the bed. "Things have happened to me, Ash, and – I want to share with you, but I'm afraid. Do you know the actors and actresses on VidStar?" He nodded, presuming she meant the general grouping of them. "They spend so much of their time being someone else for a part, some lose themselves and don't really know who they are anymore. Have you ever noticed that many of them have a lot of trouble with relationships?"

He nodded and answered, "Fireclaw has been telling me about that. She actually wants to wait for a few seasons until she's kind of forgotten by the public. That will let her find out a bit more about who she is before getting involved with anyone. She's afraid that someone would fall in love with the image of her, and this individual wouldn't be in love with her. What's worse is that she's afraid she's not much more than an image right now, although I don't think that's the case with her."

Vanalla nodded in understanding. "Fireclaw and I are on very similar journeys right now. The only difference is that she needs time to find someone who can anchor her, open her up, and give her the trust she needs – and the patience and understanding, also. See, someone is going to have to look past Fireclaw Destiny and help her find out who Tashara Sahari really is; she doesn't truly know. It's something she can't do alone. It's something ... I can't do alone."

He slipped beside her on the bed and drew her into a gentle kiss. "I will help you, and as she's already told me not all of the discoveries about who she is now were ones she was completely ready for."

"I can't say any different, and I'll be completely honest with you, Ash. My greatest fear is that some of the truths of my past might be ones ... you ... aren't completely ready for. Ones that pull you apart from me."

He thought about that for a moment and offered, "My commitment to you is an absolute, Vanalla. I've made that decision. I made *that decision* when you were just following along behind me, not really showing me who you were. It still holds. You waited for me, right?" She nodded. "Three … long … seasons?" Again, she nodded, smiling a little. "Don't be afraid, Vanalla. I love you. Share what you can as best you can, and I will accept."

"You might be signing up for a lot," she warned him.

"Oh, like you secretly being a mixed blood?" The question shocked her so much she backed up from him. He nodded and smiled. "It was a part of the dream I had. It was your face, but there was Vulpi in your fur and tail – the color of your fur. I've heard about purebred who are actually the children of mixed parents or even mixed blood parents. On the surface, you can't tell, but they truly are of mixed ancestry. Maybe, just a part of the new you I'm going to see is a part of this?"

"Dammit, cub, but if you aren't … aren't freaking perceptive!" Van blurted, shaking her head. "My … my father was a Vulpi! Yet here am I, appearing to be a purebred's purebred. It's a mask! It's a fraud! I know what I am, and now you do, too?" He slipped closer to her and stroked the fur of her cheek and around her ears. "I'm older than I look, too."

"On the surface, your beauty and vitality are beyond question, but truly knowing you, how could it be otherwise?" he asked, and she looked at him, bemused. "You have lived; you are wise; I know this. You have had many different lives to get where you are now, and you are many different aspects, voices within." Vanalla put her paw over her mouth and stifled a happy sob. "Perhaps, in some ways, seeing someone like Doctor Emma could help, but I don't know that you need to change so much as to find a new harmony with yourself. It will be hard, but everything I see about you and what you tell me about yourself seems only to be the smallest part. What you share has a depth I can't fully contemplate. Maybe, it's difficult for you, too." She nodded, still crying, still shocked by what he was saying.

"Oh, Creator," Sahni wept inside of Vanarra's mind. "He sees us! He *knows* us! Tana senses that he truly does. He doesn't understand everything yet, but…"

"Ash, Ash, please," Vanalla begged him. "Regardless of how strange it sounds, tell me what you see in me. Help me know what I am. I ask this of you."

He sat up and studied her for a moment, and then he chuckled. "It's … it's a little ridiculous. It will sound like complete nonsense. It may even make you angry."

She whispered, and her tone was not completely beyond the range of a threat. "It will make me angrier if you don't, my love. I need this – I need to see myself through *your* eyes!"

He paused, biting his lip, clearly worried. "In the dream I had, your Faelnar and Vulpi self were who you were, but being with you now, it's like a whole group. It's not how you look, okay? These are just impressions."

She saw his hesitation, and Van begged softly, "Please, Ash, tell me who I am."

"You … are so many, and yet, one. Faelnar and Vulpi mixed, yes, but more, still – one who serves, pliant and faithful, a side of yourself you were giving too free a reign before when you only followed me. There's a shade of a self as great as you at your core, almost in perfect harmony as if, together, you could fully be one. I see a shade of you in winged fire, and then some part of your spirit, brighter and closer, wreathed in life and light. There is another presence, mysterious and ancient and foreign to me, but as familiar to you as breathing. This is not a … sickness or an imbalance in what you are. It's who you are becoming. You are a collection that is becoming one, becoming whole, becoming complete."

He blinked and shook himself a little. "Sorry, that … that was a bit out there, I…" He had looked away in shame at what he thought were his random imaginings, but the look he found when he glanced back up into her eyes was amazing. "Hey, are you okay?" he asked her, putting a paw on her shoulder as she trembled.

"I … am utterly naked … before you, Ash," she confessed, her blush furs up, but only slightly. "You are in my very soul, now. You know what I am; you know who I am."

"I'm sorry that I can't express it better; I can't understand it better," he told her. "Those words just felt right to me as I said them.

It's silly of me to make such … mystical statements about who you are when I'm the cub who doesn't have a bunch of his memories."

She slipped closer to him, started rubbing his chest through his shirt. "When we are together, when we are intimate, you see things, envision other places." Blinking, he had to nod, as even now the background of an empty city office overlaid his vision, the Vulpi-Faelnar from his dreams again slipping across the face of his love. "You have helped me know who I am. I offer myself, all of me, Ash, forever so that you may know who you truly are."

Her nuzzling and kissing drew up his own desire, and her need for him was intense. Her scent surged into his nostrils and blossomed into his awareness – subtle undertones alluring him like never before. Allowing himself to let go of the moment, he fell into passion with her, their intimacy unwrapping almost a complete vision before him. As their intimacy progressed, it was as if he was following her down a path, up a hill, into a secret place, a place where she barred the door to prevent anyone else from following. It was a strange and twisting path to reach the shelter that would incubate their relationship, but it could be reached. It was mostly bare, but it was a safe place; it was secure, and she was there – every part of her, in this moment. He thought she might send him into another room so that she could have privacy and some assurance that he wouldn't take advantage of her, but the thought echoed into his mind, "Not this time, my love, my life. This time we are together, all of us, and you are my joy."

That evening, just before supper, he awoke beside her, the consummation of their union fully and totally complete, a union that he intended before that sol ended to make full and complete before Javoth and the Creator. He knew, now, that there was no way he could ever give up this amazing, complex, mysterious female that slept soundly and serenely beside him. Never had there been such a revelation of a life when he was younger, before that unassailable threshold that sealed off his memories. Yet, as they had entered the abandoned office, one mirror adorned the wall, and he saw himself – a young self, looking back at him from the mirror. It was the first time he had seen that visage, different and immature, but still very much him. It was a skinny youth, one not fully healthy – one with fear in his eyes. It was a fear, though, that was dying because he had found her, and she was magnificent.

Chapter 11: Walking as One

Javoth sat in his larger cabin having just bidden a good afternoon to Vassia. The former Vanarran Select's soul burned with the guilt and shame and loss of a life wasted to that point. There wasn't much consolation he could offer her about her past or the hidden value and meaning that lay within it. The more she told, the more of a desolation it was. It's only true value was that such a past had delivered her here with an opportunity to choose differently. The steadfast dedication to a false religion, he was discovering, was a great obstacle in finding one's way into the true one. Mistrust and the presumption of deception were everywhere, at every logical turn, and there was only one thing that allowed Vassia to hold onto that thin tendril of faith – the fact that no one other than the Creator would ever gain glory or praise or position for what she did in the name of that faith.

It gave him great pause, also, for he had misused that faith to gain himself wealth and prominence, indirectly turning the dedication and loyalty of others from the Creator onto himself. That, for Vassia, was the most deeply impactful, when he described how someone could accidently turn even the Creator's Path into a means of self-enrichment and aggrandizement. "You ... fooled yourself, then," she had told him, and he had no choice but to agree. When she asked what had broken him out of his self-made trap, he had only told her that someone with a much truer faith had confronted him and pointed out, without apology, the errors he had made. Vassia had also confessed, "Such was the way of it with me, also. It is a terror and a deep wound to learn all you believe to be a lie." Those were her last words as she had departed for the evening, the desire to share eclipsed with the need for reflection. It was a sad and morose way to end the sol, and as he stepped out onto the little porch on the front of his lair, he hoped the remaining sol's light would offer an opportunity for better.

When he saw Vanalla and Ash, once Akashar, walking towards him, their paws wrapped together in not only affection, but commitment, a smile almost immediately began to tug up the sides of his muzzle. "Dear friends," he greeted them, putting his paws on the railing. "It seems that you walk as one, now."

"You couldn't be closer to the truth, Javoth," Ash told him, smiling. "That's why we've come to see you."

"Step inside, please," he bade them, smiling. After he had invited them to sit and brought them tea, he asked, "Now, I wonder if you two could tell me what you two have discovered on the path?"

Ash deferred to Vanalla, and she bowed her head and smiled. "I wished to be joined to him, in the eyes of the Creator, and he to me."

Looking at the mixed blood's nod of agreement, he offered, "I'm so very happy for you both. I've seen this coming for a while. We all have. Can I ask what's brought about this decision, though? At this specific time?"

Ash told him without shame. "We have sealed our commitment to one another, completely and forever. For us, there can be no one else, and I think what we both learned is that we are both coming to realize more and more who we are, but this only happens for us when we're together, when we're ... close. I can see things about her and who she is that touch her, deeply. Javoth, when I'm with her, I ... I can see things about me I'd never hoped to see."

The male Lupar leaned back, understanding from Ash's phrasing that they had been fully intimate, but the commitment there was unmistakable. The two were now mates for life, and no ceremony or legal procedure would alter that in any way. "The sealing of this commitment," he asked carefully, "how long ago?"

"Only this sol," Vanalla offered in response, her earnest smile telling him that it was true. "We came to you before anything or anyone else."

"I am not the Creator," he noted, "and the Creator judges the heart and tells when one falls from the path. Absolution is not mine to give or withhold. However, you are now mates – that is clear beyond question to me. When do you plan to make the joining official?"

"Right now," Ash told him after looking at Vanalla for her nod of agreement.

"Surely, there are others who would want to celebrate with you, partake in this joy and stand by you in your commitment?"

Vanalla nodded, but answered, "While true, our *ceremony* is already complete, and we will not pretend otherwise. It would be a fraud. The others who love us have already shared the joy of us coming together, and if anything, we've been too slow in reaching this point. This is not my first joining, and my first was a grand event. Now..."

Ash finished her thought, "Now, we are here, and this doesn't seem the time or place for such a thing."

"For some," Javoth acknowledged, "the joining is an event, *the event!*" He shook his head and just laughed. "The actual life of the couple was far less glorious and regal than its celebration was." He turned his eyes on them. "Oh, you two! You are truer than that; I can tell. I think both of you fully understand that what you made is a lifetime commitment and that the physical intimacy you shared sealed that as truth. You are already joined in the eyes of the Creator, and normally, some level of ... chastisement would be on offer, but no – not here. I have never seen or heard mention of any other in your life than the one seated next to you, and you have patiently waited for this moment. You waited until you were sure of the path you walked, and that you would honestly be a good and stable mate to another. You waited until he was sure, and in that time – and I've pressed Fireclaw and even Shenaria on this – you truly sought no other. Please, Ash, understand the amazing depth of that commitment."

"I do, and I don't," he told Javoth. "I understand it happened and that it is there, still, but I can't imagine how I am that fortunate or that blessed."

"He doesn't fully know how deeply I need him in my life, but I think we're both learning that's true," Vanalla added, rubbing Ash's back. "He's very important to the *me* I am becoming."

"Mates can be a source of maturation, it's true, but they can't solve all of our issues for us," Javoth noted. "We must still rely on the Creator for that." They both nodded agreement. "Take her paw, Ash." Ash did as he was told. "Both of you have stated before me and before the Creator that you have sealed your commitment to one another, and such is sealed within your flesh and within your souls. In the name of the Creator, I hold you accountable for that until the passing from this life into the next. By your confession, your covenant is sealed, and it so recognized by the district of Shanan, the continental government of Thuratan, and by any other authority legal or familial. You are unto each other, lover, intimate, and mated. May the Creator's blessing always be upon you."

Ash and Vanalla kissed, then, and held one another's paws. "That's different than the ceremony I remember," Van commented, smiling at him. "It was lovely, and every bit of it was true. Thank you."

"Some, in these sols, don't like to pull out and use what is called the admonitory ceremony of joining, where there are no vows beyond the confession of full physical intimacy, but for you two, you delayed the ceremony far beyond its date to start with. May I ask you a different question than I asked you, before? What I asked you before was why were you coming to me, and you told me that it was to seal a physical commitment with the spiritual one. What I'd like to know, as your friend, what allowed you to open up and commit to one another? It was something so many of us have been praying for. We, who are your friends."

Ash looked to Vanalla who placed her paws in her lap and looked down. "I've had a very good friend of mine, a mentor, sit me down and tell me very plainly that I was getting too lost in my work. I have been lost in all of the details of Attoria, the planning, the legal wrangling, everything else, that I was missing my new life … in Attoria, my love. My heart is here because he is here, and the life I had needs to be on hold until we are truly joined. Even still, it can't take the place it did in the past. In the three seasons I waited, I was planning and working and orchestrating, and as you and I have spoken, Javoth – there will be periods of waiting and praying. My friends tell me that while we await the completion of the Attoria core buildings, which may be as long as a full season away, there is literally nothing that can be done."

Javoth nodded and replied. "Our little group here will not grow very much save for any defectors who reach out to us, as they have found ways to sell off more of their holdings and prolong the inevitable. Our children, though, Vanalla – they continue to learn and grow, and Ash has been a very big part of that. I sense that you can be, too."

"Only if I am here, and I am with him. So, I have been placed on a leave of my responsibilities by those who truly care for me, and they know that I need this; we need this," she breathed, hugging her new mate. "We have many trails to follow, but I want to follow them with Ash."

"For me, there's no one else," he told Javoth. "Thank you, deeply, for your kindness to us in this."

"Come by and see me after dinner, and I'll have the paperwork ready for you. Could Laxar stand as your witness? I'm sure he'd be honored."

"Your son is welcome to, and I would love that," Van told him, reaching up and kissing Javoth on the side of the muzzle as they stood.

"Yes, and … I think I'll ask you to stand as my witness very soon on that proceeding. It's time, and I love him as my son. A son … you helped bring to me, Vanalla. I am grateful beyond measure. Now, go enjoy your union, and may the Creator's blessings always attend you."

When they opened the door, they were amazed. Every Aelkinda and councilor and construction worker were gathered outside in a long line arching beyond his door. Beyond that were others Ash didn't recognize, but it was clear that his darling Vanalla certainly did. Over their shoulder, Javoth commented, "Yeah, I think you two might have just been spotted headed in my direction, it appears." He stood up straight and then announced to the silent and anxious gathering, "Ashalam and Vanalla are now joined in the eyes of the Creator." The cheer that went up was deafening.

"My goodness, Vanalla," Ash asked her, smiling and chuckling. "How did they know?"

"Uh, some of these are a little sneaky, but I think the rest just figured it out! Thank you, oh, thank you everyone! Some of you came from ... a long, long way away to see this, and I have no idea how you could have known when we ... we weren't sure."

A dark furred, serious looking Vulpi stepped up beside Fireclaw. "We were sure, even if you were not."

"Vosh," Van groaned. "You didn't like broadcast this to the universe, did you?"

"Well, someone did something of the like," a male Nephti with brilliant blue eyes chuckled, "or else I wouldn't be here."

Vanalla saw him and ran into his arms, hugging him tightly. "Oh, Dad! I ... I love you so much! What you've done for me!"

Ash walked up alongside her and just waited until the two had separated. "Ash, this is Theo. He's ... sort of an adopted father."

"I'm not anything of the *sort*," he said smugly, "I am her father, adopted, yes, but still." Vanalla nodded, laughing at what appeared to be an old and well-practiced routine.

"If you are her father, sir," Ash offered with a bow, "then I thank you and honor you for the role you have played in her life. If your advice and guidance has led her to be this amazing kit, this wonderfully kind and giving individual, then sir, I ask for your help, as well?"

"On my honor and by my pledge," the Nephti told him. "I am proud of her for the strides on the path she has made, but you, also, I sense will follow her even as she follows you. The best advice I will give you at the start of the joining is this – other than put the Creator first – at times she will lead, and at times you will. Have the grace to give way to the best guide between the two of you for the path you are travelling. All leaders who are not tyrants must do this, and it is a treasured skill and a piece of wisdom of great value."

"Thank you, sir," Ash offered, and taking this Nephti's paw in a clasp, he instantly understood that he was someone amazing. "I owe you greatly."

"It's ... not the first time I've heard that," Theo said with a somewhat mysterious air. It was one Ash didn't have time to question as other well-wishers also wanted their turns. Beyond Laxar, Fireclaw, Vassia, and the children stood three others, and they were ones that Ash could see Vanalla approach with an air of respect and honor. He could tell that Van's honor for her adopted father was absolute, but her long and loving familiarity with him engendered the teasing of family. These gathered just beyond were individuals that Vanalla deferred to almost as foreign dignitaries.

The three females stood shoulder to shoulder, one a Faelnar, one a big and impressive looking Lupar, and the other was a Vulpi. "I am truly humbled by your presence here, Nyssia," Van offered to the female in the middle, bowing. "I thank you for bringing my dear friend here to see me."

"My dear," the Lupar told her, "ever since she came to work with me, I've hardly stopped hearing about you." The comment embarrassed the Faelnar who seemed just about to burst for the opportunity to run into Vanalla's arms, her obedience to protocol the only thing keeping her from losing complete control. "It is deserved praise for the work you have done and what you will do. You have my good wishes for this and for your future, together."

"Thank you, Nyssia."

The big Lupar looked at Ash and nodded, smiling. "Ash, I believe that we may see more of one another in the future. Until then, live faithfully and well and look to the paths of light."

"Thank you, very much," he replied, bowing, and a look from Vanalla told him that he had done well.

Looking down at the Faelnar, Nyssia chuckled and said, "Oh, okay, now you can pounce on her!"

That was all the opportunity the taller than normal Faelnar with the somewhat short tail needed to hear to nearly tackle Vanalla, hugging her fiercely. "Oh, Van! I'm so very happy for you!!!"

"You got her to come here, didn't you?!" Van chided her, although laughing.

"I owe you everything, and this is the least I could do."

As they embraced, the pair wept silently in each other's arms for a pass, and Ash and the Vulpi remaining gave them that time, for the others had wandered away towards the dining hall. "I'm Dynaea," she told Ash quietly, offering her paw. "I'm watching over things while Vanalla is on her sabbatical."

"Very good of you; thank you," he stated softly. "Were you the one who ... relieved her of her responsibilities?"

"Only temporarily, I'm afraid, but Theo is hoping that this time will serve not only you and Vanalla but also that the two of you may offer some help to Trax and Shenaria, as well. New parents, you know. Besides, it won't hurt to learn some of those skills now," she told him, knowingly.

"We ... we haven't discussed children, yet – at least the timing of any."

"Ash, perhaps it would be best if you considered me not only a mentor of Vanalla, but also a colleague of Doctor Emmeniama de Kestrick. I want to be there for both of you as you go forward, together. When things even out, perhaps in half a season, I actually hope to be a part of Attoria."

"If you are a mentor and psychologist, then your presence would be welcome, indeed," he offered. "The children have had so many difficulties, and Vassia, also. If more come here..."

"*When* more come," she whispered in gentle correction. "Don't be discouraged by the seeming lack of progress in getting Vanarrans to reject their religion and its false hopes and seek a new life, here. Some of our lot have been visiting the prisons on a regular basis, and there are many, many more like Vassia out there. The ending of their sentences or the well-timed commutation thereof will pour more into your midst. These will be looking for new life, guidance, and ... they will need to go on a hike with you."

"I can scarcely take credit for what has happened here-"

"You are the fulcrum. You are that in ways you don't even fully understand, and much relies upon you. I know you see Vanalla as amazing and with a depth you don't fully understand. You, in many ways, have that same depth. You do not understand this, at present, but as the sols go on, you could come to represent the spirit and soul of this place."

Looking at the Vulpi, confused, he asked, "What ... must I do?"

"Love her. Help her. Love those who are here. Help them. It need not be overly complex. Don't become frustrated, as I've said, for in time all who are here will serve as the guides of those who come."

"Even the children?"

"Especially the children," Dynaea told him, but then smiled as she saw that Vanalla and Saletta had finally broken their tearful embrace and were approaching them, holding one another's paw. "My dear Vanalla, my congratulations are yours."

"Oh, you don't know how much I need to thank you for this," Vanalla breathed out, humiliated. "I still have so much more to learn."

"I'm sure your friend has told you that she needs to leave soon," Dynaea commented.

It was then that the big Lupar female returned after seeming to have had a good conversation with Vosh. "Soon, true, but not before we enjoy the celebration which has started in your dining hall."

Vanalla just shook her head. "How did they do it?" she asked Ash, dumbfounded, as they started to make their way to the happy gathering. "Was there just a *break glass in case of Ash and Van joining* thing I missed?!"

"It would seem so, love," he said, leaning over and kissing her on the side of the cheek. "It appears that many have longed for this, our sol." Clasping paws, the newly joined pair walked with their friends into the wonderfully jubilant celebration.

Loyal Elite Kallain de Mistral closed the door of his quarters, sighing as he stepped away. "What is wrong, my love?" his loyal aide and secret mate, Melissiana, asked him as he sat down upon the couch.

"I am bemused by the hard headedness of those in our order who resist the diminution of Sahnassa de Orturu from the status of goddess. As moderator of the conclave debate on a renewed canon of beliefs for the Sahnassites, I find it a difficult temptation to resist standing in front of them and explaining to them the certainty of their misdirected imaginings. As you and I have been in the Shade's confidence and protection for these difficult seasons, we have learned too much to believe that Sahnassa de Orturu was any kind of a goddess."

Melissiana seated herself and now drew his head gently upon her lap; it was something she always did when he was troubled. She was, truly, grateful of his frustrations in this area as she, also, shared them. The newer elements of the Sahnassites had proven more malleable when it came to the subject of their namesake's divinity, with some even going into the de Orturu archives to research. The writings of Astalla and Rothnerra not to mention those of Selena did provide much credit and honor in the direction of Sahnassa, but Triana's writings and Matreesia's did much to discount that. Even her own writings put most of the praise upon Vanarra de Gonari, a mystery of the faith Sahnassites, as a whole, found difficult to swallow. Now, however, the newer breed was tolerating it, in as much as it made their namesake just a little less godlike and a bit more Thurian.

"I feel your same frustrations, beloved," she told him. "I am Nephti, and the heart that beats within me – is it so unlike that which beat within her?"

"In a word, no," a soft voice entered the room all around them, and its intrusion made them both smile. "You have many qualities, especially your selflessness, that Sahnassa de Orturu could have truly learned from, and your guile continues to amaze, Kallain. The conclave elders will relent on the tenets of the goddess in the end. It is fear and loss of identity that drives them. Knowing this, you can redirect them."

He sat up and looked towards the corner of the room, the chair they always left open and unblocked for her to appear in, and appear she did, the smoky shade presence which Kallain preferred. "Welcome to our chambers, Noble Shade. I thank you for your insight and the influence you provide, I'm sure. Were my frustrations, alone, enough to draw you to our side?"

The visage did something that neither he nor his beloved had ever seen, she looked down in regret. "Not ... entirely. Kallain, together we have done a great many good things, and Melissiana has been the most amazing of partners for both of us. I have come to a point where those I am accountable to have required something of *me* I find difficult to obey. I have found someone, as you have one another, and ... he is very dear to me. We are now joined, but if I continue my work, unabated, I will seldom be with him. They have told me that I need this time with him and that I must surrender my duties to another, at least for a time. Therefore, I must entrust our alliance to someone else. I will still be nearby, and I am not leaving, but I cannot be there for you as I once was – at least for a time."

"I understand," Kallain told her, wrapping his paw around that of his mate. "It heartens me to know that you have found companionship. You gave this gift to us, first, did you not – before taking it for yourself?" The shade nodded. "As you have trusted Melissiana, I will trust whomever you send to me. Whom should we expect?"

The shade nodded to an empty portion of the room, and a creature of sparkling light appeared – golden facets not so brilliant as to be overwhelming, but certainly amazing and fascinating. "I am Dynaea, mentor to Vanarra, and it is I who have made this request of her – to step down for a time where she can live and love and grow."

"Please trust Dynaea as you have trusted me, and it is in the name of our friendship I ask this," requested the shade, still only partially visible albeit more defined thanks to the additional light. "Dynaea *is* greater than I."

"Only for a time," Dynaea warned. "Trust is also earned, and I will endeavor to earn yours as she has done."

"And so, we commit ourselves to you, Noble Light. Guide us and lead our way forward so that we may both see a future that is even half as bright and beautiful as you," Melissiana offered at Kallain's nod.

"The work that has been started," the glistening form told the smoky shade, "we will endeavor to complete. When the time comes for your paws to again rejoin us at this work, we will show you that we have been good stewards of your trust. Now, say your goodbyes, for I have something I wish to discuss with Kallain and Melissiana."

It was then that the shade rose and materialized fully as the mixed blood Vanarra. "Thank you for this, you two. I truly owe you, and I love you both."

The couple on the couch had also risen, and they embraced her. "Live and love, my friend. Your time of peace and rest is well deserved," Melissiana offered.

"We will endeavor to leave nothing undone," Kallain assured. After a deep and heartfelt embrace, Vanarra patted them on the shoulder and stepped away, disappearing just like a shade. When the couple turned towards the light, they saw a strange creature standing there – like a Thurian but not, with features that were beautifully delicate but with a presence and a light they both still felt. "You seem the worthy teacher. How might we learn?"

Dynaea spoke to them gently, "Attoria, for now, is in balance and grows well – all the more since that is where I have placed Vanarra and her love."

"So, her work is not truly suspended?" Kallain questioned.

The broad smile and shaking head brought out a smile on both Thurians' muzzles. "How can anyone truly stop Vanarra from *doing*? Her efforts, though, will be poured like a fountain of life into that specific community. It is we, I hope, who can help the important communities of family houses find the next steps down the path. Their way seems to have become blocked by those within their own ranks who enjoy the license to act without care or responsibility."

Melissiana nodded. "The difficulty being experienced with the overturn of the Familial Standards Relief Act. That was what barred houses from interfering in the private lives of their members."

"Interfering," Kallain mused, "or assisting. You can't be a true family house on Thuria without being able to enforce a code of conduct – standards and ethics. It was an integral part of each house's identity. May I take it, Noble Light, that you see a way for us to assist with overcoming these obstacles?"

"I do, and Vanarra was right, you do love your descriptive terms for us."

"Does the term not describe you adequately?" Melissiana asked, not wanting to give offense.

"Adequately enough, but I think that as we accomplish this task, it will be a name we can all truly share." That made Melissiana and Kallain sit up and listen intently as Dynaea began to reveal her plan.

The Consortium Pack of Business Alliance's after-party following their three-sol exposition and convention was a private affair – private and immensely decadent. Executives and corporate pack leaders had many reasons to celebrate, especially those situated in the more financially powerful houses, such as de Dothnar, de Orturu, and de Gonari. These executives had flourished after shedding the implicit, black-mailed taxation imposed by either the Sahnassites or the Vanarrans – sometimes both, in the case of de Gonari – and their ability to apply their wealth however they saw fit had become a competition for the greatest and most lavish display of prowess, prowess in nearly all of its varying forms.

In the darkened space with thumping music and equally pulsing lighting, the senior executives sat, arrayed on large couches with no less than two beautiful specimens of either male or female "aides" attending to their every whim. Not a one was accompanied by their mates as this wasn't the sort of gathering where one brought along any companion that was more than twenty seasons old and who could not immediately claim any contest of beauty simply by taking the stage. Collars were loosened and belts were not in evidence, and very little effort was made to hide the pawing that was going in both directions nor the eager consumption of rich and rare pre-Amyran fermentum easily costing the price of five lairs for "normal" Thurians.

A beautiful and seductive female Lupar cuddled up beside him on one side with a devastatingly beautiful Vulpi warming his other side, Chassir de Bosnar sipped slowly, his eyes gazing down into the clefts between soft mounds that would soon be his, later that night. "Ishara," he offered, greeting the female Nephti equally as well situated between two males, "so, what do you think of Matriarch Carinthia's efforts to get the FSRA repealed?"

That caused an uproar of laughter from everyone who could actually hear his sarcastic statement. As it died down, Ishara de Dothnar squirmed a little at the probing touches of the two lovely and muscular prowlers on either side of her. "I … I think it might just be a bit … premature – oh, you two! Stop it, now! You'll get everything you're prowling for later!" The males reluctantly backed off their more intimate assault under her dress and contented themselves with a more sedately lewd stroking near her privates on top of her clothes. "It's just not any of their damned business!" she added, angrily. "We take the big risks; why shouldn't we be entitled to the very best?! I mean, they can't lose their tails at the very next shareholders' meeting, now can they?"

Tosharn de Dothnar, the older male among them seated just in front of his peers, also enjoyed the somewhat amorous attentions of both a male and female Vulpi – trophies of beauty in every way. "Why should they interfere so long as we deliver the goods? It's not as if we were selling Thurian slaves on the market as those few were in the Shastana Shipping Group. Besides, it was our prior matriarch who paw-selected the very best prizes for herself. All of our associates are … reasonably compensated, wouldn't you say?" he asked, looking beside him. Both nodded, smiling, for indeed their pay for this "performance" was quite good.

"Well, she's enjoying the comforts of a very cold cell – Shalana is," Ishara de Dothnar spat, "and deservedly so for all of the trouble she caused. I'd dare say I plan to construct a way for her successor to follow in her path if she doesn't give up this idiotic repeal attempt. To think, because we reward ourselves and enjoy the fruits of our labors, these hypocritical and sanctimonious family leaders could actually toss us out onto our tails because a … a … really nice looking Vulpi decided he wanted to – oh, stop, you! I promised – *later*!"

Chassir and Tosharn chuckled at the clever timing of Ishara's two companions, happily emphasizing their benefactor's point by applying the now well-known "secrets of the Vulpi." Tosharn, however, also leaned up in protest. "And to think that my *preferences* would be a source of controversy that could actually deprive me of my career! Outrageous!" As if the Vulpi couple relied upon Tosharn as their protector, they snuggled into him seeking comfort. "See, my dear ones here enjoy my company and the compensation I provide them. Who are Carinthia and Pathia and Coursia to take away what we have earned?"

"They benefit very nicely by the required forfeitures of our profits we must make to them," Chassir nearly growled. "If anything needs repealing, it is their right to do that to us! Who the mange are they to deny us anything?! Oh, and speaking of that, Ishara, do you finally have that little piece of oceanfront your heart has been yearning after?"

"Next moon," she promised, stridently. "I managed to buy up the holdings company where the owner and his mate work. I have the sense that they are both going to come into a little misfortune in terms of regulatory procedure unless they are willing to accept my very generous offer."

"I've done contract work with your firm, Ishara," Tosharn laughed. "We both know that's about as likely as live sahnassas springing up from beneath the base of someone's tail. Not that those two lovely Vulpi probably don't know something really interesting to do with the base of your..." The Nephti writhed, eyes closed, as paws disappeared behind her body.

"By the moons," Dame Pathia nearly shouted, "turn it off!" Within the matriarch's private conference room in the heart of the de Dothnar keep, Kallain pressed pause on the playback of the VidStar his aide, Melissiana, had been able to acquire posing as a scantily clad server within the executive levels of the *Scandal Paws* night club. A glance back at the screen showing oversexed Ishara clearly enjoying the moment had the dame shaking her head again and looking into her fellow Nephti's face with sympathy. "That you had to stand there and witness that. I would have called up my last meal right in front of them."

"It was for the best of causes, Honored One," Melissiana told her, bowing humbly before the two dames and their matriarch. "Our associates indicate that this braggadocio is truly being backed by actions on their part and on the part of their underlings to sway and constrain our lawmakers against the policies you endorse for house empowerment. "

"Is there more?" Matriarch Carinthia asked, her expression very grim.

"You have seen the core of it," the Sahnassite Nephti offered. "What occurred after was a digression in their behaviors and a departure from any substantive discussion. I had to remove myself lest I, like the other servers in the room, became disrobed, revealing my recording equipment."

"I saw male and female servers, there," Dame Coursia commented. "All were ... compelled to remove their clothes and engage in intimate contact with these three?"

"There were, in fact, six other executives beyond these three, Honored One," Melissiana testified. "It was only this group that placed themselves in the proper location to be recorded for any period of time. I have snippets of the others, but only enough to identify them. I am also given to understand by those serving in the club that the hush payouts given by the executives' underlings make this an exceptionally prized event."

"And decidedly exclusive," Kallain warned. "Had there not been an ... engineered absence ... they would not have been short-pawed and desperate enough to look for replacements."

"Your associates' work again?" Carinthia asked. "So, what do they suggest as a course of action?"

"That we bring this information to you and ask you to decide the best path," Kallain told them. "They are enablers and encouragers of the course to a new Thuria with strong houses. They provide valuable insight and information. They are not to be the sole architects of it."

"We, as the houses," Pathia agreed, "must take responsibility for this, ourselves. We must find a way to undermine this resistance or remove it. Expose or embarrass these ... idiots!"

"It doesn't mean that we wouldn't be accepting of ideas, though," Carinthia interjected, "as you and your aide have proven yourselves truly resourceful in the past." She saw the slight look of worry in her fellow Nephti's expression. "What is it?"

Melissiana looked at Kallain for permission, and he nodded. "Honored Ones," Melissiana offered softly, "I am not a worthy vessel to provide this kind of guidance, but still, before anything is done to combat the outrageous excesses of these you see in this recording, every effort must be made to internally cleanse your house leadership. Embarrassment and exposure can go both ways, and if these feel threatened in any way, they will pursue you with equal vigor."

The elder Nephti's head turned slightly. "You believe that one of our number, maybe even we, have these same faults?"

"It is my regret to inform you," Kallain offered, "that there were several august members of your leadership present at this event. None of them are in this room, or else we would not have shared this with you. Their sentiments regarding the repeal of familial oversight on private lives may not be questioned, openly, but their presence guarantees a sort of mutual destruction should they rise in support of such a repeal. So, when you speak to the legislators directly, then these individuals come in after to undermine your words with the delegates' staff. The result is that your visits to the capital come to naught."

"The stench of Shalana's corruption lingers to this very sol!" Carinthia spat. "Names, Kallain. You observed, and I want to know."

"The names, I should think that upon deeper reflection, should not be much of a surprise. Dames Docia and Lanaria were present at this event, as well," Kallain told them.

Looking to Melissiana, the matriarch ventured, "And what were they doing, pray tell? Exactly."

The Nephti bowed her head and looked away. "They were involved … in a very intimate way with several young males in one of the dark corners of the private lounge. They were already well involved before Chassir, Ishara, and Tosharn joined in, and although I wasn't there to witness it, it was likely they made themselves … available."

"How many young males, exactly?" Dame Coursia questioned.

"I believe the count was three a piece, Honored One, at the same time – precisely."

"How could you-" Pathia asked, but then closed her eyes and swore quietly. "What honors have been stolen from us by this treachery?!"

"So long as the Familial Standards Relief Act remains in place," the matriarch reminded them, "we may not prowl into even our dames' private lives, and although I surely believe you, Melissiana, we can't take your testimony as proof of any wrongdoing. Unfortunately, if even Shalana's transgressions were only in her private relations, it would have been difficult to move against her, legally. The criminal angle was the only true recourse. So regretfully, I'm left wondering what our options are in this case."

"I am surprised that after the testimony of Shalana against these two, they remained among your number, Honored Ones," Kallain gently prodded.

Coursia shook her head. "We were *all* victims of Shalana. We were all sitting with some kind of blackmail or threat hanging over our heads. We also needed their votes to remove Shalana, and we had hoped that all of us would learn to be more circumspect when granted a second chance."

"It appeared that their appetites were very difficult to sate, Honored Ones," Melissiana noted softly. "I saw the males approach them, and very little enticement was needed to begin their activities. Dare I suggest that it may be possible to orchestrate a legitimate enforcement operation attempting to draw in these two."

"A quick glance into their medical records for … business reasons," Pathia noted. "A review of all of the dames, you understand? Moon cycle ruts wouldn't be hard to figure out, I'd wager."

"Were there any illegal substances there, Melissiana?" Carinthia asked.

"I did see some of the more common recreational drugs, including some medical grade pharmaceuticals used for the treating of sexual dysfunctions," the Nephti noted. "A high dosage of these drugs can bring on acute rut symptoms. I think it very unlikely they were prescribed for this type of use."

Carinthia stepped and started to pace slowly, her thoughts clearly focused on this issue. "Those two have certainly outlived their welcome, and the cadre of matrons beneath them has some very well educated and promising candidates." Looking at her fellow dames, she told them, "We trapped Shalana, with Kallain's help. Mightn't we do the same for these two?"

"It would take a little … careful study, but I believe I have a few contacts in enforcement I can leverage," Coursia mentioned. "I don't think it should be too difficult to trap them if we present them with the right enticements. What then, though? We've only trapped two dames and charged them with what?"

"Criminal lewdness and attempting to solicit sexual favors for money and, thereby, supporting the trafficking trade of Thurians,"

Carinthia noted. "It's a criminal offense. Possession of the pharmaceuticals, as well, would be a nice tack on. If they resist the officers, you can add battery to those charges."

"And so again," Pathia questioned, "we come only to the result of two dames drummed off our rolls? This does nothing to help us with those three monsters we witnessed or the undue influence they're having over our legislators."

"It gives us leverage over two who already have access to that inner circle of debauchery. It is the initial trap in which we can lay our next trap."

"Charging three high level executives with misdemeanors hardly warrants a celebration on our parts," Pathia complained.

"Your goal is to extinguish their resistance to the Familial Standards Relief Act," Kallain reminded them. "Gaining some leverage over these individuals is only one part of what must be pursued, Honored Ones. That leverage can only be applied in a certain way, and one must also learn how this opposition appears in front of the members of the assembly. Are their campaign funds threatened? Are they involved in a pact of mutually assured destruction should their misdeeds become known? Do they fear the newsarotzi linking them to individuals who have such poor moral rectitude? These things must be known, Honored Ones."

Carinthia's gentle pacing stopped. "There was a time in this house's history where we possessed the intelligence assets to easily carry out such an operation."

"We can assemble those assets, again, Honored One," Coursia noted. "We had many supporters in the ouster of Shalana, and many who worked with us in secret. We are mutually indebted to one another."

"There is no place of ultimate security, Coursia, in which to discuss them, plan them, coordinate them. We succeeded with Shalana, yes, but many times we were very nearly discovered."

"Matriarch Carinthia," Kallain offered, a slightly excited smile tugging up the sides of this mouth. "It is my understanding that the tours of the old de Dothnar intelligence hub have not been so popular as of late." The three of the de Dothnar matriarchy simply looked at each other for a moment and then back at him. "Perhaps, some additional historical displays in the halls of honor could help sate those desperately interested in this house's intelligence history while the *overhead* and *expense* of maintaining such a space for public tours could be redirected to something more productive. Also, I notice that certain areas of your office space seem quite crowded. It shouldn't be too difficult to relocate certain ... key ... individuals to renovated office space in previously underutilized areas?"

"But," Pathia sputtered, "everyone knows where it is."

"It will be very important to announce the closure of this space to the public," Melissiana suggested, "so that those who have a desire to visit it a final time may indulge their nostalgia. It is regrettable that your house has to realign its assets in this way, but with current building costs and increasing familial staff, there are simply few alternatives that are as ... expedient as this alternative."

"And so," Carinthia stated slowly, making sure she was following his wisdom, "this *attraction* has to be closed in favor of a more ... accessible one. One more suited to the tastes of the present sol, perhaps even one that highlights the good the matrons have been able to do in the lives of families. A ... celebration of them – plus the new history displays about house intelligence."

"A console from the situation room, Honored One," Kallain suggested. "Artifacts from Shaelen de Dothnar's office. Perhaps even interactive displays – compelling ones, as well – should take several moons to create, allow one to generate interest, and shift emphasis away from the now defunct Intelligence Hub exhibit."

"This is a very slow course you propose, Kallain," Coursia stated.

"With apologies, Honored Ones," Melissiana interjected, "it is an insidiously devious one, not unlike the planning that went into this house's protection of Vanarra de Gonari after the Meeting Den. What will appear to your adversaries, even these engaged in such misguided behavior, is the similitude of retreat, surrender. They will appear to have won the sol, all the while you have discovered the weak among their pack and will slowly corral and corner them. Patience, in this case, is a weapon."

"Your aide, Kallain," the matriarch softly noted, "is someone of our own name whose insight in these endeavors would be helpful."

"She has been my apprentice for a long time, and her assistance is important to me," he told them, guarded. "However, perhaps as a new openness towards the Sahnassites – a false hope we could offer our order – she could be made available to consult, if it is her wish."

Melissiana turned to Kallain and bowed her head, "Your will takes precedence in all I do, all I am."

"But if you were to choose in this endeavor?" he asked her, ignoring the somewhat stunned expressions of the other Nephti in the room.

"I feel the pull of my family and what it could mean for Thuria. I believe that what we and our associates work towards is a noble goal. I would like to help."

"Your allegiance is only to Kallain, however?" Carinthia questioned, her thoughts of having Melissiana in the matriarchy shoved aside.

"As mine is to you," the Faelnar told them. "You have not forgotten that even those who believe me to serve as their leader are those I will disassemble and remake into nothing more than another branch of the Creator's Path. We are steadily moving that direction, and eventually, all semblance of central direction will be dissolved. At that point, I will be without any true family, as I carry de Mistral for the sake of appearances and pretense. Since Sahnassites were once on the same path as the Foundationalists, it is … fashionable for those in our order to carry a last name."

"In time, Kallain," Carinthia asked, and it was clear that some emotional investment lay within her plea, "would you ever consider taking ours? You have been responsible for where we are, and you continue to aid us. If even the Grand Matriarch Rahnahi de Dothnar stood where I stand, she would see this, truly."

"Would you consider a relationship between me and my assistant to be beyond acceptance?" he asked her – his eyes intent and sharply observant.

"It's there now, isn't it?" Pathia noted, putting a paw on Melissiana's shoulder. "You hold each other's hearts."

Kallain closed his eyes and nodded. Melissiana did the same. "It makes me happy, Kallain," Carinthia confessed, shaking her head in relief. "I've felt pity for you these last few seasons – it is a disgusting emotion because it presupposes there was never any hope for redeeming the life you were trapped in for another. You, my friend, are giving us the way to do that for you. Your intelligence acumen and connections make you of value to this house. Your loyalty makes you of value to this house. Publicly, Kallain, maintain the name de Mistral. Privately and truly, become kept by and keeper of us."

"Those to whom I owe my first allegiance, my associates, must approve of such a direction," he told them softly. "They must know that the choice helps their cause of restoring the houses to prominence."

"Tell them this, Kallain," Carinthia bade. "There will be another, now, who stands in Shaelen's place, who takes on the role of protecting the interests of all families and especially our own. That will be you. I have despised you, and yet you were being loyal to this house – clever beyond belief! I mistrusted you, and you remained steadfast. I was galled by pride and revenge to act … shamefully, and you counseled better. You endure the most self-destructive ruse *for our sakes.* The burden of this debt has weighted me in my soul."

"I know," Dame Pathia groaned, "what you endured in dealing with Shalana. I still have nightmares about it. Your heart, though, is still with us, with this one, especially."

Coursia walked up to him and told him, "All my life, I've wondered if there were any great Thurians left or if we were all just as base and shameful as Shalana – becoming so. You answered that question for me. Please, consult with your associates; we would not presume to go against their wishes as through you, they have been of immense assistance. This is our repayment to them, as well."

Melissiana looked at the matriarch, her eyes pleading. "Honored One, if … if it is decided that we should both be of this family, would it be possible for a joining under the covering of your honor?"

"Our honor," Carinthia corrected. "Secret, initially, but it would be so." Looking to Kallain, she smiled at seeing the approval and affection in his expression towards his love. "You both need shelter after this storm."

"What you say is not incorrect, Honored One," Kallain noted, "as there are those of my order who despise me along with those of the general public for what I represent, for those they have lost in one way or another to the Sahnassites over the seasons. I will take your generous offer forward to my associates."

"In the meantime," Carinthia stated, "we will begin the *display* of pulling back, just as a wave does before it crashes upon the shore, and together, will wash away these vile monsters who treat Thurians so disgracefully."

Chapter 12: A Truer Voice

Vanarra woke up next to her lair mate in the predawn intervals of a cool autumn morning, her mind still trying to grasp how much her life had changed. It had now been six moons since Dynaea came and took over as Teldear, six moons since she had stepped a hind paw aboard the Haven. It had been six moons since she learned, for sure, that the Perratti-Lupar sleeping next to her in the tree tent was indeed her lost Ash from so long ago. With her mother, now a mother all over again with the twins she had borne Trax, there had never been any doubt or question, and her mother was exactly as she had been when Vanarra lost her. Ash, however, was a different case.

When she met him, she had suspected, but the echoes of her memory weren't clear. She remembered a skinny teen who died in her arms, not someone older – fully an adult. The gap and her inability to actually probe into his past with the tools of a Teldear made her wonder if this was Ash or just someone *like* Ash. On this side of knowing, she thought it ridiculous that she would have even doubted, but it was that she held onto that doubt for so long that gave her pause. Ash's loss, his suffering in her arms as he died, and the guilt defined her for so much of her life, and she had held onto that. When she finally touched the truth, she had collapsed – she had crumbled.

After finding her hind legs, somewhat, it had been a little unsettling being pushed from such an active role as Teldear into this quiet, rural setting, but she knew that Theo had been right in that decision. The aftermath of the realization of how kind the Perratti-Lupar truly was had shown her just how broken she was, had always been. "I'm not really even the same individual as I was, before," she thought, idly. Even the Sahnassa inside of her and Tana had quieted to the point where as the sols went by, she was more and more authentically one presence learning to love, again. Ash had sensed this brokenness in her, even through the mask of her Faelnar self, and he had loved her sol by sol, healing her. What's more, as they spent time together – intimate time, parts of Ash's life were coming back to him, and in that way, they were sharing deeply in the mutual uncertainty of changing identities.

Their commitment to one another, their union, although perhaps not formed as properly as some would prefer, was completely appropriate given the fact that back in their youth they had truly been lair mates. "He is and always has been, my mate," she thought, gently stroking the back of his head in a way she knew wouldn't wake him. She had loved Buck; she always would. Her commitment to him had been complete based on the knowledge and the certainty that Ash was dead. Ash, now, wasn't dead. "I gave my body to him, my soul to him, and so it was done – we were lair mates from that moment." Their initial intimacy in this time had actually been a recommitment to one another.

There was another and less certain aspect of their joining that was progressing towards some inevitable destiny. Ash was sharing every vision that came to him, and it was clear to her that he was now seeing the Vanarra of that time. Ash didn't recognize the figure from his visions as the Vanarra of history, but he was starting to have feelings for this teen mixed blood, wonder who she was or had been. He dreamed of being alone in the forest, afraid and cold – terrified of everything around him, and then she stood where she'd been watching him. It was as if she had appeared out of the night shadows and then came to him, kindly and earnestly. The prior night, he had dreamed of being held by her, cared for and loved.

He would try to pass it off as just a dream or a delusion – unimportant, but she could tell that these fleeting moments of another life were starting to give him the hope that there was a real past he could finally claim as his own. She could see him writing each of them in his journal as soon as he awoke or as soon after their intimate time as he felt he could without offending her.

On one of their trips into Shanandrae, she had tried an experiment. She had purchased another journal as his first was starting to fill up and wear out, but with it, she purchased her own autobiography. As far as she could tell, although he was politely thankful for the gift, he hadn't even touched the book, not even picked it up. "I don't understand, Ash," she whispered in her thoughts. "Why can't you see me? Why won't you see me?" Laxar had far less time in Vanalla's presence before he, insightful cub that he was, had understood that Vanalla and the Vanarra of old were one and the same.

Her loving strokes on the back of his head hadn't changed, but he shifted and rolled over to look at her. "You're up?"

"Sorry, couldn't sleep anymore. Forgive me, I woke you."

He looked at her form in the soft shadows of the hanging tent. "It's okay. Give me a moment, and I'll come back up, okay?"

She nodded, which he could only see in silhouette, but it was enough. When he left the tent and made his way down the rope ladder, she smiled a little as the surfaces beneath her bounced with his weight and movement.

After a few moments, though, everything became still, and although she could sense him below her, other senses appeared in her thoughts, as well. She sat, her legs crossed, her tail limp behind her, and Van closed her eyes, breathing deeply. The tent she was sitting in simply faded away to nothing, leaving her suspended in a void of deep purples and blues coursing in streams around her. These branches and confluences rippled around her, images that were increasingly common to her as she meditated. Her mind's eyes cast across them, looking for places where the flow was blocked or ran counter to what seemed the natural order. Raising her paw, she dipped into one of these stymied courses, and she caught an image of Laxar and Vassia in an argument – something that hadn't happened yet, but it was nearly certain now, and the effects of this conflict were enough to completely disrupt the flow of all events around them.

There was a strange edge to it, though, and instead of withdrawing her paw, she issued it deeper in, and more insight was gained. Vassia admired the cub, liked him, but found her former position and age difference forced her to deny herself – that, and her guilt. Minus the children, she was deeply lonely – the buildings that were going up were starting to look more and more complete, and yet there was no one new coming to live in Attoria to fill them. Laxar both feared and wondered over the former Vanarran Select, and he had even wanted to sketch her, but anxious over how such a thing might be seen and misunderstood, he refrained. "I will help them," she thought, removing her mental paw from the flows of circumstance and causality.

"Of course, you will," Ash's voice came as a soft echo into her thoughts. It was then she realized that he wasn't actually a figment of her imagination. He was real and was now seated in front of her; she could see his outline against the back of the tent, just starting to glow from the faint sheen of promised morning. "Who, though, Vanalla? Who will you help?"

"Laxar and Vassia," she replied softly as the flowing colors in her mind slipped away. "They want to care for each other, but the Vanarran Select and the Vanarran slave still overshadow their relationship. They need to find a way through that and beyond it." Van knew she had only thought the words, but he had actually heard them. What's more, he didn't know that she hadn't actually spoken because it was so dark.

He slipped in beside her and offered, "It's the work of every Vanarran who comes here, or least it will be – the promise of leaving the darkness of their past behind them in search of a new light. It will take work, though. Their age difference will be something to overcome. I can guess it will be very difficult for them."

She knew he was trying to be encouraging, but there was also an opportunity for her, lurking in his words. "Difficult is found so many places and in so many strange things. You take an interest in so many things, but there is one place where you shut your eyes and refuse to see, Ash. I have to admit that I have noticed it since we've been together."

His paw slipped around hers, and he gently contested, "Since I've been with you, I've seen more of what I think is my past than at any other time of my life. Is it something in my present I'm not seeing?"

"I don't think so. It's something ... of the past. Trax and I are both students of history, in a way; did you know that?"

"I've heard you two talking from time to time; your mother, too," he agreed.

"Certain conversations you'll listen to. Certain ones ... you always drift away – excuse yourself. There's someone in history that whenever she's discussed, you look the other way. Why?" He tensed and wouldn't answer. "I bought you the book of her history, written in her own words. You've read other books I've bought you, enjoyed them, even. This one, you didn't even unwrap the ribbon around it to get to your new journal. Why, love? Why not her?"

"It's ... just a preference thing, Van – nothing against her, really. Not a big deal." Van was quiet for a moment, and he could tell that she hadn't judged that a sufficient answer. He debated, hopelessly, within himself about what to say, and part of him just wanted to push her away and demand she let it go. Still, it was their close times, like this, when he really felt like he had a feel for his old self, whoever that was. "Yeah that's ... not true. I really don't understand it," he breathed out, the conflict within clear in his voice. "I see pictures of her, read things she's said, and I feel ... empty, lost. It's ... it's a horrible feeling; it's the weirdest thing! I feel like there's something missing in my heart – it's wrong! I have no right to feel this way! My life is FULL! I have you in it! I should be fine with that!"

"Easy, easy, love," Van offered, nuzzling against him to quell his distress. "And it's only her? Stories about Sahnassa de Orturu make you feel this way?"

"Funny thing – yes, I ... I sort of, but it's not – it depends on the story. It's a little hard reading about that time because she's in so much of it, Vanarra – she is. Hylea's journals are great, though – all those discoveries – all those ruins. I read a pretty good bit of Rahnahi de Dothnar; Flint de Gonari, too."

She was quiet for a moment and then asked him, "Do you *hate* Vanarra de Gonari?" He shrugged and then shook his head. "Would it help you if you could talk to her?"

"From beyond the grave?" he asked, sighing. "Neat trick. I mean, maybe it would have, honestly. Grand Matriarchs were supposed to be pretty fierce customers, though. You were supposed to say Honored One every time you spoke to them, and they were like revered by the family, by everyone. I mean, maybe if I could have just sat and listened to her talk, been in the audience. You know, if I was with her, I don't think I would have felt right at all about avoiding her."

She slipped away from him a short distance and then a little lamp went on, and she looked at him, a sly smile on her muzzle, but a watchful and hopeful look in her eyes. Using the new journal to cover the book underneath, she started to read. "Hi there. My name is ... well, you know what my name is, I suppose, since it's probably on the cover, but look here – let's make one thing perfectly clear right from the start. What I'm going to share with you contains a lot of pretty hard things, difficult parts of my growing up, even my adulthood. I don't tell you for the sake of making you or anyone else feel guilty or, worse, sorry for me. Don't you dare! My life has been amazing, and I have been truly blessed. I tell you because I was asked to share, and every time I've done so there have been those who told me that it helped them to hear my story. As I set out to start this, please understand that this is all I want to do, help you."

"That's ... her?" he asked, bemused and a bit incredulous.

She smiled and shrugged a bit, winking at him, and he chuckled. "You okay with it?"

"With you reading it?" he asked, rhetorically, before nodding and smiling at her. "You know, yeah. I ... there's something about having your voice in it that makes it right. Okay, yes. I think I'll be okay this way. Just promise me that if we get to something and I put up my paw, you'll stop?"

"I promise you, Ash. Thank you." He smiled and nodded at her, leaned back, and then just relaxed as she started to read again.

Laxar was in tears, and Vassia, sitting nearby, was not in much better shape as they all sat in Van and Ash's cabin. "It was her kind, Vanalla, the Selects, who tortured and punished me," he whispered to her.

"She was misguided as were you, dear cub, but look at her now. That grief weighs on her, and deep inside of her is a child who saw her friends disappear and not come back, who lived life in a different kind of terror than your own – but it was terror nonetheless. You, they would have kept you until you died of old age-"

"As a servant, as a slave to *them*," he said spitefully, in Vassia's direction.

"I'm not saying you're wrong," the former Vanarran begged him. "What I am saying is that I saw other Selects gutted right in front of me for the least of offenses or because a genetic test showed them to be too impure. My life was terrible, and I'm sorry that yours was, as well."

Ash slipped up behind his mate and offered, "You two – you are really a lot like me, but just opposite. I couldn't remember my past, and you two can't forget yours. I went through seasons of therapy and study and even medical scans and everything you can imagine, all to arrive at this – who you choose to be is just that, a choice. I didn't start to recall anything about my past until I started loving this amazing kit. You two may never be able to see past your pasts if you can't learn to trust one another or feel kindness for one another."

"And by our actions, we define ourselves," Laxar whispered.

"Creator's Path beliefs, true," Ash agreed, "but if you don't own it, it doesn't mean anything. Memorization can't help you if you keep your heart locked in a box."

Van raised her paw in Ash's direction to forestall him, but Vassia intervened. "No. It … it helps to hear this. It is a hard truth. It is the truth, though – at least for me. I was so bitter for the losses I endured, and now, I'm heartbroken by the suffering I didn't stop. Suffering like yours, Laxar. I'm sorry."

"When others from their order arrive, Lax," Ash asked, "are you afraid they'll try to dominate you like they did when you were their servant?" Again, Van almost intervened, but the mixed blood male nodded back at him. "If you stood alongside Vassia with those like yourself, do you think she would stand up for you? From what I hear, both groups might be coming here – you can't ignore this, and I know both of you. You are both dedicated and loyal and trustworthy. You've got to see that in one another."

"One of the biggest mistakes the true Vanarra de Gonari almost made was in not trusting a friend who dearly loved her," Vanalla told them, and both of them looked at her. "If she hadn't, then she would have been dead. It would have cost her the price of her own soul."

Laxar, eyes still running with tears, walked over and knelt in front of Vassia, and she slipped down to the floor, and he did the same for her. "Ash," Van whispered into his ear, smiling, "well done, my love. What do you think they'll need next?"

"I might go over and grab a little something for them from the dining hall. It's that time. That way, they can stay and talk."

"Sounds great, my love," she replied, and he nodded before slipping out the door.

After the door had closed, Laxar leaned up and looked at Vanalla. "He was right about me, about what I fear."

"I will *not* let that happen to you!" Vassia pleaded. "I've seen where that path leads, and I don't want to ever go back there, again. My eternal soul would be at risk if I ever dared it."

"And your challenge, my dear cub," Vanalla offered, "is to believe it, and to trust her."

"I have learned to always trust your council," he told her, and Vassia looked up at him, curious.

"You … know who she is?" Vassia asked him, quietly.

"I do. She is not the one you – we once worshiped," Laxar told her. "She is not the myth we created. She is the one."

They both looked at Vanalla, and she shifted in her seat a bit uncomfortably. "I have kept that secret, also," Vassia commented. "She … confronted me and turned me away from a horrible, lost path."

"I'm sitting right here, you two," Van complained.

"Then do this for us, one who we once thought of as the Great Mother. Show your true self to us both," Vassia pleaded. "Let that be the secret that binds us together."

"It must remain a secret, even from Ash, for now," Vanalla warned. Closing her eyes, she stated, "Fine. He's taking a little more time with Javoth in the dining hall. We have just a moment." Vanalla opened her eyes, and it was Vanarra who was looking at both of them. "This isn't something I can keep doing, especially for anyone else."

"No, but we needed this," Laxar told her, going to the side of Vassia and sitting next to her, clasping her paw. "This secret binds us, does it not?"

The Aelkinda nodded. "You had manifested to me, before. I longed to see you in this form once again to thank you for redeeming me."

"And pray tell, what do you see when you look at me, Vassia? Surely, I am not the holy Great Mother. You have to know that is not the case."

"No," Vassia agreed. "You are not that, but you are a gift from another age and different – far different than I ever suspected. Temple Master Lashure thought we were living in a holy time, in the answer of all of our prophecies. They were meaningless – self-invented fantasies, but you are special. Your view is longer, and so, I will ask you, please, what should the future be for us, now? We were created by those who were so misguided, myself included. I've heard some call us a mistake that needs to be erased. What destiny is there now for us?"

Vanarra walked over and sat on the small table facing where they were sitting. "My hope is that all of those who were once laboring falsely under the name of the Vanarrans find a new life, a safe life, a productive life following the Creator's Path, if they so choose, and loving and caring for those around them. Seasons from now, when the anger and memories of the purebred curse have faded, perhaps the villages of Attoria and maybe even Silarcia could be places once known for tragedies that become treasured homes for this new mixed blood purebred. Maybe, in time, some move away and live happily in other cities. Maybe, in time, others move here, those not Aelkinda. I'd always want there to be a welcome here, especially in a place that was built knowing Thurians make mistakes, but if we are together on the Path, there need not be anything that keeps us from doing good and being there for each other."

Looking at Vassia, Laxar promised, "I will be there for you."

"And I will be there for you. Together, we will help make your dreams for us into reality."

"You must find your own dreams," Vanarra emphasized. "You must find your own path. You can't build this place based solely on my vision. I'll help, but these are your choices. Never serve me or try to carry out my will."

"Your will is that we find the Creator and follow that path for both ourselves and our new home," Laxar contested. "We have no choice but to follow that path if we are to have any hope for our future."

Vanarra shook her head, smiling. "I can't see where I have any room to argue that logic."

"Who else knows your true form?" Vassia asked. "Who else knows you like this?"

"Vosh does, as does Fireclaw. Javoth, I have revealed myself to him, but I have never connected this..." and she changed back into the form of Vanalla. "With this. Does he know, Laxar?"

"If he does, he does not say," the young male offered, "but I tend to think he does not. He has spoken of the time when he left the chapel as his most difficult chapter, and he does not recall it, often. What about your ... Ash?"

"Surely the one mated to you has-"

"No," Vanalla told them softly, but firmly. "Not yet, but please, don't suggest anything and be careful of what you say. His soul has a Vanarra sized wound in it, and we've just stumbled across a way he can get past it. I read to him from my autobiography, and in that way, he can hear it without feeling pain. When he has learned more of me, who I was, he may remember who ... he was."

"His path strides across the centuries, also?"

"It was not I, Vassia, who made that choice for him. One greater than I, far greater, made that choice. Ash is a light, a special soul, and not only dear to me, dear to the one I serve." Van looked towards the door and stated softly, "He returns, and he comes with plates full of both of your favorites. He loves and cares for you both, as do I."

"If we ... were close," Laxar asked, "would he approve? Do you approve? Despite the difference in our ages?"

"You are already close, whether anyone approves. I ask you to make your commitment before you commit to the deepest intimacy."

"That was not your path," Vassia softly challenged.

"Ash and I … were already mates," she whispered, "more than fifteen hundred seasons ago." With that, they heard him entering the cabin through the kitchen door. In a normal speaking voice, she offered, "The commitment was already there."

Ash leaned in and agreed to what he thought was being said, "You two have been getting closer the entire time I've known you. In many ways, you've needed each other. You know I approve."

"As do I," Van replied, smiling in a way he couldn't see.

"We will talk to Javoth then, to Father," Laxar told them. "We will listen to his words and heed the wisdom in them."

"Good," Ash, who had ducked back into the kitchen, said, coming out with two plates of food. "Now, let's eat."

"Some for us, too?" Van asked, and he nodded. "I'll help." They both ended up in the kitchen for a moment, and she added quietly, "You already helped, too. Your approval meant an enormous amount to them. Thank you."

"How can I not? You approved of me, and that changed everything."

Within the matriarch's quarters, Dames Docia and Lanaria felt as if they were standing naked in front of the three senior dames of their house, and indeed, to some part, they were. On the large screen behind the matriarch's back was extremely detailed VidStar taken in one of the anterooms of the *Scandal Paws* night club. It was not in color as such was taken in near darkness, but every word and groan and sound played in amplified perfection as they watched. "You see that one? He's with enforcement," Pathia almost sneered. "Yes, the one finding the base of your tail so interesting, and this part is the best, just listen…"

"Oh, please, I'll … I'll give you whatever you want if you keep doing that," Docia purred.

"What if I wanted secrets? What if I wanted money?"

"All you could ever ask for and more. I'll give you whatever you ask for, for this," she breathed, huskily before the image froze in place, the dame about to reach for an intimate part of his anatomy.

"And that, my dear *dames*, is called solicitation for prostitution," Matriarch Carinthia offered soundly. "Both of you said nearly the very same thing. That's a criminal offense, and such entitles me to suspend you from your position, turn you over to the waiting claws of enforcement, freeze your family assets, and to begin to *disavow you*, officially. Now, as we all know, that would deny you any support or pension, but I have an offer to make you, one that *may* save you embarrassment and poverty so long as you do whatever we ask."

"That's blackmail!" Lanaria cursed. "You're no better than Shalana!"

"Oh no, you'll still be charged with attempted solicitation of an undercover enforcement officer – that's going to happen," Carinthia told them both. "You're still going to be removed from your positions. You see, however, it's how much *support* we give you after that's at our complete and utter discretion."

Pathia nearly growled out, "And the daring you have to question our morality means you should have both the bravery and audacity for what we are proposing."

Coursia raised her paw and shook her head, "Now, you can both just be booted out on your tails with no legal support whatsoever and the full press of enforcement on top of you, completely and utterly abandoned and alone, as far as house de Dothnar is concerned. However, our Honored Matriarch may decide to show leniency."

"What … what kind of leniency?" Docia asked, her black tail twitching on the floor.

"First, you'll be demoted to matron clerks on an estate off-continent and be required to undergo sexual addiction treatment. Your activities will be monitored to ensure you adhere to this training, and your access – while helpful to the family – will not be privileged or trusted in any way. You will retain your pensions and be allowed to retire so long as there are no other infractions with enforcement. You will, however, be on the strictest of probations. One mistake more, and we're done with you. Instead, if you keep a careful watch on yourselves, no one will ever know of the real reason for your demotions."

"What kind of *fake* reason would ever explain it?" Lanaria questioned skeptically.

Carinthia circled them as if she were letting her prey know just how trapped they truly were. "That you felt … fatigued and disillusioned with being in the matriarchy after all of those seasons under Shalana's abuse, and although you tried to put a brave face on continuing, your hearts just weren't in it anymore. You still wanted to serve the family, and so…"

"Yeah," Docia agreed. "We … we quit. Got it."

"That," Pathia contested angrily, "is a *golden prize* you have to *earn*, you stinking bitches in rut! That's payment for services rendered in helping *advance* the goals of this house instead of merely advancing your own prey count."

"Yes, Honored One, we get it," Docia sighed, closing her eyes and putting up her paw to forestall any other verbal assaults from the dames or the matriarch. "What is it you need for us to do?"

"Your secure access has already been suspended," Coursia warned, "and whatever you do know, I would strongly suggest that you keep to yourself. If you move a fur strand out of line, this offer is off the table, and you are gone. Scandal Paws hosts several gatherings of the moneyed and powerful elite, playing games with other Thurians as if they were merely toys; their executive responsibilities the justification for nearly unlimited power. I believe, based on our carefully and scrupulously gathered *evidence*, that Chassir de Bosnar, Ishara de Dothnar, and Tosharn de Dothnar are very much in your confidence."

Pathia sneered, "When they've not been enjoying being in you in other ways."

Carinthia put up her paw to hold off Pathia as she explained, "While, over the past few moons, we have been giving the impression that we had retreated on the repeal of the Familial Standards Relief Act or the FSRA, as it is known, we have actually been thoroughly examining the links between those who oppose it and those who are in our legislative assembly. You two have been either confusing or outright going against the statements we were making, and so this is obviously an activity you will discontinue. That said, however, our good relations with enforcement have made it possible as part of a plea agreement, for your benefit, to enlist your assistance in breaking these three, publicly."

"And in the process, scaring the crap out of anyone else so empty-headed as to believe the same," Coursia noted slyly. "When we crush the heads of these turf burrowers and utterly destroy them, I expect for the rest of their kind to retreat back into the shadows and stay there lest they enjoy the same treatment. This ... this is the power of a great house on Thuria – one with the ability to protect its own, care for its own, and secure their futures. This we do to reclaim the birthright of Thurians – what you denied them for the sake of your own selfish pleasures."

Docia sat down in the chair that was behind her, the one she had first sat in when brought into what she thought was a normal discussion with the matriarch. She put her head in her paws and cried. Lanaria sat beside her, and she put her paw on the Nephti's heaving back. "My fault. I ... I took Shalana's bait, led us down this path – thought ... thought we could keep doing all of it after she was gone without..." Looking up at the trio in front of them, she confessed, "We were wrong. We made a mistake. We'll ... we'll do as you ask – whatever you say."

On the bridge of the Haven, Rahnahi de Dothnar watched the exchange alongside Teldear Dynaea, Amyra looking critically at the viewer in front of them. "Real teeth there in those three," she offered, "but they are very fortunate to have Kallain's guile and prowess at their side."

"Melissiana, also," Dynaea commented, shaking her head. "Was this kind of ... negotiation common in your time?"

"Oh, it was there, but not just of this specific stripe," Rahnahi noted. "Didn't need to hold a dame's tail over the fire because she couldn't keep it low enough."

"You didn't need to hold anyone's tail over the fire, dear," Amyra quipped. "You had Dania for that."

"Sweet child. I miss her." Looking at Dynaea's expression, she answered the question there. "Dania could never fully accept those things beyond the reality she grew up with. You were there, and you saw the struggle she had. Her later seasons were ... difficult because of those experiences. They shook her, profoundly. Some can adapt to thoughts like ascension and life beyond Thuria. Not all can, and it grieves me to say that."

"She led a good life, retired from the matriarchy, and adopted several mixed blood cubs as her own," Amyra put in. "She passed surrounded by those who loved her and called her mother. I can't fault her."

"No, neither can I," Rahnahi agreed. "These two are in for a hard trail, but they can still be salvaged. You can see it. They're caught – they know that. They were in the wrong – they now know it, too. We'll keep watch over them to make sure they have little opportunity to wander, but I think dear Carinthia is right on this one."

"The real trick will be the trap," Amyra noted.

"Isn't it always?" Kylie softly put in. "However, I have some more ideas for making that trap utterly devastating and vicious, if it would suit."

"Absolutely," Dynaea replied, turning around and looking at the Vulpi Izar with a wide smile. "Cal said you were good; he wasn't wrong. Have you been keeping an eye on Vanarra … recently?"

Everyone who wasn't Dynaea shifted slightly on the bridge in a way that drew out a smile on the Teldear's delicate muzzle. "Okay, better asked this way, is there anyone here who *hasn't* been keeping up with how our vacationing Teldear is doing?"

"We probably know all the same things, save for the times we've been slipping by each other," Amyra chuckled. "What I've seen is that she's been reading her autobiography aloud to him and several other things she wrote in her prior life. He seems to be accepting of it."

"I'm seeing a little more than that," Rahnahi warned. "I've been watching Ash a little more closely. I think he's reaching a point where he's starting to realize how much he truly likes the historical Vanarra, especially when read by the voice of his mate."

"Who is, of course," Kylie put in, "the authentic Vanarra – historical and contemporary. She's just got to break it to him at some point, you know? Several others in that camp know the truth."

"Careful, careful," Dynaea warned. "We're nurturing two potential ascended beings here, not just one. Granted, Vanassa is incredibly complex and very powerful, but Ash will very likely join our ranks, as well. This is why we've given Vanarra the time she needs – to rediscover herself in his love but discover the way and time to tell him. She knows what we know, and she knows what is at stake. I trust Vanarra, and Me Sha does, as well. We just have to give her this time."

Chapter 13: The Scandal Lever

Van entered their cabin feeling hot and a little tired, or at least an approximation given the amount of work the two of them had been doing that sol. What had been a low and simmering worry nagging at everyone there was now replaced with a newer, far more urgent concern. The Vanarrans in Tanbria could no longer sustain themselves, and rather than crowd into increasingly desperate quarters in Shanandrae, the group had voted to accept what seemed the inevitable will of whatever force now directed their path. They were to be the next to arrive at the refuge of Attoria. With that news, there was now a hard press by everyone to finish the work on the town center and begin to prepare a plan for welcoming – and acculturating – the new arrivals.

All through the sol, Vanarra could tell Ash was holding onto questions, but these were questions he wouldn't ask while others were around, and when the door closed behind him, she felt it was better to face the question sooner rather than later. However, before she was able to speak, he just hugged her, held her, lovingly. "I'm going to get cleaned up, okay? You?"

"In a bit, love." He nodded and left, headed towards the communal showers for males. The realization struck as he left her. "It won't be like this, soon. We'll be living with these new arrivals." Absently, the thought came to her that she wondered if this was how Sahni was living and thought it interesting that both of them were now living apart from the rush of both society and duty. "Time to ourselves, truly ourselves, one last time," she thought, and the idea resonated in multiple ways and in multiple realities.

At that little sparking of recognition, Vanarra felt pulled to the couch and cleared her mind, sitting with her legs crossed. There was palpable tension all around her, this sol, and she felt the need to center herself. Closing her eyes, she slipped into the heightened awareness of causality and consequence. These first Vanarrans were coming, and they were heartbroken and angry, disappointed and disillusioned. There was a stark desperation that wrapped her unclear vision of who they were, a harsh fatalism lancing their pride and spilling it out of them. This, their accepting of a place in Attoria, was nothing less than true failure, and their decision to go against the Vanarran leadership meant they were all, now, without a place amongst their brethren. They were stepping out of the only society they knew, the one that had cared for and nurtured them, into an unknown. A surprising realization came to her – this wasn't all that different than those the Allarrae saved from the last moment before death and sent to Thuriana to start the colony.

"They are given the chance to ask any question and every question from the moment they arrive," Sahni's voice offered into her thoughts. "Some only ask a few, but some ask many. It helps set a foundation for them when they feel so lost."

"Been awhile since I've heard you, kit," Van replied to her inner Sahni.

"I've been busy with a child, you know?" came the amused response. "And why are you, dear Van *inside* my head, thinking about what's happening to Vanarra on Thuria?"

"Uh, Sahni, this … this is the Vanarra *on Thuria*. It's me, kit! Can you actually … hear me?"

There was a moment of silence, and she felt the questions reach out away from her. "By the moons, Van, it … it is me! It's me, Sahni I mean, on Thuriana! How in the mange are we doing this?!"

"I bet Merialla knows but hasn't told you, or she won't tell you, I'd wager."

"The ascended Nephti of mysteriousness," Sahnassa grumped. "It's good to hear your … thoughts, I guess? Is something wrong, though? Has your inner Sahni been quiet or something? Tana?"

"I get the sense that both of them are letting me be. I'm … living with Ash, now. I'm mated to him, joined. We're living in

Attoria, and no, I haven't told him exactly who I am, but we are making progress. However, in the short term, we have our first batch of new arrivals from the Vanarrans coming soon. Tanbria's temple gave up, and now they are going to be our first true refugees."

"And you were dipping into your time sense to feel them out?" Sahni asked.

"Is it a bad thing?"

"No, no – it's fine. It's something we'll be able to do very easily as ascended, and using a computer term, it's read-only. We can't damage anything just by looking."

Van thought that curious. "Is that why we can talk, kit?"

"I think that this might be a favor Vanassa is doing for us, and we're borrowing a bit of her power. Van, when new arrivals come to Thuriana, it has always been that they were allowed to ask any question they wanted for as long as they wanted when they first arrived. The answers, good or bad, removed the worst impediment, their worst fear crippling them from getting started in this new life – not knowing."

"I can suggest that to Javoth and the others. This is probably going to be a learning opportunity for all of us, but I don't want to treat it casually. Just because these are the first doesn't mean we can mess this up."

"I know," Sahnassa told her. "I think the Allarrae picked this method because it works. I would hope it works for you."

"Me, too. Tell my other self to be patient. When we join again, she'll hopefully learn something that will make her very, very happy. You alright, kit?"

"Fine, and ... healing inside, too, Van. I'm looking at this beautiful little face every sol, this adorable mixed blood between my Dasahar and me – to think that any child would have ever been looked at as lost and hopeless; I really feel how completely wrong that would be."

Vanarra smiled. "I'm happy to hear you say that, kit, and I am jealous. You were a mother to me a long time ago, and now I know just how deep that love runs. Thank you, kit. I'll talk to you later."

"Be well, dear Van, other side of myself."

Vanarra opened her eyes and found her mate, Ash, looking at her, curiously. "What were you doing, love?" he asked.

"Relaxing and thinking," she told him, smiling. "I'm trying to get a grip on the changes that are about to hit us, and I felt the need to collect my thoughts a bit."

"And, what did those thoughts collect into?" he asked, smiling a little.

"That we need to take the new arrivals, as soon as they have food and drink in their paw, as soon as we know they are alright, and pull them in and let them ask any question they want, for as long as they want. We shouldn't let the sun go down without being there for them, answering as much as we can. The worst thing for them will be not knowing, and as exhausting as it might be, it is a kindness to them."

He nodded, leaning back into the sofa. "Not knowing is hard, very hard," he agreed. "I think you're right, and you must have, too. You were smiling at the end."

"You were here, weren't you?" she asked, getting up and snuggling in beside him. "What's not to smile about?"

"I was here about ten passes, just watching you. I've never seen that kind of peace on your face. I wish I felt that way. I'm concerned by the ones who are coming here; Laxar and I talked about it. He's afraid. Vassia is, too. Everything we're trying to do might well be decided in the next few sols."

"Have faith, Ash. We are looking out for each other, surely, but there are others working on this effort, as well. Also, we have to believe that the Creator guides us. Look at everything that's come together so far, and here, the first group is coming at almost the exact moment when we are ready for them. Does it mean it will be easy? No, it does not. Does it mean that we will succeed? No, it doesn't mean that, either. I think it means that we *can* succeed. If we can, then we earn the honor of having this problem over and over again as Attoria grows."

"You sound like her, sometimes, when you talk," he mentioned, growing comfortable and relaxed in her presence.

"Who, love?"

"Vanarra de Gonari. You've been reading her autobiography and a few of those other things she wrote, and I'm just used to hearing you … as her, I guess. Besides, you're really good at laying out something and encouraging others. I watched Laxar and Vassia, this sol; they seem a lot more at peace with one another. You guide very well, Van, like she did."

"Well, she was a Grand Matriarch, so I suppose she knew a little about that," Vanalla smiled, snuggling into him more. "It makes me happy that you can see a little of Vanarra in me. I am very much a fan of her life, in terms of knowing her history."

"Yeah, Trax and I talked one time. He was really into it – Shenaria, too, come to think about it. You know, you had to be really patient with me not wanting to join the Vanarra club." She turned and looked at him, and his expression asked the question clearer than her muzzle could. "I don't know why I felt that way; I really don't. However, when you were gone this morning, I picked up the biography and read a bit of it. I'm okay, I think, so long as when I read it, I kind of imagine you voicing it; you've given her real life and color."

Van smiled and offered, "Let me ask you a question, Ash. If she … were here, would you want to ask her something? Would there be a question that comes to mind?"

"Wow, I mean, I'm not sure what I could come up with that would even make sense," he breathed, looking up at the ceiling. Then, something struck him, and he asked, "Okay, how about this? No, that's silly."

"She liked silly, sometimes. Try it."

He sighed and said, "Alright, but don't hate me. You sound just so much like a real, regular Thurian. I mean, what's it like having statues and, worse, religions spring up in your honor? Did you ever expect that would happen?"

"Not in the beginning," Van explained. "When I first started out, I was as much of a nobody as anyone could get. I could have been found dead on the trail and wouldn't be missed or cared about. Some of those I loved were treated that way. It was a … friend who took me aside and warned me that everything was going to start changing for me, though, after the Meeting Den. I was in one of the scariest, most confusing, just out of control situations, and everything was finally settling down when he hit me with the news – I was famous. I was a hero. Suddenly, word of who I was and what Sahni and I had done spread ... everywhere. My life wasn't the same."

"Oh, that had to be hard to swallow," Ash commented.

"Very, and a lot of the attention I got wasn't friendly," Van agreed. "There was a fair amount of Thurians angry about who I was, and they went after me. I had friends, though, and they helped me fight back. In time, I was pulled into this situation and that, and maybe I barely scraped through them, but at some point, you realized that you have crafted this kind of ... legacy, this wake flowing behind you. It's something that I had surprisingly little control over. Do you know that I kept – gave orders with punishments and everything – statues from being made out of me when I was Matriarch? Damned if they aren't pretty much all over the place in this time, relatively speaking. So, there is a part of me that's glad I made a difference, and I'm honored that the difference is remembered, but I'm not happy with anyone who replaces the Creator with me, and worse, if they do horrible things using my name as an excuse. So, that's the answer. How did I do?"

"Actually, not bad – makes sense given what you read. Part of me just wonders if she'd like me, at all?"

"I think she'd have an answer for you, Vanarra would. Are you up for it? Are you *brave enough* to hear it?"

"Oh, like I have a choice, now. Okay, *Vanarra*, do you like me?"

"Well," Van told him, snuggling into him a little more, "as a male, you *are truly* a fine specimen, and as mixes go, you are very well painted and a keen, *keen* hunter. So, my dear cub, yes, I like you very much on the outside. More importantly, however, I like you on the inside. Your life is anchored to the Creator's Path, and you are patient and kind and selfless. There are very few like you, and Ash – just by being who you are – you give me an immense comfort and peace that what you're doing here will add to the safety and happiness of a whole new kind of outcast. My heart, Ash, was always with those who were put out, persecuted, and abandoned; it still is. These once-Vanarrans are ... the new Anati, but you are helping the entirety of

Thurian society to do better than it has. Your willingness to sacrifice for their sakes means I not only like you, cub, I *love* you."

He turned and looked at her, accusingly. "Hey, I thought you were supposed to be answering *like* Vanarra would! That sounded more like you, I think. How am I supposed to tell where Vanalla stops and Vanarra starts?"

"Oh, now isn't *that* the question," Van chuckled, turning and licking him on the side of the muzzle as she snuggled in beside him to sleep.

The next morning, the still snoozing couple was awakened by a soft tapping on their door. When Ash opened the door, there was a Vulpi standing there he knew, but her expression was graver than usual. "Good morning, Vosh. Is something wrong?"

"Is Vanalla awake? May I speak to you both? I've learned something about the Vanarran refugees that are arriving next sol, and it's something for which we need to be prepared."

"Sure, Vosh, please. Come in, come in. Can I get you something?"

"No thank you. You are just now awakened, and it would be difficult for you. I will begin making tea for you both."

"Ash? Who is it?" Van asked from the other room of the cabin.

"It's Vosh, love. I think you'd better come out here."

"Okay, just a moment," Vanalla called back and then started to shuffle about getting out of bed and throwing on a robe. After a few moments, she saw a somewhat bleary and drowsy Ash who very much mimicked the way she felt sitting at the small table, Vosh putting two cups of hot tea down in front of both him and her empty place. "Oh, hey there," Van offered, and surrounded her secret daughter in a hug, one as gently and profoundly returned. "So good to see you. What's going on?"

"There is news that has come to us about the Vanarrans leaving Tanbria. There are thirty-five of them, but this morning, that number was thirty-seven. Two have died of starvation in that time. It is likely we will lose more before they arrive here."

"Vosh," Vanalla asked her, "why weren't we told?" The issue truly concerned her, and she wondered if Teldear Dynaea had let her attention slip when it shouldn't have.

"The Vanarrans have been starving themselves, trying to survive. All of them are very close to death; so close that we will have to orchestrate doctors and nurses into our reception plan. Fireclaw is working on that right now, but what will be getting off the transport – it is something you should prepare yourself, mentally, to face."

"Ash, go get Vassia, please. We need her input on this," Van directed him, and the pleading look in her eyes begged him to give her this time with Vosh.

"Alright. I'll find her," he told her, and then went to throw on his paw shoes. When Vosh appeared ready to divert him, Van raised her paw to hold her daughter off, shaking her head. Patiently, the dark and serious female Vulpi stilled herself and waited for Ash to depart.

As soon as he was out of earshot, Van unleashed. "Why in the mange wasn't I told about this, Vosh!? Why wasn't something done to keep that from happening?"

"The situation with the Vanarrans is desperate, Mother. They are imposing this tragedy upon themselves, and they are doing so close enough to the public eye that we cannot prevent it. These nearly waited too late before finally agreeing to relinquish their beliefs and seek shelter, here, but many of the other Vanarran temples across Thuria are in the same state. Principals have been in negotiation with them, but the Vanarrans are crumbling – too weak, now, to rise up and revolt against those who oppress them or fight back. Their only choice, so many of them think, is self-destruction. They hope the Great Mother will rescue them from this peril."

Van put her head in her paws and cried, "They hope in vain! It's so senseless, Vosh! They don't need to die?! What ... what do the overall numbers look like?"

"Worldwide, of the Vanarrans bred close enough to the standard who cannot pass as regular mixed bloods in Thurian society, there were fifty-seven thousand two hundred. This was at the start of our mission. After deaths while incarcerated and other mishaps, the number was approximately thirty-six thousand eight hundred. While some populations of Vanarrans are in better shape than those in Tanbria, most are approaching this level of distress. Given all available inputs, a final survival figure of ten thousand on the high side to two thousand on the low side has been projected. This means the worldwide population of Vanarrans, including those who are able to leave the order for normal lives, has been reduced to approximately one percent of what it was when the Vanarrans were at the height of their power."

"I … I feel sick. When I glanced in on their time-streams, I didn't pick up anything like this!"

"Amyra suspected you had started to try to view these events as an ascended, and she asked me to caution you that one of the key issues for pre-ascended is perceiving the flow of events accurately in all aspects. You have blind spots that you are unaware of, and while the information you can retrieve is, perhaps, useful, she warns that you must never consider it to be complete. There have been those known to the Allarrae who distorted the destiny of an entire galactic empire based upon the misleading evidence of prescient vision. It is a tool requiring exactly honed skill to use reliably. That is a power only Vanassa will achieve and only given significant practice."

"I … I know I need to be here with Ash – he's taking a long time or…"

"I'm giving us this moment to speak, uninterrupted. Vassia has been awake all night. I believe she suspects the news that Ash will bring to her. I believe she fears it."

"I don't doubt. Vosh, my daughter, I have to admit that I almost feel like I'm in a kind of exile here. My inner Sahni and Tana are dead silent. I'm starting to feel like one of the cast out."

"We are still here, Van," Sahni's voice whispered inside of her thoughts. "We have been just watching your progress, but it has to be *your* progress – we can't interfere. It's been amazing; you are healing inside even as we watch. It's for the best; it's not because we don't care or something bad has happened to us."

"Mother," Vosh said, her voice nearly stern and her stare direct. "I have spoken for many intervals with Amyra, Rahnahi, Merialla, and Alahari. I have challenged their wisdom *many times* on this course, and I have been persuaded that this is right path for you.

It is the right path for you, and it is the right path for your beloved Ash. His development must not be left out of consideration. According to Amyra and Rahnahi, he progresses well. Your slow path of guiding him into a knowledge of who you are is exactly what you should be doing, and the results prove that. You *must* hold fast to this course, despite the difficulty and uncertainty."

Vanarra reached out her paw to the Vulpi and stroked the side of her muzzle. "Lovely and wonderful kit, you are, my daughter."

"I will remember and cherish your words, my mother," Vosh offered, nodding. "Although the next sols will be difficult ones, Dynaea suggests that in these sols the future of Attoria will begin, and the kindness and love and patient steadfastness demonstrated interval by interval, helping these starving Vanarrans recover will transform them into the Aelkinda they need to become, that we all want them to become. I am releasing us from the temporal hover, and Vassia will be here, presently."

"Give everyone on the Haven my love, okay? Mom and Trax doing okay with the twins?"

"Essentially, in as much as new parents can be judged. It has been stressful, but they are surviving. The twins are healthy and progress well in their development, although Shonas is a better sleeper than Lithiana is, at this point," Vosh confessed. "I have stood watch over them to provide your mother and step father a respite. I find the activity pleasing, as it is a sort of guard duty with nurturing aspects."

"You might make a very good mother, Vosh," Van offered. "I wonder if that's something you would be interested in."

"Hmm... Procreation for a Terspear is not allowed by fleet law."

"Yes, but you're not only a Terspear, now. It's something to think about."

"For another time, Mother."

Vassia entered ahead of Ash, and she nodded to them. At a motion of her paw, Van directed Vassia to sit, and the former Select did so. "Ash has told me," she began, "it is as I feared it would be."

"Why would they wait so long?" Van asked, her anguish at this needless suffering plain in her voice.

"Faith, and I can understand this. If I had not had a ... profoundly disturbing vision, I would have likely stood with them, preferring starvation to compromising my long-cherished beliefs. I would imagine that the temple leadership has gone about the task of painting this place as a death camp that will be used to exterminate any so foolish as to come here. You will likely be witness to those who may have even chose this course of action because they wish to die."

"I want to disappoint them, seriously want that," Van offered, wiping her eyes.

"If we are not careful, then our uninformed desire to prove them wrong could truly kill them, proving them right."

"I don't understand, Vosh," Ash told her. "They are starving, and we can feed them. Won't that solve the problem?"

"As certainly as a knife to the heart, unfettered generosity will kill them. Their bodies have been enduring starvation for such a long time that a sudden increase of food to what we would consider normal or even sub-normal levels will reduce the minerals inhabiting key areas of their anatomy to a point where life cannot be sustained."

"Digestion ... is a pretty difficult process when you come right down to it," Van warned them. "Although the body is pretty good at it, there is a lot of water and muscular and glandular requirements needed to carry it off. These, if they match those who I've seen starving in the past, are only alive because of a delicately balanced and deteriorating orchestration of these dwindling resources. A sudden increase in intake could mean that there is not both enough of one required substance to run digestion and run the heart at the same time. Both have to work. Vassia, we have to educate *everyone* very quickly about this. We should try to set up an infirmary, something progressive where those in the very worst condition can start out, protected from too much food while they are cared for, while the doctors try to bring them back."

"As much as I hate to say it," Ash commented, "it ... it seems like we need to think about setting apart a place for the ceremonies of final rest."

"Yeah," Van replied and swallowed in a dry throat. "We're in for some really long and dark sols ahead. It will almost be like caring for newborns."

"Newborns who are burdened with disillusionment and despair and regret, hopelessness," Vassia told them, looking away. "Newborns with a lifetime of past and no expectation of a meaningful future. It can make existing truly hard to bear."

Vanalla slipped her paw into that of Vassia and whispered, "I'm sorry. I feel like I haven't been there for you; we've been-"

"You and Ash – your relationship, has been a bright spot for me. Do not regret that. It … it caused me to reach out in new directions, especially after your guidance." She was speaking to both Van and Ash, and her smile was genuine. "Laxar has been the tonic for my very soul, and I feel such affection for him. Every time I speak with him, I feel as if someone has molded him to fill the vast wounds in my heart. What's strange is that when I tell him about this, about this challenge, he will know a thing to do that I would have never thought of. He will find ways to speak to them that we cannot. When we choose the place where we will first bring them, we need to make sure they start out with some of his beautiful artwork. It's given me light in my soul when I had none."

"Then that's what we need for him to help provide," Vosh noted. "He can create visuals depicting the hope of Attoria."

They all nodded, smiling softly. "He can let them see what they'll be too sick to see by going there. He, as all of us, can help convince them they have a future," Van offered.

Chassir de Bosnar entered the precincts of the *Scandal Paws* nightclub with an air of assured conquest. With unrepentant smugness, he took his pre-arranged escorts for the night – a male and female Vulpi of exquisite attractiveness – and placed them close beside him, throwing a paw around each of them. He would have done more than nuzzle both of them, whispered some promise of the night's future erotic bliss, but the music was thumping and pulsing powerfully even in the secret lobby he had entered. When the doors of the inner sanctum of the club were opened before the three of them, even being heard at a full scream would have been patently unrealistic. He smiled, earplugs already seated in deep to prevent discomfort, and guided his two companions forward to the High Ground lounge.

High Ground was an amazingly sound-proofed central core of the club which looked down upon the revelers, if one wanted to step up to the edge and look over. Usually, he was just a bit too engaged in his own entertainments to bother with the gyrations of random singles trying to impress their dates with a show of primal attractiveness. After all, his playmates for the evening were bought and paid for, although his eyes did roam the bodies of both males and females sizing up the "common" stock for that rare find of beauty. Sadly enough, tonight, there were only his companions who met his impossibly high standards of attractiveness. He was sure they were the only ones who could properly and thoroughly relax, seduce, and pleasure him to the degree he appreciated. He made sure his escorts had earned the equivalent of academy degrees in making him feel amazing on every level.

As they took the lift to High Ground, the pressured pulse of thumping music started fading away, and he was able to draw in the scents of his companions – augmented scents, of course, but exactly what he was longing for. "Very well done, you two," he offered warmly. They were rare delicacies among a proliferation of the common – dropping those common shapes and forms from his concerns as the elevator attained its level, thirty tracks above the dance floor.

When the doors opened into the dimly lit but completely top of the line landing, Chassir's eyes widened a little as two others, also being coddled by their hired companions, noticed the new arrivals. "Chas," Ishara de Dothnar cooed – two female Nephti at her side, each one with a single paw already roaming beneath her clothing. "Good to see you."

"Well, our darling de Dothnar dames always know how to treat us," he acknowledged as he placed a considerable draft for funds into the prearranged box in the lobby, "but what are we waiting on?"

"There was a problem up here earlier – clean up, so I'm told," Tosharn de Dothnar shrugged, his arm candy also making him feel like he was the center of their universe. "However, I'm told they have a contingency space for us if this can't be taken care of."

"Great," Chas nearly growled. "I only get to get out for these sort of evenings once a moon! I'll be damned if I'm going to waste my time-"

At that moment, a small Perratti dressed in the uniform of the club appeared, looking excited which was an emotion that struck the three senior business leaders as odd. "Please, please forgive me, most honored of all guests, but I must confess that the story you were told about the High Ground being affected by a problem is incorrect – a small fabrication on our part because we hoped to bring you to our newest entertainment area, far enhanced beyond the simple hovel you have partaken in up to this point!"

"Our dear club owner doesn't think he can charge us more to stick us in a back-closet, does he?" Chassir grumbled darkly.

"Oh, no, most honored guest," the brown Perratti in the elegant uniform attested, "this has been in preparation for moons and moons! The *Deep Den* is a prize beyond count and a jewel beyond measure. It is removed from the masses so that you can be assured of privacy, and it also has special ... enchantments created especially for your likings, well, based upon what you have enjoyed in the past."

"I'd better be impressed," Ishara threatened, her two companions looking as if the transition from fawning servile escort to murderous guard could happen in an eye blink.

"I want nothing more than to show this to you! This is an exotically wonderful place which rests profoundly in your memories from this sol forward and makes you wish to recapture and relive every moment spent within the *Deep Den*. Would you please follow me?"

"Why the mange not, when you've made it sound even better than what we've had in the past," Tosharn offered. "I'm in."

"I suppose," Ishara inserted carefully, her eyes fixed on Chassir.

"Lead on, and we will see if this *Deep Den* exceeds all expectations." Without a word, the Perratti bowed and started to lead them forward to a door which none of them actually remembered ever having been there in the past. However, it was magnificently opulent and promised even better, beyond. As the small group followed their guide, they were amazed that absolutely no music could be heard whatsoever.

"These tapestries and soft hangings are amazing," Ishara noted, "and I can't even hear a bit of music."

"Soundproofing of the first degree," Tosharn noted with a sly tone in his voice. "Very ... promising for us, I would say." They all chuckled at that. Following some stairs downward, they felt themselves descending so far as to even be going underground. "Deep Den, indeed."

"Your comfort and assurance are our first and most prominent goal!" the Perratti offered effusively, taking the observation as a high compliment. Further conversation was curbed because the luxurious passage veered left and right at different times, sinuous in its path. Soon, however, they were at another door just as opulent and well finished in hardwoods and gold filigree. Smiling happily and with an air of unbridled pride and excitement, their guide announced softly, "We are here! Welcome ... to *your own private* Deep Den!"

The doors opened, and all three of the corporate executives – not to mention their escorts – stood in absolute, ecstatic shock. Ranged in front of them was a semicircular space opening up from where they were and reaching high to distant walls dressed in the finest purple cloth, favored by the most enticing and erotic of aromatic scents, soft lighting from expensively crafted stained glass lamps hanging from the shell-like roof above. What drew their attention beyond the room's complete and utter sensuous luxury was the amazing array of beautiful and naked Thurians coming to greet them. Almost as an afterthought, Ishara noticed the various stands, devices, and framings meant to satisfy almost every variation of perversity she could have imagined.

As they were swept away by the nude throng of adoring males and females, Chassir looked back at the Perratti standing by the door and ventured, "You're getting a raise, my friend! You've outdone yourself!" Turning back to the throng pawing at his clothes, the Lupar slipped free of his shirt and shouted, "Let's get this party started!" With that, the Lupar was picked up off the floor and stripped of the remainder of his clothes in an instant, doing nothing to protest or hide his excitement at the night's prospects. He laughed heartily as he saw

Ishara and Tosharn as happily treated to the same experience, Ishara already pointing at a specific device on the center stage he thought she might like.

Smiling knowingly, the Perratti exited the room and closed the door, his eyes widening to see the pathway which he had just led his guests through almost completely disassembled, its appearance returning to the underground service-way between the now shuttered night club, closed for two sols because of illegal drug activity found on the premises. The Faelnar he now worked for looked down at him, his eyes questioning. "They accepted our offer readily, and as you witnessed, showed no hesitation about joining the revelry."

"Very good. Return the night club to its prior state of enforced closure and thank everyone who helped participate as *extras* in tonight's VidStar recording," Kallain offered softly. "I will watch to see when our guests are most ready for their moment in the spotlight."

"And after?"

"Remove the faux fur pieces and return to your old identity. Ensure that you are not publicly seen in this area for four moons."

"You are most gracious, and thank you for the second chance," the Perratti-Faelnar mix offered, rubbing at the tiny inserts on his muzzle which created the appearance of a Perratti's draping muzzle fur. Kallain nodded, and soon the Faelnar had turned and was moving purposely towards his next destination.

In the halved ballroom of the Dream Star resort and spa, a gathering of law enforcement officials, house dignitaries, and several members of the assembly were holding a public news conference regarding the potential benefits to be offered by a resurgence of the houses' oversight powers, promising a major story should the ratings-hungry newsarotzi turn out, and turn out they did. Among their number, Alanar de Kestrick wasn't quite sure this wasn't a set-up. "If their idea of major is a bunch of them just talking about the old sols, I'm not going to put that up on air. Mange, they could sell it as a sleep aid-"

Just then, he was caught by something the de Dothnar matriarch was saying that almost seemed to be reading his thoughts.

"And I want to assure you that we have no intention of returning to sols where abuse and injury were considered within the rights of a house to impose on its members. While we do want there to be rewards and motivational corrections, never should any house endanger the safety or wellbeing of another Thurian. We hold the lessons taught us from history too precious to allow a return to that sort of treatment."

"Hmm," he mused as the matriarch took a drink, "referring to Vanarra de Gonari's mother without referring to de Gonari. Okay, that's not so bad."

"Forgive me, please," she chuckled softly, smiling. "I have been a victim of allergies most of the sol." There were a few head nods and light chuckles in response. "Rather, we want to ensure that those of our house, calling themselves by our family name, are acting within the strictest standards of honor and good judgment possible, regardless of their place in our society – be it the head of a corporate pack or the chair of a local babysitting cooperative. We also aim to aid law enforcement in two key areas. First, by working with Thurians to sort out their problems before a crime is committed, we can keep the incidents which trouble law enforcement from occurring. In those instances where we can't and we know crimes are being committed, crimes like Thurian slavery, embezzling, influence peddling, and others, we can work as strong partners with law enforcement to make sure that the guilty are punished and our laws are upheld."

"Sounds lovely," Alanar mused, becoming bored again.

"And to that end, we became aware of several individuals who thought themselves nigh untouchable, beyond the law in every respect. We, at present, lack any legal ability to work and guide them as a family should, and so we were left with no other alternative but to cooperate with enforcement."

Alanar had reached his limit on quiet listening, and now although he knew his lovely Emma would probably sear his hide for it, he stood up. "Grand Matriarch, Honored One, has there been some sort of raid or enforcement action we should know about?"

"If you'll kindly turn around, you'll all notice the line of enforcement officers in the back. If I could impose upon you all to remain silent as we dim the lights, I believe we will have something for you that is particularly news-worthy in just a moment."

The Lupar enforcement chief stood up then alongside her and added, "I also want to make the point to you that the operation you'll witness tonight is conducted by *enforcement* only. While the house of de Dothnar provided us information and assistance, they in no way operated as more than citizen observers and reporters of illicit behavior. They will not be judge or jury of the accused."

"I would offer that we are willing to play a supportive and nurturing role," the matriarch pointed out, "helping those families impacted by these events or by those who wish to seek counseling to help keep them from future illegal activities."

"And such would be very much appreciated," the Lupar chief noted. "Now, my officers are going to kneel facing the back wall, which will open, and at this time I would ask you to all check your photo and VidStar equipment to ensure that it does not create any additional lighting or sounds. Also, I would ask that, no matter what you witness, please do not make any noise until my officers have everyone actually in custody. Finally, and this should go without saying," he offered mostly in Alanar's direction, "if anyone interferes with the actions of my officers they risk being arrested, as well. Everyone who will be taken on the raid tonight will be considered innocent until proven guilty in court. Any misunderstandings?" The room seemed to offer him agreement as cameras and recorders and PawLinks were all silenced.

Chassir was enjoying the most sensuous and erotic time of his entire life; it was like every individual there had no other purpose than to outdo one another in trying to make him and his fellow corporate demigods nearly drown in pleasure. Clothes had been discarded by everyone, long ago, and in a haze of drinks and the most amazing sexual high, he simply looked around and laughed as the music pulsed around him. Tosharn had a line of Thurians of every type and stripe bent over with him behind them, satisfying himself one after another. Ishara, he thought, might actually die of pleasure – two strong females fixing her in place on a vibrating saddle that had been specially equipped. She had reached the heights of ecstasy so powerfully that she was now a moaning, babbling, nonsensical mass of female fur. He was only slightly more coherent as the next in a long line of seductive females knelt in front of his chair and began trying to prove their superior skill in bringing pleasure. As his head lolled back, the room seemed to spin, and Chassir felt himself about to pass out in the most exquisite ecstasy he had ever known.

All at once, everything ceased – the pleasure, the music, the darkness. There was a weird emotion radiating off everyone around him, only Ishara's babbling incoherence was the sole remaining constant. Looking down, he saw the beautifully skanky Vulpi-Perratti mix with her head up and looking away at where the wall had once been. Swallowing in a suddenly dry throat, he turned his head to look where the curtains had been, where the wall had been. His mind simply couldn't conceive of what his eyes were telling him; it was like they had been transported to another place – some hotel ballroom somewhere. What's worse, is that his addled brain started to pick out individuals in the crowd he knew – competitors both internal and external and newsarotzi, especially the ones he hated.

"Whaz ... this?" he asked, not bothering to cover himself as he stood up. Looking around, he saw that – save for the furniture – the room he had been in was simply gone, and in its place, some enforcement officers stood guarding the exits while others were already taking members of the confused and stunned group into custody, slipping binders on those on the periphery, including his two chartered companions for the evening. Groaning, Ishara had finally removed herself from the "pleasure saddle" and was starting to drink in the scene, as well, but its full impact hadn't hit her, yet. A glance in Toshar's direction caused them to lock eyes, and realization passed like a lightning bolt between them. They had been set up, and by the number of lenses and recording devices pointed at them from the full half of the conference room, they both knew there was no amount of money that would fix what was happening.

Chassir finally had the presence of mind to cover himself with his paws, even though he knew it was already too late, his head throbbing and blush fur screaming to full height, and the silence ... the silence was deafening, soul-destroying. His head clearing, he finally realized that whoever had set this up would have wanted to be here to see it, and rapidly, as Thurian after Thurian nearby him was led away in binders, Chassir scanned the crowd who was still taking still images and VidStar of the eerily silent sting operation. He saw a smirking and well-pleased Alanar de Kestrick, clicking off image after image especially focused on him at the moment. Eyes drifting further around, he saw the enforcement chief – someone he had bullied and intimidated through his connections in government. There were also assembly delegates there, ones who had never been to one of these gatherings.

Finally, his eyes came to rest on the de Dothnar Matriarch, and the two locked their gazes. He could see in her expression a flood of information – so much that it was overwhelming in its clarity; it was nearly as if she was speaking directly to him mind-to-mind. "You thought that you were beyond the reach of any paw; you thought you could keep our houses from stopping you, keep us weak, forever." Her chin raised up in just the least bit of haughty pride. "You did not." Binders were now slipped about his wrists, and his paws were pulled behind him. His head ached in the sharp tumble of pleasures being washed out so quickly with anguished shame and defeat.

As he was led away, he wanted to scream; he wanted to threaten, but the silence had stuffed itself into his ears and into his muzzle, making it barely possible to breathe. "This … this night, every corporate pack leader is going to hear about this night! They'll … they'll all cower and hide! Nothing … will stop the houses, now! Nothing!" Only his mind could make noise, an echoing din in his head, but no protests could fall from his muzzle even as he was led away through the far door into the darkened hallway.

Watching the last prisoner being led out the door, Alanar turned around to face the podium once again. "Remind me to never get on your bad side," he thought, looking at the group arrayed there.

"What you've seen, tonight, is the result of the cooperative work of several law enforcement and prosecutorial departments in the government along with the informational assistance of houses de Dothnar and de Gonari," the enforcement chief offered. "This sends a very clear and unmistakable message – Thurian trafficking will not be tolerated. Those who sell themselves and those who would purchase their services are equally worthy of both their shame and the legal punishments dictated by our justice system. We will be conducting raids not unlike what you've seen, but many of them will be different.

Those of you in the trafficking trade should be on notice, that as of right now, you will never see us coming until it's too late."

"Question!" Alanar piped up when the big Lupar on stage took a breath.

"Yes?" The answer was given in such a way that the patient tolerance of the chief was obvious to everyone.

"I couldn't help but notice a few … corporate pack luminaries among the bunch you happened to snag tonight. How was their presence *arranged*?" Alanar knew they weren't there by accident, and his gaze was flicking across everyone on stage to figure who had wanted to take down three of the biggest corporate heads in town.

The chief shook his head and responded, "Their presence, to be clear, was arranged by themselves. No one was forced into our trap; our *Deep Den* could have been left at any time. Instead, everyone you saw appeared to embrace the illegal activities most readily. A full record of those apprehended will appear on our department TransNet site, per our standard operating procedure, by the end of next sol."

"If I may?" the Grand Matriarch asked the chief, who nodded, and all attention swung around to focus on her. "We have information regarding far more than these you saw, tonight, participating in schemes and activities that are unworthy of us as Thurians entrusted by others. As to the source of our data, I will confess to you – with deepest regret – that some lingering practices fostered by our former matriarch resulted in several internal disciplinary actions. The individuals, including two low level dames of our house, have been completely relieved of their responsibilities and sent to psychological counseling. However, they provided information which, after an internal review, we realized had to go to enforcement – there was simply no alternative."

It was again Alanar who was one of the few in the room who were brave enough to go up against the power standing on the platform, especially since their claws were still blood-soaked, figuratively, by raking the pelts of the business elite. However, he pressed his question quickly as he sensed the other newsarotzi around him wanting to join in the questioning. "Exactly how much of this information has been turned over to enforcement and exactly how many others have been implicated?"

The chief raised his paw and shook his head. "Regretfully, that wanders into the realm of several, highly sensitive investigations which are now being managed in our offices, so I must decline to comment at this time."

A mixed blood Nephti-Faelnar in the back beat Alanar to the next punch. "If that's so, why are we here, tonight?!"

"As enforcement and servants of the public, we are bound to ensure that those honest Thurians who pay our salaries understand that we will go after those who are trafficking in enslaved Thurians, those who offer sex for hire, many of them not by their own choice. In truth, while we knew that there was the possibility of several prominent individuals compromising themselves tonight, there were no guarantees. As I mentioned earlier, no one forced or misled these individuals to come to this *party*, nor were they forced to stay once they understood what kind of gathering it was, as our internal surveillance VidStar will attest."

"I'd love to see that," Alanar chuckled, just loudly enough to be heard.

"That and all of the statements tonight from those participating is, unfortunately, evidence that must come out at trial," the chief responded.

"Matriarch?" Alanar pressed, but then shook his head. "My apologies, Honored One. Grand Matriarch, your house took a prominent role – at least in providing information. Is this something your house plans to continue?"

"We will always observe the law, and such was the burden our internally disclosed information laid upon us. However, my deepest wish is that we could have spoken to every single individual on the other side of that barrier, tonight, seasons and seasons ago. We could have gotten to know them, growing up. We could have helped direct them away from influences and decisions that, tonight, crushed in on top of them. I take no victory or joy from anyone going into the paws of enforcement. It's a failure, for all of us. I only wish my paws weren't tied behind my back keeping me from helping as families once did."

"In all fairness, families did a lot of things in the past that weren't so … helpful," Alanar posited aloud, "Honored One."

"Very true," the Grand Matriarch agreed, "but in correcting those injustices, as a society, we created others. The chief and I have been talking, recently, about an improved balance between enforcement's responsibility and house oversight."

"If I may, Grand Matriarch?" the chief asked, politely. Looking into the crowd he said, "Throughout my many seasons of enforcement, I usually only see the times when Thurians' lives are falling apart. I see it far too much. I wish I didn't have to. I wish my officers didn't have to. I believe that the houses understand where the boundaries need to be, but if they just had these necessary powers restored, I would happily submit to them as a member of a house, dues and all."

Chapter 14: The Refugees of Privation

Vanalla listened to Ash read off of his PawLink as she got ready for a very different arrival sol than they had originally planned. "Chassir de Bosnar, Ishara de Dothnar, and Tosharn de Dothnar have all been suspended from their positions at their respective firms, and the governmental accounting office is now actively investigating all three for impropriety. Early challenges to the legality of the sting operation that netted not only these three prominent Thurians but seventy-two others have all been struck down by the courts, but individual challenges by the defendants in resulting court cases can try to re-test the legality of the operation. However, experts are asserting that the resulting evidence provided by many of the now incarcerated is making those sorts of legal maneuvers patently irrelevant."

Vanalla shrugged on a medically sterilized top as she offered, "Which is a nice way of saying that we're finding out you're so guilty, how we found out isn't going to matter anymore. Seventy-two, huh?"

"Yeah, says they are ... well, now. Professional escorts and prostitutes, some who drove in from cities more than a hundred courses away for the opportunity to participate in the activities at *Scandal Paws*. Guess that will knock down the sex trade in the area for a bit."

"It might, but moreover," she offered, now pulling up the draw-string slacks, "our entire corporate pack executive community is now scrambling for cover. The moment that legislation to restore the house's authority to look at the private life of its members comes up, they have two choices."

"What's that?" he asked.

"Either shut up and let it happen or quit their house and look like they did so because of their own *Scandal Paws.*"

"Scandal Claws, you mean," Ash put forward as he sat the article aside and began changing into his own medical garb. "What was supposed to be a soft and pleasurable touch just ripped a bunch of lives apart."

Van secured the mask in front of her muzzle and then lowered it, letting it rest on standby around her neck. "Heard some things about those three, though. They weren't innocently living it up on the primal side; there was a lot they were doing to harm others. This," she offered, picking up the portable viewer with the article, "was just a part of it."

An urgent knock came on their cabin door, and Vanalla stepped over and opened it to see an anxious Fireclaw waiting there. "You guys ready? They're only a few passes away."

"We are," Ash offered, coming out and standing behind Vanalla.

"They're not going to arrive in the main core – we'd never walk them as far as they need to go," she told them as the pair exited their cabin and started following behind her. "We're going to put them up in the boarding lair, which might as well be our hospital until we can get them well enough to start building residences."

"Yeah, I kind of have the idea that we're going to be doing that while they recover," Ash asserted.

"You're not wrong," Fireclaw admitted. "We're going to get some help for you, too, though. Van, however…"

"I know," Vanalla told her, putting a paw on her shoulder. "I know where you need me."

"Thank you," Fireclaw offered softly, patting Van's paw before walking on. "I think we all thought this would be different at the start. We had a time telling the children that they couldn't welcome the new arrivals – that it wouldn't be safe for them."

"Which *them*?" Ash asked.

"Yes, both. We'll have to be damned careful that we don't pick up any diseases they are carrying. The conditions I've heard about," Fireclaw sighed, "really, really bad."

As they approached the boarding-lair, Van blinked in surprise, and Ash was just as amazed. There were literally scores of medical staff ready to assist the new Attorian residents to their hospital bed and begin their recovery. "What's the count now?" Fireclaw asked Laxar, who was standing near the entrance at a computer terminal.

"They're only five passes away, but..." They all walked up closer to him so he could tell them. "Our count is now thirty-three," he whispered. "Two have died during transport."

Fireclaw swore darkly to herself and then looked at Ash. "I'm sorry, cub, but that one's on you. You ready for that?"

"I am. We found a place that won't infect the water table; there's a lot of clay. We even have four dug out, so ... I'm grateful it's not more," he told them, sadly. "If someone can give me at least a name or something, I'll put a marker on the graves."

"I don't know if we'll have that," she told him. "We'll try."

Vanalla caught a look from Fireclaw, and it made her smile softly. "You've changed so much," Van offered into Fireclaw's thoughts. "You are willing to give everything to them, and wow – that is now who you are."

Fireclaw hugged Van, holding her as she cried a little. "And I have you to thank, Great Mother, for leading me there. Thank you for letting me lead this; as you did in your time, please help me to do in mine." Van patted her on the back, understanding that the allusion to the "Great Mother" was meant partially as a joke and partially in real seriousness. It wasn't intended as worship so much as it was filled with reverent respect for the Grand Matriarch Vanarra de Gonari who walked hidden in their midst.

A Vulpi couple walked towards them, then, as the embrace ended. "So, they'll be arriving soon?" Alanar asked.

"Only a few passes, now," Laxar offered from nearby.

"Emma," Vanalla stated, "it's so good of you to be here for us. As soon as you can give us anything to go on, we'll follow your word."

"We'll work together on this," Doctor Emmeniama de Kestrick asserted. "The key messages here are hope and a future. Stay with those phrases; it may be the only thing they can retain in their condition. Keep it simple, very simple, at this point. I've already instructed the rest of the staff."

"Yeah, and I'm going to be ... behind the scenes," Fireclaw noted. "Damn well wouldn't do to have them seeing someone who looks like a close match to their Great Mother right from the start."

"We'll take care of things, kit," Van promised. With that and a mutual paw squeeze on their shoulders, Fireclaw stepped back into the operations control center. Lifting her mask onto her muzzle, Vanalla turned towards the entrance of the boarding lair and just waited.

The first vehicle to arrive seemed to appear less than a pass later in a flurry of flashing lights. "Ambulance," she acknowledged as Ash and Vosh followed her down, the hover already landing. "Excuse me," she asked the assistant driver as he lowered his window. "Can you tell us about your patient?"

"He's ... he's not a patient ... anymore," the shaken mix blood told her. "I ... we tried."

"Okay, if you have a mortuary bag, please go ahead and use it, putting any identification you can find into its outer pocket. Pull up over there, and Ash here will be around to collect the body for burial. We already have a place approved for that."

"Yes, and ... I'm sorry. We really did try very hard," the Pantera-Lupar told her. She patted his shoulder and sent him away so the next vehicle could pull in. It, also, was another casualty, and it and its following ambulance were all ushered into the holding area for burial.

The next vehicle pulled in and landed, and Vanalla asked hopefully, "Your patient?"

"We've got him on fluids and a very carefully balanced electrolyte regimen," the Perratti driver told her. "He's stable, and I think – minus not really wanting to live – that he's actually going to. You have a place for him?"

"If you can unload him and bring him into triage, we'll take it from there," Vanalla told him. "Vosh, if you'd assist?" Vosh nodded and followed the driver as he exited the vehicle. In a few moments, what seemed to only be the shadow of a Thurian was being pulled out of the back, his fur thin and brittle- looking as dried leaves. As they began to carry him up, he stirred awake, his sunken in eyes blearily searching around him.

"Where am I?" he whispered, but such a hush had fallen over the staff that his words could be easily heard by most nearby.

"You are in Attoria. Welcome," Vanalla told him, almost as quietly.

"I do not wish to live. I want to die," he told her, the heartbreak making it nearly impossible for Van to speak. It was everything she could do to withhold the healing force inside of her from latching onto this poor Thurian and performing a miracle in front of everyone.

Vosh looked back over her shoulder and told him, "That is a temporary wish and one you only have because you know of none better. You will have a future here…"

"You do have hope."

Vanalla's soft words to him and the shedding of a tear gripped the Thurian lying on the gurney. He looked at her, some small spark of who he might have been long ago presenting itself in that sunken in face, in those dark and distant eyes. "We were told the … Attorian hope was only destruction."

"I am not destroyed, and you won't be either. Please, be patient with us, and we will show you the hope of Attoria is a future for you and yours, not an end."

"I … can try," he offered, seemingly lost in her eyes. Van quickly closed hers and then nodded, Vosh and the assistant ambulance driver following the directions of Emma at the top of the entrance stairs.

They all watched and assisted as the next few ambulances brought in two more living and two more dead Vanarrans. Sadly enough, Ash had learned that even his preparations weren't enough, and he had retired to go and begin digging the fifth grave, a task made at least mechanically easier thanks to a commercial digger. As the transport came in with the ambulatory Vanarrans, it was clear that they were only in slightly better condition than those who had lost the ability to walk for themselves.

"Please, please, we're so hungry," one of the females told them as Vosh assisted her inside. "You have food, right? Food?"

"We do," Vosh told her softly, "but if we were to feed you now, the shock to your system would kill you. We will supply nutrients and fluids to your body gradually so that you can recover enough of the right body chemicals to eat and not perish."

"But ... you do have food, right?"

"We do, and when you are well enough," Vosh promised her, "you may have your fill. Help us heal you now, though, and be patient."

Van and Laxar, along with many of the other volunteers, helped frightened, hungry, and desperately defeated Vanarrans into different rooms where doctors and nurses were already waiting for them with venous fluids. Each one was a walking horror, fur falling out, faces sunk in – many of them just didn't look Thurian anymore. It looked like flesh that had been wrapped tight on top of a fake skeleton, and those paw-ful who spoke were speaking from souls long shattered beyond recognition.

When all were settled in their places, Van went to check on Fireclaw. She found her in the far corner of the boarding lair office, alone, crying. When the soft paw wrapped around her shoulder, the words started to come out. "I've never seen ... suffering like that! I never knew it was possible. Did we do this to them? Did, Vanarra?" she whispered.

"We didn't. We stopped them from harming others, but what they had been doing for ages in secret, the lives they have harmed-"

"You're not saying they deserved this, are you? You wouldn't wish this on Vassia, right?"

"I don't, but the innocent are harmed when someone discounts the life of another, and these innocents weren't even those they intended to harm," Van explained, sitting beside her on the little corner couch. "What's worse, many of those who perpetrated the purebred curse are still imprisoned, still fed three times a sol. They haven't suffered near what these have."

"How will they ever come back from it?" Fireclaw wept, despondently. "No one can."

"They can, and they will, and it will be the love you show to them that helps. It's the love everyone shows them that will help. Sadly enough, I've seen Alanar talking hard with Emma when she's had a moment. I think he hated the Vanarrans, and now he sees what's left of them. It's not always a good thing to see those you opposed defeated like this."

"How many graves up there, Van, before we even have all of them here? How many more sols like this?"

"More," Van sighed. "Dynaea spoke to me a little earlier, mentally. It will be more. Several more temples are trying to hold on far too long. She also told me that a Vanarran temple on the Luratan continent was first thought to be abandoned, but instead..."

"They were all dead."

"They were all dead, yes. They killed themselves rather than surrender to come with us. It's not what I wanted."

"Then why can you not stop it?!" Fireclaw demanded harshly.

"Because we can't stop individual choice. Dynaea told me how she had tried to stretch their food supply, send them encouraging messages to help convince them to come to Attoria. Nothing worked. Finally, when enforcement wanted to come in and pull them all out – yeah, that's when."

"Does this place even have an honest hope, Van?" Fireclaw asked.

"It does. It's my greatest hope that we won't start with the bare minimum, but with these, we might have about one fifth of what we would need to make a viable Aelkinda colony. We are only at the first step – survival. We need one hundred and fifty, minimum, coming back up to full health. Second step, contributing and belonging. We need for them to feel like they are a part of this community. Third step, living and earning; we need this colony to be self-sufficient. Finally, we need them joining and breeding and raising kits and cubs. I believe we can get there, and what we saw come in this sol is some of our raw material for that dream. But they are more than that, you realize?"

Fireclaw just looked at her, confused. Van continued, "Do you realize that your future friend, your confidant, and maybe even your mate are among these who you are showing kindness to? You realize that this sol begins your investment in their next step? These are charitable cases you can push off on someone else. The only way you will win them over to survival is to give to them out of your own soul."

"I want them to all know me as Tashara, not Fireclaw, not the Great Mother. I want to know all of their names like I know the children."

"They, in many ways, are all your children now. Yours to care for."

Fireclaw circled Van's paw with her own. "Ours to care for."

Dear Diary,

There are many things I thought beyond the realm of possibility for me to write in your pages. Most of these things, such as my falling in love with the most wonderful of Thurians, my betrothal to her, and the beginning of our lives together, are wonderfully positive. I still feel that my giving up my former job to come here to this new start, to Attoria, is a truly good thing. However, this sol, Diary, has been hard. I dug seven graves with a commercial digger, and then I wrote down the name of seven Thurians whose lives ended because they starved themselves to death in the name of their goddess. I went into my shop and made temporary markers for them. There is no one but me to honor them; everyone else is working to keep the twenty-eight remaining souls alive.

As I look down at the names on these graves, I refused to put their Vanarran titles on them. I think that, since it was their religion that misled them to starve themselves, such wouldn't be appropriate. This sol, I'm burying everything about them, including their futures. It's such a waste. That's the hardest thing about this for me. These almost-skeletons I buried – I looked at them – they were little babies once. These were kits and cubs that crawled around wanting nothing more than to be loved. They could have grown up into artists and musicians and professionals and teachers, but no. Now, I'm standing over them – eight tracks of clay and dirt between us, life and death between us.

Although it's not my charge to judge who the Creator might catch and who the Creator might not, a part of my spirit tells me these are lost. Buried in thick clay, packed in tight, nothing of what they were – not even the water and biological material they were made of are really even going to re-circulate for maybe millions of seasons. Who knows? Their lives were meaningless. I pray mine will be better, and I pray those shells of Thurians in our boarding house will choose to have better lives than what lies in front of me right now.

With this done, I'm going to go clean up and try to find Van, help the others. I felt that I had to do this, first, though. If this diary is ever found, then at least these Thurians will have some small purpose – if only to warn others what not to do.

Buried this sol in Attoria: Avanna, Daniella, Carastar, Dishan, Ishanic, Corleona, Dalvatan.

May the Creator's forgiveness find you, sorry. May there be some second chance for you. I'm so sorry.

Emmeniama de Kestrick saw Ash, the one she first treated as Akashar, coming from a small rise where he had been working all sol. Her connection to this mixed blood was deeper than she wanted to admit, and although she and Alanar were very happy together, part of her still felt the pain and uncertainty from three long seasons of attempting to help this mixed blood recover his memories. At the moment, also, it seemed that she had precious little to do. Most of the new Attorian citizens were sleeping, a delicate balance of nutrition flowing into their veins. She had just finished up a long session talking with Fireclaw or Tashara; the former Vanarrans dying had hit her hard, and after spending a life in a profession obsessed with health, beauty, and vitality, the desperate physical situation of the Vanarrans had been a psychological shock. Doctor Emma was glad she was taking her sabbatical here, away from the forms and strictures of the hospital. Here, she could simply help, and as her former mixed blood patient made his way up the entrance stairs of the boarding lair, she called out to him.

"Hello, Akashar," she offered, smiling at him.

Surprised and shocked by her greeting, one he had heard so many times as a precursor to some deep inner investigation, he stopped and stared up at her. "Oh, Doctor Emma! They ... I knew you were here. It's Ash, now."

"I know," she told him, coming down to his level and sitting. "I ... have to admit that I missed greeting you after you were gone."

He looked at her, curious. "You see so many patients, Doctor. I'm surprised that I would stick out."

"I saw you for three seasons straight, and very few have tried so very hard as you did. None of them have been as dedicated as you were. I let you go in the confidence that I had done everything for you I could, and that you had spared nothing of your soul in trying to do what I asked. We prize patients like you, Ash. The truth is, I missed you. I was going to catch up with you later, but I saw you coming from ... up there. You had to bury them, didn't you?"

"Yes," he replied.

"I'm not your doctor anymore, Ash, but ... I find that my life – or the way I've chosen to live it – has left me with few real friends. Both of us, now, have someone to fill the part of our lives in the role of a mate." He looked at her, curious, with just a bit of a smile at one corner of his mouth. "Alanar asked just before we came out here."

"Oh, congratulations Doctor!" he offered warmly, his happiness for her genuine.

"Thank you, but would it be okay if you called me just ... Emma? Could I be your friend, Ash?"

"You're already Vanalla's," he told her, smiling. "And I owe you so much. You know you can have whatever you'd need from me."

"How about a few passes here, on the steps, telling me what you're feeling?" He nodded, but he commented, "I really don't have to tell you, though. I can do what I've always done." Pulling out his diary, he surrendered it to her.

"Ash, I'm not sure I should. You did that for me when you were in therapy with me. I no longer have any medical reason to invade your privacy like that."

"Just read the last page, and it's not an invasion of privacy if I'm giving it to you." Nodding, she took it, flipped from the back searching forwards until she located the last written page. Sitting there in the small light fixed on the arched awning, Emma read. After she finished it, she closed it and held onto it for a moment.

"I … agree, Ash. I agree with you. We've got twenty-eight in the building behind us, and I'm just aching inside wanting to help them, worried I won't be able to. Worried that none of us will be able to break through all of the seasons of trained hatred. Has Van ever told you what happened when some of them were in the hospital?"

"I didn't, not yet," Van chuckled from the top of the stairs. "Can I join?"

"Yes, please. Has … has Ash ever let you read his diary?"

Sitting down on the other side of her mate, Van replied, "He has, on occasion. Something I should see?"

Emma offered, and with a look in Ash's direction for approval and a nod in response, she gave it to Vanalla. "Last entry."

Van flipped through and found the entry and read it. Tears dropped from her eyes and fell on the paper, and she wiped them off. Closing it, she offered it back to him and leaned into his neck. "So sorry, love," she whispered.

"This … this is helping," he told them. "My love and … a good friend. What were you going to tell me about when some of the Vanarrans were in the hospital?"

Emma nodded and said, "Well, it was shortly after the Sahnassites bombed the temple, and several of the Vanarrans were in Shanandrae recovering. I … well, I thought I could interact with them and try to help them through their recovery, and one of them went for me – like trying to kill me."

"What happened?"

"Well, your darling mate was there, and I'm not entirely sure, but I think she pushed her stun prod into the frame of the bed; shut him right down!"

He pulled away a little and looked at his mate, curious. "Guilty," Van replied, sniffling, wiping her eyes. "Yeah, totally guilty on that one. Messed up a perfectly good stunner, too."

"I was grateful for it," she told them, but then reached for both of their paws. "Just as I'm grateful to think of you both as my friends, now. I have a three-moon sabbatical, and I'm going to stay and help.

I'm not only here to help these who have arrived. I'm here to help you, too – I want you to know that. You were there for me, Vanalla, and I want to be there for you."

"You've done so much for us, Emma. It's kind of you," Van offered, clasping the Vulpi's paw.

"I don't want you to ever have to make another journal entry like that, Ash," Emma told him. "I'll do everything I can, okay?"

He nodded, and the three embraced, sitting on the steps.

There were very few, if any, of the Vanarrans Vassia knew in the group who had arrived. Vidiana, however, was one she did know. She hadn't recognized her, at first, but the bleary eyed, delirious mixed blood had locked eyes on her for only a moment before passing out, and then it clicked. Now, she sat beside that bed, watching the drip, drip, drip of fluids making their way into the desiccated flesh of someone who had once fiercely challenged her for her position in the Shanandrae research establishment.

Her mind awash in memories, she didn't see the eyes flicker open and then slowly turn upon her. It wasn't until the husky whisper – as close to a growl as the owner could manage – came to her ears. "Betrayer!"

Turning to face her accuser, she asked, "Why, Vidiana, would you call me that? What reason do you have or cause for you to care?"

"It is the cause of ... the Great Mother. We were faithful. We refused to ... I refused to surrender."

"And yet you are here, now," Vassia commented softly. "You didn't choose to stay and die as the others did on Luratan."

"Outvoted by ... cowards," came the bitter protestation. "Too weak to fight their foolishness."

"You'll find they made the braver choice – the wiser one. If the Great Mother truly approved of what we were doing, tell me, how has she rewarded our faithfulness? She didn't keep the Sahnassites from destroying our sacred temple in Shanandrae. She didn't prevent a tanker full of fuel from obliterating the children we had bred. She didn't keep our secret vengeance against the purebred from finding its way into their paws, did she? She didn't stop the healing all of those we poisoned. She didn't bring food to you as you starved, and she didn't protect you when you were set upon by those seeking vengeance for what was done to their children, did she?"

Looking into the pain filled eyes, Vassia could tell that she'd hit her mark. "Either she doesn't exist and we were fooling ourselves, or guess what – she didn't like what we were doing. I think, no ... I know we got it wrong, Vidiana. We got everything wrong. The only reason I'm here and not in that bed or dead is because I was sent to prison. Many of us were. Several of us were sentenced to death, and they died."

"Holy martyrs," Vidiana contested.

"Fools!" Vassia spat. "They sat in their cell and gushed out their faith in the Great Mother, but when the sentence was carried out, they were *gone*! Call me faithless, call me a traitor, but I've found a path that works for me – a path I can believe in."

"That of Creator's Path heretic?"

"Creator's Path *faithful*. I've known nothing but misery my entire life and swallowed it all as sacred duty, and my path was like crawling over sharp stones sol in and sol out, and now, I have companionship. I care for others, and they care for me. It isn't a duty; it's kindness! It's more selfless love than I could hope to have at any Vanarran temple."

"You should let me die, heretic," Vidiana said, fatigue now claiming its hold over her.

"They should kill us all; it is only by *heresy* we're even alive. It's only by the heresy of the mercies taught in the Creator's Path that they suffer us to live." The shell of a Thurian slammed her eyes shut angrily, her grimace only fading as sleep once again claimed her.

Vassia stood and departed the room quietly. There, a short distance away, Vanalla reclined against the wall, alone in the deserted hallway. Walking over, she bowed her head. "Great Mother ... her faith was in her imagined version of you, but it wasn't anything more than a projection of what they wanted, what they ... what we were trained to want. I'm sorry. I don't know how many of them will even try to stay alive. If they do regain their strength, they may try to overwhelm us and turn this into the re-genesis of the Vanarran cult."

Van looked surprised for a moment and then shook her head. "You ... sly predator, Me Sha! Darn you if you're not good!"

"I'm sorry?" Vassia questioned.

"Let's just say that I'm not here by accident, Vassia. I have a feeling that the concerns you just offered are why I'm here – living here, actually. Wow," Van breathed. "And I thought this was all about me and my life with Ash – mostly." Looking at Vassia's confused face which was forced to echo Van's sly smile, even if she didn't understand it, Van explained, "There is someone who leads me, teaches me, and he has for many, many seasons. I thought ... wow, I don't know exactly what I thought. See, part of what I do is on the surface, just small things, but here I can get in deep with these individuals, like Vidiana, help turn her onto a better path. I can help, and the doubts you have about being able to influence what they choose are something, specifically, I can help with. Now, it's been a long sol for you my faithful *friend*; why don't you get some rest. I can stand watch for a while."

Vassia, still smiling softly, nodded meekly and was about to walk away when Van grabbed her shoulder. When her eyes flashed back to Vanalla's face, she was no longer looking into the eyes of a Faelnar, but the eyes of a mixed blood. "I love you, Vassia, and honor you for your bravery in the face of what she said to you, and what they all may say." The impact of seeing the reality of her once Great Mother drew tears from the once Vanarran Select, and those silent tears turned into sobs of joy as Vanarra held her in a loving embrace.

When they parted, Vassia mouthed, "Thank you." With a nod, the mixed blood's image disappeared replaced again with that of the Faelnar.

"You will rest well tonight, dear friend. Take peace as my gift," Van bade. Smiling, Vassia bowed and departed. "She'll be one of the very few who gets to know the truth of me, but we need at least a few. Now, as to you," Van thought, entering the room with the sleeping Vidiana, "I'm a little curious as to what your story is." She could feel Tana starting to reach into the subconscious dreaming of the pathetic mixed blood lying in front of her, the drip of venous fluids the only thing keeping her alive. "It's not my goal to control you," she told herself, "but it is my goal to make sure you listen to me."

Vidiana blinked awake and startled. She had no idea where she was. It was clear she was in some kind of office or its lobby, but she didn't remember how she got here. Sitting up and looking around, she was in a chair obviously slouching before from being asleep. There was an administrative desk, but it was empty. However, there was conversation coming from down the hall from what sounded like two females. She wondered if she should dart away through the open door, but it looked desperately cold outside, and looking down at her own body, Vidiana realized she was wearing a jacket. There was something vaguely familiar about the scene outside – almost as if it was a landscape she should have recognized. It seemed barer and smaller than it should be. She was studying it so intently that she didn't even recognize when a large form entered the room.

At a soft intake of air through a muzzle, she turned and saw a large gray mixed blood, a pure-mix between what appeared to be Lupar and Nephti. This one was very serious looking, but not unkind, she reasoned. "I hate when the weather is like this," the gray one groaned as she sat down. "Always gives me a headache. Van is just finishing something up; she'll see you in a moment."

"Thank … you," Vidiana replied, uncertain. "Van?" she thought. "Van who? What is this? Where am I?" There was something familiar about the mixed blood seated near her, now studiously attending to her work.

It was then that what Vidiana could only define as a "presence" came into the room, demanding her attention. Looking up, she beheld a mixed blood Vulpi-Faelnar, a young adult surrounded by the air of complete command. "Good morning to you! I'm Vanarra Anasto. I have some time for you now if you'd like to come back."

Faced with the young version of the Great Mother, there was nothing else she could do but stand and reply, "Yes, thank you. Thank you very much."

As she followed the mixed blood into her office, Vanarra asked, "So, I've heard that you have been dealing with some hard times lately, not much in the way of food or support."

Beginning to wonder if this was some type of lucid vision, Vidiana answered honestly. "We were ostracized and kept huddled together without food or any way to get out. Some of us ... didn't make it."

"I'm very sorry to hear that," Vanarra replied sympathetically. "Times are tough for our kind, but that doesn't mean they are without hope. Juice?" The mere word made Vidiana's mouth water, and she nodded – both eagerly and humbly. Taking the bottled juice as politely as she could and downing it in full, by compulsion, widened Van's eyes a bit. "I ... I see."

"Thank you. I'm ... I'm sorry."

"Kit, are you hungry right now? I mean, *really* hungry right now?"

Her blush fur riding high, Vidiana responded, "Yes, I am. I'm sorry."

Vanarra bit her lip a little and said, "Just this once, okay? Come back here for me." The two, at the Faelnar-Vulpi's direction, left the office and went down the hallway to the back. Going to one of the open commercial kitchens compartmentalized opposite the tall shelves, Van reached into one of the large cooler units and pulled out a plate of food, slipping it into a warmer. After a quick pass in which neither one of them spoke, the plate of food was pulled out, its smell and appearance causing Vidiana to literally tremble with need.

Van took the plate, snapping up some utensils and a napkin in her paw, and walked over to one of the long tables. Setting the place with practiced ease, Vanarra offered, "I'll get you a drink, and eat as slowly as you can, right now."

"I'm sorry, so sorry," Vidiana apologized, magnetically drawn into the seat. "I've not had any food like this for ... for so long." The hungry Thurian just seemed to be mesmerized by the sight of this incredible setting in front of her while the Faelnar-Vulpi got a drink for her.

Van placed the drink before her and said softly, "Go ahead, kit. I don't know what else I can do for you, but I can, at least, feed you here and now."

Tears starting to roll down her cheek fur, paws trembling, Vidiana took up the utensils and slowly speared the most beautifully caramelized tuber root her eyes had ever beheld and brought it to her mouth. The impact on her psyche when she took the first bite was devastating – nothing else existed, and no food had ever tasted as thoroughly and magically delicious as that did.

Almost coming out of fugue state, Vidiana beheld the mixed blood manager of this business wiping a tear from her own eye having seen the profound effect simple food had on this stranger. "I … remember being hungry like that. I was hungry a lot, growing up," she confessed aloud. "Much of my hunger was … unnecessary."

It took a compelling effort to form a question and not, once again delight herself in the wonder of this meal, but Vidiana asked, "Unnecessary? I don't understand."

Van waited, perhaps thinking, until her guest had recovered from the experience of another morsel of food before she answered. "I … didn't know it at the time, but when I was young – after I lost my mother, there were wonderfully kind purebreds out there who were looking for me. They knew about and regretted everything that happened, and if I had shown up at their door, one door in particular, I would have been adopted immediately as a daughter and loved and cared for. I didn't know. I thought I was doing things the only way they could be done, and I was wrong. I thought I could only rely on myself and others like me. There I was wrong, too. I almost froze to death, almost starved to death. I could have been in a bedroom in a nice lair somewhere, studying and trying to prove to everyone that I was worthy of a chance. I hid from the world, instead."

Vidiana once again consumed a bite of something else – roast grazer, while she contemplated what Vanarra had said. "Sometimes, you don't have a choice. The world puts walls up and keeps you inside of them."

"True, sometimes, but I've learned to guard myself against the walls that weren't put up by them but, rather, were put up by me. I hid from those who would have helped me. Mercy from the world is sometimes hard to find especially for some of us, but it's there – it can be found, and it can be earned. I denied myself any chance at it because I told myself that all purebred were evil, that all purebred were the same. I vengefully hurt them when I should have been winning their trust. A little humiliation can go a long way in the cause of saving you – keeping yourself fed and with a place to lay your head. Now, answer me this, can you read?"

Vidiana humbly nodded. Van added another question, "Do you have any place to stay?"

"I do; I'm just … hungry," the humiliated mixed blood answered, not sure of the answer she just gave, but it seemed to fit her reality.

"Okay, then here's the deal we will strike. I will start you on a trial basis in here with some light stocking and organizing – doing inventory of things that are easy to reach, that sort of thing. There's no shame in that. It's how almost everyone starts. Now, after some of our events, we have left over food. Most of that has gone to an orphanage I support, but the truth is that sometimes we have so much overage that even they can't take it all. Part of your pay will be in food because if you are weak and malnourished, you're going to have a hard time working. Now, let me be absolutely transparent on this point – you may not steal. If you steal, I have to let you go. If you are ugly to or don't play well with the other members of my group – the ones already here, I will have to let you go. We'll work out a schedule of *payments* to slowly build you up, but before long, I hope that you'll be strong enough to earn your place in this, a new community for you. I take it my group here is not what you've been used to?"

"What I was used to … failed," Vidiana admitted. "We … we believed so passionately and firmly that, even now, I don't want to give up my beliefs. I'm not sure I can."

"I understand that, but sometimes, our beliefs are informed by the situation we're in. Here, you'll find the opportunity to seek out new ideas and test them, even as you test those you hold to. Be certain, though, that here, whether purebred or mixed, all are equal in terms of treatment. No one is to take advantage of you because you are of mixed parentage, but the purebreds, also, are not to be slighted in any way – past histories are forgiven here, all histories. Do you think you can live with that?"

Vidiana thought for a moment, the chords and harmonies of this dream seeping into an awakening mind, allowing her some view into her own real history, her past as a Vanarran. "I can. I can try."

"That's all anyone can ask of you, but understand that the standard of how you reply to that question is how you will be judged – not on any other merit. Now, finish up, and I'll check back with you in a moment."

"Thank you, Great-"

"Van will do, sweetie. I'm not great. I just try. You do that, too, now. Just try…"

Vidiana's eyes blinked open when her arm was gently jostled by a brown and gold Faelnar changing the fluid linc. "I'm sorry to wake you, but I needed to give you some more. Your vitals are improving. That's good news."

Having an almost instinctual loathing of a purebred's touch, she grimaced and wanted to resist. "Just try…" the words filtered back through her consciousness. "She is doing something that keeps you alive," her own voice told her. "For what that's worth," she shot back, internally. "Maybe it is worth something, and … need to pee."

Her blush furs sailing high as possible on her thinly furred face, Vidiana admitted, "I … I need some help; I … need to urinate."

The Faelnar's eyes widened, and she smiled. "That's a good sign! Do you think you would be able to walk if I support you? I could wait and attach the next bag when you get back." Humiliated, Vidiana nodded, and Van started to gently cradle the nearly starved female into position.

"She's so gentle with me," Vidiana's mind couldn't help but observe, "and her kind touch is not revolting." A tear borne of self-realization slipped down her cheek as she was helped to a standing position. It was the beginning of her heartbreak at the possibility that all she had given her life to and all she had tried to do was, in fact, wrong.

Ash sat in the cabin, alone in the dark as rain poured overhead, his eyes pouring in time with the streaks of water down the curved panes of glass. Almost without realizing how she had gotten there, he felt and smelled the presence of his mate alongside him. It was a scent that seemed familiar, yet foreign, with undertones of complex association deep inside of his soul, but the first blush of something, that at times, was shockingly unfamiliar in a way. Tonight, because of the wetness of her coat, the undertones were stronger, and he felt his soul opening to her more readily.

"I can sense you're sad, cub," she whispered. "I'm ... sorry that you have had to do such hard things in the last few sols."

"I can understand," he stated softly, "why some truly feel the need for children, and why some don't ever want them. What pain there is to bear someone from birth only to have them waste the gifts life offers – all while you watch, while you care."

"Not if *you* were their parent, my love," Vanalla offered consolingly. "Nor I, for that matter. These should never have been bred for the sakes of creating some magical new species that will solve Thuria's problems. You, however, dear one – you will be a father to these now, I think."

"Too late for all of the ones I saw," he breathed, his voice quavering, "and for those you saw, too, right?"

"The ones that you laid to rest, yes," Van admitted gently. "Vidiana has just started to see her way clear to a new possibility, and what's strange is that ... no matter how old you are, you need a father figure to be in your life, someone to lead you when you are lost. Maybe the interpretation given our ages and theirs is *friend*, but for all of their following of their Great Mother, they forgot the father. They forgot steadfast male leadership by example and the pillar of faith upon which not only his life is built, but that of his family. You are my pillar, Ash. So much has happened to you, and yet you are still good. You are still kind. You are so kind that your heart aches for those you cannot help, who are beyond our help. I love you for that."

He leaned into her and asked, "So you think there is hope?"

"I do." Her nuzzle was accompanied by just a hint of a nip at the corner of his ear.

"What would *Vanarra* say?" he asked, feeling a need to tease her back in some way. There was only a slight pause before the answer came, and the slightest change of accent accentuated the difference of the "speaker."

"For season upon season, cub, I *offered* help to those who needed it. I *offered* healing or escape or kindness. Not all accepted, but I could never deny at least offering that help when I saw the need.

I am not going to be completely ignorant of the Creator's part in this, but by my choices and the Creator's power, lives were changed. I wept for joy some nights surrounded by the orphans I had been able to help. I still think of every one of them. My nights of sadness for what had happened to me and the special ones I loved were softened by the knowledge that I had preserved a life, nurtured a life, helped blossom a life into full bloom. That boarding lair is now full of those same needs. They are the orphans, now, and they are nothing but. Cub, what you feel is what you feel, but what you *will* feel and come to know is greater. Accept that from someone who has lived long enough and travelled far enough to know it."

Reaching over, he turned on the light and just looked at her. His brown and gold Faelnar with those beautiful golden eyes just looked back at him, smiling softly. "I turned on the light ... half expecting to see her there and not you," he remarked, amazed. "This is something special about you, love. You make her so real inside of yourself. I'm ashamed to admit it, but when you talk like her, it ... it really touches me." He then looked at her, apologetically. "I'm not asking you to be her. That would be wrong."

She reached around him and turned off the light, and that special voice spoke to him again. "I am who I am, dearest love, and if these words reach you and give comfort to your heart, then there is nothing I would want more." Her gentle touch and caress spoke to him of her affection and love and desire to give him joy and peace, and as she took him in her arms and started to nuzzle and kiss him, a remarkable transformation seemed to happen. Her scent, for the first time, when it grew from her increasing desire, didn't rise as one – with both the overtones and undertones surging in time with her arousal. This time, to his amazement and surprised joy, the undertones he found more deeply comforting and touching leaped above those he had known before as prominent when being with her. They utterly eclipsed and dissipated to non-existence like the falling of a wall. His soul, as if wanting to run into the very center of her own, was instantly and whole heartedly committed to their union.

"My love!" he pled at a whisper and caressed her in return, showing in every way his need for her.

"I have loved you always, and always I will love you," came back the whisper perfectly in tune with the tenor and tambour of shared heartbeats, and that released everything that Ash had been and Ash was now into the joining, and love and soul mingled between them like never before.

Chapter 15: Rediscovered Countries

The next morning, Ash awoke in the warm darkness, the fur of his chest being rubbed, and his nose filled with the scent of his beautiful mate. "Which one?" he wondered, inwardly.

"Sorry, love," the voice came, that other voice – the same sound but not the same intonations. "You were stirring, and the stars around you, too."

"Strange words," he chuckled, "and a strangely amazing and comforting moment that, if Doctor Emma had anything to say about it, *should* be profoundly disturbing. Am I learning that my lovely Vanalla has ... two sides? That two individuals inhabit the mind of this one body? When we made love, I ... felt things *so* deeply inside of myself, about myself. I saw past barriers I'd never seen through before, and I felt this love for Vanarra, but she was so much different – younger. I love you, though, Vanalla."

"*Though* is not right nor is it needed," the voice softly told him in the darkness. "Does the way I speak to you sound familiar at all?"

He looked over at her, and all he could see was the reflection of her eyes in the darkness. "It's ... beautiful. It's ... home!" he said, tears running down his cheek fur. "What's happening?"

"Slowly, over time, I've been letting you see me, dear one. At first, I had to wear a mask, a mask that hides me like nothing you've ever seen before. All of my features, my colors, my scent – all was hidden. The mask would never hide my heart, though – it cannot hide that. I have been yours since I saw you hiding in the woods, oh so long ago." A vision came to his mind, terrified feelings as his mind's eye looked this way and that through a forest, but then his eyes came to rest on her, on the Faelnar-Vulpi with the eyes that speared into his soul, froze him not with fear, but with wonder. "Do you remember that sol, my love?"

"I … I do. The fragments – I've seen this, parts of this when we were together, just moments but never the full." He reached for the side of her muzzle and kissed her, and the scent in his nostrils was no longer the Faelnar alone, but that of a Vulpi was entangled and mixed within intensely complex smells which came from her. Soft, shimmering lights seemed to come from around the sides of her form, outlining one that wasn't merely Faelnar any longer. The tail that lofted up above her as she lay on the bed was thicker and fuller – almost that of a Vulpi. "Am I losing my mind?"

"No, my love. You have discovered it. The secret of how this came to be will take time to explain beyond what you have learned since we were parted, so long ago, since I … could not save you."

There were other mental images now, images of being curled up beside a very worried looking Vanarra, eyes blurred by tears and … by pain. There was a hospital and a squalid room in which they huddled as his vision got darker, and one intense spasm of pain that tore his mind away from her – it's echo in the dream a scream from his own muzzle, the grief at leaving his love. "I … I remember," he breathed out. "I was ill, very bad. You were there, weren't you, and…"

"And I lost you," the voice wept, head burying itself in his shoulder and neck.

"Then, I woke up, and … I couldn't remember anything. I couldn't…"

"But now, can you?" she asked softly. "Can you remember my love for you? Can you remember the dark nights spent as bright sols in the great library, the Pinnacle Center archive? Can you remember our home there? Our secret lair?"

"Vents, the vents were important to – I became – no! I studied air systems and felt…"

"Even though you thought you didn't remember, you still did – at some level. You also knew me and hid from my story until I told it to you. Until I spoke in this voice, and until I told you how I loved you again."

Ash was trembling as he held onto her. "Oh, please, please, don't let this be a dream! Don't…"

"It is not a dream. You lay beside me now, my dearest love, seventeen hundred and more seasons beyond that of our first life on Thuria, back when we were shunned and held down and hurt. Back when we were the starving ones, when we were the ones seeing our friends and … loves die."

"The orphanage," he remembered, "that … horrible place. They were all starving there. I left – no, I was thrown out, alone. Then, you were there!"

"And now, I am here. Now, I love you again. Forgive me this deception, my love," she pled softly at his neck. "I could go no faster than you could in letting you know who you truly were, who I truly was."

"You waited for all that time for me to try and figure myself out…"

"Because the key to unlock your memories was … me. Even I didn't know that, Ash. I hoped, but I didn't know," she told him as he held her lovingly at his chest.

He looked at her body which now seemed to be rippling with soft light. "What is this … glow I see from you?"

"It is the light of my becoming, of what's next for me. It is the me that will come after me slipping into being in small ways, right before you."

"Please, no! Please," he begged, holding her. "Please don't tell me I lose you … after all of this?!"

She pulled away from him, but she was smiling at him. "No. I am here for you. I am here for *this* life of ours together, my love, and I feel that our lives – long that they are, will stretch even further than we might think." He held her paws as soft light started to filter in through the sides of the blinds at the windows. "Night and darkness are ending, Ash, and you have still so much more to discover, even beyond this night's wonders."

"When the light comes, what will I see?" he asked. "Will I see the brown and gold Faelnar or … will I see the Faelnar-Vulpi – which will you be?"

"I will be both, my love, but if you wish, I will show you my true self. Know that, in this time, I cannot be that way when we are around others who do not know of me. They must always see the Faelnar; they must always see, hear, and smell Vanalla, only. You will know I am there, though, and when we are like this, you will see me, dear one."

At that moment, just enough light seemed to come into the cabin to illuminate her form in the softest beauty. It was enough to hide from view her own inner light and start to express her shape in the way all others were seen. His eyes drank her in, hungrily. The way the light shimmered across her fur and framed the beautiful elegance of her tail. The soft, sleeveless shirt she wore couldn't hide the magnificence of her curves, but it was the love in her eyes that held him, entranced. The eyes and the lines of her face were the only thing about her that remained from Vanalla to Vanarra, but they were indefinably *her*.

"You are there, and you've been there *all the time*! Why ... why couldn't I see you?! Why didn't I know?"

She could hear the desperation in his voice, the sense of failure that he should have somehow known it was her far earlier, and she reached her paw to the side of his muzzle. "No, love. You were not to know. A paw that guides us saw fit that you would come to this time and not know, that you would grow without those memories of bitterness and loss. In this time, you never were treated as less because you were a mixed blood, were you?"

"No, those ... at the Creator's Path chapel I went to loved me and adopted me as their own. They showed the greatest kindness to me. I wouldn't be here without them. Were you here all along," he asked, "watching over me?"

"I was not, my love, but the paw that guides us loves me as his daughter, and now, I sense, you as his son. I think it was his paws and those of the Creator who guided you. You are no longer a teen; you are an adult with a rich, warm, and caring heart – a tender heart. You learned this because others were kind to you, and you learned patience, too, didn't you?"

"It ... was so frustrating not knowing who I was," he told her, "and even now, I feel uncertain. I remember ... being Ash, no – being *Ashalam*! That was my name, wasn't it?"

"It was. That first self waking inside of you is waking inside of this new one, but the two of you are not the same as you were, are you? You are more than that. I can tell."

"I … I can tell how beautiful you are," he breathed out, the ever-increasing light now giving her form more depth and definition. "Oh, I wish this sol could have come so much sooner!"

"It could not, even though I have wanted that more than you could know. After all, you did not know I was here, but I knew you were there. I watched sol by sol and waited, and I could tell that this night, when you had started to hear my voice as my voice and know my scent that this is *our* morning. The darkness that fell over Shanandrae Commons has lifted, and you are with me now."

"Joined together in love even before," he remarked, wonderstruck and warmed in heart. "I fell in love with you … all over again!"

"Never a greater compliment was paid to me, and never a deeper touch have I felt in the depths of my soul," she whispered, leaning over to him and kissing him deeply. The love they had experienced before was manifested a thousand times over as they again came to one another, offering themselves up as living incarnations of their love.

After their loving was complete and both rested, he looked at her still wonderstruck by the fact she lay before him. "I love you, Vanarra. I love you with all of my heart."

"I have loved you for so long, and I love you more now than ever. We'll need to leave soon to help in the boarding lair."

"I don't want to leave you."

"We'll be together, but I must put back on the Faelnar mask, it's true," she admitted. "And we can't talk about anything other than our lives together, now. We can't be overheard."

"I'm not sure anything else matters more than our lives together, now," he agreed.

"True, but there is more than you could possibly imagine, and just as you have changed in the time you've been growing, I have been changing, and that history will take time to unravel for you. You will have to be patient, my love, when it comes to answers and explanations."

"I've waited this long, my precious one," he told her. "I can wait a little longer, just don't leave."

She nodded and sat up, and as the first strong light of the early morning speared into the cabin, she looked up at the ceiling and again returned to hues of brown and of gold and of a tail thin and long. Looking back down at him, she smiled, and her voice resumed its more modern aspect when she next spoke. "We have to face this morning and the mornings after, and we have to help those who may not even want such a thing."

"Is that why you or ... we are here? To help them?"

She chuckled and shook her head, slipping off of the bed. "*Patience*, you! Still, in some ways, yes, what you say is true. Now, I'm going for a shower, and so should you ... *after me*," Van warned when she saw the look in his eyes.

"As you wish, my love, and ... thank you. Thank you for everything."

"Thank you," she offered softly coming to him. "Thanks and a new life for us both, my love."

Ashalam watched her leave and just laid back, trying to sort through all of the thoughts breaking freshly in upon him – wonder and mystery all but erasing the sadness of the sol before.

Soon after, Ash followed the one he had known as "Vanalla" out of their cabin and down the trail that led to the main central core of Attoria's buildings. "You're staring," she softly challenged.

He came even with her on the path. "It's so ... amazing and complete, Van – this camouflage you wear. I know you have this lovely and wonderful tail, but I just can't see it! Not that I don't admire this one, but really, utterly fantastic!"

"Now, now, keep your voice down. A few know of my secrets, but not very many, and we couldn't very well explain what you were talking about when I'm not supposed to be known in this time. The truth is my tail is still there, but cloaked in every critical way, just like the rest of me. *How* will take some explanation, and in point of fact, there will be many, many explanations, my love. We can't do them all right now. I don't think we can do them all this moon, truly."

"So long as I get to stay with you, I'm okay," he said softly, taking her paw. "It's how it was. I wasn't okay until you were with me and took care of me."

"It worked the other way, too, and you have, my love. Even now – in this moment – your touch and patience and love … so much. I just hope you…"

"Hope what, love?"

"I hope you can accept my apology, Ash. There was so much I learned, not even a season later, that would have saved you – kept you by my side."

"But from what we've read, about all you've done – would that have still happened if I was with you?" Van was silent, looking down at the path. "I don't think so, either."

"That doesn't mean I don't need you, now," Van whispered to him, her voice nearly desperate.

"I can see that, but what I don't want you to feel is … regret."

"I can feel nothing but," she told him, shaking her head. "Oh, the nights without end I would go to sleep just begging to be let back into those few moments where I could have protected you from that Vulpi or where I could have listened to my instinct and taken you right out of that lair without leaving you to get worse. Where I could have known about the free clinics or the emergency numbers where we could have gotten real help for you…"

"But you would have never met Sorla. You would have never met Gorta. You would never have become … you, right?" he asked.

"I need you, Ashalam. I need you, and I always have."

"I'm glad you found someone to love you after I was gone," he told her, seriously. "I would have never wanted anything for you but for you to be loved. He sounded like a great cub, the best."

"Yeah, and I'm ashamed of what I did after you were gone and before I got serious with him." His questioning glance was met with her shaking head. "When we're alone, I can tell you about it. I can confess there, but there are tasks ahead of us. Do you see her, waiting for us?"

"Vosh?"

"She knows me, but her presence at the door tells me that we're needed."

The moment Van and Ash were in range of Vosh, she stepped forward and hugged her, whispering something into her ear that Ash couldn't hear. "You, too," Van softly uttered back as she leaned up. "Now, what's going on?"

"Vidiana has been progressing very well through the night, but she has asked for you, specifically, as soon as you are available."

"Curious," Van remarked. "Vosh, is everyone else…"

"Still alive, yes. Only one deteriorated mildly during the night, and that was because of an allergy to the medication he was receiving. The issue has been remedied, and he is being very closely watched."

"Is there something I can do? Just … sit with them or something?" Ash asked, and Vosh smiled at this.

"Certainly. I believe the first male we brought in would benefit greatly from your gentle presence," she offered as calmly as ever. Ash sensed there was another word she wanted to add to that sentence, but she withheld it. Still, there was no mistaking the shine of excitement and joy in the green eyes; it was something he had never seen before, and a half smile cocked up his own muzzle.

"Okay, sure. Just … give me a moment with Van, okay?"

"By all means," Vosh replied and bowed slightly to him.

After she had stepped away, he asked, "Why have I never seen her act that way before? It's like she…"

"She does," Van told him. "Secretly, Vosh is my adopted daughter, although much different than you or I, in truth. That makes you…"

"Her … secret step father?" he asked.

"No. *Father*," Vanalla insisted to him. "She is starting to fill the voids in her life, the one for a male role model parent, for example."

"She's always seemed – I don't know, a little … distrustful in the past? Cautious?"

"Vosh wasn't sure how you would react when I started revealing who I was and the truths that brought us together in this time. I think that she's made up her considerably intelligent mind that you'll do well. She loves you, Ash. That's something you have to understand. What's more, not that a need should arise, but if it does, she can defend you. She can defend all of us."

"Much different than you or me?" he asked, looking down the hall at the Vulpi standing some distance away, supposedly out of ear shot of their whispers. Vosh then looked right at him and nodded, slowly. "Wow, she has good hearing! You do, you know?" he said, whispering to her. The Vulpi canted her head in acknowledgment.

"Like I said, much different, but loves you and would never harm you. Her whole being is with us, unreservedly, and our mutual trust is absolute. In time, she will reveal to you her own truths, but for now, go with her. If she says someone would benefit from your words and presence, Vosh is not likely to be wrong."

He leaned over and kissed her on the side of the muzzle. "I am surrounded by wonderful mysteries," he happily confessed. "I love you, Van."

"You, too." She returned his kiss, and then they were parted, Ash nearly jogging down the hall, anxious to speak with his newly found daughter.

"I'm so, so happy for you, Van," Sahnassa inside of her wept softly. "I wish you could feel how profound the changes are in you that I feel. Tana senses every bit of it, and what's more, I think even myself on Thuriana can even sense this. She'll want to speak with you soon, I know it."

"So many to pay attention to," Van chuckled aloud, softly. "You … have seen me through to this sol, dear kits, and however Tana can do it, please, please send my love to Me Sha."

"I already have it, Vanarra," a soft voice came from the shadows near her.

"Theo!" she whispered in surprise. "I had no idea you were here!"

Stepping out, the familiar Nephti said to her, in humored admonishment, "Oh, as if *here* is such a firm and certain state. You are beginning to sense that *here* doesn't just have to be one place, are you not?" he asked, reaching out for and embracing her.

"I know – totally strange trying to dip into the time stream. Vosh told me I wasn't seeing everything."

"Very difficult task, but imagine that what you are seeing is a long-distance view, distorted by the heat or fog. Your view isn't clear, and you know that. You need to know it here, too, but that doesn't mean that in every way, this view is useless. You, my daughter, are a prodigy. Be careful," he offered, parting from her. "However, don't be so careful that you don't actually try."

"Okay, and ... thank you, Dad. Me Sha," she offered, leaning her head on his chest as he held her again. "I so wish that you could stay with us and help us."

"Why?" he asked. "You are doing very well for yourself! Dynaea is certainly keeping up her end. I see nothing that begs correction or adjustment."

"Especially when I look through Sahni's memories, when you came back to us, everything that was going wrong just got better."

"Ah!" he noted, pulling away from her and slightly bending the knees of his Nephti form to look at her, eye-to-eye. "But you are *growing up*, you see! This is no different than when a child is hurt or scared, and in comes the parent to make them feel better. You know what it is like not to have that, and now you have had that, after a fashion, from me. All of those here around you, Vanarra – she who walks in light tinged with fire – are your charges, now, and you are bringing that sort of comfort and peace and direction and help *to them*! You do not need for me to do what you are, so ably, capable to do for yourself. It doesn't mean I won't be there if you need me. It doesn't mean that I won't ask you to work with me in the future. It does mean that I will let you be you, even as you become more than you could possibly imagine. I will train you, yes, but then ... I will trust you."

Her eyes held him in utmost appreciation and thankfulness. "Like you ... are trusting me now. You didn't relieve me of my command as Teldear, did you?"

"I sent you to the next most important place – not only for yourself, but for Ash, Vosh, and all of these others," he countered. "What a joy to see this in you, this ... awakening! Now, regretfully, I must be far less *here* than I am right now. I am proud of you, and you are doing amazing."

"Thank you."

After a gentle kiss on the side of her muzzle, he stepped back into the shadows and disappeared. Her heart immeasurably lifted and encouraged, she turned towards Vidiana's room.

Vanalla stood looking carefully at Vidiana as she waited for a reply to her assertion – ugly though it was. "You hate us. You have to. You have no choice."

"Who told you that?"

"It's simple logic," the nearly bedridden mixed blood contested against the purebred Faelnar she saw in front of her.

"Simple logic is often incomplete logic," Vanalla said as she sat down on a stool beside the bed. "That's why it's so simple. Like a child's drawing, it has the form of reality but is incomplete and not to the proper size and dimension. The world is *complex*, and so in many cases, its logic must also be." The listener seemed slightly dumbfounded by that specific response.

"How…" she tried to respond, but Van put up a paw finger.

"However, take as evidence several more complex truths to feed your logic. I am living here for the express purpose of helping you build a new life, and I've left friends and family, actually, to do so. I've left a job I loved and honors I appreciated. I have taken on this responsibility not knowing if there is the slightest chance I can be successful. The same can be said for everyone here, Vidiana. The same can be said for all of us who greeted you and now take care of you."

"There is no reason for you to. You owe us nothing, and we did nothing to earn any care from those of pure blood. If anything, shouldn't you be glad to be rid of us?"

"Many are, I know that. Especially those who have been trying to help their children through recovery. It is very difficult. However, I have my own reasons for being here – my own reasons why I think letting you have a new start is important."

"Why?"

Van sighed and folded her arms. "I know you see me as only purebred, but my heart has always gone out to those mixed bloods, especially back in the sols before equal treatment was even attempted. I've read it, thought about it, and I might as well have lived it. Understand that my heart breaks when someone is just ... written off as useless because of something they couldn't control. I could not control being what I am, can you say any differently?"

"No, I ... I am this which you see," Vidiana agreed. "Were it possible, in these times, that I could become a Faelnar like you, I would be free. I would just walk away and start a new life where no one would hate me, no one would despise me, no one would-"

"No ... one ... does. Not here," Van softly interrupted. "That is why there *is* an Attoria. It is the ultimate sign of forgiveness and restitution. More than fifteen hundred seasons ago, purebred forced mixed bloods to kill other purebreds to keep mixed blood *Anati* under their paw. That happened on this ground. Now, those who are here have but one goal – to take mixed bloods who have become their own kind of purebred, give them a home, help them flourish and grow. Even though there are many purebreds in the world who do hate you, many of them still donated to create this new opportunity for you. The more of you who come, the more chance there is of building a lasting community."

"What can there be for us other than slavery? Servitude?" Vidiana posed. "Our lot can't be better than those puremixes we kept, could it?"

"Here, you have every opportunity to build a life. Here, in Attoria, there is freedom, compassion, knowledge, and a real chance at self-reliance. We've built a plan that you can follow exactly or that you can modify. It starts with small farming, woodworking, metal working, and learning the skills to supply your own needs. It gives you a way to begin producing items others will want to buy – produce, products, and other things. We have ways and means to get the items created by your paws out for sale, and the funds come back here. They come back to be used by the community, to spread the hope to others who could join you."

"Would they ever take the risk of allowing our numbers to grow? For us to grow strong?"

"Would you and those like you ever make the same mistakes as before?" Van softly challenged. "If the desire by those who come here is to retake the mantle of the Vanarrans than this place will become like the ones you left, and all of the help you see will leave, and you … will starve. Your kind, despite the best efforts of those who want otherwise, will disappear from Thuria, leaving it poorer than it might have been."

"Remove us from the surface of the world, and what would truly be lost?" Vidiana challenged. "A pawful of outcasts in a single village against all of Thuria has nothing to offer."

Van smiled knowingly, her expression incredibly compassionate. "Hard failures and weakness can create their own special types of strengths and successes – unique and vastly different than anyone else now living. Yes, this will be difficult for you. Yes, you will not live at the standards you enjoyed even less than a season ago – but you were living a lie. If there is anyone who should be able to dispel their own self-delusion, it will be your kind. You have all nearly perished for it, why not live and hold that lesson precious? Why not prove that, despite the worst and smallest of starts, your kind – a new kind: the Aelkinda, have learned the meaning of honest truth, and self-truth more than anything else?"

There was something about the way the Faelnar had spoken that resonated, deeply, with Vidiana. This horrible failure was their uniqueness. This second chance was their uniqueness, and the vision dream with Vanarra now slipping back into her thoughts. "So, our second chance would define us, allow us to define ourselves anew?"

"Unlike anyone else in the history of Thuria," Van stated, looking towards the wall. "It is a terribly awesome responsibility and a sacred trust given from those not yet born who would follow behind you. It is the effort of planting grains and harvesting them now that will, in turn, become new seed sown into the future – some Aelkinda many seasons from now achieving greatness in a way that neither of us, sitting here, can even begin to imagine. Will it be a world record in athletic sports? Will it be an invention or medicine that helps or even saves millions? Will it be the unfailingly steady paw that guides others through the toughest of times? I don't know. It truly could be."

"Farming, then?"

"Amongst other things," Vanalla answered, smiling softly. "An ongoing food supply is truly the most basic of necessities, but that will be accomplished, and then there will be other opportunities. Shelter, for the present, is taken care of, although it will have to be maintained. You have the potential to become a beautiful and vibrant community that is not only self-sufficient, it can create art to express itself. Even those things have value outside of Attoria. Paintings, figurines, statues-"

"No more statues," Vidiana swore. "Especially not to our *Great Mother* who forsook us in our time of need."

Vanalla was silent for a moment considering her. "Certainly a good idea, I'll grant you, to not produce those, but might I ask that you not consider the long departed Vanarra de Gonari an enemy to you. I think there is the very strong possibility that all of those who called themselves Vanarrans misunderstood her – fundamentally misunderstood her."

"How would you know?"

"Have you read her autobiography? *In my own words* is a very-"

"It is heresy! It is a fabrication of the houses to…"

"It was in her own words, written under her very paw," Van countered. "Did you know the original, paw-written version is on file at the de Gonari archives? It's been verified against other paw-writing of hers that has a perfect chain of custody?" Vidiana's head cant in mild surprise made Van nod. "Any chance the Vanarrans fostered what just might have been a little willful blindness on who Vanarra de Gonari truly was? What she believed?"

"Before, I would have nearly ripped you apart because of such heresy. Now, honestly … I don't know. What's … your name? I don't think I ever asked or you ever told me."

"Vanalla Ashallo. For convenience, I'm called Van, and you?"

"Select- no, I guess that's not true anymore. Vidiana, I guess, is my name."

"If you don't like it, you can change it. You can change a lot about yourself here, even how you feel about Vanarra de Gonari. Looks like your bag needs changing. Let me go get another one."

As she got to the door, Vidiana asked, "If … if you had that book…"

"I think I can get my copy from my cabin and loan it to you. I want it back, okay? You can't tear it to shreds if you disagree with it."

"No absolute promises," Vidiana replied to the joking taunt, trying hard not to smile. Vanalla seemed to be very honest with her and very sympathetic. Regardless of how much she used to disagree with the purebred's point of view, she was a purebred who was being kind to her, and her long training in detecting subterfuge or falsehood told Vidiana that the Faelnar was telling her what she truly believed. Intelligence and hope mixed together with a kind and caring heart were also nearly irresistible to someone who had spent moons suffering hunger, isolation, and hopelessness. "I will do everything I can to prevent harm to your book, however."

"Thanks. Do we slip in a facilities break right now, too?"

Vidiana nodded. "Yeah, I … I seem to need that again. Hunger is … it's really starting to bite at me."

"I'll ask them to rerun your blood work and see if you're ready for that. Nothing would make me happier than to get you eating again."

"Vanalla … thank you. Just … thank you," Vidiana replied, her blush fur at full. She would have said more, but the exchange had been exhausting to her, and she knew that once she had emptied and her bag was reconnected, sleep would soon come.

"Hey, kit," Vanarra's voice called to Vidiana, and a gentle paw touched her arm. "You okay?"

She twitched awake and tried to sort where she was. It was the warehouse Vanarra had shown her. Sitting up and looking around, she realized what she had done, fallen asleep during lunchtime. "Oh, my goodness! I'm so sorry!"

"No worries, kit. I checked; your work is all done. What's up with you, though? Tresk told me that you almost fell asleep the moment you finished eating, and that was after working like your tail was on fire or something." Van slipped into the chair next to hers. "Is there a reason why you ... need to sleep here?"

Worries and fears slipped back into her mind, worries about being hunted by purebreds and harassed in the middle of the night, where they lived being pummeled with rocks and firebombs. Those like her had needed to sleep in shifts, and those who tried to sleep during those attacks couldn't. "Not ... safe to sleep..."

"Where you are, now? When you go?" Vidiana felt the hopelessness nearly shake her head for her. Vanarra rubbed the bottom of her muzzle thoughtfully. "That's ... that's a tough one."

At that moment, a purebred Nephti female, a young one, walked into the room. "Oh, sorry, Van! I didn't mean to interrupt."

"No, no, Sahni. Maybe, just maybe, you might be able to help." Looking at Vidiana, concerned now as well, the Nephti pulled out a chair to sit right beside her boss. "It's not safe where Vidiana is sleeping at night, or at least it hasn't been. I need some time to get her worked into something long term."

"Hey, I ... I might be able to help with that! My little complex has a guest lair that we can rent for a pretty decent fee. I've got a fair amount – maybe half a moon's worth – that I could put her up!" Vidiana almost instantly shrank back, looking afraid. "It would be alright, I promise! I could take you from there to here and then we could go back together."

"Sahni's complex isn't a matriarchal estate, but it's a good, safe place. What are you afraid of, kit?" Van asked. Shyly and humiliated, Vidiana pointed at the Nephti. "What?! You can't be serious!"

Sahni put her paw on Van's shoulder. "Think about it, right? Maybe someone like me has been doing horrible things, making her feel afraid, threatening her."

"I know, kit," Van chastised, but it wasn't solely directed at the Nephti, a piece of it was for Vidiana. "That said, I will vouch for you, and that should be more than enough! You took care of me, Sahni. You ... you took care of me."

Vidiana was struck by the truth of that to the very hollows of her soul. "It's right," she breathed, her head falling in time with ears and tail. "You did. I ... I should have remembered that."

"Hey, hey," Sahni offered, gingerly picking up Vidiana's paw. "She's done the same for me. It's what binds us together, despite the other differences we have."

Vidiana's vision clouded over for a moment, and another voice slipped her out of sleep with a start. "Hey, I'm sorry," the female voice said soothingly, "I just wanted to check on you. It was my turn."

"Sorry, Van-" Vidiana began, but then her eyes focused on someone who was like Vanarra de Gonari, but not quite. Her angle of view was also wrong, and Vidiana realized that she was laying down looking up at this stranger. "You ... are not Vanarra."

"Nope, I'm not. I look a little like her, though," the Vulpi-Faelnar admitted as she checked the fluids bag. "I was actually called Fireclaw Destiny, at one time, but I've given that up. My new name – well, it's my old one, really. I'm Tashara. I actually came to visit you because your lab work came back, and I have some good news."

"Lab work? I ... I don't remember-"

"I think they took it from you while you were asleep, actually," the mixed blood commented. "The news is that we have a little solid food for you to try. Not something really rich or sweet and not a lot of it, either, I'm afraid. Just a bit. You'll probably drop right back off to sleep after a few bites, but the good news is that you won't actually die from being fed. There's nothing to fear. They're being very conservative and careful. You could have potentially eaten several intervals ago, but they wanted a second look just to make sure. You seemed to be pretty deeply asleep, maybe dreaming?"

"Did ... did I say anything?" Vidiana asked, curious, but she had to swallow because the thought of food was making her mouth nearly flood, and she was trembling.

"Not that I could tell, no. Now, I've been told I have to take you to the facilities, first, then I have to change your bag to a new one, and then we can try to eat, okay?"

"I ... I really want food, something ... badly," Vidiana nearly begged.

"Yeah, and that's why they sent me to do this. I completely stink at self-discipline and control, and I've been burned enough times that I know that when Vanalla tells me something, I'll lose my tail if I don't do it."

The statement struck Vidiana with a twinge of humor she hadn't felt in a very long time, and she chuckled to see the face so much like that of her once Great Mother looking so embarrassed. "I ... I will endeavor to learn your lesson, then. I will do as you say we must."

"Thank you. I screw up and do the wrong thing – I just hate that!"

In a pawful of passes, Vidiana was sitting up and eating as a babe from the proffered spoon from Tashara – or Tasha as she had explained Van had shortened it to. It was a grainy soft mass with just traces of a meat like taste that under most circumstances would have probably been utterly disgusting to her, but Vidiana's starved body gave her almost unfathomable ecstasy at the consumption of actual food. After only a few spoonfuls, however, Vidiana realized the need for the care that had been taken bringing her back up to some level of normal body chemistry.

"I ... I want to keep going, but I feel shaky – little ... dizzy. Need to stop."

"You did awesome," Tasha told her. "You only had one more spoonful, and I was supposed to stop you if you wanted any more."

"Don't think ... that would be such a good idea," Vidiana admitted. "I ... I don't think my body is keeping up with it, so well."

"Well, you may experience some discomfort, some pain, rather, when your digestion actually tries to start up again. I'm sorry about that. They tell me that it will go away, but the doctor will be coming in to help you with some pain meds for that." Eyes closed, the former Vanarran nodded, her face already scrunched up a little, wincing at dull pain coming from her gut. "I ... admire you. I want you to know that."

"Ad – admire what? Nothing about what we've done or our pitiable state..."

"Yes, but you're not giving up. You're facing it. It's been better than I've done at times in my life. Some of your companions down the hall are not doing as well as you. It seems as if they've not only lost hope but refused to even think there could be."

Despite the slowly raising background of pain distracting her, the thought that she was doing better than some of those who could actually walk in was disturbing. "When ... after I'm awake again and not ... hurting like this, can you please ask Vassia to see me?"

"I'll do my best," the Faelnar-Vulpi stated as she put her paw on the paw of the thinly furred female, squeezing it gently before stepping off into the hallway. Looking up, she saw Ash waiting for her, looking at her carefully in the otherwise empty space. "You, dear Ash, are wondering something. I wonder what is the thing you are wondering about? Wonder if you'll tell me?"

"*Wonder* if you'll get tired of that word," he chuckled. "Sorry, it's probably nothing. I just ... learned some things about Vanar-Vanalla, rather-"

"You had it right the first time, big cub," Tasha whispered softly, smiling. "She is exactly that. Damned, I wonder what all of these in this place would think if they knew that they were being tended by the Great Mother, herself. I'm glad you know, Ash. Many of us have been pulling for you."

"So, do ... do you know how I got here-"

Tasha put a paw finger in front of his lips to stop him from speaking. "I probably don't know much more than you do, and second, she will tell you when you're ready. Now, as for me, I would be a lost, ruined has-been named Fireclaw Destiny if it wasn't for her, and later, I will tell you how she told me who she was. That, at least, will give you a good laugh."

"But you came to trust in her?" he asked.

"With my life," Tasha told him. "With ... with my soul, Ash. She took my meaningless existence and gave me the chance to do something meaningful, and here we are, together."

"Thank you," he told her, smiling. "I've missed so much of her life."

"She missed you ... for all of it. I mean that." Tasha's words as she patted his shoulder and walked away truly struck him. Ash knew that for whatever time there was between the old Shanandrae Common's squalid waiting room and when he was found and taken to the new Shanandrae Commons, over seventeen hundred seasons had come and gone. He wasn't aware of the passage of that time, and there were no more memories beyond his blacking out, laying on the floor gasping out his words to the young Vanarra. Strolling towards the entrance of the boarding lair, he considered how different life had been for her. She had lived every one of those seasons. "She missed you … for all of it." The words echoed in his mind, and looking around, he saw a copy of *In Her Words…* laying with a note that it should be passed to Vidiana when she was well enough to read it.

Curious, he went over and picked it up and started thumbing through it. Much of it he remembered, for they had shared most of it, read from Van's own muzzle. However, as he flipped to a certain chapter heading, he realized it was unfamiliar to him. "The ashes of my first love…" was the title, and as he started scanning the first few sentences, he realized very quickly that Van had skipped over this section, entirely. Taking the book and folding it under his clothes, he slipped up to an unused room he knew of, one intended as something halfway between storage and an access passage to some of the boarding lair's support systems. Finding a comfortable nook in the little industrial space, he started to read.

"You've come to the very chapter that has caused me to put off writing any sort of autobiography until it's nearly too late. This is because, honestly, other than losing my mother, the loss of my dear Ashalam was utterly devastating in my life. If you doubt it, there were six sols between the sentence I just wrote and this one. Nothing is as raw to me or unsettles me like that. Very little is as debilitating to me as pulling up the memory of him dying in my arms – the memory of how I was never permitted to see him afterwards. My Ash was murdered, and that is all there is to it. He was murdered by an uncaring, bigoted, and ruthless group of hospital administrators that we were just so unfortunate as to attempt to rely upon. Nothing grieves me more than knowing that there were doctors who *would have helped* him. Bless them, and curse me for not knowing. Curse me for telling a kind and loving transport driver, now a dear friend, to take me to that awful and hateful place known as Shanandrae Commons."

"Don't think that I haven't enjoyed and been thoroughly grateful for a wonderful life with the one who was once known to me as Fanassaragatti de Caterra who became Buck Harlock and then Buck de Gonari. Buck healed as much in me from losing Ash as was possible for any male to heal, but it was just impossible to ask my dear Faelnar mate to bind up all of the enormous wounds of my heart. There is only one who can, and he is lost to me forever. Ash was the first real, honest, dedicated love based on shared needs, dependence on one another, and genuine attraction that I had ever experienced. He is and forever will be my first true love. I had, secretly, before I met Buck, sought out lovers who reminded me of him. I made love to them in his name, ignoring who they were and offering all of my love and passion on the altar of my heart in the name of my beloved Ashalam."

"It was only when I came to love Buck that one key fact burst into clarity for me. I wasn't honoring Ash; I was hurting others. I may have had a somewhat less than positive effect on a few joinings – early on. I regret that, horribly, now. I may have truly hurt those who would have loved me because sometimes what I was doing wasn't all that hard to figure out. It took me seasons and the love of a wonderful Faelnar and a dear friend to steer away from this course. I finally did learn, and I finally took all of that misplaced honor and, instead, realized that I had only been truly honoring my dear Ash by one act and by one act alone – taking care of the orphans in Shanandrae. I am – to this sol – deeply happy when one of those we helped comes back to me. Very few have gone astray, and some now even work for me as members of this house. I love them and honor them for their kindness."

"You see, they'll say something – one little thing, and it will make me think of him. For a split instant, Ash lives. Maybe not in truth, but in my heart he does, and because I helped an orphan become not so much an orphan, Ash lives a little in everyone we helped. Then, my dear Sahni reminded me that the orphans I had helped came in all shapes and sizes, herself included. It might have been a bed I purchased or a medical procedure I paid for when someone needed it. At the time, it didn't seem like the hugest deal in the world, but collectively, many other cubs and kits benefited because there was something Ash's passing did to me; it made me nearly incapable of just leaving someone aching and hurting. It doesn't mean I was forced to do it when they didn't want help, were too proud, or were too dedicated to self-destruction. Those were few. Many needed help and were just grateful for it."

"I don't tell you this to make you think of me as any great Thurian. I tell you this because losing Ashalam hurt like nothing else in my life. If my pain can help others, can yours? It's completely a choice, and I would be a liar of the worst kind if I told you I always made the right one. I have seen ones who took the hurt and pain they experienced and turned right around and inflicted that same pain on others, almost as if to say you are no better than I am, and I will pass along my pain to you which will make my pain less. No, I won't do that. It doesn't work. At one time in my life, I tried. I never regretted anything more, and my dearest and closest friend was borne out of saying goodbye forever to that impulse."

"I won't lie to you. All of these pretty words help, but they only help – they don't fix. I lost Ash. I was in some part responsible for what happened to him. If it is within your power, fiercely protect and care for those you love. Listen to every impulse that says they need you and ignore what would distract you. I was distracted by our nightly chores and ignored the testimony of my own eyes, and I was blinded by my own self-imposed ignorance. Save him or her, please. Save the ones you love. Protect them; please take it from me that they are worth everything in the world. No acts of generosity or kindness in their name, much less acts of selfishness, will ever bring them back."

Ash closed the book and looked at the outside light streaming in through a small window. "Now, I am back. Oh, by the moons, my poor kit! No! You … you weren't responsible for it," he groaned as tears pricked at the corner of his eyes. "I was the idiot! I said something stupid that got me nailed by that Vulpi! Van, you never saw it, never heard it, but I did!" He held his head in his paws and cried hard.

Just then, a soft and supportive paw landed gently on his shoulder. By its strength, he knew it to be a male, and what little his nose could tell him was that the scent was Nephti. Looking up, shaking, he stared into an older Nephti's face, one he recognized after a moment. "Theo?"

"Yes, my dear cub, it's me. I knew this moment was coming for you, and you need someone other than Vanarra to help you through it."

"I … I caused all of her pain!" he wept.

"You did not!" Theo offered, coming to sit right beside him, putting a paw on his back. "The Vulpi who hit you could have decided not to hurt you for something as common as a tease about the Vulpi mating drive. The hospital administrators could have let you into the emergency room, and the doctors could have actually made half an effort at saving you as opposed to just sort of using you as a free practice for when they had a real patient. Your world could have been more accepting of mixed bloods and not required you to work in horrible conditions just to feed yourselves. Your choices were important – choices always are, but you can't steal away the full responsibility for something when you don't actually own all of the choice in the matter."

Ash looked at him, confused. "It's true," Theo asserted. "I know how we are sometimes – males. There are the useless instances of our gender who won't accept responsibility for anything as theirs, but then there is the other kind, one for which you seem to be a lifetime member. We destroy the importance of the choices others had in our lives for two reasons. First, we think we should have been clever enough to find the one tiny path through all of the obstacles others put before us – despite the fact they should never have done so in the first place. If you've ever watched athletes on the track, running and jumping over obstacles, you will see them fall or miss, and they've practiced those very obstacles hundreds if not thousands of times. What about just living our lives? It's never the same obstacles on any sol. Do you understand?"

A bit more collected, now, Ash nodded and offered, "How can we prepare for what's new, when what's new always changes?"

"We can never completely prepare. We become the best we can, make ourselves as ready as we can to face the world, but we can't foresee everything. Not even I can do that. Now, the second reason is we take responsibility for everything is because that presumes we had the control in the first place – total control. It's the same argument, just turned inside out and backwards. You don't have that kind of control, and I don't. So, you could have altered what you said, yes. I think you've already learned how to control that. The great truth out of getting injured is you learned not to make silly comments about the Vulpi mating drive. Meanwhile, in the seasons intervening, Thuria learned not to despise, torture, hunt, or kill mixed bloods. They learned the lesson so well that now, in this age, Thuria is giving the Aelkinda, the former Vanarrans, another chance – a second chance here with you. Which, Ash, is the greater learning?"

"How do you know that?" Ash asked, putting his paw into Theo's. "How ... how can you know all of these things?"

"I'm not from around here, friend," Theo answered, looking up and smiling. "I'm not even Thurian, actually; I hail from another place entirely. Now, there's a thought you probably didn't think you'd have to deal with when you were up on that hill with the digger. Besides, you were in such distress over things you had so very little control over. You needed some comfort and a little perspective."

"But why me, then?"

"Because I brought you here, Ashalam," the Nephti beside him told him firmly and without any chance of argument, his stare fixed into the mixed blood's inmost being, it seemed. When he saw that the truth in those words had finally sunk into Ash's soul, he looked at the far wall and continued. "I met your dear Vanarra seasons and seasons after your so-called passing and learned how much she had been hurt by the injustice of your loss. In time, I've watched her grow. I've watched her becoming more than even she can imagine. She is a prodigy, but she is held down and held back by wounds deep within her. I am healing those wounds, now, by bringing you back to her side, back into her life."

"But ... but why without any memories?!" Ash asked, confused and now, even angry.

"When I pulled you back, I looked at you. I looked into you for quite some time, Ashalam *Aganastar*. You see, I know the name you don't even know about yourself. What's more, I learned ... Vanarra isn't the only prodigy. She can tell you more of what this means, but part of it is that I could have pulled you out with all of your memories intact, and you would have been horribly lost in this new time. There's someone you'll be able to meet who can tell you what that's like, but unlike her, you were young – very young. You needed time to find yourself as an adult and grow. The self you left behind more than seventeen hundred seasons ago wasn't going to be all that helpful – hatred and fear of purebreds was something you left behind."

"Vanarra was in that blindness, too!" Ash countered.

"No, no she wasn't. She was always there. Even when I had not yet caused her to return to this world, you were looking for her as much as you were looking for your memories – your career, your expertise, the way you act and help others all swirled together in and around her. Oh, how you are going to realize that more and more in the sols to come! Also, think about the way you were protecting something invisible to you, something that kept you out of relationships ... until now. Until she unlocked everything in you."

"You did that to me, too?"

"I put the walls in place, but you burrowed through them together. I did not pick your path, but being with her helped. I did everything in my power, Ash, to bring you here to this moment where you are ready for her and where she is ready for you. That was actually a lot of work! She's grown, Ash. She's amazing. You – not to be too blunt about it – are just sort of starting out. You've done very well and on your own, too. Now, you'll need to do well with us helping you."

"I don't think I understand," Ash admitted.

"Understand this. Are you happy to be alive and be with her?"

"Yes. Yes, I am. Thank you for that."

"You are welcome. Everything else is a detail that you will come to know about in time, but know this, Ash..."

"What?" he asked, uncertain.

"Existence is far more beautiful and far more complex than you could have ever have guessed, and what you are building here, what you are helping to build, will change this planet's future in profoundly good and meaningful ways. Your life is far more now than it might have been before."

"From ... from what I remember, my life as an Anati outcast wasn't filled with much more meaning than simple survival."

"True. Now, I saw where you stopped. Read the rest of that chapter downstairs where they can see you, and then, perhaps, join her for lunch."

"Will you be coming?" Ashalam asked, starting to feel a connection and closeness to this male that he had never really experienced with anyone, before.

"I'd better leave it to her to tell things to you. You can tell her you read the chapter, but I would prefer if you didn't tell her I slipped in to help you. Let's keep that between us; just consider the insight, okay?"

"Is she truly your daughter? I mean, originally?"

"I adopted her, and not her, alone, Ash. Now, go on."

Theo stood and offered Ash his paw, and Ash took it, feeling an amazing gentle strength helping him to stand. "Thank you." Theo nodded, and he watched as Ash took the first few steps away. Then, Ash looked behind him. The Nephti was gone.

Chapter 16: Agonized Veracity

Van left the dining hall in search of Ash. She'd been busy around the boarding lair helping with their patients, many of whom were improving greatly after a kind of understanding had been reached between Vassia and Vidiana. It was something she knew she had contributed to allowing Vidiana to see, in dreams, what life was like with the real Vanarra. She hadn't fully unchained the former Vanarran's mind while in the dreams, only allowing her to "remember" she was a cast out mixed blood with no place to go and nothing to eat. However, the memories and impressions in the dreams were following Vidiana out into her waking world, and the knowledge that "They might have simply gotten everything wrong about their Great Mother, turned her into something she truly wasn't" was a very profound admission for the former Select who had called Vassia a traitor.

Now, Van set about trying to begin the process of revealing the full truth of who she was and all that meant to her beloved Ashalam. Her view frustrated, she reached inward and asked – by impulse and emotion – for Tana to show her to him. She found him sitting off in a rather delightful spot, some distance away from the boarding lair near the modest sized river that flowed at the outskirts of their current settlement. As she came upon him, she could see he was reading, but she couldn't see what. Suddenly, he turned, hearing her approach, and the title caught her eye. Van's heart caught in her throat for a moment, but he smiled. "In her words?" she asked.

"Yeah," he admitted. "You … kind of skipped a chapter. I read it. Did you bring something?"

She smiled, feeling a little nervous, and slipped the pack off of her back. "I got us a few hot things from the hall. I'm sorry I didn't find you earlier."

"You were busy, and it gave me time."

She slipped down beside him, and seeing the page he was on, she closed her eyes. "Having written an autobiography was ... a mistake."

"I don't think so," he disagreed. "Unless it's not true?"

"No, no, it's true – everything's true. My embarrassment and ... sadness that you learn about what you meant to me from a book is-"

"You're telling me, Van. It's okay. I was actually pretty upset by what I was reading, and it took me a long time to think through it. I ... read this and immediately blamed myself."

"No, Ash, please," Van softly pleaded, shaking her head. "You – of anyone – weren't to blame. I-"

"Blamed yourself," he countered. "Just like I did. Dammit, Van, was it really either of us? Wasn't the world around us at least a little responsible."

"Maybe, but the world didn't know you and love you – I did. My ignorance cost you everything."

"And my poor judgment cost you my being there. The Vulpi who got me in the gut – she did it because I made a comment about her sex drive. It was a dumb thing to do, and I've sat here thinking about it, I know why I did it. I hated her because she was a purebred. She could work her way up and out of being disavowed; she had hope. We didn't. I was a dumb, immature male who offended her, and she took it out on me."

Van looked at the ground for a while before saying anything else. "What she did was wrong. I won't regret the stripes I gave her."

"What I did was wrong. Then, out of pride, I toughed through the pain until it was really too late. I ... as much as anyone, deserve blame, but not all of it. I'm sorry, but the hospital staff – we didn't control that. The doctors? No! The society that put us where we were living, where we had to? It was like that when we were born. Millions of decisions over thousands of seasons crowded in around us, and a really horrible thing happened. I'm now here," he offered, putting his paw in hers, "and I'm with you, and you're with me."

"That makes me really, really feel good, Ash," Van told him, leaning into him.

"I'm glad, but … can you please tell me how I got here? Who did it?"

Van relaxed and leaned up against the tree, angling her head to the sky, her eyes closed. "You met him, already. My dad, my adopted one."

"Theo?" he asked, and she nodded. "I thought he was just a Nephti?"

"More, cub. He's more," she told him, and her eyes opened. "Up there, high above us, is the little envelope of atmosphere that keeps everything here living and safe. Beyond that, the sun, the moons, the planets, the stars, the galaxies – more than we can possibly imagine. Beyond that, there is even more. Our universe is not the only one. There are others. From one of those others, that is where my adopted daddy is from. Theo just looks like a Thurian, and he looks that way and then another and then another, as many different forms as you can possibly imagine and many you can't. That's what he can be. His kind live a very long time, and he's the one who leads not only his kind but many, many others."

"You … have a dad from outer space?" he asked, carefully.

"Not so hard to believe. I'm here, and you're here," she told him, looking at him, her gaze holding him fixed. "You … are a poor liar, Ashalam. He talked to you already, didn't he?"

Ash shook his head in resignation of his failure to keep this from her. "He asked me not to say. I … I was pretty messed up when I read that chapter you wrote about me. I had a lot of guilt about it. He … actually came and sat beside me. He told me he did it, brought me here. He told me why."

"How much did he tell you?" she asked, her eyes studying him.

"He told me you were becoming something – that you were some kind of prodigy, but a prodigy at what, he didn't go into." Looking at the wariness in her expression, he hung his head and apologized. "I'm sorry I hid that from you."

"I should have expected it. There was no way he was going to let me tell you when he was the one who made the decision. Theo does many things, but one of the things he does really well is own up. I've admired him for that, and I still do – maybe even more now," she mused, relaxing her appraisal of him. "Oh, Ash, there's so much ground to cover. If I just come out and tell you, it's going to sound crazy – it may even make you doubt my sanity or worse … doubt me."

"I love you, Vanarra," he whispered. "Truly. Please."

"You love … a little more than half of me, actually, but something very loud inside of me," Van nearly complained, "is telling me that's not a fair statement. Do you remember the stories of Sahnassa de Orturu, Vanarra's – my friend?" He nodded. "She was my friend, and what's more … she is still."

"She's alive now, too?" Van nodded. "Same kind of thing as me or more like you?"

"More like me. You skipped a big chunk of time when Theo pulled you forward, and it's time that Sahni and I have lived through. Sahni was there for me in a way that no purebred ever was, cub. You remember how we were treated, how we were made to feel less than fully Thurian because our mommas and daddies weren't of the same stripe? Sahni, more than any other purebred I had ever met, ignored all of that. She was my employee, and then she was my friend, and then, she was a friend like none I'd ever known. We were close. We are … close."

She turned and look back at the river as she continued. "Our whole lives – from working together as comparative kits until we were both Grand Matriarchs nearing the end of our reign. She came to me one sol and told me she was terminally ill. It would be a long process, so I thought, but then she up and disappeared – some thought she killed herself."

"Yeah, I remember that from some other book I saw once. She was supposed to have gone out in a boat and – hey, wasn't that what you did in the end?"

"Hard to meet up with a spaceship in the middle of Shanandrae Park. Theo … picked us up, restored us and lengthened our lives. However, when I started learning of all of the little ways he and my friend had started manipulating me and my life, I got … angry. I got really pissed off, truth be told. I wanted to leave them all and just – I don't know. I stormed after Theo demanding an explanation, an apology – something stupid like that."

"What happened?" he asked, gently coaxing her, holding her paw.

Van closed her eyes and softly told him. "He … he showed me … who he really is. Oh, Ash, he's ancient! He's powerful beyond words – he's light and time and this amazing presence. When it's all wrapped up in that Nephti covering he wears, he hides it. One true look at who he was changed me forever. That was the first change. Then, he reunited me with Sahnassa, and we spoke. I couldn't help myself, Ash – I still felt betrayed by the fact she did things and didn't tell me at the time. Theo, although he didn't do it directly, introduced Sahni and me to something … unique. Something that would allow us to actually live each other's lives, each other's histories as if I was Sahni and she was me."

"Really?" Ash asked, and Van looked at him, curious. He was reeling. "I … I just don't know, Van! That's fantastic – I mean, you'd know everything about someone; there wouldn't be any secrets."

"There aren't," she told him, and that got his attention again. "There are no secrets between Sahni and me. In fact, there was such a depth to the sharing that, just after it happened, I thought I was her, and she thought she was me. We lived each other's lives and so … yeah, we were *that* confused. I guess, in a way, Ash, Sahni and I are still confused, but the confusion is part of who we are becoming."

"I don't understand. You don't know who you are, now?"

"I know who I am, and I know who she is, but who we are has become confused in the sense that we are mixed together. I have lived her full life, and she mine. I have a lifetime and beyond of her memories and experiences. It's shaped who I am, cub, don't you understand that? I am this … balance between Sahnassa de Orturu and Vanarra Anasto. I'm quite a bit more Vanarra because that's who I was originally, but the things I think and know and love – all are deeply touched by her."

"Does … does she love me?"

"Yes!" Vanarra offered so happily and expansively that, for a split instant, Ash could actually see that other soul inside of hers. "I love you, Ashalam! I truly do!"

Vanarra shook herself a little and stared back at Ash's stunned expression. "Ash..."

"I saw her! Just ... just for a moment there! I saw her! Wow, and ... she wasn't kidding – I could feel something from you that wasn't you! She loves me?"

"Oh, my dear Ash," Vanarra said, more in her own voice and mannerisms. "How could she not? She has lived *my life*, and she knows what I feel when I look at you. She knows our story and has lived it right along with us. I lost you, cub. She lost you, too. When we have some time and when we can have some privacy, she'll be able to tell you in her own words why she loves you. For short periods of time, and I'll put off exactly how I do it, I can cause her to appear alongside me, and it's not just like she's a puppet. It's really her – authentically her."

"I don't doubt it," he said in amazed wonder, looking into her eyes. "It's like for this ... moment ... I saw her in you!"

"Yeah, occasionally, she gets excited and jumps me. Which in fairness, I probably do that to her wherever the physical Sahni is."

"So, is it like this battle all of the time? Fighting for control?" he asked, concerned.

"No, no, please Ash! You mustn't think it's like that. She and I became so close because we care about one another so very much. We found that we needed each other, and we can act together – most of the time. I guess this is what Theo means, in part, when he says we are a prodigy. That first sharing of lives led to others, and now we are very deep into one another's souls. We truly are mixing together, and that mixing will lead to something. It won't happen for a while, yet, and so I think we could have a nice, long life here on Thuria together, if that's what you still want?" Van asked, suddenly getting worried.

"It ... is a lot to take in, but in a sense, I'm ... I'm glad you found someone to help you. It makes up for me not being there, at least a little. So, what will it lead to?"

Van looked as if she wanted to race ahead and tell him, but then something seemed to stir in her, and she shut it down. "Ah, I have to be ... have to be careful about that. I might be just a bit too keyed up talking to you, and my control isn't great right now. I've learned that it's best to not lose control. Please, let me share what's coming for me for another time."

"Are you going to be okay? I mean – now and then?"

Van smiled and hugged him. "I am. I am. What about you? Here I'm talking all of this stuff which just has to sound like so much craziness!"

He leaned back and just shook his head. "My life when I woke up – that was ... crazy and scary. This, honestly, is the first time I've heard any explanation of who I am, why I was brought here. And yeah, what you are saying is crazy, but that doesn't mean that it isn't real. So, I was what you needed?"

"Yeah. You, and ... and another. My mom, Ash," she told him softly. "She's now back with me, also. Shenaria."

"Oh, wow! Wow! That's ... that's!!! I mean, wow, Van! Wow!" he nearly shouted, his face drawn up in an exuberant smile. "Oh, now I get it; I do! I remember all of those times you talked to me! I remember the *pain* you felt, and now you have her back! You do! I'm so happy for you!"

"Oh, cub, my cub ... my Ash ... my Ashalam. I love you so much," Van whispered, falling into him, nuzzling into his shoulder.

"Excuse me," Laxar's voice softly intruded upon their revelry, and Ash looked up at his fellow mixed blood wondering how much he had heard.

"Oh, it's alright," Van reassured him. "Laxar here figured me out all on his own, the scamp! He knows exactly who I am, and what's better, he keeps my secrets."

"I told Father I would come and speak to you. Father wishes for me to seek your ... blessing, I guess."

"For you and for Vassia, in a joining?" Van asked him, a bit of her feral smile showing through.

Laxar's slight blush raise fur didn't track with the confidence in his voice. "Yes, in our joining. He is, of course, concerned for our ages, and sadly, his ... patience is failing him slightly. He was going to walk over here. He's right over there."

"Ah," Van offered. "He needs a little reassurance that this is the right thing for you both. Okay, cub. Ash, if it's okay, would you mind if I went over and talked with him?"

"I … I think my brain is full – I better stop," he joked. "I love you, though, Van. Please know that I love all of you."

"Thanks," she offered, and again he could almost see the difference in her, the two voices joining as one in the body before him.

Once she was away, Laxar sat down beside Ash, his eyes still fixed on his mate. "She is … magnificent."

Ash then turned and looked at Laxar, the Thurian far more mixed than he, represented a middle ground between his bi-species lineage and the indistinguishable combinations of the Aelkinda. By the pose of his head looking at his retreating mate, Ash felt he witnessed a kind of bow or reverence in it. For a moment, he wondered if the young male actually desired his mate, as in a hunt, but he was here asking her assistance to enable him to join with another female. Confused, he tried to get a sense of what Laxar was feeling, and trying to take everything in gave him the impression of worship or honor.

"Lax, you've known about her … a lot longer than I. Can you tell me about it? How you met?"

"Sure," Laxar turned to him, his expression pleased, but there was a dark side to the possibility of sharing such painful memories that tempered that expression. "I've actually wanted, for a long time, to tell you. I love Vanarra, but not as a mate would. I hold no place in her heart equal to yours, nor would I try. However, we do share something very deep – she rescued me, saved my life, and then gave me a new one."

"You are not alone in that," Ash offered, putting a reassuring paw on Laxar's shoulder.

"Brothers, then, by the gifts she has given us, if you would have me as that, Ashalam," his fellow mixed blood offered, tendering his open paw.

Ash was struck by the love and earnestness he saw in the younger male's expression. Laxar had always been his friend, but the Lupar-Perratti could tell that the affection and kinship in the stare he was receiving was absolute. There was nothing he could do; such had to be returned. He placed his paw in the offered one and clasped it tightly – the two males using shared demonstrations of their strength in careful alignment to one another to convey respect, trust, and commitment. He felt a deeper bond with Laxar than he ever had before, partly in the honor of being called a brother – something Ash had never considered possible. He also realized that although Laxar had these experiences, he had kept them hidden until it was safe to reveal them, until the once Akashar had been found and returned into being as Ashalam. "I love you, brother," he offered.

"I love you, brother, and I am honored that you would accept one such as me."

"One such as you?" Ash pressed. "Laxar, you're amazing! The art you create and – cub, I just have to tell you – your smarts! You are always polite and kind and respectful, maybe even when you shouldn't be!" The compliment bent his new brother's head down in shame.

"It is ... my past, Ashalam; that is the cause of my shame."

"Can you share that with me?" came the soft question. When Laxar looked uncertain, Ash offered, "I promise you two things. I won't love or care about you any less because of what I hear. My past wasn't all that great either, and I will share that with you. Second, you have my silence. No one will know."

"Many do know, and I do not always know who," the young male said quietly, his head still looking at the grass beyond their hind paws. "As more and more of those who used to be Vanarrans come here, they will know. It will be known by all, eventually."

"It will not be me who tells it, and it will be me who stands back to back with you, guarding you," he insisted, renewing the clasp that had weakened under the weight of Laxar's guilt. "You are my brother, now. You are my family, now. We protect our own."

Laxar's eyes looked at him with nearly the same reverence they had held Vanarra in as she had left them. "Then, I will tell you, and your kindness is the greatest gift to me." Relaxing and putting his paws in his lap, the young male closed his eyes and began to recount everything he could remember about his life in the service of the Vanarrans.

Vanarra returned from her extended conversation with Javoth regarding the future state of his ward and son. It had been a difficult conversation, at times, because there was always the fear of abuse lingering in the Lupar minister's mind, and very few had more room to apprehend such fears than Javoth. He had taken in a much younger Laxar, one whose emotional wounds and tortured life were still very fresh. Javoth understood the enormous temptation that posed and had invested many long sols and moons building his ward and eventually his adopted son to the point where hopelessly compliant service wasn't the only thing he knew or understood. Javoth now saw the taking of Vassia, an older female and former Vanarran, as mate as deeply troubling and full of peril.

It had only taken a couple of intervals to remind Javoth that nearly all joined couples face that very same peril, and for as wide a range of reasons as there *were* couples. It wasn't difficult to argue for Vassia's humility. Her soul had been crushed and now reformed, and although sorely tested once again by these new Vanarrans, she still remained strong in her outward focus and empathy. Her deepest empathy and grief was for Laxar – someone she had actually seen in the Vanarran temple that was destroyed by the Sahnassites. The dismissive way she had treated him as a thing and not a Thurian left her in awe, now that she saw artist, sculptor, guide, and confidant in him. Given all of this, Van had posited that it was actually Laxar who needed to be careful, lest his pain and Vassia's guilt combine to place her in the role of an abused lair mate.

After a brief prayer, they had parted with Vassia and Laxar's union all but complete, and Javoth finally at peace with the matter. Only then had she turned her attention outward. Tana's sense had told her that while matters in the boarding lair were still a work in progress, there were no emergencies requiring their tending – although Vidiana would experience another dream early tomorrow morning, thanks to Van. Fireclaw, still forming a new identity as Tashara, was working with Laxar trying to learn how to paint. As always, he was the most patient of teachers even when she was not the most patient of students. Vassia was praying and meditating, obviously trying to come to peace given the difficult sol with those who still considered themselves Vanarran shunning her as a traitor. The children in the camp were being tended to by Vosh, and all was well there.

Only when she turned her attention back towards her own cabin did she feel the sorrow and distress and worry coming from Ash. "Oh, no! I've … I've not kept track of him like I should! Why? What's wrong?!" She tried getting Tana to sense, but it was difficult for her. Ash's own potential towards ascendance sometimes made her perceptions difficult. Carefully and quickly, she made her way to their cabin and found him sitting on its small porch. She could tell that he had been crying, and what broke her heart was the fact she could tell his grief was still very much with him.

"Ash? Love?" she asked softly as she approached. He only acknowledged her by putting his head into his paws, still grief-stricken but now his frustration was also truly making itself present. Part of her recognized the signs of his unhappiness being exactly how he would have reacted, but that gave little comfort. She made her way up the steps and sat beside him on a nearby chair and simply waited.

Although it seemed like an eternity to wait, Vanarra did as Tana had the barest sense that he was somehow pulling himself together enough to talk to her. "I'm not sure … I'm not sure I should be here!" he finally said, clearly grief-stricken, and Van's heart sank, thinking that something had happened to make him suddenly regret being in this time.

"With … me?" Van asked softly.

"No! Any of us!" he groaned, looking up. "I'm … I'm terrified that Attoria is a mistake, Van! That all we're doing is pulling together a bunch of Thurians who would be better suited to a penitentiary and trying to pretend that they can form a free and just community! It's … it's madness!"

"What happened, please, Ash? I'm … I'm afraid," she admitted, and she was.

"You know – have you heard Laxar's story?" he asked, looking at her with near accusation.

"I *know* his story very well, and I've helped him overcome it," she asserted softly.

"He's not over what happened to him, Vanarra," he swore at her, nearly angry, but at a warning glance from her, he corrected. "Sorry, Vanalla. I … I just – how many more like him are out there!?"

"Not as many as I would have hoped," Vanarra confessed leaning back and looking at the sky. "Many were among the first to die for any reason. Laxar lived on borrowed time until he ran. I take it he told you his real history because now, you know who I am and … who you are."

"I called him brother, now," Ash told her, "and he the same, but then it kills me to hear what happened to him – he's had more broken bones, more wounds, more … more torture – I don't know who would have had more."

"I am healing him, bit by bit, love," Van offered. "Those scars will fade in time, and he will be as healthy as he can be. I've done much for him already."

"You can heal?" he asked her, curious.

"Something I have to be very careful about how I do it, but yes." She looked at him and smiled. "You do love him! You love him, otherwise you wouldn't feel so torn up over how he's been treated!" Ash nodded, looking a little resigned, his eyes drifting away from her. "The real villains among the Vanarrans have already been put down – if not by me by others. Do you know who is coming to us?"

"Were they the ones who treated him like some kind of … amusement?" he asked, frustrated.

"They certainly didn't think much of ones like Laxar, but they are ones who don't have that blood on their paws."

"What's to say that they won't start to abuse him – damned, even his mate! What's to stop – he's just so … vulnerable!"

She reached over and put her paw on his shoulder, gently rubbing it. "He was even more that way when he was first freed. He's come a long way, Ash. He'll come further still. They all will."

"What is going to stop something secret from starting up, Van, something where ones like Lax and … maybe even like me are bullied, intimidated?!" he nearly growled, but then caught himself.

"Damn, I ... it's those memories of – Theo was right. Oh, damn, *Theo ... was ... right!*"

Ash bowed over and wept bitterly. Vanarra felt confused and wondered what Theo had said to him that broke him so utterly in that moment. The hard crying continued for several passes as she kept a paw on his shoulder, but slowly, Ash seemed to come to himself. She slipped out of her chair and gently held him, gathering him up as rain began to fall and shepherding him inside, her true self revealed the moment the doors were closed behind them. She took them to their bed and relieved him of his shoes and loosened his clothes. Slipping in behind him, she cradled his body, spooned against him, just holding on as she felt him weeping silent, tense tears that tightened his gut as waves of grief overcame him.

Slowly, as the intervals wore on, the grief finally subsided, and a drifting Vanarra came to her senses. A gentle nuzzle along the side of his head told him she was awake, and his voice, strained by such an intense emotional catharsis, rasped out, "He was right about me."

"I don't understand, love. How was Theo right about you?"

"That if I had been brought into this time with my memories intact, I would have been ... I would have become someone else, someone so much more bitter ... lower than I-"

"I'm so sorry, love. That's the difficult bit. Theo is more often right than he is wrong, and he does what he does because he cares about us. It's difficult to accept when he says such a thing, even harder to believe it."

"So, you call him father, Vanarra," he asked, "is that why?"

"One of many reasons," she confessed, repeating it as she pulled in closer to him. "One of many reasons. Even placing me here, I didn't believe it was actually for my good, but here we are, and here I am. I can help keep that which you fear from happening; I and those who work with me – and you, too. I was called the Great Mother by these very Vanarrans, and hidden among them, I will be like a mother to them in many ways. That is my cause, my love. The Aelkinda can become my gift back to Thuria in payment for the horrors the Vanarrans and Sahnassites did in our names – mine, and that of my beloved Sahni."

"Wasn't your fault," he told her, compassion and understanding and certainty rich in his voice.

"Neither were your feelings when Laxar told you his pain. Just make sure that tomorrow, he knows you still love him as a brother."

"I will, Vanarra. I will."

Vidiana stepped from her room in the boarding lair, her walking cane still giving her just a bit of support. Over the past few sols, she had regained some of her strength. Of all of the former Vanarrans, she was reported to be doing the best, which was strange to her. Often, when she would close her eyes in one bed, she would reawaken in another – from the boarding lair to the guest lair at Sahnassa's complex. There, she would go and do a full sol's work at Celebrations by Vanarra, and then go home again with the Nephti in the evenings. Laying her head on the pillow there seemed to bring her back to where she was now. It didn't happen every night, but it was more often than not.

What's more, her time spent in this *world of the past*, as she liked to think of it, was illuminating. She was getting to know the "The Great Mother" as a regular Thurian. It was even accurate to say that the two had become friends, also with Sahnassa. Van had a lot of practical experience and was very plainspoken, but the Nephti was as accomplished at intellectual pursuits and at familial politics. With them working together, it was easy to see how much of an effective team they were. The others in that office – Flint, Tresk, Saiphar, and Sheffer – understood and respected the place the two had found with one another.

Then, she was here – weak, crippled by starvation, and loosed from the moorings of her faith that had held her secure her entire life. This persistent dream, this alternative to her current sufferings, gave her hope. She had even read some of Vanarra's history *In my own words* and found it not sacrilege or desecration or heresy – it completely matched the Van she had met in her dreams. When Vidiana awoke, she often wished she had been able to ask the "Great Mother" why their order had been abandoned or how these dreams were happening, but when she was in her dream world, those questions didn't seem important.

It was a minor frustration and a puzzle, but next to the task of making it down the hallway to visit the others of her order still recovering and offer them encouragement, the task she took on now was monumentally enormous – Vidiana wanted to go outside. All of her "dream life" talking about her new start there was making her curious about this place of Attoria in which they had been landed. The boarding lair was nice, new, a bit utilitarian, but not unlike new government buildings she had visited on occasion – too new to have any amenities but complete in all other respects.

Stepping out of the rounded doorway onto the landing made her wonder why there wasn't anyone tracking her progress. A quick turnaround brought Vassia into view, looking at her carefully but giving her space. She had hated the former geneticist because she had not gone through what they did – she had taken the faithless way of running and hiding here, safe and well fed, while the true worshipers starved. She smiled and motioned with her head that she would appreciate the traitor's company. "After all, I am a traitor to that way of life, too," she thought.

"And so, what are you doing?" Vassia asked quietly, coming up behind her. "I hope you are not planning to make a run for the path out of here so you can resume starving yourself."

"No, I'm … done with that, for now. I don't see the point, honestly."

"That's a surprise – a very quick change for someone who, not even a moon ago, was more than willing to starve herself to death for the Great Mother," Vassia's challenge was gently delivered, but there, nonetheless.

"I have little integrity or beliefs to rely upon, anymore, but what I do know from *In my own words* was that if all is as it states, we understood our Great Mother very poorly, and it's hard to understand why we did."

"I've been giving that some thought over the last few moons," Vassia offered. "We became a system of self-perpetuating belief and power, training the next generation to train the next generation to train the next – as equally lost – generation. The Perfected One was a dream, some kind of psychotic episode, or worse, an excuse for incompetents who wanted to give our kind, the mixed blood, equal rights and honors."

"But we are not mixed blood any longer, are we?" Vidiana asked. "Males and females of our kind will sire males and females of our kind with equal fertility to the purebred, not those of mixed breed."

"Yes, I know," Vassia complained. "I helped make that happen, and you were the beneficiary of our injections, as well?" Her companion nodded. "So, that's it, then. We are now a kind, a *purebred* kind-"

"No! I wouldn't call us that!"

"Then, what?! What term would be accurate enough, yet not polluted with our own Vanarran self-aggrandizements? We, you and I, were told that we are the throwbacks to the purest ancestor of all mongrel species, but we're not! We're a manufactured, genetically engineered equivalence between all kinds."

"And the name I've heard for us, the new ... curse to match the term *Anati?* Aelkinda? Is that what we are to call ourselves in shame?"

As they slowly made their way away from the boarding lair, Vidiana's eyes were touched by pure sunlight, and she was forced to shut them and trust the guiding paws of Vassia. "That name has started here, and it's not yet a curse to anyone!" Vassia nearly growled. "Oh, we may make it so, but it is not a curse in and of itself."

"Then what do you call it, if not a curse?"

"A blessing – mercy and grace mixed together here in a place called Attoria. It's a place we can decide who we are and be all that we can be."

"If not for the Great Mother, then who benefits from our service and achievements?"

"We do," Vassia asserted, guiding her charge to the small pavilion at the center of the Attoria village core. "We are our means and our ends, if you like. If you'd like better, we are the means and ends of our Creator, and that version of peace and harmony is very attractive to me after the seasons of what I've been through."

"Creator – a myth!"

"Great Mother – a myth, also? If you had the chance of serving a myth that put you into slavery and kept you blind, had you inflict horrors on the innocent both in and out of your own group or one who only demanded kindness and love towards all others, which myth would you rather serve?"

"There have been horrific atrocities committed in the name of the Creator, Vassia," Vidiana stated as she was helped up the steps of the pavilion. "Clan wars were fought, thousands died!"

"And our ecumenical parents, the church of the Foundationalists – what was their death toll? What was ours? How odd that splinter movements from the Creator's path that took two different directions to wander from the path have killed so many while those still on the path have harmed almost no one. Sahnassites and Vanarrans are equally lost. Here, here is a seat for you," Vassia directed, and the two sat, Vidiana's eyes finally starting to clear given the shade.

"All very well then, for the Sahnassites as they may simply recant their beliefs and appear indistinguishable from those around them."

"Not so, entirely," Vassia warned, closing her eyes. "I've heard more than a few stories at this point. Sahnassites carry a different kind of stamp than we, but they can be seen. Even they have been hunted. Still, you are right. Attoria is our only refuge, for now, the only place where we can find safety."

"What … am I seeing, Vassia? I … I guess that is where we came from, but what is all of the rest of this?"

"Oh, we are in the park pavilion of the village core of Attoria. Down there is a memorial to the Vulpi who were slain by the Foundationalists long ago."

"Our new home is the site of a … massacre?"

Vassia shrugged. "Thuria is old, and there has likely been a killing of some kind at nearly every place your hind paw would tread. Still, it is a warning for us. Now, yes, that is the boarding lair, and there is a civic meeting den. Over there are the greenhouses and planting supplies for farming and raising crops-"

"Is that what we are to be? Slaves upon a farm?"

"Slaves do not own themselves, whereas we do. We will farm for ourselves, and then we will farm for export, and we can specialize however we'd like. Attoria is in a favorable band of climate and location for many kinds of crops. The valley is quite fertile. Before the Sahnassites purchased it and ran everyone else away, all of this was productive farmland even to the base of the mountains."

"We are on Sahnassite land?" Vidiana questioned darkly.

"We are on *our* land, and the price was paid for it. The Sahnassites have no hold here, as I pray the Vanarrans don't, either."

"You are quite serious about this *new start*, aren't you? What's to say that some … vengeful group won't come over those mountains and wipe us all out in the middle of the night? Then, there can be two lovely markers next to this pavilion, I suppose, so that would be a plus."

The sarcastic comment not sitting well with Vassia, she fought not to shout. "I have enough assurance that we are protected that here is where I live," she grated out carefully.

"And that … protection falls away if we return to our Vanarran worship?"

"You would want to?"

"Yes!" Vidiana nearly shouted. "I've known nothing else than to worship the Great Mother! Now, I feel as if I can finally do that properly as I understand her better."

"She was a follower of the Creator's Path. How will you reconcile that with the worship of her?"

"If that means I must worship the Creator to honor her, I will. I am not stupid, Vassia; I know we got it wrong, but I … I don't think I can abandon the reverence and appreciation I've invested a lifetime into! I just can't."

Vassia considered this for a moment but then responded, "Well … don't. Do you want to honor her? She perpetually gave others a new start, and she held them accountable for making good on it. A new start here means that you may worship her if you wish, but you may not demand or impose that belief upon another as they cannot demand or impose their way upon you. You, also, can honor her by hard work making this a better community, making it survive and prosper."

Vidiana looked at the floor of the pavilion, conflicted. "I wish we had just one of her statues here, something to focus our devotions around."

"In time, maybe, but they wouldn't be like ones in our old temples. If I could choose, I would pick the one I saw in the emergency room of Shanandrae Commons Hospital. I remember what it said. All ages, all stations, all kinds, all creeds, all welcome, all aided, all healed and departing whole – our duty, our calling, our goal."

"Do we think she actually said that?"

"It is recorded outside of her autobiography, but yes. There is adequate proof from the dedication VidStar – the words come right out of her own muzzle."

Vidiana sighed and put her head back, the fatigue of walking this far affecting her. "I told that … purebred, Vanalla, that I didn't *want* any new statues, but it is something my soul keeps grasping after, and it's gone. I would walk to the statues of her and pray to them, ask questions. I thought I heard answers in my heart, but…" There was a haunted look in her eyes as she opened them. "Some of our number bled out their own blood on the hind paws of our statue trying to convince her we were seriously devoted to her. I feel so lost without that image to focus upon."

Vassia thought long and hard as Vidiana rested, nearly panting, closing her eyes again. "Say I could get a statue … made. Say there was a place for us to put it. Would you seriously want to go and throw yourself at its hind paws and beg for reason from an inanimate object? Do you really think that, after all we've been through, the spirit of Vanarra de Gonari would inhabit it?"

"No, but … I wish it was a place that I could go to seek wisdom. What's truer now than even before, I wish I could find it. That purebred Faelnar, Vanalla. You know of her?"

"I do. She is very wise and very kind," Vassia offered, wondering if the once Vanarran hadn't seen through Vanarra's mask to some degree.

"She also seems very well versed on the historical Vanarra. Does she truly have deep knowledge on that subject?"

"She does."

Vidiana closed her eyes and lowered her head, tears running from the corners of her eyes. "What a beautiful image that is. A statue of our Great Mother, as she truly was, and an authority we can ask for guidance. A counselor into this new way of life would be there for all of us to consult and take comfort in."

"This would separate the image and the mystery from the history, you realize that?"

"I do, but I … am … desperate, and I can't understand how your soul has found any peace in this new reality, Vassia. I truly don't!" Eyes were wiped and turned towards her, searchingly, and Vassia felt nearly denuded by that stare. "What have you done that has allowed you to put all of this behind you?"

"I haven't," came the admission. "I, however, have come to look towards the leaders of this place such as Tashara, Javoth, and, yes, Vanalla to help guide me, and … if I must be fully open with you, my heart has found a home in the arms of a loving male, one not of our kind, Vidiana."

"What … is he? Purebred?!"

"No, he was … was one of the servants of the temple. He was one of the few of that number to survive the Sahnassite annihilation at the Center for Thurian Perfection."

"He survived that blast?!"

"He fled before it happened," Vassia confessed. "He sought safety and found it, and he has grown into so much more of an amazing individual than I could have ever guessed our lowly servants capable of. There is *nothing* about him that is lowly, and much about myself that is, Vidiana. Yet, he has loved me, and I have loved him. We are to be joined."

Vidiana looked at her, dumbstruck. Her mind reeled at how this would destroy the very breeding program Vassia herself had worked on for decades. Her fellow Aelkinda sighed and nearly groaned out her protest at Vidiana's all too obvious shock. "There has been no talk, whatsoever, of *progeny* since – like all of our servants – he was sterilized upon reaching sexual maturity."

"It could be reversed," came the untrusting answer.

"Then our genetic engineering would make any children of ours fully Aelkinda. The only genes of his which would be allowed to survive would be ones which are like our own."

Vidiana sat back at hearing this news, her revulsion at Vassia's choice momentarily forgotten. "Mixed bloods can be used to … father or mother our own?"

"Our own? What does that mean? Vanarrans? Devotees of the Great Mother. I'll remind you that this one manufactured positive does not, in any way, reverse the fact that nothing has protected us while we were besieged."

"But here we are, with this ability-"

"An ability that would come to bear meaningful fruit in, what, a few dozen centuries? You and I and our plans will be long dead by the time it will even matter! Do you know how few of us I expect to survive long enough to live here? To build a life? Stop thinking the way you used to think, Vidiana, please! This is one … minor advantage and not the only one we'll need to survive! Put away any dreams of dominating this world! We are fortunate to still have any place in it!"

"You sound defeated."

"I was defeated! We defeated ourselves! Had it not been for the continuing kindness of those we used to despise we would all be defeated and dead and not even having this conversation! This cub should have hated me, but he was kind to me even when he was afraid of me, and when he learned how beaten down I was he could have… he could have…"

Vidiana seemed to get a small inkling of the reason why her once fellow Vanarran had come to love one of their lesser servants. "Taken revenge on you." Vassia nodded and wouldn't answer further, looking away. There was quiet for nearly three full passes until Vidiana finally uttered, "But he didn't, and you love him for it, and in turn, he loves you." There was only the faintest of nods to signify agreement, but it was there. "So, this … is what it means to be mentally unstable. I mean me, not you. I say I don't want a statue then I do, and then I accept defeat and then I don't, and then I curse your heresy only moments before envying it. None of us is … right, Vassia. Not one of us. The only anchor in our world is gone, and we have no other skills left to cope by. This Vanalla, can she be trusted to guide us and guide us well?"

"She can be trusted with our lives and, perhaps, even our souls," Vassia told her softly. "No one knows the *truth* of Vanarra de Gonari – our Great Mother, other than she. If there must be this tie to our pasts, if we cannot live without it, only she would use such power to help us. Not even Javoth, the minister of the Creator's Path, would I trust with this, although he and Vanalla may oppose the idea."

"Tell them we have no other place to grasp our paws. Tell *her* we are lost and need that help to even conceive of a future. If she can truly know the heart of the one we called our Great Mother, then she will be listened to."

"Would you follow her as your Temple Master? Would you desire to?"

"You said she is trustworthy. If she is both trustworthy and wise, perhaps … perhaps she can keep us from wanting that."

"I will try, Vidiana. I promised myself that when you and the others came here I would listen, and I would try." She reached for and found the paw of her once former Vanarran counterpart and was surprised to feel a thankful grasp being returned.

Chapter 17: Revisions of Nurture

Sitting in the civic hall's main chamber, the small leadership council of Attoria sat around the circular table, each trying to come to grips with the proposal Vassia had made at Vidiana's request. Javoth was shaking his head, clearly disturbed by it but making some effort to think it through. Vanalla looked like she was just utterly struck and nearly horrified, and Tashara was looking at Van, as was Vosh. Several of the others, Ash included, watched from the seats surrounding the table.

"I ... I am finding it very difficult to come to some kind of peace with this suggestion," Javoth admitted. "Did we not just finally put the Great Mother away – disprove her by her absence and her lack of aid for these poor souls? Why would we resurrect her, create another statue of her? Why would we assign someone to speak on her behalf? Are we not just re-instating everything we have been charged by the whole of Thuria to abolish?"

It was Vosh who spoke. "In Thurian ages past, archivists accomplished in the knowledge of a historical figure would take on that role, play-acting as another individual to educate – teach a lesson. It is clear that the Vanarrans who would become Aelkinda lack much true knowledge of the historical Vanarra de Gonari, especially regarding her faith."

"Vosh," Van contested. "You can't mean that I should sit behind this statue and pretend to be-"

"There would be no pretending," Vosh offered, and Van looked at her, stunned. "This is a form of historical interpretation and education. If someone were to ask for holy guidance, there would be none to give because the Vanarra, of old, never gave such guidance. She could tell about her life, what she hoped for, and what she fought for. These are concepts sorely missing from the minds of those in the boarding lair I have interviewed."

"What's to keep them from just worshiping the statue, again?"

"If I may?" a soft male voice answered Tashara from the periphery, and she nodded, inviting Laxar forward to an open space with no chair. "The statues at the temple were set upon pedestals or on altars, were … huge and made the Great Mother seem larger than life, even exaggerating her features. A statue that was realistic, one that conveyed the honest truth of her spirit that was no more than her true height could face the viewer eye to eye, as she would have done. There would be no pedestal because the piece could be installed with its hind paws on the floor."

"Then where would Van sit?" Tashara asked.

"I … perceive that she could acceptably sit in front of the statue and to its left or the viewer's right. This is not a position of honor, and such would be left empty."

"No," Javoth contested, looking at Vosh who spoke. "The risk for recontamination of their-"

"Our lives *are* contaminated, Javoth," Vassia offered softly as his son stepped back, dismissed by Tashara's head nod. "I have been reading about the village of Lasrihal. Do you know if its history?"

"I do," Javoth replied after a pause, leaning back and seeing the parallel, although he truly didn't want to. "But I put statues in front of Thurians for them to worship, and that was wrong! I don't want to commit that failing again."

"If I may?" Ash asked, following Laxar's example, and Tashara also nodded for him to take the open spot. Van tracked his movements, uncertain. "Javoth, this would not be that failing, it would be a service to them. There are enough books and documents which are historically accurate so that anything Vanalla offered, in terms of history, could be verified as correct. We're not trying to further their bad beliefs, just correct them. We can't deny they have them, though, and we can't deny they haven't spent an entire lifetime looking at giant statues which misrepresented her."

"And talking to someone near a statue that is a bit more … reasonable, you think, will help them let go of their beliefs?" Javoth asked, and the thought, said in that manner, felt more convincing to him, cooling his doubts. "Should we … have someone watching and monitoring?"

"I will," Ash offered. "She's my mate, and I'll protect her and help her."

"We're going to have to come clean about this to our sponsors, enforcement, everyone," Tashara warned. "They don't want any signs that we're actually restarting the Vanarran religion. I'll have to work with some of my folks to shape this in our newsletter and press releases. Who is doing the-" She looked and saw Laxar nod. "You sure you are up to this, cub?"

"He is up to it," Vassia promised. "He will have as much help as he needs."

Tashara looked at Van and asked, "What do you think? We're basically volunteering you for this, it would seem. Is it something we need to give you time to think through?"

"I … I would like a little time, yeah," Van softly stated, and Ash nodded, returning to his seat. "I don't disagree with their needs, but *we* need to be so very careful at this point. We need to think where to put this, will it serve the needs of Attoria as it grows, will it actually anger the ones we're trying to help?"

"There are a lot of questions, I know. However, when Vidiana – who I am sensing is starting to have a true change of heart – asks for this, I believe she is asking for help. She is not asking for us to restore the old ways. She does not, nor do I think she could easily accept a statue like the ones we knew before. She … needs a reality to ground herself in, and the *reality* of Vanarra de Gonari is a good place to start."

Grabbing a little something off of the kitchen's counter instead of going to the dining hall, since she had awakened later, Van slipped outside into the morning air and began making her way to the secret studio that had once been where Attorian Vulpi were enslaved to their de Caterra masters. "How patterns do repeat in a place," she breathed into the air, hoping that this time they were taking the antithesis of the prior pattern and making the freed and self-deterministic Aelkinda of Attoria.

When she arrived at the entrance, she found Vassia sitting there in a light robe, smiling and tending a fire near the entrance. "You do this often?" Van asked.

"It's one of my favorite places," she confessed. "It is important that I remain nearby for Laxar, but keep a little distance between us, after…"

"How far have you gotten?" Vanarra asked softly, as she sat beside her watching the fire.

"We have begun to share the pleasures of one another's company, now that we have announced our commitment, but we are not engaging in the final intimacy until that commitment is sealed. It is funny, however. I don't feel as if life will be any different for us after the official ceremony."

"I don't know if there is any ceremony, or any act – for that matter – which will make your union more complete. I can tell that you two are already a mated pair in every sense of the words save just the public commitment. However, save that for the other side of making those public vows, Vassia. In the end, it will leave you with nothing to regret."

"In this specific instance, regrets I understand and would hope to avoid," Vassia offered. "I still feel the sting of your words when I was in the wrong."

"I'm sorry I-"

"No, I needed it. I'm just gratified to be where I am now and who I am … And whose I am, also." Vassia watched Vanarra's preoccupation with the fire and noted, "You are fearful of some regret, too, aren't you? Vidiana's idea still does not sit well with you."

"There are some points of it that are good that I can agree to, yes, but I do not like – I cannot even conceive of a statue that would make the former Vanarrans not want to bow down to it. I don't want to see them bowing down to me."

"You had best prepare yourself, then, in that regard. Many of them might, at first. However, what Laxar has told me is that he intends to execute the statue in such a way that it will be difficult for these once Vanarrans to place their old ideas upon it."

"It's a finely drawn line he has to straddle," Van commented. "They have to like it enough to not go and create something else on their own, but it can't fill them with holy awe and wonder so they hit the floor and start pledging themselves to it."

"Come, Vanalla," Laxar's voice called from the entrance. "Let us see if I am up to the task."

As Van stood and walked inside, she didn't revert from her Faelnar form until Vassia had assured her, "There is no one else here."

Vanarra turned towards her and changed into her mixed blood form in the same instant. "How is he going to do the face in a way that they won't see me sitting right there? We can't have them doing that, either!"

"Maybe part of the power of the statue is the reality of your being there," Laxar put in as Vassia helped Van remove her coat. "Maybe they will trust the words that come from your muzzle as Vanarra because they can see a fragment of your true self shining through."

As a robe was slipped onto Vanarra's shoulders, she contested, "And then they'll write about the miracle of how the Great Mother's spirit possessed a mere Faelnar and redirected them back onto the path of world domination." With the robe open, she looked at Laxar and opened her paw to him, palm up. "How is this supposed to happen? How are you supposed to-" She was going to ask him a question, but his eyes had grown very wide, and then he had slammed them shut, turning away. "What's wrong?"

"I have what I need," he told them. "Vassia, please, escort her from here. I have to get this out, quickly! I can see all of it, but it might not last!"

Vassia quickly redirected Van to change out and then, indicating she should remain silent, escorted her from the room. They were outside of the studio back at the fire before the Aelkinda female allowed anything to be said. "What was that about?"

"I have learned that it is the way of things with him and his art. The inspiration is seized and then must be worked through in silence and solitude. He asked me to model for our own private piece of artwork, and the moment I had sat upon the bed, he shooed me out, eyes slammed closed. What resulted made me feel more female than I ever have, and it was the most beautiful reflection of my love for him, and in it, his love for me. If the work he has seen is even half what he did for me, for us, then it will be all we need it to be."

"Sure he doesn't want to like have me try a few things at least, different poses?"

"He was watching you the entire time, and if he hadn't seen exactly what he needed, he would have asked you to stay, but he has seen the answer, and once he has it, there is no need to see more. Seeing more, as he says, is only noise and delay. What we do for you and for Attoria, here, is too important for that. Trust me, my redeeming mother, and we will not fail you."

Uncertain, Van tested her senses within, and Tana and her inner Sahnassa agreed. "Very well, Vassia. I trust you both. If I am needed, though, call for me. I will do whatever he needs."

Vassia wrapped her arms around the now Faelnar and promised, "I think I saw just a part of what he did, and if so, I'm sure it won't be necessary. However, if something happens, we will call, but until then, please give us this space."

"Alright. You staying with him?"

"I might join you for breakfast if you haven't had any. I think it would be best if even I didn't disturb him for several intervals. I also want to tell Vidiana we are progressing along the path she suggested. If she asks to speak with you as you are to be the interpreter, I would suggest agreeing and hearing her out. As unstable as her mind appears to be, it has a logic which agrees with the rest of them and may serve as a template."

"In case I need to know how to be appropriately mad, just to match them?"

"Yes. Just as you did with me, if you'll remember."

"Vassia, I love you, and I love Laxar. I'll do anything I can to help."

"Then, let us go and see what we can do while the artist takes his time. I will return to him about mid-sol with a meal."

"Sounds good. Let's walk by the cabin, and I can pick up Ash. We talked for a long time last night."

"Vosh showed him something interesting?"

"Almost too interesting, but he's very happy and very motivated now."

"I look forward to hearing it," Vassia answered, motioning that they should proceed, and proceed they did.

"Thank you for coming, Alanar," Tashara said, standing along with Javoth and Vassia to greet the Vulpi reporter and his mate. "And you, as well Doctor Emma."

As the Vulpi couple entered the Attoria Meeting Den, the central administration building, Alanar replied, "Our pleasure. I was curious how things were proceeding here, but I've been so busy covering the house rights story that it's been difficult to find the time. I take it you have another development?"

"Everyone still doing okay?" Emma asked, clearly expecting bad news.

"Thankfully," Javoth answered as he motioned for them to sit, "we've not lost anyone else after that first horrible sol. Everyone else is growing in strength and is now on solid food, which is a great benefit. Some are even beginning to move about the boarding lair and the area of the village center, but not much further. They are still very weak when compared with other Thurians."

"I take it their mental condition is only … serviceable to keep them living," the psychologist asked.

"We are seeing improvements there, but…" Tashara hesitated a moment before continuing, "That's why we've asked you to visit. We've received a request or a suggestion, you might say, from one of those recovering. How much access have you been granted to the Vanarran temples?"

"Before their fall," Alanar offered, "almost none – other than looking at the outside like everyone else. However, when the one in Carantra was investigated by enforcement and everyone was found dead, I did get a look inside. They all died laying around a statue of the Great Mother, in the room in the center atrium of the temple."

Vassia nodded. "It doesn't surprise me. As Vanarrans, we were taught to idolize the Great Mother, follow her example in all things leading to the coming of the Perfected Ones, the new species we helped bring into being. All of our deepest training was done in the presence of that statue or in the presence of the Perfected One's statue. When faced with crisis or hopelessness, there is a longing in those of us with that background to see the three-dimensional image of the Great Mother, or more properly, Vanarra de Gonari."

"What I saw in that temple *wasn't* Vanarra de Gonari," Alanar contested. "It was a ... gross exaggeration of her, especially in the front and hips."

"An exaggeration of her motherliness, and while Vanarra de Gonari is ... recorded as being well endowed," Vassia admitted, "it is clear that – yes – she wasn't like that. However, those statues still bore a likeness to her that we believe we can use here to help former Vanarrans adjust to a new reality. Can you come with us?"

They all stood, and Alanar and Emma followed the trio down the entrance hallway to a closed door. "This, eventually," Javoth explained, "will become a library, but for right now, we intend it to be a place where former Vanarrans can reset their understanding of Vanarra de Gonari and what she stood for." Both he and Tashara opened opposing doors to reveal what was a now a very meditative space, and in the center, lit by a light from the front, was a statue.

"Wow, just ... wow!" Alanar commented, walking forward. "That's an amazing piece, and the pose is very compelling."

"Questing, in a way, for help," Emma noted critically, "or asking a question – it's very evocative! It's like she expects an answer of some kind."

"It is not at all the way we were raised to see her," Vassia stated, stepping in and standing between the two Vulpi. "The first time I saw it, it stunned me. However, it is a very authentic likeness and varies drastically from what we were taught to admire."

"Still has a nice chest on her, though," Alanar quipped, and Emma looked at him sternly.

"I believe those measurements have been confirmed via the historical record as completely accurate," Javoth chuckled, seeing her disagreement with his smart-alecky comment. "There was an exhaustive amount of work to render her exactly as she was. She's about fifty or so in this interpretation, and so she's still relatively young."

"So, the idea is that by letting Vanarrans or former Vanarrans see this interpretation of her, and…" he paused, looking at the books on the nearby shelves. "Ah, her own auto-biography and several of the more – well, what's considered the more reliable works. You're hoping that this will help them learn not to worship her?"

Vassia stepped forward and took a position to the left of the statue, facing them. "Our thought is that those who come here need a guide to help them understand what they're seeing, someone to answer questions – an interpreter, if you will."

"Would they stand there?"

"I don't know that such has been decided," Javoth noted. "However, in close proximity has been generally agreed."

"You said a historical interpreter," Doctor Emma mused. "Does this mean that it would be a speech they would give or would they answer questions? Some of those questions might be quite harsh and … risky."

Tashara walked up to and looked at the statue. "I think the individual we've chosen for that work is up to it."

"Vanalla Ashallo," Emma stated firmly.

"That has been our thought," Javoth confessed. "She's very well versed on the history of Vanarra de Gonari and has a bit of history in dealing with difficult cases. However, I would prefer it that her name not be recorded, to protect her and her family from interest."

"If she messes this up," Alanar told him directly, "she'll get a lot of interest. Still, I can see the point. So, we'll call her a well-qualified and well-trained historical interpreter, someone who…"

"I think it's safe to say," Emma told her mate, "that she is someone who has not only the facts but the disposition to face down the most zealous former Vanarran and claw down their mistaken beliefs and misinformation point by point."

"Fair enough, but it doesn't mean someone here or someone who sneaks in here isn't going to tell the world who she is. How's security been?"

"Surprisingly good. Not a lot of interest, honestly, in running down a bunch of the non-guilty Vanarrans who were starving and about to die."

"That's good to hear, Tasha," Emma replied.

"Do you ever miss being called Fireclaw Destiny?" Alanar asked her, crossing his arms and just looking at her, bemused.

"You know ... no. I'm not going to say that I don't get a little nostalgic at hearing that, but it's more the life I had, not the life I have now."

"They're talking about a comeback," he challenged gently. "The intercontinental team is looking a little young this go around. Muzzles are buzzing about it."

"Yeah, because if I did it, I'd be *entertaining* to someone," Tasha noted a bit darkly. "I'd be back in the thick of the rumors and awful gossip, and at the end of it – I just don't think I'd have anything more than I have right now. Right now, as you know, we're at this really incredible delicate time here in Attoria. It's why we're trying this." Pointing at the statue, she continued, "This is what I have to get done right now – making sure that this first little group of nearly starved Thurians can find a way to live here and build a new life, a life which harms no one and makes all of Thuria accept them as equals."

"It's hard work," Javoth put in. "They are so damaged. I had one of their assistants – although slaves would be a better word – in my care long before this. It took seasons to undo some of the harm they had done to him. The challenge we're finding here is that every one of them has the same damage – the ones here, and the ones yet to come here."

"I don't know how many more you'll get," Alanar warned. "Death tolls are starting to mount up quickly. Some places are doing better than others, but-"

"We need to buy some time, and we need help for that. Alanar, I don't know – Thurians have been so generous already, I don't know if they can give any more, but if someone actually brought bundles of food to those Vanarrans who are still living, that act of kindness might help them decide to come here."

"I'll walk through the boarding lair and tell that story," Alanar promised. "Also, Flame Blossom wanted me to tell you that if you needed her, she would be there for you."

"See if she can help get them here. Raise a little to feed them and offer transport. These – the ones who came here – were so weak that we couldn't even start to work through their issues until now."

"It would be better if you could get them before they completely collapse and lose the will to live," Emma asserted softly. "I know how hard you've had to fight to keep these living, and … I can see where this might be necessary, may even be helpful. Please offer your *interpreter* my help if she needs it, alright?"

"Done, and like I said, we want to be open and transparent with everyone who gave us their money and support. That's why we called you here."

Alanar looked at the statue and asked, "I suppose you also don't want to tell me who the artist is."

"He is Laxar," Vassia explained, "and I'm very proud of the amazing work he does."

"He is the former Vanarran servant I told you about, and he's the one I've raised as my own son. He's a self-taught artist, and he's very gifted. It's our hope that, like him, there are many who are coming to Attoria who are as equally gifted – who have something to give to Thuria, not take from it."

"A noble sentiment for all of us," Doctor Emma offered. "Is Vanalla here?"

"No, actually. She and her lair mate went back to Shanandrae to talk to Trax and Shenaria. They are thinking about moving here and building a place, nearby."

"With such young children?" Emma asked. "Isn't that a concern?"

"I think Vanalla will make sure that things are doing relatively well before she agrees to it. Steps like this will facilitate, eventually, those not of Vanarran heritage to move and flourish here."

"I don't know how anxious I would be, as a purebred, to move here."

"There will be that fear, Alanar, but there might be an initial step where some mixed bloods move here, and in time, their purebred friends might join them," Tashara suggested. "We're hoping that some of us can blaze a bit of trail, there. It's actually good, we think, for purebreds and mixed to interact with the ones coming here – the ones who were so isolated and insulated from everything else in the world. This, Attoria, can be their safe lair to start learning how to relate to others who aren't like them."

"I hope this works, Javoth," Alanar offered. "I agree with what's been said – they didn't ask to be born into the crazy places they were born into or taught the crazy things they were taught. It's up to them, though."

"As it must be," Tashara stated. "As it should be."

As Vanalla walked into the entrance of the Attoria Meeting Den, she kept her eyes closed relying on both Laxar and Ash to guide her forward. "This shouldn't be happening," she told them. "I can't believe I'm going to see a statue of me that Vanarrans will want to bow down to and worship. Laxar, I know you did your best."

"I think you need to see this first, Van – it's very different," Ash told her gently. "It will be okay, I think."

"Oh, Ash, there can be a long time between seems okay and gets really not okay in a very bad way."

"Well, we're here," Laxar told her. "Tell me what *you* think."

Vanarra opened her eyes and was stunned, stunned in three ways – once for each of the souls who shared her body. Tana was struck by how accurately Laxar had sensed every nuance of the impression she tried to radiate to him, and beyond by what he had added of his own accord. Sahnassa was electrified to see the expression at the core of their friendship – the pleading and guiding look that had caused her to volunteer to help Vanarra serve food at a business where she had just been turned down for a job. It was the Vanarra who had encouraged her, helped her, and who had cared for her. Vanarra, in her inmost self, saw a part of her own mother there, her father, and her own soul at a time when she had finally put away the bitterness from living as a mixed blood.

"Oh, Laxar, you precious soul," she breathed walking towards the figure. "How do you do this, see these things?"

"I have been looking for the authentic Great Mother all of my life," the young artist told her. "She saved me and healed me and brought me to my home and a father I love and respect. Every memory of you is here in some way, all I could manage. Vassia says I ... exhausted myself too much with it, but it had to come out the way it did. This requires nothing less."

"You have done more for me in this moment than you can possibly know. The ones I am and the one I will become love you for it, Laxar." She went to him and surrounded him with a loving embrace.

"When I saw it," Vassia's voice played into the room as she stepped in from the hallway, "it hit my very soul. Looking at this image should prove to any Vanarran that they are wrong about you; we were always wrong about you. I will want Vidiana to see this soon, and with you in the room."

"That's ... that's just going to be so strange," she breathed. "How do we do that?"

"Well, whilst I can swear Vidiana to secrecy, I believe, with relative assurance that she will keep her word, I don't believe it would be wise for the others of our former order to know you are the speaker in this room," Vassia offered, walking over and lightly embracing her lover and soon to be mate.

"Well, how do we prevent it? I can mask my scent with the changeling cloak abilities Tana can provide, I suppose, but my appearance..."

"A mask," Ash told her. "We've talked about it, Javoth, Tasha, and I. Kylie is going to play seamstress, and so we know the job will be done right. As for your scent, I would suggest that we use incense to cover that. There was a type used at Vanarran temples, and approximating it here will help ease the transition to this view of the Great Mother."

"I ... remember that smell," Laxar commented, his ears rising along with his tail.

"It had a certain place in our ceremonies," Vassia commented quietly.

"I don't get it," Ash asked. "What was so special about it?"

"That specific incense was formulated to stimulate both the male and female receptors that look for heat scent. It's not a heat scent, but it is close enough that it can cause the same fuzzing of the mind, so to speak," Vassia told them. "Vanarrans equate that smell with religious experiences."

"I don't want this to be a religious experience," Van warned Vassia.

"The former Vanarrans coming to see a statue of the Great Mother? Unavoidable. However, that is yet another tool we can use. There will always be incense here, but even from the first, we introduce a secondary scent, one buried beneath the primary one which – over time – will become the primary one. As time goes on and their understanding matures, the scent will change. As we bring in new groups of former Vanarrans, we'll have to adjust back and forth, but as you can keep perfect track of who needs what scent, the scent can change to the individual."

"Clever plan," Van commented, "and with Kylie's help or even by ourselves, we can change the air in an instant. Okay. That does seem to make at least a little sense. I ... I am willing to try."

Vidiana approached Attoria's civic Meeting Den with Vassia at her side. Over the past sols, she – as had the rest of the once Vanarrans – had grown strong enough to walk short distances around the village core and were growing a little listless and wanting for something to do. While none of them had the stamina to put in a full sol's work, they had, at least, been seeing to their own needs without constant help and supervision. All of them knew what they were supposed to be doing – namely starting to set forth on a new life in this place that had been prepared for that purpose, but in their souls, their own purpose was lacking. There were the whispered conversations filled with the desperately toxic desires of returning to what they knew and wanting "it all back." That part warred inside of her, too, and the only hope she had had of ending that contest lay before her.

"Very well," Vassia offered, breaking her out of her internal struggle. "You're here. Go in, and turn down the right hallway. You'll know it when you see it."

"What will I know other than what I suggested?

"An experience that shook me to my foundations even though I saw it come together. An experience that touched me in ways I could not escape."

"We will see if a cobbled together statue and a pretend Great Mother are any comfort to those whose hearts have been emptied."

"We will see," Vassia agreed and stepped back to let her walk in.

Vidiana walked into the structure, finding the doors in front of her and to the left of her securely closed, but the door to the right was, indeed, open. Looking in that direction also brought a scent to full recognition, something that her nose – desensitized to smells thanks to the antiseptic atmosphere of the boarding lair – missed until it was trapped by the space she now stood in, concentrated. It seemed to peel away the blinding and concealing aromas she had lived in and slept in and plunge into her mind and heart and body. "Temple incense," she breathed out, savoring the feelings of elation and purpose that were conditioned responses. She nearly wanted to fling off her clothes and run forward into the worship of the Great Mother and the Perfected One, but the strangeness of the little hallway kept those feelings under some degree of control.

Stepping carefully and almost stealthily down the hall, Vidiana came to a sheer curtain that had a part in the middle, and there, behind it, was a figure standing and lit from above and in front. Cautious, the lifelong Vanarran poked her head through the slit between the two sheets of overlapping purple blue material and was stunned to see the image of the Great Mother looking at her in entreaty. A trickle of uncontrolled urine slipped from her body and spread coolness down the insides of her legs before she had the presence of mind to control it. Still, she was reeling – trembling in something akin to holy excitement and awe, but her own lack of control shamed her into an emotion that overtook her before she could mount any defense – anger like she'd never felt in her entire life.

Shamed and betrayed by what was in front of her, she raised a paw, claws expressed, and reared back to deliver as powerful and destructive a strike as she could manage, but a penetrating female voice from nearby commanded her, "Stop!"

Vidiana crumpled to the floor as if her heart had refused to beat two times in a row, and she was gasping and shaking on all fours.

Her voice ragged and distraught, words tore from her muzzle. "You were our Great Mother! You abandoned us!"

"I was never yours," came the answer. "The sect of the Vanarrans took my life and my history and perverted it to their own ends. Even the image of my own body was prey to their lie."

At some level, Vidiana knew that the voice she heard might be coming from the Faelnar she had singled out, but that fact had diminished to insignificance in this interchange. The voice wasn't one of a historian or archivist; no voice of a disinterested third party would carry the intimate hurt and revilement that this one carried. Turning her head up and looking at the statue, she could see the outline of the Great Mother's breasts beneath a simple top she wore. Their size, indeed, was nearly svelte in comparison to the statues she had seen all of her life. Vidiana came to a kneel and looked at the unmoving female's hips; they, too, were slenderer than the facsimiles adorning most of their temples.

At this vantage point, the statue in front of her seemed to be making an impassioned argument, and the voice giving words to the silent visage seemed to understand that intrinsically. "Have you even studied my history? The things I wrote about myself? What words did I give you that made you think I wanted to be your god?! Wasn't I clear in telling you that the Creator's Path meant everything to me?"

"We ... We were taught that book was heresy-"

"Then I, make no mistake, am that heretic. There are writings from Flint de Gonari, the Grand Matriarch Rahnahi de Dothnar, and the numerous others that tell you the stripe and color of my faith. Why did you ignore them? Why did you ignore me?"

"It ... wasn't our fault; it was what we were taught."

"It is your fault if you still continue to believe it," Vanarra de Gonari said so firmly that the statue's lips nearly seemed to move and the eyes turn upon her as Vidiana struggled to her hind paws. "You have made my name your name and turned that name into a curse. The purebred curse is Vanarran, and that is my name – not yours! It's mine! That was a name that started out being called by a mother who wouldn't kill me just because I was born different. Thousands and thousands again have died because of the Vanarrans. Thousands more purebreds were poisoned and scarred forever. You call me a Great

Mother. What kind of mother brings these kinds of plagues into the world?" There was an uneasy pause before the next question was asked, "Why did you do these things in my name?"

There was a long moment of silence that stripped layers upon layers of resistance from the walls of the once Vanarran's heart. It was as if the owner of that voice had seen deep into her hidden past, her most secret soul, and found that Vidiana had been responsible for atrocities – ones done in secret, ones done so that even her fellow Vanarrans did not know of it. "That ... is why you starved yourselves. All of you here know what you have done, and that guilt demands you justify yourselves by wrapping holy purpose around acts that were callous, hateful, and utterly criminal." The soft delivery of that accusation ripped a gash in the middle of Vidiana's soul, leaving her bare in a way she had never been, even when in the temple of the Great Mother and the Perfected One.

Her heart ached in a way it never had, as if its own weight would cause it to collapse in on itself. "I'm ... I'm sorry," she whispered out, "truly sorry."

There was a deep sigh and then a voice of one who sounded as if she was trying her best to be patient. "By the moons, I hope you are. Those were beautiful kits and cubs you hurt. Did you and yours forget that I fell in love and joined myself to a purebred? I didn't think they were ugly or perversions of some imaginary perfected form; my love was beautiful. I found grace and magic in his form and in his soul all our lives. You cannot find forgiveness in any way until you let go of hating those who look different than you do."

Vidiana's response was something between a chuckle and a sob, "But we are now this form! We have made ourselves to be this way, and if we mate, our children will be as we are! We are marked upon the world. We are now the cursed!"

"You are only if you demonstrate no ability to change your mind. I have had those who stood against me and refused to do what they should, but the moment they made up their minds to choose a different path, I forgave them. I became their friend. I even became their ally and supporter. All that is needed to change a Vanarran into an Aelkinda is a choice – a choice to believe that there is a future without the driving rage of hate to push it forward. You need to think about that; you need to think about that a good long while, and when you make a choice, make it a good one. Attoria isn't only a village. It is a new start. Come back after you've thought about what I've said. Tell me if I am wrong or if I'm right about you."

After a moment's pause of paralyzed indecision, a distraught and utterly shaken Vidiana almost staggered from the room, nearly trying to run away as she made her way down the hall. As soon as she was out of the range of hearing, the lights came up, the air instantly cleared, and Vanalla – sitting just to the right of the door – was joined by an alien presence looking at her wide-eyed.

"My!" Dynaea exclaimed in honest astonishment. "I've heard of tough love and could have even been accused of using it from time to time, but Vanarra…"

Standing up and removing the black hood and cowl which had so adequately hidden her from Vidiana, Vanalla turned back into Vanarra and offered without apology, "She wanted to hear from the Great Mother. She heard."

"Almost so much that I sense she is on the edge of mental collapse."

"You should also sense that Vassia is talking to her, relaying her experience – which was much the same, actually. Sometimes, we Thurians need to be shaken and shaken hard to break us out of self-assurance, and I have never seen more self-assurance than I saw in the Vanarrans and Sahnassites when I first arrived here. This is the equivalent of taking someone who tortured children and convincing them they were wrong to do so."

"I won't dispute that point," Dynaea agreed. "It's just … jarring for me to hear you speak like that."

"Focus the discussion on how they betrayed me?" Dynaea thought about that for a moment and nodded. "It fits. They worshiped a fake me – a made-up me. Kylie and I were talking about the Asteravans one night, and she mentioned the honor and reverence those of your kind hold for Angela, the first Teldear. The difference is that all of the Asteravans can see her now, talk to her – learn why she is great, not just make something up."

"She has mentioned you, you know?" Dynaea said, biting her lip a little. "She's … impressed."

"Well, Kylie gave me more than enough reasons to think well of her, and you for that matter. I don't know, Dynaea, I really don't. There were hundreds of important figures in Thurian history, and this bunch uses us as a fodder for their beliefs. It does make me angry. It's like I was used, not unlike the way I was when males treated me as a plaything without my permission. Here, I wasn't drugged unconscious, I was dead – to them, anyhow. We were just as helpless to do anything about it. I wish the Allarrae had permitted a Teldear to follow Sahni after her time was over."

Dynaea smiled wryly. "Ah, you can be sure that Me Sha is enjoying a bittersweet victory as such was his vote. A perpetual presence on Thuria is now an unquestioned certainty across the highest levels."

"I wish he had just made it that way," Vanarra complained, screwing up her brow in confusion. "Couldn't he have?"

"Me Sha does not retain that title by being an autocrat and demanding others do as he says. He guides the consensus and provisions the recovery when he knows that the best choice hasn't been made. Right now, ones who opposed him on it, Nyssia to name a name, are deeply rethinking their positions, and that's why…"

"That's why Saletta is studying with her!" Van nearly blurted.

"It gets better than that," Dynaea offered. "Your former commander, Dassalil, the one you called Old Redwing, is the daughter of a Supreme Council family deeply opposed – originally – to allowing the Teldear to remain a part of Thurian society. Saletta is being an excellent ambassador for your kind and their promise, but the time you spent serving beneath Dassalil was as much an ambassadorship. Having spoken with her before coming here, it appears she has advocated very strongly on behalf of your kind."

The amusement in Dynaea's expression drew out Van. "What? What happened?"

"Well, let's just say that when Dassalil came up against obstinacy, she got a little … hot."

"Like flames or something? I thought she couldn't do that."

"It seems as if she ascended during the argument."

Remembering how much energy was released when Lyshantor had ascended, Van shook her head in surprise. "Wow…"

"It made an impression – in the floor and in the wall and ceiling, yes, but in her parents, also. She told me to tell you, when the moment was right, that you brought out the best in her, and she never realized it."

Vanarra threw back her head in a good, hearty laugh, shaking her head. "I guess she did beat me after all."

"And she gets to blame you, dear. A sweet victory for her all around," Dynaea offered.

"Well," Van countered, closing her eyes and reaching out with Tana and Sahni, "from what I can sense of Vidiana and Vassia, my little bit of fire in her direction helped."

Dynaea closed her eyes and replied, a little stunned, "You know your kind well." Opening her eyes, she bowed to Vanarra and said, "That is the highest compliment I can pay you as Teldear, especially when I can feel the very future of Attoria turning on this moment."

Chapter 18: The Turnings of Trust

Half a moon later, Van felt as if she actually saw Dynaea's statement becoming a reality. Without exception, every one of the former Vanarrans had come to her in the statue room and walked out a changed individual. In all of them, she felt an identity as Aelkinda and, as importantly, an identity as Attorians forming within them. Some had been to see her only once, and some multiple times, but all had now acknowledged the faults of how they were raised and how such was not how the historical Vanarra would have wanted them to live.

Ash, in his own way, had been contributing. A few males had cautiously joined his little work crew learning skills to repair and upgrade the buildings and other structures in the village whilst coming to a deeper knowledge of the Creator's Path in the process. They questioned him, and he answered – never pressuring. Tana, within her, felt that two or three were reaching the point where they would make some kind of commitment, leaving the Vanarran tenets behind forever.

Several of the females and some of the other males had taken to working in the greenhouses and fields, beginning the work of growing food for themselves – the first fragile beginnings of being able to support themselves, live independently as they never had before. This simple work was teaching them that most of their lives had been spent siphoning off of the works and labors of others, producing nothing. Here, though, was a seed which by their care and tending was turning into that which would sustain them, and in time, others.

Vanarra, as Vanalla – her Faelnar form, sat in the central village gazebo watching the happenings as she enjoyed the rarity of a solitary lunch. While it wasn't commonly known amongst the Attorian population that she was the one who answered on behalf of the statue of the Great Mother come Vanarra, she had still been sought out as an individual worthy of asking council or perspective or guidance. Some of what she said to them felt as if there were echoes of things she said when she was the boss in Celebrations by Vanarra, a matron, a dame, and finally, a Grand Matriarch. While the niceties of elected leadership had not yet been chosen among them, it was as if all in the village were turning towards her to guide them.

"It's not a bad thing, Van," her inner Sahnassa told her. "You can truly help them, and you want to. It's the truest definition of what a Teldear is at their best."

"As, what, their leader? Their Grand Matriarch?"

"Why not?" Sahni told her, her presence almost seeming to sit alongside Van as she ate. "I did that, and I can tell you that I was a better Grand Matriarch and everything else because I was a Teldear. The insight you have and the larger perspective are especially important. That's a good thing, actually."

"Oh, why?"

"Well, because Tana has picked up on Vassia starting to move in your direction. She and Laxar have had a rather impassioned discussion, and I believe she will be seeking your advice. Yep, she's trying to find you."

"Okay, so I guess I eat quickly and then sit up and don't slouch so that she can see me."

Sahnassa chuckled, fading back into Van's thoughts. "Wouldn't be the first time you had to cram down a lunch because someone wanted your help."

"Guess not," Van observed, but then a memory sparked, and she laughed softly. "Oh, right! That was you at least of a couple of times!"

"And see where I ended up," came the whispered jest.

Van finished her lunch quickly and then picked up a paw-held viewer reviewing the current funding and supplies available. It wasn't half a pass later before Vassia coughed at the bottom of the gazebo stairs and asked, "Vanalla? I don't mean to intrude on your time alone, but Laxar and I – mostly I, need your help."

"Come on up! I have some time. Something wrong?" As Vassia mounted the steps she didn't speak, but rather came to sit alongside Van, looking at the floor, her blush fur raised. "Okay, question answered. Tell me, Vassia. If I can help, I will."

"It is difficult and embarrassing for me, and far too embarrassing for Laxar for him to bring this to you. He has begged me not to, but I see no choice if I am to live with a clear conscience."

"Would it help to frame things up a bit?" Van asked, setting down the viewer. "Why is it so embarrassing?"

"It involves the way in which Laxar and I relate … intimately, as a male and female would. Since our joining, only a few sols ago, we have been truly becoming more and more revealing of ourselves, and before I realized it was happening, we were falling into a pattern that is starting to burden me with guilt and doubts."

"The beginning of a relationship, especially a committed relationship, can be a very difficult time because you are learning what fantasies and dreams your new mate will accept and which they will have difficulty with. It can create some feelings of rejection, actually," Van observed.

"Which I do not want!" Vassia spoke passionately. "I do not want to make him feel as if I am rejecting him, but I do not want to abuse him, either."

"Tell me. What is the source of this?"

"The Rites of Servant Reward. Do you know of it?"

Van sighed and looked away. "I remember from when he explained to Emma and the others at Shanandrae Commons what was done to him for both rewards and for punishments. Yes, what was done to him then was abuse."

"Then you can understand my reluctance when he wanted to coax me into doing many of the same things," Vassia whispered before unburdening her soul about all of her fears and regrets about repeating any aspect of what had happened to Laxar in the temple when he was a servant of the Vanarrans.

Vanalla's advice was simple, in the end, and her acceptance of the uniqueness of their union was plain. "I would advise talking to him, apologizing for not understanding his needs, and offering to give him the gift of love however he desires. Tell him what has been provided, and offer to do the rites for him."

"And he chooses?"

"He chooses. That doesn't mean you can't make choices, as well. For example, maybe the robes might be a bit much. Maybe any clothing might be a bit much."

Vassia bit her lip as her blush fur raised. "Interesting," she commented softly. "Thank you for your help. I was afraid."

"I know. There was a reason, and this isn't settled. When faced with actually following through on what he asked, he may not want to. However, if my sense of him is correct, he will." Van's knowing smile deepened the blush already present on Vassia's muzzle, and she abruptly stood and bowed.

"I seem to have responsibilities to my mate I must attend to. If you will excuse me?"

"Certainly," Van replied, almost keeping the feral grin off of her muzzle.

"And thank you," Vassia offered, but then at a softer volume offered, "Great Mother." Van smirked as she watched the quickly retreating back of the once Vanarran move with purpose in the direction of Laxar's cave studio.

However, less than a pass after she was gone, there was a male's soft cough from the bottom of the steps. "Callanar?" she asked, turning towards him. The older, graying Aelkinda was somewhat shy and – of all of the Vanarrans – had needed only the slightest prodding to realize how his old beliefs were misdirected. She sensed, too, that he had long ago come to this realization himself but had no avenue to pursue any other alternative. She had found him, however, in the past few sols growing bolder and more questioning, and from the tone of his first statement, Van could tell that such would also be the case this sol.

"Good morning to you, just barely it appears," he chuckled good naturedly.

"I do like an early lunch," she admitted, noting that the time was almost mid-sol. "It's a habit from a long time ago."

"And, as I have witnessed from my window, you also seem to favor giving advice."

"I will offer help when asked, Callanar. It is what I should do."

He nodded as he accepted her open paw as an invitation to come and speak with him. "To judge by Vassia's speed and the considerably higher loft in her tail than when she first approached you for an audience, it seems she found your advice quite satisfactory."

"That remains to be seen," Van admitted. "It might help. I hope it will help."

"The more I hear you speak, the more you sound like the Great Mother I encountered in the administration building – the civic Meeting Den, so it's called, I think."

"You encountered someone who has knowledge of Vanarra de Gonari, but you were looking at a statue."

"Was I, I wonder?" His question, like his look, was probing.

"You're searching for something, Callanar," she pressed gently. "What is it? That is what I wonder."

Deflected from an easier line of questioning, he looked away. "I have spent my entire life as a Vanarran. I was born a Vanarran, raised in the Vanarran traditions, trained and schooled as such, and I served my order as a Vanarran. All the while, I doubted. I would never say it aloud, but I always did. I didn't feel like we were being carried forward by some holy and noble purpose. I felt more as if we were some kind of cobbled-together wheel rolling down a hill – all parts of it moving towards the inevitable. The sustainable perfected species of which I am now a part was supposed to be the bottom of that hill."

"I don't understand."

"You see, I received the gene therapy that made it possible for me to reproduce unassisted, have children like me. I had become – as all of our legends attest – a Perfected One. There was only one problem with that," he noted, looking at her.

"What?"

"I wasn't," he smiled ruefully. "Every morning, getting out of bed, I would be halfway down the hall and realize that I'd forgotten something important. Something I needed for the sol was left in my bed chambers, and I had to return for it. Thankfully, I usually remembered what it was, but more than a moon after the injections, I was still doing that. I wasn't perfect." He looked away with an expression of amusement. "I wasn't even average, some of my order would say. Then I realized the truth; it was all a lie. The wheel had rolled down the hill and come to rest, the prophecy had been fulfilled, and all we did from that moment forward, it seemed, was to utterly come apart – hardly the perfection we were promised."

He looked at her, seriously, and continued. "Then, we were rescued from our own ignorant devotion to a lost ideal, and I do appreciate that, but I find myself again questioning this new world, this Attoria, I find myself in. I look around," and he did so to emphasize the point, "and I see yet another circle, and I wonder is this another wheel being formed? Then I look to its center, and here are you. I felt the impact of what was said to me in that room of the Meeting Den! I don't deny that! I agree with it!" Callanar's words were an impassioned growl, belying his inner torment. "Our beliefs were false beliefs! Our lives were false lives!"

"But you wonder, now?"

He looked at her with an almost predatory ferocity, like a long-caged animal now freed who refused to ever again submit to its former confines. "I wonder if it is not you who will place us again upon a wheel, push us off, and if it is not we who will again come to some pointless spot at the bottom of some hill. If it is not us, then it will be our descendants who do! And you, as a purebred – you, who should have the greatest cause to be angry at and despise us, are sitting here in the middle of this great circle and dispensing advice. It is not just advice, and we both know it! You are dispensing *direction*! I cannot help but ask myself are you setting us up for yet another long fall. Are you doing it using the forms and echoes of our past failings just to make us fodder for the next one?"

She looked at him and nodded, which stunned him into silence. "I use the forms and echoes of your past failures to make sure you never fail again in that way. All history is a pathway, Callanar. All history has a flow. There will always be forward movement of some type guided by the collective choices that are made. My only intent is to keep that movement from repeating the history that defined the Vanarrans. Vanarra de Gonari never intended for you to follow her as a goddess or priestess or whatever. She lived her life, made her contributions, and then it was over. Do you see how that statue in our Meeting Den is different than all of the ones you used to know? Ours is a real size, not exaggerated or distorted. There is a lesson in that I hope everyone here learns."

"What would that lesson be?"

"That none of us is to be worshiped because none of us are worthy of that. None of us, though, can't be helped, can't be loved, can't be guided to be selfless, caring, and everything we would hope. Free, also, but only free in the respect that we do not do harm to others, by omission or commission of an action. This doesn't require a statue of a long dead female, Callanar! It only requires the recognition of something greater than we are!"

"A new god or goddess set above us?"

"I believe in a Creator, but it doesn't have to be that for you. It could be the growth and health of your community. I'm not going to define it."

"You say that, but yet you already have a high priest? Is that not the function this ... Javoth is fulfilling?"

"Javoth is a minister, but his is not the role of high priest. Have you asked after his past?"

"I have not," Callanar replied, a little brusquely.

"Do," she plead with him softly. "He is a broken soul, like any of us. He is just a broken soul who is giving to others, trying to seek forgiveness, and striving to love those around him more than he loves himself."

"And so, does that mean he would look at us in ... what, disappointment?"

"His greatest disappointment was himself. He found a way past that, but it was difficult. If you find yourself on a journey and the way isn't known to you, would you not wish to speak to someone who has gone ahead of you?"

Callanar's countenance settled into an introspective stare. "I can't refute that as good advice, I suppose." He then looked at Vanalla in a very lost way. "We ... need advice from someone, don't we? Desperately?" Van just canted her head at him. "We are aching inside for it. We are burning up for want of it."

"Some of you are burning more than others," she bespoke him in the gentlest of ways. "Some of you carried the burdens of questions you were not permitted to ask, and now you can't take on those kinds of burdens ever again. You need answers; deserve answers, and I and everyone else here will do what we can to provide such."

"But ... what after you leave? What then?"

"My life is in Attoria, Callanar. This is now my home." Truly shocked he put the back of his paw to his mouth and just looked at her. "You thought that we would just get you well enough to farm and fix buildings and then leave? No. We've committed ourselves to this. My adopted sister and her husband are moving here with their two children, soon." His eyes started running with tears.

"No!" he breathed out, feeling suddenly utterly unworthy of the sacrifice she was describing.

"Yes. I will be there, season upon season, for those who join us. I will nurse them to physical health, just as I helped with all of you. I will answer their questions – either like this or in that special room of the Meeting Den."

"And this will be your life? This will be its purpose to be here resurrecting us from the stupidity of our own delusions?"

"Find me anything more meaningful to do, Callanar, and I will," she challenged him. "My children, if I am so favored, will grow and learn alongside yours. I will share your successes. I will share your failures. I will offer you whatever help I can. The hope of Attoria is my hope also, and it is my responsibility, just as it is yours."

The stunned Aelkinda shook his head. "And what great purpose could merit such sacrifice. What is that hope? What will it bring?"

"Aelkinda who live and work and love and laugh alongside Faelnar, Nephti, Vulpi, Pantera, Perratti, Lupar, and all of the other mixes in this world. Aelkinda who contribute and give for no other reason than it is the right thing to do. Aelkinda who take a broken start and turn it into a tradition of service and achievement. Aelkinda who will make the good they do so great that the sins of the past will be acknowledged, understood, and then ... forgotten."

"Even the Great Mother could not claim such amazing beneficence!" he breathed, truly awed.

"And I will not be in this alone. Fireclaw Destiny was a hugely popular, if not infamous at times, primals star. She has forsaken that life and will be here, also. You have met Tashara?" He nodded. "That is her. My Ashalam, Javoth, Laxar, and a host of others are committing to the same."

He turned away from her and held onto the rail behind his back, his chest heaving in great waves as he wept. The soft paw that lighted upon his shoulder nearly made him wail. "We don't deserve this! We don't deserve this kind of sacrifice; we don't!"

"I can't tell you every reason why I know that is not true, my friend, but I believe that if I were to take the sum total of what Aelkinda could add to the cultural wealth of Thuria over the next one thousand seasons, what I and the others are giving up would be more than a fair trade. As I said, find me anything more meaningful to do, and I will."

"I'm sorry," he replied. "I'm sorry for accusing you in the way that I did."

"Don't be." She pulled his shoulder back so that he again faced her. "You have every right to be unsure of us and what we intend. You've had a lifetime to learn that. What I hope is that the time ahead of us will be different. I hope that, sometime in the future, we can collectively make a commitment to be there for one another; that will be the sol when the real hope of Attoria starts to come true."

"It ... is a lot to consider," he breathed, still reeling – this new ground very uncertain beneath his hind paws. "I will make you this commitment, Vanalla Ashallo. I will consider it."

"It's all I can ask," she replied, closing her eyes and bowing slightly to him.

"Good sol to you, then," Callanar offered and then stood and made his way towards the dining hall where several other of the former Vanarrans also making the trek joined him and began what looked to be a very serious conversation. Van watched them go, each one wearing the various clothes that had been donated during the then

"Fireclaw's" fundraising drive, just as Callanar had on. She leaned back and closed her eyes, asking for Tana to let her see them without her appearing to stare at them.

Her consciousness hovering over their conversation, she smiled, hearing Callanar's astonished explanation to the rest of his cohorts. It appeared as if he had been selected as the most articulate and learned "doubter" in the group and had been sent to question the one whose words had impacted every one of their group so thoroughly. "You can do this, Van," her inner Sahnassa offered. "You can be their Great Mother."

"But different than their version, before," she replied. "All I want to do is help them get a new start."

"It's what you're best at," came the reply, "and what we will do for them and for as long as we are able to, my friend."

The rest of that sol came and went with a somewhat notable degree of seclusion on the part of the Vanarrans-come-Aelkinda. Upon the next morning, Tashara caught her coming out of her cabin, Ash indicating he had been asked to take care of some kind of project.

"Hey. Something's going on. Our new arrivals were having a very private and very intense discussion over breakfast, and it's making me anxious. Please tell me that super-sense of yours didn't fall asleep and miss something."

"I think this sol will be a good one," Van reassured her. "I think our friends might have come to a good place. Say, would it be out of line for me to ask you and Javoth to join me for an outside lunch at the gazebo? Say an interval before mid sol or so?"

"I think I can manage it. I'm ... anxious, Van. We have a lot riding on making this work, and as far as I can tell, they all – to a one – went back into the boarding lair."

"It will be alright, but..." Van's head inclined in a certain direction to draw Tashara's eye. "I think I might need a little private discussion time with him, and he's hesitating because he sees you and me together. Don't worry, okay? I'm paying close attention. We're going to be alright, kit. I promise."

"You're the boss. Talk to you later." After a brief hug at the shoulder, the Vulpi-Faelnar mix walked away, and Van made her way towards the Meeting Den.

Just as she reached the door, Laxar joined her. "Good morning."

"Good morning to you, cub. Everything okay?"

"I'd like to speak with you, in private, if I may."

"Certainly. No worries; statue room okay? I was going there in case any of our friends wanted a consult."

"I guess that's me," he replied, following her the rest of the way in silence until the door was closed. A padded bench along the back wall near the door was where they came to rest. Van's gentle stare made him blush and look at the floor until he could actually utter the words he wanted to say, trembling and breathing hard as he did so. "Thank you. Thank you for talking to Vassia and telling her how important it was for me to be ... rewarded by someone who..."

At that moment, he slipped to the floor in front of her and put his head on her knees and wept. "Oh, cub, dear cub," Van offered consolingly, her Faelnar appearance dissolving away as they were alone, her paws reaching for his head and stroking the fur behind his ears. "You deserve to be loved in the way that you need; you dear soul. You deserve nothing less." His eyes looked up at her, his blush fur at full, and he raised up slightly as if he was about to speak. "It requires no apology," she preempted him, "and there is nothing, cub, nothing at all for you to be ashamed of. So long as you two do what every other mated couple should do – namely keep those moments a private thing between the two of you, there will never be any shame in this."

"She touched my inmost soul, Great Mother! She ... closed places in it that were open and wounded! It was like I was bleeding inside and never knew it!"

"And it wasn't the Great Mother who did that, was it? It was your wonderful, caring, and devoted mate," Van told him. "She came to me, as you know, and she was afraid that if she did what was once done to you in the past, it would harm you again, but it did not, did it?"

He shook his head, crying. "I feel so loved! I feel so happy!"

Van's eyes ran with tears hearing the desperate tone in his voice, as of someone almost dead from thirst who finally finds all the water they will ever need. "I love you, cub," she offered, leaning over and kissing him on the top of the head. "You will always be my own, of my family, in the way that it was in the old times. Ash and I will always, always love both you and your precious mate."

He laid his head back on her knees breathing out thank you after thank you, until nearly an interval later, they emerged from the door of the Meeting Den. "I guess no others wanting their time with the Great Mother."

"Father, maybe?" he asked, seeing Javoth walking towards them from across the circle.

"Yeah, looks worried. Our guests have been acting a little secretive this morning, and it just might be something Javoth is inclined to have some concerns about. I'll talk to him, but in the meantime, can you please go get Tashara. I think we'll all need to be here around an interval or so before mid-sol."

"That's not long from now."

"Hurry, then – without visibly appearing to rush. Just go directly; you should have time."

"Yes, and again, with all my heart, thank you."

She gently took his head and kissed the top of it before allowing him to slip away. As Javoth walked up, he noted, "My son seems to be very grateful to you."

"He is. As you might expect, there are small difficulties that crop up whenever any committed relationship is new. It's alright now, and something he'd rather keep private."

"Details I would probably not appreciate?" he asked, mounting the steps and taking a seat opposite her.

"You might, but out of respect for Laxar, I keep his confidence. If he needs to, he will ask. However, I believe he is happy as is Vassia. I don't know that anything else can or should be done."

"Yes, about doing things," he offered softly. "I am concerned that those new to our number might have something in mind for this sol."

"You are concerned?"

He closed his eyes and bowed his head slightly. "I do not wish to think this way, but they already outnumber us greatly."

"Something which will only get more noticeable over time," she commented. "Have you been talking to any of them?"

"Almost all of them have been to see me as I understand the same is true for you."

"It is. Every one. What do they talk about when they come to you?"

"Much of it is … doctrinal. The Sahnassites and Vanarrans were splintered off of the Creator's Path, and in doing so – especially over time – they departed from the tenets of the core faith. In as much as speaking with Laxar has prepared me for this, it has been a true challenge unraveling so much misinformation and spurious traditions, so much that was – it's difficult to describe it. It's like the Creator's Path teachings were a fabric, but in undoing the hem of it, they pulled strands apart, cut off what they didn't like, and added their own threads to create something which is now barely recognizable. Callanar has been somewhat difficult, perhaps the most difficult. He doubts the Vanarran faith and appears to have done so for a long time, but now he places those same doubts on the Creator's Path. He has been difficult to help."

"Much the same here. I've spoken with every one of them. Basically, it's been more about tearing down the false Vanarra and trying to build a new one – the historical version. Same thing – they took what they wanted and added in bits and pieces – not to mention a few dozen cup sizes," she chuckled.

"I've noticed that. I have also noted that even though they speak with both of us," he posited carefully, "they seem to have a greater affinity for you. As conversations have progressed, I notice them looking to you as more than just a symbolic authority – a referential one. I'm beginning to believe that they may seek you as more than just an amateur archivist."

She canted her a head a bit and asked, "What are you suggesting?"

"That they may desire a new Great Mother, and they may desire to reset their stories and mythos based upon you. This could get very lost very quickly. That, however, is not my biggest fear. My biggest fear is that they will outright revolt and take control. Then, our safety may be in danger, and eventually theirs also."

"I don't think that is where this is going," Tashara noted walking up the steps with Laxar. "They are up to something, but taking over and restarting the Vanarran religion? I don't see it."

"Neither do I, Father. My conversations with them have been interesting, but they have been asking more questions about Vanalla than anyone else."

"Which is a relief, if you'll pardon. I'm glad that they didn't just latch onto me for the fact I look like their super awesome spirit mommy of the large chest size."

There was a chuckle from the rest of them as the last two arrivals sat. "Seriously, though. Do we have any definite ideas where this is going?"

"None and-" Van stopped in mid-sentence. "What is my crazy cub doing now?" she asked, watching Ashalam haul a big round metal fire pit insert towards them. As he drew close, she asked, "Cub, for the love of Shasta's pouch – what are you doing with that?"

"I'm just doing what I was asked, very humbly and very politely but very insistently to do." He finished hauling it into position several tracks from the bottom of the steps. "There. Now, they asked me to wait here or … up there, rather."

Van motioned him up to sit beside her, and she hugged and kissed him lightly before her eye caught movement. "Whatever it is, it's beginning. Play it cool, everyone. Don't make any assumptions, or worse, accusations." A long row of Vanarrans dressed in their brown robes, the robes they had arrived in, made their way in single file, orderly proceeding from the boarding lair to the path leading to the gazebo.

"Anyone else praying right now?" Javoth asked, clearly nervous.

"Vassia is with them," Laxar noted, confused. "What is she doing?"

"I think she's showing unity with them, maybe in a way she felt she needed to," Van commented. "She's right behind Vidiana at the end of the line. Patience everyone, hear them out."

"They didn't seem aggressive in the least, earlier," Ash noted, his voice a bit calmer than Javoth or Laxar.

The line of Vanarrans proceeded down the path and broke formation only to make a straight line right beyond the fire pit Ash had placed there. Then, silence reigned for a few moments until Vanalla spoke to them. "What is it we can do for you?" she asked.

Callanar stepped forward from the group and stood at the bottom of the stairs looking up at her. "We have discussed with every one of our number, Vassia included, and we are agreed." Reaching under his neck, he unfastened his robe and removed it, revealing the standard work clothes beneath. Holding the robe over the fire pit for a moment, he told them, "This sol we will commit to you by our solemn vow that we will never again call ourselves Vanarrans. We are the Aelkinda of Attoria, and that is the *only* way we will be known."

All of the others likewise removed their robes, showing themselves similarly attired underneath. To a one, they surrounded the fire pit, some standing two deep, but their arms were outstretched to hang their garments over its metal basin. Callanar looked back at them. "For this vow, we have but one and only one requirement."

"Name it," Javoth requested.

"We will become members of this community only if *she* leads it," he absolutely demanded, pointing at Van with his free paw. "This we have all agreed and will accept no other."

Van looked at Javoth who seemed very concerned by this and turned to face Callanar. "Counter condition," she proposed. "I will always be here to offer guidance, but I am not a replacement for what you used to worship, and if I were to lead you, I would do so only as Attoria is forming. There must be a mechanism for choosing a leader and limiting that leader's power."

"Agreed," Callanar stated firmly, but then looked to Javoth. "We gave serious consideration to asking you, noble preacher of the faith, but it was decided that our faith and our governance – while interrelated – should not be the same. You have been our light of doctrinal truth, but it is Vanalla who has given us the will and reasons why we should live here, why this Attoria matters to us and why it is not only for our survival but our very great hope. Would you agree?" he asked.

After a few moments, Javoth slowly nodded, seeming to have come to the decision with difficulty.

"It is done then," Callanar offered, dropping his robe into the metal basin, being followed immediately by the others doing the same. Several books and papers were also pulled out and added to the pile. "Vassia, if you would be so kind?"

She stepped forward and looked at Laxar apologetically. "It was a step I needed to take, and … I was the only one who could actually do this." She turned, knelt, and set the hem of the nearest garment ablaze. The fire grew slowly and smoked black and acrid as the synthetic fabric started to catch.

"Okay, so … my first bit of direction as your leader is to have us all get away from that thing about twenty paces or so. It's going to smell."

There was a bit of chuckling as they all stepped away and formed a group together. "I sense a … (cough) … refinement may need to be made to that particular bit of ceremony!" Callanar offered, waving the smoke from his eyes as the wind blew it. "Although a bad smell is appropriate, considering…"

"Would you have all new arrivals do this?" Javoth asked.

"It is something I thought right," Callanar stated. "With these robes and our former doctrine being destroyed, we've severed our ties to that belief and our pasts. I don't know if all of us are fully ready to embrace the Creator's Path, but we are fully letting go of what we knew before. Oh, and to that end, *Leader*," he stated, addressing Vanalla. "Here are a series of letters signed and encoded in such a way that those still of the Vanarran faith will be honor-bound to appreciate their authenticity. These are to all of the temples we know of or where we know someone who is a member there. These state, categorically and earnestly, what we have learned in Attoria, that this is a place a refuge, a place of hope, and a place to find a new future."

"Thank you, Callanar. That will certainly be helpful. Tashara, can you please make sure these get where they are supposed to go?"

"As you say, *Leader*," came the response, picking up on Callanar's honorarium.

"Leader?" Van asked. "I'm not sure of that as an appropriate title. It could mean many things, and I wish-"

"What?" Callanar questioned.

"Kept by and keeper of. It's what I want for you, for me, and for all of us. We are not only a village of individuals, are we? We are becoming a family, I think."

"It would serve," Vidiana noted, her eyes widening. "We placed our faith in the perverted and misshapen image of the Great Mother, but what she really was in her time was *Matriarch* – leader of her family. We are not big enough for both civil and familial government, but you have said it. I would – I feel the need for that, even if my family is led by a Faelnar."

"I feel that same need," Javoth offered, looking to Vanalla. "I have given some thought to our discussions over time, and we've spoken about the benefits Thurians have missed in the absence of families."

"Well," Callanar noted, "maybe here is where we try such a thing. Kept by and keeper of is of deeper meaning and moment than a mere citizen. We also, some of us, may choose a new faith, but we need a deep tie that transcends that freedom and still maintains us."

"That is the definition of what families have been and what they are to be," Vanalla told them, and her manner of speaking in that moment was striking. It was the calm and absolute assurance of someone who believed to her tail-tip in what she was telling them, and her conviction held them spellbound. "Families teach us that while we may have different vocations or preferences or even faiths, there is a connection and interrelationship we share with one another. It is primal; it is deep; it is instinctual, and it is something that is truly and utterly Thurian. We are keeper of and kept by, kept by and keeper of – there is no wrong order for that when it is said. If it were possible, both should be said equally because they are always true, equally. We then take this familial relationship and seal it with a promise of truth and valor and steadfastness. Honor to all, honor from all, honor above all. It is our pledge. It is our requirement. It must be our identity as individuals, as well as a community. It is who we are, what we are, and what we must be," she gently conveyed to them, her voice falling to almost a whisper at the last.

Callanar's lower lip was quivering, and his eyes were gaping with astonishment. "Hon ... Honored One," he whispered, but then said louder, "Yes, Honored One."

Tashara reached forward and placed her paw upon Van's shoulder. "Honored One."

"Honored One," Vassia offered, stepping forward and stating it evenly – fully supporting but also fully demanding.

"We will see," Vanalla told them all. "We don't have any grand designs here other than becoming a community, a family who works and lives together – all of us for the benefit of the others more than for ourselves. Leave those kinds of titles alone, for now. Think of me as the village matriarch, if it suits. If we were to ever gather enough of us together to be called a house, we would have to seek the approval of the other houses. However, if that is the direction we wish to go, I can help make sure we don't do anything that would – of itself – disqualify that goal. Now," she said with a sly smile, "there are plants that need tending, fields that need preparing, and some letters which need to be delivered. Let's get the work done … and eat dinner together."

"Like a family?" Laxar put in.

"Like a family," Vanalla agreed, and there were many hugs intermingled with thanksgiving before the group finally departed to begin their work on the future of Attoria.

Seven moons had come and gone since the first set of robes were burned in the central circle of the village of Attoria. After the first group of twenty-nine Vanarran garments and their accompanying religious texts had been incinerated, more refugees came, convinced by the letters of appeal offered by Callanar and the others. After the construction of a more permanent monumental fire pit soon after those arrivals, it's first use hadn't waited for more than ten sols before fifty-nine more robes were added to those of the first group – no Vanarran robes remained anywhere in Attoria. To a one, no Aelkinda existed who had not been before the statue of their once Great Mother and been brought to a new understanding of who she truly was. For some, it was a quiet and thoughtful transition, but many were as fierce and raw as what Vidiana experienced.

Later, when they were shaken and uncertain, they would come to notice that it was a purebred Faelnar who led them, but it wasn't one removed from the duties of the sol. She got down in the dirt, planting and weeding. She helped sew donated cloth into garments and sat with them when they were ill, but mostly, she just listened. Some, at first, wanted one of their own number as a leader, one like them. Callanar and the others just asked for patience and that the new arrivals watch the Faelnar, sol by sol. "She … treats us like her own, as if our importance exceeded any concern of hers," one had said.

"That is why she has become our matriarch, in *fact* if not in official title," Callanar and the others had responded. Inside of ten sols, there wasn't a one of the new arrivals who had not pledged themselves to follow her. Within twenty more sols, the Attoria village was starting to take shape as a legitimate working and breathing community. Five sols later, a group of one hundred and seventeen refugees was brought in, and as before, the Attorian Aelkinda cared for them, the gentle direction of Vanalla Ashallo leading them forward.

As Vanarra, in Faelnar form, waited in the gazebo, she looked at the numbers of new arrivals passing back and forth before her. "Seven hundred and fifty-seven, with more coming," she thought, as now familiar sounds came to her ears. The banging of hammers and all other manner of tools continually buzzed in the background as new dwellings were coming into being to house their ever-rising numbers. While some of Tashara's contractors were certainly among their number, those were doubled by the paws of Attorians wanting to contribute to building their own future.

"It takes shape now, the future does," a familiar voice called to her from the bottom of the steps.

"It does, Me Sha," Van replied, knowing that he would have erected force barriers to keep both his presence and any evidence of it from view. "It's so good to see you!"

The male Nephti with the piercing blue eyes walked up to meet her and hugged her, earnestly. "It is very good to see you, my daughter, and good to see you doing a Teldear's work!"

"Constantly worried, though," she told him, breaking away.

"Worried? About what?"

They sat together, and Van took a moment to compose herself. "When I started this mission, it was made *very* clear to me that there were to be no big heroes. You see what's happening here? I don't think we're going to get to some magic number where they'll just take over leadership. It feels like they want me to lead them … for a long time."

"You are the Great Mother, their *authentic* Great Mother, now," he told her. "What that means, though, has been completely redefined, but redefined by you! You are shattering any idea of what they understood authority and leadership to be. Your rank as leader is what you use to *serve* them, give to them. Is Ash happy with this arrangement?"

She looked at the floor, her blush fur rising. "He's proud of me, Dad. He's … proud of me. He's told me that."

"As well he should be," he offered earnestly. "Understand that there are huge heroes like the Heroines of the Meeting Den, the Most Honored of All Matrons-"

"Oh, stop!" Van whispered, frowning sourly, one corner of her mouth twitching up because she knew it was a tease.

"This time, I believe it to be different. They could call you the Founder of Attoria, but you're not – at least as far as the public knows. That was Fireclaw who became Tashara and then disappeared into the normal workings here. They could call you the Great Mother of Attoria, but it wouldn't be apt since you are *clearly* a Faelnar – a purebred through and through."

"So how will they remember me?"

"What are you doing? That is how they will remember you. Also, consider the very reason this place exists – it is to recover from the mistaken actions of idolizing someone. That is a lesson you have taught, that you can continue to reinforce, and that you can document clearly and concretely so those coming behind you have no doubt about you and your intentions. I would think that … later on, you know, that you consider putting that sentiment in stone somewhere around here. This spot is becoming more and more what it should be – the center of this place not only physically, but spiritually, in a way. See that gap there?" Van nodded. "A good place for a chapel, I think."

"A good place for a very firm and unmistakable warning, too," she considered aloud. "I … also want to remember Flint in some small way. When … when they're ready, I want them to build it exactly to his original specifications. Nothing bigger, nothing grander."

"Javoth would agree with you, I'm sure."

"But Theo, I am really worried about doing the wrong thing here! My … Sahni and Tana all felt right about this course, about me being leader here, but it still could go horribly wrong! What do I need to look out for? What should I be doing?"

He looked at her and gently shook his head. "I didn't raise a daughter who needed guard rails her entire life. Do you realize that by sending you back here I was not only approving of your readiness for *this specific mission*, but the Supreme Council was, as well, doing the same and in vast majority?"

"No easy answers, then; I have to make the decisions," she stated softly, looking away, but then cut her eyes back at him. "Not … unanimously, though."

"Nyssia was unconvinced, but then again that was why it was important to pair Saletta with her. I believe that my colleague – while willing to go along with my choice, thought that others, such as Dynaea, might be better. In a way, Nyssia is having her way, yes, with Dynaea taking the lead on the larger planetary matters, but she has confided to me, privately, that she now believes in you. She has grown quite fond of Saletta, and not as a curiosity or worse, as a pet, but as a friend and, perhaps, even a … daughter, of sorts."

"What did Saletta do that made the difference?"

He looked at her, a little regretful. "It isn't a good story, in some respects. Saletta served out a prison sentence on a world for taking the risk to save someone's life who was considered disposable. Nyssia offered to free her, but Saletta would have none of it. Your former dame realized that her presence in that cell was causing a slow change, but a very critical one. She was in that cell for more than a season, by your time measurement. Everyone … everyone in that prison knew her and came to love her. Moreover, her story leaked out to the populace. In anger, the government had her executed."

"But she's not dead! I saw her!"

"Nyssia allowed Saletta to think that if she chose to face the sentence, it would be the end for her, but as I swapped a dying substitute body for Saletta's when I renewed her, Nyssia did the same once again. Allarrae live, as you know, for a very long time, and it is easy – far too easy, sometimes – to believe that we have found *the* right way, that our view of the universe is correct and fits all possible situations. When she saw your friend face death by impaling because of what it would mean to the oppressed and powerless, her respect for your dear friend and for you and for Thurians grew. Grew *substantially*."

"What a brave, brave kit," Van breathed. "Is Saletta okay, now?"

Theo nodded. "I think she got a sense of exactly how shaken Nyssia was with her willingness to sacrifice, and Saletta felt the affection and respect. I believe it has put them together in the way that you and I are together."

"So, she gets a … mother?" Theo nodded. "That means Saletta can or … will ascend?"

"I would bet on it," he replied, knowingly. "And the two of you – well summing that up a bit – will have new and marvelous adventures you can't even imagine as of yet. It may even come to pass that I have you acting as senior Teldear if or maybe when I grant her that title. In truth, Nyssia has already mentioned it."

"Wow! That … that is very happy news, Me Sha!" Van whispered, rubbing tears from the corners of her eyes.

"I thought so, too, and … it will help temper the warning I have to give you and the work that comes from it. Everything I see of Attoria is working well and in order, but the outside world doesn't know that. They are becoming worried by ominous signs and unanswered questions as more and more *Vanarrans* head to the *isolated Vanarran Enclave* of Attoria. This Attoria has, of course, been paid for by the generous donations of peace-loving Thurians, even those Thurians who donated despite having their children and other loved ones harmed by that evil cult."

Van listened to what he was saying, and then it clicked. "The Newsarotzi."

"Right first time. The political scene is relatively stable, and the houses are moving just slowly and carefully enough to escape their venom. So, ratings-starved Newsarotzi are now looking for something – anything to keep their ad revenues up and their shareholders happy. It didn't take them long to go to their archival recordings of those wonderful sols of yester-season when ratings were clawing right through the ceiling and advertisers were locked in a wholesale bidding war to get half a pass of time on the local news. Oh, for those glorious times when the Sahnassites were tearing into the Vanarrans!"

"You, Me Sha, are pretty cynical, sometimes," Van observed. "Has it really gotten as bad as all that?"

"The gathering of news, unless it's paid a flat fee from taxes and its budget is made inviolable, doesn't stand any real chance of not being driven by such forces. Even Alanar's leadership has been pressuring for him to stop *soft-pawing* Attoria. A number of other news organizations are beginning to chafe that Alanar is the favored son of the leadership, here. They are even starting to suggest that he might be part of some deeper conspiracy to mislead Thurians as the Vanarrans recover, regroup, and rally for an even more damaging strike straight to the soul of Thurian society."

"Great stars, Theo! Really?! Damn, that's incredibly low, not to mention absolutely inaccurate and unfair!"

"In the absence of facts, theories abound, and it is the nature of all who fear pain and those who profit on their fear to vigorously invent potential dangers. We all know those who can't help but be unhappy. Solve all their problems, and they yet bemoan their happiness and cower. It is a difficult truth, but as Rahnahi said…"

"Ignorance feeds fear," Van observed. "We have to open up, explain what's happening here – show what's happening. That's … going to take some coaching and prepping of our citizens. There are still some who are very new. Asked the right questions, and-"

"And you'll get the truth as they see it. That's the problem – they can't be helped *or* coached. They can only be told of what is happening and asked to participate. They should participate honestly, even if it is damaging. A work in progress is not finished and is necessarily imperfect. That describes Attoria very well. Thurians will expect to see imperfection even though you are very happy and a little proud of how things are going. You can be – you know. Well, that and you're awesomely well taught."

She shook her head. "Theo!" she groaned, leaning into him. "Well, I can certainly tell we're going to have to start a donors' newsletter of some type – something I'm sure Tasha knows about or can find out."

"Don't forget Dynaea," he warned. "They can help, but it's up to you to manage the situation on the ground. Oh, dear Van – my daughter. This time is specifically why I wanted you for this. Not only are you the right leader for all of these," he asserted, motioning expansively to the groups of Aelkinda walking back and forth between their duties, "but you are also the right leader to manage the outsiders. If you need me, let me know. I can help, but…"

"I think I know what I have to do, Me Sha," Van told him, nodding her head. "Newsletter, group discussions with our citizenry, our … family, and then an open visit from several in the newsarotzi segment. It won't make them happy, though, if we prove there is no story here."

"Maybe, you can prove to the right ones there is a story here and a good one. To the wrong ones, work with Dynaea. Perhaps, she can dig up a little freelance corruption – a juicy bone to throw their way."

"I will. Thank you, Me Sha," she offered, reaching around him and hugging him. With a wink, he was gone.

Chapter 19: Preset Agendas

The Hope of Attoria," Tasha breathed aloud as she looked over the first version of their newsletter. "I hope it captures what you wanted."

Van picked it up and looked at the hard-copy that had been printed out in the administration building. "Vidiana?" she asked, pointing at one of the amazing sketches Laxar had done.

"Her story, about how her heart turned from the Vanarran way and found a better path. She's not a bad speaker for this place, and she introduces the feeling of family that's become a part of that, *Honored One*," the former primal star teased, knowing that she could get away with it.

There was as smirk returned for her trouble, but Van kept reading. "Not bad, *Fireclaw*."

"Oh, you're just playing ugly, now!" Tasha complained.

Van chuckled and continued to check through the document. "Current numbers, current stats – including deaths? I suppose we should. It's not many, but that should prove a little chilling to the hot pursuit of a wildly resurgent and dangerous community of Vanarrans. What's the distribution channel?"

"The entire donor list, but the way these things work about a fifth will be returned. We need to find someone either in the Aelkinda community or a volunteer who can do a little relationship management and so on. What is it?"

"They aren't waiting," Van sighed. "Kylie just piped into my head and let me know we're going to have a couple of newsarotzi poking into our business here, hiking in."

"Hikers? Really? The border fence for this area is courses away."

"Secret cameras, microphones – all at the wood-line in about three quarters of an interval."

"They from a major station?"

"Freelance, looking for a quick pick-up, a nice package story, probably full of shadowy figures, half-heard conversations – enough to create fear and angst. I ... wonder."

Tasha watched as the Faelnar started tapping her chin, clearly in deep thought, and she looked at Van warily as the edges of Van's mouth started to turn up. "Uh, that look scares me to freaking death, Van! Stop it!"

"What?"

"That damned sly smile of yours! I saw it one too many times in the freaking Shanandrae Commons hospital, and now look what's happened to me!"

Van chuckled. "I'm not thinking about you, oh fiery one. I've got my eye on the couple coming in our direction." Closing her eyes, she considered aloud, "She's outfitted pretty well, but the poor cub. He's not a strong hiker, and those power packs are pretty weighty. Also, as these two are potential threats to those I protect, I think I'll order a light back scan." Tasha sat, a little awed that in the few moments they were sharing, most of two Thurians' lives were being placed under a magnifying glass. Van's eyes were closed as she could now interpret the backscan largely in real-time. "Not a bad sort. A little desperate, the two of them – hence the stunt. I wonder."

When Van opened her eyes, Tasha was standing up and staring right at her, and she walked dead in front of the Faelnar. "You're about to change their lives, aren't you?!" came the harsh whisper.

"I'm going to do the same thing for them that I did for you – offer up a choice."

"Are you sure you're headed the right way!?" the black on black Pantera with worried brown eyes hissed as he stumbled behind the nearly snow-white female Lupar pushing her way down what appeared to be not much more than a grazer trail in the forest, a darkening sky above them.

"I am," she said, confidently, holding up her PawLink with its extra power pack and antenna assist attached. "Just like the last two times you asked me since we jumped the fence."

He just shook his head, regretting more and more his decision to help the freelancer, Malliana Dorsi, get "covert VidStar of what really goes on in the village of Attoria." At this point, he suspected that the village was host to a lot of eating and sleeping and bodily functions, and not much more. He had his own doubts about how much of a concern a group of several hundred former Vanarrans could actually be. Everyone knew they were here, and enforcement organizations from all of the surrounding districts were constantly on the alert for any trying to escape the "Vanarran Reservation" as some had called it. He had done freelance VidStar work for a long time, but usually just as an add-on videographer at press events or program shoots or the like. As he stumbled on a root going across the ground and strained to recover, he wished desperately to be back at his last video shoot – a commercial for a fur dresser. The females there were trying to be appealing, and in fact, certainly were.

It wasn't that Kennar didn't find Malliana appealing so much as she had stung him quick with her no nonsense, not paying for poor results philosophy. She seemingly wasn't interested in anything more than a story. "Damn," he swore again as loose pea gravel gave way under his hind paws, causing his stride to lengthen to an almost painful distance, his elbow actually scraping an outcropped boulder as he tried to right himself.

"You alright?" Malliana asked, clearly becoming wearied by his performance. "Should I have hired someone else?"

"I'm beginning to wonder!" he replied hotly. "After all, there wasn't a damned thing about all of this extracurricular crap on your ticket." It was a point she had to concede, and it meant that he just had regular paw shoes as she was equipped with the latest hikers that went almost all the way up her ankle.

"That's why the pay is nice," she told him, glancing over her shoulder as she pressed ahead. "But if you get hurt, and I – ah!" Suddenly, there was no ground to walk on, and she was suddenly falling for about three tracks when her hind paw struck a stone banging her joint hard and making her yelp as she tipped forward into a muddy stream bed. The rest of her body banged into the ground so hard it knocked the wind out of her, and her vision swam. Just while she was trying to right herself, she heard the Pantera behind her yell in surprise and heard a mass of sounds as things were loosed and felt to the ground all around her, one of them banging into the back of her head.

"Oh, ow!" she groaned out, her whole body aching. She wasn't sure, but she thought she heard stifled curses through clenched teeth from the male behind her. Lifting, with some effort, her muddy muzzle from the mire, she looked back to see the Pantera lying on his back, holding his arm. The amount of pain he was in recommended itself to her when she tried to flex and move her right hind paw. "Oh, dammit! Oh, that … the freaking hurts! I … I think I broke it!"

"Yeah, freaking surprise that!" he spat back. "What I get for trying to run to catch you! Mange ridden crap! That … has to be broken!"

"How … bad, I wonder?" she asked, largely concerned about herself, but turning over allowed her to see him trying to take the same kind of inventory. Feeling along her leg, she was at least comforted by the fact that no bones were poking through the skin, and although it was swelling, there weren't the gravelly sensations of a bundle of broken bones. "Mine is a clean break, I think. Still in place."

"Same … same here, but damn it hurts!" he wept. For a while, neither of them spoke as wind began blowing around them. It wasn't until the rain began actually pelting them that they started to apprehend their true danger. "We … we have to get out," he told her. "Look where we are. Stream bed. That – if that's a lot of rain…" Almost in response to his words, the skies opened a harsh torrent straight down upon them.

Malliana watched as the stream started to fill in the Lupar-shaped impression she had just made. Looking towards the walls of the stream bed, she blinked as the realization struck her. "Flood … line," she screamed at him, pointing.

"We have to get out of here!" he repeated.

"No shit!" she screamed back. "But I can't walk!"

Reluctantly, he moved towards her, keeping his throbbing forearm in the middle of his chest. Reaching out a paw, he grimaced as they both strained, trying to get her to a standing position. As he jarred his injured arm, Kennar almost screamed, but to his credit, he didn't let her drop again into the muddy soup all around them.

Once reasonably stable, her injured right paw hoisted above the ground, she watched in despair as the Lupar-shaped impression started overflowing, the downpour driving all surrounding water into the little pit she had made by falling in. "We … we have to go! This is going to fill up!"

"Yeah, no shit, like you said," he growled back at her. As they both desperately looked around, they could see no other alternative other than making their way downstream. "We're screwed!"

"We can still try – but … the gear!"

"It's all busted and scattered all over!" he told her, looking around. "I can't see any of it!"

She sighed realizing that part of the contract she had signed made her responsible for any accidental losses in his equipment. At least, she thought, they still had their packs. "Which direction?" she asked.

He looked up and down the stream bed, and from his viewpoint, the walls only got steeper, upstream, but downstream there looked to be some better chances. "Let's try this way," he told her, and slowly, they started to slog along, the rain still pelting hard upon them. Every few steps, one of them would yelp as an arm or leg was jostled, but progress came to them – if slowly. As water actually started to stream around their hind paws, they looked at each other, now uncertain if their survival wasn't already out of reach.

"So, I told him," Callanar explained to the two other Attorians, "that we have been extraordinarily blessed, despite all of our wrongs over the seasons, to *have* a place to shelter in. He told me that he wished himself dead, and I told him that I understood that feeling."

"Twas one I shared," Vassia agreed as she looked beyond the new pavilion that sheltered them from the appallingly heavy deluge coming from the skies. "I wanted that several times."

Vidiana nodded, shaking her head and looking up at the wood-textured plasti-planks above them. Above that, she knew, was at least a couple of tracks of sloping soil and freshly planted grass. "It's not that loud, this roof."

"It's why we went with the naturally terraced ceiling. Seemed like a bit of an excess for a mere pavilion," Callanar agreed, "but it's keeping us nice and dry and able to enjoy a conversation. We built it and were given the freedom to do so as we saw fit. I plan to tell our despairing new arrivals that. I mean look around at all of the things that we, with our own paws, have built! These ... these things are uniquely ours!"

"Laxar's designs are ... startling," Vidiana conceded. "Dear, please forgive me any slight or rude comment I said about you two. You seem very happy together."

"I find our relationship more fulfilling than anything I've ever felt in my life," Vassia noted, looking away and smiling, her blush fur riding higher. "He's been like that bridge to me, a way across that I – wait! What – is that just grass blowing in the wind?"

Callanar stood, looking intensely at the area. "Grass doesn't have white fur! There's someone in the stream bed!"

"In this rain?" Vidiana croaked. "That becomes a real gusher during a downpour! I watched it once as we were putting the roof on that! Come on!"

As the three of them darted towards the stream, they could now hear the cries of those trapped below. "Help! Help us, please! Help us!" came a panicked female's shrill voice.

Running up to the edge and squatting to look over, they could barely see the white paw desperately jutting above the surface. "We're here! We hear you!" Callanar shouted back to them. "Vidiana, I can't see them without falling over myself. I think I remember an emergency box we rigged inside the bridge. See if you can catch a glance where they are and maybe find some rope!"

"I will!"

As they watched Vidiana sprint for the bridge, Vassia turned to him. "Callanar, if I lie down flat, I might be able to reach her without hazarding falling in. Can you hold my hind paws?"

"Let's do it," he told her, and soon she was edging towards the side seeing the white paw jutting up at random and erratic intervals. However, as she came closer, a large trough of dirt sank down beneath her. Callanar pulled her back just as a huge plug of soil dropped into the bed, a scream issuing from beneath them as it fell.

"Again!" she demanded over the rain, and he agreed. This time, as she crawled, she could see her intended quarry down the narrow trench this mini-landslide had created. "I see her! I see two of them!" she called back. Looking down, she saw a terrified face looking back up at her, her paws grasping tightly to an exposed root that was the only thing keeping her from falling back down into the rapidly flowing brownish black waters below. Well below her, a black Pantera male braced himself against the stream bank as well as he could, but the waters were starting to flow at a volume that could easily dislodge him and carry him away.

"I have rope!" Vidiana called to her.

She turned back and yelled, "The one below is about to lose his hind paws! Anchor the rope and throw it over just to my right side! I'll try to reach the one above with my paw!"

Looking back at the female, she screamed, "Pull up hard and grab my paw!"

"My ... my leg is broken!"

"Push with your good leg!" Vassia demanded. The statement struck the white Lupar as just common sense enough to work, but she realized that if she did as she was being told and missed, there would be no hope for her. "I will catch you! I will catch you if you go now!"

Frantic and panicked, the female Lupar did what she was told and nearly howled with pain as two sets of expressed claws sank into the flesh of her arm – a desperate move which had allowed the female above her to get a good and solid grip. Just then, a rope flew over the side towards the male below who was literally beginning to slip. Just as his hind paws went, he grasped the rope as the females above watched.

"Pull us up! He has the rope!" she shouted back, but now there were two sets of paws, one on each of her legs. Gently and slowly with Vassia trying hard not to wound the female Lupar any further, the two were hauled up. The first moment she could let go, Vassia did and went under the other female's armpit, blood clearly on her claws as they swept past her vision. In a moment, her other arm went under the female's other shoulder, laying her head alongside.

"Oh gods, thank you! Thank you! Kennar! Please, save Kennar!" she yelped as both were finally pulled further away from the edge.

"Tie it around you!" one of them shouted down at him, a mixed blood Lupar-Perratti.

"He can't!" Malliana shouted back. "His arm is broken!"

"Hold this and get ready to pull when I call up!" With that, the mixed blood was over the side using the rope to guide him down. Several long moments went by with nothing being said until there was a very strong shout, "Pull us up now! Quickly!"

With seven Thurians pulling at the rope, it rose swiftly and then stopped. "About a track of slack, please!" They gave it, and the aspect of the rope changed, now angled out. "Okay, pull slowly!" came the direction, and again the word was heeded. Ashalam's head appeared first, and then he helped the black Pantera onto level ground.

"I ... I was going to die! I was going to die! Thank you; thank you!" the shaking male bleated from the ground next to Ash.

"Let's get them inside," Callanar called, gently helping the female to her hind paws and offering his body as support. "Can you go get her? We're going to need her."

"I will," Ash replied and patted the chest of the male. "You're fine now. We'll take good care of you. Go with them, and I'll bring some more help."

As the pair was helped away, they watched Ash turn and head towards one of the cabins barely visible in the distance. "Her?" Malliana thought, fighting to think through the pain of her broken leg. She was grateful that Kennar was curious also.

"Her?" he asked Callanar. "Who is he going to go get?"

Callanar made no answer until they were under the shelter of the boarding lair. "She is the one we look to for leadership in this place, guidance, and she knows a great many things."

A worried glance passed between the two new arrivals as others from inside the lair brought towels and tried to help rescued and rescuer alike. In a few passes, both were settled in different rooms on the second level and awaited the coming of this leader or guide as ice was applied to her broken leg. Malliana tried to shake off the pain and think, tried turning on the journalistic part of her mind which was wilting beneath the pain she felt. It wasn't something she could manage for even a few connected ticks. "There, there," a soft voice comforted her. "Do you have any allergies, kit?"

"No, not ... not that I know of."

"Okay; I'm going to give you something to blunt the pain. Just try to relax." In a pass, a cool sensation at her upper arm told her that she was being given an injection, and her strained breathing started to lessen almost immediately. "That will help. Now, I'm going to cut your trousers off of you. Don't worry. We have something for you to wear when this is over."

"Thank ... thank you," Malliana said, finally coherent enough to actually start to look at this visitor who still wore a cowl over her head. "Who are you?"

Golden brown paws pushed the cowl back, and a purebred Faelnar's face greeted hers, and the appearance of a full purebred amongst all of the mixes and super mixes she had seen since being rescued was a little jarring to her. Golden eyes appraised her, kindly but fully. "My name is Vanalla. And you are?"

"Malliana Dorsi," she confessed and then instantly regretted it. "So much for a fake identity to cover us in case we get caught," she thought.

Vanalla took the scissors and started cutting off the female's pants, working her way from the hem of the lower leg up towards her groin. As the scissors cut, the Lupar felt a little anxiety as they came close to her injury. "And so, Malliana Dorsi, why did you and your companion just happen to be in the restricted fenced off area around Attoria?"

The scissors were so close to the aching and biting pain in her leg that she was a little too terrified to answer with anything other than the truth. "I'm a freelance newsarotzi!" The admission was made with some degree of stress as the metal sheers were kept carefully away from the injury. Although the questioning wasn't an interrogation under torture, it wasn't hard to wonder about the possibility.

"Freelance, meaning you go looking for a story, package it, and then hope there's someone to pay you at the end. At the end, unless you've already got some money down from an interested party who wants you to find a story, right?"

The cutting of the trousers was now very close to the Lupar's intimate areas, and a slip could cut more than just her underthings by accident. "Yeah, yeah, please … please be careful!" Malliana begged.

"Be still and answer quietly – that will help. I still have the other leg to do," Van told her, and the Lupar's head sank back into the sheets as the scissors finally snicked through the waistband material.

Once again, the scissors were positioned near her uninjured leg's hind paw and began their journey up. "So, you are a freelance newsarotzi here in search of a story. Well, you will probably find one, I suspect." The easy admission caught her off guard, and she leaned up to look at the Faelnar carefully working to remove her soaked trousers. "I'm glad they put down towels before laying you down. It would have gotten your bed all wet."

"My bed?" she asked. "Aren't you going to call for some kind of medical evacuation or…"

A nearly stern look in her direction as the scissors were again poised near her crotch silenced her. "Not sure. It's a broken leg, not a heart attack, and that will keep for a bit. If I can scan it and see that it's a pretty simple break, it would be better to just immobilize you and give you something for the pain and swelling until the weather improves. Then, we can arrange transportation. I presume that somewhere beyond the fence-line you have a vehicle?" There was a feeble nod as the snick went through her waistband. "Let me get your tail free," she was told and endured the humiliation of feeling the soft paw of the Faelnar working in behind her and loosing the fasteners near the base of her tail.

In a moment, she was lying there in just her under-things below the waist line, blush fur up so high it nearly hurt. The golden eyes studied her leg very carefully before she raised up and retrieved a portable scanner. Slipping the components above and below the injury, Van explained, "One of the benefits of having a sponsor who was a professional athlete. They know about field-ready medical gear. So, let's have a look." Van looked into the scanner as the female tensed, trying to stay still. "You can relax and breathe, kit, it's good enough to manage that. Looks ... doesn't even look broken, actually except ... right there. Yep, simple fracture – won't be hard to set, not that painful. You were very fortunate. We can take good care of you. With any luck, you'll be able to rest here for a few sols, and then we can help you retrieve your vehicle and perhaps have someone drive you both out to ... where? Shanandrae?"

"Yes."

"You know, if you just sneak in here, all brazen, break your leg, get trapped in a flooding creek, get your leg fixed up and just ... leave, there isn't going to be much of a story, is there?"

"It's something," the Lupar said weakly as the scanner was put to the side.

"Yeah, but you've got no depth, no details," Van told her, as if in mere casual interest. "I mean, don't take this the wrong way, but you being solid white and your camera mount being solid black, you two weren't just going to dance in here among us undetected. Did you really intend to just skulk about on the edges, get VidStar, and whisper tensely for the viewers about what you were seeing?"

Malliana looked up at her, eyes wide and mouth agape. She started to speak, but by then, Van had positioned herself below the ankle of the injured leg. "Hold it right there. Not a good idea to lie to someone who is about to set your leg. Brace yourself now. There's going to be some serious pain for a tiny bit – oh, but first," Van said, turning to the door over her shoulder. "Vassia, could you please let the camera mount know that we're about to set Malliana's leg. She will probably not be all that quiet about it. We don't want him to panic."

A muffled voice came from behind the door. "Fair warning appreciated – he's already arrived at panic. Ash is trying to calm him down. Give us a pass, and I'll let you know."

"Thank you, Vassia!" Van offered.

"Was she?"

"One of the ones who rescued you, yes."

"No, I mean, yes, but was she once a ... Vanarran?"

"Once," Van repeated softly. "In the middle of the town center, they've erected a fire pit where those who decide to renounce the Vanarran ways can burn their robes, their scrolls, and their sacred texts."

"They've done that?"

"Everyone who is here. We're sort of between batches of new arrivals."

Vassia's voice came from behind the door. "He wants to see her."

"He's not going to see me, I'm nearly freaking naked. Can you open the door, please?"

Van shrugged. "Sure."

Once the door was opened, the brown eyed Vassia looked down at her. "Pardon me, I'm going to yell," she warned the super mix. "Kennar, dammit, I'm nearly naked, and they're going to set my leg. Can you just chill out, please?!?!" she screamed.

There was a long pause, and a somewhat feeble shout back returned, "Oh ... okay."

"I think he likes you," Van told her softly as the door was shut.

"Yeah, not the most attractive of Lupar pelts here," Malliana croaked as her head fell back. "I generally do my reporting from off camera."

"You shouldn't be judged by that," Van told her. "I very much doubt Kennar is judging you by that. He shows the anxiety one would have over a close relation or even a ... mate."

"Please, he has to hate me. I drug him into this."

"That you may have," Van contested as she positioned herself, then the leg, and then her paws, carefully. "But then you two went through a harsh trial together. For a while, you were all each other had. That makes impressions on males ... and females."

"He's not my type," Malliana offered dismissively. "Wrong species for me."

"And yet I have joined myself to a Lupar Perratti mix," Vanalla told her. "I looked past his outside, which I still have to admit I find really attractive and looked at the kind soul on the inside. Now, you can't answer back right now."

"Why?"

"Because I need your tongue safely in your mouth with your muzzle shut. I need you to brace yourself for the pain. It should only be a few ticks, but … it won't be good at all. Ready?" Malliana, trembling, nodded and leaned back, grasping the sheets on either side of her. "One, two, three," Van told her and pulled. The female Lupar's whole body tensed and arched slightly at the pain, but the Faelnar's movements were quick and exact, and in only two ticks, the pressure was released, the pain going with it.

Malliana, however, was reduced to tears. "There, there," Van told her as she started to wrap and splint the leg for support. "That was perfect. I could tell. Nothing to be afraid of. With a little patience and a little exercise, it will completely heal." Despite these reassurances, the Lupar kept quietly crying whilst her leg was wrapped. Van slipped up to the Lupar's head and put a paw on top between the folded back ears and gently rubbed. "What's wrong, Malliana?"

"I … I came out here to … get VidStar to make this … place seem secret, and … scary. Now we're hurt, and you're helping us, but I still don't know if I can trust you and-"

"Yeah, we've been too quiet and inwardly focused. It's a lot of work helping a whole community that was misled their entire lives find a better path, especially when they come to us in such bad condition. It's difficult to do public relations and that job at the same time. In time, you will understand that it will be alright. You won't know that or trust us until you see that you can. As for now, try to get some rest and … don't you come unhinged when I set Kennar's arm. Okay?"

"Okay," came the whispered response as the Lupar looked down at her leg, properly and completely bandaged.

"If you need help getting to the facilities, call for Vassia. She can help you." An embarrassed head nod was all she got in return.

As Vanalla left, Malliana stated "Thank you" as best she could, to which Van also offered a gentle head nod as she left the room.

"*Good* morning," Kennar croaked sarcastically as he found his employer sitting on the sheltered front porch of the boarding lair. Her leg was raised, and she was sitting in comfortable clothes. "Sleep *well?*"

Looking up, she saw him cradling his arm in a sling. "I guess you didn't," she replied softly.

"No!" he told her in a harsh whisper. "I have spent the night terrified as any sane purebred should be to be in the presence of these, of these…"

"Yeah, of these … what?" Malliana asked, looking out at the goings on in the town core.

"Who the mange knows?!" he rasped, bending over and looking at her, his fear and anger mixed in a way she couldn't bring herself to echo.

"I don't know, but the one who sat up with me all night, helped me, comforted me … she is a good soul. Vidiana, her name is. Weren't you tended to?"

"I … wouldn't let them," he said with a disgusted snarl as he attempted to carefully move into the seat next to hers. It took him a great effort to do so without banging his arm, and even then, he shifted this way and that unable to settle it.

"You need to let them give you something. Didn't Vanalla see you?"

"That makes NO sense!" he cursed softly. "I don't know why she is here, but the rest of these – do you remember that story about the Pantera these kinds poisoned? I take that seriously – she could have as easily been my mother or my baby sister."

Malliana leaned her head back and looked at the roof covering them. "These rescued us, and according to enforcement, all of the ones who actually did the poisoning have been locked up, and I might also add most have been killed in jail by other inmates. I'm not sure if that matches your version of justice or not, but these didn't."

"That's what they want you to believe, but if not these, what about others who will come here?"

"Because," a soft voice said from behind them, "the ones coming here are only the ones who are willing to forsake their lost religion. Say what you will, but even coming to Attoria is admitting that the Great Mother and Perfected One will not rescue them, don't care for them, or don't exist." They looked up and saw Vanalla walking across the porch to meet them. "I have good ears."

"So, they commit heresy by coming here?" Malliana questioned.

"They do. They are all immediately considered dead to the rest of the Vanarrans, even as those die of starvation and isolation. The … richer pockets of the order can last awhile longer, but most cannot. Those who were *truly faithful*," she said, "have died in their faith, and that saddens me greatly. Many more will die, still."

"They have caused enough pain," Kennar charged, "I'm not sure that they don't deserve it."

"Once someone has recognized that they have fallen from the Path and repented, they are to be given forgiveness," Van confronted him, gently. "Would you deny them that? Would you have someone deny *you* that were you walking in their tracks?" His disgusted grunt and look away from her made her frown. "I heard you refused any treatment last night. Do you know what that means?"

"No," he replied back curtly, not looking at her.

"That you're a damned idiot and a bigot, not to mention being an outrageous, flaming hypocrite," she flatly complained, and he fixed his gaze on her in surprise. "Vidiana treated your friend here all night, and although I was told she was *challenging* at times, there were words exchanged that were actually honest and grateful. I realize you are afraid, Kennar. Everyone else here is afraid, also, and works so hard for this, Attoria – their very last chance. Your behavior emphasizes that fear, and as the leader of this community, I have justification to confront you with that." His gaze dropped at her insistent stare. "Callanar volunteered to stay awake and help you, and you kept that door barred like you were keeping out wild forest stalkers! He's a good soul! He deserves better gratitude than that, better treatment than that. Are you a member of a family, Kennar?"

"Yes, de Grassith," he told her, looking back into her penetrating stare.

"Kept by and keeper of – it's what all of these are learning! Don't think yourself superior to these, either – in the last few hundred seasons, all of Thuria damned well forgot it, too – including the families! Here, it is being reborn, actually practiced. Here, that is being lived out. You spent a night of useless pain – not to mention some swelling all because you weren't willing to trust. The Vanarrans have learned the lesson in the hardest way possible that their decision not to trust purebreds and trying to walk over them was their greatest mistake. Most of the ones known as Vanarrans will be dead, and there will be only a bare fractional percentage of their former number who survive." He was about to speak, but she raised her paw finger at him. "Before you say good riddance, I would demand that if you would truly advocate for genocide, you move your ass out of our chair and hit the trail! Is genocide of these who saved you when you trespassed against them what you would really advocate?"

He closed his eyes and shook his head. "No. I'm ... I'm sorry. I was afraid, and-"

"You still are. I can see that. *Ignorance feeds fear* between individuals and in communities. Callanar is beside himself wondering what he did wrong in talking to you. Would you be Thurian enough to admit the truth to him? Would you?"

The blush furs on his face rose, but also those on Malliana's. She reached out a paw to him, resting it on his good arm and told Vanalla, "It is my fault we are here."

"He took the job – his choice, his responsibility. You chose differently last night, and now how do you feel about Vidiana?"

Malliana replied, "She's ... lived a hard life, and she told me some of what the order did to them. I didn't know."

Van nodded firmly before speaking. "Kennar is ignorant of those facts and is so by choice; so, I ask you again, would you be Thurian enough to admit the truth to him?"

"I'm ashamed of myself," he replied. "I will. It is my fault."

"You have no cause to hate anyone here ... except for me," Van told them both, "because I can be a mighty big pain in the tail." The self-deprecating humor made both of their moods lighten. "This is going to be so hard for those outside of Attoria and those within. To save them, we've had to remove them from the presence of other

Thurians, break the sieges of their temples so they can eat and come to some new understanding of their lives. We have created, though, a wall – a barrier in doing that. It is needed, and yet it costs us your trust."

"What if someone volunteered to tell your story and observe, honestly, what was going on."

"Would that story sell, Malliana?" Van queried. "It has very little fear or blood in it."

"It has enough. Vidiana told me of the ones buried on the hill."

"Thirty-seven, now," Van sighed, going and sitting in a chair opposite the two. "Too late for them. Children up there on that hill buried, as well. Find me their guilt if you can. Breaks my heart if not my soul thinking about them. They deserved none of this…"

"Is that why you are here?" Kennar asked.

"I'm here as a volunteer, or at least that is how it started. However, what you choose at the start doesn't always mean that's what you get to become. You see, oddly enough, I am quite the expert on Vanarra de Gonari – the historical one. I have had very frank interactions with many if not all of those here disabusing them of the mystical Great Mother and introducing them to the real one. That … knowledge and willingness to argue it out with them somehow earned their trust, their respect. They made me their leader here. I'm not sure I deserve it, but it doesn't really matter – it is so. The fact that I've missed how the outside world would come to fear us is a miss on my part, I think."

"I only promise to do my job," Malliana told Vanalla, "but I will do it honestly."

"And we'll be honest with you," Vanalla reassured her. "And you…"

Her gaze fell again, somewhat balefully, on Kennar, and he responded, "I … would appreciate it if Callanar could come and help me. It would be very kind of him, and I owe him an apology."

Vanalla smiled and nodded. "Very well, and he's becoming quite adept at medicinal herbs and mixtures that are helping many ills here. They helped Malliana last night."

"Thank you, and thank him, please," he told her.

"You can do that yourself. I'll go and get him. Now, as for the two of you, I have a PawLink. If there is anyone you need to call, please feel free, but talk quickly – only StarSats out here. It gets expensive."

Van walked away from them, and the two of them looked at each other. "What do you say?" Kennar asked. "Do we call someone to come get us?"

Malliana slowly shook her head. "She's … not wrong. She can accuse you, but last night, I felt the same way."

"Then why did you talk to her, this Vidiana?"

"My curiosity got the better of me. The stories here are deep. I had ten sols to get this story together for my commissioner, and what I was going for was shallow, fast, real sensational crap. It goes something like this: here at the mysterious Vanarran refuge compound, those Vanarrans who accept the generous donations of well-intentioned Thurians are using this so-called new start as a means to rebuild their operations and potentially, come back stronger. Who knows what evil is being planned in the Attoria sanctuary?"

"Is that what you truly think of us?" a male Aelkinda asked from nearby.

Malliana looked at the shocked individual with understanding and apology. "That was the story I made up in my mind sitting at a comfortable desk in Shanandrae, and then I came here, was rescued by all of you, and spoke with Vidiana. That story … is gone now. I'm still trying to figure out what the real story might be. You are?"

"Callanar," the male Pantera said, eyes downcast. "To whom I owe a really big apology and," Kennar grimaced as he moved his body, "a little help, please!"

"*Now*, he accepts my help!" Callanar sighed. "I suppose so, although much of the good of what I could have done will be far harder because you've put off treatment for so long."

"I'm sorry," he replied, "but Malliana is right; we've built up this whole idea of how things would be here based on what we knew."

"And what *did* you already know?" Callanar gently cradled Kennar's broken arm and held it as he added, "Before even deciding to come within the borders of this place?"

"Only what I knew growing up. Be afraid of Vanarrans – don't look them in the eye, don't speak to them. There are those who have offended them, and bad things happened. Then, there was everything on the news about the poisonings, the weapons."

"It's not a good picture, I'll admit, and I was a part of that past, of that … mindset," Callanar agreed. "Arrogance was taught as a weapon of fear, and sometimes, that fear was intentionally validated. It is a sin for which we owe many seasons of penance, but so many of us are dying that maybe that will stand in its stead."

"I don't know that such will work among the population," Malliana offered. "Kennar is right; these thoughts we have are just the logical extension of everything we experienced."

"Those of the Vanarran faith are placing their hopes in nothing at all," he told them as he inspected and gently palpitated the arm. "There's a fair amount of heat in it, potentially just swelling but maybe infection starting. I'm going to have you drink a fair number of brews, I think, just in case." As he rummaged in his leather bag, he pulled out several vials explaining, "I was a chemist, actually, and sometimes a consultant for things like pharmaceuticals and other drugs. It was my responsibility to help brew the … narcotics that made initiates feel such rapture when worshiping the Great Mother. My doubts started early, you see. As initiates, we didn't even know we were being drugged – we thought everything we were feeling was divine bringing us to a deeper knowledge of our inner purpose. Here, drink this – it's for the swelling. Now, I'm going to rub some liniment into your fur. It doesn't smell very nice, but it will ease your pain and keep any surface infection in check. I noticed both of you carry quite a number of scrapes and nicks from your misadventure. Make sure you check yourselves. In fact, you should be checked for parasites – Attoria, as any wooded place, has its share."

Malliana softly told him, "Vidiana helped me with that last night."

Kennar's blush fur raised, but the Aelkinda shook his head. "It's worth the embarrassment, my friend. Let me check you after this, and you'll feel better for knowing." The Pantera sighed and nodded, still ashamed. "It's okay. Keeper of and kept by – it's what she's teaching us."

"She is pretty interesting," Malliana noted.

"I can't easily put words to her meaning here," Callanar explained, shaking his head as he rubbed the sweetly pungent mix into the Pantera's fur. "She is a heart, a nucleus that we have always lacked. For ... seasons, it's odd – we were raised on the distorted knowledge of Vanarra de Gonari, but Vanalla has set us to rights on that score, but it's hard not to tell ... sometimes..."

"What?" Kennar asked, confused by the wistful and wondering expression in the Aelkinda's features.

He sighed and resumed rubbing the arm. "I'm not sure I should share that."

"Trust goes both ways," Malliana offered. "If my sources thought I would tell on them, I wouldn't have sources. I'll keep your identity a secret."

"So you say," Callanar agreed, releasing the arm and looking at her. "I spent every moment of my life praising, serving, and venerating the Great Mother. What ... what if one greater than her is actually walking the ground with us right now? What if someone greater than Vanarra de Gonari is here, now, and walking in Faelnar form – not to be worshiped, but to be *followed*, to be *learned from*?"

"You think Vanalla is that?"

He looked into Kennar's eyes a little hopelessly. "I cannot say. I can tell you that she inspires a kind of loyalty that makes me want to follow her as some of the houses of old followed the great matriarchs of history. See, that was yet another piece of knowledge that was denied us! We didn't know and weren't taught anything about the great houses and their histories."

"She's got the teeth of the old matriarchs, I'll say that," the Pantera groaned as Kennar pressed and tended his arm.

"I've listened to the wisdom of Rahnahi de Dothnar and some of the writings of Vanarra de Gonari, and may you be forever protected from the outright ferocity that was in the claws of Amyra de Gonari defending her family. What she did to the de Oterbythe matriarch still gives me pause," Callanar confessed. "But she was always doing so for her own family, and Vanalla ... stands for us."

"She does at that," Malliana agreed. "She darn near bit a chunk out of Kennar's hide for keeping you out last night."

"It was deserved."

"Don't think that I don't carry a few scars and claw marks with her name on them," Callanar assured them. "Vanarran heretics wanting to become something else can still be very thick skulled, and she'll cut you to the bone – verbally – for any sort of nonsense, especially that *superiority* and *arrogance* we used to carry around with us so undeservedly. You can tell, though, that she does it because she doesn't want us to fail, and she doesn't want us to succeed being as utterly deluded as we were. She has committed to be here with us without end – she will never leave here; I truly believe that. Only her death would break that oath."

"Think about it," Kennar commented, looking at Malliana. "What if they actually had a matriarch here? A matriarchy? Damn, but that might not be a bad idea – might be very reassuring to everyone else."

"How so?" Callanar asked.

"Well, one thing she said to me as she was raking me a new fur pattern was that all of Thuria forgot about how houses worked. The thing is, they're starting to get it back, remember it, implement it. Last moon, my dues went up to five percent of my pay, and I paid it – gladly. I have a matron checking on me, helping me work out problems and find new jobs," he explained, nodding at Malliana.

"Yeah, bad call on this one as far as she goes, but he's right, Callanar. There have been some serious shifts in the order of things, and … I've even applied to one of the old Lupar houses starting to reassemble itself. It's de Vassar, and they had about dwindled away to nothing, but some of those of the original blood had held onto parts of the old family legacy, and now, they're trying to grow it. It's kind of exciting."

"We were taught that the old matriarchal houses meant that our kind, the mixed bloods, were kept stuck as second class or worse."

"But Callanar, it was Amyra and those like her that helped change that," Malliana contested. "It might have been true at one time-"

"But it's not true now," Callanar offered with a knowing look.

"Like what used to be true with Vanarrans is now not true…"

"With *Aelkinda*," he told them, saying the word which such polish and pride that his sense of ownership and responsibility was unmistakable. "Not here, in *Attoria*."

"The Vanarran – I mean the home of the Aelkinda?"

"The home, Malliana, of any who wish to stay with us. Vanalla's own sister, her mate, and their two children are scheduled to move here within a moon – their lair is nearly complete. Tashara lives here – a very ... interesting Vulpi named Vosha, also. There is a minister of the Creator's Path, a very wise Lupar named Javoth, not to mention Ash and Laxar and others. That is the true secret of this place, the secret we find about ourselves as we sit around and try to understand our new lives. We do not want to live alone anymore. We want those who are not like us around – as difficult as it will be to become used to it. We *need* those differences, not to require everyone to be the same, but to simply take care of one another."

"Some of the families are trying to favor the root species – de Dothnar being Nephti, de Bosnar being Lupar," Kennar offered, "but in large part, that will be impossible now. It may be their heritage, but with mixed bloods, families will be made of others than that of any purebred species, and if that is so..."

"What of their mates?" Callanar asked. "If she be Lupar and he a mixed blood with Faelnar, would a Faelnar house deny them?"

"That answer to that is now no, officially," Malliana told them both. "Such was decided last moon at the first house convocation in a generation – a secret one that I happened to sneak my way into. Grand Matriarch Carinthia de Dothnar argued the point far beyond any question. Several would-be leaders of houses were thrown out of their posts for even arguing for purebred-only houses. Made for a good story, and good pay, honestly."

"It was a wise choice," Callanar affirmed, "and one I am grateful for. It means the dreams I hope for this place we might some sol have."

"Such as?"

"Attoria as one family or mostly so, anchored in the Aelkinda but open to all," he told them. "Open ... to all."

Chapter 20: Familial Relations

Shenaria sat up straight looking out the window of her new studio in the front of her lair, hearing Trax playing with Shonas and Lithiana, trying to lay them down for a nap. Before her stood an empty canvas on a new easel. Beyond the large windows of the new lair was an amazing sunset peeking through the trees and mountains of the pass that led into the valley where Attoria lay. It was all so new, and having been granted a tour around the village, Shenaria knew that both she, Trax, and her little ones shared the biggest single-family dwelling outside of the boarding lair. Even Vanarra – or Vanalla as she was known here – didn't have a larger place.

What's more, she had met the paws who had made it, the paws of former Vanarrans now Aelkinda, souls who were so kind to her and lived in accommodations far less than those she and her family had been afforded. This had been disquieting to her. Similarly, the absolute deference shown Vanalla was something that Shenaria wasn't quite prepared for – without question, she was their leader, and they honored her as greatly as any matriarch. She felt an uncertain worry pervading her spirit and hoped that her fears weren't true, and that if they weren't true now, hoped that they would never come true.

"Hello, Mother," her daughter's voice said softly from the doorway. "Forgive me; I didn't want to startle you."

"Oh, no … you know, just trying to figure out what to paint, that's all. It's my first piece since packing everything, and I want to have *something* to show Laxar, get his help or whatever."

"Can you actually paint through all of that worry?" Van asked softly, closing the door and changing into her true Faelnar-Vulpi self.

"Can't they still see you through the window?"

Van chuckled, "Taken care of. A little innovation from Kylie, one of the many new features she's woven in here."

"This place, daughter," Shenaria breathed, standing and turning to face her, "is amazing, and maybe it's too much."

"It's actually not as big as the lair Trax and you shared in Shanandrae!"

"It's a continent next to any other lair here, and you know it."

"That worries you," Van observed coming and sitting on the couch and offering the spot next to her. Still trying to work out what to say, Shenaria hesitated and then came and sat uneasily. "That worries you a lot, and in ways that are difficult for you to say."

"Yes, absolutely," the gold-on-gold Faelnar offered, "and I'd really appreciate it if Tana explained it to you because I'm not sure that I can get the words out without creating an awful mess."

"Alright," Van agreed smiling, and she slowly shut her eyes and appeared to concentrate. "Uh huh. Yes. Oh, I see. Well, that's interesting."

"What?" Shenaria questioned anxiously.

Van threw open her eyes and smiled deviously at her mother. "That she refuses to poke into your head and try to explain what's bothering you because telling me is part of the process of becoming unbothered by it!"

"She told you I was worried!"

"I could sense that without her, but she confirmed it, yes. However, I don't want to ever lose the ability for us to talk, Mother. That's too important to me. Just out with it – I'm a big kit."

"Maybe you're getting too big," Shenaria warned. "That's what's bothering me. Answer me, kit, why do I have this tremendous lair – I know it's only tremendous for Attoria, but that's the question."

Vanarra nodded and answered. "When you and Trax were willing to come here with the kids, I told some of the Aelkinda. I didn't think much of it, but in a few sols, they came back with plans, plans that put this place to shame, actually. I pressed them on why they wanted to build so large a construction for just one family, and they answered me that they wanted to show their gratitude for what had been given to them, and what I and many of the volunteers are helping to bring about – a true second chance for them. It was ... enormous, and they had planned such artistry in here that it would have been more a shrine than anything else."

"And?"

"I called them on it; reminded them why they were here. I've never let them so much as add a door pull to our cabin, and I think your coming may have manifested some pent-up demand. Gratitude, I told them, was one thing, but worship was another. That, when we look at the Thurians walking around us, is not what we are supposed to do. So, we negotiated, and here you now have what we negotiated, but more importantly, you have the model of lair that will be built for every family with children."

"Oh!" Shenaria bleated. "That's ... good, I suppose!"

"I think so. In the meantime, I think that our collective skills have gotten to the point where we can actually attempt to build the Creator's Path Chapel, and I do mean *chapel*, not some magnificent edifice to hold thousands. In point of fact, we're thinking about having size limitations for dwellings and places of worship written into the laws of Attoria. Creativity, yes, and the desire to better one's self are certainly things that need to be done, but massive lairs for a pawful to live in are a disgrace. The private lairs of some of the Temple Masters were temples in their own right. Not all, not the ones in Shanandrae, but elsewhere it certainly was true – embarrassingly so."

"I am still worried about the honor they show you, about the ... deference they show you. Is that or ... should I say, *why* is that alright?"

"Attoria is beginning at a very interesting time and in a very special way," Van told her mother, snuggling into her. "City and family are being born at the exact same time, and it is all they can do to keep themselves from giving me the actual honorarium of Honored One when I speak to them. They want it. They want it the way Thurians around the world *should* want it. They want it in a way that, thanks to our two accidental guests last month – the two newsarotzi I told you about – will cause the Grand Matriarch Carinthia de Dothnar and her aides to visit Attoria in just a few sols."

"What? Why?"

"To interview the Thurians here, speak with them, and speak with me. House de Dothnar has been at the front of bringing back the families to power on Thuria, and believe it or not, the subject of Attoria has come up in some of their larger gatherings – those with other houses. Dynaea and I have already talked about this, and we've discussed this with Amyra and Rahnahi. To allow Attoria to grow without the essential bonds of a family invites something less desirable to come in and take its place."

Shenaria leaned into her daughter and relaxed, but her voice was laden with regret. "I fear where there is no cause, daughter. You are so much wiser than I."

"No, no – Me Sha and I have discussed this. He's leaving the implementation to me, but he is offering his advice – Dynaea, also. She's been speaking with me or the other way around nearly every sol in the evenings. What I'm telling you only sounds good because there have been so many discussions and questions and decisions and consultations that went into it. Maybe, at an outside chance, I could have come up with all of this on my own, but I doubt it. So, if you see your daughter being elevated in a new matriarchy, then please know that it isn't only of your daughter's doing."

Shenaria reached up and massaged the spot between Vanarra's ears that she knew her daughter liked, and Van crooned. "Smart, noble kit. Thank you," the gold-on-gold Faelnar told her, tenderly.

"Well, I have to get you to agree to it; I'll need you as a matron … or more."

"A … what?!? You're not serious?"

"Mother, you starved and then faced down death for the cause of giving a pathetic mixed blood a chance at life. Besides the fact that I love you forever for that, it makes you qualified. If I am to be the matriarch here, I must make choices about who leads and who follows, who serves and who supports. I know you have everything inside of you *already* to be not only matron, but matriarch."

"You, my dear and horribly biased child, are completely out of your mind," Shenaria told her, chuckling, returning to rubbing between her daughter's ears. "I can't believe it."

"Then you must believe me," Amyra's voice sounded into the room.   "I'm sorry, dears, but family politics always makes me interested."

"Nosy is more like it," Rahnahi's voice interjected.

"Oh, you two are already here," Van complained although still not opening her eyes or diminishing her smile, "ruining the perfect moment. Show up, already."

"The real reason," Amyra told them as she materialized in a chair opposite them, "is because I've missed my time with Shenaria and Trax, and I'm not really willing to give that up."

At that moment, Trax nosed out of the next room quietly closing the door behind him. "Oh, I wondered if that was you! Good to see you! Dinner's on, then?"

"Indeed, good sir," Amyra offered, nodding to his courteous bow, and then said to Van whose eyes had slit open slightly, "In your absence, Rahnahi and I have taken to having dinner with them every few sols. Don't see much need to stop."

Rahnahi's form appeared in another chair opposite them and explained, "I've really enjoyed playing with the little ones. I never did that enough after becoming a matriarch."

"So, that's why you stopped coming to the library," Van accused softly, almost drowsily.

"Indeed," Rahnahi agreed. "Also, I'm going to hazard a guess here that, although I agree with my learned peer and, well, peers, rather that you would make a good matron, Shenaria, I'd bet Van knows of someone who is actually a more passionate advocate."

"Can't get her to shut up in my head," Vanarra complained, and she reluctantly turned and looked into the golden eyes of her mother. "It's Tana, Mom. She sees it. She knows that you have something that is truly needed here, and she's been candid enough with me to tell me it's something I'm ill equipped for."

"You're dreaming, the lot of you," Shenaria charged, but then the gold stone around Van's neck appeared and surged to a fiery radiance. "Okay, okay, okay! No need to singe the fur off of me, Tana, please!"

"Sorry – told you she is passionate about this. I don't understand it totally, and in truth, I'm not sure she does either, but that's why she's Tana – her insight is different, more instinctual against the flows of time than mine is. She feels time like you would feel vibrations or hear music. You, for whatever reason, clarify the sound she hears – and that is about as much sense as I can make of it. I just know that I love you, Mom, and I know that you can do this."

"What say you, Trax?" Amyra asked. "What's your opinion, good sir?"

"She's Shenaria. What else is there to argue?" he asked, shaking his head and smiling. "I live with her every sol, and every sol she's still the most amazing miracle. She has no limits on what she will give."

"I hate to break this up, but we're going to have a visitor or … visitors? Interesting," Rahnahi put in. "We should step out, Amyra, but dinner afterwards, okay?" Her eyes were firmly on Trax.

"Sure thing," Trax promised. "I've been practicing your favorites, and with Ash and Laxar helping, I have the real stuff fresh from the forest and from the gardens here."

"Hurry this up, dear," Amyra warned in Vanarra's direction. "The danger of getting between Rahnahi and good food hasn't changed with ascension."

"We will. Who is it?"

"Callanar," Rahnahi offered and after disappearing, added, "with guests you'll recognize."

As the knock sounded, Amyra told them, "We'll be close by if you need something, dears." Then, she also disappeared.

"Come in, please!" Shenaria called after looking at Vanarra to make sure she had changed back and assumed a somewhat more dignified pose. Callanar slowly opened the door and smiled when the gold-on-gold Faelnar offered happily, "Oh, Callanar! Please, come in! Come in!"

"Thank you, so much! I actually have a couple with me who wanted to have a discussion with our Matriarch."

"It's not official," Van told them, but Malliana and Kennar were already being led into the room.

"From what we've heard, that might well be coming," Malliana said as she entered, and seeing Vanalla and the others made her smile, widely, and caused Van to rise from the couch. "I'd not realized how much I missed all of you!" The two embraced, and Shenaria warmly clasped paws with Kennar, Trax soon following.

"Come, come, sit! I see you came legitimately this time!" Van teased. "Tasha told me that we had a request from you, last sol."

"I would have been here earlier with them, Matriarch," Callanar professed, "but we became embroiled in our own greeting and in talking with the others, and ... time just slipped away from us."

"It's okay; it's okay. I presume another night or so in the boarding lair wouldn't kill you? We've got a couple of rooms free after our most recent batch of new arrivals filtered out into their own lairs."

"They're going up really quick," Kennar observed. "I'd swear the gardens have doubled in size since we left."

"Something close to that," Van agreed. "So, what knits you so close into family politics these sols?"

"Well, in all honesty, we were both called before de Dothnar's senior leadership and asked a lot of probing questions about what happens here, about our report, and about everyone we spoke with. From what I could tell, they took the report positively. It ... also got me thinking, and I'm thinking about something I don't think I could have imagined two moons ago. I spoke with Kennar, and he's thinking the same thing. We have an offer from the station lead at Newsarotzi Nine. Alanar doesn't want the assignment because his mate's practice is in Shanandrae and because he got dumped on for being too favorable here. The pack leads at Nine are wondering if you would entertain the notion of a live-in correspondent?"

"As a part of our community?" Callanar asked, a little bewildered.

"That's the thought," Kennar assured them. "Nine has always been favorable, I think, and they field a lot of questions they'd like to be able to provide answers to – between commercials, that is."

"Since I packaged the report for Nine, only, it's made them something of the authority, and there are those who have an interest in getting updates every sol on the goings on here," Malliana explained as Van motioned them all to sit.

Callanar shook his head in confusion. "I find it hard to believe that someone, not of our number, would be so interested in matters here that they would want to know of new things *every single sol*!".

"There are hundreds of different aspects to cover," Malliana disagreed. "The very next batch of Aelkinda who come here would be enough for six moons of stories, let alone the buildings going up and everyone else who is here. Add on the potential formation of a matriarchy – there's no way that's not going to interest a good set of Thurians."

"Thurians who are also rediscovering their own familial roots," Trax agreed. "Also, Thurians who are trying to develop some familial roots for the first time."

"We would have to get the approval of the leadership here, however, to proceed," Malliana stated, looking Van square in the eye.

"Probably talking about quarters a lot smaller than what you're dealing with right now," Van warned. "This size is for families with children, at least for now."

"That cabin where you and Ash live; is that like what we would have?"

"We?" Van asked, smiling up at Kennar, to which he blushed.

"For *each* of us," Malliana patiently clarified.

"Well, if it is not together, you would probably be put together with another citizen. These are two individual cabins, but we are trying to economize – use space wisely. That is unless you two would prefer to bunk together."

Kennar looked at Malliana hopefully, but she looked back at Van. "I think we would *learn more* from doing as you suggest – bunking with another citizen of Attoria, I mean."

"Alright," Vanalla answered. "Probationary period – that's how you'll start. You have a moon to impress me with not only how well you report but how well you contribute to the community. I may lead, but you *will* see me getting my paws dirty with anything anyone else is being asked to do. I've actually worked the digger for the last few graves up there, just to give you a flavor what I might ask you to do."

Malliana's and Kennar's eyes widened appreciatively, and they both looked at Callanar. "It is so, even against my arguments and those of others. Many of us stood there stunned as she did it. We watched our leader serve even those who can never repay her for her kindness in granting them their great rest." His eyes were blinking trying to hold back tears. "Also, she … *sang* to them."

"And you say there are no stories here!" Malliana breathed out.

"Understand that there is only a certain amount of invasiveness I'll allow. I don't want life here to be on VidStar camera thirty intervals a sol all season long," Vanalla warned. "We need some firm ground rules – simple ones, but firm."

"I have to ask first, don't I?"

"You do, but if there is something you see that is expressly in the moment, you can, but it had damned well better be the exception rather than the rule. If I feel that it was an unfair invasion of an individual's privacy, I will ask to have it back as a condition of your remaining here. Also, remember that we're dealing with a sword that has far more than just one edge. Featuring individuals prominently, at least in this phase, may cause risks to them and to the community that I won't be comfortable with. Again, our story here *is* community and family. Shouldn't that be enough?"

"Can I get you singing?" Malliana asked, and Kennar nodded.

"Your camera may not be insured for such risks, but if I choose to repeat the rites I performed for those we lost, then you are welcome to. Don't merely feature me singing, however – those in their final rest and those who mourn them are the greatest part of that. Just, please dear kit, try to show the truth in the kindest way you can. There are enemies a plenty outside of this valley."

"I wouldn't be here, Vanalla, if I didn't want this to succeed," Malliana told her. "I think it can. I think it will, but telling the stories to those who can't come will make things better for everyone."

"As we discussed," Callanar agreed. "Matriarch, I agree with her, and I've come to trust her and Kennar, as well. I would hope that this would be permitted."

Vanalla stood and faced both Kennar and Malliana, who sat somewhat close together. "I charge you then, joining us here isn't simply a new address, it's a commitment. It's a family. It's-"

"The very same thing she's told all of us," Callanar interjected to the pair who seemed surprised by Vanalla's impassioned delivery. "It's *our* last and best hope, but in the end, it may well be for the peace and joy of your spirits in addition to our own. This is certainly not a Vanarran community, and it is not an Aelkinda community – it is *our* community, yours and mine and everyone else's."

"Nice adaptation!" Van complimented him. "We needed that. Now, do you two accept that responsibility?"

"I do," Malliana offered, nodding.

"Kennar?" Van asked after seeing him hesitate.

"I ... am a member of family de Grassith, but I feel more at home here. What do I do?" he asked.

"For now, accept on your honor and on the honor of your house, and in time, Kennar," Van reassured him, placing a paw on his shoulder, "we can find a path forward for you, together."

"What do I say? Yes?" he asked.

"How about an old form of promise – some still use it now," Trax suggested. "It's *on my honor and by my pledge.*"

"Then, I accept the responsibility, Vanalla ... Matriarch, on my honor and by my pledge."

Vanalla nodded, smiling. "Then on behalf of our family, I welcome you. May this family be your joy, and may you be so to us."

"Wait," Malliana asked, "does that mean I have a family name now?"

"Perhaps," Van offered. "I meet with the Matriarch of de Dothnar soon; we'll see what comes of it. As for now, why don't Callanar and I take you to dinner with your new family."

"It's just about time for that, isn't it?" Callanar noted. "Shenaria and Trax, will you be joining us?"

"I just laid the little ones down. We'll eat here tonight, but can I see you tomorrow? I want to start cataloging some of the herb remedies you've rediscovered."

"Ah, yes; that would be most welcome. Alright, come on new *family members*," he offered, "let's go."

"See you later, my sister," Van told Shenaria, giving her a hug. "And you, Trax."

With that, the group left, and as soon as the door was shut, Rahnahi was standing behind it. "I thought that would never end! Alright Trax, let's get to cooking!"

The house motorcade of de Dothnar made its way quickly down the fast trail, its group of six house enforcement escorts riding alongside a single, sleek black limo-hover. Within, the Grand Matriarch Carinthia de Dothnar questioned her head of intelligence and his aide, Melissiana, about their destination, less than an interval away.

"Satisfied with the security arrangements?"

"Yes, Honored One," Kallain offered. "We have had teams infiltrating their perimeter during the night, and all have reported being in assigned positions within the last two intervals, as discussed. If there had been any deviations to this, of course I would have informed you."

"Satisfaction goes both ways, Kallain," Carinthia warned. "My concern will be what will happen if they are discovered. If the assets we placed in the area, if my memory is correct, were to all present themselves at once, it would look like an invasion of enforcement units. I hope we have emphasized adequate care not only for our own lives but for the other lives inside of Attoria."

Melissiana nodded, answering, "I interviewed every team myself, Honored One, at Kallain's request. All have a clear understanding of the priorities of this mission and its engagement protocols. We are here for a peaceful purpose and a purpose that may well make history. I have made sure that our team understands that tragedies are not the way we wish to make history this sol."

Coursia nodded beside her matriarch. "Not far off what I've told the others riding with enforcement, Honored One. As usual, please forgive our prodding, Kallain."

The Faelnar raised his paw in understanding. "Such checking between each of us can only serve to better the results of this attempt, and my trust in my team and in my matriarchy allows no presumption of perfection upon myself or any asset we employ. It is a fair question, Honored One, and as fair to point out that none of our teams experienced any difficulty reaching and maintaining their concealed positions. It also appears that the leader of Attoria is keeping to her word, as well. There is a notable lack of activity, especially on the perimeter. Traffic is very well confined between the key buildings, and even their communal meal times have been shifted to ensure we don't have an ... unexpected interaction."

Pathia cocked her head a bit. "Please forgive me, but I've been – as you know – working on other assignments for our house. Attoria's leader, might I ask what we know about her?"

Kallain nodded to Melissiana who pulled out her data pad. "Vanalla Ashallo, species Faelnar, age is approximately forty-eight seasons. Her coloration is brown and gold. She is joined to a Perratti-Lupar mix named Ashalam – no known last name. At present, they have no children, and a sister, brother-in-law, a niece, and a nephew who now live with them in Attoria; this was a recent move of no more than a few sols ago." As Melissiana continued reading through the details, Pathia's expression became more and more frustrated. "She served as a volunteer at Shanandrae Commons Hospital where she assisted with patient care and counseling-"

"Stop, please," Pathia bade. "That's her history, her education, her travels, yes. Still, what do we know about *her*? The reports I've read say that the former Vanarrans relocated to Attoria have come to revere her as a matriarch and follow her leadership. Those somewhat sterile details don't do much to explain why this has happened, do they?"

"It suggests, Honored One," Kallain offered, "someone who demonstrated leadership in several venues prior to this one, especially in her work at Shanandrae Commons. You look for a leader who understands sacrifice; she opened her lair to and adopted as sister a female found abused and beaten in a construction site. There are even more than adequate reports that what was viewed as the self-awakening of Fireclaw Destiny and the turnaround in her career were in some part orchestrated by this Vanalla Ashallo. There is not a mark of any kind on her enforcement record, and based on these factors and the reports – as you say – that have been coming out of the various news outlets, it is clear that Vanalla Ashallo has a very deep understanding of Thurian interactions. According to psychologist

Emmeniama de Kestrick, Vanalla's expertise was often sought on not only the most difficult cases but the most dangerous."

"Dangerous?" Carinthia questioned. "I don't remember that."

"Honored One, the good doctor reports that Vanalla had a special insight that let her know when patients were volatile, and that actually saved the doctor injury or death when Vanarrans were brought there after the raid on that temple. The stories, although grudgingly told, regarding Fireclaw's – shall we say – redirection onto a more generous path, indicate a profound understanding of how to manage difficult Thurians."

Pathia took the data pad offered by Melissiana and flicked through the pages. "There isn't much here on the official record before her return to Shanandrae. Her … schooling was remote, and nothing specifically indicates she was being trained in counseling techniques or familial management or matriarchal law. Charismatic leader, perhaps, but is she really matriarch material, Honored One?"

"The answer is no," Carinthia offered, shrugging, "but neither was I when I started, if you'll remember. Her foreign work – time in Tapricia and Luratan. It looks like difficult work. Not a lot of praise or official recognition. That's what houses used to do."

"It's what we're now doing again, Honored One," Coursia offered. "The truth is that we have very little to go on as regards Vanalla Ashallo other than what has been stated in the report and then this – she has proven capable to this point of managing the affairs of Attoria. Our own questioning of the freelance newsarotzi points to activities that even I have started to emulate."

"Is that why you were digging a ditch in the rain, last sol, Dame Coursia?" Matriarch Carinthia added.

"It was needed, and I could help. Afterwards, I heard more from our family members and felt more connected to them than I have in a long time. While, yes, it is the job of the matrons to have their paws on the various families and individuals in our charge, I honestly felt ashamed by some of what I was reading about this Vanalla. The Attoria Logs being written by Malliana Dorsi and published on the Newsarotzi Nine TransNet site continue to contain – amongst the other bits of Attorian life, insights into Vanalla's character. Do you know she's actually helped bury the dead, Honored One?"

"Have there been many deaths in Attoria?" Carinthia asked.

"Only, Honored One," Melissiana answered, "in the new arrivals. Sometimes, starvation and other illnesses have taken too great a toll before the Vanarrans decided to leave their temples."

"The report I read said she had actually sung over the dead after helping to bury them," Coursia offered. "Honored One, they posted VidStar on it. There is this mud-stained and mussed Faelnar standing beside a large number, quite a crowd of these *Aelkinda*. Her singing moved all of them. It moved me. She was singing something that was reported to be from the ancient Nephti tribal period, a lament from the time of Alahari."

"So, a knowledge of history then, too," Pathia observed. "The ancient roots are not a bad place for anyone being in the matriarchy to start."

"That is another point found in her favor, Honored One," Melissiana explained. "Her knowledge not only of tribal history, but of early golden age matriarchal history is also extremely well informed. In point of fact, examining this sol's most recent entry in the Attoria Logs speaks to several conversion experiences where Vanarrans who were still firmly convinced of their beliefs were soundly countered by someone with a very keen and specific knowledge of the facts of Vanarra de Gonari's life. It is my own opinion that it is this Vanalla who intervenes and helps contradict the mis-learnings of the Vanarrans."

"Interesting," Carinthia mused. "Could there be anyone better for this place? What of our quiet allies, Kallain? Do we have any sense if they hold an opinion on this Vanalla?"

"It is my understanding that they firmly approve of her in this position, Honored One, but the decision to bestow fostering upon them to create a legitimate family house is completely upon us."

"Enough facts and enough theory," Carinthia charged her two intelligence team members. "Give me your gut on this."

"I doubt Attorians could have been more fortunate in finding a guide, Honored One," Melissiana stated at Kallain's nod for her to go ahead. "What I gathered from speaking with Malliana is that this Vanalla intends to spend the rest of her life in Attoria, helping them, and that such loyalty being shown by a purebred when the history is what it is…"

"Yes," the matriarch agreed. "Yes, she would be both symbol and sacrifice and pledge, all in one individual. Kallain?"

"The Attorian situation continues to unfold, and over the next season as the deepest pockets of Vanarran funding run dry, the population there will continue to grow. I for one, Honored One, do not think that in the existing family houses all current matriarchs could reach her level of achievement or success given the difficult circumstances there."

"Yeah, I'll be honest and say that I'm not so sure I'd be up for that mission, and like you said, Coursia, you've already learned a bit from her. Okay, high expectations, yes, but without any other candidates showing up, I think it would be in our interest to foster good relations, at the least, if not foster directly Attoria and its current leader. However, let us see how the visit goes…"

"Agreed, Honored One," Kallain replied, and Melissiana also nodded.

"Are you nervous?" Shenaria asked her daughter, dressed in the nicest of the clothes that had yet been turned out by the paws of those immigrants to Attoria. The two were standing in the administration building entrance waiting for the Grand Matriarch and her party to arrive, the cool winds of the sol lightly blowing around them.

"I've been a matriarch longer than she has," Van chuckled, "but I do want this to go well."

"Kallain and Melissiana will help?"

"They'll play their part," Tashara offered, "but they can't do more than that. Not something that we can mention, either, actually."

"Mother is exceptionally proficient in negotiations," Vosh stated firmly.

"I will agree with that," Vassia offered.

"I didn't negotiate with you," Van contested. "I *threatened*."

"I listened," Vassia countered. "Is Javoth coming?"

"He's inside with Ash and Laxar making sure we're ready, but we're dealing with matriarchy, so it's only us kits, and best that it is just us kits in the know," Vanalla told them.

"Speak for yourself, daughter," Shenaria breathed. "I am scared out of my wits that I'm going to do something wrong!"

"Grandama, you are most wise with a strong heart," Vosh told her. "I do not perceive any inordinate opportunity for you to create issues."

"Yeah, probably my department," Van warned. "Kylie says they will be pulling into sight in three, two, and one. Hang tough everyone – this is where it gets interesting."

Shenaria watched nervously as several of the enforcement hovers sped ahead and surrounded the entrance, house guards exiting with their weapons clearly ready. Her daughter simply stayed in a relaxed standing pose, watching with some discretion how the vehicles were deploying, a barely perceptible head shake noting an error in the deployment. It was clear that as the matriarch's limohover halted and the problem was immediately corrected, Kallain or someone in that vehicle had seen it also.

"They require practice," Vosh said without perceptibly moving her lips.

"Yeah, new for them," Van thought back to the group as the limo hover slipped under the newly upgraded hover landing in front of the building. Immediately, Kallain and Melissiana exited, taking stations to the left and right of the open door, with Kallain offering a paw to the Honored Dame who now exited. When her hind paw touched the ground, Vanalla and her contingent knelt and bowed their heads.

"Oh!" an older voice said quietly. Soon, two more had exited the vehicle, including the Grand Matriarch.

Once those hind paws had stopped moving, Vanalla spoke. "It is our privilege to welcome you to Attoria, Honored Ones, and we are so very grateful for your visit."

"You greet us with profound honor," Carinthia replied. "Please, rise."

They did, and Van asked, keeping her eyes slightly averted below the eye level of the matriarch. "If I might introduce myself and my party to you, Honored One?" Van asked, addressing only the matriarch this time. The gentle head nod from the elder Nephti came with earnest interest, and that nod was echoed as each individual was named. "Vosha Terspeara, my aide. Tashara Sahari, our head of public relations and fundraising, formerly known as Fireclaw Destiny. Vassia, one of the first Aelkinda to join us here and of great help to us. Shenaria Lasser, my adopted sister and mother of the first family here, and I am Vanalla Ashallo, at your service Honored Ones."

"Well met," Carinthia complimented. "Kallain, if you would be so kind?"

"Yes, Honored One. The Grand Matriarch Carinthia de Dothnar, Honored Dame Coursia de Dothnar, Honored Dame Pathia de Dothnar. My aide and mate, Melissiana de Dothnar, and I am Kallain de Dothnar, chief of house intelligence."

Carinthia nodded and offered, "It is good for you to have us here and to pay us this honor. One would be led to believe that you understand house protocols to near perfection."

"We try to pay all owed respect and courtesy, Honored One, and we have watched your accomplishments over the past moons with great interest and enthusiasm."

"It is very much appreciated."

"If it would suit, Honored One, we could go inside and offer you some refreshment after your long ride," Van suggested.

"I think I will ask my seconds to follow that course, but I would like to walk a bit with you … up there," the matriarch told her, pointing to the cemetery at the highest point in the village.

"As you request, it is done. Please," Van said over her shoulder, "would you escort the Honored Dames and our other guests inside?"

"I would like to follow you, Honored One, at a respectful distance if that would be alright," Kallain told her.

"Vanalla, you may also choose someone to accompany us. I offer this out of mutual respect."

"My gratitude, Honored One. Vosha, if you would be so kind as to accompany Intelligence Chief Kallain de Dothnar?" The brief nod was the only answer that was provided. After a few passes, the various groups separated with Van and the matriarch starting the walk which would bring them to the cemetery away from all of the others, save a large contingent of very nervous house guards with Kallain and Vosha following behind them.

After travelling in silence for a few steps, just enough to put them beyond the easy hearing of others, Carinthia asked, "So, Vanalla Ashallo, leader and might become *matriarch* of these here, do you have any idea why I called you out to go to this place with me?"

"Would you entertain a very candid answer, Honored One?"

"I would welcome candor, actually," Carinthia spoke easily, "I see so little of it these sols."

"Honored One, other than you might have a deep-seated dislike for some of your house guards, who are about to come out of their fur with anxiety, I believe you are showing an immense amount of trust in all of the citizens of this place, and you know well that they are watching you. By choosing the cemetery as your first stop, I would also guess that you would place some degree of honor and respect on those friends and colleagues they lost. In addition, because you called me out – specifically – you might just be putting a great big underscore under that Vanalla is leader trend that's been building for some time."

"Not bad," Carinthia noted, looking at her a little surprised as they started to mount the base of the hill. "Am I doing wrong by any of those?"

"I believe the trust is well placed, Honored One, simply turn and look around." Carinthia did so, and Van pointed as she explained. "The administration building, about half smaller than it is now, only those five cabins over there or so, the boarding lair, a few of those tool sheds and resource buildings. That's all they started with, here."

"From satellite, we counted a far greater number of cabins and workshops, planted fields and gardens, not to mention a new lair that was larger than the rest. Is that yours?"

"No, Honored One. I still reside in that cabin right over there – one of the originals. That is actually my sister's place, and it's only larger because it is the template or model structure for what will be the standard family dwelling here."

"Meaning that as families come into being, they can upgrade their lodgings."

"Families need room to grow, Honored One, and this family, this group of Thurians is working very hard, desperately so, to make Attoria work. They realize that without this, there is no future for them."

Nodding in understanding, Carinthia turned and started to make her way higher up the hill. "I felt that way when my house was on the edge of disaster. It wasn't quite so true for us, I suppose. If de Dothnar fell apart, I could go out and try to get some job in what I studied, but it would take a great chunk of my soul and darken the rest of it forever. Here, it seems as if the future of this place will either mean life or death to those who come here."

"These are a worthy group of Thurians, Honored One, and every individual has forsaken their old beliefs and committed themselves to make this place work. What's more, that commitment has no option but to extend itself to one another – if they succeed, it will only be together."

By then, the pair had reached the posts surrounding the field of interment. Carinthia scanned the ground and asked, "How many?"

"We hit forty-one in the last moon, Honored One. It was a small bunch of refugees, and half of them starved before coming here, or they died just after arriving," Vanalla told her. "The ones who survived have been paired with others in cabins who are nursing them back to health. We keep the boarding lair as clear as we can since we never know when we're going to have others coming to us."

"By the Creator's great mercy, what horrors you must have seen. Why would you ever want to stay here?"

"Because, Honored One, I have never known a time when so many who were so lost needed so much help; with these, that help can come from almost nowhere else. This is why Tashara asked for the donations and why we fought to have this place come into being. They need help; they are lost. I coordinate their activities, help direct them – I even argue with the new ones about what they think they know about Vanarra de Gonari and what they don't know."

"What is the greatest thing they do not know?"

"That Vanarra de Gonari *loved* her family, Honored One. She stuffed herself and another mix blood into a hover and charged into the de Gonari estate, risking their own lives to save the life of her matriarch and dames. She stood like a shield between those who would harm her family and those who were her own. It was … instinct for her. It was love that called her to do it. There wasn't any master plan for a master race. There was family and faith and that was all. That … that's what they're missing the most."

"The matriarch of de Gonari could stand to spend a few intervals in your presence, Vanalla Ashallo. The Vanarrans aren't the only ones who need to be disabused of misguided beliefs."

"If I may serve, I would be happy to offer that gift, Honored One. My heart, though, it is here."

"To watch this come to be all around you, and to help that happen – to serve those here so as to ensure it does," Carinthia mused, looking all around. "Your citizenry is very disciplined. I've not so much as seen shade or curtain move while we have been here talking." Vanalla giggled slightly. "What is funny?"

"I've spotted six of your perimeter guard as we walked, Honored One – I'm sorry."

"You have got to be joking! Very well then, call them out!"

Vanalla stood erect and pointed straight over the interment field. "I caught a reflection twice straight ahead of us, there." She then moved a quarter turn to her right and pointed some distance away. "Two guards, at least, standing behind those trees which are too small for them, actually." Turning another few degrees, she pointed again. "There! Oh, caught one moving that time – or shall I say a second time." Turning to her left, she noted, "And there – now that we have the higher ground, their cover is compromised. Over here I see two more, and there, two more again. How many is that, Honored One?"

"Up to about ten or so; it appears we need a bit of polish on our field maneuvers. And yet, again, I do not see any movement from the lairs. Could you call all of them here if I wished it?"

"I could not call all of them here, Honored One, because they were ordered not to, however, if you were to extend your paws in front of you, raised, and lower them beside you spread wide, they would interpret this as a summons, and they will obey you. I would, however, suggest bringing your head of intelligence into this discussion so that the somewhat nervously repositioning and – oh, please just get to some good cover!" Van actually shouted in frustration at the pair of house guards she had last pointed out.

"I take your point, dear." Kallain, standing at the base of the hill walked up, a chagrined look upon his features. "I have to say that I am somewhat disappointed that our resources have been observed so quickly."

"My apologies, Honored One," Kallain offered. "I have observed Vanalla easily discerning several of our positions. Might I ask where you acquired such skill?"

"A period of time having to be very observant for my own safety far away from here."

"What I wanted to alert you to, Kallain, is that Vanalla has instructed her citizenry to remain in their dwellings and out of sight unless I make certain movements to call them here. I have not seen them. I wish to. Would you please communicate that when I raise my paws and lower them, we will be approached by..." She looked at Van with a questioning expression.

"More than half of the Aelkinda here, plus several others, Honored One," Vanalla supplied.

He looked at the matriarch with concern. "I am unsure of the security risks this would cause to you, Honored One. I do not recommend it."

"At this moment, Kallain, there are – how many live here, Vanalla?"

"One thousand, two hundred and twenty-three, Honored One."

"We are outnumbered, and if all wanted harm to come to me or the rest of the party, we would be ill equipped to turn them back, even with our weapons. We are already exercising trust, but I can't build relationships with a village population I cannot see. Please, if you would step down the hill and make sure that we are alright and no accidents will ensue. If you can gain that assurance, please return and let me know. Is there anything you would need to do, Vanalla?"

"Already done, Honored One," Van told her. "When you wanted to pursue this, I did this gesture with my left paw. That let Vosha know that you are considering seeing the Aelkinda. She's alerted them to be ready and how to approach in a non-threatening way. They will come single file and stand beside and behind her wherever she stands. She will be their gathering point."

Looking to Kallain, Carinthia stated, "I believe we are starting to see the mutual benefits that this relationship would bring. Where, may I ask, did you learn this paw signal?"

"Vanarra de Gonari used it and ones like it throughout her time as Matriarch, Honored One. It's in her autobiography. It seemed a good, non-obtrusive way to communicate."

"You are well studied on her. Please, Kallain, see to it." With a nod, he was away. "How would you confirm for your aide that I wish to have them here?"

"Right paw down, three paw fingers spread on my leg, front or back – twice. It confirms the message, Honored One."

"Fascinating. With such discipline, you could mold them into quite the power," Carinthia probed.

"Or, I could see to their protection, reassure them, Honored One. The Vanarrans were always disciplined, hierarchical, and they venerated female deities. While they have renounced their faith, their culture and predispositions towards needing leadership have placed me where I now am – in their eyes."

"They *want* to call you matriarch, have you become one for them?"

"I will let them tell you in their own words, Honored One, but yes. I am growing weary reminding them that even though they use the term to describe me, it isn't official."

"Such isn't beyond question," Carinthia told her, turning back to look at the interment field. "I think it likely. Do you know the fostering laws?"

"I've studied them, Honored One. It was an essential part of Vanarra de Gonari's history as – during her time – de Kestrick was fostered, and that was almost true for de Oterbythe. Real close one there."

"Then you know the pathway by which you could hold that title in truth. Good. It is a relief that I'm not having to cover the elementary ground for you. I don't mean to give out false hopes, but I feel, already, as if I am speaking with a peer. Maybe someone who exceeds my abilities in touching those of my house – that would be a better description. I've read how you … farm with them, tend wounds, nurse their sick, and counsel them. You have even buried them, and if the stories are true, you have sung over these graves?"

Vanalla lowered her head, showing a bit of blush fur. "I am required to answer yes to that question, Honored One, to maintain my honesty."

"Would you sing that song for me, so that I may hear it? The very song you sang for them?"

"If I must, Honored One," Van deferred, but Carinthia opened her paw and raised it, suggesting she start. Van sighed and turned towards the graves and bowed her head. In a clear, soft voice, Vanalla started to sing…

Kay tess serrat? Kay tess a suinah?

Presse anisana, presse unteraroo.

Kay tess serrat? Kay tess a suinah?

Un treeful los pettera. Balleth unteraroo.

Un lay unger, Un lay avoara

Balleth kay a porta, presse unteraroo

un neefa unger, un neefa unger

Con balleth unteraroo, unteraroo, unteraroo

Dorsa es con santhi, sella el, salla el?

Un corsa unteraroo, unteraroo un kay, un kay

Vanalla stopped singing and looked at the matriarch, and tears were running down her cheek fur, her mouth agape. "That! That was ancient Nephti!"

"*Alahari's Lament*, Honored One. Do you know it?"

"I had once memorized the words in primary, but I do not remember the meanings. Do you?"

"I do, here is what those words mean…

What are you doing? What is its meaning?

Those beneath the soil, those under the roots.

What are you doing? What is its meaning?

You have done wrong, hiding under the roots.

I was to protect you; I was to love you.

You are lost to us, under the roots.

I was your protector, a comfort for you as protector.

But you are under the roots, under the roots

Do my words have meaning to you, to you?

if my heart is with you, under the roots, forever, forever.

"I would hope that as few as possible come here and lay beneath these roots, Honored One," Vanalla told her. "It seems weaving this group of onetime cult worshipers into a family, a house, is the best way to give them an identity, interdependence, and a reliance on one another that will stabilize them, preserve them, and make them a gift to Thuria – never again a curse."

The matriarch wiped her eyes. "Your voice is beautiful, Vanalla, and the message is very apt."

"Matriarch," Kallain offered, "I have chosen to order our guards to holster all arms and to keep them holstered until I signal differently." Looking at Vanalla, he warned, "They can very quickly be unholstered if there is trouble."

"My own want no trouble. They have had enough of it," she told him and then turned to the matriarch. "It is on you, Honored One. Summon them if you wish it."

"As you say, Vanalla." Turning around and facing the village, she raised her paws in front of her and to the sides, paws up and open. After a few moments, she lowered them slowly to her sides, wide, and added a gentle bow to the motion. By the time she raised up, Carinthia could see streams of Thurians, Aelkinda, walking towards one another forming a single line which started to make progress to them.

"This ... is curious," Carinthia noted. "Why bring them this way?"

"Triggered by your action, I would have to tell you, Honored One, how to bring them. Travelling in single file at a slow walk, they pose no threat because everyone can see them – there is no option for concealment. They are being viewed on all sides as they progress, and one doesn't hide behind another. All walk with their paws out of their pockets, and their clothes are simple. They are also unpocketed, if you'll notice."

"Un-pocketed," Kallain repeated, curious. "Why?"

"At certain times, it allows us to hold discussions without distractions. It is also a sign of openness that all you have is what others can see – nothing is concealed other than what is required for modesty."

The matriarch watched as the assembly formed, but how they formed was interesting to her. They weren't in ranks like a military unit, and they were bunched together like a normal crowd. Each maintained arm's length from the other, following the contour of the base of the hill. When they were all in place, Carinthia turned as Van moved beside her. In one fluid motion, both Vanalla and the entire population of Aelkinda and those who had come with them bowed.

"What ... what is the meaning of this, Vanalla?" Carinthia asked, not as a demand brought by insult but almost in desperation.

"We show you the respect that is due a Grand Matriarch of a noble house, and we offer our gratitude for your visit, Honored One."

Carinthia shook her head and just looked at Kallain. "Bid them rise, please, Vanalla – these Aelkinda of your charge."

Vanalla rose and clapped her paws once, as the rest of the village had their heads bowed to the ground. All raised their heads and rose, their paws at their sides. "Even now, Honored One, they maintain a seeable distance around them. They keep paws to the side in plain view. They know that trusting them is difficult, but they will do anything that is necessary to demonstrate that they are worthy of trust. If it is discipline, then discipline. If it is consideration, then that also."

"We have much to learn from you," Carinthia stated quietly. "Learn of you and from you. May I address them?"

"They will listen attentively, and they are honored by your visit, Matriarch."

Carinthia turned and took a couple of steps down the hill, drawing closer to the throng – this "open crowd" who were facing her. "I am the Grand Matriarch Carinthia de Dothnar, and I have received many honors in my time, but my soul has never been touched by any other honor the same way you have. I thank you for that with deepest gratitude. I do not wish for anyone to live in tyranny, nor under the rule of another without consent. I know this place is where you must be, but I would have your assurance that you would wish to proceed with being more than just a community, that you would be a family. That is what I hope to learn."

A male Aelkinda took a step forward, and Vanalla offered, "He is Callanar, and he has been given the right to speak for all of those assembled. May he?"

"You are Callanar?"

"I am, most Honored One," the male Aelkinda replied, bowing his head.

"And all here and those not here have given you consent to speak on their behalf?"

"They have, Honored One, as they will signify."

All of those around Callanar offered up, "Yes, he speaks for us," and they nodded, and that affirmation filtered through the crowd.

"You seek to turn your community into a *family*, Callanar. Why is that?" Carinthia asked.

"As former Vanarrans, we once had our religion which bound us together. Although misguided, and we see that now, our shared faith gave us unity, and that unity is something that we have struggled living without. We need those close ties to one another to feel as if we belong."

"And yet you call Vanalla – someone not of your heritage and one Vanarrans used to shun – your matriarch, even though she has not been confirmed as one – why?" she challenged.

"Because, for us, it is so in fact, even if not in law. Honored One, of all of us, she is the greatest … *servant*. Of all of us, she has the wisdom we need and the discernment we respect. She is fostering those talents in those underneath her and in ourselves. Much of what you see here, all around you, even us, we would name as that which came from her guidance, her gentle paw. She has contested with every one of us, and in every case, her knowledge and her arguments have prevailed. Yet, she is always kind to us and always defends us. In short, there is no one else among our number or those we know of we could respect more, who we would wish to follow, and wish to serve beside." Callanar turned to the rest of the assembly who nodded in agreement.

Carinthia looked at Vanalla and quietly spoke, "Honored One – you bring real truth to that title. I've always thought of that honorarium as something I needed to live up to, and here the title actually seems to be running to catch up with you."

"You are too kind, Honored One," Vanalla stated and turned to Callanar. "You know that you could have another, whoever you-"

"Our decision is made, unless you directly and most emphatically refuse," Callanar stated, nearly with defiance.

"And here is the state of things, Honored One," Vanalla offered. "I do not want to refuse what they ask of me. I want to serve them and help reverse what, in the end, was never their fault. Those who set their hind paws upon this path are gone – gone and dead."

"Beneath the roots," Callanar interjected, "and beyond our reach to hold them accountable for the lies they taught us or the things we did because of those lies. We have undertaken several attempts – the more stubborn among us, myself included – to disprove what she has told us of the one we once called our Great Mother. No source has been denied us, for many of them we knew from before but refused to entertain. Now that we do, we simply cannot refute what she says. Honored One, she goes through the pains of argument sol in and sol out, wrestling the falsehoods out of us, exhausting herself for our benefit. Can you wonder why such loyalty surrounds her?"

"I do not wonder," Carinthia told him, firmly. "I do not. Callanar, you do realize that the matriarchy, if formed, will be feminine in gender. Your position as speaker-"

"Forgive me, Honored One, for interrupting, but that is not important. The choice of me was only for this sol and because those females who could have treated with you better than I are tending to our newest members, our most fragile. They, also, have our respect and the respect of every male member of this community. So, since it is not possible for me to be a part of the organizational leadership of a family that we wish to create, that is why I speak. I will gain immeasurably if such a choice is made in favor of giving Attorians a family, but I will only do so as a family *member*. As is the case with the males of your house, we shall seek leadership opportunities in the other areas of our lives. We follow the traditions set forth in Alahari's time."

Carinthia shook her head. "I am touched, Callanar. While we try to coax and cajole and convince *modern* Thurians that they have a need for a family, that they should contribute substantially to it – you are already living that here. Grant me time to see with my own eyes, across moons – mind you, and to have my observers also record faithfully what is happening here. Malliana's TransNet logs are already providing much of what I would hope to see, but with my family representatives here, two goals will be accomplished. First, we will accumulate the proof needed by the other great houses to instantiate your family in the convention of family houses. Second, and I pray this will be the case, that our own learn from what appears to be your most excellent of examples. If I may take my leave of you and meet with those in your administration building, I will begin this effort."

"Thank you, Honored One," Callanar offered, and he knelt. When he did, the entire assembly did, as well – all except for Vanalla and the matriarch.

"Extraordinary," Carinthia breathed in Van's direction.

"They are a family I would be proud and honored to call my own, even if I did nothing more than cared for the trails here, Honored One." Turning to the assembly, she told them, "To each other and to our duties. Thank you. Please return as you came."

The matriarch watched spellbound as the group stood and took that direction as law, executing it perfectly. In less than five passes, there were again only the four of them in plain sight – the matriarch, Vanalla, Kallain, and Vosh. "I am overwhelmed. I only … dreamed of what it meant to see a leader in the stripe of Alahari. The honors they pay you are like those they paid her! Did you teach them this?"

"I did not, Honored One," Vanalla told her as they started to walk back down the hill. "This … they came up with on their own. Sadly, they are a beautiful and very spiritual community who were misused for so many seasons. They have a depth and beauty that amazes me every sol."

"Have you given any thought to what Attoria's family name could be?"

"It has come up in discussion, Honored One, as you might imagine. They want to defer the choice to me, but I have not given in to their wishes to create such a name. It is already bad enough that they call me matriarch; if I give them a family name, then it will be even harder for them should something bad happen and there be no family."

"Start giving thought to it," Carinthia stated. "Do as you have already – finding a word that will bring them together in the spirit I saw this sol. I'll tell you the truth, Vanalla, far more candidly than I should. We need this example, what's starting here. We've successfully argued for our rights, those of family houses, and we have legally won back much of what was lost. We cannot say that for the spirit of our families. It is a struggle as Thurians try to reconcile why they surrender their freedoms and independence for the responsibility of a family. Our matrons are doing good but not well. They are contributing, but even they lack the true vision and true spirit. If we could create that here, if we could take this … Attorian family and use it to inspire the rest of us, that would be great indeed, Vanalla. Vanarra de Gonari's shadow is long as was that of her peer, Sahnassa de Orturu, but they had their families given to them. In many ways, you and I must create our own – from different starting points, true, but still."

"You believe, Honored One, that there is a possibility the convention of houses will approve?"

"Right now, in form and in manner, I am largely the convention of the houses. The rest are so weak or are so used to following that what I say has enormous weight – at least for now. Find the name to call your own, Vanalla. You will need that name, I believe."

"Thank you, Honored One," Vanalla bade, and extended her paw to indicate that the matriarch should proceed ahead of her. "I will join you in a moment, if I might speak to my aide?"

"I'll await you inside, and please, if you could ask Callanar to join us, I would like to know more of him," Carinthia questioned, and Van nodded.

As the matriarch disappeared inside, Kallain walked by her. "You never cease to amaze me, Noble Shade, and I can see your time was well spent."

"Get on in there, cub," Van chuckled, softly, knowing that Kallain had kept his muzzle pointed towards the door so the perimeter guards couldn't see what he was saying nor hear his whisper. "Don't want her asking you why you tarried."

He smiled back at her and continued in. "I agree, Mother," Vosh said quietly once beside her. "Your sense of how she would react was well and truly accurate."

"You would have interpreted the gathering as a threat, I know, but she saw unity and discipline and most importantly, community. How's it gone inside?"

"Grandama has been the very unwilling center of attention since Coursia and Pathia wanted to know why she chose to come here. Her explanations have given them as much inspiration as was just imparted to the matriarch."

"My mom," Van sighed, shaking her head and smiling. "Please, bring Callanar here by telling him that he impressed the matriarch, and she would like to learn more from him of this community. If any are with him, remind them that they, too, may well be called on in the future if they wish to."

"I will," Vosh offered and turned on her heels headed towards one of the cabins in particular.

"You do have to look for him a little. Don't make it too polished," she told her daughter, mentally. Vosh turned slightly, swishing her tail in a visible sign of annoyance that made Vanalla chuckle.

Chapter 21: Pinnacle Rhymes

Intervals later, Vanalla found herself walking in the darkness in nearly that same spot, her way lit by the safety lamps around the central village core. It had been, in many ways, an exhausting sol, but in some ways, it had been truly rewarding. "It's as if all of the wrong that was done in our names can truly be undone, and the curses that were a part of this generation can be made into blessings and hope," her inner Sahni whispered happily into her thoughts. Tana agreed, but there was also a wellspring of pride in Shenaria for how she had performed.

When Carinthia asked for testimonials as to why Vanalla would be the choice to lead this family, her mother had taken the first opportunity to unburden her soul-felt gratitude not only about how *Vanalla* had helped her recover and open up to the nurses, but how she had sacrificially stepped out of the way when she realized that Trax and Shenaria felt a genuine attraction to one another. Notwithstanding that the gold-on-gold Faelnar hadn't been able to stop crying as she told the story, after just a few ticks, Carinthia had held her paw over her muzzle and wept silently as she listened. Coursia and Pathia were simply staring at Vanalla in amazement, and when Shenaria spoke about how she had been adopted as a sister – that was enough to send one of the young matrons of de Dothnar up to Vanalla's chair to hug her, that matron having been disowned under similar circumstances by her once best friend.

By then, Callanar arrived, and he spoke in such practical and clear minded terms that his words had as much of a dramatic effect on the de Dothnar matriarchy as Shenaria's emotional confession. When he had finished, there was no doubt in anyone's mind where this decision should go, and even Coursia's most vigorous challenge as to their prematurity of assigning the role to Vanalla before the true confirmation brought an answer that distilled away all doubts. "There is no other among us who has touched every soul, rescued us from our false beliefs, as she has. She mediates between us and stands as a shield over us, even as her own paws see to our needs alongside our own. Alahari, in her own time, could claim no better than what Vanalla now does for us."

She had just come from seeing him, allaying his anxiety that he had gone too far, been too strident or hadn't inserted the appropriate honorariums frequently enough. The words she had spoken to him, she knew, would at least allow him to sleep that night as his anxiety was so great. Being older, she sensed that he had little in terms of aspirations for finding a mate, but there was already a friendship and kinship between them that Vanarra, beneath the Faelnar skin, treasured.

"Uh oh," Van breathed as Tana touched her consciousness, and her steps were immediately directed away from a meandering path back to her own cabin towards the main administration building. Her eyes saw another shape making its way in that same direction, and as subtly as she could, Vanarra increased her pace to meet with the female Aelkinda. Unfortunately, it was only a few steps in front of the main entrance. Tana felt the possibility for strife and division and a fraying of time strands away from the solidity of a good future into the diffuse morass of far less desirable alternatives.

"Vidiana," Van called. "Good evening to you. Is everything alright?"

"After this sol, I'm not sure how it could get better, but I remembered something that I wanted to pull to read in the matriarchal law should we have need of it."

"Angling for dame already?" Van teased and leaned into the female in a way that spoke to the close friendship that had been developing between them.

"*That* is not your fairest judgment," came a somewhat soured response, although the sides of the mouth did tug up slightly. "In listening to those two dames discuss with their matriarch, I have to confess to being lost, Vanalla. It bothers me, the various accords and compacts of which I know nothing. I feel uncertain when such is unsettled before me, and I – what is that sound?"

Van listened, and she heard it, also – a very feminine mewl coming from in front of them. "It would appear someone *has* come here before us," Van offered, dropping to a whisper.

Vidiana's eyes, ears, and nose worked very quickly, and it took not more than the space of a few ticks before she frowned, her back fur raising up. "Our new *purebreds*," she growled, starting to take a step forward.

Van leaned in front of her and tapped her own nose, to which Vidiana reacted in confusion for a moment before understanding the Faelnar's meaning. "Oh, I don't mean you!"

"I know, but you are now very angry. I want to know why before you *do* anything."

"Can't you smell it? Don't you know what that is?"

"Of course I do," Vanalla told her. "Heat scent, and specifically from … oh, a Lupar female and a male Pantera."

As a male's grunt came to their ear followed by another soft mewling plea, Vidiana looked at Van in outrage. At nearly a whispered shout, she blurted, "You can see by the flicker of light what room they are in! They are desecrating the-"

Van shook her head. "You can't desecrate something that is … not … sacred. That room may be important to you, but it is not truly sacred, is it? The sacred thing I am worried about is right here." She pointed at and gently touched the Aelkinda's chest. The look of hopeless frustration caused Van to add very quickly, "It's not a great decision and not one I can approve of so easily as they are not legally joined. Still, I can claw no stripes here. Although I could have chosen differently, I made the decision to pursue my joining not in front of others, but in the sacred embrace of my lover."

"I would never fault you for that decision!" Vidiana told her. "You and Ash are the most marvelous of joined couples. No one could fault you in your commitment to one another."

"Well, I sense another commitment has been made," Van suggested. "These two who snuck so boldly onto our territory for the express purpose of damaging our reputation are now here, living with us, committed to that. They are committed to that, *together!*"

Vidiana's eyes widened in realization. "They commit to each other ... in the room where we commit to this community?"

"Not in the same way, surely," Van offered, biting her lip a little in amusement. "However, I believe they will become our family, and that they aren't there by accident. Did you watch them in the proceedings this sol? They could tell that this opportunity to make our community a family is significantly greater, but before they can be one of us, they have to deal with what has been between them for some time now."

"Yes, I saw them holding one another's paws, but only when they think we are not looking," Vidiana supplied, her anger softening. "They will stand before us as a mated pair?"

"And will we accept them or accuse them, Vidiana. How would you like to be treated?"

Vidiana was quiet for a few moments and then nodded. "I can see their love, and they have tried to hide it."

"It's not dishonesty; it's fear. This is something that they thought they couldn't ask for, even though ... they could have," Van told her. "If they had come to me and asked to have time in that room for that purpose, I may have questioned them, but I would not have said no."

"In your paws then?" Vidiana asked, and Van nodded. "I will exercise my patience, then, regarding the learning of matriarchal law I suppose."

"Not to say you have to, but Vosh has much of what you need in her cabin." The pleased smile radiated a new light from inside of the Aelkinda. "You really like her?"

"We all do. As with you, she delivers the truth. You are ... nurturing compassion, but she is fact. At times, we have need of both. Thank you and good evening to you ... Honored One."

"And to you, *Dame* Vidiana, and ... if this comes true for me, know that such will become true for you. I must have you at my side," Vanalla told her. Vidiana's eyes grew wide, and she blinked back tears. She bowed low to Vanalla and then departed, headed in the direction of Vosh's cabin. "Vosh? You have a visitor coming," Van told her daughter, mentally.

"I was following the conversation, as you might expect. I have found and materialized an appropriate volume for Vidiana. She is a wise and loyal female, Mother. I like her. I like Callanar, also."

"You're allowed, my daughter. Now, let me go clean up this little issue inside. Give me a warning if anyone else comes traipsing in this direction."

"I will."

Vanalla slipped towards the front of the building, and with Tana's help, her movements became utterly and completely silent.

Vanalla walked through the entrance of the Pinnacle Academy Library, what had been in Vanarra's time the Pinnacle Center, and she looked up at the large statues adorning the atrium. Seeing the one of Lyssia de Oterbythe she breathed out, "Lyshantor. I'm so glad you continue to be, but I remember you like this. I wonder if those who knew me from this time will ever get nostalgic for who I was?"

Slipping up the steps toward the main library, she saw it was relatively full of students, all quietly and intently working on their studies – some together in little groups or some all alone. As she stepped soundlessly past, almost no one looked up to see the brown and gold Faelnar dressed in a business style robe which meant to imitate the traditional style of matron and dame robes common on Thuria. Almost none did, but one or two looked up and studied her for a moment, and one Lupar male leaned down and whispered to his companions who all stopped and looked at her. Seeing them, she nodded, and they nodded back – conversations obviously concerning her reverberating back and forth amongst their number.

"The time is coming, Sahni," Van told her inmost self, "where we won't be able to walk around without being recognized."

"It *was* nice to be able to do that again," Sahni agreed, "but it's not you. They need you now, Van. You know it. I know it. It's why we're here, this sol."

"The next step in fostering after the matriarch's visit – only a moon later, didn't take long did it?"

"She was impressed. They all were. I thought-"

"And there she is," an old and gruff voice near the reference desk rumbled out. "That Faelnar who just might become matriarch of all of those poor lost souls in Attoria."

What sounded like a near insult, in terms of its tone, to the poor Perratti male behind the reference desk, only served to make Van smile and turn to face the one who had spoken to her. "Drayash!" she screamed in a whisper, seeing him looking at her with his own gleeful expression.

Walking over quickly, she embraced the old cub and then held him back to look at him. "Cub! You've lost twenty seasons since last I saw you!"

"Well, I ought, I'm healthy now! Healthier than I've ever been, I think, thanks to Missy!"

"Missy?"

"Yeah," he told her companionably, "Professor Doctor Mysnala de Gonari, formerly of an un-housed last name, and my one and only!"

"Cub!" Vanalla bleated softly, tears pricking at her eyes. "Joined?!"

"More than a season now. We wanted to hunt a bit before committing, work things out, but we're very, very happy. I want you to know that my life started turning around the very moment you stopped and prayed with me, dear kit. I've never forgotten that."

"They got your medication and all worked out, right?" Van asked.

Drayash dismissively waved his paw. "That was the *how*, but not the why – at least not to me. Missy has always wanted to meet you. She's up getting ready for some big to-do in the tower conference rooms, but now that I see you gliding about in those lovely robes, I might have an inkling of exactly what the to-do is she was hesitating telling me about!"

"Well, I've noticed that I've gathered a few sets of eyes just walking through here," Van commented, motioning with her head towards the student groups. "However, you see that *rather* tough-looking Vulpi? She's my aide."

"Don't suppose you'd have many problems with security then," Drayash said appreciatively as he sized up Vosh who was, by her glare alone, dissuading a couple of Pantera females from approaching them. "The way she moves would scare off a ravenous stalker!"

"She nearly glows in the dark with that *don't mess with me* aura, true," Van chuckled. "A very serious, very straightforward kit, and very close to me, as are you."

"Dray?" a female voice called quietly. "Who's that you're talking to? I thought you'd be making your rounds again?"

They turned around to see an adorable, petite elder Faelnar who could have easily been mistaken for Saletta in her later seasons, although Van noticed that this one was still endowed nicely up front. "I was, love, I was, but when I saw this dear kit enter the premises, I TransCom'd to Charlis and asked him to take the turn. Love, this is Vanalla Ashallo, and this is my lovely and dear and kind mate, Mysnala de Gonari."

At the mention of Van's name, the Faelnar was surprised and put her paw over her heart. "My dear! I … is this the – she's not that-"

"Ah, you'll need to forgive my dear one, here," Drayash offered softly, amused by his mate's reaction. "Being a learned doctor professor means occasionally that her words get all tangled up on the way out, you see?"

The elder Faelnar's blush fur shot up, and she stepped right in front of Drayash, looking up at him, fiercely. "I'll find words soon enough for you, you rogue! You scamp!"

"Oh, will you? Will I need to go fetch a dictionary for them or will you use the little small ones regular Thurian folk can understand?"

Vanalla chuckled at how easily he consterned her, but then quickly added, "It is my honor and pleasure to meet you, Doctor Mysnala. Thank you for keeping watch over Drayash; his health and happiness means a lot to me. He was the first one I met after coming back to Shanandrae."

Van's friendly manner seemed to put the female at ease, and "Missy" finally settled down enough to get a full sentence out. "Thank you. I've spent a whole career being able to stand up in front of anyone and just lecture away, but this one always catches me off guard!"

"Which is funny given what he does, don't you think?" Vanalla asked, and she had the pleasure of seeing the confused look followed quickly by wide eyes and then a laugh.

"I suppose so!" she replied, trying to control her volume. "You've been the subject of so many conversations – especially with the role you are playing in Attoria. However, my mate also credits your … intersession with helping him regain his health. I've done what I can for him, as well."

"He looks in top shape, Missy! What are you doing?"

"Oh, herb drinks and raw vegetables and not the first drop of fermentum in moons!" Drayash complained.

"Dear cub," Vanalla offered, putting her paw on his shoulder. "Please, stay with it. You look so good; it makes me so happy to see you well."

"See Missy, kind then and kind now to me. If anyone knows what it means to be family, it's this one," he said softly, nodding to Vanalla.

"He has always spoken about you and the questions you raised and – hey, there is something you might want to see."

"Really?" Van asked, curious.

"Yes, sure!" Drayash agreed. "A little redecorating project that's been undertaken since you and I last spoke."

"Okay, I'm interested. You two lead the way!" As Drayash slipped his paw around that of his mate, all aspects of Vanarra felt the love and warmth between the two Faelnar as they walked. They were feeling it so fully that Van barely recognized where they were going. "Dray, you … are you taking me to the-"

"It's not an altar anymore. It's something much better. Missy's been working on this."

"I have a longstanding disagreement with the Faelnar who runs the de Gonari family archive and Halls of Honor, if you could even call them that," Missy complained. "This is my own little effort to combat her distortion of history." When they turned down the hallway that had been made in the archive to give easier access to the secret lair of Vanarra Anasto, Van's mouth dropped. All of the worshipful art had been replaced with real-life images and displays – some she recognized immediately as being like the ones in the Windston museum so many seasons ago. "Oh, Doctor Mysnala," Van breathed in wonder, "this is amazing! I ... some of these things look so familiar!"

"A lot of it is the rescued work of Arani de Bosnar and the other curators who followed her in the seasons after Vanarra de Gonari's disappearance. While the displays in the hallway here are quite real, take a look here! These are three dimensional projections that allow you to see larger displays that we don't actually have room for down here." Van shook her head, marveling at what appeared to be a whole additional room beyond the large dark frame on the wall. "The room is not really there, of course, but the artifact imaging is taken directly from the historical items themselves."

"My ... what an old Racerra 3000," Van swallowed, shaking her head, ancient memories replaying in her mind.

"The Meeting Den was the genesis for so much that has happened in Thurian culture and history," Missy explained as they turned around and saw another three-dimensional projection of Vanarra's in her old matriarchal headdress, her own features staring back at her. They continued to walk, and Van couldn't mistake the love that had been poured out and into what she was seeing. However, as they turned the corner, a display came to life which nearly stopped Van's heart.

"Tana!" she breathed. There, rendered in near perfection by the most exacting imagery was Tana de Gonari standing, looking stately and beautiful in the traditional dress of a dame from that period.

"I ... I talk to this one, sometimes," Dray confessed. "It's strange to be able to see her like this."

"I'll say," Van replied, biting her lip and fighting back a tear. "She looks so real."

"Oh, but that's not the best part. There was an archive recording made by Lyssia de Oterbythe of Vanarra's secret home," Missy explained as they stepped forward, and the curtain in front of them parted, revealing her onetime lair exactly as it had looked the night she had left it. "If you are a fan of the history of Vanarra de Gonari, I think you are going to enjoy this."

Missy pressed a control, and the hallway light dimmed. "What you are about to see," a deep male voice announced, "is a three-dimensional recreation of an archive record made by archivist Lyssia de Oterbythe shortly after the rescue of the Vulpi and the fall of de Caterra. With her rights and place assured, then Matron Vanarra de Gonari led her father, her step mother, and archivist Lyssia through the ductwork from the children's section into the lair she had found and occupied as a young teen. It was in this lair that Vanarra Anasto hid from the world until the unfortunate death of her first love, Ashalam. When you listen, remember that all of the voices you hear are completely authentic. Only minor quality enhancements have been made to the recording to give it the correct spatial sense."

Four nearly solid figures appeared in the room, and immediately Van was shaking her head as she looked at herself, Lyssia, her own father, and her step-mother Fillesse. For a moment, they were still, and then Lyssia started to move and speak. "This is Archivist Lyssia de Oterbythe recording the secret … lair, the hiding place of the young Vanarra Anasto when she was alone, after her mother had passed. Matron, can you please tell us about this space, describe the things in it?"

Van watched her own form come to life and start to point out and explain items all around. "Well, here is my bed. It's made out of two bed-sheets sewn together and stuffed with pillows I took from … all over. The blankets and coverings I … well, stole from the garbage of department stores. I stacked some clothes I used and other things here – kind of my closet. Here's a stunner, a knife – like I said, those were hard times. Here … is my music player and … wow, my first Rahnahi book! It's really the archive's copy, I suppose, but … it was my first. I've … marked in it – sorry, Lyssia."

"That's fine. It's been replaced many times over, I'm sure. It's now an artifact I would want to preserve, however. Go on, what else?" virtual Lyssia prodded.

"The rest of my library is over here. Books about reading and writing, history – I read them all. Oh, and here's a book about sex. I suppose I was interested in that, too. Some … religious books. Wait, I wonder what's in this box." After taking the box and opening it,

Van shone the light into it. "Well, oh no," the virtual Van gasped covering her muzzle with her paws. "I ... I'd forgotten."

"What?" her long dead father asked.

"Dad, do you remember this pattern?" Van asked him, teary-eyed as she held up a small, woven blouse and pants and presented them to her father.

As he held them and looked at them, the expressions changing on his face brought Fillesse close to his side. "What is it, love?"

"It's ... my – Shenaria wove this for her. We ... we didn't have much money, and she had to make the clothes. This was made after I was taken; Van, you were obviously older."

"Uh huh," Van cried. "Exactly eight seasons old. My mother's paws touched that; my mother's paws made that – for me!" Vattar walked to his daughter and held her, and the two cried, gently cradling the clothing between them.

The image froze, and the figures faded away, the male voice returning. "Matron Vanarra de Gonari would later assume one of the greatest and most controversial mantles in Thurian history, eventually becoming the Legendary Matriarch of house de Gonari who helped save hundreds at the Meeting Den resort as a mere *Anati*. She played a pivotal role in the freeing of the Vulpi enslaved by house de Caterra, helping also to bring about equal rights and treatment for mixed bloods. She stood in the siege of House de Oterbythe as matron, later helping that house recover from the treachery which almost destroyed it. Her legacy and contribution to the rights of all Thurians have been unequaled in the long span of Thurian history. As you depart, take note of the displays to see what she treasured and held important. Vanarra de Gonari, who has been described by the noted author and scholar and poet Rahnahi de Dothnar, as the best example of what Thurians can be if they will only love as much as she."

The curtain closed slowly as the lights raised. "Missy," Van breathed, nearly unable to speak and choked with emotion. "Just ... wonderful, okay?"

"It's touched many that deeply, and even though I spent months working with the technical team to get it to work," she explained, "it still touches me. The ... matriarch of de Gonari was here earlier and saw it. She didn't say anything. She just walked away quietly. I think it struck some kind of place inside of her she didn't expect."

"I can sympathize!" Van chuckled, wiping her eyes. "Oh, that's wonderful."

"Beats what you saw the last time you were down here," Drayash offered. "When we were all scared and running for our lives from both the Vanarrans and the Sahnassites. Now, here you are, dear kit, trying to help them pick up the pieces. I think Vanarra de Gonari and Tana would have been very proud of you."

"Kind of you to say," Van told him as she stepped over and lightly hugged them both. "Thank you for taking the time to show me this. It means more than you'll ever know."

As they started to walk out, Missy confessed, "I really hope it meant something to the matriarch. She reacted very strangely – just looking at the displays on the way out, scanning them. She has to have seen these pictures hundreds of times, but…"

"Maybe she was seeing them in a new way, love," Drayash offered.

"Well, I guess I will get a good read on her in a bit," Van suggested checking her PawLink. "I'm scheduled to meet with that bright batch in just a few passes."

"Is it true, dear kit? You seeking to be matriarch for all of those ex-Vanarrans?"

"They need a family, Dray. They need that security. They're looking to me, and … I have to help them. These didn't do anything wrong, not really – they deserve a second chance, and the best second chance we can manage. We didn't do well with mixed bloods back in Vanarra's time. I'm hoping we've learned to be more forgiving, now."

"We'll see," Missy said, doubtful. "There's been a lot of harsh talk about Attoria I've been shushing as I make my way through the library. It's gotten worse the last few sols."

"Word leaked out of what I'm here for," Van sighed. "This could get interesting. If something happens, Dray, stay back. I can take care of it – whatever it turns out to be. I want you and Missy to live many long seasons together, alright?"

"I'll TransCom it in, but … as you say," he told her, worried.

Vanalla stood, calmly, in front of a half circle shaped table where no less than five matriarchs had been interviewing her for the last two intervals, Carinthia de Dothnar sitting in the center. To her left were the matriarchs from de Gonari and de Bosnar. To her right sat the matriarchs from de Orturu and de Khaetria. To the once Grand Matriarch Vanarra de Gonari, hiding behind the mask of Vanalla Ashallo, it had been an interesting and engaging session in multiple ways.

At first, the matriarchs had started out polite, with Carinthia being the most engaged in the questions, the rest simply content to sit and listen to the answers. However, Van's answers were always replete with historical references that applied to every family represented. She had some inner amusement revealing to these would-be leaders of houses how their families had worked together and cooperated to achieve gains that were mutually beneficial. This clearly caused some level of confusion and discomfort amongst their number. Each event she cited between two houses was something that either one matriarch would dispute as being historically inaccurate or another might claim complete ignorance that such an event had occurred.

A break had been called for a quarter interval after the entire purpose of the "interview" seemed to get lost in the historical debate, Carinthia finally realizing this and calling a halt. The dames sitting behind their matriarchs also disappeared and started making calls immediately during the halt. It was a very different group of matriarchs who called her, once again, to stand before them. Carinthia spoke first. "We are now called back into session – yes, Matriarch Tessia of de Gonari?"

The older Faelnar turned towards Vanalla and contested, "You, young one, in the last two intervals have provided more historical clarity for my house than I've been able to sort out during my entire tenure. It … points out a rather fundamental misunderstanding not that you have, but that we have, of our roles as the leaders of these houses."

"This is true for me, also," the matriarch of de Orturu breathed out, shaking her head. "I didn't believe you at first, but I had my staff check the private archives of the matriarchs, and as far as they can tell, you are right in everything you say. I think ... we might have all just had that experience." Somewhat surprised head nods circulated around the table with varying degrees of discomfort.

The de Gonari matriarch nodded and then turned to Vanalla. "You are an exceptional historian and archivist; your knowledge of family history seems unparalleled, although I have a few archivists amongst our number who are just itching for an opportunity to spar with you on certain subjects. Having historical knowledge doesn't automatically equate to an ability to run a large pack like a family house, manage its interests, and develop the resources necessary to further a house's goals. How would you answer that concern about your experience?"

"Honored One, as the charitable organization formed to create and further Attoria as a refuge did include a number of certified accountants, accredited architects, and the consultancy of several medical professionals, including Doctor Emmeniama de Kestrick," Van answered, disassembling multiple arguments at once, "it was always a presumption, and a correct one, that no one individual would have the sum of experience required to foster such a ... unique undertaking. Such wasn't my belief in my own abilities, either, when I volunteered well before knowing how I would be asked to serve. The decisions required to run a house are the sole accountability of the leader of that house, but that leader would not be even counted as such if she didn't understand the requirement to gather other options and ideas and test them, try them, and not only in her own thoughts, in the hearts and minds of those she trusts. In many ways, this openness to not only serve but to hear is what seems to have drawn the Aelkinda to begin to support me."

"*Begin* to support?" Carinthia disagreed. "They consider a matter of fact, my peers, despite any decision we come to here, in this place. As we all transition back to a more traditional way of running our houses, we are finding this type of universal consent to participate in the familial oversight of one's private life something we can only dream of! Vanalla is being offered that willingly and freely without exception by every member of the Attorian community!"

"I'm not so sure that is a complete positive," the de Orturu matriarch warned. "There are many of us who worry about zealotry now in any form, especially by those whose order once caused so much harm to my family and to others. How would you answer that, Vanalla?"

"You speak to a very specific … fear, Honored One, or should I say worry? It is one that would be directed at either my willing or unwilling or oblivious ignorance to the creation of a new Great Mother for the Aelkinda to worship, especially in relation to their desire to follow me, specifically. Am I adequately expressing the concern?"

"You said it right the first time," the de Bosnar matriarch refuted, passing an almost accusing look at her Nephti counterpart. "Fear." The tension in the room increased as the verbal accusation split itself half between Vanalla and half between the de Orturu matriarch.

Stepping out from in front of the small lectern she had been given, Van walked towards the de Bosnar matriarch. "I understand," she stated. "It is my fear, as well. However, in your own history, the formation of your house began during what specific event, if I may ask, Honored One."

"The Famine of Desecration," the de Bosnar matriarch responded. "Lupar could not have survived unless there was a central familial authority to pull the tribes together and insure the necessary food wasn't hoarded but shared."

"Survival. Survival created your family, Honored One – the need for it. Honored One?" she asked, turning towards the de Gonari matriarch. "In the legends of the de Gonari, to which event do they attribute the formation of your family house?"

A dame leaned up and whispered in the matriarch's ear, and then she answered, "I'm led to believe that is was the clan wars in the eastern region of the Rician continent."

"Indeed, Honored One. The wars had ravaged the male population until there was a true danger that the generation living then would have been the last. The family stopped the war and, in time, brought back a sustainable population to the region." Looking at the de Khaetria, she gently stepped a few tracks away from her and asked, "Your family, Honored One?"

"Disease, a horrible plague among the tribes," the Vulpi answered, clearly haunted and very directly seeming to identify with the story. "Population ... decimated. No one tribe could survive alone, but the leaders – the chiefs – would never agree. The families of the various tribes gathered without the chiefs and made the decision."

"Thank you, Honored One," she offered in a gentle bow to that matriarch. Slowly, she turned to the de Orturu matriarch and only asked the question by raising her eyebrow fur.

"The fire. The Burning of the East. A monstrous blaze that destroyed nearly all of the tribal lands after three seasons of drought on Thuratan."

"Survival, Honored Ones," Vanalla replied, slowly stepping back to the lectern. It was a subtle sign of disapproval of the de Orturu matriarch's challenge, but still, her next words answered it. "All around this planet, Vanarrans are dying. During the time we have been speaking, maybe none – I would hope – but more like several if not tens and twenties have died of starvation. In some of the temples that died out completely, we have all read reports of cannibalism. As desperate as the situations that created your family houses, those who have fled to Attoria have faced equal desperation and tragedy. They have tried clinging to one another, hoping that by their mutual agreement they could survive without any sort of central infrastructure outside of government. This, they have found impossible to do. They need the security of *belonging*, and they know they need help learning to live again. They have fears, also. Fears that Attoria will fail and there will be no home for them, nowhere to belong."

Vanalla said nothing else but only looked to the de Orturu matriarch who, after a moment, wouldn't meet her gaze. "Of course," she sighed, seemingly disappointed in her own inability to see that answer. It was a sign in Vanalla's mind that she was redeemable. "Of course, they are zealous for the stability you represent. They are scared to death, aren't they?"

"Oh yes, Honored One, very much so. They *know* they need one another, and they *know* in their bones they need a family. They had one, before – as distorted, twisted, and perverted as it might have been, it was their family. They understand how the distortion was wrong. They understand how their upbringing was twisted from that normal Thurian experience. They understand all too well, the perversions that culture wove into their lives, every sol. All of those failings they understand, but even with those horrors stripped away, the need to follow along with others who care about you and whom you can care for is inescapable. If I am not chosen or even if I was taken away from them, their needs would drive them to choose another. This is not about me, Honored Ones; it is about them. I understand the dangers of creating a female figure for them to worship, but more importantly, they do. Still, they understand the need for family exceeds almost any other concern, save basic survival."

"Well answered," the de Orturu matriarch stated, looking up. "I swear to you, Vanalla, I have no idea what is happening here. I thought that we were here to interview and question you as a potential matriarch in the fostered community of Attoria, but I am completely being ... *schooled* by you in my own position!"

"I apologize, Honored One," Van said, bowing humbly. "I do not mean to offend in any way."

"No, dammit!" the de Orturu matriarch stood up. "You're not offending me! I'm..." It took a moment for the older Nephti to gather herself to explain, closing her eyes as she did, her paws splayed open on the table. "I've learned more about my own history and the history of these other houses in the last two intervals, and now, I am reminded that we all share the exact same heritage of need your Attorians are experiencing. You challenge me in a way that I feel I really need to be challenged! That, alone, makes you equal among our number and makes me desperately wonder what in the Creator caused you to become that which you are!"

"They need me, Honored One," Vanalla answered. "It's not much more complex than that. I will do everything I can to serve them, to heal them, to help them. I want them to survive, and I want them to fully live. I dearly and truly love them – every single one."

The de Orturu matriarch sat down just looking at the table, her eyes dropping tears to its surface. "Got it all wrong," she murmured.

The Vulpi beside her put a paw on her shoulder. "I think we all have. I think ... that's where we lost our way so many seasons ago. I..." The de Khaetrian matriarch's ears shifted direction. "I'm sorry; I hear something ... odd."

Slowly, she stood up and walked towards the windows behind her. "What?" she asked, curious.

Vanalla stepped around the table and went to her side. Below was a group of protesters, about four hundred, chanting and waving signs. "Why are they here?" the matriarch asked as her peers and their attendants joined them at the window.

"Because of me," Vanalla offered. "Because of this. It's amazing how history echoes, Honored Ones. Many seasons ago, others stood where we do trying to find a way forward for mixed bloods, and below the protestors gathered."

"Yes," Carinthia stated. "The *preserved tail* is still in the select archives. That was a very violent confrontation if my memory serves."

"I very much hope this one will be different," Van told them before turning on her heels and walking towards the room's exit.

"Wait!" Carinthia shouted. "You certainly don't intend to face them! There are hundreds of them down there!"

"I will face them, Honored Ones, even if it meets with your displeasure. Below, I see a movement based on fear and hatred and potentially a few other things. They wish to make their voices heard, very well. They will hear mine as well, defending my family."

As Vanalla resumed her walk to the exit, the matriarch of de Gonari called after her. "Vanalla! Matriarchs don't just risk themselves in confrontations like this!"

At the door, she turned about. "With all deference, Honored One, Amyra de Gonari would strongly disagree." With that, she was gone.

The de Gonari matriarch turned and looked at her peers, shaking her head. "The ... Grand Matriarch Amyra's stand before the mixed blood terrorists in the Mercy Garden!"

"And how will we be counted on this sol, my peers?" Carinthia asked, and the group just looked at one another.

The protesters had been gathering in the nearby athletic complex for nearly an interval, making signs and organizing themselves, a great number of poster and banner supplies already pre-staged. A somewhat small and skinny Lupar male had looked through the list of suggested messages and found nothing that he agreed with or felt that he could say from his heart. There was no quick slogan or witty quip that he could paint onto a board that would echo what he was feeling. As a child, both he and his parents had been terrorized by a Vanarran chapter in their neighborhood that demanded not only to be recognized as equals but as superiors. His own father and mother had been intimidated into always yielding to them in every part of their lives, in traffic, out walking, at every interaction. He felt he was the reason why. When he learned the truth about the purebred curse, it felt like his fears were confirmed.

Finally, "I am afraid of you" is what he placed onto his poster, not in red, but in black. Once he had finished putting the post and supports on the back of it, he moved into the area where the protestors were gathering. "Vanarrans have no place!" and "Attoria isn't justice!" and "Hold them accountable!" were just a few of the signs he saw around him. Others looked at his sign and whispered to their neighbors, but largely they didn't say anything to him. "I'm afraid of you, too," he thought, sighing.

"That's not what we intended to have on these signs," an erudite Lupar, strong and keen, said, upon observing his sign.

"Do you want me to throw it away?" he asked.

The male looked both it and him up and down and almost laughed. "No, keep it. It works for you." Seeing the snickers and chuckles around him, he wanted to just leave all of them, but just as he was hesitating, the call came for everyone to gather. The Lupar who had appraised both him and his sign as mutually pathetic now stood before everyone on the raised platform. "We have just verified that the leader of Attoria is being interviewed in the Pinnacle spire right now, and this is the opportunity for us to make our voices heard about the amazing injustice being done to all true Thurians by allowing such a harbor of terrorism and religious extremism to exist! We're leaving now, and everyone keep up." His eye rested on the skinny Lupar, sneering a little as he added, "the best you can. Fine, let's go."

Humiliated but drawn along by the tide, he held his sign facing downward while others were already starting to wave theirs above their heads and chant the slogans that had also been on the leaflets. In a quarter interval, the group of four hundred had situated themselves squarely in the middle of the archive entrance walk in the clear view of the spire conference rooms. With a little coaching from the head Lupar, everyone finally started shouting and repeating the same slogans, and hidden amongst a forest of other signs, Tymar de Bosnar finally held his sign aloft and chanted along. In his heart, Tymar regretted ever joining the protest is it seemed completely pointless to stand outside and yell insults at a building.

One or two times, he saw academy security, especially the older cub he liked, looking on their activities with disapproval and some level of anxiety. Yet, they didn't interfere. After a few passes, something strange started to happen; the protesters' volume seemed to become muffled and then fall away, signs starting to wilt like sun-dried flowers in a drought. Looking up the path, confused, he saw the reason why. It was a brown and gold Faelnar approaching them, alone; her slow, dignified step spoke not of any fear or intimidation – only purpose. It was clear some in the group recognized this Faelnar, and as he stared at her, he thought he might, also. There was a Newsarotzi story on Attoria that showed a nearly mud-caked Faelnar much like her working alongside a bunch of the Vanarrans as they weeded and planted a garden or crops of some kind.

Her eyes weren't fixed on any specific point or individual, but still, she made her approach undeterred by either their number or their appearance. The chants fell away to almost nothing as she came to within ten tracks of them – her steps not slowing, and the group parted and allowed her to enter their midst, forming an anxious circle around her as she halted. All around her, every Thurian seemed stuck, as Tymar was, in some combination of shame and awe.

As the sounds of the protestors dropped to nothing, the Faelnar simply turned and looked at the group, her eyes seeming to take in every single one of them, and her appraisal of Tymar made it feel like a searchlight had been shined into the depths of his soul. None of the others could truly claim not to have been affected by this Faelnar's gaze. It was only her softly spoken command that impacted them more. "You wanted to have your voices heard, but you dropped to absolute silence at my approach. You want your messages to be understood, but none of you have your signs where I can see them. So, please, at least let me see those."

Even though this was not an elder Female, the anxiety and shame in the air were palpable as the academy students raised their signs only to chest height, the bottom of the posts soundly on the ground. "Now, in every group, there is a leader. Who is it? No? Am I to guess then? Well, you leave me only the superficial to consider, but I think that should be enough." Her eyes swept around again, and she began to describe what she saw. "Wardrobe from the most expensive boutique on the Rician quarter of Shanandrae but very unsure, no." Her eyes went to Tymar, and a touch of sympathy hit them. "Very carefully acquired second-paw clothes, well cared for, and not a designer piece among them. You're too busy for it." Her eyes then darted to movement, and she observed stepping forward, "But you ... designer labels two seasons old, confident air, disdainful and challenging expression. Yes, you'll do. So, what are you *really* protesting, here?"

The keen Lupar hadn't flinched at all, and Tymar observed that her ability to pick him out of the crowd, while exceptional to everyone else standing around, seemed to only be the barest qualification allowing her to treat with him. "Don't pretend that we don't know what you're doing in Attoria – resurrecting and rearming the Vanarrans so they can finish what they started, dominate Thurian society and eventually eliminate all other kinds, even the mixed bloods."

"Those are the Vanarran aims, it is true," the Faelnar agreed, "and every Vanarran still within the confines of their temples and properties should still be regarded as holding those views and as a true threat."

"Then you agree with me!" the Lupar struck back.

"I believe those are the *Vanarran* aims. The Vanarrans are named that not because of their biology or genealogical heritage – they are only named so because of their *beliefs,* true?" There wasn't an answer, and it was clear the commanding Faelnar took silence as an answer, regardless. "Oh, so I see. It is impossible to take a child, then, an infant of their breed, raise it to know nothing of *Vanarran* beliefs or *Vanarran* agendas and have it come out as anything other than a *Vanarran*; have I correctly stated your point of view?"

"You are trying to tell us that such a blatantly misleading hypothetical is even possible? Of course, an insular environment controlled to perfection can create an individual of any stripe of belief!" he retorted, coming towards her.

"I'm trying to tell you that such a blatantly obvious hypothetical isn't hypothetical at all!" the Faelnar contested with enough ferocity to cause the male to stop and everyone else to take a step back. She whipped around her head and looked straight at Tymar, her voice tempered but insistent. "You, please, show me your sign – hold it high above your head." Reluctantly, he did so. "Thank you," she offered. "This exceedingly *honest* sign I could place into the paw of every member of the Attoria community without exception, and it would be true. Although it might take some bravery for them to admit it, they would have no choice but to agree that such was true for them. It would be so in many ways. First and foremost, if faced with those who still hold the Vanarran beliefs, they would be absolutely terrified."

She raised her voice and swept the crowd with her gaze as they murmured in confusion. Her voice sailed above the rumble, "*Anyone* who severs themselves from the Vanarran order or causes others to do so is under the unquestionable threat of death! Yes, it is death for the heresy of showing such a lack of faith in the Great Mother and the Perfected One not to endure in this *time of tribulation*! To undermine the faithful – that puts every volunteer and donor under that very same threat of death! So, they would look at one of their own breed with fear and horror because if something happened to empower the Vanarrans once again, every individual in Attoria would be afraid for their lives and with good cause!"

The Faelnar's voice quieted and then she looked at them, her expression saddened. "Second, they would hold that sign … and look at you. They are afraid of you."

"Why?" Tymar asked, his voice a clear tenor. "I've spent my whole life *afraid of them!* Why would they ever fear me?"

"Because of this. Because of an outcry to take from them the only safe home they know, their only opportunity for a future. No one was using Attoria before – the Sahnassites who have so easily and safely faded back in amongst your numbers simply left it abandoned, overgrown. It was the site of a massacre of Vulpi by mixed bloods, but in the end, we all know that the massacre was staged by the de Caterra – by *Faelnar!*" She pointed at her own chest. "I am not de Caterra; I am not a monster! They are not monsters, either! They are working twenty-four interval sols weeding gardens and tending crops and trying to become independent again because they are so fearful that the benevolence we thought we learned seventeen hundred seasons ago might vanish. Just as mixed bloods were once considered automatically guilty of every possible disgrace and base instinct, the Aelkinda – the new name they have chosen to call themselves – are terrified that Thuria will forget the lessons of her past and wipe ... all ... of ... them ... out."

Turning around and facing the protest leader, she asked him directly, "Is genocide what you desire? Do you want to murder them or, by neglect, allow their deaths to occur at other paws? Is that what you really stand for? Is that why you are here?"

"It's not why I am here," Tymar told her, stepping forward. "I just don't want to be afraid of them like I was growing up."

"Then come as a visitor and meet them," Van told him, gently. "Ignorance feeds fear. If you come to know someone is harmful, then you don't fear them – you understand and work against their aims. If you learn, however, that these are just good souls, wounded and needing help, might you not lose your fear in favor of a better calling? Wouldn't it be worthwhile to try?" He looked at her earnestly and nodded. "What about the rest of you? Here you are, protesting at a meeting where former Vanarrans are trying to do the very thing so against all of the old Vanarran teaching and beliefs – have a family to rely upon and an inclusive family that has me in it, mixed bloods, others of different species – even Lupar."

The group looked uncertain, but the Faelnar turned her gaze back to the one she had identified as their leader. "I place their lives in your paws. What is your choice? Genocide, tolerance, or compassion?"

He looked at her, searchingly. "They really have changed? They were raised with all of these crazy beliefs, and they can just forget them?"

"Forget, not at all. Is it possible to not forget, though, and still change? Hasn't that been so for at least some aspect of your life? All of your lives?"

He looked away and nodded. "I thought my father was an honest Thurian and faithful to my mother. I learned he was having orgies in exotic clubs until he was busted."

"Then you have been hurt and grievously so by those who raised you," she told him, and the gentle raising of her eyebrow fur brought forward the next conclusion.

"Like the ones who raised them," he told her. Looking around, he told his group, "Just ... put the signs away. We were wrong to do this. I was wrong."

"It is *never* wrong for your voice to be heard, to ask difficult questions, but you have done the right thing by listening to the answers. You all deserve honor for that, and you," she stated, turning to look at Tymar. "You are a rarity in this world, and your honesty and willingness to share your heart do you great credit, cub. I admire you for that." She had the pleasure of seeing his blush fur shoot skyward before continuing, "Now, my name is Vanalla Ashallo. For the present, I am the leader of the village of Attoria, what hopes to become the family of Attoria. Go to the Attoria Donations TransNet site and mention that you want to visit, and we'll arrange it. Please, if you come, come with an open mind and an open heart. Draw your own conclusions, but only on what you directly observe – please don't let others scare you or use you. Good sol to all of you, now, and thank you."

Numerous soft utterances of "Thank you" treated her departure back up the walking path to what everyone could now see was the full gathering of matrons, dames, and matriarchs who were in attendance at the meeting, waiting not one hundred tracks away. Upon approaching them, she stopped and bowed. "My apologies for the delay, Honored Ones," she stated, "and my earlier statements which may have been less than respectful. I will return to do whatever is necessary to help reach a decision."

"The decision has been made, Matriarch Vanalla. You only need to tell us of the name your family will be known by," Carinthia told her.

The other Nephti matriarch added, "And commit to help us relearn what it means to be the matriarchs of families, not of … organizations."

"In as much as I can help you, I will upon my honor and by my pledge," she told them, and all of them nodded in witness of the vow. "Our family has met regarding the subject of a name, should we be so favored. Collectively, after much discussion, they have chosen *de Kyvara*."

At this, the de Gonari matriarch seemed to startle. "Hearth fire? The one set by a female for the use of her tribe?"

"I don't understand," Carinthia stated. "The word is unfamiliar to me."

"It is a word in the old Faelnar tongue from the tribal period. It refers to a practice when some of the tribe would go hunting, the ones tending children would ensure that fires were lit specifically for the returning hunters. When lit by a male, it is known as *kyvarar*. When lit by a female, it is known as *kyvara*. It is a very good choice, to my mind, when there were so many I had worried were being considered."

"I know," Vanalla replied, now freed from the use of the honorific because of their declaration of status. "Some had wanted to use variations of my own name, and I wouldn't let them – and just so you know, the vast majority of the group was deeply opposed to the idea. Other names in various languages were considered for concepts like hope and forgiveness and honor, but this name suited us all as it has been a common practice every moon for there to be a town bonfire. I am the one who generally lights it, but they felt that such a name would suggest my place with them, Vanarra's rightful place in lighting the way for mixed bloods, and Alahari's for lighting the way for us all."

"Well said, and I think so long as the heritage of that name is made clear to all who follow, the young, that would be an apt lesson," the de Bosnar matriarch said.

"And a powerful symbol," the de Orturu matriarch agreed. "As I asked earlier and required of you, I would hope that you could assist us in learning what it means to be a better family."

"I would be honored to host you at any time, Honored One, but ... just be prepared to get dirty," Vanalla warned, smiling, and to that the de Orturu matriarch chuckled before formally greeting her newest peer. "In honor, then I greet you, Matriarch Vanalla de Kyvara."

Chapter 22: When Shadows Fall

Waiting with a somewhat anxious version of patience, Callanar watched Vanalla returning to the village in her hover, Vosh riding alongside her. In short order, the vehicle was parked, the two said a few words, and Van started walking towards the front of the administration building where he had been waiting. As he watched her approach, her expression told him absolutely nothing. She was the same resolute, calm, and centered individual she always was, but as she drew close enough that a reasonable speaking voice was halfway possible, he quickly proved that he was not. "May I call you Honored One, officially or ... are we yet delayed again or..." She didn't stop walking, but entered the building, signaling for him to follow her which he very quickly did.

They reached the room where the statue of Vanarra de Gonari was kept, and she directed him to close the door. "Well?!" he begged.

"They have confirmed me as matriarch of the house de Kyvara, a house under the very light fostering of de Dothnar," she told him evenly, and he easily noticed her lack of enthusiasm.

"And this ... is what we hoped for, was it not?"

"Yes, but there was something more to it, Callanar," she told him, inviting him to sit with her. "We, because of our situation here, are experiencing a more authentic version of family than I believe the rest of Thuria has experienced in generations. I find myself conflicted, pretty deeply, about what has happened."

"Please explain; how so?" he asked.

"We are starting from the very root by which all houses began, the need for survival. We rely on each other for survival, plainly."

"We rely on you," he told her, "but you could theoretically abandon us and seek opportunities elsewhere if you were any other Thurian. Yet, I truly believe you see our survival as your own."

"The existing houses lost that, Callanar, somewhere along the way. Our story ... inspires them and reminds them of what they forgot. Do you know that the matriarch of de Orturu wants to come here and work alongside us in the field? Someone nearly dripping with gold and bangles and bracelets and house crests and the like."

"It has been discussed among our number, I'd have you know, that we have no such honors to place upon you to show our love and respect for what you mean to us."

Van looked at him and just shook her head. "That's it, though. They know and I know how all of you feel towards me. I don't need one single glass bead to prove that to anyone, certainly not to remind myself. Yet, do you and the others feel as if you should, over time, bury and bedeck me in the same trappings as they?"

Callanar sat up and chuffed a bit. "I ... might have said yes until you asked me in *that* manner. Now, I sense that it is not only what you do not want, but that you sense some inherent evil in it, some deep problem."

"I have seen how matriarchs from Amyra to Vanarra to those I stood before this very sol dress, and all I see when I look at what they are wearing is potential kindnesses that could be shown to those of their own family and those who are in need – withheld. It's very true that the ceremonial jewelry of a house is accumulated over time, but what was lost in order to accumulate that? I have a fair idea of what it feels like to be one of their number, but what I am here doesn't feel anything like that. I don't want what we have here to ever become that. Do ... do I have the right to cause that kind of change?"

Callanar looked at her, curious. "You believe that if you set this example, the other matriarchs may choose to follow you?"

"I wonder at two things. Say that they make a gift of jewels so I will have something to wear, but I do not wear it. Say that I sell those jewels so that we can have another building, safe coverage for a bad winter or poor crops, what then? Secondly, yes. Our story here is very compelling to them, the other matriarchs. They have members who have to be convinced that families matter. Here-"

"It is all we have, and it matters greatly and without question," he interjected and then looked toward the statue of Vanarra de Gonari. "Dear Creator, could it really happen? Could the definition of what family means be borne anew from such poor vessels as we? You, Honored One-"

"I am as poor a vessel as anyone here. Yet, the responsibility, Callanar – that is what gives me pause! It could happen that we don't really influence anything, but the future doesn't have that feel to it."

"I am glad that I am not the only one who senses the moods of things to come," he commented.

"What does your sense of the future tell you?"

"That you will be not only our matriarch, but more, and that this which we do will not be small."

"No, and that is my fear. Turn the clock fifteen hundred seasons ahead, Callanar, and will they revere me as you once revered her?" Vanalla asked, pointing at the statue.

"I would hope they would learn our lesson – the very lesson that brought us into such dire circumstances. No one will ever let us forget it, will they? It will always be a part of our very fur, the skin beneath it, the blood, the bones, all of it. We are now Aelkinda, yes, but we were formed in our mother's wombs by the misguided paws of the Vanarrans. That is a legacy that will forever be with us, just like the purebred curse will always be with us, collectively, regardless if the individuals here are guilty or not."

"So, the hope is that the tragedy that spawned this age will prevent tragedy in a future one, by its example?"

Callanar shook his head and sighed. "I don't know that we can armor the future sufficiently from here in the present. We can only do what we can do and try to tell them. You know more about Vanarra de Gonari than any of us. Do you think she took steps to prevent the twisting of her legacy by our former faith? Do you think Sahnassa de Orturu did?"

"No. I don't think they saw the seeds of this germinating in their own time, honestly. They were just living their lives and doing what they thought needed to be done. I think they knew they were living in an extraordinary time – don't get me wrong. That, we couldn't have missed, I mean, even if we were there. That's not to say that they couldn't have done things had they known."

"What do you think they could have done?"

Vanalla shook her head and pointed at the statues. "Nothing bigger than that, ever. The giant one in the Yarveas at the Meeting Den occurred while they were both alive. They were both dames by then, but they and those who led them as matriarchs should have taken greater responsibility. See, maybe that can be part of the Aelkinda legacy, as well. Honors so ... overblown have to be avoided, not because they impact those living now – it's what it will mean to the generations to follow. Teach history lessons without worshiping or deifying those who lived in history. That can be part of who we are, written into our charter."

"Certainly sounds reasonable, and it would touch back on your first point – no jewelry dripping from the matriarch."

Van nodded, looking at the far wall. "No *Halls of Honor*," she groused. "Instead, you get a museum, and that museum is open to any who would want to look. Anyone can question the historical accuracy or bias of it, and the bad is shown with the good. Families should accept the difficult lessons and not only concentrate on the moments of supreme house glory. The matriarch is what she should be – the chief servant of the house. That is how she should be judged."

"As you are," he offered. "You ... love us, and we don't deserve it. I know that. Do the members of these other families think that same thing about their own house leadership?"

Vanalla shook her head. "Do you know that in Amyra's time, if one of those ... baubles fell off the matriarchal jewelry and a mixed blood found it or was found with it, the mixed blood would be put to death?"

Callanar was silent and sighed. "I have a darker observation than that. If the matriarchs in Amyra's time were more like what you suggest, then such would never have happened. Not only would there have been no jewelry over which to grow angry, mixed bloods would have been welcomed from the start."

"How so?" Van asked, looking at him.

"If you love your family, and they make a choice to join with someone who is different, why does that cancel out your love? Why is that a dishonor? Vanarrans were raised under the strictest breeding restrictions. I understood all of the reasons for it; I fully believed in how it maintained our holy purpose, but then I saw my first female Perratti when I was young. Everything about her form utterly captivated me. My leadership noticed and made sure I never saw her again. We hated … what was different. You embrace Ash, who is so unlike yourself but still wonderful in his own way, and then Vassia has her love for Laxar – you accept that, also. If they were more like you, Vanalla, there never would have been persecution of a single mixed blood."

"Perhaps," she mused and then turned to him. "I enjoy these conversations with you, Callanar. Your insight is valuable to me."

"A high compliment as will it be to call you Honored One in public. I hope I haven't disturbed you now by not doing so." She shook her head. "Thank you, although I suppose that in the future, such conversations as these will need to be held with your dames."

"Callanar," Van breathed, "you ever read the history of Siflin de Oterbythe?"

"The name sounds vaguely familiar, but I can't place it. Who was he?"

"A Perratti manager of the Meeting Den at the time of the tragedy. His performance during the crisis wasn't entirely superb, and for a long time, he couldn't find a place to work. His matriarch finally solved the issue by taking him as her aide, and in the end, he was the one who was sent to face down the Grand Matriarch Amyra de Gonari regarding the treachery of Geistana de Oterbythe. Later, he and the matriarch became extremely close – never intimate as far as we know, but he trusted her, and she trusted him. There was honesty between them unlike she ever had with any dame, and she told the Grand Matriarch Vanarra that when she was a dame, I think. I want you for my aide, Callanar. These conversations can't stop. I need them, but this is only if you are willing."

He closed his eyes and wiped tears from them. "You honor me more than I can say. Shouldn't your – shouldn't Ash be considered before me?"

"We are mated, and that relationship defines us, and I treasure it. It also limits how we can safely interact in these types of situations. I would rather be his lover and his mate and not his boss. You, however, are the very definition of loyal and honest. You represent the feelings and emotions and thoughts of everyone so well, and they respect you. There will be dames, and one sol, there will be matrons, but for now, Callanar will you help me?"

"I owe you and the others who gave us this opportunity everything, and so yes, I will, and I do so gladly and gratefully, Honored One."

"Very well. Let's go share this news with the rest of the community and start sharing our philosophy for how a matriarch should serve her family."

"As you command, Honored One, so I will do," he said humbly, standing up and bowing to her, deeply.

"Good afternoon, sir."

The older male Perratti looked across his papers at his visitor and nodded. "Good afternoon, Specialist Shadow. Please be seated." The dark red-furred Vulpi took a seat across from his boss in the Shanandrae capital office overlooking the river. "I suppose you were a bit surprised to be recalled from the Luratan assignment."

"Yes, sir. There were a few … loose threads that I still needed to trim up." The displeasure in Shadow's voice was evident, but his superior ignored it.

"Specialist Ice can take care of those, Shadow – at least the ones which were strictly job-related. The key objective was already in your paws, and honestly, I have an assignment with a bit more sensitivity that you might be a match for. What do you know about the village of Attoria?"

"Only the barest details," he answered casually as he took a drink that had been left for him by the assistant. "It's the only safe refuge for Vanarrans, created by a charity foundation sponsored by Fireclaw Destiny. It's kept a pretty decent public image by communicating with not only its donors but with the newsarotzi in general. It's still not fully independent in terms of providing for itself, but it's tracking positively – experts say two seasons, maybe, before they can self-sustain. No major crime or even minor that I've heard of, and a recently fulfilled desire to join the ranks of family houses. That's been granted, and their new matriarch appears to have been significantly impressive to those of the other houses. So, again, it's a pretty quiet subject, as far as I've heard."

"Well, yes," the Perratti offered, shifting a little uncomfortably seeing how well-read Shadow was on this subject. "While a peaceful Attoria is the common perception, the government and certain … key individuals have some doubts about that, especially given what's been witnessed in the other self-created Vanarran refuges around Thuria." The Perratti stood and went to a world map. "Here, in western Thuratan, three thousand plus Vanarrans started raiding warehouses, supply transports, and various retail stores for supplies. Here," he indicated, pointing to Ricia, "we found an entire city infrastructure *voluntarily* supporting the Vanarrans with food and supplies, only to find out they were being blackmailed with the release of a neurotoxic gas. Here," and he pointed to somewhere else on the map, "No less than five thousand armed Vanarrans took over six villages in the rural sectors, conscripting them to provide food, shelter, and other supplies. That took the military to pry them out, and there was a lot of blood on the ground when that was done – of all kinds."

"But there's a difference here, sir, isn't there? Attoria was never a Vanarran temple or outpost; its property was purchased by the supporting foundation."

"It's true. However, at every other Vanarran enclave we've checked so far, without exception, there have been significant criminal enterprises in play – ones intended to bring the Vanarrans back to some semblance of their former power and influence."

Shadow looked at his boss, curious. "I thought all of those instances had been dealt with … in a very *final* way."

"Indeed, they have," the Perratti replied, sitting down. "There are only a pawful left to check, and that's where Ice and Steel are going next. As you, they have the right to fulfill their mission with the full privilege of final sanction. So, that will leave only those Vanarrans still trying to subsist in their former temples, those in hiding, or those living in Attoria."

"I've read that those in Attoria no longer consider themselves Vanarrans. I believe the term is Aelkinda that they now prefer."

"There is great concern, Shadow, that what we're being told and what the public has been told may not adequately represent what is actually happening. As so many other self-created refuges have turned out so badly, there is great doubt by those in the core intelligence council that Attoria is – at its heart – any different."

"I see," Shadow sighed, relaxing back into his seat, his keen blue eyes still fixed at the Perratti. "So, infiltrate them, learn their secrets, and if I find anything of a serious nature – what assets will be standing by?"

"Under the most dire of circumstances, aerial bombardment is available upon request, essentially leveling Attoria and killing everyone in its borders," the Perratti explained. "Of course, it wouldn't be a direct military mission but rather the *accidental* crash of a flyer transporting high explosives."

"How much explosives?"

"Enough to make a crater where Attoria once was. With their numbers peaking above twenty-five hundred at present, it's not like we can afford to risk a direct military assault. Access to that valley from the ground is problematic, at best, and if they have become armed with some previously undetected munitions, it could otherwise be quite a standoff. A lengthy and costly ground campaign would be difficult to sustain."

"How has public relations managed the other situations?"

The Perratti leaned back and looked somewhat askance at the Vulpi sitting in front of him. "Military training accident, here, a dam failure, there. Maybe a fuel tanker crash or two. Scattered abroad and at different times, it's not enough to truly raise suspicion. A little funding of the local newsarotzi and other persuasive influences have also kept their eyes fixed elsewhere. We're managing to dampen the TransNet traffic on this, so it's conceivable that the rest of Thuria might wake up one sol to find that there are no free Vanarrans left."

Shadow looked at his employer critically. "Meaning that, based upon what I've heard so far of their survival rates once in enforcement confinement, it wouldn't be too long before there wouldn't be any Vanarrans … at all."

There was a pause before the answer came. "While not a direction, Shadow, the intelligence council maintains that as an option, or at least, a potential outcome."

"Genocide, Director?"

"If it was a rogue nation state, family house, or corporate pack, we wouldn't hesitate. Five hundred seasons ago, there were no Vanarran Select. If Thuria returns to a peaceful state and there are no Vanarran Select, that's a price the government feels willing to pay. There may even be some truth to the rumors that their need for domination was a part of their genetic breeding program. If so, then as unpalatable as it might be to us, extermination may be our only alternative."

"I see, sir," Shadow replied, finishing his drink. "What's my cover story?"

"A potential donor wanting to spend a few sols in Attoria to assess the situation. Assistant will have the papers for you, just outside, and one other thing, Shadow."

"Yes, sir?" he asked as he stood.

"There's a Lupar female there, Malliana Dorsi. Although not officially part of the mission, she is someone we'd like you to keep an eye out for. She's the daughter of a representative, and he's … concerned that she has been co-opted to some cult-like purpose."

Shadow's head canted a bit as he asked, "Isn't she the chief correspondent – the newsarotzi responsible for sending the press releases and other stories about Attoria?"

"Specialist Shadow, for someone who knows only the *barest of details* about Attoria, you are remarkably well informed," the director complained. "She is at that, and we're not at all sure that she hasn't chosen to stay of her own volition. However, if something questionable is happening in Attoria, it's quite possible that such may not be true. Extraction is … preferred, especially if you have to exercise full sanction." The director held up an envelope, and the Vulpi took it, opened it, and extracted the image of the Lupar female. "Extraction without undue *interaction* is also preferred, Shadow," the director growled. "I do find it difficult to explain, to some parties, why paternity tests are a part of our on-going expenses."

"None have come back positive, I trust," the Vulpi replied smugly.

"None yet, Shadow. I'd like to keep it that way or, better still, not have to pay for them in the first place."

There was only a chuckle as the Vulpi left the room.

Aboard the Haven, Teldear Dynaea sighed, "And I was having such a good sol."

"Sadly, he is not wrong about some of the other sites, as you well know," Kylie noted. "They have good reason for suspecting any concentration of former Vanarrans isn't so former in their long term aims."

"Vanarra doesn't believe any who are now living there have the faintest desire to return to what didn't work. Not all are prepared to embrace the Creator's Path, true," Dynaea contested, "but she and I agree. It's just not in them."

"They have been treated with exceptional fairness, kindness, and patience," Amyra offered, appearing behind the Teldear and putting a paw on her shoulder as she sat in the command chair of the bridge. "Their loyalty and gratitude have been cultivated, and that has choked out what's sprung up everywhere else. There are thankfully a few thousand Vanarrans who are being sheltered privately, in hiding."

"They are going to stay in hiding so long as those stories keep appearing on the TransNet," Rahnahi offered, her voice the only indication of her presence. "Every one of the ones I have visited is terrified that execution waits for them the moment they step out their front door. Bless the kind Thurians sheltering them, but if we can't get those worthwhile refugees out of hiding and into Attoria, we're going to have suicides."

"Rahnahi?" Dynaea asked, and at that, the Nephti appeared. "Can we start thinking through a way to influence these to come to Attoria?"

"If there is an Attoria left there," the former de Dothnar matriarch sighed. "Crashing a big flyer full of explosives right into the village core could really and truly ruin their sol."

"You were listening in?"

"I was there, Teldear," Rahnahi commented. "I read them both, and we have a problem. Neither of those Thurians so blithely talking about the extinction of Aelkinda are bad. They believe they are protecting Thuria as a whole."

"While true," Amyra contested, "and I can understand their bias, it was a horrifyingly casual conversation to watch."

"Without doubt," Dynaea agreed. "Kylie, inform Vanarra – see how she wants to distribute the news to our inner circle living there. How long before Shadow appears at the Attoria doorstep?"

"He's scheduled for the morning, tomorrow," Kylie reported. "We have to put together some idea of how to manage this before then. We should-"

"Oh, I hate when you stop talking like that!" Dynaea swore, standing up and walking towards the distracted Vulpi-Izar.

"Yeah, and this time won't be any different," Kylie sighed. "We have a dignitary coming. Nyssia's super-cruiser just hailed from the pulsar. She'll be here in a matter of passes."

"Don't you sometimes wish that Theo was the only Allarraen?" Amyra queried.

"Nyssia can be trouble, yes, but she's still accountable to Theo," Dynaea offered. "We'll just have to see how this plays out."

In less than ten passes, the two figures were appearing on the bridge of the Haven. Once again, Nyssia appeared as a female Lupar of nearly daunting size, but this time Saletta appeared exactly as she had all of those seasons ago on Thuria. Dynaea, in her normal Asteravan form, bowed low and offered, "Supreme Councilor Nyssia, we are deeply honored by your visit."

"That was very politely offered, Teldear," Nyssia nearly chuckled, her formality only breaking slightly allowing a gentle smile and a soft lilt in her voice, "however forced as it may be. Please know that I am not here to interfere with operations beyond what is absolutely essential. Might I ask a few moments private consultation?"

"As you wish. Kylie, if you would please lock out main conference one once we are inside?"

"I will," Kylie replied, nodding. As Dynaea and Nyssia left the bridge, Kylie asked quietly, "Hey, kit, not that it's not totally wonderful to see you, but what's going on? Why's she here?"

Saletta's expression was completely apologetic. "She's not telling me, either. I know she had a long talk with Theo, though – she mentioned that much. After that," the small Faelnar offered, shrugging, "she called up her cruiser, we boarded, and set course for here." Her steps, however, were bringing her to stand right in front of the other Faelnar who was simply looking at her, smiling and trying not to cry. "Hello, Honored One!"

Amyra wrapped her arms around the diminutive female and held her close. "Oh, dearest child," she breathed, crying. "You saved my life, you remember?"

"I've tried to avoid long knives ever since, but it was so worth it!" Slipping away, she just looked at Amyra and shook her head. "Seeing you so young is amazing! It makes me want to go find my matron's insignia and get started on some project for you! Oh, and you! I can't believe how you look! I … I apologize-"

Rahnahi sighed and walked over and hugged the kit, as well. "Yes, yes, I know. I'm not fat anymore."

"Don't let her kid you; she still eats well," Amyra teased, taking her former matron by the arm and leading her towards one of the rest areas. "So, truly no idea what's going on here? We have just hit a snag with the government potentially wanting to erase Attoria if they find anything not to their liking, so Nyssia's timing is…"

"Truly and utterly her own," Saletta sighed as she followed along. "With Theo, he shows up when things get desperate or when he can truly help. He may be there before, but you won't see him. Why and when Nyssia does things is as much as a mystery to me this sol as it was when I first met her. One sol, she just changed into that Allarrae dragon form, and I walked around for the next three sols hoping not to get eaten. Although, as I actually say it aloud now I seem to remember Dassalil dropping by sometime soon after that. She wasn't half as terrifying as she might have been had I not been scared furless by seeing Nyssia slither about." Kylie hummed in the back of her throat. "You suspect something?"

"I do. Dassalil was Van's prior commander. It seems like Nyssia has been doing a lot of follow up on Theo, Thuria, and Vanarra. Were you able to listen in on any of the discussions?"

"No, but Dassalil was very kind to me and seemed to know a lot about me already – I guess Van must have mentioned me or something," Saletta offered, sighing. "Like I said, I was politely dismissed for the core of their meeting, not unlike now, of course."

"Has it been all bad?" Amyra asked, concerned and sounding protective over the matron who had saved her life. "Even Supreme Councilors have to treat others with respect."

"No, no; it's not that. Please understand that she's never been disrespectful. She is as mysterious as the sol is long and a lot more private than Theo, I think. What's more is that, little by little, I get the sense that we're working well together. I'm certainly not even *close* to her on any scale – evolutionary or ascendance or intellect or whatever, but lately, she's shown some real concern for me. She's listened, too – really listened," Saletta stated as she sat down on one of the couches in the lounge. Looking at Amyra, she shrugged. "She's reminded me of Kinnessa at times, oddly enough. She won't let you know exactly how much she likes you, I think, because she must think it important to keep some kind of distance."

"It's a balancing task for all leaders, true," Rahnahi stated. "I like to keep my trainees close enough to know what's going on with them but far enough away that they feel they have to pull their weight."

"Trainees? What for?" Saletta asked, smiling.

"We train the newly ascended of Thuria and of Thuriana, and I expect for *you* to be in our classes at some point, my former matron and future student," Amyra told her.

Saletta just shook her head. "I can't even imagine! So, please, can you tell me what's going on here? I'm curious. I don't get to hear that much – other than Van got joined!"

A half interval later, Dynaea appeared at the door, having to wait a moment for Kylie to stop her explanation of the Vanarran and Sahnassite decline. However, after that story, they all seemed to notice her at once. "My apologies, but I have a request from Supreme Counselor Nyssia that I am entertaining, and tentatively, I've agreed, but as the subject of this request is you, Saletta, she would like for you to join her in the landing bay to discuss it."

"Seriously? The landing bay?" Kylie asked.

"And this is to be a private conversation," Dynaea warned. "In all respects."

"I'll go," Saletta stated, standing. "I just knew something was up with her. She's been acting even more mysterious than usual on this trip."

"And that's why I love that kit," Amyra sighed. "Face forward. That's what she does."

"You taught me," Saletta acknowledged, nodding, as she walked towards Dynaea. "So, should Kylie just TriGate me out?"

"You are actually going to exit the Haven via the landing gangway, level one, aft section. Kylie will light-guide you."

"What's your favorite color, Saletta?" Kylie asked.

"Purple. Why?"

"Look into the hallway," the Vulpi offered. The lights in the corridor had all gone to purple in one direction.

"Oh, thanks! It's beautiful!" she breathed. "Okay, if I don't get to say goodbye, I love you all, okay?"

With that, she was gone, and Rahnahi took a hard look at Dynaea. "You ... are really unsure about what you were asked. That doesn't inspire much confidence."

"I have my issues with that, sometimes," Dynaea admitted. "But nevertheless, I'm bound by secrecy on this one. I can't tell you anything, and even I was told relatively little."

"Well, I'll dampen my audio sensors in the bay, but I'm not closing my eyes completely," Kylie warned. "After a little time aboard the *Defender*, I learned never to do that."

A few passes later, Saletta stepped carefully down the purple-lit gangway as it lowered to the floor of the landing bay. She didn't see her mentor anywhere, and so she decided to walk into the most open part of the bay. As she stepped about twenty tracks beyond the outer edge of the Haven's hull, a voice echoed around her. "You are very trusting of me, Saletta. I don't feel that I have adequately returned that respect."

"Theo vouched for you, and Theo saved my life," she offered. "You've never harmed me, and you've saved me when by accident or ... on purpose I was going to get myself harmed or killed. You've been kind to me." Just then, the outline and substance of a deep blue-black dragon appeared, occupying the space that would have been occupied by Vosh had she not been spending most of her time as a Thurian and very little in her native Terspear form. With something to focus on, Saletta approached the huge beast watching her intently.

"Do you remember the first time I appeared to you this way?"

"I do," Saletta stated, her blush fur raising as she remembered the experience. "I was … a little shy – well, terrified around you."

"And even then, when we had so little history, Saletta, you trusted me. You respected me. You didn't resent me."

The creature closed its eyes and seemed to be uncertain if not deeply troubled. "Nyssia, what's wrong? What have I done?"

"You, Saletta, have done absolutely nothing meriting reproach or correction. In my own eyes, I cannot say the same. I opposed our deep involvement in your culture. That means that I voted against the Allarrean fleet coming to save your world."

The eyes opened and looked down at her, expectant of a response. "I'm sure you had your reasons," Saletta offered. "To me, they are mysterious, sometimes, but you always seem to have good reasons for what you do."

"Reasons that now have drawn into sharp focus, knowing you as I do," Nyssia responded softly. "It was Theo who asked for me to take you on as a protégé, and I agreed to it … with great reluctance. Do you remember that I gave you a name in our language?"

"I do. You don't use it very much. It was *Tanliki Danashi*. I think you said it meant I was your student."

"*Teacher's pet*, but expressed in the way I said it, it literally means *the little pet of the teacher*. It was a name that relegated you in my mind to an indulgence due my leader, and it also implied that I had been burdened with you as a punishment." There was a long pause, and the creature hung its head. "It was a shameful thing for me to do, and I regret it. I slighted you every time I said it, and sometimes my reasons for not telling you something or being mysterious around you were … poor. I even orchestrated your capture, in a way, to prove to Theo his belief in you was ill founded. Then, you were utterly willing to sacrifice yourself. Saletta, I apologize to you for this offense and for all of the others. Supreme Counselor Nyssia of Allarrae, ancient in life and legacy, I may be, but I was wrong about you – wrong beyond justification and wrong beyond any rationalization for my actions."

"I forgive you, and … I'm sorry I was a disappointment to you."

The creature's eyes opened, and she nearly glared down at the diminutive female. "No! You exceeded my expectations, and I am just ashamed that my initial appraisal of you was so poor. Do you know that I never *once* looked at your history until you were captured? To me, you were just some random furry little being tossed into my life without my true consent. I finally read your file, and then I didn't believe it. I … exercised counselor privilege and back-scanned you to the point you were born. I, Saletta, know everything you have ever done or said – and I was ashamed of what I had done once I learned of it. I look at you now, and I truly grieve your losses. I know that you took the blade meant to kill the one who now is ascended. You nearly died for her. You did die for those you sought to help. To them you did, at least. You had no way of knowing I would save you."

The self-doubt and contrition coming from the Allarraen drew Saletta close, and she touched the front talon of the creature with both of her paws. "Even now, you care for me more than you do yourself. When Theo saved you and changed you so you were renewed and long-lived, do you remember what you felt?"

"I … I do," Saletta confessed. "I felt how he cared for me, his kindness and concern for me. It … it changed me."

"I have never shared with you in that way, and I never even considered it. I want to, Saletta, but in order to share I must first answer the questions I have about myself and about those with whom I used to agree – those against you and your world," Nyssia told her. "I need to press Theo with hard questions, and those answers are important to me. I'm not trying to be mysterious with you. I…"

"You need time," the Faelnar almost whispered. "You may need more than that, it sounds like."

Curiosity made the regal beast cant its head. "What would I need?"

"I am not sure I have any right to tell you, but after your questions are answered, if they can be answered, you should spend time here."

Nyssia's gaze turned towards the roof, and on it appeared an image of Allarrae, the home world. "I so seldom leave it. I have sought to know every crevice of its existence, in all dimensions and in all times. I thought Theo somewhat ... eccentric for spending the time he does away. My cruiser runs my errands, brings me those I want to see. I came here for that event the ... the joining, yes. I realized afterwards – I enjoyed that trip. I need to spend time in Theo's company, see what he sees, and learn to become what may best serve you, Saletta. I, when I am worthy of such trust, would ask you to become my Teldear. To get ready for that, I want to leave you here for a time in the care of the ones who love you the most."

"My family. My friends," Saletta breathed. "I ... want to count you among that number, Nyssia."

"You will; I promise – only when I know how to be a better fulfiller of what that truly means."

"If any place can teach you that, this one can. If anyone can teach you that, these can."

Nyssia dissolved into the Lupar who had come with her. "I will seek Theo's permission before I do, but on your recommendation, Saletta, I will ask. My ... presence may not be appreciated here. When I come into a discussion, especially with those who are not Allarrae by birth, I think it gives me undue influence."

"With some, true. Still, what is your appraisal of Teldear Dynaea?"

A sly smile crossed the Lupar's features. "Nice enough, but – what's that phrase you use? Oh, she can stand on her own hind legs."

"And Vanarra could actually stand on her hind legs and arms."

"Of all of these, you respect her most. Love her the most?"

"Perhaps, we always love and honor the ones who save us, Supreme Counselor Nyssia," Saletta offered, bowing gracefully and respectfully.

"I have so much to learn from you, my teacher."

"Kept by and keeper of. Kept by and keeper of," Saletta told the Lupar as she gently embraced the Allarraen for the first time.

A few passes later, Kylie announced to the group in the conference room, "I think Saletta wants back in."

"How do you know they're done?" Rahnahi asked.

"Well, someone of Saletta's general mass just rapped on the side of the hull. I felt it. Opening communications panel." In the boarding area, Saletta pressed a newly appeared communications control on the hull.

"Kylie, you can restore all local sensors. Our conversation is over," Saletta reported and then squealed in surprise when she found herself suddenly standing back in the conference room. "A ... little warning would be nice!"

"Sorry, dear," Amyra told her. "I was a bit worried about you."

"She was pacing," Kylie complained, "inter-dimensionally."

"Saletta," Dynaea interjected. "I need to know your decision."

"If you will have me, Teldear Dynaea, I would love to serve your mission here in whatever capacity you have need of me."

"Nyssia ... doesn't want you as her pupil, anymore?" Amyra asked, confused.

"Nyssia and I have come to an understanding, and we need to have some time on our own," Saletta told her former matriarch. "I believe, though, that for the first time, she understands the value that Thurians offer. Our families make us strong, and in recognition of how important mine is to me, she has offered me time to spend with you. I accepted."

"That was what I expected," Dynaea stated, smiling. "We would be happy to have you, Saletta."

"She also might be coming back at some point to learn how our families and culture work, first paw."

Dynaea's smile became a bit tense. "That ... was *not* what I was expecting! We would be happy to have *you*, Saletta."

There was a chuckle from the diminutive Faelnar. "And not her! Oh, I can certainly understand your anxiety, especially based on what I just heard – namely her resistance to helping Thuria."

"Among other things – many other things. Supreme Counselor Nyssia is very … insular, and that's being nice."

"Being nice to her is changing that, and she is actually working through a lot of things, I think. I would love to help her, and I think that she will help us."

"Believe it when I see it, I'm afraid," Dynaea sighed, "but I couldn't be happier if it becomes true. There aren't many factions among the Allarrae, but a change of heart on her part would be very much welcome."

"We can but try. So, what kind of things can I do to help?"

"Well," Amyra offered her former matron, "you see there is this secret agent who is coming to Attoria, and if he doesn't like what he sees, he might just cause it to get blown off the face of the planet."

"Oh! Well, now!"

Van sat with Ash in the administration building, in the small conference room which had been refitted as the matriarch's. It enabled Vanalla to sit behind a desk with up to six others at the table that was slid up against the front of her desk. Ash sat there, now, working on a piece of equipment while Van sorted through papers. "Ash?"

"Yes?"

"Just got a note from Dynaea that says we are going to have a government visitor, a covert government visitor."

"We talked about that," he noted, not looking up. "They weren't going to stay out of our fur altogether forever."

"Bit more menace in this one. If he sees anything like a weapons cache or secret underground stores of nerve gas, they're going to drop a flyer full of explosives on our head. Turn this place into a crater."

"Well," Ash chuckled, "I guess we better hide the secret lair." Then, he put down his tools and asked, "Don't they have enough to do? We have visitors come and go from here nearly every sol."

"Ah, but I guess they believe every one of them is duped, I suppose," Van sighed. "Some more detail here. Let me read through it, and I can tell you more."

"Alright," he agreed and started working again, but movement in the corner of his eye caught his attention. A diminutive Faelnar with a strangely familiar face if slightly varied coloring was slipping into the office with them. What struck him was that it was someone from their joining reception, but he remembered her being taller. When he was about to greet her, she held up her paw and quietly slipped into the seat across from him.

"And now we have a visitor, I hear," Van commented without looking up. When the visitor didn't respond, she finally looked up.

"Hello, Honored One," Saletta told her, smiling.

"What?!?" Van nearly cried in surprise and then sighed and shook her head. "Tana hid you, the scamp! Oh, Letta, it's good to see you!"

The two stood and nearly pounced on one another in a deep and complete embrace. "Oh, Van … missed you so!"

"But what are you doing here?!" Van asked her after one last tight squeeze. "Does this mean I've got an Allarraen hanging around outside or in some nearby dimension?"

"No. Nyssia's cruiser just left orbit, and I'm very sure she's on it. Ash!" Saletta reached up and hugged the Lupar Perratti who had joined them. "I hope you are doing well, too!"

"I'm … surprised to see you," he told her, looking down at her as they parted. "I'm sorry, but I kind of remember you being a little … taller."

"I'm afraid it's an inside joke, hun," Van warned him. "When Dassalil dumped me off here, I didn't know it but Saletta was sent here as a planetary scout to give me the details, only she disguised herself by taking every feature I knew about her and sitting it on its head. This really is what she looks like, but I have to say, Letta, aren't you, like, a little concerned to be showing yourself exactly as you were?"

"Why no! See, my name is Lettanalli Cassiarri, and others have told me that I bear a striking resemblance to Saletta de Gonari, but maybe it was that talk show host from a generation, ago."

Van looked at her critically. "You really think everyone's going to buy that?"

"Well, you won't, but everyone else will, I'd bet."

"Well, you get your first test," Van warned. "Callanar is about ten steps from the door having seen you enter, no doubt."

"Who's he?" Saletta asked.

"Head of our constables and Van's immediate aide as matriarch," Ash warned.

"Excuse me!" a male voice called from the entrance to the office. "Oh, my goodness. I'm so sorry, Honored One. Was this visitor ... expected?"

"This visitor, no," Van told him. "However, she is someone who has always been very close to me – a good friend. Please, meet Lettanalli Cassiarri, but you can call her Letta. Letta, this is Callanar de Kyvara."

"Hearth! No! *Hearth Fire!*" Letta nearly gasped. "Beautiful! Is that ... the family name here?"

"For the entire village minus kindly visitors such as yourself," Callanar offered, bowing.

"And you ... are the Honored One?" Letta asked, her eyes wide with expectation and hope.

"Indeed," Callanar said proudly. "She is our Matriarch, Vanalla de Kyvara, and when our period of fostering is over, it is exceedingly obvious that she will become Grand Matriarch Vanalla de Kyvara."

"I'm proud of you, Van," Letta offered very softly, but then she looked at her, curious. "No ... shoulder piece?"

"Not for this family," Ash explained. "Van and the others believe that it is better to have the matriarch be a more active paw in the community."

"We're still small, kit," Van explained. "Jewels and the like– distance, not a good thing for us. But still, we take care of each other."

"I'd ... I'd love to be part of that again, Van, if only for a time."

"Well, I wanted to ask you. What brings you here? I thought you were being mentored by someone. A diplomat?"

"Should I go?" Callanar asked, a little worried he'd overstayed into a private conversation.

"It's okay," Letta offered kindly. "If you wish, I'm fine with it. Please!"

"Let's sit," Van offered, and they all took seats. "Now, I'm completely startled you are here, but I'm still really happy about it. I'm just confused, though. What brings you here?"

"My mentor and I are actually taking a break right now. See, I'm afraid that she thought of me as something of a burden and, well, a joke, really."

"That's exceedingly unkind," Callanar interjected, and Van just looked at him. "It's just you are so well spoken and seem quite intelligent. Besides, you are held in the esteem of our matriarch, which does you no small favor in my eyes, as well."

"You are very kind, Callanar," Letta told him. "That was how things started off, but over time, it has changed. Van, she ... apologized to me and gave me this time away as a way to ask forgiveness and because she had to do some real soul-searching. She is going to speak with the one who sponsored me into her service, and I believe that she is going to come back a different Thurian. Also, I should warn you that I told her if she truly wanted to understand the meaning of family and look to someone who could teach that even to someone as learned and skilled as she, she needs to come to you, Van."

"My stars," Callanar commented. "I like you already! So, you are looking for a place here, among us?"

"Exactly!" she replied, and it was clear that she was already liking Van's aide. Turning to Van, she asked, "If there is anything I could do to just work with you again for a short time, in some capacity, could you see your way clear to permit that?"

"Well, you won't be starting as a dame, my dear," Van warned. "Those spots are already taken, and we don't have matrons quite yet. We're still working up to that. We're trending well, but we're still running below the break-even."

"But surely there's something, Honored One?" Callanar pressed.

"Oh, there *will* be something," Van promised them both. "But I think that it would suit for you to work, perhaps, at Callanar's direction. If there is even a chance that you might become a long-term part of this community, there's a lot you need to catch up on. There's a lot you need to learn, not that you won't pick up on it very quickly."

"You are so right about what I need to learn, Van," Letta offered, humbly. "While I was being mentored, I was very much out of touch. What I've heard of this place and its promise, its ... hope is very encouraging, but I am ignorant of a great many things."

"Since taking the position of aide to the matriarch," Callanar told her, "I have not been able to tend the herb garden and make the medicines we need. I have some help in that area, but we are very much focused on all of the key necessities of survival. I was just telling the matriarch, last sol, how frustrating it is to have the resources we need to survive, but very little of us available to expand those opportunities which may bring us independence."

"He's right. These medicines and remedies may well become the major export of this community," Van told her, "helping it to self-sustain."

"So, that would be a good place for me to help?" she asked.

Ash just shook his head. "There is no job here that isn't important. Every job matters, and sometimes we cross over and do different things when there is a need. They are long sols."

"If this is what you choose for me, Van, then you have my whole heart until I am recalled. I ... I think that will be some time."

"I'll want to hear more about that," Vanalla told her. "I'm a little disappointed in your mentor."

"Please, don't be. She came to a place where she realized that I wasn't a burden and that I could do more than she thought – that I was more than she thought. When she realized it, it broke her, a little bit, inside. She talked to me very directly about it; she was very painfully regretting her actions. I think she feels as if she needs to be mentored before trying to do that for me or anyone else."

"Wisdom is sometimes expressed by the tasks we turn down or put aside until we are ready for them," Callanar reflected. "Starting you in the herb garden will give the others of our family an opportunity to meet you, talk with you. Every sol, we have a lot of pulled muscles and minor injuries. If you have a gentle manner and a kind touch, you will be very happily accepted by them."

"He speaks the truth, as always, and Letta, he has my trust. You know what that means," Van told her, and the Faelnar solemnly nodded. "He will set you up in our community with a roommate. It's how it is for everyone here."

"I'm so excited, Van, to be here, and Callanar, I hope to be a help to you and to the others here."

"Then we are ready for you to start?" he asked, and she nodded.

"Dinner is at 21:00, kit. Come over to our place tonight so we can talk a little more, maybe after. Callanar, thank you. She's a dear friend."

"I can see that, Honored One. I believe that in a very short time, she will be so to all of us. Shall we?" Saletta nodded, and they all stood. Saletta embraced Vanalla and Ash a final time and then smiled at Callanar and followed his direction to leave the room.

Just before he was out the door, she called to him. "Callanar, we have a visitor coming tomorrow. More details tomorrow morning early, but please make sure you come here early. There are some complications with this one."

"As you wish, Honored One."

Chapter 23: The Teldear's Method

All settled, kit?" Van asked as she invited the Faelnar into her cabin, Ash standing as she entered.

"Oh, yes. I love my lair-mate! She was so fascinated by the fact I wanted to come here, mostly about your history."

As the door closed, Van asked, "So what do I have to *remember*, now?"

"That we, when we were young, served in the same corporate pack, one run by the de Gonari. You were my supervisor, and I worked for you. I didn't mention which one, by the way. I said that there was a scuffle at work, and that I was almost killed, but you helped me, saved me. And … now that the door is closed, I know that it is Vanalla de Kyvara I serve, but might I see my Vanarra? Or our Vanarra – sorry, Ash!"

"I don't mind a bit," he chuckled as he walked up and embraced her. When they parted, Vanarra de Gonari was standing in front of them.

"*My* Honored One!" she breathed, and the two friends hugged once again. Then, to their mutual surprise, there was another Faelnar in the room with them – a gold-on-gold, standing silently and smiling warmly at the diminutive Faelnar. "Tana?!" Saletta breathed in awe.

"She's been busting to do that since the moment she knew you were coming, *and* she still didn't tell me!" Van complained, and the silent figure waved a paw dismissively in Van's direction, coming close to and embracing Saletta.

"Tana!" the new arrival bleated, suddenly overcome with joy and love and acceptance and affection. "I love you, my friend! I love you, too!" Tears streaming down her cheek fur, she added, "You … passed the test that I couldn't." Slipping back, she looked into the almost puzzled expression in the golden eyes. Saletta's eyes cut to Van's and back to Tana's, nervously. "Look, there is something I've wanted to tell both of you, and as I think Sahni is-"

"I'm right here," a new voice stated as, in shock, they turned around. Sahnassa stood a short distance away and approached Saletta, hugging her. To the confused expression, the Nephti answered, "Tana is letting me out for a bit, as she believes that this is very important to all of us. I think she senses some regret in you but doesn't know why."

Saletta took a step back and nearly bumped into Ash, but Ash stopped her and held her paw, having her sit on the small table in front of their couch. "Thank you, Ash – this helps. In Nyssia's service, I had a lot of time for self-reflection and, even though she might have been trying to pick at me a bit, she did point out something I hadn't thought of. When I was very old in my life before, very near to the end, Theo came to me, but I felt like I was falling; I was … afraid. It didn't last long, but I think it lasted long enough for Theo to realize that I didn't – I couldn't make the type of choice that you made, Tana. Maybe, I wasn't right for it, this joining that's happening between you three. It's just I … I wanted to say that … that I'm sorry I failed you."

Van's eyebrow fur sank, and she mentally called out to Kylie. "Find out real quick if Sahni can get someplace safe. We need to be one for a moment."

There was a brief pause, and Kylie answered, "It's the middle of the night on Thuriana. You're clear. Alahari and Lyshantor are keeping watch. I'll shield you from the rest of the camp."

With no other warning than the slight pause required for that exchange, all three of the figures in front of Saletta merged together and glowed with an intense golden white light. Saletta slipped free of Ash's grasp and fell to the ground in front of the glowing figure of Vanassa. "Saletta!" the figure admonished her with a voice that seemed to echo all around them. "You are *always* a part of me. Our souls have touched, and nothing can ever change that. When I kept you, before, from fading away, you saw into my soul and I into yours.

You are *not* unworthy, my dear one. You are worthy of becoming exactly what you were meant to be. Saletta, you have changed the heart of an Allarraen, and that is no small feat. Tell me, noble soul, how you can be unworthy. Tell me how you can sacrifice yourself for the lives and freedoms of others and not be worthy. If it would be of service to you, I would gladly take you into myself, and we would be one." The figure knelt down and looked at the overwhelmed Saletta, gently lifting her muzzle so they saw eye to eye. "You won't need that to become amazing. You won't need that to be happy. You won't need that to be forever loved and adored by me. Please, precious friend, know that is from my heart, and no part of it – before or after my final becoming – has ever regretted your presence for a moment. I am always honored you chose to call me friend."

Vanassa slipped her embrace around Saletta, and the petite Faelnar's eyes were wide open, eyes amazed and awestruck, fur standing on end, body helplessly rigid, tail standing straight out. The glow around Vanassa expanded and took in the helpless Saletta, and for a few moments, they remained so, Ash shielding his eyes to look. After a moment, the glow faded, until Vanarra was herself again, gently supporting a nearly unconscious Saletta onto the floor. "Ky," Van said aloud, "thank Sahni for me. Letta needed that." Looking at Ash, she asked, "You … okay?"

"Jealous!" he joked. "I want a glowy super-powered self, too!"

"And that's why you're my mate, cub," Van chuckled. "Don't laugh too hard, though. Amyra and Rahnahi say you're right on the cusp of the thing. Sadly enough, you'll need to go on vacation if you do that."

"Really? Why?" he asked.

"You … might do worse damage than a flyer full of explosives, actually. Ascending can create a pretty large power discharge in real-space."

"Really? How bad?"

"Blew up a lair, and that was with someone really skilled blocking part of it," Van told him. "Saw that one, myself."

"Oh."

"Yeah, oh," Van chuckled. "So, if you start to see the light, kind of head the other way mentally and come tell me, 'kay?"

"Promise. How is she doing?"

"Starting to come around. To answer your next question, I shared a bit of our love for her and some of our power. I helped move her forward a bit."

"You leveled her up? Cool!" Ash exclaimed as Saletta's eyes started to focus, following his voice.

"You've being playing VidStar games with Trax again, haven't you?" Vanarra accused.

"Only a little – not much time for that."

"Van?" Saletta asked, her head turning and searching.

"Right here, kit."

"Thank you; I ... I felt so guilty about that."

Van sighed and shook her head. "Nyssia may have had a change of heart, but she hurt you by insinuating that you were unworthy. I wanted you to never feel that way again."

"Not ... not now," Saletta agreed, sitting up. "I saw ... I felt..."

"What did you see?" Ash asked her, and she just looked at him, mouth agape.

"I don't have any words for it. It ... it may take seasons for me to think of them. Van ... Vanassa touched a dark part of my heart and just..."

"You didn't deserve to carry such guilt and pain, and certainly not because of us, kit," Van told her, rubbing her paw. "We love you too much for that."

Jayanar Bonario, or *Shadow* to his professional associates in the same business, slipped the expensive envelope out of his suit pocket and examined it again as the chauffer drove him past the somewhat less than impressive security gate which marked the outer boundaries of the Attoria refuge. It hadn't been needed, and it was the only proof other than his word and that of his uniformed driver that he had any business crossing the territorial border of the village. It had only been one lone Lupar guard, as well. Without doubt, his driver could certainly have ended that individual's existence had he put up any fight whatsoever, but a quick conversation – barely a stop at all – had sent the sleek black limo hover again on its way.

"Not really security at all," he mused, putting back the now unneeded envelope into its resting place. "Just a fence and a mild-mannered guard to keep away the curious, that is unless there is a more malevolent layer of security backing that up closer in," he mused.

"Driver," he called up to the governmental security driver in the front seat. "I don't expect that security guard was all they have. Be cautious."

"Yes, sir," the driver replied, dutifully, and their speed tapered, allowing Jayanar to more carefully observe the forest beyond as they made their way. Intensive searching and examination, however, augmented with several sensors in the specially modified hover, showed absolutely nothing beyond trees, bushes, and the occasional forest grazer. "Idyllic," he thought, sarcastically, his true assessment starting to drift down to the extremes. There were no mines, trip-wires, or any sort of automated surveillance detectable as the vehicle made its passage; this meant that they were either expertly hidden and shielded or simply not there. "Insidiously clever or hopelessly naïve," he considered. Then again, the mere presence of nearly twenty-five hundred former Vanarrans – supposedly former – wasn't exactly an attraction for the curious.

Although reports suggested that public generosity towards the Attoria project remained quite high, the opinions of most Thurians were quite dark when it came to the Vanarrans, themselves. A steady diet of Newsarotzi stories and enforcement reports illuminated how the high ideals of Vanarran perfection had degenerated into thievery, blackmail, and intimidation. He would have wondered how Thurians could separate Attoria in their minds from all of that, but the primal star sponsors of the village made the distinction how such would be the fate of all Vanarrans if there was no Attoria. Frequent, if potentially tainted, reports were circulated out of Attoria describing the long sols of hard work the refugees were enduring, but how that community was forming with them nevertheless. It showed how

Attoria was not only striving towards self-reliance but starting to trend in that direction.

For the remainder of the trip into the heart of Attoria, Shadow kept close observation with both his eyes and the instruments at his disposal in the modified hover. "No, nothing along the trail," he considered when they broke out of the trees and into the village center. He strained to look for the difficult to see, the unobvious, and atop a hill, he thought he spotted it. It was a lone individual, Faelnar by the looks of her, standing facing a fenced area, her paws resting on the top post. What attracted his attention was that the female seemed to be shouting or singing – what it was, he couldn't tell. "Part of their secret religion?" he wondered, throwing his thoughts back into the captured archives and *extracted* intelligence, but there was a lack of ease in finding a match between the tableau atop the hill and anything that he had read about or been briefed on.

Once the vehicle turned, he attempted a quick gauge of the village's size and tenor, comparing it with the covert StarSat images. "Exact match, with the administration building there, but ... a new building going up across the way." There wasn't enough of a building there for him to place it, and unlike in commercial building practices, there existed no placard to explain what structure was being raised.

As the hover slipped down to its skids in front of the administration building, he changed his focus from the place to the Thurians, immediately cataloging every individual in his vicinity. It was easy as there were not many about, but he still exercised caution as it had been made clear by many previous experiences that a moment's distraction could easily cut short both career and life in his profession. As he stepped out of the door opened by his chauffer, he found himself looking down on a gold-on-gold Faelnar whose eyes met him with a nervous anxiety that almost made Shadow wince.

"She's afraid of me," he thought, curious. Aloud he offered, "Jayanar Bonario, Representative Agent for the Intercontinental Shipping and Sourcing Consortium."

"I am Shenaria de Kyvara, Dame of our family," she replied, but it was clear that her anxiety was unabated by his introduction. "I am to show you inside."

"Please, Honored One," he put forth in his most respectful and gentle manner. "Lead the way, and I will follow." She said nothing but turned and started inside. In body language, he could tell that she felt that safety was inside, and that instinctively put him on his guard, his paw smoothing his suit coat above the easily accessed military projectile weapon located there. Its firm resistance beneath the expensive fabric of his suit reminded him that he had not even been searched or scanned for any weapons.

Beyond the first entranceway was a small, circular room with hallways leading away in three directions, and it also accommodated another member of this community who was not of Vanarran ancestry – one he knew immediately from the dossier files on Attoria. "Tashara de Kyvara. You must be Jayanar," she greeted, her smile as carefully controlled as the rest of her body language suggested. He clasped with her warm paw and quickly took her in. The former athlete was not in her top performance trim, as he had seen from the images in her file, but the additions were in the right places – to his eye. When his eye made its way back to her golden ones, he detected a measure of disapproval in his appraisal.

"I am, and it's very good to meet the famous Fireclaw Destiny face to face. Your performance records still stand, to this sol."

"Hooray," the mixed blood offered in a deadpan flatness of tone that indicated she had little if any interest in those pursuits, as her next words completely confirmed. "Tashara is who I am now; who I was before spent way too much time just trying to please herself."

"You had a history of charity work, as I recall. Quite generous, actually, while using that name."

"Not all of the time, and not that I'm proud of. I once spent more than one million in an evening on my own birthsol party."

"The … story about that is something of a legend," he noted, "after your first season."

"Yeah. Now, I spend every sol looking at Thurians who nearly starved to death, so imagine how I feel about that," she gently challenged, but then changed subjects. "The matriarch had a regular duty this morning she had to perform, but she should be returning shortly. Would you like to wait in her office?"

"I'd be grateful, and as grateful to enjoy your company," he said smoothly. Shadow knew that his natural physique and regular work-out routine served him well, just as his exceptionally replete resume when dealing with the opposite sex of any type or species.

"As you wish," the female replied, her eyes meeting his just long enough to let him know that Tashara found him exactly as she expected she would. They started to go down the center hallway when an open door down the right side caught his attention.

"Pardon me, but … might we have a look down here?" he asked.

Tashara shrugged slightly and stated, "No issue. Please, what did you see?"

"This door down the right side," he told her as they walked. At the end of the hall, a dark-furred and intimidating female Vulpi appeared and walked towards them. He tracked her eyes intently as she approached, looking to see which doors she had a concern about, but her eyes were only for his guide.

"Tasha," the Vulpi told her. "Matriarch Vanalla was delayed at the graveside. It will be a few more passes than expected."

"Everything alright?"

"One of our new arrivals – his mate did not survive," she whispered in the mixed blood's ear.

Shadow's quick and attentive ear caught it, although he could tell the volume wasn't meant for him to overhear. "I'm so sorry," Tasha said, sadly. "So many in that last group."

"I know," the impressive female Vulpi stated. Looking at him, she nodded a quick bow and offered, "My apologies for the delay and for interrupting you."

"Okay. Shenaria will want to go up there. You'd better tell her," Tasha directed, and the Vulpi nodded and left them.

"Something wrong?" he asked, walking into the room with the Vanarra statue.

"The ones we are getting now … are very unhealthy, starving as I said. Our first groups were bad, but then it got better for a while. Now, it's getting bad again – the number who are too far gone by the time they get here. It breaks my heart."

"Interesting ... statue," he commented, looking at the life-sized and reasonable accurate rendering of Vanarra de Gonari. "Drawn to more realistic proportions than some I've seen, before."

"The only one of its kind, here, and even that's something of a concession. When Vanarrans come to us, they've forsaken their pledge and faith, but the shadow of the Great Mother looms pretty huge over their lives. They have been taught, season upon season, to worship her, completely ignore parts of her history, and use her name and form as an excuse for all sorts of horrible things. Nearly all of them end up coming here when they learn of it, early on. Matriarch Vanalla sits right there and watches, listens, and when they start to talk to the statue, she answers."

"She answers as the Great Mother?" he questioned.

"No. Matriarch Vanalla was a student of the historical Vanarra, a very diligent student. There's never been any lie or half-truth she hasn't been able to call as just that, and she quotes Vanarra de Gonari back to them. Some, it only takes one such encounter. Some, it takes several. All of them, eventually, are finally able to leave their misguided views of the Great Mother here and take up an understanding of the real history of the Faelnar-Vulpi behind that statue. See there, these are some of the Grand Matriarch's own auto-biographies."

She picked one at seeming random and offered it to him. Taking it, he flipped through the book and examined it. His eyes told him, quickly and exactly, that these were newly purchased copies a number of seasons ago, but that continuous use had nearly worn them out. When he got to one section, he stopped, seeing many circular stains on the pages. "Tears?" he asked.

"Let me see?" Tasha asked, and then looking at the book, she nodded. "It's around this part where Vanarra is talking about her faith in the Creator. It's something few Vanarrans have ever been allowed to read."

"No ... hold outs, then?" he asked. "No one clinging to the old Vanarran ways?" The challenge was gentle, but it offered an opportunity for Tasha to quickly gloss over or dismiss the key fears brewing in Shanandrae.

"That's something very few understand who don't live here and don't know about the Vanarrans in detail. If someone who is a Vanarran comes here, they can no longer call themselves that. It is an unforgivable offense to break faith with the other Vanarrans and live in *the village of heretics*. The mere act of coming here means that they can't ever go back," she explained, shelving the book. "You needn't take my word, though. My understanding is that you'll be staying a few sols?"

"That's what my sponsors have requested," he demurred smoothly with just a hint of enticement in his manner, hoping that at least one of those sols might be spent in the close company of the exceptionally attractive mixed blood. The near revulsion in her eyes and step backwards disabused him of the possibility of that occurring.

Her next words indicated a desire to correct both of his assumptions. "Specifically, I only mean that you will be able to talk to whoever you want and go wherever you want. No restrictions."

"Really, that's most generous," he said, not believing a word of it – after all, her tail still had loft in it. "My sponsors will most certainly approve."

Quietly and in a way that nearly disarmed his façade, she asserted, "I hope so."

"Tasha?" a female voice called out. "You in here?"

"Honored One, we're down the hallway here," the mixed blood replied, looking relieved and making for the door. In a moment, they were standing in the hallway, a brown and gold Faelnar in a kind of natural woven vest over her somewhat average looking blouse making her way towards them. For a moment, Shadow thought she must not have been the right individual until he recognized her from his dossier on this mission. In confirmation, Tasha bowed to her and stated, "Honored One, the guest you told us about is here. This is … Jayanar Bonario."

"Yes, from the ISRC pack, I hear," came the polite and nearly friendly greeting.

"Honored … One?" he asked, his eyes quickly roaming up and down her form, as well, locking onto a joining bracelet around her wrist. When his eyes returned to hers, she nodded, a smile of gentle tolerance on her features. Her body, while quite attractive, was dressed in clothes which seemed more apt for gardening than the regal affairs of house leadership. A look into her face, however, disabused the observer very quickly that clothes made the matriarch; her Faelnar face had both a historically classical aspect combined with a serenity that spoke to a depth of experience far deeper than what her dossier suggested. "Here," he thought, "was a Faelnar to be reckoned with." "Forgive me," he offered aloud, "I'm not used to seeing Matriarchs dressed … casually."

"Well, it's how we roll here, and it's different than what you've probably been told. My guess is that you'll experience a lot of that while you're here," she told him, her voice rich with casual familiarity but only because the one wielding it carried herself with what appeared to be unshakably confident grace. The intent seemed to be to put a visitor at ease without surrendering to stereotypes for how members of the matriarchy should behave. "Shall we all go to the office? Have a little chat?"

"Please, you go first," he said, presenting the lead to both females, but only Vanalla – the matriarch – took his offer. "You lose either way," he thought, somewhat smugly, regarding the female who trailed behind. "Either I see yours or you see mine." He kept his tail just a touch higher than it should have been and kept a gentle rhythm to it that was a proven trademark of his – also an effective tool. In a few moments, they were in a rather humble looking office, its old wooden desk sitting at the head of what was nothing short of a fold up table when viewed by a quick glance at its base. Vanalla took her place behind the desk, offering a nearby seat to Shadow.

"Thank you," he proffered graciously. "A very lovely office, Honored One."

"Functional, which is what is prized around here," Vanalla explained. "Give us a few, Tasha, please."

Turning around he attempted to give her thanks for her time with him, but the female left, her tail and ears laying disappointingly low, and taking a sigh, he realized that his show had not been well received. "Well now," he started, "very interesting place here, Honored One."

"A home for those who need it," Vanalla explained, gently seating herself. "Also, in private, we can dispense with the honorariums. Besides, if I'm ever called that, I would have liked to have earned it first. I apologize for my tardiness; I have become part of a little tradition for some of my family."

"Certainly understandable," he agreed. "A matriarch's duties are many and varied."

"And now include you and your visit. I read your introductory TransNet e-mail – from your office, I mean. They said you would have something to give me?"

"Oh, yes," he replied, fishing the envelope from his pocket. "It contains a series of requests regarding my visit, as such would help me complete my assessment of Attoria, for investment purposes."

Taking the envelope, she eyed him steadily. "I would suspect that your assessment will mean a great deal to every life here."

It was an odd response, one which seemed to suggest some recognition of his underlying purpose. "Clever, this one," he thought. Aloud, he attempted to shift away from that subject. "We certainly hope that the funds we can invest in Attoria will be of benefit to everyone here. It's my understanding, however, that we would only be adding marginally to the existing storehouse of resources."

"Most of which we keep in reserve or hope to return. There's nothing that the residents of Attoria wouldn't like more than just being able to leave these precincts without fear for their very lives," she said, laying aside the letter once she had done no more than glance at its contents. "Everything seems in order, Jayanar. For the purposes of discovering the truth of Attoria, I grant you unlimited access to any and all facilities within our borders. You may also speak with anyone, and I've asked them to speak with you at least as much as they feel comfortable. That said, I dearly love every soul here, and please do not think that harming or threatening any of them would be something I would let pass without incident."

"For the sake of business, there shouldn't be any need for such a ... dire warning," he commented, trying to tease out her true meaning.

"For the sake of business, no. There are many kinds of businesses, and different individuals conduct their affairs in different ways. For some, the lives we are harboring here seem ... pretty cheap – disposable, forgettable. Out of more than fifty-seven thousand before their decline began, less than eight thousand Aelkinda are still alive. There are around twenty-five hundred or so, living here. While none in Attoria are now able to subscribe to the Vanarran religion, we don't believe that the remaining five thousand or so are all following their failed beliefs, either. We've heard that some have fallen prey to Thurian traffickers, and mercifully, some are being hidden by good and noble Thurian families. Still, it's not a place they can live for very long. Attoria represents the only outpost where Aelkinda can survive. It is their only hope."

Leaning forward, he commented, "Not that I hold the view, but there are those who were remarking that these were just an invention of the Vanarrans, and they weren't part of the natural order of Thuria."

"And so," Vanalla asked him, "faced with these living *aberrations,* we become like the de Caterra of old? We practice genocide on a whole class of Thurians who, through no fault of their own, were born different than the rest of us? In this sol, we think of ourselves as so advanced because of our open heartedness towards mixed bloods. We may even look with a little bit of swelling pride upon a mixed blood who attains high office. There, there; how noble we are, we think. How tolerant we are, but then there those who used to sport brown robes and shun us as lower creatures, harm our children and pervert our justice. Now that they have been utterly humbled and made powerless, are we really going to be any different than once we were? What will we do, push them into shadow and hope they disappear? I do hope we can do better."

He cringed, inwardly, at her use of his codename, and it seemed as if she had walked an almost perfect line between appearing to have discovered his purpose or having just stumbled upon such because of her beliefs. He sat back and thought for a moment before answering. "I consider that something worth hoping for," he countered, "but how are other Thurians supposed to integrate these back into society?"

"Forgive them. Care about them. Adopt them as family," Van suggested. "It's what I've done. If someone falls from the path and confesses their failings, then they are to be welcomed back into a relationship with us – embraced by the Creator in love, isn't that right? This isn't a game to us, and it's not a pastime. It's simply life. Still, perhaps subjects just a little too deep for us right from the start. The essentials of this moment are that you are here and welcome to do what you need to in order to fulfill what you were asked to do. There is a new cabin which has no residents, as of yet. That's being granted for your use, alone. It is a unique luxury here, as no one has a lair to themselves. Tashara is your appointed guide for the evening to help you get oriented to the schedule here. If there is a problem or issue that you need help with, she'll know where to find me or the right individual."

Vanalla stood, and the sense of dislocation Shadow felt was keen. This matriarch wasn't in her position for no reason, and her conversation had been genuinely surprising, if not disarming, in a way. Still, standing to reach out and clasp paws with her, he remembered that her vision might not match the vision of the others harboring here. If that was so, her earnest sincerity just might abbreviate her life span by a considerable margin. "A pleasure to meet you, Honored One, and from what I can see, the title is well-deserved."

"Tasha will be waiting outside, I think. Good sol to you, and I hope to see you at dinner," she told him, bowing slightly to him. He returned the gesture and slipped back from the table, taking his steps away at a measured, even pace.

Upon exiting the door, he found the attractive mixed blood standing and waiting, clearly exercising her patience as she greeted him. "Your bags have already been taken to your cabin if you'd like to go and settle in."

"I think I'd like that very much," he offered, nearly in a seductive growl. Without much in the way of tail loft or ear lift she started along her way, and he had to admit that her hind quarters, while most certainly attractive, were not quite so appealing with every step forward laced with tolerant indifference to him. It was yet another thing that unsettled him, and he quickly caught up to her, coming alongside. "You don't seem ... thrilled by my presence here."

As they left the building and walked across the village center and towards the residential section, she sighed and answered him. "There's nothing wrong with your presence. Anyone is welcome to have a presence here if they want to learn about or, even better, contribute to what goes on here. What I find very difficult to stomach, even from a guest representing potential benefactors, is the *show* you are putting on. I used to do that for stadiums full of Thurians, and so I know how it's done – for males and females. I know exactly how to walk, how to sway, and exactly how much to raise my tail. I pretended to be sexy for them, and I wouldn't have cared anything about them. You'll forgive me, but I suspect the same about you."

Shadow felt a little cut to the quick by this assessment but looked at the mixed blood critically. It was difficult medicine to take, but her somewhat embarrassed and nearly hopeful expression tempered his response considerably. "Forgive me," he said quietly. "I meant no disrespect other than what such a … rude presentation signifies – interest in you, and I won't lie – you are attractive. I was hoping that would at least be a little interesting, that is unless you've already found someone here who suits you. I see that the matriarch has already paired with someone – one of the refugees, then?"

"No. Someone from Shanandrae she knew. They were trying to put together a relationship well before Attoria was even dreamed of," she offered as she angled towards a certain cabin, its roof and timbers visibly newer than most of the ones nearby to it. "As for me? No. I guess I'm still trying to figure if I can trust myself to make a good decision. As I said, I spent far too much time in my past having affairs, even scheduling them for certain periods of the season – flirt during this time of the season, seduce them by when, how long to enjoy the romance before breaking everything off so it wouldn't get in the way of my career. I used Thurians. I don't think very much of myself for that."

Her candor and clarity threw his own life and choices into stark relief, and a shade of self-doubt leapt through his psyche before he banished it and found an appropriate follow-up question. "And is being here helping you? Have you found some kind of … special respite from the feelings of guilt you have?"

"Nothing more than what intervals upon intervals of hard work alongside Thurians who are just trying to survive would bring," she told him, stepping onto the deck of that particular cabin – its newly constructed smell radiating out from it like a beacon. She stepped to the railing and looked out over a newly cleared field to her right, more than a dozen Aelkinda working and tilling and pulling weeds. "They … they say I'm too hard on myself," she whispered, nearly, not looking at him. "They say that the work I've done to help them has far more meaning and that those I used participated of their own free will."

"It does take two to have a hunt," he stated evenly, slipping beside her and keeping his distance in recognition of her pensive mood.

"Yes, but I had this big sign spray-painted into my fur that said *I'm famous*, and it drew them in like I was the wounded animal. They never understood that they were the prey, my prey. They had a choice, yes, but I had more responsibility because of how many looked up to me, and until I met Vanalla, Jayanar, I never lived up to it."

"You've known her for a while, then?"

"Ever since I was hospitalized for having a little kit charge into me – what a klutz I was. Then I blame and even sue the kit and her family and the stadium. I … I don't know what you do but understand that anyone who has tried to get close to me would probably still be subject to the whims and fancies of the Newsarotzi. The stains of fame in my fur would wipe off on them, and that's a lot to live with."

"Fame couldn't have been all bad. You have a lot of achievements, after all. I happened to look you up once I stumbled across your image on the fundraising part of the Attoria TransNet site. The VidStar highlights recorded in the TransNet data wells paint you as a … pretty fierce and even dangerous competitor."

She smiled, but only on one side of her mouth, away from him, although his careful observation of her could detect it. "Fierce, yes. Dangerous, perhaps. The most dangerous thing was my pride, though. It actually almost cost me my career. Pride can be a good thing in that if you set a bar for yourself, you don't want to drop below it. The moment I had pride in myself by comparing to other Thurians, that's where I lost it. I feel good about my time as a professional athlete. I grew a lot. It got me ready for other things, like this. Did you ever think that you'd see this in your lifetime?"

"Not … specifically," he queried, thinking this an interesting window into her psyche, and in turn, maybe the psychology of Attoria as a whole. "What do you mean?"

Her voice was capped a such at low volume that he nearly had to strain to hear her, and he did lean closer as she spoke. "Thurians of

... any kind starving themselves, feeling as if they have to. Thurians for whom, literally, there is no safe place outside of living in hiding or coming here. The joy these feel being here – you'll see, Jayanar, you will. This is a hard place to live; they are out there, sol in and sol out, doing back-breaking labor, and yet when you sit with them tonight, eating dinner, it's like they wouldn't give it up for the world. You get the sense it's something – some kind of kinship – they've never had before. Being a Vanarran couldn't give it to them. Attoria can."

"Which means?" he asked softly, very close to her.

"Nothing," she told him, stepping back just a bit. "It doesn't mean anything special or unique. These are just normal Thurians. They want to live in safety. They treasure that. They find comfort in family even when things are difficult. How does that make them different than any of the rest of us?"

"If true, then they wouldn't be any different."

"Save for the fact that so many who could join them are kept from coming here, even if they want."

He looked towards the field, breaking his eye contact with her. "What about the ones of their kind who ... don't want to come here. Should they be made to come here?"

"Yeah," Tasha sighed, leaning on the railing. "The death numbers are staggering. They're wiping themselves out, almost completely. Only those special enough to survive will make it here. Of those, some will die because they made the choice too late. Those who remain have something that all of those others did not. These are special Thurians, Jayanar, in that way at least. I pray that, in time, Thuria is patient and tolerant enough to allow them to show us *how* special."

"A ... *better* Thurian?"

"Not so much, but a lot of the right kinds of kindness and compassion and patience pulled together in one place. We have members who aren't Aelkinda. They have the same character traits that many others do, across the world. Here, those just seem concentrated. That kind of family; that kind of community, isn't made out of *better* individuals – not a perfect species but a good one. One that will do wonderful things – honorable things. I can't sum it all up for you. You'll have to get to know them. For now, just settle in to your cabin, and then I'll come and get you around 18:00. That's when dinner is. We'll be eating at dining hall alpha; that's also where Vanalla will be. She tries to rotate between them to give everyone a chance to see her and ask questions if they have need."

"By far the most accessible matriarch on record," he noted, but then he bowed to her, slightly. "Thank you for excusing my rudeness, if you would be so kind as to do so."

"I will." Then, she surprised him by sauntering up close to him, letting her tail brush his shoulder, and then slipping down the stairs and away a few tracks appearing to be the hottest of potential hunts. Her head looked back over her shoulder, and her expression was as alluring and sensually seductive as any had ever seen. Turning on her heels, she walked back to him, her manner as candid and honest as before – the entire façade of her interest in him shattered. "So, a good show then?"

"You certainly haven't lost your skill or your appeal, but ... your point is also taken. 18:00 for dinner, then. Meet you here?"

"Or somewhere else if you're looking around. Just be careful, okay? No one wants anyone to get hurt here, but this is a working farm with somewhat primitive tools. Just make sure you're paying attention to what's around you."

"I'm ... rather good at that. Thank you," he offered, and then, she nodded and left him. Turning around, he reached for the door to the cabin and gently opened it. Not that he thought it probable that such was rigged to harm him in any way, but it wasn't advisable in his line of work to lower one's guard. The scene which greeted him was completely as expected – a new cabin with bare and thrifty furnishings, his unopened luggage placed out of the walkway. Walking in, he saw the bed was made, towels were provided, and there were even a small set of toiletries available. "Only lacks for a candy on your turned-down sheets," he commented softly, pulling a device from his inner coat pocket. Sweeping it around the room, he looked at the small display. In all quarters, wherever he aimed it, the device showed negative – no devices or transmissions. "Nothing more than the wood and the tree screechers."

Putting that device back into his pocket, he reached for his first piece of luggage and put it on the bed. A quick visual and touch check showed that it, also, had been undisturbed and unmolested.

After a moment, a different device was placed on the nightstand and switched on. After watching it for a time, he sighed – no one else was in the proximity of his cabin. No one had sneaked up to take a peek at the newcomer or try to sort out his purpose. After tapping the signaling device inside the cover of his luggage to indicate his successful and safe arrival, Shadow changed clothes from a suit to something which was slightly more in line with his surroundings. Hanging in the closet were work trousers and a shirt, very much like all of the ones he had seen worn by those who worked the field. The material was basic, sturdy, and functional as was its fit, once he had tried it on.

Once done, he had donned a pair of athletic paw shoes and stepped back onto the small porch of his cabin. He had only been inside a quarter of an interval, but it was clear that the work he was seeing in the fields before was authentic. More rows were plowed – an ambitious number for having such done manually, and the clearing teams had more than made a dent in what the plow had yet to reach.

It was at this moment that Shadow just relaxed and looked around him, listening, as thousands of observed nuances filtered through his memory and found their places. Every inflection of speech and conversation, every action and reaction, and every visual he was seeing or had seen. Shadow had a talent for sniffing out the signs of a concealed menace based on just a few moments' observation. Usually, it's presence was like an undercurrent which was hiding beneath the surface. In time, that undercurrent could be traced and frequently right to the menace, itself. The dangerous presence would always leave traces it couldn't fully hide, even in the best of circumstances.

What Shadow sensed made him shake his head in confusion. Not only was this place utterly devoid of any kind of detectable dark undercurrent of menace, there was an undercurrent of supportive benevolence. It was as if a master criminal had turned to the good and placed all of their knowledge and resources into supporting their community. The center of this current of benevolence wasn't all that difficult to sort, either. It was their matriarch, Vanalla, who seemed to bend the very space around her just with her presence. Replaying their conversation in his mind, he realized how exact her words actually were. She left open the gaping possibility that he was somehow vital to the safety of all of the lives in Attoria without explaining how such might be. He wondered if she had resources in government intelligence who had warned her of Shadow's posting on this assignment.

Making sure his door, which had no lock, was closed, he started walking towards what seemed to be a different set of older buildings, one surrounded by a small but very interesting garden. The fragrant herbs that met his nose were instantly cataloged – not a one matched any psychotropic or controlled substance he was aware of. Tapping on the frame of the open door as he leaned in, he saw a lone Faelnar, a petite one, looking in a concerned manner at a bunch of different herbs laid about on the table. Her study of the herbs was so intense that she didn't seem to acknowledge him until she stood up straight.

"I have come to an incontrovertible realization – an … essential truth," she said as decisively and fervently as one could imagine.

"And what … would that be?" he asked, a little incredulous.

"That I don't have the foggiest idea what I am doing." Then, she burst out in laughter. "I'm sorry – I'm just so completely out of my element here! Lettanalli Cassiarri. I'm new here, and you can just call me Letta."

"Jayanar Bonario," he replied, meeting her offered paw and clasping it. "I guess … I'm new here, too. What brings you to Attoria?"

"Well," she explained as she released his paw and leaned against the nearby table. "I was doing an internship, and … it didn't quite work out. My mentor and I had some problems, and after a while, my mentor realized the problems were hers as was the need to go seek some counseling."

"Oh, my," Jayanar breathed. "So, you were without a situation?"

"Well, not really. My mentor noted that I kept mentioning my friend Vanalla, who used to be my boss a long time ago. She was aware that Vanalla had settled here – frankly a bit more than settled, actually."

"Oh, how do you mean?"

"I think she's found a place and role in life that suits her. She loves to help others, help them heal from emotional wounds – I think she went through some really bad stuff as a young kit, you know? Somehow, she found her way out of it, and it just gave her this perspective, this way of helping."

"Sounds almost *mystical* in a way," he gently prompted.

The petite Faelnar shrugged and turned back to the small piles of herbs. "If kindness and wise council are mystical, then so be it. She's willing to give a lot of herself. Callanar – he's the constable here and the herbalist I'm going to study with – said that he distrusted her and her motives until he realized that Vanalla intended to spend the rest of her life here, helping them in any capacity." Picking up a twig with little flowers in it, she sniffed and then sneezed, shaking her head as she put it down. "I ... whew! That's nasty. Anyway, she was just sort of helping them unwind all of their misconceptions about Vanarra de Gonari because she's such a history buff. However, with all of them feeling so lost, Vanalla was just someone who did something for them that no one had ever done before."

"What was that?" he prodded, feeling like he might lead her inadvertently to sharing something damning.

"Give herself to them, completely. She has a mate, and he's also promised that he is going to live here with them for the rest of his life. I ... respect them for that. I get the feeling that the Aelkinda feel more than respect for her. They honor her, and that's why she became their matriarch."

"They do seem to reverence her, in a way," he noted, walking alongside the Faelnar and looking down at the piles. "I ... think I've seen that one in salads, before."

Letta giggled. "I'm not risking it. I need a book or a data pad or something. I only worked in offices for the last little bit. I used to be much better about this, but it's just been too long. As far as Vanalla goes, I think it's just honor. I think that – how did Callanar put it? They threw themselves at the hind paws of a statue for their entire lives, and it got them nowhere. Worse, some of their brothers and sisters did horrible things."

"Horrible?"

"He said unforgivable, actually."

"Said it, and meant it," Callanar offered from the doorway. "My apologies, but I just wanted to see how you were getting on."

"I … am a big fat loser, Callanar," Letta offered sadly. "I swear to you I spent all kinds of time in the woods long ago, watching presentation after presentation – I mean, I used to pride myself on this, but it's just all gone out of my head! I've been away too long."

"It's not a problem. You're here. You're willing to help, Letta. It will come back to you," he offered comfortingly and then turned to the visitor, offering a paw to clasp, which was accepted. "I'm Callanar de Kyvara, the matriarch's aide and erstwhile head constable for the village." Releasing paws, he swept his own above the piles and added, "Formerly, I was the herbalist of the village, but the other duties I have now make that very difficult. Letta has graciously volunteered to help me in this."

An intense internal measuring was occurring in Shadow's psyche as he took in his first close contact with an Aelkinda from Attoria. His impression, despite all of the files on their training and breeding for specific characteristics was that he had been holding the paw of another Thurian – not something otherworldly. "The herb garden is lovely," he offered, his mind still collecting datum. "Can you tell me about the herbs?"

"Absolutely. Here, let's start over with this one." As Callanar led the way around the room, he – to the right amount of detail for visitors – rattled off the name and basic purpose. Letta looked as if she was remembering things from time to time, based upon what he said, and the smile drew larger across her features. In only a few passes, all of the plants had been named and described.

In observing the subsequent conversation between Letta and Callanar, Shadow felt a little disconcerted. "Why the mange am I here?" he started to ask himself, although he – at some level – knew the answer, but the concerns that had set him upon this journey initially seemed to have so little foundation in fact, at least so far. If there was a great and menacing secret lurking in Attoria, he was reasonably convinced of the fact that such wouldn't be found within this herb garden. Even as they talked, he scanned outside, looking for contraband narcotic plants or even signs that they grew naturally. There was nothing.

Chapter 24: Of Light and Shadow

He was puzzling over what he should do next when a whimper came from the doorway. Turning around, he saw an Aelkinda female clutching her stomach. He reached out a paw, which she gladly took. "Callanar?" he asked.

"Vassia?" the other Aelkinda asked coming alongside her, Saletta doing the same.

"I … I just feel so sick to my stomach," she explained. "I … I took a nap and woke up feeling this way."

Callanar groaned in frustration. "The doctor's gone for the sol, too."

"Vassia?" Letta asked. "I'm new here, but I might be able to help you. My name is Letta. This ever happened before?"

"First time," came the somewhat scared reply.

"And … I'm sorry to ask, but do you have a mate?"

"I … I do. Laxar," she explained, wincing as the Faelnar started to press a point, hard, on the female's wrist. "I … wait, I can feel – what's happening? What are you doing?"

"A slight sugar imbalance caused by malnutrition just might be depriving your system of what it needs for you to not feel dizzy. Is that part of this?"

"It is, but – it was, but how are you doing this?"

"Using a trick someone showed me a long, long time ago. It is useful for curing motion sickness or reducing the symptoms, but it can also be helpful when you have ... well, gestational distress."

"Gestational..." Callanar mused, but then trailed off and looked at Vassia wide-eyed. "My stars, Vassia! Could you be? Are you?"

"I'm ... I'm close to my time, and it hasn't happened yet. I ... maybe?"

"Let me smell your breath, kit," Letta asked, and a quick sniff in the muzzle told the little Faelnar all she seemed to need. "You ... have got a lot of planning to do because Attoria is going to be getting a new resident. Was this something you were hoping for?"

"Hoping for, but we never dreamed we could – not without help!" Vassia stated, completely shocked.

"Well, my dear one," Callanar offered, starting to smile. "Perhaps the help wasn't needed. If this works out, you'd be the first – the first in all Attoria, yours and Laxar's." There was a quiet moment where she just looked at him, sobbed once, and then accepted his embrace and that of the small Faelnar.

"Congratulations," Shadow told her when they parted. "I take it this was a surprise."

"It is. Oh, Laxar will be so happy about this – we were so worried."

"Well," Letta told her, "now that Callanar refreshed my memory, there's a special little mixture I remember making. Can you help me, Callanar?"

"Certainly, certainly! What did you have in mind?" he asked, and soon the two were whispering, pulling together and grinding up herbs and other stocks stores in the open walled cabin.

"Would you like to sit?" Shadow asked, feeling he needed to play the role of the polite stranger at the present moment. The stool he offered was accepted by the trembling female. "Is your mate ... Aelkinda?" he asked, quickly adding, "Only if you don't mind telling me."

"No, no, it's fine. He's not – actually a mixed blood who used to serve in our temples. The others treated him very badly, and the truth is, even I might have once or twice. When I came here, I was so lost, and he accepted me, gave me companionship, for … forgave me," she said softly, looking down. "It's something I still don't feel worthy of, but he did. His kindness touched my heart and ended so many doubts I had. He's much younger than me, but in some ways, he's so much wiser. His heart follows a truer path than mine ever could."

"Are there many of them here, who used to serve in the temples?"

"No," she said softly. "None."

"None?"

"None, sir," Vassia told him. "If they are not in hiding, I don't know if there are even any more who exist. Vanarrans … would have cut their kind down when the needs of the Selects became dire. It's horrifying, but it's why we wanted to have a child. We'd hoped some small good, some honor could come from his unique escape. We do hold out some hope that maybe some survived and were taken in, but we have not heard anything of the sort."

"Well, congratulations and best wishes," Shadow told her, his objectivity feeling more compromised by the moment. Walking behind Callanar and Letta, he told them, "With … apologies, I need to go. Thank you for your time."

"Oh, certainly," Callanar offered, turning around, bowing. "Very good to have you here."

"I agree. See you around!" Letta offered, but she was very much into the grinding she was doing and paused only for a moment to say it. With that, Shadow left their presence and headed towards the open fields, trying to find some thread of concern or incongruity that his perceptive and observant mind could latch onto. He knew that his superiors, the director especially, had sent him out here believing there was a strong possibility of something illegal and dangerous to society happening here as had been seen at the other Vanarran retreats. Even in his experience with them, the way they operated and worked was so different from what he was seeing here. Those Vanarrans had hoarded weapons, technology, funds – all to support their ability to return to what they were. The ones here had nothing other than what charity built for them, and they seemed happy to have it.

A couple of intervals later, Shadow had successfully traversed all of the key areas of Attoria – every field, every residential quarter, the common buildings, and even surveyed the decent amount of forethought that had been taken to manage the sanitation needs of the village. Everything that was a part of the sol-in and sol-out life of this Aelkinda refuge was visible. He had been greeted many times, asked about what he was looking for, and thanked profusely for his expressed desire to inform investors about this village and its aims.

Subtle probing in conversations brought out nothing that was the least bit concerning or significantly inconsistent with what he had been told, earlier. Did they enjoy being here? They were profoundly grateful, even if some were regretful of what resources had been wasted or left behind in their former lives. Does anyone still hold to the old beliefs? No, and had he seen the fire-pit in the village center where they burn their robes and scrolls and books related to the Vanarran way of life? What's so special about Vanalla? She cared about them when they didn't deserve it and dedicated her life to them, even being as a purebred. Was she a character that they felt admiration for, even reverence for? Admiration, certainly, and loyalty, but they refused to be trapped by worshiping a mere Thurian ever again.

It left Shadow feeling frustrated in a way he seldom felt on missions. Staring across a modest sized lake on the edge of the village, he relaxed and tried to assemble all of the varying impressions in his thoughts. The sense of overarching benevolence hadn't wavered in strength, but it had been refined. It was truly directed mostly at the matriarch, but there were others who were held in high respect, this Laxar, for one. He was a prized treasure to them because no others of his kind, temple servants, were known to have survived anywhere on Thuria. None of these were worshiped or seen as mystical, just giving or forgiving, in Laxar's case. The purebred and other mixed bloods who had joined were considered a part of their number, not special for good or for ill.

"Usually, by now," he grumped to himself, "I can tell if a place has a hiding stalker. This place feels like your average sleepy town with not even the occasional affair or petty theft or vandalism to compare with. Boring, honestly." His eyes then flicked to movement, and he saw Tashara coming towards him. "Well, not *all* of it is boring," he noted, looking in her direction and smiling. "Besides, it's early, yet. Something dangerous may yet raise its head." When she comes into polite speaking range, he offered, "Hello, Tasha. Good to see you."

"Ah, so you learned my short name," she said, smirking. "It means I get to pick yours, you know?"

"Short name?"

"One of the matriarch's idiosyncrasies, but in all honesty, it does make our conversations with each other feel a bit more relaxed. Some hold to it; some don't. Ever been called *Jay* before?"

"Ah, no. Tashara it is, then. It's a lovely name – surprised you didn't use it in competition."

Her smirk increased slightly and then softened to a neutral expression as she looked towards the lake. "No, I pretty well sold off all of the pieces of my identity when I joined up with the league. Tanatta Fireclaw was who I scraped off of for a portion of the name. Check the histories, you'll see she abandoned it because she picked the name for fire-bombing a factory and clawing the face of Lyssia de Oterbythe. All of that came out after she died, of course."

"And the Destiny part?" he asked.

"Sheer bravado and self-aggrandizement – telling the world to look at me, I'm important. Crappy choices upon reflection, but what's done is done, I suppose. How did your tour around the village go? I presume you didn't stay in your cabin all sol."

"Yeah," he sighed, leaning back against the tree and letting a rock he gathered fling towards the water. "I saw all of it. Didn't talk to everyone, of course, but it felt like more than forty or so. Very friendly sort. They keep talking about a few purebred who are out here. Do you know who they are, other than the matriarch?"

"Well, there's Javoth de Bosnar, our Creator's Path minister. There are Malliana and Kennar, but you'd know them from the TransNet blog posts. I think they went camping or something – kind of a couple, now, by the way."

"Really?" he queried, the *camping* excuse gathering his attention.

"Yeah. Sweet cub and kit, for sure. They're back tonight, I think. Might see them at supper which it's just about time for, by the way," she noted, looking at him. "Kind of just chance which dining hall they'll go for, but they usually check in with Vanalla, and she'll be eating at ours. Your chances are better than average, then, I'd suppose."

"Thank you. When I came in," he added, "I noticed someone standing by that fence up on the hill overlooking the square. It's the only place I didn't get to."

"If you want to come up tonight with the matriarch, she'd probably be okay with it. It's our garden of final rest – truly not much of a garden, more of just a place right now. She goes up each night and sometimes during the sol to sing over the graves. There are always a couple dozen or more who go up with her."

"I ... I don't know that I saw them."

She canted her head, looking at the flyers dodging back and forth over the lake. "They might have been kneeling or something of that ilk."

"They kneel to her?"

"No. You see, the graves are the graves of the ones who died on the way here or died soon after coming here. Thankfully, we haven't lost anyone we've been able to heal up. Many of the Aelkinda are now Creator's Path, and they mourn the lost who were once their friends and companions from before. There is an undercurrent here, and I was wondering if you had picked up on it."

He tried to hide his interest, as this was exactly the kind of thing he was looking for. "Well, no. I guess not. All seemed pretty normal to me."

"Really? Very little about this place is actually normal. There's not a stitch of selfishness, no crime, overflowing with self-sacrifice, and it's utterly bathed in humility – that didn't like attract your attention or anything?" His expression told her that he hadn't seen what she was talking about. "It's *guilt*, Jayanar, plain and simple. No one living here poisoned a kit or cub. No one here murdered anyone. We know that from the seized records. They are trying to forget their former lives, but realizing just how much they once had, what they did with it or allowed others of their number to do, it just kills some of them. They can't talk about it. I don't know how long it's going to hang around, but in this generation, I think they'll carry it to their grave."

"And, the matriarch singing allows them a way to express that guilt."

"In her presence, with her understanding. In a way, it *is* forgiveness, as much as she can grant it to them. In the end, it's the Creator who has to be offered repentance. Javoth is a very busy minister. He does a lot of counseling. He's really helped them, but I think it will always be ingrained in who they are."

"I … guess it will," he agreed softly. "I think I might know a little of how they feel."

"Don't we all, cub. Don't we all. Right now, however, I'm getting a little more hungry than I can stand. What say we head for the dining hall? It took me a little bit to find you. We won't be the first ones, for sure."

"Fashionably late," he chuckled as he followed her open paw pointing in the direction of the dining hall. "Thank you. Such a short time and such a thorough education."

As they walked, Tashara commented, "Not what you expected?"

"Let's say that I had been given different impressions," he offered, evading the question slightly.

"Yeah, there's a lot of misconceptions going on around this place. Malliana and her cub, Kennar, were about scared out of their fur – although it did have something to do with the fact that one had broken an arm and the other a leg sneaking in here."

"Really? How so?"

"The edge of the stream bed collapsed on them, and they toppled in – and speak their names and here they are! Hey, you two! Have a good time?" Tashara called to the black Pantera and white Lupar making their way towards the same communal building.

"Pretty fair," Kennar offered, shrugging.

"We didn't get a good forest grazer count," Malliana sighed. "We might have been a little distracted, but I swore we were at the right place – dusk and dawn."

Tashara chuckled. "I've been distracted like that, before. It was great!"

The blush furs on both purebred shot up, and Malliana's brow furrowed. "Tasha! Darn it! In front of a stranger?!"

"You guys aren't a state secret," the mixed blood chuckled as she opened the door for them to enter the roiling atmosphere of the dining hall. "Come on in and get something good for your trouble."

"You're trouble," Kennar complained, and then looked at Shadow. "She is, you know?"

"I'd already picked up on that," he said smoothly and was pleased to see her pretty face smirk and knew she was tempted to whack him on the hind quarters. Instead, she was left just shaking her head as they entered.

"Come on, trouble cub," she told him once they had entered. "Let's get our food, and then there's a seat near the front for us."

"I hope that they are not planning to make a big announcement or anything. I was … kind of hoping to keep a low profile," he whispered.

"Strange, given how many you spoken with," a strong female voice rumbled in his direction. Turning around, he was met with a very tough and imposing Vulpi female.

"This, Jayanar, is Vosha de Kyvara – or Vosh, if you prefer. She's also one of the constables. She was likely keeping tabs on you just because you're new," Tashara explained.

"No offense was meant," the female Vulpi told him, "and you'll be relieved to know that nothing is planned that would draw undue notice in your direction. In all fairness, however, your presence as a newcomer has drawn the normal amount of attention. Tashara, Vanalla asked me to pass along that she will be a few passes late. It seems as if Trax and Ashalam were exceptionally successful in identifying where the forest grazers are migrating."

"Dammit!" Malliana groused. "Rotten chances for us."

"You had your fun in the woods; don't complain," Tashara teased, and again blush furs were sent sailing. Shadow smiled outwardly while grimacing inwardly – this was more secondary school lunchroom chatter than the banter thrown around in a secret army barracks or in the dens of religious cultists. As the teasing went back and forth, he scanned the room. The same jovial companionship just beside him was echoed throughout the entire hall. He looked carefully from face to face, and he struggled to find anyone who was unhappy or discontented or angered in any way.

The female Vulpi was at his shoulder. "You … are a good observer. It is an excellent skill to cultivate."

"And what did you observe about me and what I was doing, this sol?" he asked.

"You were simply collecting information. Coming behind you, I asked the nature of your questions, and you seemed to be trying to determine if any lingering remnants of the Vanarran religious practices exist. They do. They are all here, in this hall and in this village," she told him.

"I … don't see any of it, and I didn't see any, earlier."

"You see *them*," Vosh told him. "*They* are the result. Even though these have disavowed Vanarran practices, the Vanarran religion put them here, and put far more than these to death – either self-imposed or at the paws of others." There was something about this Vulpi that commanded an almost immediate respect from the professional side of his background – here was an equal, perhaps even someone who carried the right of sanction at one time.

"You a former member of … *the pack*?" he asked.

"I had a military role," Vosh told him. "I still retain my ranking, although my records are not available for viewing. My service record is … exceptionally confidential."

He was amazed that they could have this kind of conversation in public, but the background noise of conversations created a bubble around them that shielded any details of what they might say. Only facing muzzle to ear made it possible to hear correctly. "Sealed then?" She nodded. "Understood, but still, I have a job to do."

"I know, and I will let you do it, unimpeded. I'm only interested in preventing harm to all of these. However, should you have need of me, I am an available resource."

He nodded to her, answering. "Quite polite of you," he offered. "The same in return." She nodded and was away. "Military intelligence," Shadow pondered. "That's certainly not a good sign. They beat us to the hunting grounds! Already embedded here for likely moons and would have reported if there was a conspiracy, surely. Damn, this soup looks weak," he grumped inwardly. Oddly enough, at that moment, a tray was placed in his paws offering a soup that upon a brief smell was very far from weak. His mouth was instantly salivating. Bread was also offered to him of a considerable size, larger than was offered in restaurants, and he looked at Tashara in confusion."

She almost had to shout back. "They have so much work to do. They can't do it on empty stomachs!"

"Doesn't it cost quite a lot?" he asked as they maneuvered to their appointed place at the table.

"More and more is grown here. Our imports are down fully forty percent from when we started, and we're trending very nicely." He nodded as that number roughly matched what he had been briefed on if it was a little more conservative than what the Director's notes had offered.

In short order, he had been seated at the side of the beautiful mixed blood, Tashara, and after a quick blessing over the food done for the entire table by Javoth de Bosnar, the group commenced eating. After sating the edge of his hunger, Shadow looked round. At that moment, he saw the Matriarch of House de Kyvara carrying a tray of food and working her way down to a table in the middle of the room crowded with others. She spoke to several others on her way to her place but then settled in amongst a bunch of the ones who had been working in the field not two intervals earlier.

Leaning over to Tashara, he noted, "Not the conventional sort of matriarch."

"Too true, but this is a family that needs its matriarch to be in their midst – one of them. The very last thing we would do is place her on a pedestal in front of them, make her unapproachable."

"Other family leaders seem to cultivate that distance, engender that mystique."

"Not her, and I don't know if you've heard, but other matriarchs have been coming down here and nearly taking classes from her. Just because the houses have done a thing for seasons and seasons doesn't mean it's right. In some ways, Vanalla is almost reinventing the Thurian matriarchy if you look at some reports, and honestly, it's all to the better from what I've heard and seen. After all, what use is having a family if you can't approach them – be a family!"

He could just see her listening intently to someone as she ate her meal, but then almost had to cover her mouth as someone said something funny – nearly causing her to spit out her food. The rest of the table was in fits of hysterical laughter, and the smiles were so infectious that even Shadow found himself smiling a little. He glanced over and saw Tashara looking at him, her expression appreciative and, for once, not distant. It was as if she was saying, "And now you can see it. That means I might actually be open to knowing you better."

"I'd never know she was a matriarch if I hadn't been introduced," he commented, "at least, seeing her like this, but her skills in other areas seem their equal or better." The compliment was something he hoped would draw her out in a number of ways.

"I can't dispute that. You'll see more after dinner if I can catch her. Like I said, she's going to sing for them."

"You're coming to the memorial?" one of the Aelkinda across from him said, and they struck up a conversation which lasted until Vanalla was heading back up behind them with her empty tray.

"Matriarch! Honored One!" Tashara called to stop her, and the hurried matriarch halted in her tracks, just behind them.

"Hey, Tasha, what's up? Enjoy your afternoon, Jayanar?"

"Very … instructive," he told her, nodding.

"Jayanar would like to join you tonight for the memorial, if you don't mind."

"Well, better put your tray up cause I'm almost late for the gathering. Oh, Salanar, you can come, too, cub!" She addressed her comment to Shadow's conversation partner who, humble, bowed to her. Looking back to the mixed blood, she stated, "I need you to get the skinny from the cubs on the grazer herds. I want to try to track where they're going and keep any new fields we make out of their way."

"Does this mean we'll finally make pastureland?" Salanar asked, the young male excited and hopeful.

"Yes, yes, but don't imagine that some of the … side work from that endeavor will be all that pleasant. After all, a good grazer herd produces a lot of *fertile output*. You should have heard those crazies over there wanting to sign up for it!" she said, looking back to the group who were getting up and seeing her nod and impish expression in their direction made them all chuckle again and wave to her. "Meet you outside," she told Jayanar. "Sala, can you please escort him so he knows where to go?"

"Oh yes, Honored One." With that, she was away.

After the trays of food had been disposed of, Shadow found himself in the solo company of the young male, Salanar. "Callanar told me that you were visiting, potentially bringing some additional resources to us."

"Potentially," he replied, "but the outlook is promising. The matter is not, as yet, decided."

Salanar bowed and looked embarrassed. "Such kindness is really an amazing gift. Even if the decision is no, it still is deeply encouraging that you are willing to spend time with us. Not long ago, death was my single future, my only future. My order then lost its leader, and we ... wavered in our faith. We accepted the offer of shelter here, and then we found so many others whose faith had wavered and even fallen. It's a hard thing to let that happen, to let go," he told the Vulpi stranger. "I've been reading the Creator's Path, and I think that's where my heart is going. Do you have a faith?"

"I ... like to keep an open mind."

"Better than what we did, surely," Salanar offered as they walked towards the base of the mound. "We worshiped a lie in the Perfected One and the Great Mother. We never questioned it until it almost killed us."

"You seem to esteem your matriarch, if you don't mind the observation."

His blush fur rose, and he smiled. "Old habits, to an extent. She represents a lot of really wonderful things to us. She has sacrificed herself for us, and the more you see her work and lead, the more you realize that she has amazing ability. There was never a Vanarran Select to equal her. Even the stories of the Great Mother fall short, especially when confronted by history. I mean, please understand, Vanarra de Gonari was a good Thurian and a strong influence on her time, but there were many things she did early on that were quite bad. She didn't live a life of unvarnished purity."

"Well, neither has your matriarch, I suppose," Shadow challenged, gently, trying to get a rise out of the young and impressionable male.

Instead of getting angry, he laughed. "She'd be the first to tell you that! However, that's what makes her special to us, in a way. Her ability really is beyond question when it comes to leadership, and we need someone like her. Otherwise, we'd fall apart. Secondly, she … loves us. She's granted us family – something we never had. I know she's in no way supernatural, but she is extremely special to us. She's someone we're profoundly grateful to have – that's Callanar's way of putting it. I agree."

"You talking about the matriarch again, Salanar?" one of the others near him in the gathering group asked.

"We have a visitor, this evening. He's been invited to come along. I was just giving him background."

"You were here last time, Salanar. If you keep this up, she'll think you're hunting her," one of the females teased, gently, and he smiled, embarrassed.

"She is, of course, spoken for – Ashalam is her mate," he told Shadow.

"Oh, don't let her fuss you," the first said. "We all look up to her." The female nodded, and just then they had to stop as Vanalla was approaching them. "Honored One, good evening!"

"Good evening! Everyone meet Jayanar, our visitor?"

"Just a bit," Shadow stated.

"Good. We can do more later, but I think we should get up there. This is going to get tricky as the evenings start to come earlier. Jayanar, you beside me. We go together, and the others will follow in a double line." As they started to walk up, all of the Vulpi's muscles tensed and his senses became alert because he was now isolated at the head of a line of what might be religious fanatics alongside their leader. Reaching up to his shirt, he felt for the military grade projectile weapon stealthily holstered therein. When he touched it, Vanalla cleared her throat slightly and whispered, "You know, you are about the most paranoid cub I've met in a long time. I promise you, my singing isn't great, but it's truly not that bad."

Slipping his paw down, he replied, "Just some other experiences I've had in my profession make me ... cautious in certain situations."

"You seriously need a new job, cub. Adrenaline rushes come at a premium, and sometimes that bill comes due."

"For the right cause, it can be well worth the risk," he offered somewhat candidly. If she didn't know from the first that he was not what he appeared, knowing that her constable, Vosh, clearly could identify him made him exceptionally nervous, despite her reassurances. It was a little brazen of him, and he knew it, but he wanted to get a reaction from her.

She simply shook her head. "Sometimes, in search of the next rush, the cause's rightness becomes secondary, and innocent Thurians get hurt or worse. Please, make sure you're not one of them, okay?"

That turn of viewpoint was surprising to him, and as they reached the top, he answered, "I'll do my best." As he stepped off to the side, placing himself in a position that offered the maximum possibility for escape, Shadow realized that her statement cut both ways. She was concerned for his safety, yes, but also concerned that he not become someone who placed the thrill of the chase above the lives of others. Watching her take each paw and gently embrace every individual as they came up, he studied them as each of the twenty or so took their place on a grass-woven mat over a cement platform, kneeling as they did so.

Soon, all were in position, and Vanalla made her way, forward of the pads' center, right next to the fence. She turned and faced away from them towards the graves. For a few moments, they were all quiet, the sounds of the night being all that could be heard. Shadow looked across the hill down at the village, and it seemed that even activity there had been silenced to grant special reverence to this moment. He remembered a little time spent on an army base and how everyone became still at a certain sounding of a drum and horn that occurred every evening. It was an eerie moment if you didn't know what was going on, but to everyone else, it was a requirement of normal respect and honor.

For a moment, Shadow felt a bit ashamed at his earlier angst until the piercing keening, perfectly on key, broke the night silence in two like a knife. It startled him so much that he nearly reached for the weapon he had checked on moments before, but as his eyes looked for a target, he only saw the form of this Faelnar matriarch of Aelkinda, her arms spread low and head raised up, thickly accented words pouring from her mouth in a song of mourning, in a song of loss. Her very voice seemed to bend the air around him and, with it, reality. All around him, the Aelkinda were pitching forward, tears falling from their eyes as she sung for their ignorant dead, those who died without ever realizing Attoria's promise, lost in their Vanarran ways.

Although he knew it was something Vanalla did sometimes two times per sol, the grief in her voice seemed new, the loss tender and raw, and the agony of the ancient words was shockingly genuine. There was no need to know what the words meant, the weeping around him teasing tears into his own eyes. Faces came back to his memory – faces his right of sanction had ended, silenced forever. None without just cause, but all that he had lain down in their great rest could have been sung the same song now breaking through the tough shell around Shadow's heart in a way he felt completely unprepared to meet.

Then, it was done – the song ended, the mourning silenced. Peaceful evening sounds were all that remained, and the matriarch stayed at the low fence, her paws spread on the top run, head bowed. For nearly a pass, there was silence, and then she straightened. As one, the group stood, turned, and started to make their way off of the hill. In less than a pass, they were together, alone. Slipping up alongside her, he offered, "That was more than I expected. Touching." The words came out with a bitterness he hadn't even realized was there, but now that he had said it, he could grab onto it.

"Don't resent that the song touched you," she chided him. "There are shadows darkening many hearts, cub. Mine is no different. I sing to these, yes, but my heart burns for those I've lost, as well. This grief they feel – it's real. Our grief meets here, mingles together, makes us seem less … foreign to one another." He didn't answer, and she sighed. "Well, at least you can put in your report that their matriarch sings every night to a bunch of graves at a fence. Should be a bit entertaining to them."

"To whom?"

"Well, your investors, of course. Makes me wonder who is backing them, though. Must be a very interesting group," she observed. Glancing down the hill, Vanalla added, "We'd best get down. I see Vosh with Tasha. Something they want me for."

She stepped away and started back down the hill, Shadow following at a distance. He didn't like how he felt, and it seemed like he had been shoved, face-first, into his own emotions – into the responsibility for all he had done. It was something he did resent, despite her pleas for him not to. Emotions like regret clouded his judgment, slowed his reactions, and they were a far cry from the fast high of erotic pleasure in the arms of a female or the thrill of the predatory chase. He felt like she had done this to him on purpose, and it made him angry.

When he reached the bottom of the hill, he was a fast boil closing in on boiling over, but his eyes caught those of Tashara, and the look of understanding quieted his soul a bit. "It's okay," she mouthed. "We'll talk."

He almost growled that she knew what would happen to him, but the promise to relieve the pressure mounting in him was enough to stay his claws, for now. "What's up, kit?" Van asked Vosh.

"The feral grazer herds are having a problem. There is a ranging pack of prowlers that have just crossed the ridge and are going to tear them up before we can ever coax them into a pasture and start settling them in."

"Damn," Van spat softly. "We need a hunt. We need to take out that prowler pack and get those animals in a pasture of some kind soon after. Can we stop work on the field for a bit?"

"We could," Vosh noted. "About five sols, tops. It's about the same amount of time that we'd need to get a basic pasture in place."

"Talk to the dames; visit them tonight, Vosh. Let them know."

"Should we break out the teams early?" the dark Vulpi asked.

"No. Let everyone have their sleep. We'll push it hard in sun but I don't want any of ours swinging hammers or sawing in the dark. I want a rush, not a panic." Turning around to Jayanar, she said, "I think that the graveyard got to you, and I can guess you have a lot to say to me, but I can't right now. I have to take care of this and my family. Tasha, can you please … take care of him?"

"I'll do my best, Honored One," she offered.

"Very well. Jayanar, if you'd like to take down prowlers tomorrow, you're welcome to join the hunt. Dining hall, 06:00 intervals. Weapons provided, but only if you have experience."

"I do, excellent experience," he said, a little proudly. There was no way he was telling her that it was hunting other Thurians fleeing or flouting the law, and there was no way he was apologizing for his life.

"The team would welcome it. Good night to you."

As Van turned away, Vosh approached Jayanar. "I would prefer it if you were on the hunt tomorrow. We could use you. These grazers are our best hope for starting a herd of our own and, eventually, supplying our own needs."

"I heard the time. I will be there." She bowed to him and left, Tashara and Jayanar just standing together in uncomfortable silence.

"Your cabin, maybe?" she asked carefully. He started walking without answering. "What happened?" came her gentle question as she came up alongside him.

"The display … up there – and what she said," he nearly growled.

"Yeah, it bit down on your soul; I can see that. You're in pain."

"I've been in pain," he growled. "This is … worse." He found it exceedingly difficult to form any word without yelling, without striking out.

When he reached the threshold of the cabin porch, she asked, "Can … I come in with you? You need to talk to someone right now. Yell, if you must, but talk at the very least."

Her concern for him was stroking his fur in the wrong direction, and so he turned on her. His eyes fell across her shoulders, the swell of her breasts, her hips, her lovely tail, even her musculature hiding beneath the soft and downy fur. Her irises were dilated by the darkness but also by an interest in him. "At … your own risk," he told her, "and it might be substantial."

"I'll risk it," she nearly whispered and followed him inside. As she closed the door, he was just staring at the wall, clenching and unclenching his paw fingers into fists. "Rage," she breathed. "That's what I see, but you are still in control. I think that's an achievement as angry as you are." She turned around and clicked the lock on the door, and when she faced him, her arms raised, and her eyes widened at the military grade weapon pointed at her chest. "Please. I don't want to hurt you," she pled in a whisper.

"Prove it," he told her, his teeth grating together. Then, to his astonishment, she brought her paw-fingers to the buttons in the center of her blouse and started unbuttoning them slowly, maintaining eye contact with him the entire time. Keeping the weapon on her, he noticed her body position, the set of her ears and tail, the dilation in her eyes. She lowered her arms behind her, and her blouse fell to the floor. With her arms raised again, she turned around slowly, her back to him. Carefully, deliberately, the paws lowered and went behind her back in full view of him. Tail fastener popped, and then with a slight lowering motion, she turned both herself and her skirt so the fastener holding it on her hips was facing him, and she sideways to him. The fasteners were released, one by one, and putting one paw in the air, she then let go of the skirt and let it fall to the floor, her other paw joining the first in the air.

She stepped out of the skirt crumpled at her hind paws and stood in front of him with the dark black of her underthings the only variation from the rest of her fur. She repeated, softly, "I don't want to hurt you." As angry and aggravated as he felt, as on edge and danger-ready as he felt, he couldn't deny the absolute beauty standing in front of him.

"You ... wanted nothing to do with me before," he challenged. "Why this?" It was an opening, if she wanted it, to tell him this wasn't a proposition – just the only way she could prove that she didn't want to hurt him.

"Before," Tasha uttered, "your interest in me was ... a joke, a play. You didn't feel any emotion for me, really, I don't think. You are truly angry right now, and as I've said, I know that place. I know that as if I had grown up with it every sol; I did know it a lot more frequently, not so much now. Still, I can see how afraid and angry you are. I don't know what she said to you or what you saw, but she found a weak spot behind the show you were putting on for us. She came really close to the real you, maybe, I don't know – you don't have to tell me. I'm afraid that, if you leave here, you … you could hurt someone – you could hurt yourself, Jayanar. I don't want that."

"You … care for me?" he asked, almost with a sneer, but it wasn't as much of a sneer as he had wanted it to be.

"I don't know you more than one sol, and not even a full one at that, but I know where you are. I … I can see it," she replied, her own lips drawing above her teeth. "I've hated like that. I was afraid I would lose everything, and I turned into a monster. I'm prepared to do whatever I can to save you from that." She lowered the shoulder straps of her support top and let it fall to the floor, his eyes falling along with it until he looked back up in shock and appreciation for her beauty. "And I won't lie, cub," she said, reaching for a fastener on the side of her underthings, "you are a wickedly keen cub. It's … it's also-" she started, but then her scent hit him.

"Your time," he breathed, and she nodded. "Well, I guess with so little in the way of … possessions, you don't appear to be as much of a danger as I thought you might be."

The gun lowered almost in time with the falling of her last piece of clothing. "I … am a danger, Jayanar. I'll warn you that is something I can't deny. However, I might be the kind of danger," she told him, "that you might just come to enjoy." She looked, her eyes pleading, at the gun in his paw. He holstered it and then removed his outer coat, the gun going with it. "Thank you," she told him, as she slowly approached. Reaching around her, he held her in his arms and kissed her deeply, her body warm and yielding to him in every way.

His eyes opening intervals later, Shadow held the naked female sleeping beside his bare body, their passion utterly consuming both of them until they succumbed to fatigue in the early intervals of the morning, a gentle rain storm softly lulling them to sleep. She groaned next to him and stirred awake. His arms grasped around her, holding them together. "Jayanar," she whispered, "you were wonderful; you *are* wonderful."

"Not so bad, yourself. I … guess you have no problem finding companionship here, though, right?"

"No, not really," she turned around so she could look him in the eyes. "I won't lie to you. You aren't my first – maybe not even my thirty-first, but all of those were when I was a primal star, in fact, fairly early on. I haven't been with someone like this in maybe ... ten seasons."

"A damned tragedy, Tasha. You are nothing short of inspiring, and may I say your stamina is admirable, to say the least."

"Not an event they will ever make a formal competition, I'm afraid," she chuckled. "It's not how they began, you know? The primals?"

"Oh, how so," he offered, nuzzling her.

"Well, there were a few standard events, but it was the hunt afterwards that was the exciting part. You see, only champions were allowed in the hunting grounds to find a mate. Think of it, like beasts in the woods, Jayanar. You pick up my scent; you hunt me down, and ... you take me – if you can."

"I guess then this was a successful hunt," he offered, awash in the feelings of her and that he felt for her. Looking into her eyes, however, he remembered why they had come together, and his expression became apologetic. "I know ... you didn't want this, at least not at first, but you were right, Tasha. I ... I would have done something."

"I'm sorry she hurt you," Tasha offered softly, nuzzling back into him. "I don't think she meant to. Do you know what it was that she said that touched so much pain inside of you?"

The emotions were a little more distant, and so they didn't overwhelm him as they had before. Her close companionship next to him also dampened the ill effects, but he had to still lean back and look at the roof of the cabin. "It is hard for me to say, Tasha. I'm thinking back through it, now, and she didn't do anything other than show concern for me, I guess. Then we got to the top of the hill, and they all were so sorrowful, regretful." His jaw clenched, and his eyes slammed shut. "I don't like ... regret. It's pointless."

"I don't disagree," she told him. "It doesn't mean that it's not there. I've ... walked away from a lot of regrets. I did some damned stupid stuff, cub. My experience in the hunt is part of that."

"I noticed you had a very good technique," he complimented, the pain fading away as she cuddled into him.

"Thank you. Not that proud of how I got it. I scheduled hunts, you know? I would win my season, sometimes lose it, and then go to the parties after with my mouth just watering for the right male. I'd find one, beautiful and rotten, and just make him mine. We'd be together and date and have fun, and then as training camp for the next season came due, I'd pick a fight and make sure that the whole relationship just blew up and blew away. I'd come back to training camp ready to kick tail to keep my mind off of how lonely I really was, even when I was with someone. I was alone because I knew I would get rid of them. It was a horrible way to live."

"Alone covers much of my life," he told her. "And there are times when I have to do something I don't want to do, but the greater good demands it."

"What greater good?"

"Greater good of the job, I guess – what I'm assigned to do. In the end and with a great deal of good chance, the job is done and over, and off I go – onto the next one. I'm not sure how long I can keep on going or even if I should, sometimes. If I don't do what I do, I don't know who will, but still, do I have to? Maybe that's it, Tasha. Maybe the regret of it all got to me, seeing theirs. Maybe Vanalla suggested I should find something else because of something she noticed about me. Maybe that's why I was so angry."

"Because it felt like she was saying what you did didn't matter?"

He shook his head. "Because, like those poor souls on that hill, if something doesn't change, I could be like them, buried with regret."

"Which souls, the ones lost or the ones who mourn them?"

He sighed and admitted, "I'm not sure that being either would be any better than the alternative. Maybe ... that was why I was so angry."

"Yeah, Vanalla plain out excels at helping you see when your life doesn't have all of the meaning it could, to put it politely. It ... hurts. I've never hated anyone more in my life, until I realized she cared," Tasha stated with a faraway look in her eyes.

"She's why you changed?" he asked.

"Yeah," came the soft reply. "She committed to me as a friend, and she surprised me more than anyone else I've ever known with how much she knew, how much she cared, and what lengths she was willing to go to in order to help others."

"Is that what she is to everyone here?"

"Not all, and not all in the same way, but more often than not – yes. What time is it?"

"Only about four or so," he told her. "I'm wondering if I should get up to go on the hunt with them – the wild prowlers, they said."

"They won't this sol because of the rain. They'd prefer a dry morning, I think. Besides," Tasha said, her eyes hungry as she looked into his. "I think that you just might be sleeping in tomorrow."

The wanting look in her eyes continued to dissolve any remaining anger or confusion he had and bury it beneath a rising passion for her. "Sounds like a wonderful idea," he agreed, pulling her closer and again becoming lost in the wonderful feel of her body against his own.

Chapter 25: Shift at Mid Sol

The PawLink buzzed an irritating pulse of repeating vibrations in the attempt to get someone to answer it. Tasha, who was closer, rolled over and picked it up, Jayanar stirring beside her. "Hey look, cub," she told him. "Looks like work wants a status report."

He groaned and put up his paw, and Tasha gently placing the device so he could read it easily and wouldn't accidently drop it. "Thank you; so considerate." Cracking open his eyes, he read the "overt" message desiring a status report, but then saw sourcing information indicating it was urgent that he reply. He tapped out a quick acknowledgement, but he knew that wouldn't hold them for long. "I'm sorry, lovely one; I've been here less than a full sol, and they seem to think I'll have every answer for them in a few passes.

"You need some time?" she asked, and he sat up, nodding. "I have to go into Shanandrae this sol for several donor meetings, so I need to get up. Okay if I wash up in your shower?" Again, he nodded. Leaning over, she licked him on the side of the muzzle. "Thank you for trusting me and letting me help you."

"I hope it wasn't all charity," he commented, smiling at her naked back as she stood.

"Oh, no," she chuckled, looking back over her shoulder. "I would be lying if I didn't say thank you for quite a bit more than that, too."

She smiled as she walked away, leaving him smiling as well. Bending back down to look at his PawLink, he repositioned himself so he could sit up against the rough-cut headboard. Keying the controls for secure satellite communication, he put his paw pad right where it needed to be in order to permit the device to work – his physical touch was required to allow it to continue in secure mode, once selected. He keyed out an initial report. "Shadow on station; nothing out of the ordinary to report." Adding the correct check-sums to the end of such a message, he sent it and waited for confirmation.

"Request you confirm illegal Vanarran activities as soon as possible, including status of potentially abducted Lupar, Malliana."

He shook his head and replied, "Malliana present, but doesn't appear to be under any duress or undue influence. No illegal Vanarran activities observed – mostly farming and other basic chores. Small ceremony each night to mourn their dead. Will continue to investigate and look for opportunities to scout any restricted areas, when identified. To this moment, no place requested has been denied access."

There was a longer pause this time before the reply. "Proceed, Shadow. Advise immediately if decisive action required. Advise if any support is needed."

He thought for a moment and then replied, "Forward source and additional details regarding potential abduction case. Forward any new information beyond initial brief that may direct towards any illegal activities or secret locations within the borders of Attoria refuge. Will continue to converse with residents to establish social norms or any potential Vanarran influence."

The response took a moment, once again. "Source of report for Malliana is her father, Representative Kaliashik Dorsi. Sensitive issue – take great care, regarding. Will research and forward new intel as available. Next report no later than 29:30 this evening, local time."

The signoff signal was sent and the communication stopped, leaving a somewhat befuddled Shadow to think through his mission, what he'd been asked to do. The initial statement gave a lot away – StarSat tracking surveillance simply assumed that he had already witnessed some kind of illegal Vanarran activity when he'd witnessed nothing of the sort, and he was starting to agree that the Aelkinda walking around him were no more Vanarran than he was. The report regarding Malliana was interesting but also suspect. It could, of course, be a parent who legitimately reports a child missing, but a parent who disagrees with a child's decision is quite another matter.

All of this led to two possible interpretations of his mission. First, the intel showing that Attoria was a place fomenting a Vanarran resurgence was sound, and the evidence had just been cleverly hidden from him. He would search and eventually find a massive cache of money, weapons, drugs, or some other kind of contraband which had no place in the paws of simple farmers, and that would be that. Yet, Shadow was aware from his reading that there were times when central got the intelligence completely backwards if not just flatly fictitious, and as he considered it, the one case in question was where Representatives of the Assembly were supposedly supplying "verified" information. "I'd believe the kidnapping and brainwashing story more easily if her father *wasn't* an assembly delegate," he reasoned darkly.

Just then, Tasha opened the door to the bathroom and came out in a towel. "You're up next, I suppose," she suggested.

"But darling," he countered, "I'm only going to spend the sol working in the fields, am I not?"

"Yes, but you shouldn't go out there smelling like *me*, should you?" she asked, smiling wickedly.

"Oh, I suppose not," he groaned standing up, and her eyes were instantly on his body once again.

"You are … a very lovely cub, Jayanar," Tasha offered, biting her lip a little. "You'd better get in there fast, or you'll have to explain to someone why you didn't get *any* work done at all this sol."

"There are worse fates," he said, taking her into his arms and kissing her deeply. Releasing her, he shook his head, "but I suppose a donor meeting is important."

"It is, and you are, too. Are you okay this morning?"

He sighed as he released her. "I suppose. I will choose to believe, for now, that Vanalla didn't intentionally goad my emotions. We'll just have to see how the rest of the sol goes. Will I see you tonight?"

"You won't," she sighed, sitting on the bed. "It's an overnight trip as I'm looking to finally sell my place in Shanandrae. I'll get something smaller – still upscale, for when I visit, but that's all I'm really doing right now is visiting, and I'm going to auction off a lot of my junk to help feed and clothe those who are here.

He walked over to her and licked her gently on the side of the muzzle. "You are a wonderful, wonderful female. I look forward to seeing you whenever I can."

"And you, my sweet, are a truly lovely cub." The lick was returned, and Shadow gave her a last opportunity to watch his hindquarters as he left for the bathroom.

Less than one full sol later, Shadow found himself creeping quietly through the woods alongside the Vulpi female who had impressed him so much, earlier. Being with her was a comfortable feeling, as if being near a professional skilled in your own trade, as she clearly was. There wasn't any hint of romantic flirting or even any attraction between them other than those who understand the deadly business that is a continual part of the work they are asked to perform.

As they slipped downwind of where Vosh thought the predators were hiding, Shadow stayed keyed into his environment. He looked all around, not only for signs of the prowlers that were their targets but also for anything that might lend any credence to the supposed reason for his mission – justification of an attack that would destroy Attoria. There had been nothing. During the sol, he had worked besides scores of different Aelkinda of every age and description, pulling weeds, tilling fields, and planting crops. All had been friendly, and to a one, all had been humble about their aspirations. "I … just want to live long enough to be old." "I would like to have a family, one sol." "I only want to pay my own way and give back because of the wrongs those of our kind once did." "I'd like to see children playing here."

All of these were the hopes of the refugee, not of the bitterly defeated. There was never a desire to return to the way their lives had been. When carefully asked, nearly all admitted to some kind of torture they had undergone or the horror of seeing those they grew up with disappear – slaughtered because they failed to live up to the standards of perfection set by the Vanarran eugenics program. Many seemed to be almost completely happy despite their life of hard labor, and when asked, he had watched his namesake cross their expressions, darkened by the way their life was, and one had actually fallen to his knees in tears in front of him. Death was their only remaining birthright, and it was painful to accept that one's shape and fur color would always mark them as infamous and despised.

The love and care and dedication of Vanalla, who had joined him in the sol's work alongside those she led, was nothing short of pure magic to them. She and the others like her who should revile them gave them hope that some Thurians could accept them, and the more Shadow engaged with them and seemed to rely on them, the more he could feel their appreciation for him growing. He could understand, seeing Malliana and her beau, Kennar, working and taking images for the TransNet posts, why they wanted to stay.

The wind rustled around Vosh and blew stiffly against him, as well. It settled, but it created a din and racket in the trees all around, one which covered a quick question to his counterpart. "Is the reason you stay, why you want to remain with the Aelkinda, because they appreciate you so much as a purebred?"

"I stay because Vanalla is here, and I owe her much. However, what you speak of is pleasant and fulfilling in many ways. The mixed bloods and purebred here have noticed that these refugees expected no kindness, expected to never know peace or even have a future of any type in front of them. When they realize that you truly do like them, see past their breed, their hearts are open to you, and they have no more secrets before you. Trusting them will cause them to love you because they have all lived what it means to never be accorded such an honor."

She had whispered the words just loud enough for him to hear, and the dying wind caused her to cease lest she be heard by their prey. "That's all this is. That's why Malliana is here, as well," he thought to himself. He had been able to talk to the Lupar for a good half interval, and she talked about how she and Kennar snuck in, how they hurt themselves, and how terrified they were. He could hear both her embarrassment at having acted so terrified and mistrusting, initially, and how the Aelkinda welcomed her despite that mistrust. Now that she had their loyal friendship and they hers, her life had changed.

He remembered her explanation as he kept a close eye on a draw between some hills that looked like a good place for the prowlers to choose. "I go back to the capitol and see regular Thurians, and that's it – I'm just a regular Thurian. Others pass me on the path without acknowledging me. Here, I'm special. They all know me, and they – to a one – are kind to me. I'm being really selfish, I know, but I can't get enough of that. It also makes me not want to disappoint them, but that has made them all the more appreciative. I help get their story out – I help tell it. It's humbling to realize that someone else – all of these – see you as a kind of life line. They hope my news articles and posts will help keep them safe. I hope they do. I truly hope that."

When he had asked if there was anything else, outside of this appreciation and gratitude, that kept her here, she had taken him by the arm and away from the others. "I have to tell you that ... I'm also here because here I know my father can't keep me from being with someone like Kennar. I know he doesn't like it. I know it makes him angry, but I love that Pantera. I don't know why I do; I just do! He ... makes me feel everything I'd always hoped I'd feel from a male. I was attracted to him even before I came here; that's why I kept choosing him for my videographer. Being here gave us the freedom to ... explore. To be together, as a couple. We never understood – either of us – how good it could be. I know that's not going to convince a single investor, and that it's really silly, but if you wonder why – that's why."

The thought that not only he but his Director had been manipulated by a father wanting only a certain future for a pet daughter made him angry – especially angry if he failed to find any evidence of Vanarran practices or aims in the village. Genocide was a heavy toll to extract for the sake of kicking one's child back onto a path of your preference.

A paw gently touched his leg, and he looked up, having lost his focus for a moment. Ahead, in the shady draw covered by vegetation, two wild prowlers, rogue males, were making their way out and moving in the direction of the grazer path from their preferred wild pasture to the best source of water nearby. Vosh glanced at him, and her eyes then cut in such a way that Shadow knew which one of the two was his target and which was hers. Both raised their hunting rifles and began the process of aiming and at a silent – almost subliminal – signal, the two shots were fired so close together they sounded like only one. Both predators jumped in different directions, howling with pain, but they both faltered and collapsed, blood pouring from their chests onto the ground.

"Heart shot," Vosh commented. "It was the quickest for them, I decided."

"Probably already dead," Shadow agreed. "Excellent aim."

"And you," she agreed. They both stood and started to walk towards their prey. "Prowler meat isn't fit for consumption, and so we'll set a fire in camp and burn them. We'll create drag stretchers behind us and stay on the most even path. It will be tough work, but we can get them back without attracting other predators or carrion eaters."

"You've thought it through."

"May I ask a question?" He nodded. "You seemed distracted just before the predators emerged. That's uncharacteristic for you."

"My ... task and the beliefs of those who sent me aren't proving to be as they said. It concerns me. Someone gets the wrong idea about this place, and something bad can happen, if you follow."

"I do," Vosh agreed. "I think that what we just did is being repeated across Thuria, but with those of the Aelkinda breed as targets – guilty or not. I think that Thurians are failing as they failed with the mixed bloods, but this time, it is worse. De Caterra never truly approached fully wiping out all mixed bloods, not in a statistical sense. Aelkinda, very easily, could be washed from the planet. These here know that, and that shapes their gratitude."

"There was much the Vanarrans did to recommend hate towards their number."

Vosh shook her head, stooping over to look at the two dead animals. "In actuality, their crimes are minor. They injured many children, but nearly all could be completely returned to good health. They bribed and intimidated, blackmailed and pressured – but the number of actual murders that can be attributed to their number outside of their own kind is less than two hundred. Less than two hundred over one hundred and fifty seasons. In contrast to the purebred de Caterra, who killed tens of thousands of mixed bloods and enslaved those of our breed in a shameful way to leave nearly all of those so controlled as emotionally crippled and dependent, the Vanarrans were amateurs. Their greatest crimes they committed against their own, and by those numbers, they approach the de Caterra in infamy."

"What are you saying?" he asked as he stopped down to look at the huge gaping maw of the dead predator.

"For which crimes would Thurians take such offense as to condone or even commit genocide? Do they find righteous outrage avenging dead Vanarrans by killing peaceful Aelkinda? Or, do Thurians just long for someone to hate who can no longer fight them? Were they bullied for so long that they will now slay those who dared such intimidation? These are darker sols than anyone suspects, especially when another group is as guilty or more than the Vanarrans. Those are walking free – largely unscathed."

"Sahnassites," he agreed. "Some of those who were highly ranked in that organization are now in pretty decent positions, not doing poorly."

"Those who weren't found guilty of a crime are free to live as if Sahnassites never were, regardless of their real actions or leanings. Aelkinda bear the marks of who they are in their fur. They can't escape it. I wonder more about the dark souls of the invisible Sahnassites than I do about exceptionally obvious Aelkinda. Come, let's start on getting these out of here."

"Alright," he replied, but his mind was churning. Vosh had spoken strict and exceptionally supportable logic – at least to his way of thinking. As they assembled what would be required to drag the carcasses back to the village, he began to wonder about Kaliashik Dorsi. He began to wonder, and he began to plan.

As he expected, the secure PawLink in his possession was flashing, demanding answers, by the time he returned to the privacy of his cabin. He remarked as he picked up the device and keyed in the correct sequence how empty the place seemed without Tasha nearby, how vacant. "Maybe that's my life," he brooded as the device came to full readiness.

Keying in, he attempted to preempt the flood he knew would come. "Extensive interactions with many members of the community plus most of the sol spent hiking the terrain around the village continues to point out nothing that is of concern. Primary focus of community, at present, seems to be removal of predators in the area, recapture and domestication of feral livestock, and planting of the roots and vegetables that must be grown before the cold season. Other than activities supporting these endeavors, nothing else outside of two assistants to the matriarch and two assistants to Creator's Path minister have been observed."

The next message that came was from the director who was clearly having his own doubts. "The story we are getting here continues to get filled in with additional information indicating extreme danger from Attoria – and you're not seeing anything? Are you sure that Malliana Dorsi is not under the undue influence of these individuals or is being kept against her will?"

"Quite the opposite, sir. Additional discussions with Malliana Dorsi indicate that her presence here is partly because she has fallen in love with a Pantera and doesn't wish to live with the disapproval of her father. The couple appears happy, engaged in the community, and under no duress whatsoever. Sir, what are the chances that our intelligence and monitoring departments got this one sideways? I mean the whole mission?"

There was a pause before the response. "Most of that intel is not coming from internal. Most is coming from Representative Kaliashik Dorsi's office. Internal intel tracks more with yours, but the representative claims to have inside sources."

"Strongly suggest a better vetting of those sources, if possible," Shadow put in as tactfully as he could. "Orders from this point?"

"Significantly intensify your investigation. We have to be right about this one, and we have to prove it."

"Understood – covert imaging and recordings have already been made, but I will significantly explore and search for any other activity. Afterwards, please send other resources if secondary confirmation is required." There, that had torn it. He had basically told his boss that if he didn't find anything, he should send additional resources who would find the same thing – guaranteed.

"Doubtful that will be necessary, but still, press hard! Regarding the representative's resources, I will make some discreet inquiries."

The channel closed leaving Shadow frustrated. There was still a good amount of time, a couple of intervals, before the evening meal, and he did take his director's instructions to heart. Putting the PawLink back in its holster and then returning it to his belt, he headed outside once again. Work continued in the fields, the most obvious scene representing the village's occupation, but across the field he saw the mixed blood, Laxar, walking along its edge, in something of a rush. When he got to a clump of trees, he stepped behind them and disappeared. The Vulpi's hind paws started moving almost before he reasoned out what he was doing. Laxar's movements were furtive, secretive, hurried, and that was to Shadow like a blood marking a leaf or patch of ground to a wild stalker.

It took him about a quarter interval to move around the large field in such a way as to not attract attention, slipping into the woods and paralleling the fields' edges at a distance where he couldn't be spotted. When came up behind that patch of trees, he noticed a well-worn path leading behind them. Turning, he started down that path, trailing after the mixed blood who was no longer in sight. However, the freshly crushed plants near the edge of the path indicated his presence not long prior. "If there's going to be anything secret in this place, this is where it will be – at the fringes."

His pursuit led him what felt like nearly a half track away from the field where he'd started with nothing but path and trees and shrubs as accompaniment. No automated monitoring tools were in evidence, and he wondered if the path would go on well out of the valley until he came upon a hillside cave with a metal door. "What are you doing back here, Laxar?" he asked himself, trying to puzzle it out. Laxar was the artist of the village, supportive of many other key aspects, but that was his primary role, or ... his cover. Slipping up close to the door and slipping out his military grade projectile weapon, he pondered, "Although the isolation needed by an artist would be a valid cover for several activities."

Carefully trying the door, he found that it was very subject to infiltration – smoothly oiled and not locked or wired in any way. Slipping inside, he wondered what he'd find – Aelkinda who were packing weapons for sale, guarding them, manufacturing narcotics. His stealthy entry was aided by a passing cloud that darkened the already dim forest behind, and he could tell that no one was in the space he was trying to enter. Closing the door behind him, silently, he then crouched and moved to cover on the near side of the room behind a worktable. Looking up, he surveyed the room.

It was, in many respects, exactly what one would expect in an artist's studio – shelves and containers and works in progress, finished works, all lit by dim lights from above, lights that could be made brighter, but Shadow wasn't complaining. Beyond that, there was a door with more light flooding in from behind it. It was interesting in that it appeared to have almost a rocky or rough look to it, as if – when closed – it would blend into the wall. There was even a tapestry slid to the side to cover it. "If there is anything in this village worth hiding…" he thought, slipping the door open and removing his weapon. What he saw, at first, seemed to confirm his suspicions.

Laxar had his back to Shadow, bent over some kind of frame, and working on something the Vulpi couldn't see. Scanning around the room, he saw curtains draped from the walls all around, and the floor had been finished to a high shine, the stone meticulously polished. Slipping a paw to look behind the curtain to his left, he saw assorted boxes, smaller ones, stacked neatly and well-organized. Just then, the polishing sounds stopped, and Laxar went rigid, his ears rotating around in Shadow's direction. There was the metal click sound as Shadow slipped the safety off of his weapon, and somewhat to his surprise, Laxar slowly raised his paws, dropping what he had in them through the frame to the floor.

"I see you know what this sound means," he told the frightened mixed blood whose ears were standing straight up although his tail was on the floor, hovering just above it. He even thought he could see individual fur strands standing on end.

"In the … temple, I heard it a lot more. It always meant someone was going to die."

"Turn around slowly," he ordered, and Laxar did so, his body visibly trembling. "It doesn't have to mean that, this sol, but I want answers."

"Yes, sir," the mixed blood replied in a very timid voice. "I … I have a mate. I have a – I just found out I have a child, sir, please."

"Like I said, I want answers. I was sent to search out Attoria, yes, but I'm looking for dangerous things, secret things. Do you have any of those here?"

"Dangerous, no," Laxar admitted, his head lowering in shame. "Secret, yes. I'm sorry."

"It's better that I know and that you show me," Shadow told him. "That's why you're going to start by closing and locking this door behind me. Then, I want you to pull every curtain back so I can see what's behind it."

"Yes, sir," the frightened male replied. "Please ... please don't kill me." He begged even as he complied, the Vulpi struggling to keep an eye on both his prisoner and the seams of the curtains, looking for movement. The sound of the locking door almost startled Shadow, turning and facing Laxar with the weapon. His pathetic captive only closed his eyes and trembled, a small pool of urine collecting at his hind paws.

Shadow started to feel more than a little regret for this – he had held hundreds of Thurians under the muzzle of a projectile weapon, and he knew those who played at being scared, those who planned, and those could face the threat with complete and unnatural poise. Laxar was terrified to his core and acted as if he knew death was certain. "Pull them all back, Laxar. Let me see everything. Are we alone in here?"

"Yes ... yes, sir!" he bleated and then struggled to do exactly as the Vulpi had ordered.

"Not so quickly. I don't want to be surprised by someone, now, that might end very unpleasantly for you." Laxar did as he was told, panting and seeming as if he was about to throw up with fear. However, in a few passes, all of the curtains were pulled back. Only rock wall had shown behind them, smoothly cut, but visibly solid. "Stand in the middle of the room, your paws on that frame, spread out. I'm going to search you." Again, there was instant obedience. It took only a few moments with a standard enforcement frisk to find out that all the mixed blood had was trousers that were wet in the front.

They were alone, it seemed, and Laxar was unarmed. Stepping back, he ordered, "Turn around. Now, I'm going to lower the weapon, but keep it in my paw. I'm very quick; I'll warn you. Now, what is this place?"

"It was a … it was a gift to me by Vanalla, sir," he replied softly. "She saw that I was interested in art, and she gave it to me."

"And I suppose these are your art supplies?" Shadow asked, incredulous.

"May I show you, please?" he asked.

"Carefully, if you value only having the holes in your body you started with," came the casual warning.

"I've been shot before, and I do not wish to repeat it."

"When was that?"

"Fleeing the Vanarran temple. I ran away and got as far as the edge of the trees on the other side before I was hit. I … I limped away and found help," he said, opening boxes all across the top of each stack. "These are all paints – oil based, mostly. These were donated, and this was thought to be the best place to keep them."

"Open the fourth box down, third stack. No, that one," the Vulpi ordered. Again, it was presented to him. He took it, opened the cap, and squeezed out a little of the substance. Although Shadow's knowledge of art was somewhat limited, the pungency told him it was exactly as advertised.

"It's a good shade for the flowers that climb the trees on vines," Laxar offered softly.

"Let's look at a few more," he ordered, and curtain by curtain, stack by stack, they checked the inventory. "What's this last pile?"

At that point, Laxar lowered his head, blush fur high, and tears streaming down his cheek fur. The boxes were different than anything else in the room – the oil paints, the synthetics, the brushes, the markers, the chalks, the canvases. These were marked with labels more suitable to a hospital, he thought. "I said, Laxar, what is that last pile?"

"Please … please don't make me tell you, sir. Please," the mixed blood begged quietly.

"You have no choice. Look at me." Laxar looked up to stare straight into the barrel of the Vulpi's weapon, pointed right between his eyes.

"They're for me!" he confessed. "I use them – they're used on me!"

"You don't seem particularly sick?" he challenged. "What's in them?"

Humiliated, Laxar took each box, opened its lid, and sat it at Shadow's hind paws. "Half of this I'd expect to find in an emergency ward and half at some kind of natural medicine place," he commented, looking at the long needles intended for use in holistic nerve therapy. "These are all used on you? How? Are they used on anyone else?"

"No, no one else but me. I'm the only one … like me who is here."

"Like you? I don't understand. Tasha's a mixed blood – I've seen others?"

"No, sir," Laxar replied, facing the floor. "I … was a temple servant of the Vanarrans. They did things to me. That's why I need these."

"Explain," Shadow quietly insisted.

"If … if the Selects were pleased by one of us, then they would take us for something called the Rites of Reward. I believe the common term used to describe what they did was … sexual molestation and torture."

"This was done to … you, cub?" he asked, Shadow now starting to feel a real pang of guilt for everything in the last half interval.

The nod was slow and painful. "Since … since I was a child, sir. I obtained … permission from Vanalla to have these things so that I and my mate could … re-enact those rites."

"Why would you want that?" Shadow found himself saying.

"There was no reward in those rites. They did it to assuage their guilt, if and when they ever had it. Afterwards, after such intimacy, we felt such love towards them – love they never returned. Now, my mate does this and loves me. I know it's … weak of me, but it is special to me. No one knew except for my mate, my matriarch, and myself until this sol."

"Laxar, I want an honest answer, and it is an answer I *will* hold you accountable for. Is there anything illegal or dangerous happening in Attoria?"

Laxar, still trembling, raised his paw and pointed a finger at Shadow's weapon. "Other than the rifles used for hunting prowlers, that's the only one of those I've ever seen here. No one here has ever been harmed, and I don't think anyone here really wants to harm anyone else – by the Creator, I hope that's still true."

Shadow realized that Laxar was praying that the Vulpi wouldn't harm him. Holstering the weapon, Shadow nearly snarled. "It's not what I get off on, cub, but I have my orders."

"Do those orders involve … killing?" Laxar asked.

"Only if I need to protect myself or others," he explained. "Now, I'll have to tie you up and leave through the woods."

"Why?"

"I've threatened you in a way that your matriarch will probably not appreciate," Shadow told him, as Laxar timidly got to his hind paws.

"What you did just now, what were you looking for? What were you afraid of?"

Shadow carefully considered the male, debating whether to end this conversation and render the mixed blood unconscious, but that had a high price. Now, he held out a very thin hope that Laxar would keep his confidence. "I've been sent because someone thought Malliana was kidnapped and because there are those who suspect Attoria hides secrets of a new Vanarran insurrection."

"What have you seen? I've lived here a long time now, and I've not seen it. Have you seen it?"

"No, actually. It's been the most damned frustrating assignment I've had in a good long while. They normally assign me to places where they know trouble exists. I … fix problems for them. I'll be damned if I can even find one small instance of trouble here – it's the most rapemating perfect place to live I've ever seen."

Laxar shook his head. "Life is hard here. They struggle – work long intervals with no pay but survival."

"Yeah, and how amazing it is to see nearly every former Vanarran as stunned as I am that they are happy and content with their lives. I don't understand the orders of those who sent me."

"Please forgive this, but I don't want you to go. You seem not to think little of me for my ... weakness."

Shadow shook his head. "You lack experience, Laxar. Your weakness is a minor thing against the weaknesses I've seen – narcotics, sex, gambling, crime, conspiracy. I'm sorry you were treated that way in the temple; you clearly didn't deserve it. I'm glad you've found a way to make peace with it."

The Vulpi hadn't been looking at the mixed blood while he said this, but when he finished, he looked up to see Laxar staring at him in wide eyed wonder and joy. "Thank ... thank you, Jayanar. I always thought others would ... revile me for this."

"I wouldn't share it, as it deals with the relationship you have between you and your mate – and that's the only reason why I wouldn't. Laxar, I'm sorry I made you tell me."

"The way I feel right now, sir – I don't feel that way. I'm glad. You've ... you've removed an enormous amount of guilt from my life."

"Life has enough of that. So, did this ... happen or not?"

"You and I had a discussion, and ... I guess you startled me," he said, pointing at the front of his trousers. "I have a change of clothes, though. I won't tell anyone."

He felt gratitude towards the mixed blood he really hadn't felt with anyone else in a long time, and along with his attraction and potential affiliation, maybe even love, for Tasha, it made him exceptionally reticent to allow anything bad to happen to anyone in Attoria. "Did we damage anything when we were looking? I'll help put it right."

"I'll change clothes – I keep them in the next room."

"Can I come with you? I won't watch you change, but I saw a lot of art. Would you mind?"

"Not at all! Not at all!" Laxar nearly effused. "Please!"

They were watched by Vanalla, Malliana, and Kennar as they returned across the field, Shadow noticed, and the Lupar and the Pantera seemed very involved in trying to convince Vanalla of something, and it was clear that the matriarch wasn't in full agreement. In fact, her expression towards Laxar and Shadow was a little desperate, which was amusing the Vulpi. Laxar stopped him about a hundred tracks away, however, and turned so his back was facing Vanalla and the others. "I ... would appreciate your silence about what happened, please, and about my issues," Laxar asked softly.

"I held a weapon on you and threatened your life – without cause, it appears. I'll hold your secret as you hold mine."

"Jayanar, I ... I hope you stay in Attoria. It may not be possible, but I think you fit in or could, you know?"

"I don't know what I'm supposed to do next. My job keeps a very chaotic schedule, not to mention assignments, but I appreciate the sentiment. Let me ask you something, Laxar. If I happened to find others who were in your position in the temples, do you think you could help them?"

They started walking again, and Laxar just shook his head. "I would do everything I could, but I don't know that you'll find any. We were the most disposable of all."

"They treat you well, here, Laxar, I've noticed it. Even in the short time. The others…"

"The others know that I am likely to be the only one, ever, who was their servant. They work to allow me time to do my art. Ask Callanar about it."

"Hey cubs," Vanalla called out now that they were close, and Malliana and Kennar seemed slightly irritated by the interruption. "Did you give him a tour of your studio, Laxar?" she asked.

"Yes, Honored One," Laxar replied as if he done just that with no weapon ever manifesting in the process. "Jayanar was very kind to me."

"His art is extraordinary," the Vulpi complimented, "and I think he is, as well. And how are you two this sol?" he asked the couple standing to the side of Vanalla.

"Frustrated," Van answered for them when they would not. "Look, you've unburdened yourself to me. Tell them – at least you'll have their support."

"What is it?" Laxar asked.

"My *father!*" Malliana spat. "He's sending me notes and just sent the regional enforcement officer to the village center. He's treating me like I'm in some kind of cult and brainwashed and demanding to haul my tail out of here without my say so because *I'm in danger; Attoria isn't a safe place!*"

"Doesn't actually mention me, at all," Kennar softly complained. "It's like I don't exist."

"Dammit!" Malliana swore. "I'm here *because* it's a safe place. I'm here *because* Kennar is here! I want to be here with him. I ... I want to be here, and yet he acts as if this is some damned horror VidStar, and all of you are going to grow fangs and horns and go after me – rip me to shreds."

"You can't just ignore him?" Jayanar asked.

"Her father is a representative," Vanalla explained. "It makes his ranting a little more potent than your normal overprotective and somewhat controlling parent."

"I'm not going. I'm not going even for a little while."

Something clicked for Shadow at that moment, and he realized the components of a strategy. "Then ... don't," he suggested. "In fact, you might take some care to have Vosh or someone else looking out for you."

"Really?" she asked, curious. "You don't think I'm in actual danger, do you?"

"I have reason, based on my experience, to offer you some degree of concern. Representatives have been known to make requests of certain government agencies, including the military and intelligence services, to perform extractions of desired individuals."

"He might abduct me?!?!" Malliana screeched, furious. "Really?! He would freaking do that, too! Dammit, I'm not a baby kit!"

"Regardless," Vanalla offered. "Jayanar may be right, and that somewhat *forceful* overture by the enforcement chief could just be the opener. I'll speak to Callanar and to Vosh, but I want you two in the center of the village. I want the others around you to know that you're worried of intruders. Right now, we only have Jayanar visiting, and so that makes for a really thin visitor's list. Anyone else found here shouldn't be here."

"Yes, Honored One," Kennar agreed. "Jayanar, thank you. I … he doesn't want this, between us. He's made it clear."

"The old prejudices die hard, Kennar."

"Hard, but not fast, sadly. Alright, you two. Cut along and get that done. Don't bring sorrow to us by having something happen to you, okay?"

Malliana was crying but embraced both Vanalla and Jayanar before she left with Kennar. "I feel such pain from them," Laxar noted. "It's awful."

"Yes. I … was wondering, Honored One, when would we see Tasha, again?"

"She's coming back, tonight. Did well, based on what I've heard, but she was stopped and questioned by enforcement. Something's up, and I'm worried. We hang on by threads here, and there are a few out there who I know would like to cut us away."

"We'll have to see," Jayanar sighed and nodded, before turning away.

Shadow shut down his communications with the director, a gnawing sense of dread in the pit of his stomach. The director had told him that, despite the lack of evidence, the representative was demanding that the fiery purge of all life go ahead as soon as his daughter could be rescued from the clutches of this evil group. "If you pull the trigger, Director, you'll be wiping out what I can see as only a helpless group of refugees just trying to scrape out a new life for themselves. Regardless of what other former Vanarrans are doing, these deserve to be judged on their own behavior, and from what I can see, that behavior is completely innocent."

There was no commitment, in turn, that even Shadow's life would be spared if the purge of the village was ordered, although his director told him that he would try to warn him when they had reached the point of no return – when Attoria's final destiny had been set. He was up and pacing in the small cabin, and every sense he had of the place was that there was nothing beyond what his eyes had seen – no criminal enterprise, no unexplained phenomena, no undercurrent whatsoever. "And they will still wipe this place off the map leaving two thousand burned to death. No hope for those who were once Vanarrans." It burned him inside, making him angrier and angrier until a knock finally broke his concentration.

"Jayanar? Is that you?" a soft female voice asked, and he darted to the door and opened it.

"Tasha! Come in here, please."

"Sure, sure," she replied, bemused and a little concerned by his behavior as she closed the door behind her. "What's wrong?"

"I have a question, and I need an answer from you. This is very important to me, and I'll know if you're lying." He stood very close to her, holding her by the arms and looking straight into her face, and it clearly unnerved her.

"What do you want, Jayanar? Tell me! You obviously want to know something, and you think I and everyone else are keeping secrets from you – so just ask, dammit!" she demanded, her arms crossed and eyes snapping.

"I want to know the truth of this place, Tasha!" he demanded with equal ferocity.

"You've seen it for three sols, and yet you refuse to accept it! What the mange did you think you would find? Okay, so you want to know the truth?" she spat, mocking him, tearing herself away. "How about this? Attoria is actually under the protection of space aliens from another dimension who are benevolently ensuring that Thuria allows some of these Aelkinda to live because they believe that they – as everyone else – have value." His expression with her was unchanged in its anger. "Okay, fine – not good enough? Let's try this! Attoria is actually the long-held secret plan of a group of de Caterra who survived the purges and are living among us as a *secret society* with Vanalla as their chief agent in this, the final part of their master plan."

She walked right up to him, nearly close enough to touch noses and stated, "How about this? Fireclaw Destiny was nothing but a tool of Vanarrans and their puppet who put together this Attoria solution when things started going badly for them. Every word said to you, therefore, by me and everyone else here, is a lie – a lie we all agreed on, a lie we all coordinated with absolute perfection, and when we build up the Vanarrans numbers back to that of a fighting force, we'll use that to take over Thuria and extinguish all other life, you know ... because... Oh, and that means that when you leave or we kill you, I get to become the new Great Mother, around all of these Perfected Ones. Would you believe that, Jayanar? Could you?"

He nearly drew back his paw to cuff her, but her expression was too saddened and disappointed in him for Shadow to strike. "Fine, and so why do you think I'm here?"

"You were sent by someone who wanted ... justification for a specific point of view, and they're hoping you'll find it. They didn't send you out here to waste your time; you are too good at what you do to – so they believe we are all so awful. If we're awful, they'd have justification to do something ... bad." He took a step back, looking at her, his eyes hard. "Oh, no. That ... that is it, isn't it? Oh, no." She walked across the room and sat down on the bed. "Destroy Attoria and all who are in it, and the Aelkinda will die off. No. These are living beings who don't want to hurt anyone. Jayanar, please, I know you have a decent mind, better than mine. Who would that serve?"

He looked away towards the window, not enjoying seeing the beautiful mixed blood so despondent. Questions which had been simmering on the edge of his consciousness as frustrations or annoyances at this assignment raced back into the center of his mental view and tumbled and jumped like gymnasts in a chaotic display until it was as if time suddenly ceased, and they were all in position. They were all in place. The picture in front of him fit. The picture in front of him made sense. The picture in front of him looked behind his director's chair to forces in the government, ones with reputed ties to the Sahnassites.

"Do you have a hover?" he asked, but she didn't respond. "Tasha, dammit, do you have a hover? There might not be a lot of time."

"Time enough to die?"

"No," he said, walking up to her and lifting her into his arms, her warm body yielding to the concern in his eyes, the understanding that finally registered in them. Distance dropped between them, and he could tell that although she still held secrets, as any female does, the truth of her life in Attoria was nothing more than he had witnessed, and her love and life were nothing other than what she had represented to him. "No, time enough to save you."

"Please, let's both go to Vanalla before you do anything."

"I don't see what good that will do, Tasha. When all is said and sorted, she's just the matriarch of a tiny group of refugees – no political connections, no *real* house power or authority."

"Don't discount her. She can help – I know it." He looked doubtful, but she insisted. "She can. Maybe buy you time or something. Please!"

"Fine," he said, "but you need to put a double guard on Malliana, tonight. Hide her. She might be the only thing keeping all of you alive."

A few passes later, they were seated in front of the matriarch of Attoria, with her paw rubbing the bottom of her chin. "Okay, so ... if you count our survival as an investment, I can say that you didn't exactly lie to me, and you're bringing this to me, now. That's good. Thank you."

"What do you think you can do, Honored One?"

"They won't move until they have Malliana?" she asked, and he shook his head. "We can keep her safe, and we can seriously add to the dissuasion factor. I don't know if you noticed a rather mild-mannered Nephti driving in this evening?" He shook his head. "The Grand Matriarch Carinthia de Dothnar is here. I'll have Malliana take a picture of her and put it on TransNet. Government intelligence is sure to pick that up. She can also invite several of her fellow matriarchs. I can't keep it up forever, Jayanar, but I can buy you that time, at least."

"The more family and corporate pack leadership you can put into this space will shield you, and I'll telegraph that information as I leave."

"There are other levers I can throw, as well, but I have to know what you are going to do?"

"I have ... certain training and a few contacts to leverage. I suspect a hidden mover in this. The entire time I've been here, everything I've seen and heard has made sense. What hasn't made sense to me is the increasing ardor on the other end of my communications for me to rubber-stamp Attoria as evil and dangerous so they could just destroy the place."

"If you've got suspicions, cub, please, let me know."

"I think we have Sahnassites – or former Sahnassites – trying to finish off their old rivals, settling old scores. I can't prove it. It's a hunch, Honored One, and my hunches have a history of being right."

"I'll take your word for it," Vanalla replied seriously. "Okay, that's worth a couple of additional notes to our other resident matriarch. She has someone trustworthy who was on the inside of that organization. I think she can feed you intel. Whatever support you need, Jayanar, we will back you. Our survival is in your paws, cub."

He stood, nodded, and then headed out the door, Tasha following him. "I want to go," she told him. "I want to help."

"You have a LoftStar PawLink?" he asked, and she nodded. "Stay here. If it looks like it is going to go bad, I'll get a signal to you. Get everyone out of the village and dispersed to the areas well away from here in the valley. That will hopefully, at least, save a few lives. Please, kit, I care for you, but this is bigger than we are. I need for you to do this." Her growing reticence at what he had been saying all but melted, and she stared up at him.

"Okay," she agreed. "Please, understand that I care about you, and … I really want to see you again."

Taking the activator for her hover, he agreed, "I'd like to see as much of you as possible." The quip made her smile, and she kissed him deeply.

Chapter 26: The Workings of a Matriarch

Any doubts Shadow may have had about Vanalla de Kyvara being an authentic matriarch were erased not two intervals after he left Attoria and approached the outskirts of Shanandrae. Although he had his own ideas about how to pursue things, he had felt a growing sense of dread until the quick message from Tasha came. Putting the vehicle in auto-drive he read it, finding it to be a TransNet post that had been echoed by the Shanandrae Newsarotzi noting that two visiting matriarchs, from de Dothnar and De Gonari, were already in Attoria helping to plan the next phase of its future and how their houses could be brought into closer alignment. "Political cover. Nice," he thought. Vanalla's actions threw cold ice water on whatever force wanted to end Attoria. "It won't be possible to firebomb Attoria with visiting dignitaries," he reasoned.

While that indemnification from attack – although effective – was only temporary, the other piece of the message was actually far more tantalizing. Kallain de Dothnar, once Kallain de Mistral was a de Dothnar Faelnar and had been head of the Sahnassite order at one time. Now, he was the primary force behind their rapidly and effectively reassembled house intelligence service. It was even suspected that he and his cohorts were using the old de Dothnar intelligence hub. The amazing fact behind this now well-known intelligence sanctuary was that knowing of its existence did nothing to help the house's opponents. Its location was simply inaccessible to anyone who wasn't an invited guest. Although he and his director's department had been scouring private VidStar images taken on tour, it was soon quite obvious that with the addition of new technology and new staff, the de Dothnar intelligence hub had returned to service as a formidable force in espionage.

He was to meet Kallain de Dothnar not on the de Dothnar estate, but in a secured building used by one of de Dothnar's corporate packs. Although he knew he must stay focused on this desperate gambit that ran nearly counter to the orders of his director, meeting the secretive Kallain was a professional privilege granted to very few beyond the confines of that house's senior leadership. He promised himself that he wouldn't swoon or act over eager in the presence of someone whose reputation was so substantial, but it did lend enormous credibility to whatever information that was going to be passed to him. As he thought through it, Vanalla's ability to reach out and garner the help of an almost legendary intelligence resource with very little notice again showed an acumen he had suspected upon first meeting her.

"Dammit, it's completely likely she knew exactly who I was and what I was there for," he reasoned.

Thinking back to her comment about his presence, he was nearly sure of it. "I would suspect that your assessment will mean a great deal to every life here." She wasn't wrong, and what's more, she had not only seen through the whole ruse of his cover but allowed him to play it through. Vanalla had laid back and given him a free paw to investigate where he liked; that translated into one of two options. First, she knew there was nothing to hide and acting as if there was, being defensive, would have only thrown confusion and unwanted suspicion on all of Attoria. It was also possible that he was still being masterfully turned and directed, moved into the position she wanted to keep his eyes off of something horrible and deadly to all of Thuria. Yet, at this moment, it seemed far more likely that he and his director and potentially even more in his organization were blindly following the course laid down by an unseen and desperately malevolent paw.

Approaching the office complex, he played back through all of his previous missions with the Vanarrans in his mind. In the Vanarran complex on Ricia, he had come upon several pallets of neurotoxic gas canisters. These were present when the armed Vanarran guards had challenged him, to their ultimate demise. However, as one of the Vanarrans had died, he had seen the mortally wounded mixed blood look up from the floor at the pallets and shake his head, his expression stunned and unsure as if he had never before seen those canisters in his life. Agents Ice and Storm, in turn, had shared somewhat similar unexplained moments of confusion or surprise on the part of Vanarrans where they were sent to investigate. Arms and high explosives were present in those facilities, but they weren't tucked into places that made sense – an armory, a storeroom. Rather they had been mixed in amongst food or supplies of other kinds as if one expected to find a military grade rocket launcher sitting between the canned creele and tuber roots.

Pulling Tasha's hover into the privileged spot next to the lift in the parking garage, he looked around, and seeing nothing, stepped out. A quick walk to the double glass doors later, he was stepping inside the standard, metal elevator which seemed to be a trademark of business buildings. However, after following his instructions to select the twentieth floor, he noticed that the lift stopped on three and its back entrance opened. In walked a Faelnar in an expensive and couture-perfect business suit. From the department file images, he knew he was in the presence of Kallain de Dothnar. "Greetings to you, Shadow."

The use of his codename meant that Kallain knew exactly what Jayanar was and for whom he worked. "An honor to meet you, Kallain."

Pulling out a thin, grazer-hide satchel, the Faelnar explained, "We have been working this case, it seems, from two different directions, but I must admit that until now our biases were crossed."

"Oh, how so?"

"Your organization seems unusually and impractically successful at finding illegal activities at Vanarran outposts. Would it interest you to learn that four sols ago, we intercepted a shipment of radioactive isotopes – weapons grade, being smuggled *into* Attoria?"

"That … is news to me," Shadow admitted.

"In the intelligence community, we sometimes lack in the discipline of sharing key information, and that is what I want to rectify." He provided the satchel to Shadow as the lift arrived at his destination. When the doors opened, Kallain put a paw finger to the end of his muzzle and raised his paw to bar the door. The door closed, and Kallain pressed the selection for the parking garage. "I regret this will be a short interview, but I must ensure that I do not create any more suspicion in our adversaries than is necessary. In short, what you will find is that one of my former Sahnassite brethren, Loyal Elite Prime Chuffar, has insinuated himself into the inner circle of a Lupar Representative Kaliashik Dorsi. Not only him, but others in high places. With help from a small and loyal band of followers, he has been extracting incriminating weaponry from Sahnassite facilities and depositing such in Vanarran locations moments before you or one of your representatives arrive. Therefore, Vanarrans are guilty and, given other provocations to make them immediately hostile, the inevitable battle ensues leaving all Vanarrans destroyed."

"And your bias?" Shadow asked.

"That Chuffar couldn't have turned into so desperate and evil a creature, and that our prior Sahnassite facilities had been emptied. It seems that the ball is still in play, and I had hoped that the game was long over."

The door to the garage opened, and Kallain reached out a paw which Shadow clasped. Silently, the Vulpi turned and went his way, his prize now in his paw.

Later that evening, Shadow was living up to his call-sign, hiding in the darkened corners of an atrium ceiling above a residential lair's study. The effect, he supposed, of this peculiar architecture was intended to make the broadly curving and shallow dome above disappear beyond the walls, much as the sky would above the walls of a garden, and with the lighting effects and décor which complimented that theme. It was the most difficult room of Representative Kaliashik Dorsi's estate and lair to penetrate, and a careful examination of the plans provided by Kallain provided one and only one way in or out that was undetectable, but it was, at least, a way. Now, he was here, and if information from a couple of other departmental sources was correct, the very Nephti he was hoping to catch with the Lupar owner of the lair was on his way.

Within a half interval, just as he was starting to get restless, the doors of the study opened and the very two individuals he was hoping to see entered the room, and Shadow's readied paw-finger touched the capture button on the evidence recorder, taking its feed from an electronic microphone he had placed earlier to perfection in the center of an expensive floral arrangement.

"I've waited long enough for an explanation," the Nephti demanded. "Why has government intelligence not captured the evidence required to end Attoria and burnt it to ash?"

"My daughter is still there, Chuffar," the representative explained. "Not to mention that over the last few intervals two matriarchs have placed themselves within its boundaries with their staff, and there is word of two more matriarchs flying in tonight. There is no course now other than patience, according to the Director of Intelligence. Our paws are bound, for now, on this matter."

"I've provided you everything you need to know that Attoria is a transfer point for weapons grade radioactive materials. The blasted agent should have been able to validate the fact within six intervals of showing up. Every one of them carry a radiometer as a part of their standard equipment."

"Yes, yes," the Lupar sighed, sitting in a comfortable chair and pouring himself a drink. "The director stated that his operative detected nothing of the sort. He told me that he had been all around that entire valley and nothing had given the operative the slightest hint that anything was amiss."

"I can guarantee you," Chuffar blustered, "that the agent is utterly incompetent! My sources say that the radioactive material was there!"

The Lupar shrugged. "Your evidence hasn't been wrong in the past, Chuffar, but maybe there was a hitch this time. Besides, radioactive material would do Attoria exactly how much good?"

"In the right paws, they could receive an amazing remuneration for it. They would live quite comfortably, all the while planning their eventual return to power. You know how they are, Kaliashik. Their thirst for power and domination is utterly unquenchable. If that contraband gets away from Attoria then you could lose an entire city!"

"That may be, but I'm not taking action while five matriarchs and my daughter are there!" Kaliashik told him, sternly. "Be patient!" The representative cooled his temper and drank a sip from his drink. "We know that Vanarrans are unsalvageable, and it's only a matter of time before they – with your help – will no longer be a species on this planet. They will be gone, Chuffar – dead and gone. In time, the rightful order reasserts itself, and no one gets harmed, but if you haven't noticed, the houses are regaining power and now hold much of what they used to have."

"Such shouldn't be their purview," Chuffar contended. "They are a relic of a bygone age and pointless to the exigencies of the Thuria of this sol and interval. What use has going backwards ever served."

"We'll see, but right now," the Lupar warned, "we don't have the luxury of unilateral action. Now, the interval is late, and this is an exceptionally inconvenient conversation. My flyer for Luratan leaves very early tomorrow, and as I am the key member of the delegation trying to secure a trade deal that is very much in our favor, I would like to arrive rested and prepared. Attoria will wait until it is only a minimal casualty count that will pay, and my daughter will not be among them. Her bastard Pantera lover – one can only hope."

Chuffar seemed to realize he had pushed enough and that pushing more wouldn't be useful. "That is all I can ask, I guess. However, if your Pantera problem does manage to escape, I'm sure that something ... innocent can be arranged, if you would like."

Kaliashik looked at the Nephti carefully, intently, for a moment before asking the question that would doom him. "Quietly?"

"Cheaply, as well. In fact, I'll warrant that such can be had for under ten thousand or so – no one need ever know. It would help to have my resource on retainer."

Kaliashik picked up his PawLink and keyed for a few moments. "Fifteen thousand transferred. Have to have a little for yourself, you know. Don't worry about these Vanarran bastards. We'll get them. No problem."

Chuffar looked around the room at the dome and sighed. "I suppose so. I've always admired this room, Kaliashik. Very peaceful and, as you have said, very private."

"My own little de Dothnar intelligence hub," the Lupar chuckled. "A little space of tranquility."

"It's like having a piece of the outside indoors. I really must look into building something of the sort for those with whom I associate. Our needs are increasing now that those of the Elite Order are growing in number."

"You'll have to let me know if you want to," Kaliashik offered, standing. "I can send you the plans. Now, let me see you out."

With that, the two quit the room, and Shadow turned off his evidence recorder. It was the work of a few moments to retrieve the microphone and then make his way back through the claustrophobic mechanical spaces towards his waiting hover.

The next morning, Jayanar Bonario stepped into the receptionist's office for his director, and her Faelnar eyes lit up in surprise. "Jay," she breathed, "the director has been in a fuss about you all morning – tried to reach you and didn't like your message very much, telling him to wait."

"Had to be done. Is he in?"

"He is. Central military intelligence is also in there with him, and they are conferring – or so he said. Ah, he'll see you now."

"Thank you very much," he offered the attractive Faelnar with a short bow. In a moment, he had entered, and the elder Perratti was sizing him up.

"A bit surprised to see you, Jayanar. This is Vice Marshall Admodar of the military intelligence wing. We've been consulting together about the Attoria problem, trying to determine the best way to carry it off, given the circumstances."

"Circumstances, sir? I'm afraid I don't understand."

"Horrible problem," the Pantera Marshall explained. "Radioactive isotopes and four matriarchs huddled in around them, unknowingly, we presume. Exactly where are they located?"

"I believe those specific isotopes are located deep within the de Dothnar intelligence hub, unless I much miss my guess – well out of the reach of any in Attoria," Shadow commented, and one could have heard a strand of fur strike the carpeted office floor at that moment.

"You'd better explain yourself, Shadow," the Perratti almost growled after a moment. Nodding respectfully, the Vulpi removed the satchel from underneath his left arm and presented it to his superior. "What's this?" came the question as the fasteners were released, papers and other evidence being removed and mentally cataloged.

"A gift from someone else in our business, namely Kallain de Dothnar."

"Head of their intelligence service," the director acknowledged, a little surprised, as he rifled through the material. "Dammit, he found them?"

"Yes, sir. He found a group of individuals trying to smuggle the isotopes into Attoria without being seen ... without being seen by the Attorians, especially. You see, sir, in a number of my previous assignments, it's always been something big – a biological or chemical agent, drugs, or weapons that were the pretense for sending in our forces to take down the Vanarrans."

"Not much of a *pretense*," Admodar countered. "It's more like *solid fact!* Every operation we've been a part of has seen the items we were warned about present as described, within the Vanarran precincts."

"Yes, but considering *exactly* where we have found some of them, don't you think it's curious, Marshall? Artillery shells in the larder, military weapons in a janitorial supply closet, and according to this, the plan was to smuggle the isotopes into an artists' studio."

"But we heard it was some kind of ... secret cave?"

"It is a cave, but that's all it is. I've looked around every part of it myself, scanned every corner. It's not large, not imposing, and dare I say not at all secret," Shadow nearly chuckled. "Every single individual, including visitors to Attoria, knew exactly where Laxar's art studio was. I watched him paint – it's not a cover, and every supply in the space is art related. I'd swear to it." Shadow smiled inwardly, given the minor lie he was using to protect Laxar's secret.

The director was to starting grind his teeth, something he did only when he was really angry, and the Marshall wasn't much better off. "If what you are saying is correct," the director managed after a few moments of tense silence, "then we have been *played!* Placed into the position to eliminate Vanarrans who might not have even known what was there? Who might not have even been conspiring or doing anything illegal in the smallest degree!"

"It's too fantastic," the Pantera Marshall contested. "For every operation in the last ten moons has been exactly as Kaliashik's sources had said."

"And who are his sources, sir?" Shadow asked. "How well have we vetted them?"

"Not well enough," the director sighed after having looked through more of the papers.

"And as regards Representative Kaliashik. I'm afraid I have a very unflattering report to put forward to you on that score. It's in his own words. Here, please listen. The other voice you hear will be the former Loyal Elite of the Sahnassites, Chuffar de Dothnar."

Stone-faced, both senior intelligence leaders listened to the conversation recorded in the representative's lair not fifteen intervals ago. When the recording was over, there was again a silence in the room that hung for a long time. "I seriously mean to get those sorry bastards," the director finally spat.

"Geornan," the Vice Marshal said, barely above a whisper. "He's made us out to be murderers – they have; he and whoever he's working with. Either that, or it's criminal incompetence. Chuffar and this ... and now a slice? A slice on his daughter's fiancé? Seriously?!"

"So it would seem, sir. What are your orders, Director?"

"Oh, do wipe that damned smug expression off your muzzle, Shadow!" the director complained.

"I'm sorry, sir. I don't think I was."

"He wasn't," the Pantera offered, shrugging.

"You don't know him half as well as I do – he was, on the inside! So, how ... how much does anyone else know of this affair – of our ... mistakes?" the director requested.

"The Attorian matriarch, Vanalla, was expecting someone from intel to be sent down, and I could tell almost from the moment I arrived that she suspected me. Knowing that, she still opened the whole place up to me, anywhere I wanted to go and anyone I wanted to talk to – no restrictions. I saw Malliana and her fiancé, Kennar.

They seemed both happy and there of their own free will. When I started to pick up a scent that all of this was a set-up, I confided high-level details to the matriarch to get her cooperation. Her uptake rate from simple facts was frankly amazing. She apparently has much more in terms of resources then I first suspected."

"Kallain de Dothnar is almost never seen outside of the intelligence hub," the Pantera noted. "We thought that all they could do from down there was cut out paper dolls and do puzzle books. We were dead wrong. What you've got laid out on the table here, Geornan, is some damned fine intelligence work – well sourced and clearly presented and on par with anything we're doing. Shadow, did he give you any indication that he was willing to work with us further?"

Shadow nodded, answering, "It was a brief conversation, but he mentioned that we'd been working the same case from different sides. The documents in the satchel and enough leads for me to follow up on were excellent cooperation, already. I received no indication that he would be willing to do anything more, but he was willing to go this far."

"If he has the isotopes, which we have to recover," the Vice Marshal explained succinctly, "he has one more thing to do. Furthermore, he knows the source of at least some of the leaks of these critical weapons and contraband. Unless he's developed a need for radioactive controlled items…"

"A house has no use for those," the director offered, shaking his head, "especially when he knows that we just heard he has them. It's likely a matter of making a request for a meeting, his terms, of course."

"Can't argue that. He's been in the driver's seat while we've been taken for a ride by someone else. What's worse, if we don't expose Chuffar and Kaliashik soon, who knows what other venues he may find, and we'd get buried in the process. Damn, we still might get buried by the media if he has them ready on standby. If anyone bothers to go back on those other Vanarran raids with any detail, our paw will be looking pretty weak. Shadow, you've had an excellent head on this. Suggestions?"

"As matriarch of a little over twenty-five hundred in Attoria, Vanalla de Kyvara has developed enough influential connections to bring all of this into our paws. She possesses enough information to badly damage our operations and credibility, as does Kallain. They are choosing not to do so, which I'd take as a mark in our favor. What's more, we could decide to pursue Chuffar and Kaliashik on our own, and yes, with what we've recorded we could bring them in, but their operations might only be momentarily headless, not dismantled."

"Key point, that," the director agreed. "Someone has got expert and covert sourcing for some very dangerous items; regardless of how they are using them, we need that stopped, and stopped quickly. In the meantime, I'll pull Ice off of her clean-up duties and question her to see if she's seen anything that matches this intel. We'll also put a stop to any more planned raids – logistical problems as an excuse or whatever."

"It will buy us time, but not eternity," the Pantera in the crisp military uniform disagreed. "What's the next step?"

"You don't decide the next step until you've defined the outcome you want," the director contested, shaking his head. "In the end, I'd like to see us clear of this business as far as culpability for the raids where innocent Vanarrans might have died. I want to tie that one around these two bastards like a noose."

"This might also allow us to free ourselves a bit from the continual interference of the Assembly," the Vice Marshal remarked, shaking his head. "Not a damned sol goes by without some staffer from representative X or Y showing up with something to be checked into. Most of it is political sniping, using us for that purpose. All the while, mangy crap like this is going down – it's senseless!"

"They are becoming the bane of all of the agencies, I'm sure. Maybe that's why Kallain can achieve such a score so quickly – he's not tied to anyone but a matriarch." The Director's observation gave them all pause, and they all nodded. "Damn, well, if that's the endgame, how do we get there?"

Shadow spoke up. "I go back to Attoria, tell the matriarch what we've found. She has her own intelligence assets, as well. We see if we can work together on this. After all, four matriarchs and their staffs are now calling Attoria their home – at least temporarily."

"We know our desired end-game. I wonder what hers is," the Marshall pondered aloud.

"We need to know that. We've stopped the bleed, for now, and we need to check to make sure our own assets who are capable of carrying out future raids are stood down and can't be interfered with. Who knows where these bastards have their claws. If any of the things we'd planned go ahead, we'll be staked out on the ground and left for dead. You'd better get after it, Shadow. We'll have a full time here just trying to put the safety back on."

Nodding at the intense frustration in his director's eyes, Shadow didn't doubt the statement in the least. For moons, his unit had been gearing up and executing these assaults so frequently they had become routine – and that routine had to stop, at once. "I'll be in touch, sir," he told them, standing.

"Just one more thing," his director warned. "Share no more than you positively have to, but understand that some transparency is required. We're not dealing with the opposition any longer; we're dealing with potential allies. Act accordingly."

"Yes, sir," Shadow acknowledged and quit the room.

In two intervals, he was returning to Attoria in Tasha's hover, and he pulled into the administration building just as Callanar was walking out to see him. "Jayanar?" the older Aelkinda asked. "What are you doing back? They'd told me you'd gone."

"Am I not welcome?" the Vulpi joked, smiling at the surprise and greeting in the elder face.

"No, you certainly are, but there's quite the little meeting in there," he noted, pointing back towards the building behind him. "Five ... count them ... five matriarchs meeting in council, their seconds also!"

"Where's Tasha, is she around?"

"She's with them, acting as the matriarch's aide whilst I'm gathering you. Vosh found out you were coming, of course."

"She's quite the individual," Jayanar acknowledged.

"Agreed. Also, I was to bring you in as soon as possible upon your arrival," Callanar offered.

"Then we'd best see to it. Thank you, my friend." In a few moments, Shadow had been shown into the inner conference room, again the desk with its conference table forming a "T" shape with Vanalla sitting in her place in the company of a seated Faelnar, Lupar, and two Nephti. Behind them stood their senior dames, but that was something Shadow knew only because he had read the dossiers of the primary house leadership in the area. All of them were without their rank and signs of office, dressed in clothes very much like those worn by the rest of Attoria. Still, seeing the other matriarchs bringing themselves to Vanalla's level and seating themselves in front of her spoke immense volumes to him. Vanalla was in charge here and potentially with greater influence than any other single matriarch or house member in this room. This, without question, was not a meeting of equals.

Vanalla looked at him, and behind her stare, he sensed an enormous depth and intellect that she had kept masked from him, at least partially, during his first visit. He reasoned that if Vanarra de Gonari herself had been seated at the head of this table, the awe caused by her piercing appraisal of him would have been no less. This phenomenal magnetism of the matriarch and utter trust she fostered were so great that he felt like bowing before her even minus the title, and he did, regardless. They had all stopped speaking the moment he had entered the room, and the silence in the room was heavy, expectant, anxious.

"Matriarch Vanalla de Kyvara," he greeted, addressing the most senior member at the table as form required, even if she wasn't officially the most senior according to the old forms.

"Jayanar," Vanalla greeted. "Welcome back, and I am glad to see you. I presume you come with something to share with us?"

"I do, Honored One … Honored Ones." His eyes momentarily caught those of Tasha standing behind the matriarch and to her left, Callanar taking the position again on her right. The nervous excitement was masked in the Vulpi-Faelnar mix, but there was enough there that it gave him hope. Finally, Vanalla nodded, and he stood. "I originally introduced myself to the matriarch and the others here as Jayanar Bonario, and so I am. However, in certain circles of the government intelligence service, I go by another name – Shadow. I was sent here for the express purpose of locating contraband material and confirming its presence. That confirmation was intended to be the trigger for a raid disguised as an accident which would have devastated Attoria, killing all or most of those who live here."

The matriarch of de Dothnar blinked. "Uh, I'm presuming you didn't find anything."

"I found an artist's studio, and a very ... good soul. I frightened him and invaded his privacy, Honored One. For that, I am sorry, and I apologize."

"He's said nothing but good things about you, but I thank you, nonetheless. Please, continue."

"Thanks to the timely intervention of your intelligence services, Matriarch Carinthia, I was able to confirm that Attoria is innocent of any wrongdoing. My leadership is taking steps to dismantle the operation that was meant to go against this place, in addition to any others that were in the planning stages against *any* other so-called Vanarran outposts. We have reason to believe, based upon new discoveries, that our intelligence channels regarding the Vanarrans and Attoria have been compromised."

"Reasons to believe are fine," Vanalla stated, a little admonishing in her tone. "Proof is far better."

Shadow nodded and placed an evidence recorder in the middle of the table and pressed play. "This is the once Loyal Elite Chuffar de Dothnar of the Sahnassites and current Representative Kaliashik Dorsi, Honored Ones," he said, talking over the voices for just a moment. Everyone in the room listened to the conversation in rapt attention.

When it was over, the matriarch for de Dothnar said softly, "Disavowed." It was a statement in judgment, a decision instantly made. Looking at the others, she shook her head. "We were trying to give those of that order our patience and understanding as they transitioned. This ... this means that Chuffar is working restore the hold Sahnassite paws once had on our house and Thuria, in general. I *will not* let that happen again."

"I understand," Vanalla offered, "but we must forestall specific action against these, for now. Just as you've told me had to be done with Shalana, taking down Chuffar will be a task of equal measure, I think. *Shadow,*" Van emphasized, calling him by the name as if it was his professional title, "I take it that, based upon your return here, your leadership has a certain willingness to cooperate with us?"

"He does, and there are more in the military who are on our side, Honored One. They are equally appalled by the potential of having been misled into harming those who did not deserve it," he explained.

"There's more to it than that," the matriarch of de Orturu offered. "The governmental raids have had an intense chilling effect keeping good Aelkinda away from Attoria in fear of their lives. They won't come here because they believe that hiding in the basement of a lair is better than coming to live in a place where they could be an easy target for mass murder." The de Gonari and de Bosnar matriarchs looked at her, surprised. "We … have reports from our dames and matrons that there is a fair amount of sheltering going on. Runaways have been found hiding in Creator's Path chapels and churches. The faith is creating a network to house the refugees safely, but they will not leave to come here. There could be as many as five hundred to a thousand on the different continents in this situation. That's to say nothing of the fact that other Vanarran installations are just scraping by, far too terrified to do anything."

"Is there any hard evidence gathered by any of your assets, Honored Ones, indicating that any of those installations are in any way dangerous?" Shadow asked.

Vanalla spoke for the group. "There have been ones that were – and so not every raid was unjustified. However, out of those who are left – no. De Gonari has actually been offering up their services as independent observers to that task. The Vanarrans only need convincing the way to Attoria is safe. De Dothnar has been secretly providing some basic food and relief supplies. However, we really need those individuals here. They won't come here if they can't feel safe in doing so. That's the price of my cooperation, Shadow. It doesn't take a genius to see that the military and governmental intelligence services have a lot to lose if word of their accidentally misdirected raids come to light. I leave it for my peers to mention any other prices they have, but lives come before reputations in my book, any sol."

"And in mine, also," Carinthia de Dothnar offered. "I would like ongoing cooperation and information sharing between our intelligence services and your own, but I can't require it."

"I believe, Honored One," Shadow explained, "there would be a willingness now for this. Our desire is to not only bring down the specific actors in this case but also significantly decrease the number of times our services are used for political purposes and not for the defense and protection of our citizens. The prevention of any additional loss of life need not be stated; our regret for those misjudgments is sincere."

"Then so will the repayment be sincere. Instead of determining how you can kill them when someone has falsely implicated them, we need for your group to get them here in safety, and military assets could be a significant help to that," Vanalla stated firmly. "A formal airlift has credibility, but it should also include transporting those sheltering to and from Attoria as confidence for those refugees."

"Based on my meeting this morning, I don't believe we would have difficulty with military asset usage. As I said, the shock that such could be perpetrated against us was … severe. My director wished to convey his most heartfelt apologies, as do I." He wasn't looking at any of the matriarchs at this point, but rather at Callanar. "I am sorry. We should have found out sooner."

"If I may?" Callanar asked, seeing as the apology was directed to him. Vanalla looked to her peers and then nodded. "For hundreds of seasons, those of my old order placed ourselves apart from the rest of society, and in the end, they had no compunction harming those they disagreed with. Collectively, we deserve no better, but we would be very grateful of it. As we would be grateful to be considered friends and not enemies."

"That's already true for me. I think it can be true for the rest of those with whom I work. I think we can agree to your terms, Honored Ones."

"Very good," Vanalla replied, but then turned back to Callanar. "Given what we just heard from the recorder, I want you to rearrange things so that Malliana and Kennar are in the center of our village. Tell them why. Tell those around them why. Take the recording, with your permission, Shadow?" He nodded. "Were you there when the recording was made?" Again, he nodded. "I … I may ask you to speak to her later. This will be very hard news."

"Her father will go to prison," Shadow acknowledged. "I understand."

"It's more than that," Vanalla contested softly. "Her father has betrayed her very soul by wanting to kill her heart's love for selfish cause. There is no house disavowal, of course, but she will disavow him in her inmost self. Nothing could be worse." Shadow looked at the other matriarchs who were hanging on Vanalla's every word. This, he decided, was why they followed her lead; her insight into the Thurian soul and articulation of the ways of honor and truth were magnetic. It was a trait missing from any leader he had ever known. Vanalla turned towards the others at the table, and she bowed her head to them. "My fellow matriarchs, thank you. Your presence has helped to preserve us, and I think your stance over us in this time protected us like a shield. You have my deep and most profound gratitude."

"You've – by example," Carinthia stated firmly, "shown us what it *means* to be a matriarch, and our houses are already the stronger for it. We want to continue to help. Just reach out where we may be of service."

In a few moments, the meeting was dismissed, but Vanalla indicated that Shadow should talk with her alone. Getting up from her desk, she walked up beside him. "And so, here you are, back in Attoria. I'm sure that your director could have sent someone else down or come himself. Why you?"

"I have my reasons – developed some ties to this place, and I had to return Tasha's hover, Honored One."

Vanalla chuckled and shook her head. "It's just us, now – forget the titles, cub. You know, the hover could have been delivered," Vanalla softly challenged. "She told me that you two got along very well. She's been lonely, Shadow, for a long time now. I think you have, too."

He sat in a chair at the table in front of her and admitted, looking at the far wall. "Lonely and also tired. I think that many of us will be taking some time off if or when this is settled. There are a lot of sleepless nights ahead of us looking into the faces of those we might have falsely condemned."

"The guilt is only with the guilty, cub," she said, placing a paw on his shoulder. "You were performing your job to the best of your ability, and I don't know about the others you serve with – only you. They have to search out their own hearts. That said, I showed you Attoria as it really was, and you made your own judgment. You spared us. If you had been given a reasonable opportunity to do so in the other assignments, the same heart and mind would have made the same call. I'm confident of that."

"I've never met a leader like you, before," he told her, turning around and breaking the contact. "I thought it was religious fanaticism or cultish loyalty, but no, you're just a really damned good leader for all of these. Callanar nearly worships you, but he doesn't because of the respect he says he owes you. Others feel the same. I think … I could come to feel that way, in time." He looked at her, unsure of why he had confessed so much of his own feelings at that moment, but her expression told him that his words would never be used against him.

"Vosh has done well here. Maybe, just maybe, your director might find it useful to check in with Attoria from time to time – through a designated proxy. You could find a little rest and a bit of a respite from being so lonely, from time to time."

"Your lives seem very active here; I don't know that I would get bored," he commented, smiling. "Always a lot of work to do."

"A little easier now that we aren't trying to orchestrate things around you. If you will forgive this, I have to admit getting you riled up on purpose; I had a good idea of what would set you off. So long as you didn't go out that first night you were here and run across our intercept of the radioactive contraband, we were okay. Now, that could have been a knock down shouting match with me, maybe even coming to blows, but you and Tasha seemed able to solve the problem. In case you're wondering how we did the intercept, we actually created another cave nearby to Laxar's – a fake entrance that just had rock behind it. Fools spent half an interval trying to key a secret panel. There wasn't any – it was a rock."

They both laughed a little as Shadow chuckled thinking that through. "I bet they were surprised."

"To find a bunch of really pissed off Nephti standing there, holding them at stunner point, ready to hand them their tails if they dared anything – you bet. Now, when you and Tasha started warming up to each other, I had to send her away so that you would get the look at Attoria you needed."

"Does this mean that … Tasha and I aren't allowed to…"

"Associate, yes, of course you are allowed. Although as I'm sure your director would point out, I'd prefer if you stay mission-focused for the time being. Taking down Chuffar and dismantling his network isn't going to be easy. He's one of those Sahnassites who refused to quietly transition to a new life, and Vosh suspects that he has many others ready to stand in his place if he falls. On that score, you still okay being paired up with Vosh?"

"She seems exceptionally capable. She doesn't…" His worry was evident, and it made Van smile.

"She's fine with being just friends, and she was aware that you and Tasha might have found something together. She's the protective type, not the jealous type, but be damned certain of the protective part; it's no joke."

"She's admirable for that reason alone. I … respect her."

"And she, you. Still, there's a lot of planning to do and quarters are tight because of the other matriarchs. I doubt Carinthia and her group will leave tonight, and so I have to put you up with someone if you're staying the night. Tasha … requested the honor. Same cabin; it's where I told her to go."

Shadow's blush fur raised minutely. "I think it is I who would be honored."

A few passes later, Shadow had walked from the administration building, again greeted heartily by multiple Aelkinda who all wanted to know how his visit was going. "Very well, and in fact, we may be able to leverage our resources to help those in hiding reach Attoria, safely." The reaction to this was almost tear strewn; several of them outright hugged him. Where was he going now, they wanted to know. Going to visit Tasha, well, then they would see him later, and gratefully, they departed. He was nearly riding an emotional high as he came up to her cabin door. What was behind it, waiting, made him both excited and gave him pause. He had lied to her, threatened her, and terrified her. It could have even been construed that he used her, to some degree. He would have to be careful here, he realized, and there was nothing he could assume about her.

Tapping on the door, he received no answer, but at a bit harder tap, it came open. He walked in and closed it behind him. She was sitting on the bed, looking at the window, and worry was in her features. "Tasha?" he asked.

"Shadow," she replied. "I … I like that. I know Jayanar is your real name, but I like the mystery in it. Did she tell you that she sort of … wound you up and sent me in your direction to cover over the capture of the-"

"She did. I can only be so upset, Tasha. It wasn't like I came here without false pretense," he offered, edging closer.

"Yeah, and then I … then I loved you, and I didn't know if you would know that I meant it, that I was attracted to you but just cared about you, I don't know why, but I do," she stated in a rush, still not looking at him. "And then, I didn't know about you." She looked at him, her eyes searching him, desperately. "Was I just … part of the mission or did you actually feel anything for me?"

"I was doing my job, and it was part of the mission. What I find so difficult to grasp right now is how I could have come to feel so much for you while we've been apart. I can't understand how one Thurian could hold so much magic for me? I held you in my arms, yes, and I was angry, but you changed me, Tasha. You showed me what I have been starving for – moons upon moons or worse, seasons. You truly cared for me; I could tell that. You didn't want me to get hurt, Tasha. Do you know what that felt like afterwards when I realized that I still entertained the notion that all of you could die? That I would make that decision? How … could I not care for someone like that?" he asked her quietly. "There have been others, and I'll admit that I just used them for my own pleasure; I can't deny it."

"Nor I, as I said. Would you forsake the opportunity for any others, for me? Until we know if this is real between us, and it really works out?"

"I cannot be the kind of mate you might like, at least not right away. My job puts me in dangerous places, far away and for long periods of time. It asks things of me I must do. Tasha, killing is one of those things."

"I had guessed. Can you tell me why, though?" Tasha asked.

"Not specifics, but in general. I kill to protect myself. I kill to protect others. I kill to stop a crime. I don't like doing it, and I hate when I have to – I regret every single time, but I'd kill Malliana's own father if he tried to hurt her. I'd kill someone who intended to harm you, or Vanalla, or any of these here."

"Protector of the pack," she breathed, looking up at him. "It is the sacrifice needed for a safe life, and it's why I love you, I think. The burdens you must carry … I would make them lighter, if you'd let me."

"You already have. Imagine … imagine how I would mourn, Tasha – how I already mourn the innocents I might have killed. A few hundred right now, maybe, but if Attoria had gone up in flames, it would be two thousand more that I would see at night when I close my eyes." She leaned in and kissed him, gently, on the side of the cheek. "So beautiful and so kind. Tell me, Tasha, was it your mother who was Faelnar?"

"No, she was the Vulpi. Why do you ask?"

"I … wondered if it was the Faelnar in you that attracts me so much. Vanalla-"

The mixed blood bit her lip with a smile. "Are you crushing on the matriarch, Shadow? And here I was hoping that I was the reason you wanted to come back to Attoria."

"You are," he replied sternly but then smiled. "Your matriarch may be the most singular leader I've ever met. I wondered if it was because she was a Faelnar."

"No. De Caterra proved long ago that no breed has the corner on wisdom. Vanalla is special all on her own."

He nodded. "I can see that. I feel that, if I were to look to her as my leader, I would be serving someone the likes of which hasn't been seen since the times of Vanarra de Gonari. To serve someone like that means that I might never have to have these kinds of regrets, ever again. To love you and to serve her – that is a life too good to even hope for."

"If that … is what you want, you dear cub, perhaps it can be. Vanalla helped turn my life around, turned me away from being a selfish spoiled brat playing at being an adult. Fireclaw Destiny was who I was. It's not who I am, now. The journey from who I was into who I am started with Vanalla. Damn, you'd have probably shot me if I was still that kit and I said what I was really thinking at the time, filled with lots of *who the mange do you think you are* and *you're never getting away with it* and all. Now, I saw you, and you were hurting. That's all that mattered."

"What she said hurt because … it was true," he confessed, "and standing there watching those souls I had already written off as dead mourning their own dead with Vanalla singing over them – it shook me. It shook me in a way I've not recovered from, and I'm not sure I want to. I'm not sure I should."

"Was … that the only thing to shake you?" she asked, looking up into his eyes, her pupils dilated wide and her scent rich on the air.

"No, and in your arms, I found life like I never have before."

"Find it with me again, love. Find it with me, please," she breathed, reaching up and kissing him full on the lips, a long passionate kiss that hinted at how her previous time with him was guarded in comparison to how she was offering herself up to him now. It was a sacrifice that demanded he sacrifice of himself in the same way – more than an exchange of intimacy or biology, Shadow felt as if his very soul was being touched by her. There was the hesitation, the moment of resistance knowing that he would be forever compromised in this moment, forever held captive by the beautiful golden eyes pouring their light into his own, the feelings capturing his whole being in this moment.

"No, I don't want to be alone anymore," he nearly screamed in his mind, and he released every inhibition and pain and pretense, wrapping himself in her soul as much as he allowed himself to be wrapped and surrounded by her lovely and amorous body. She was a huntress worthy of him, and he a hunter worthy of her – and it was this realization that struck him into such a deep commitment that it made him cry silently as he held her against his body.

Tears of release from torment and pain and guilt streamed down his face from eyes that had never cried since childhood. He felt hot tears soak through his now naked shoulder fur, and he realized that she, also, had surrendered all. There was pain unique to her profoundly public life that in this private moment he could nearly sense from every strand of fur, every muscle and sinew of her body. She was trusting him as she had never trusted anyone before, and her longing to be loved in anonymity for who she truly was eclipsed any joy that had ever been gathered from being loved by millions.

After a few moments, their souls had opened to one another, blossomed as if dead flowers resurrected and blooming anew. Both struggled to hide their tears until they saw the tears of the other, and they both knew instinctively what it meant. Knowing that they could finally be what each other had longed for and thought was impossible made their love truly love and not just a sexual act. It wasn't Shadow or Jayanar or Fireclaw Destiny or even Tasha who was a part of that most perfect of intersections, alone, it was everything they felt themselves becoming, and everything they hoped they might be.

Intervals later, a rain storm keeping them wrapped in one another's arms, he woke against her body, its warmth and softness and pliancy making him instantly fall in love with her all over again; he nudged her softly with his muzzle. "Sorry," she breathed, coming to.

"No better than I," he admitted. "I never knew what love was until I met you. I never knew."

"Nor I," she agreed. "There is no one else for me, now. No one else whose Shadow I'd rather rest in, dearest cub."

"There is no destiny better than the one I hold," he offered, and she kissed him. "What now? I wanted to talk with you and find out if you felt as I feel, but what of those who need us?"

"Vanalla has everything in her paws, at present. She passed me a note during the meeting. She said that both of us had done what, for the present, needed to be done. She told me this was our time, Shadow. Our time."

"To serve someone who cares so completely for you; what is it like, Tasha?"

The mixed blood looked at the ceiling. "It holds me to a standard where I dare not fail because I don't want to disappoint her. It is strange to love the one you serve like family, like a parent or an older sister. I never doubt her; it doesn't mean I don't question her or that she ignores my advice, but I never doubt that she cares for me. I've lived long enough with her to know that can't be questioned. She's fully committed herself to me, just as she's committed herself to those here."

"Must be extraordinary," he mused, stroking her face.

"It is, cub, but I'll tell you a secret. If she thought you unworthy of that trust, she would have arranged it so we would never have had time together – before or now."

"What are you saying?" he asked, curious.

"That she had you at almost the moment she met you, and that she could tell you were a Thurian worthy of her time. Shadow, she's committing to you, too. Just like me, she knows you have a life that won't be easy to leave, but just like me … she's patient with whoever is worthy. She doesn't trust irrationally; she doesn't trust everyone. She knows. She just does. With you, she knows the same as she's known with me."

Shadow didn't know why this made everything he had gained with Tasha perfect, why it made him feel a hope he'd never felt before, but there was a life here amongst these Thurians that he could just taste, and he wanted it as he never wanted anything before, and she was before him, and she was that new life. The Vulpi unleashed all of his passion and love, once again, into the core of the mixed blood, wanting with every fiber of his being for his life in Attoria to become a reality.

Chapter 27: The Plan for Knowing

Shadow followed behind his boss into the secure meeting space in the de Dothnar matriarch's keep. Within, they found the director of military intelligence, the matriarch of de Dothnar and her key dames, the matriarch of de Kyvara with Callanar and Vosh, along with the matriarchs of houses de Bosnar, de Orturu, and de Gonari. Most notably, seated at the head of the table, was Kallain de Dothnar with his loyal assistant and mate, Melissiana, key dames and seconds of both. Kallain approached them and bowed. "Welcome to you, Director Geornan de Oterbythe and Jayanar Bonario. We sincerely appreciate your attendance at this meeting."

The elder Perratti took the offered paw and clasped it. "A pleasure to meet you, and my thanks for your solid assistance. We look forward to more cooperation in the sols to come."

"Very good. Good to see you, again. My apologies that our last meeting was so short, but hopefully this will make up for it."

"I look forward to it, and thank you," Shadow offered.

Kallain nodded. "If you'll join us at the table, we are ready to get started."

The group took their seats, and Shadow's eyes went to those of the de Kyvara matriarch. Her quick eye roll made him smile, slightly. She had predicted this meeting was going to be difficult as spies had little willingness to trust one another, but in this instance, in her own words, "They had little choice."

Kallain started the meeting, formally. "I want to thank everyone for your participation and your partnership. I know that sharing between organizations such as ours is not something we specialize at, but based upon what we captured being brought into Attoria, we're hoping that everyone can put aside organizational boundaries for the greater good."

"To that point," Shadow's director was the first to respond. "I would like to know a bit more about how radioactive isotopes were intercepted by Attoria when Attoria has very little sophisticated technology to speak of."

"Director," Matriarch Vanalla offered, smiling, "you are correct about our technology, especially that of our population, but we do have friends, and those friends have been of great assistance."

"As I'm sure you're aware," Matriarch Carinthia noted, as gently as possible, "Matriarch Vanalla has served as an ally, an inspiration, and as assistance to us on numerous occasions. The houses you see represented here are now allied, in large part, thanks to her efforts and example. To that end, we have provided technical and informational assistance along with skilled house guards to supplement that which is available to her house."

Carinthia nodded to Melissiana who was waiting for her cue. "Director, we have witnessed the numerous governmental raids occurring against Vanarran sites for some time now, and our desire to assist house de Kyvara was actually directed against someone who might have been Vanarran trying to slip something into their borders. As you are aware, the Attoria population is seen by devout Vanarrans as heretics and traitors. There was a credible threat, and hearing of the kinds of material found in the Vanarran raids gave us sufficient justification to install monitoring appropriate to that threat."

"Wait a moment," the director interrupted. "You are saying that you've installed nuclear monitoring equipment on the trails leading into the Attoria valley because of our raids?"

"Indeed," she told them. "That and providing a reserve guard force to react should an intrusion be detected. It wasn't the most thorough defense, but given the terrain, it was a reasonable and inexpensive one."

"And you just happened to have nuclear monitoring equipment available to you?" the Vice Marshal asked, his Pantera nose wrinkling up a bit in doubt.

"We do.   Are you familiar with the FireWall Security corporate pack?" Melissiana patiently asked, and the Marshal nodded. "That is catalog item ABX-2834, and as de Dothnar are key stakeholders, it was not beyond our abilities to petition them for six of those units to guard the three major approaches to the village." She saw a question in his expression and answered preemptively. "Two per avenue of access, Marshal. We judged redundancy to be desirable under these circumstances. We also employed chemical monitors, from the same pack, as well as some other heat tracking and security devices to cover potential non-mechanized means of entry to the valley."

"Interesting, but I suppose reasonable," Director Geornan noted, "given the circumstances."

"And barely in time," Kallain noted. "The devices registered the radioactive spike ten intervals after being placed. We were exceptionally fortunate and very nearly not."

"And so how did this intercept play out?" the Vice Mashal wanted to know.

Melissiana continued her narrative. "The intruders chose to park their vehicle far away from Attoria, and so there were three intervals of hiking required to get anywhere close to the village. Our forces located their vehicle, but we undertook to capture the remaining two guards, successfully. Scans of the vehicle and confiscation of certain planning documents made it clear they were headed towards a cave that is an outer part of the Attoria village."

"It's an artist's studio, now," Shadow noted. "I've seen it, myself. Pretty simple."

"Indeed," Melissiana noted. "I've visited it, also. Once their target was known, it was possible to make TransCom contact with the administration of Attoria, and a plan was quickly formed to hide the true entrance to the cave and suggest, through deception, that the actual entrance was about seventy or so tracks away. That was within the margin of error for the point finder devices we suspected they would be using."

Vanalla spoke up. "We mobilized really fast with a bunch we had in the mess hall and grabbed rakes, picks, shovels, and cloths – anything we could think of. Well, with only about two intervals to work, we did a pretty good job. We put little solar-powered guide lights into the forest for a ways, created a fake path, covered the real entrance, and about the time we were finishing up, de Dothnar's guard arrived. We housed them in the real cave and waited for the intruders to find the fake one. It worked. They must have beat on the non-entrance for ages trying to open it. They got so distracted and made so much noise that it was very easy to surprise them."

"We have all of them in our custody at the moment," Kallain stated evenly, ignoring the raised eyebrows save for adding, "which is our right given the restoration of house powers act. We considered this an attack against an allied house, and so we exercised our right."

"Which means they're still alive," the Vice Marshal stated firmly as an expectation which had better not be found to be incorrect.

"Of course," he stated, nearly dismissively. "However, I will tell you that they are not in the best of health. Recovery is ... possible, given appropriate care."

"Please," Carinthia warned the increasingly uncomfortable intelligence leads, "we caught these individuals delivering *nuclear material* into a site we were asked, in good faith, to protect. There are few exercises of our authority that could be more legitimate than this. They are alive, and that is all we are required to provide. We could turn them over to you, and they could die a half interval later, and we would have fulfilled our obligation. It may be a truth you are uncomfortable with, but it is a requirement of a Great House on Thuria to protect those who are your own and those on whom your promise rests."

"For all of this ... gentle treatment," Director Geornan asked, "has there been any positive intelligence gain – or was this just revenge and punishment?"

Melissiana stood and walked around the table, putting a small file in front of each attendee as she spoke. "The treatment of these individuals, as you describe it, was *only* oriented towards positive intelligence gain, and such is in these folders I am now providing you."

Dubiously, the two senior intelligence leads popped their folders open and started to read. "New Windston?" Shadow asked, curious.

"Indeed," Kallain replied, his expression open and communicative, a far change from his more defensive reaction to the two intelligence chiefs, and a quick flick of his leader's eyes above the page told Shadow that Geornan had noticed that, as well. "We were able to extract details from them that not only suggested New Windston, but based on acquired VidStar surveillance from certain locations, allowed us to confirm it. We even were able to retrace their vehicle's movements back to that area based on forensic study and comparison with that same imaging."

A quick eye flick in Shadow's direction was his boss's direction to continue the line of questioning, as their challenges of house intelligence authority had met a stony reception. "So, what you're saying, is that the nuclear material originated in New Windston?"

"I do not feel comfortable in calling that the origination point; only the point at which we have first evidence," Kallain stated quite candidly.

The director closed the file once again, ready to get some additional strikes in, if he could, against what he considered interlopers into his space, albeit not amateurs. "Edge surveillance then, routes out of town?"

Kallain's defenses were again up. "Checked, obvious precaution."

The director's eyes were now resigned as they glanced in Shadow's direction, and so he stepped in. "And so I take it that none were found – no entries or exits of that vehicle for quite some time before. But then why the concern with noting New Windston as the origination point?"

"The vehicle history is not a perfect match. There is a full course of travel before the vehicle ever reaches its first VidStar capture point. On page three, you'll see how close those are."

Shadow looked at the diagram and thought, furiously. The concentric circles and arcs and vectors showing the location of the surveillance equipment to first catch sight of the vehicle were no more than one tenth of a course from one another. Regardless, he reasoned, Kallain was not a fool – nor did he suffer them, it appeared. The additional course had to be taken as accurate. After all, they had the vehicle and could have pulled out its movement logs from the maintenance subsystems. While they didn't track location, they did track operational times and speeds. Flipping back and forth between images of the vehicle from different vantage points, he quickly did the math in his head.

"Dammit," he said aloud, stunned. "There's a hidden facility somewhere in this city." Realizing he had sworn, he apologized. "I am sorry for that."

"There is nothing to be sorry about," the matriarch for de Gonari stated firmly. "You have the singular advantage of being observant, intelligent, and focused on the goal of efforts."

Both senior intel chiefs squirmed at the implicit insult, which Shadow felt was somewhat deserved. It was clear that since family houses had regained their rights, they were going to be fiercely protective of them. Vanalla jumped in. "Look, Shadow's seen it, and we feel if you look at the information, you will, also. Please, accept our sharing of this information with you for what it is. We need your help. While we were able to sift the information to get to this level of detail, we lack the requisite experienced field operatives to pursue it. Even if we did, we would likely wander into jurisdictions we have no right to operate in. Although we ask your acceptance for the work we have done, we are more than willing to turn this part of the operation over to you. You, as we, have good reasons to run these individuals to ground."

The director leaned over the table and looked at her, and it was his first attempt at candor. It appeared that if the matriarchs were going to pick and choose amongst them, Shadow's director was going to do so, also.

"I accept that," he offered in an almost friendly tone. "I won't attempt to hide from you the very obvious fact – we are smarting badly over having been caught in this trap and the potential harm we might have done without cause. We do have the motivation to proceed. However, there are certain requirements for our cooperation. First, as you say, it is our field agents who will pursue this, and yours are not to accompany or pursue their own operations. The last thing I need is to have an operative on either side harmed by friendly fire."

The de Bosnar matriarch raised up as if to go after the director, but Van's stare in her direction and a raised paw, begging forbearance placed the matriarch, reluctantly, back in her chair. Vanalla spoke. "None of us want that. I think that is true for all of us. Also?" she prompted.

Shadow watched his director carefully and realized that the old Perratti was starting to like this new matriarch, and his directness was not a show of disrespect, but trust. "We need the intruders turned over and the contraband material. It's not a point we can negotiate on."

Van's sweep of eyes around the table landed on Kallain who nodded and then to his matriarch, who also nodded. "Agreed. We believe we have obtained everything from them we can, and although they have been injured – mostly in their capture, if you'll forgive that – you may be able to learn more from them." The de Gonari matriarch seemed to chafe at this, but Van looked in her direction and responded, "One of the great benefits we have in this case is an excellent chain of custody. The sooner these items and individuals make it into enforcement's paws, the better the case against them."

"If you can provide that, what would it be?" the Vice Marshal asked.

"All VidStar recordings in real time of the captured individuals in an unedited format," Kallain told him. "Only the time of their interrogation has been omitted. Otherwise, the continuous feed from their cells should be more than enough validation of who you will be taking possession of."

"Helpful," the Pantera replied in a grudging compliment, and Kallain nodded.

"Now," Vanalla broached gently, "to the subject of repayment for our services to you. We can all recognize the difficulties from a public relations viewpoint, here, at least the potential problems. The raids have blanketed Thuria with fear, as far as potential Vanarran refugees are concerned. Genocide is exactly what the perpetrators of these deceptions wanted, and even if we catch them, doing nothing may result in death through starvation or desperate measures for those who remain. We seek your assistance for a very public and open airlift of Vanarrans to the safe haven of Attoria, a haven you and those in government can promote and validate."

The Vice Marshal leaned over the table. "Don't mistake that we understand what you have saved us from, and it is something we can entertain *after* we have the issue of this contraband and its source resolved. I have no desire to extinguish the lives of all Aelkinda. I believe that what you are proposing would be an extended process, but it is something that we could support. We would support it once the source is found and taken care of."

"I would be grateful for that," Vanalla offered. "I also have another request, but it is just that, and you may refuse it. While we will not interfere with the remainder of this investigation, we do wish to participate, if only as observers, but as direct observers. It was our home that was almost burned for no reason. We cannot leave this fully in the paws of others. I don't believe we should – but I can't both promise not to interfere and demand something which you might not be able to accommodate. Hence, it is a request."

"It is one we think important," the de Dothnar matriarch added, and the other matriarchs nodded, as well.

Both the director and the Vice Marshal looked at each other; Shadow knew instinctively what they were thinking. The combination of houses de Kyvara, de Dothnar, de Orturu, de Gonari, and house de Bosnar created a formidable and powerful entity which now had bargaining and persuasive influence the likes of which hadn't been seen in several hundred seasons. Such a request, in the past, they would have politely turned aside, but the expectant eyes looking at them across the table could not be denied.

It was the director who spoke, softly. "We have to take certain practicalities into consideration. We don't want to create a communications link that can cause our agents to be traced as they make their way through dangerous circumstances."

"One of our constituent companies designed an in-ear TransCom which is not being released to the market," Melissiana noted, pulling out a small case and stepping forward, offering the case to Shadow. "Instead of using standard communications which require a live connection at all times, this one works a bit like a messaging service.   Through an ultra-low power wrist com which uses specifically ranged convergent energy fields, the signal is only strong enough to be detected ten courses away.   If you'll pardon me for saying so, an intruder to any location would likely be picked up on scent well before then."

"Messaging service, you say," Shadow noted as he took out the device, glancing at his director for permission.   At a nod, he slipped the device into his ear, finding it actually secure and comfortable.   Placing the wristband on, he observed, "Very comfortable in all respects. How does it work?"

"Touch here to listen to any messages that have been stored for you. It will quietly alert you to a new message, and then, you have to check."

"What if there's something important that has to get through?" the Vice Marshal asked Melissiana.

"In covert operations, interruptions can be fatal, as I'm sure you know. The wearer must choose to check for messages in order to receive them. What's more is that in certain situations, such as hidden installations, there are add-on repeater modules that will self-destruct after a set period of time which can use pipes, conduit, or even structural beams as an antenna. The repeater units are magnetic," she explained, offering Shadow one out of her pocket. "Not difficult to conceal and very difficult to locate by electromagnetic and radio frequency trace. Once a specific wavelength and frequency are used by any of these devices, it cannot be used again for a minimum of one sol."

Shadow touched the listen area of the band and heard Matriarch Vanalla's voice. "We hope that this will help you, and that, in turn, we can help you succeed."

He looked at her and nodded, "Your compliments are appreciated, Matriarch, very much. I wonder if the repeater units could also double as demolition charges."

Kallain tapped the bottom of his chin for a moment as he looked upwards, mulling it over. "I believe it would be possible to increase the reagents, perhaps selecting other ones, which would at least serve in an incendiary capacity."

"I'll take three," Shadow stated, pressing the record button. The matriarch, seeing what he did, took a medium sized TransCom offered to her by Vosh, and then she hit the play button. "I'll take three" played clearly in the room with only a little deterioration in voice quality.

"Voice compression is used to reduce the signal impact, but it is still clear enough to be understood. What you just heard would haven't been more than a tenth of a tick, at most. The transmission, as it is digital, is also encrypted."

"I'd like to get one monogrammed, if you don't mind," Shadow added, again touching the record button.

They all looked at the matriarch. "Not yet," she told them. Then, a red light appeared on the device, and she touched it. It played again, and she stated, "About one third of a tick, that time. It's very good at picking up whispers, as well."

"I should certainly hope so," Shadow offered at a barely audible level. After a moment, Vanalla pressed the switch, and Shadow's whisper was surprisingly loud.

"It doesn't hurt that we are literally listening from inside of his head. Transmission of the vibration through the bone helps, as well. However, please don't snack while recording – it's really very loud, and … kind of gross." That drew a chuckle out of several in the room at Vanalla's joke.

"Impressive," the director commented. "I'd like to do a little field testing with a few of those units, perhaps after leaving from here."

"Agreed," Kallain stated. "I would like to orchestrate a follow-up by secure LineCom no later than 21:30 this evening, if at all possible. We have the case of items ready for you, but the reagents will only dissolve the electronics. It would be tomorrow morning before we could provide repeaters that would be useful as incendiary devices.

"Given the advantage we currently have – in that the opponents, whoever they are, do not know where their colleagues are – we should consider a start tomorrow for this operation," the director noted.

"I'd concur." There were multiple head nods in agreement with Kallain's and the director's assessment.

"Then, I shall wish you a very good sol, and we will be in touch this evening by secure LineCom," the director stated, standing along with the Vice Marshal and Shadow. "Honored Ones," he stated, bowing, and at their collective nod, he left the room with the Pantera and Vulpi close behind.

With the cases provided by Kallain riding in a trailing vehicle, Shadow sat next to the Vice Marshal and across from his boss in the limo hover. When they were well away, the director finally spoke. "Well, isn't that something?"

"Yeah. Changing age of time we live in," the Vice Marshal sighed, nodding.

"Sirs?" Shadow asked, unsure and seeking clarification.

"Never has there been the gathering of power in the houses to the degree I just saw," he told them. "The houses never came together to demand action from the government for such an operation."

"Historically, Geornan, they didn't need us. Now, we also find ourselves needing them. They know the mistake we made, and there is that tacit, unspoken promise to keep it reasonably under wraps if we help them."

"It means more than that," the Perratti director charged. "It's an alert that the houses intend to combine and improve their intelligence assets, ongoing. These devices are a nice share, I suppose, but I want them checked out before any of our team uses them. A few intervals aren't a lot of time, but it's all we have."

"And the question is who gets sent into New Windston, Director," the Vice Marshal charged, his eyes flicking to Shadow.

"Yes, it's not hard to see how strongly they were hinting their preference in that area. I dislike being told which assets to choose for which mission, especially by outside amateurs – as professional-like as they may be, but still…" He looked out the window for a moment and then flicked his gaze to Shadow. "Any objections to the assignment?"

"No, sir. It seems … interesting."

"Interesting and dangerous if that matriarch buzzes in at a bad time."

Shadow looked at his director and suggested, "Of all the familial aristocracy in that room, Vanalla de Kyvara is the only one I'd listen to, but I *would* listen to her. She's very clever and dead straight about what she has an aim for, and in the end, it's pretty admirable. There's no chance she'll ever be covered in gold leading a family of refugees, but she does so all the same. Besides, her political acumen has to be commended."

"Better with us than against us, you think?" the director asked very incisively, and Shadow's slow nod spoke volumes. "Doesn't mean I won't be on my guard, but if they cover over our oversight and somehow parlay this into a win for us – against the terms we discussed earlier, I'll consider her on the friendly list. However, I won't substitute one overbearing and trivial set of patrons for another."

The Pantera shook his head. "She's setting the trail markers right now, and although de Dothnar's matriarch clearly has the most power in that room, you could feel it – Shadow is right. Vanalla has the gravitas; they listen and follow her, even to pulling out of Shanandrae and standing next to her to slow us down – good thing, but quite the show of influence."

The director sighed and nodded. "It's done then. Not saying that we can't or won't adjust our positions later, but for right now, we're playing on the same team."

Shenaria slipped into the administration building and made her way to her daughter's office in the back, surprised to find her seated with multiple Allarraen visual display viewers hovering in mid-air, and what's more, she was not in her Faelnar form, but it was her – the true Vanarra. "Hey Mom," came the cheerful voice. "Just finishing up. We got back about a half interval ago."

"I'm a little surprised to see you working like this," Shenaria offered, concerned. "It would take a little explaining to-" Van flicked one of the screens into the air, and it grew large and faced the gold-on-gold Faelnar. It showed a proximity map of the administration building and the space around with no one else anywhere near except for Shenaria and Vanarra. "Well, that would cover it, I guess. It's just such a shock to see you like this. I ... I know you are there, love," she said approaching as the screen slipped back into position in front of Van. "But I've really gotten this weird mixed up idea about you now. This *you* is my daughter, and I love you. The Faelnar you is my friend and benefactor and matriarch, and I love you."

Van smiled as all of the viewers collapsed back into one on her small laptop, disappearing from the air. "Either way, I'm really the winner, right?" she asked.

Shenaria sighed, shaking her head, and walking to embrace her daughter, pulling Van's head against her own chest in a loving and motherly hug. "I love you, either way. I know. There are all of these sides to you, now. You, Vanalla, Vanassa, Sahnassa, Tana, and even more – so Kylie and Amyra tell me. Is it true that you were known, at one time, as she who walks in light?"

"It's true," Van said, making no effort to remove herself from her mother's embrace and reaching around her, even, pulling her closer. "Sahnassa's one was better, though – she who walks in fire."

"So, you'll become she who walks in fire and walks in light?"

"I guess, but I don't know for sure," Van said as she released and looked up at her mother. "I'm ... sorry that I'm not just your daughter any longer."

"You will always be that, trust me. I have it on good authority," Shenaria told her, smiling softly. "I was just going to ask you how things went?"

"Well, from their perspective, we're all playing on the same team – at least for now, and now is really what we need. The other sols are just the other sols, and we'll worry about them when they come up. It looks like they've chosen Shadow to do the infiltration, and that's a good thing. I think a lot of him."

"You're not the only one," Shenaria agreed, taking her daughter's paw and helping her stand. "Tasha seems to think on him a lot, quite a lot!"

"I don't doubt. She's been really lonely, and now, she has a little fire back in her life. I have a good read on him, though. He's a good soul, and I think that he'll join us. I think it's just a matter of time."

"Tasha said that she thought that he was becoming attached to you, as well. What does that mean?"

Van shook a little and changed back into her Faelnar form. "Well, it's not like a hunt, but individuals like Jayanar seek to follow deeply committed and trustworthy leaders – basically someone who is a good pack leader. He's not done poorly in this respect; his present leader, Geornan, is not bad, but I'm kind of showing off a bit. It doesn't hurt that many around here give me a good report."

"But ... if I understood Saletta correctly, one of the things you're doing here in this time is trying to correct the impacts of your life before, when you were matriarch before. Isn't there a concern that – I mean we talked about this, I know, but-"

"But you're worried, Mom, about your kit, right?"

"I am," Shenaria offered, shrugging. "Can't help it, and maybe this is because Saletta's expressed the concern."

"Not surprising," Van noted, but not unkindly. "See, I actually don't want to remove the effects of my life or Sahni's from this time – not completely. I just want to make sure that those individuals who used us as an excuse to undermine the houses and the Creator's Path are checked. In large part, we've done that. The problem is that we now have consequences from eliminating the Vanarran and Sahnassite cults, namely and especially everyone here. This is part of those consequences, but let me tell you a secret." Van's offering came in time with standing and taking her mother's paw in her own and slowly walking towards the door. "This time, we're taking steps with the foundation of Attoria to make sure that they will not revere me as a deity. Last time, I was just being the best matriarch I could be. Now, I know I have to be more than that. I have to be a matriarch who is only remembered as that, and nothing more. The miracle at the Healer's Grave, the freeing of the Vulpi, the rescue, and all of those other things were allowed to grow legendary."

"To these Aelkinda, here, you are terribly important – maybe too important," her mother challenged softly. "At least that's what Saletta is worried about."

"You like her, don't you?" Van asked.

"A lot. She's becoming a close friend. Trax is very happy to have her here as well, and the kids take to her like she's family."

"She is that, to me. She is right to be worried, and so am I. However, all of us can take comfort in the fact that the Aelkinda have learned the lesson of worshiping Vanarra de Gonari, and how wrong that was. Talk to Callanar or Vassia if you want to get a read on this – ask them that question, and you might appreciate their answers. Saletta might, as well." As they reached the door, Shenaria looked at her daughter and blinked, never fully used to the smoothness with which she transformed into the Faelnar who had first welcomed her in this new time. "Ash still coming to dinner tonight, or is he working late with Trax and Laxar again on the next series of cabins?"

"What do you think?" Van chuckled. "He would sooner die of exhaustion rather than rest while someone's lair needed finishing. He's not alone, though. Callanar and the others are very dedicated, as well. Oh, and you should know I got a call earlier. Lallie and Dexer were wondering if they could come visit, maybe help a little, too."

Vanalla chuckled. "It was Racea and Ariasta last moon. It was really good to see them. Think there's any reason those two are coming?"

"If I had to guess, I think they are looking for advice from you or from me, just maybe. I think they are thinking about finally joining. Also, I think they miss you. I think you've been a special piece of magic in their lives."

"Hover approaching," Van warned her mother, "and it's someone we know. Shadow. Stay here with me?"

"Of course," Shenaria offered her daughter. "I love you, Vannie."

"I love you, too, Mom," Van replied as she watched the fast sports hover swoop in and settle just in front of them. When he stepped out, Vanalla nodded a bow to him and offered, "Welcome, Jayanar. What brings you to see us?"

He bowed low in front of her and replied, "Honored One. May we step inside?"

"Please, could you walk with us to my cabin?"

"Certainly." She could tell he wasn't thrilled by this as far as his mission was concerned, but his curiosity was piqued.

"Shall I tag along, Honored One?" Shenaria asked.

"I think so. I don't think our mates will be showing up anytime soon," Van sighed as they started to walk. "I take it that your department has made a decision?"

"They have, Honored One," Shadow replied quietly. "The infiltration is tomorrow, early morning, and because we appear to have developed a good working relationship, they are tapping me for the assignment."

"You'll have to be exceptionally careful. Even Shadows can be spotted."

"That's just it, Honored One. You seem to have a knack for quite a number of things, and I get the sense that you know more than you are letting on. You wouldn't have pulled all of the matriarchs together on a hunch, and you wouldn't have so masterfully directed that meeting, either, without some foundation for it. Actually, both of my seniors sitting at the table felt as if they'd been put on a lead and led around the yard."

"I truly didn't mean to offend them," Van told him, sounding a bit regretful. "I just wanted their help. They and you are the legitimate way to bring criminals to the attention of enforcement."

"It wasn't offense so much as I believe they were stunned by the cadre of houses you could assemble on command and how quickly they responded to you, Honored One. It was ... impressive."

"A little oppressive for them, I get that," Vanalla sighed. "I didn't want to flout house power in front of them just for the sake of it or a cheap thrill, but this is important, and time is short. In time, they'll find that I don't have much ambition to leverage their services and abilities, but as someone was trying to trick you into annihilating us..."

"I see your point, Honored One," Shadow replied. "This ... is yours?"

"Yes," she replied, smiling at him as he just stared dumbfounded at the exceptionally modest sized cabin.

"But Dame Shenaria's residence..."

"As we stated before, cub," Van warned him, "everyone in Attoria shares, and as yet, Ash and I don't have children. Probably a few seasons down the trail for us. I owe the others my full attention now, and tomorrow, you'll have mine. I have some idea of what you'll be getting into, and there will be a few experts close to me who can help. Vosh, for one, but I have a few others on-call who can help you." As they entered the cabin, Shadow closed the door behind them. "I apologize. It's not as clean as I would like."

"Leader of the entire village, matriarch, and executive director – for all intents and purposes – in an alliance between multi-billion holding corporate packs."

"It's all I need, and I'm content. What about you, for tomorrow? Do you have everything you need?" she asked as she sat down, her Dame sitting alongside her, close. Dame Shenaria was the adopted sister of the matriarch, so it made sense. "What about the equipment we provided? You seemed to take to it well enough."

Shadow looked at the ground in consternation. "They ... have yet to approve it, and the way this kind of analysis goes, I doubt I'll have it by tomorrow, Honored One."

"You're just damned lucky I have a few good friends," she told him, reaching over the side of her couch and pulling out a box and giving it to him. "In ear piece along with three separate charges, should last the whole mission. There are three repeaters set up to do exactly as you asked, go up in flames when you trigger them – hot enough to ignite magnesium so don't get singed. What bothers me about this are the infectious diseases. Now, I'm hoping our Sahnassites splurged a little and have a way of killing off all the bad stuff, but that's going to have to temper your plans."

"What do you suggest, Honored One?"

"I hope they would have a furnace where the bad stuff could be incinerated under some really serious heat, like the temperature of burning magnesium, for example, but if not, you'll have to be doubly sure. Burning amongst a bunch of paper board boxes and so forth wouldn't do it. You've got the possibility of nuclear material, as well. Gotta be careful about that, cub."

"I will be. However, destruction of this facility would be a significant blow to them, Honored One. That's the key line of reasoning."

"I can see the strength of that, but you are one cub. What kind of facility are you suspecting might be there?" Vanalla asked.

"We are thinking in the under levels of a warehouse, office complex – small one, as that is all that New Windston has."

"Exactly, but think of what's come out of there. The truth is, doing the math on this has driven Vosh nearly crazy and then me, because of her. We got the numbers from Kallain on what he intercepted, and it wasn't good. It also wouldn't be hidden in a basement or warehouse unless the building were lined with lead, and that might have just attracted attention. The truth is, that Ash goes to New Windston every now and again, and minus the private lairs, he's been in every retail establishment, in every floor of most of them. Everyone is friendly, and he's never been denied entry anywhere. He's been to most, if not all of the stockyards and supply stations in the town. So have lots of Thurians, when Kallain reviewed the surveillance images."

"But that doesn't tally with the small area, in the city, where the material emerged from, does it?"

"There are private lairs in those areas and small hover garages."

Shadow shook his head. "A hover garage wouldn't house all of the material we suspect has come out of there."

"I know," Vanalla offered, pulling out a data pad from a wooden side table and presenting it to him. "That's what drove Vosh crazy. That's what drove her to drive me crazy enough to ask my peers to cough up every geological survey of this place in their archives. Look at image one."

"A map," he observed, zooming the document in for detail, "showing New Windston, the ruins of the original city, and … highlighted here, the Windston historical museum site?"

"A private lair is there, now – a rather decent sized one, yes. The city of New Windston is built in and around where the museum once stood. Now, flip to image two."

He did so, and his eyebrow fur raised. "Mines?"

"From over three thousand seasons worth of mining. Back in the fossil fuel ages, much of this area was probed for precious metals and fossilized fuel. No fuel was ever found, but there were enough veins of precious metals and pockets of jewels to justify substantial sub-strata exploration. Now, the next three images show different mine systems from different times, and the last image overlays everything."

Shadow just looked up at her in shock. "It's a guess, but it fits the facts, cub," Vanalla stated softly. "Also, a little quiet recon by Vosh of some of the areas over those supposedly inactive tunnels have found two *active* ventilation ducts – fans of some kind driving them, and they are monitored. She had to dash away super quick because someone tried to find out who she was. Now, hunters are in there from time to time, and Ash recalled that many of them complained because they felt the land owners – some *foreign* company – ran them off for trespassing even though the land isn't marked."

"Why wouldn't it be marked?"

"A big sign saying *don't come in here* usually has the opposite result. They rely on word of mouth."

"But where is the final lair where all of that material is stored?" Shadow asked.

"Last image, please. That's the recovered geological survey that was a part of Dame Dania de Dothnar's final report on the Meeting Den. It's not a solid piece of igneous rock like everyone has thought. Igneous just means volcanic, and volcanoes, even ancient ones, do more things than form rocks."

Shadow shook his head. "Natural caverns deep within the mesa where once rested the famous Meeting Den?"

"Yeah, had me shaking my head for a few intervals, too. But if you can't find anything through normal searching…"

"Extraordinary searching will have to do," he said, flipping back through the images once again. "It's at least plausible. I have the tools with me to look for intrusion countermeasures, but if I find them around something small, I'd probably ignore it – unless I happen to realize I'm not looking for a huge storage facility but maybe only a door."

"Keeping an eye open for all possibilities, right?" she asked, and he nodded. "Tasha wanted to see you, but I've got you set up with Ash tonight. I'll be spending the night with her, and Ash will be waking you up and taking you into town."

"I'd prefer to take my own hover."

"Leaving it with us means we can preposition it based on input from you. Ash's old beat up delivery hover won't attract attention as he has business in New Windston that morning, anyway. He has a reason to be there – that beautiful, slick ride of yours doesn't so much, and it will stand out amongst all of the farmers' and laborers' vehicles like the sorest of paw fingers. Don't worry. I can guess what they equipped you with. I will make sure that no one will be pressing any buttons they shouldn't – besides, it will likely be Vosh who drops the vehicle or picks you up in it."

"Is she a competent driver?" Van nodded, assured. "*How* competent, exactly?"

"She knows vehicles like no one I've ever seen. She has a feel for them like they are a living part of her soul. She knows exactly how much to push a hover and when to push. Bringing that hover in will give her a bit of practice with it. She won't need much; that I promise you."

Shadow sat back and sighed. "You are, of course, correct. I had hoped on hiding it somewhere, but this will at least solve that problem."

"Once you're into … wherever you're going, Vosh will be running interference on the entry point, if needed for pick-up, but something else she can do is enhance your communication. She'll have a number of small auto-drones with her. Each of them can place a relay where we believe it will do the most good. In point of fact, since your beauties are so special, I'd suggest you consider saving them for when you are definitely in an interesting spot."

"That implies you'll be able to track me," Shadow almost grumbled. "If you can, someone else can."

"Like the rest of the tech we showed you, you own when and how that part works. Also, the tracking signal jumps frequencies in a very difficult pattern, as well. If they don't know your frequency, they can't triangulate you. Vosh also had an idea. One of those drones can transmit a very loud visual and audio signal – camera images in real time. We'll give them something to look at that's not you. That thing will be screaming like a tree screecher. If anyone has any security, it will be watching that."

"This is a heck of a support team. Can't say I've ever had one like it, before," Shadow told her.

"Cub," Van told him softly, looking at the floor. "We don't want you to fail. Someone tried to end us, and that's a problem, obviously, but we want you back alive. You were just going to go it alone, weren't you – no help, no support, just you?"

"It's frequently how things go," he confessed.

"It's up to you. I've told you what we're doing, but you can choose to ignore it and not use any of our help. I won't force our help on you, but I will, at least, offer it. Okay?"

"It's a good offer. I'll see how things go."

"We'll stand by. Ash will be by to pick you up at about four intervals before high night if you want to visit Tasha. You have that time, at least. You don't have to trust us, Jayanar. Just come back."

He nodded. "You are the most undemanding matriarch I've ever met. You must have quite a job to keep the others in step."

"They know how to wield power without my help. It's caring about how they do it that they've needed some practice in. Go on, now."

"Thank you, Honored One," he said, standing. Looking down at her, he added, "And … I mean that."

"Thank you, and good hunting."

As he walked from the matriarch's cabin, he said quietly to himself, "I certainly hope so."

"Ready?" Ash asked softly as Shadow slipped into the seat beside him, the cold chill of what was still night on the air.

The warmth of the old hover felt comforting as a somewhat keyed up Vulpi slipped in beside him. "Never better."

"Good. Now, we're going to work our way around and come from a slightly different direction. We won't make it totally obvious that we're coming from Attoria," Ash said as he started moving them forward. "Vosh checked out the trails, so we'll have an easy go – no construction or accidents to hold us up, make us late; if that's okay?"

"Sounds like you've planned it out," Shadow offered, his expression fixed and stoic.

"Yeah, the easy part," Ash replied. "I wish you didn't have to go alone, but…"

"It's best. You and everyone else here has offered enormous help, but this is my job. I'm well practiced at it."

Ash nodded as the village disappeared behind them. "Believe me, I understand that. I am qualified at carpentry and cooling systems, maybe a little hunting. It's a discipline you've studied many seasons to perfect, I'd wager."

"No desire to play secret agent?" Shadow taunted, gently.

"Never one of my strong suits. I've had to do some really crazy things for work, repairing the systems on top of those huge buildings in the center of Shanandrae. Got caught in a lightning storm once and jumped off the roof to a balcony – that's about as out there as I've gotten or ever hope to get."

"You can manage a firearm, though," the Vulpi prompted. "If it came to defending someone, like your mate, would you?"

"With my life, but if you mean taking someone else's life, only if I had to. Only if I was left with no other choice."

The Vulpi closed his eyes and nodded, "That's pretty much the job description for what I do. No one wants to leave orphans and widows in their wake, but if they intend that you should die, the choices are not always what we would hope."

"If someone's shooting at you…"

"You shoot back. For you, always shoot back. For me," Shadow told him, pulling his military projectile grade weapon from its holster on the side of his body and checking it, quickly, before replacing it, "I have to make a call."

"I understand, a little. Alright, I won't bother you if you want to rest. If something comes up, I'll wake you," Ash offered.

"Just one thing. What's it like being the mate of a matriarch?"

"Something else, my friend," Ash breathed. "I loved her before, but to see how the others now love her too, it's…"

"Troubling?" Shadow questioned.

"No. Validating. I knew she was great before, even when she was just a hospital volunteer. She was smart then; she's smart now. She was kind then; she's kind now. I'm honored to know her, and that was before anyone started calling her Honored One. Don't mistake; we still nip at each other from time to time, but she's convinced me about this place – Attoria – and these Thurians. Mixed bloods like me didn't have it easy a long time ago, but only de Caterra wanted to actually exterminate us. Now, there are those who want to repeat what they tried to do, only now, they are a lot closer to succeeding. There's like less than ten thousand Aelkinda. I looked up in my history book – even with de Caterra at full strength, there were still two hundred thousand mixed bloods, worldwide, at the least."

"It is a cause you two share, it seems."

"Yes. That, and we truly trust one another. I love her, and she loves me. I never have to be alone. Look, she told me what you were planning. She's also told me that you can reach out to her during the mission. Talk to her. It's okay. Lean on her, if you need to. She's good for that. Besides, I'm sure Tasha won't be far away from the receiver set the entire time."

"What's your take on her – Tasha? Former primal star? Speaker for fundraising and relations for Attoria?"

Ash smiled. "She's been one of Van's projects. Kit has come a long, long way. I don't know if you're ready for something longer term, but I think she is. She'll wait, I think, if you need her to, but understand that she doesn't look at you in any way as being disposable."

"I certainly hope not to be, but yes. She's made me consider things that I have never considered before, doubted I ever would. Would there be much work for a secret agent in Attoria?"

"Vosh stays busy keeping an eye on things; I'm sure she'd like help, but … what you find out is that those qualities which make you good at something can make you good or amazing at other things, too. Forgive me for saying this, but being around you is a little intimidating."

"Because I'm a killer?" Shadow asked, a little distantly.

"Because you've held some really difficult decisions in your paws and made the call. I received a lot of questions from the others, the Aelkinda, who wanted to know if you would join us. I think they were starting to look up to you, a bit. You're a very practical leader and a protector. Anyone who is afraid can feel that. Callanar makes a good constable, but sometime, in the future, we may need someone tougher than a constable. If the gates open after this mission and lots of Vanarrans start coming our way, they won't come to us as Aelkinda. They'll come to us as Vanarrans, like I said. Firm paw might be a good thing."

"You're afraid of the Vanarrans?"

"Only an idiot wouldn't be," Ash confessed. "Damned scary stuff some of them did. Those here have renounced it and proven faithful to that word. Everyone new, however…"

"Is a commitment unmade," the Vulpi completed. "I see. There are no easy answers here, are there?"

"With Thurians, never, and here … yeah, maybe even less. We will always need help making the hope of Attoria a reality."

Shadow was quiet for a moment, and it was difficult to slide away from the fact that he found Ash's suggestion very palatable, especially since it would allow him to obtain a dream long thought outside of his possible orbit, namely that of a lair, a mate, and one sol, a family. "Something to consider, Ash. Thank you."

"Fair enough. Now, I'll watch things and drive. Rest, please. I want to make sure that you are good to go when I drop you off."

"Thank you, again, my friend." Shadow leaned his seat back and closed his eyes, everything about the mission momentarily put on hold as he knew this part, resting and being ready, was as much a part of his job as anything he would ever be asked to do. As he drifted off to sleep, part of him half dreamed that he was in Attoria, already, working to keep the peace. It left him with a contented feeling that was as much a lure into the abyss of sleep as anything ever could be.

"Shadow," a male voice whispered to him, a light paw resting on his shoulder. "A block away it gets dark. Can't see you get out."

The Vulpi was awake, and his eyes surveyed the area in front of him carefully. "Approaching the point of observation?"

"Once I'm beyond the light, yeah. I'll go and camp in their overnight restaurant, and then get back in to catch a little rest. It will tally up. You ready? You have everything you need?"

"I do, Ash. Thank you. Keep safe."

"Yeah, you, too," the mixed blood offered, pulling the hover to a stop. Having already checked the door on his side to make sure that no warning alarm would sound, he slipped it up and nearly sprang out onto the trail, slipping away into the hedges quickly and beyond, into the forest. The delivery hover slipped forward as if nothing had happened, drove forward through the next three lights, and then came to a stop in front of the flashing lights of a diner. In a moment, an appropriately trail-weary mixed blood stumbled out of the hover and made his way inside, taking a seat at a window and appearing to order his breakfast.

A very soft chirp in his ear alerted him to a new message. Pressing play on his wrist-control, he heard the recording. "I take it my cub dropped you off alright?"

Pressing record, he whispered back, "He did. Looks like he's enjoying a nice breakfast. Wish I was him. Starting to scout the area. I'll let you know." Moving under the cover of darkness and the screen of the hedges, the Vulpi made his way along into the heart of the area where the vehicle that had smuggled out the radioactive isotopes departed from. A difficult issue was gauging what kind of place could have contained a hover of the size that had been used. Even if the items were only staged here, and the matriarch's hunch was wrong, the vehicle would probably not have been left in the open. Looking at his PawLink, he scanned for traces of radioactivity. What had been smuggled out was toxic, and there was the possibility that if inadequately shielded, he might pick up a trace.

After an interval of moving around the area and getting its measure, he slipped back into the woods a bit and pulled back up the matriarch's charts. Morning, while showing no visible signs of eroding his cover, was only a half interval away, and a protracted stake-out wasn't what he was hoping for. With the low-light setting on his PawLink, he looked the documents over carefully, as he had intervals before.

Mentally, he remarked to himself about how seeing something on a chart did poor justice to visualizing the same. Most of his skill and trade dealt in StarSat images or covert VidStar recordings made by vehicles capturing every aspect of an area as they drove through. This kind of antique knowledge wasn't in vogue with him or his peers, but as he held the charts, now, he had to concede that they offered more insight than everything his own organization had collected and collated about the mission. Scanning north of the trail, he saw that one of the old tunnels jutted out towards a lair, behind it. StarSat showed this has a simple domestic lair with a modest hover garage behind it.

"Still," he thought. "Worth a look." Quietly creeping through the woods, he pressed a control which activated his augmented eyewear. Immediately, he froze. The magnetometer reading was going higher than it should have. Looking to his left, he saw a TransCom-enabled wildlife camera with night vision. He wasn't in its field of view, but it was pointed back towards the lair that was his target. Carefully, he worked his way behind the property, and every fifty tracks in an arc pattern, he found the same sensor array. Every one of them was pointed towards the lair.

"Mange, what a passive array," he thought. Taking a few tracks back from this perimeter, he climbed a tree which put him reasonably high above the canopy and with an unobstructed view to the back of the lair. He had disabled his scopes for the climb, but now that he was in a good position, he looked down on the garage and the somewhat generous grassy area behind it. Flipping from setting to setting, he almost went blind as the amount of trans-sight illumination, something only security sensors would use, radiated out from the garage like a small sun.

It wasn't long before he was back on the ground. As he held onto a tree, thinking, a strange rumbling vibration came to his ear as if something heavy was passing by – only there wasn't anything around him. He shook his head. He knew it was mechanical. He knew it faded in and out as if something coming towards and then away from him. It was something, he realized, that he felt mostly through the tree and his paw pads resting on its surface.

Mentally, he clicked through his list. There was a lair with a fairly well-hidden garage behind it. Tree cover made it difficult if not impossible to see the garage without climbing a tree or risking detection by the wildlife camera array. There was a vibration that came and went – smoothly, mechanically. "Damn her," Shadow spat. "She's very likely got it dead on accurate, but there's no way I'd breach that property without some kind of back-up." Slipping back well behind the detection radius, he made his way back to the hedges, morning's light starting to streak the sky.

Touching record, he stated, "Searched the area, found the farmer's lair to be exceptionally well monitored. Can't approach without being spotted. Your suspicion about a tunnel is probably correct. I felt something pass under my paws while I was behind the lair in the woods."

He sent it and just waited while he tried to figure out what to do. After a moment, there was the soft chirp that told him a response had been stored. He keyed play, and it was the matriarch's voice. "Well, it was a good guess. You know, that tunnel wasn't the only way in there. If you work to the east, one of those other tunnel ends might have a well or entrance or ventilation. Just an idea."

"Worth a try," he thought, and then he was grateful for the light offering up just a bit more detail of his surroundings. Almost before he understood why, he was approaching an object which had snagged his attention. He thought it a stump, at first, but it appeared a bit too uniform and oversized for the trees in this area. The closer he got, the more he became convinced what he was seeing was made by Thurian paws. Slipping the cover off, he looked down a long, dark hole which went down about ninety tracks. There was some water pooled at the bottom, but as he took out distance viewers and paired them with his high intensity UltraBright, he saw some kind of wires running through the middle third of his view. In his pack, he carried enough rope for one hundred twenty tracks.

Before committing to such a rash endeavor as going down into a long, dark hole which he might have to climb out of, he wanted some other proof this was a part of the tunnel system. Touching record, he gave his position in grid coordinate, bespoke what he'd found, and what he thought the depth was, asking for confirmation.

Vosh's voice came back to him as he prepared the rope. "Elevation of the mine in that area suggest eighty to ninety tracks below ground level is accurate. Your position correlates to what we see, as well. This appears to be an entrance."

"I'm taking it. Don't know if I can reach you once I'm inside."

Just as he had finished anchoring the rope, the response came back to him. "Take the red repeater and put it at the bottom of the hole. It's got a good chance of keeping you in touch with us for a bit longer."

He was grateful for the message as he mounted the top of the pipe-like hole going underground. "Nice having the help," he thought to himself as he started to lower himself carefully, slowly, below the surface.

Chapter 28: Shadows in the Dark

There wasn't any reward quite as sweet as realizing that the investment of hard physical labor – what it had taken him to lower himself into the hole – had paid off. About ten tracks off of the bottom, a tunnel stretched in two opposite directions. Reaching a hind paw down, however, he got his first piece of bad news. There wasn't a ground below the water that he could feel. Taking out his UltraBright, he tried to see into the water, but it looked like another long, dark hole beneath him. Shining into the tunnel brought a better result, however. The ground was still covered in about a track of water, but there was a ground beneath it.

"It will have to be easy and slow tracking," he thought. Swinging back and forth allowed him to noisily splash onto the floor of the tunnel going north. Getting his bearings, he prepared to move out, but then remembered the repeater. Taking it out, he clipped it onto a section of wire supports right next to him. When it burned, it would just go into the water leaving his rope intact.

"I'm now in the tunnel, and it looks like the maps are accurate. It will take me some time to walk through this. The tunnel is partially flooded."

About fifty tracks down the tunnel, the faithful chirp in his ear meant he'd gotten a response. It was Vanalla, this time. "We found another map, one of the ones that wasn't clear enough to include with your original set. It looks like you are in one of the lowest parts of this area of the mine. Hopefully, as you progress, the water line will drop."

He nodded to himself and answered, "Hope so. Let you know in a bit."

Progress, although louder than he would have preferred, was at least steady, and another hundred tracks found the matriarch's words coming true. He had entered a main back-bone of this mine through a side tunnel that had dropped off the main level, and he could see a relatively flat surface ahead of him. "Looks good. I'm heading back to where I thought I heard the vibration."

Continuing forward after making a left from his original tunnel, he was grateful and wary of the sounds of air blowing through the mine. There was, at least some chance, that the sounds had dampened the cacophony of his arrival, but it also enclosed him in a very tight envelope of awareness. Still, he pressed forward, keeping his light on its lowest setting, pointed at the floor.

After nearly five hundred tracks, by his reckoning, and increasingly visible signs of ancient occupation, he arrived at what appeared to be a cave in. Looking at it, though, puzzled him. With the amount of debris on the ground, there should have been a large, gaping hole above him where everything had fallen away, and yet the ceiling, what he could see of it, looked as stable and well packed and supported as everything he had already seen – even more so as he had made more progress. A bare rock in the pile was exposed to him, and so, curious, he leaned his head up against it, resting the length of his ear along its surface.

He heard a humming sound that was so potent he nearly flinched. It only took him a moment to realize what it was – a cyclic hum of electrical power. It was close, on the other side of this supposed cave in. A glance at the magnetometer and electromagnetic spectrum in his portable viewers confirmed it. There was something on the other side – potentially an industrial grade light fixture on a wall, perhaps something else – that was buzzing away, supplied by power. This grew his excitement for a moment, and for the next half interval, he tried to move parallel to it and find any method of entry. Every single access way on his map had been blocked by faux-cave-ins.

"Damn, who knows how thick these things are," he wondered, looking at his diagram. The main tunnel, the backbone of the mine, so to speak, was more than fifty tracks away. There could be that much or more in terms of debris, but he doubted it. Still, it wasn't the kind of risk to take so early in the mission. Slipping back about fifty tracks from the tunnel, he keyed record. "This is starting to look like you might be right. The central path in the mine is electrified. Someone is using it, but they've blocked every entrance. I can't gain entry without giving them intervals of sounds of me digging. Probably not the best idea."

After a few moments, he wondered if the transmitter could actually reach out of here, but a little chirp in his ear nearly made him smile. "Cub, you backtrack to that entrance tunnel of yours, go three more down on the left, and there's a wider tunnel leading north. Vosh thinks there's a natural cave you might use that could bridge the two mine systems. That would at least get you closer."

"Sounds good," he answered back. "Signal is clear, surprisingly so."

When he was just about at the tunnel entrance she had indicated, there was another chirp. "Well, we might have flown in a couple of little drones and landed repeaters above your head. As you make progress, we'll reposition them. It's not perfect, however. Messages are taking longer between us due to error correction and loss of signal. Keep sending, though. We'll keep helping."

"That was a long one," he remarked, mentally, but he knew that every part of it was essential. "Damned comforting to hear that voice." In a few passes, he was reaching the end of the northern tunnel she had specified. Smiling as he shone his light at the end of the tunnel, he saw a metal grate covering another hole. Looking down, he could see why the miners stopped here. Although there was a rough and rocky face that might work as a way down for an individual, groups of individuals or worse, equipment, would have stood little chance. "They probably just burrowed around."

The grate wasn't difficult to dislodge, and in moments, he was slipping down the rock face wall using his climbing instructors' standard litany of "three-points of contact" to lower himself the ninety or so tracks to the surface of the cave. Once he was sure he had a good stance, he shone the UltraBright all around. The ground was very uneven and rocky, slick and slimily smooth in places and seemingly unweathered in others. His prior experience with caves was something during training many seasons ago, but scanning around the ceiling, he found seams where water leached in, pulling down long and thin stalactites made of a translucent white material, and whatever had dripped down them through the centuries had made the shining slick paths through the otherwise rocky maze.

He shook his head and pressed record. "I'm in a beautiful cavern, large. Looks like it runs mostly parallel to the main branch. I'm going to try to find a way across."

Several passes later, he was about half way across the cavern when he heard the chirp in his ear. Pressing play, he heard Vanalla. "Wish you could take pictures, but if your PawLink was found, it might tip them off as to how you got in. We still have you at about the same depth and moving in the right direction. Keep moving forward."

The traverse was long. When he was about three quarters to the end, he asked, "Ash make it back to you okay?"

Not too long after, he was approaching another drop which appeared to have been caused by a cave in. "Cub is fine. Think he likes you. How's it going?"

"The end of this thing is a drop, maybe twenty or thirty tracks. Might be another tunnel down there moving away. Compass says I'm still going north. I'm going to slip down and have a look."

He did that, although his descent wasn't anywhere near as graceful as his first had been, and he ended up picking himself off a pile of loose debris, partly of his own making, and dusting himself off. Moving forward, however, he found a small and somewhat natural tunnel where someone had attempted to shift the debris to the side, but it was only a rudimentary attempt.

There wasn't a reply, and he wondered if he had finally gone too deep. After only a pawful of additional steps, he realized he was coming up to some kind of metal grating. It had been clearly fixed into the wall very firmly, attempting to keep someone from entering the cave he was in or the mine. "I'm up against a metal grate blocking the way, just like there was at the other end. This one is dug in. Last one just lifted away."

He studied it for only a moment, it seemed, until a chirp gathered his attention. "Hey, cub. You are considerably closer to where they might be at this point. Take a good look, first, and be careful of any noise."

"It wasn't as if I was just going to blow it up," he complained softly – without transmitting that. However, Matriarch Vanalla had a point, and he knew it. He had been shining his light around, but now he studied the bars even closer. He didn't see anything, but the uneasy feeling he had was underscored by the matriarch's warning. Leaning back, he accidently shone his light beyond and glanced something that made him angle his light back. "Wires," he sighed. Reaching into his pack, he pulled out a telescoping tool that was insulated and extended its reach beyond the bars. Slipping the thick wires out of the dust and dirt that had been used to hide them, he noted, "Heavy gauge, meant for high power."

Carefully, he slipped the tool back and pulled out another one, a small fluorescent strip which glowed faintly in the presence of an active electromagnetic field. For a moment, nothing happened, and then it glowed so brightly it nearly blinded him before again winking out. Shielding his eyes, he waited, and ten ticks later, the pulse returned.

"Nice. Takes more than ten ticks to breach it, and there you go – fried," he scoffed. Although it was a simple technology, it was quite difficult to defeat. First, he couldn't just cut the wire as systems like this frequently measured the current to make sure that such hadn't happened. If he did that, guards would be sure to come. Taking the telescoping tool out once again, he lifted both wires out of the dirt uncovering them all the way. As he did so, he couldn't help but smile. Both of them had been bent or run over by something which shaved off the insulation about a track inside the grating. After a few passes of work, he had managed to tease the rest of the insulation off of one wire and, using the fluorescent strip as a guide, time it so that on one cycle, power went through the bars and on the next, through the connected wires, a broken stalagmite providing more than ample pressure to maintain contact.

Between cycles, he clipped both wires with heavy duty cutters in his pack and then moved on to working the bars free. Again, he was pleased to find another short-cut had been taken that made his job easier. While it did take him more than ten ticks, two of the bars slid back and forth very easily, and with the right leverage, both broke free. Now, there was enough room for him to put his pack through, and eventually, himself with a little groaning. After a pass of collecting himself, he gently put the bars back into place so that, from a distance, very little evidence would exist that they had been tampered with.

As he put on his eyewear and looked for any kind of security illumination, he clicked record on his wrist. "Instinct is your gift, Matriarch. The bars were hot and likely monitored. I shorted the wires a track away and got through the bars. There's damn well something here."

A chirp after he had collected his gear and started making his way along the path made him smile. They certainly weren't falling asleep on the job. "Glad you're alright," Tasha's voice told him. "Stay focused, cub. Now that you found proof of active monitoring, Van is pulling in more resources – quietly and securely, but having them on standby."

"Damn if she doesn't plan ahead. Good to hear you, Tasha."

"Thanks, cub," she told him as he reached another area with a false wall of rock and rubble. "I'll pass this back to her, but … I'm thinking about you, praying for you, too."

He didn't record anything for a few passes but rather listened, carefully ensuring he didn't disturb something that would make a noise. He had to strain to hear it, but there was the electric hum sound all over again. Slipping back nearly to the grate, he sent back, "Thank Tasha for me, please. I can tell I'm again paralleling their tunnel. Looking for a way to move further north. This tunnel looks just east and west."

In a few passes, a chirp came back. "Maps say that almost exactly seventy tracks east from the place where the cave connects the two mine systems, in the tunnel you are now in, there is a shaft going down three levels. Bottom level connects, the rest don't. This … is from a paw drawn map we found, really old, but … it's sourced decently."

He searched, pacing off the distance carefully and then feeling along both walls, he searched for any sign of a break. Tapping gently, he came across a section of rock that was anything but. It wasn't large, but it was some kind of plastiform simulation of a rock wall. The camouflage was exceptionally well done, and from the point of view of the grate would have been completely impossible to see.

"Someone's gone to a lot of trouble to hide the way," he told them, softly. "This will take some time to check out before I can breach it."

When he was halfway through his inspection of the false door, the chirp sounded in his ear again. It made him smile, and he intentionally kept it waiting a little until he had finished his review. The little chirps reminded him of a mythical creature in his story books as a child – a small, leathery flyer with multifaceted skin like little green and blue jewels that was a cub's pet on a distant world. It would come with messages tied to its leg, and in turn, the cub would return his answer the same way. The little beast had the ability to fly through walls like some kind of spirit, and it was incredibly fast once in the open air. He imagined it lighting on his own shoulder and chirping to him. Then, it would jump down to his wrist, raising its little hind leg up for the removal of the message.

Touching the play button on the wrist control, he heard, "We are here for you as long as you need us," Vanalla told him. "We're not going anywhere. Also, we are proactively orienting a few drones ahead of you to the north, under cover, of course."

Mentally stroking the imaginary little beast for its patient service, he touched record to give it its message. "Thank you for that. It would be a pretty dismal place down here without being able to hear from you. I've cleared the fake door and am opening it up. I'll head down three levels and then back up. Contact you then." And, with that, the little beast was on its way. He had the mental image of Tasha waiting at the window watching as his imaginary little creature swooped in and landed obediently on the matriarch's desk. Vanalla would, of course, appreciate the little creature as much as he did, as she had given it to him.

As he carefully opened the door and looked down the shaft, its attached ladder along the back, it struck him how real his fantasy actually was. This little beast in his ear, technological though it was, came from Vanalla, and that was after his own organization and their inevitable distrust and inefficiency failed to ensure such necessary support. She had seen the evidence in front of her, seen the need, and insured he would have it. Some part of her had seen that he didn't want to be alone, and this had prevented that.

An interval later, he was working his way back up a similar shaft having disabled two more security systems, both active but not impressive in any regard. It was clear that whatever was being defended was presumed to be, to the most part, secure by virtue of its inaccessible nature. There had been some care taken to insure any intruders were detected, but the deterioration on wires and other little clues alerted him to the fact that once high and polished security was now ill maintained. It was running on whatever strength it had possessed when set-up and when maintenance had ceased several seasons ago. Checks through his special viewers rendered no proof of a replacement system – something using trans-visible light, for example – to cover the failings of an old, original system.

As he entered the horizontal shaft indicated on the matriarch's maps, he quietly listened. A pulsing, thrumming sound now interrupted the near silence which had been his constant companion, save for the matriarch's messenger whispering in his ear. He made his way closer to the sound where he was sure it would pick up. "I'm going to let you hear something. I'm back up the shaft, and there's some kind of equipment. Listen…" He placed his ear against the wall, and the sound grew more intense. He let it play for about twenty ticks and then leaned away. "What do you make of that?"

He searched back and forth for some kind of entrance, following the noise. He almost missed the chirp, but as he had been expecting it, he retreated and pressed play when he was in a space where he could reliably hear her. "Cub, we passed that to some resources we have access to, and that's a CycloDyne medium power reactor, model fifteen eighteen. It's clean, but it can be pushed into overload. If it was, the resultant explosion would be … significant. It would approximately equal about fifteen of the military's mark eighteen standard explosives charges. Yeah, I know, a bit of macabre numbering from CycloDyne. So, there is an option readymade, if you want to use it. Our reads put you right up against the base of the mesa that houses the Guides statue, just like the maps say."

"I think I can get in. On the off chance I can't hear from you once inside, how do I overload it?"

After a few passes and taking care of some necessary private business, he got the answer as he was eating a meat bar from his pack and taking a drink.

"Strangely enough, set the reactor on full, which you should be able to do from the engineering control. Then, make the cooling system inoperable – our guess is one of the repeaters into the mechanical control housing would be the ticket. You'd make it physically impossible to cool the reactor. Then, destroy the engineering station – no way to shut that off. Cub, if you take this option, I want you to look for another way out other than the caves. I think we can air drop escape supplies to you if you can get high enough. If you're that close to the reactor to hear it like that, and it overloads, the caves won't survive. Time to overload would be about ten passes."

"It's an option," he told her. "Thank you. If I can get in, we'll see if it is my best one. Wish me luck."

When he had found the entrance, he pressed play one last time, just in case he had missed the chirp. "You have skill, experience, and determination, cub," the matriarch told him in a voice which conveyed her sincere appreciation of him. "Luck is something you will make. We'll be listening."

"Exactly the sort I'd like to put my allegiance behind," he thought, and after he had examined the door for alarms or traps a good long while, he pushed through.

"That's it, he's in," Vanarra stated as Tasha and Kylie watched alongside her, aboard the Haven.

"Kylie," Tasha asked nervously, looking at the tactical readout, "how many guards in there with him?"

"About thirty."

"One … Vulpi against thirty of them," Tasha sighed, nervously shifting back and forth as her tail darted this way and that.

"Those are long odds," Van seemed to agree, but then added, "for the Sahnassites, that is. You are probably not going to want to watch what happens next, kit."

"No, I want to see this. I want to know exactly who I've invited into my lair bed … if he survives, that is."

"He will, but unless I miss my guess, once he learns what they're planning to do, he won't let one of them walk out of that place alive…"

The noise was potent where he was, in the dark and musty little room. The reactor had to be close, that was something that wasn't hard to miss, but changing the settings on his night viewers, he was able to get a clearer picture of exactly where he was. It was, for lack of a better description, an equipment closet. It had an arching outer wall through which he had entered that was paralleled by an arching inner wall with a door some distance along its axis. Light was spilling in underneath from a lit hallway, and he held his breath as paw steps made their way down the hall, quick shadows appearing and disappearing against that light.

Feeling relatively secure after searching the room for some kind of camera, he started to examine the equipment stored all around him. Some of the items were admittedly janitorial in nature, cleaners and sprays, but in another section, there were boxes of replacement parts for power equipment, what he guessed was the reactor and power grid replacement parts. Most of these were small and in carefully labeled bins. Some of the larger components were corralled in bins which were labeled, reserved for energy conduit or plumbing and the like. "But why this door to the cave?" he wondered, looking back at the way he had come. Opening the door, he brushed his paws along its edge.

A steady breeze pushed air under the door and out into the cave. Looking to the side of the door, he saw a workbench with electrical repair equipment, and the "exhaust door's" purpose became clearer. As well protected as it was presumed to be, based on the obstacles he had overcome, it would probably be a little convenient to take advantage of whatever was driving the positive air pressure of this facility to clear whatever fumes were bothering you. Closing the door, he could feel the draft intensify until he had fully closed and sealed the door. It had been only a port, not a true door, and so its presence made sense to him. So long as a mechanic didn't come by any time soon, Shadow reasoned he could likely remain in the space he was in.

He also thought that it might be a good time to think about some useful thievery or sabotage. Knowing his own inventory, some basic items from the workbench such as a power meter and soldering laser were added to his possessions. If he did have to sabotage the reactor, he thought about the parts that could be used to quickly repair it, and those were quietly escorted out of the storage room and far down the shaft he had entered from originally. "Door entered into an electrician's workroom of some type. Doing a little clean out," he said to the "pet" messenger. "Removing some tools and hiding a few key repair parts for the reactor." He was going to add to that, but the chirp met his ear.

"If you have time, cub, we should establish if you can transmit from inside the facility. You also might want to think about putting one of the incendiary repeaters near some key materials near where you entered. In case that place is wired like an electromagnetic shield through its walls, that door you found might be the only way to get a signal to you."

"Not a bad idea. Stand by," he told them. Removing one of his two remaining repeaters, he touched the control switch to on and then placed the repeater on top of a thin metal cabinet of solvents. If the device melted through the aluminum, there would be quite the fire and fumes sparked by the contents of that humble cabinet. With the port closed, he touched the record button and quietly asked, "Repeater is in place. Can you receive me?"

After about a pass, he heard the response, "We can receive you. How read you us?"

"I hear you, and I'm proceeding into the facility. I have this repeater hidden in a place where when it catches fire, it will do some real harm. I'll try to place another repeater soon." Slipping close to the inner door, he listened carefully, not hearing anyone. Slipping out an attachment for his PawLink, he probed under the door with a micro VidStar camera. What he saw was a curving hallway with double doors not twenty courses away.

As he had no interior plan for whatever facility he was in, this first move was the most crucial. He was in information gathering mode, true, but he was also the hunter, now. Shadow knew that whoever these bastards were who had tried to smuggle contraband into Attoria as a tool to destroy innocents were going to have their blood adorning his muzzle by the time this sol was over. There was no forgiveness; there was no remorse. Now, there was only the hunt. Now there was only stealth.

Looking in the other direction gave him what he was searching for, a clear hallway with obvious cover ahead, another storage room across the hall. Looking back up at his own door, he could tell there was no lock, only a simple door pull as he saw on the door opposite. Slipping the door open noiselessly, his ears attentive, he made his way quickly across the hall in seemingly the time it took to blink. Entering the far room made him react almost automatically without even processing the thought. The Nephti who was bent over working on a piece of electronics only had enough time to turn around before he was battered by a strong paw across the side of his head – a blow delivered with exact perfection which stunned and disabled his opponent. One injection later, the Nephti was out and being stripped of his clothes and identification.

All of this had taken place under three tracks of vertical height and in less than twenty ticks. Although the plasti-shield wall halfway down the room had registered in his thoughts, it was nothing more than an obstacle he was avoiding, an exposure of his cover he was preventing through quick stealth and guile. In three passes, the Nephti was seemingly gone from the room, his naked body now carried across the hall and deposited into the cave; he would sleep out what would likely be the remaining intervals of his life. The clothes he wore were now Shadow's, granting a measure of concealment to the Vulpi as he moved around. He was glad that both he and the Nephti he had just replaced shared a similar coloration and bulk of tail, even if the shapes weren't exactly the same. From a distance, the disguise would pass.

Now, Shadow's keen eyes guided him closer to the large glass windows which promised potential exposure, true, but also his first full look at the place he had managed to infiltrate. Quickly scanning for any movement, his eyes darted around as he slid the equipment the Nephti had been working on into a position which gave him a better vantage point and, what was better, a reason for being there. Shadow found it difficult not to just gawk and stare dumbfounded at what was in front of him. The facility was a massive storehouse the size of a whisk field, full of goods in boxes and various raw materials organized around a central core. Coming into the core was a track from which items were being removed from railcar by crane, a team of five individuals coordinating the effort. All of them were dressed as he now was.

Slipping back into cover, he tapped the record button. "Massive bay the size of an athletic field with a rail car that comes into the middle of it for deliveries, some kind of tram. At least twenty-five if not thirty tracks to the ceiling, largely circular in nature with varied rooms. Feels like the lowest level. More later."

He had made it into the warehouse and was well along the arc of the wall before the chirp timidly returned. "Acknowledged." A smile tugged up the side of his muzzle. She knew when to keep it short, and he imagined that she would already be passing that information along to Vosh and others – maybe even his own agency, regarding what he was finding. There was a spine along the wall which suggested a lift system, and getting into a vantage point to safely watch it, he observed that his hunch was correct. There only appeared to be a single button with the indicator lights showing the lift at its lowest level. Scanning to the side, he looked for options – stairs or a concealed crawlspace.

Sadly, he could see nothing, but with the lift being on the ground floor, he took an inspiration and went with it. Stepping towards the elevator door with the warehouse goods obscuring his traverse, he pressed the button and stepped to the side, prepared to dash away if he'd triggered an alarm or if someone was in the lift. Thankfully, the door opened and then closed with Shadow now inside. Looking at the control panel, he saw what looked like to be access controls and a numeric keypad. Shaking his head, knowing that his unwitting benefactor probably had a code to get the elevator moving, he looked up and found the emergency exit. Flipping it open, it wasn't a moment more before the elevator was empty and any sign of his presence was gone.

"This is better – out of sight and out of mind, and with the freedom to go where I will," he mused, looking at the long ladder stretching up from beside him. Slipping over, he was just in time to dismount the lift car before the doors opened once again and someone else wandered in. Watching, nearly holding his breath, Shadow looked below the lift and found full confirmation of his hypothesis. "First level – stores, supplies, and subway. Let's see if lair goods are on the second level."

Making the climb with ease, his long intervals of physical training paying dividends, he was gratified to see that the first level was the only one which didn't have some kind of alternative access from the elevator service duct. Looking up, his technologically enhanced eyesight granting him nearly a mid-sol view of the shaft, he counted seven levels, including the first at a height of what had to be nearly one hundred tracks. "Amazing," he whispered into the recorder just after getting to the landing on the second level, "there are seven levels to this place. Construction looks like something that was brought in, railcar by railcar. That big garage behind the barn makes much more sense, now."

Keeping pace with one rising elevator and using it to mask his noise as he climbed, that dangerous and intoxicating sense of enjoyment started to infect him, a force which he knew both drove and endangered him. He was here, in someone's inner sanctum, in a place they never expected anyone to infiltrate, a place they believed completely safe from discovery. With the right contacts and brave action, he had penetrated their defenses and was now prowling through the heart of their forbidden and prized rangelands. They had threatened his tribe and his love, and now, he would hunt them in their own camp, leaving no one alive within, ending the threat, forever. Forever, that is, if they were still a true threat.

Touching record again, he whispered, "They didn't think anyone would ever make it this far. All security inside the facility has dropped away. Going to have a look at the top levels."

At the sixth level, he slipped back out into the attached workroom to the side of the elevator service-way and was edging up to the door, about to slip the VidStar camera out and explore a bit when the chirp sounded in his ear. "They are likely to have higher levels of security, especially around the prizes. We also need a favor, cub. Any chance you can get as high as you can, maybe start thinking about scoping a way out – for later? If you signal us there and stay there, we'll be able to triangulate you, tell you how high up you are."

The matriarch's temperance tamped down the thrill of the game and helped remind him that returning the way he came wasn't an option if he chose to set the reactor to critical. He needed a way out, and he needed a way that he could get out in about ten passes. Looking down the shaft, he sighed. "Damn if she doesn't have a point." Having to climb the distance could consume most of that, which meant if up was his way out, the elevator would have to play a role. He had watched them now, several times, and they were relatively swift, making the full vertical traverse in well under a single pass.

"I'll work on it. Ping you back in a few," he told her before slipping back out to the ladder. In a little over a pass, he was in a work area at the top of the lift shaft, a room which seemed to "crown" the entire facility within the rock. "I'm at the top," he told her. "I'll search around up here for a few passes while you check. Like you said, looking for alternatives."

Other than the machinery for the elevator, there wasn't a lot of equipment to look at, but there was one large red door that attracted his attention, it's frame imbedded in the outer wall. Slipping close to it, he saw that it, indeed, was alarmed and strongly barred from any entry, with levers and a control panel seeming to indicate a very armed security system to what appeared to be, by the diagram, a stovepipe tunnel up and out of the facility. Moreover, he felt a suction of air around the edges of the door. There was a chirp in his ear again, just when he was starting to want for it. "You, dear cub, are almost half way up the Meeting Den mesa. I'm hoping they have either a way out to the side of the mesa or, perhaps, even a way up. You seeing anything?"

"Indeed. It's well barred and alarmed, and it looks like it leads up, not out to the side. I might be able to make it up to the top if I can take the lift to the level below, hop out here, and scramble up the ladder. Still, that will just leave me trapped on top – unless I want to jump."

Working his way back down into the lift shaft, he had made it down to the fifth level by the time Vanalla responded. "We'll leave you a present that will make the descent a lot more plausible. I'm presuming you've played around with that kind of toy in the past. Just leap off of the opposite side away from where you came in. When that reactor blows, if that's what you choose to do, the side with the mines is going to be hazardous in the extreme. I'm also going to relocate support resources into a clearing you should be able to make."

"Will do," he replied. "Going to continue to check out this lift shaft I'm in. I didn't see another one on the opposite side of the facility. I think this is... hold on." His eyes caught sight of another platform opposite the lifts, barred by a railing. "See something on the opposite side of the shaft I want to get a look at."

As he pulled a coil of synthetic cord from a pouch on the side of his pants, he realized how much he was trusting the matriarch, not to mention her equipment. If someone was able to eavesdrop on their electronic conversation, he'd completely given away his location, but his intuition told him that the residents of this place had no idea he was inside. A search for the missing Nephti hadn't even seemed to kick off yet, but he knew that he had limited time available to him before someone would begin to suspect the mechanic's disappearance wasn't easily explained away. Securing the line to his specially constructed belt, he set up the rigging system which would catch him if he fell. The other end was connected to a good, solid post well anchored right beside him.

Once this was done, Shadow had the daunting task of making two nearly perfect jumps, each one about eight tracks wide. He had to land perfectly, at least the first time, as his target was a cross support between the lifts with only about a half track available to stand on. While in shape and knowing he was theoretically capable of both leaps, he still had more than fifty tracks below him threatening him very firmly if he failed to judge his steps correctly. With the correct amount of lead strung out to his side, Shadow sprang into the air and landed perfectly, spinning around a vertical support a bit like an exotic dancer he had seen on another mission. It wasn't especially graceful, but he was safe, his security line dangling easily behind him.

Just then, he heard a sound from below and saw a shape in the pit he had just leapt over starting to make its way swiftly up towards him. Biting his lip to keep from swearing, he unholstered his knife and sliced the line at his hip, tossing it hard away from him to clear the cab. With less than a tick to spare, his smoothly sheathed the knife and made his second leap, his tail feeling like it had been brushed by the leading edge of the rising lift. His landing, this time, was even less graceful since he had hurried. He almost bounced off the railing before catching himself at the last moment.

A whirr above him caused him to scramble up and over the railing without thinking, his tail again feeling like it was being brushed by the descending lift which sailed below him towards one of the lower levels. Shaking his head, he thought about telling the matriarch but then thought better of it. He was now facing what had gathered his interest moments before the terrifying necessity of complete concentration for the jumps he had made – the security system switch panel. Smiling, he knelt beside it, recognizing the model as one he had been trained on regarding best infiltration techniques, and what's more, the largest physical item in his back-pack was specifically designed to accommodate this purpose.

In less than three passes, his portable viewer allowed him to see everything that was being seen by the numerous security cameras around the facility. In point of fact, he realized that he had been very fortunate. The lift access on the first level was clearly in the range of one of the cameras, but his disguise had likely helped him. Now, however, there would be no problem. An exceptionally well-designed program he had just loaded into the electronic "brain" of the security system caused it to selectively hallucinate. His software hack was as far beyond "loops" of recorded VidStar as it was simple images placed in front of security cameras. Now, he gained unparalleled access to information and freedom of movement.

Black bands with a certain pattern only visible to the Ultra-violet range of the spectrum, something the cameras picked up, ensured that whenever he moved through the field of view of the camera, his presence would be edited out of that portion of the image. These were now around his hat and on his upper arms. They disappeared nicely into his stolen uniform, blended exceptionally well. He could certainly be seen by anyone directly looking at him, but for someone who was relying on the camera system to catch him, there was no hope.

What absorbed him so utterly, however, were all of the images of the facility. There were camera feeds from nearly every portion of the facility, and it allowed him to count how many individuals shared this space with him. Touching record, he breathed, "I'm into their security system, Vanalla, and ... this place is something else. From the lift, I make this place eight levels if you include the elevator loft, but I see labs, storage, armories, barracks, workshops – it's like a small city contained in one underground structure, kitchen ... everything. The amount of funds required to create this, and in secret. They were creating their own de Dothnar intelligence and operations hub, right beneath the statue of the guides."

The chirp sounded in his ear. "How many you think are in there with you, cub?"

"Counted twenty-seven so far, to judge by the cameras. Twenty-eight given the one I encouraged to take up caving as a hobby. What are you thinking that we should do about this place, Matriarch?"

He had finalized his tampering of the security system when the answer came. "Cub, they've tried to annihilate an entire village of innocents, and no one can easily reach this place – not many chances for making a mistake here if you need to destroy everything. However, like I said, destroy it well if you do."

"The reactor," he thought. His director had also told him that if the collection of items he located was too dangerous, his sanction was fully and completely approved. "Still, twenty-eight dead, by my paws." There was a moment of regret that was touching him, and he thought through what this would mean. Knowing that his organization had been duped by these very individuals made him angry, but he was also sick of killing. In this case, he believed it had to happen – the cause was undeniably just, but there were so many times when it hadn't been. "If I kill here, it's justified. If I leave Attoria and keep doing what I've been doing, it … it may not be. It may never be, again."

"Vanalla," he stated quietly. "I'm … tired of killing. I will look, thoroughly, and make sure that this place is a threat and there are no other options before I take any action, but if I see the threat, I will do what needs to be done. After, I don't want to again, never again, after this. I'd need a place that would make that true for me."

He disconnected the equipment that he could take with him and closed the panel, leaving no sign of his activities. He was making plans to jump back across and slip down to level four when the answer came. "Cub, you are already part of us; you know that. There is a time where the soul gets tired of killing and needs a refuge. There's space for you here, cub. I'll face your director and anyone else I have to. Just make sure you come back so I can."

Although he knew it was a blurring of his focus, Jayanar felt hope rising inside his soul unlike anything he had experienced before – a peaceful life, a meaningful life, and a full and loving life in Tasha's arms were suddenly possibilities outside of the nerve jangling, adrenaline-spiked life of prey and predator. There was a matriarch, also, who commanded the family he would become a part of – someone good, honest, noble, and dedicated selflessly to the work of shepherding those others had wanted to kill. Callanar came to his mind, and he smiled. He liked the Aelkinda, very much, and as he thought about it, there wasn't a one he had met he didn't like. "Grateful Thurians aren't hard to like," he observed.

"I will try, Honored One," he told her, his commitment clear and firm in his voice.

Chapter 29: The Renovation of the Guides

Passes later, his traverse into the middle floor of the facility was complete, careful jumps putting him back on the access ladder side of the lift shaft. Listening carefully at the door he didn't hear or see anyone, and looking on his PawLink, he scanned the security cameras. Most, if not all of the ones he had seen earlier were on the third level, having a meal. Carefully, he popped open the hatch and looked around. There wasn't anyone there, and so he exited, standing. Looking around at the three doors, he saw warnings that made him swallow. There were three main laboratories on this level – one bearing the mark of nuclear materials, one bearing the warning of chemically toxic substances, and one bearing a marker for biological hazards. Scanning around the doors, he looked for anything that would have prevented entry, but then remembered from his initial leap into the lift that there was a credential reading system.

"I am on the fourth level. I've got nuclear, biological, and chemical labs all here, but no controls on the door, no alarms."

Looking into the windows and glancing around for possible concealment or cover took him a few moments, and just when he was about to push the door open, he heard a chirp. Playing the message, it was Vosh's voice. "Intelligence states that at other Sahnassite facilities in the past, they were more prone to use light or laser tripwires at hind paw level – on a different security system."

His eyebrow fur raised as he recalled a detail mentioned in his initial briefing. Looking down, he pulled the door open in the nuclear lab and looked to the left and right inside. Sure enough, small posts beside the doors faced each other right where he would have pushed the door opened or stepped. "Good save, Vosh. Stepping over it, now."

He entered and then started making his way around the lab, recording with his PawLink as he went. Finding a manifest in the corner, he looked through it, shaking his head, recording as he went. The items presently in inventory were far less daunting than what had been previously stored. The shipment meant for Attoria had been the last of their most significant inventory, and he sighed, seeing items which had been confiscated at several Vanarran facilities as supposed contraband. "The list of our failures, all clearly marked."

Realizing that there was little left of value in this lab save for some low-grade material which might be useful for triggering sensors or calibrating instruments, he decided to move to the biological lab taking the same care to enter as before. Here, the lab was exceptionally well-stocked – numerous vials were racked and sorted behind heavy glass and an airlock which required specialized gear to be worn when passing through. "Hear this, Vanalla. Nuclear manifest is about empty, but biological is chocked full – Calnar-B, Altian-X, Zephar strains ZYK and RTK. They've got a lot of them. I see Lasset-12 and Perco's Curse – there's not a disease or bioweapon I've heard about that they don't have. Moving to chemical lab."

After he had entered the chemical lab, he heard, "Tell us what you see, and we'll analyze it. We can talk when you get to cover."

"Practical, as always, my dear Matriarch," he said to himself before pushing the record switch. "Manifest in chemical is just as bad – waist high canisters of diasposene, metritholine, venom gas, again, another who's who of dangerous chemicals. They appear very well stocked."

It was then that he heard movement in the lift shaft, and he ducked behind one of the counters near the door. He cursed to himself thinking that his fortune was ending too early and that he would likely have to either disable or kill whoever this was entering his level. There was a soft ping just before the door opened, and two Nephti entered the lobby already engrossed in a conversation. "Loyal Elite Chuffar, you know that they caught the export of the shipment. They might have traced it to the access lair. We can't have them snooping around there – it's incredibly exposed if someone gets too nosy."

"It's been there for more than a hundred seasons without detection, and very few of the Sahnassites ever knew of it. We are the privileged few. To everyone in the town of New Windston, it's just another lair with keep out signs. Anyone curious has been taken care of, and we've even spread rumors in town of it being haunted. We never have visitors; I don't think this changes anything. We'll take the virus out and then move it to a safe lair some distance away. In a few sols, we set up our courier, and the laced envelope is delivered right to the administration building in Attoria addressed to their so-called Matriarch. She opens it, and the infection cycle begins. Zephar RTK will kill everything in Attoria, and we will make sure that no one comes or goes for the fifteen intervals required."

"It is an exceptionally short-lived plague, true, but effective," the other Nephti agreed. "Is the courier to be one of ours?"

"No. That is unnecessary. There are a bunch of shiny new faces who take the box containing the envelope the last course or so for us – keep our paws clean. The courier's trip is one-way, either way."

"Loyal Elite, the use of Zephar RTK will bring intensive enforcement and special investigation services down on this area. Our abilities to move freely will be impeded for some time to come."

"A necessary consequence," the overweight Nephti acknowledged. "Destroying the hope of Attoria and everyone involved in the project will ensure that the Vanarran influence is destroyed forever, and their legacy will be non-existent beyond this generation. None of them will ever attempt to congregate again and build any such blasphemous community. Now, come in, and I'll point out the strains to use. Our dear doctors were just finishing up their lunch and will be joining us shortly."

The moment the two were through the door, Shadow was making his escape and had returned to the lift access-way. Moving up silently to the top floor, again, he touched the record button. "They are about to export Zephar RTK from the facility. They intend to use it on Attoria and enforce their own quarantine until everyone there is dead. I guess the decision is made, then."

Slipping out into the top level hallway, he saw a plush and very worshipful space, one adorned with what appeared to be old statuary of the perfect forms of a Nephti, Perratti, Pantera, Lupar,

Faelnar, and Vulpi, metallic and shining. "Foundationalists, that's all you are," he said to himself, remembering the "perfect forms" from a historical text during his academy seasons.

The chirp then came to his ear. "Yeah, cub. I ... I don't see a way around it. We've looked at everything you've told us about, and the reactor is the only way. It will create a fire that will basically melt the inside of that place, rupture every canister of everything and incinerate it. This is just another reason why the mine is not an escape route. It's got to be the top. We're putting a gift up there for you. We think we've found the hatch – you'll find it nearby."

Slipping out of the worshipful space where the six perfect forms resided, Shadow made his way back to the lift access shaft and began the long trek down to the reactor room on the first level. There was a burden he felt as he went down each rung of the ladder; he had watched the individuals living here for several passes as they went about their normal duties. Maybe not all of them were malevolent bastards like this Chuffar, individuals willing to unleash a plague on an entire village without much concern. Maybe some of them were like the ones in Attoria, following because they felt they had no other choice but wonderful souls once freed from what bound them. When he reached the bottom of the shaft, he asked softly, "Vanalla, can you put Callanar on. I ... I have to ask him a question."

In a few passes as he watched for a safe opportunity to leave his hiding place and make his way to the reactor room, he heard the elder male's voice. "I am here. Please, ask anything you like."

It took a few passes for him to actually ask his question as chance provided him with the opportunity to move out of the shaft, unseen, through the hallways and into the reactor space. The security cameras were, of course, ignoring him and thus defeating the primary nervous system of this hidden facility, but he was again careful as once more, trip wire sensors watched the thresholds as a secondary measure. "No security system is worthwhile if its presence and workings are clearly understood," he thought. However, once again concealed in a closet, he asked his question. "Sorry for the delay. Callanar, I find myself in a place where I must again destroy others to save lives, but there were so many mistakes with the Vanarrans, before. There were all of you who were in the same position as many of these – just following along. I find it difficult not to draw the comparison, you know?"

As Shadow waited for a technician to complete an inspection of the reactor, he wondered how the elder Aelkinda would react. In a few passes, he had his answer. "Each sect had their own special programs, those elite few who know the dirtiest secrets, the real and horrifying truths. The closer you get to the secrets, however, the less likely you are to find those who are innocent of their purpose. It sounds like there is no closer place to the heart of those secrets than where you are. Now, I can't give you absolution, my friend, not because you don't deserve it, but because I don't deserve to give it to you. We can only thank you for making such hard choices on our behalf, whatever the outcome."

Shadow nodded, longing to be in Callanar's presence to thank him directly, but he replied, "Thank you, my friend. Van, better get those arrangements for me into position, I'm placing a charge in the coolant controls after I set the reactor on overload. I'd prefer to delay that, but it looks like I'll have to lay my paws on it. It will be a race, then. Hope the lift is available."

Making his way stealthily out, he crept behind the pipes and placed the repeater he had just retrieved into the heart of the control system for the coolant system, noting with pleasure that it was right above the pump motors. After burning through all of the control systems, the melting metal and plastics would invariably foul the motors, requiring replacement in order to repair them. Just when he was making his way to the control panel to set the reactor on overload, he heard a chirp.

"Vosh has an idea," Van told him, and then he heard the Vulpi's voice. "Go to the panel, reach underneath and disconnect the speaker. Then, press the safety alarm test button and set the reactor output to full. Then, within three ticks of one another, execute the increase and release the alarm test. The control panel will enter demo mode, but the reactor status will change, just as you asked. Wait until the reactor temperature is at least three hundred but not more than five hundred. Leave then, and when you are at the top of the elevator shaft, destroy the coolant system with the repeater. The overload will be inevitable."

Raising his eyebrow fur, he had to give it to his fellow Vulpi. She'd apparently researched the reactor's weaknesses after identifying which one it was, and as he did as she asked, he was amazed to see the control console do exactly what she had said it would. Going around the reactor's side, he checked an electronic temperature gauge, and true to her word, it was steadily rising. Looking at his PawLink made him grimace, several individuals had just exited the elevator on his level and appeared to return to the job of unloading and sorting the massive haul of equipment on the tram bed. Again, he would have to skirt the edges of the room. Also, likely he would have to wait until the elevator was clear before risking an approach. Glancing back at the reactor panel made him smile.

"I owe you, Vosh, all of you, really – the reactor temp is climbing." Just then, a black flash on his PawLink screen made him duck for cover, the security override software warning him when someone was close. Back in his closet, he peeked out and watched as a female Nephti came, took a data pad, and again made notes, checking the reactor settings. Shifting her weight back and forth, the Nephti seemed uncertain and then headed towards Shadow's secret hiding place. Slipping back along the side wall, every muscle tensed and aware, the predator ready and willing inside of him, he waited until the door had opened before slicing a hard paw edge out into the Nephti's throat whilst grabbing her shirt and pulling her inside. A hard punch to the side of her head rendered the female unconscious and helpless, but to make sure, an injection went into her neck. "Better for you, anyway, poor kit. Sorry."

Slipping back out he checked the temperature and winced. It was four hundred ninety and on a steady climb higher. Without waiting to see how fast it was rising, he slipped out of the room and moved down the outside ring of hallways until he had no choice but to reenter the storage area. In nearly plain sight of the others, he casually made his way towards the elevators. "Hey, Maracu! You finally decide to stop napping and get to work?!" a voice called to him. He raised a paw for a moment and kept walking. He could feel interest turning towards him like searchlights, others in the group turning to stare, but just then there was a loud clank of metal on the floor and a yelp of pain. The "searchlights" swiveled back to see what ill had befallen their comrade, and before anyone could look back in his direction or cared to, he was in the elevator.

Pressing his badge to the reader, he keyed the top floor and smiled as the lift started a smooth traverse as he had commanded it to. Seeing a switch, he waited until he was between the sixth and seventh levels before shutting off the lift. Its warning bell sounded out, but now it was too late. He was up and out and into the shaft and making his way quickly up the ladder within a pawful of ticks. In less than a pass, he had reached the emergency hatchway and pulled it, setting off even more alarms. Looking at his PawLink, he pressed the "detonate" control, and then both of the repeaters he had with him triggered. In the wireless feed from the security system, he could see the flashes of light in the back of the reactor room, and switching over for a moment, he could even see smoke coming from under the technician's door where he had first entered the facility.

Switching back to look at the reactor room, he saw fire blossom over the control panel, and in just a moment, he saw a massive outgas of steam just as a pawful of stunned Nephti charged into the room, scalding them into retreat. The flinging of debris sailing through the room as the motors tore themselves apart made him shut down his paw link and enter the tunnel. As he climbed, he keyed record, "The reactor is done for, just saw the coolant system rip itself to pieces. Hope you are ready up top."

He was nearly at the end of the shaft when he heard the reply. "Our gift is up there, cub, just look where Vanarra is looking for it, and then follow that line off of the mountain." He had no idea what she meant until he threw the hatch open and realized where he had exited. He was literally standing between the two giant matriarchs. Looking up, it was easy to find the mixed blood and follow her eye line. Running forward, he found the black backpack waiting in the tall grass right where she said it would be. Scooping it up, he kept running, the far edge of the mesa some distance away.

As quickly as he could, he put his left arm into a strap, then the right, even as he still ran at a good pace. Shadow felt as if he could feel the ground trembling beneath him as he ran, shuddering as something horrible happened deep underground. Clipping the belt around his waist and cinching it tight, he realized that everything was in order and, what's more, the edge of the cliff was coming up on him fast. Just then, it felt like the entire surface of the mesa was lifting up, and glancing over his shoulder, he saw a gout of smoke and fire blast out of the base of the statue where he had just left, and leaning forward, he sprinted ahead at his best speed.

Hurtling at a fully committed run, he dove into open air as a massive wave of pressure seemed to sweep up from behind him, and in the micro-ticks as he fell, looking at the mesa behind him, he saw more gouts of flame spew from the face in his direction. Pulling the release, the glorious wing-chute opened above him slowing his fall. With only twenty or thirty ticks of air time left to him, he was looking quickly for a landing space when he noticed a flashing light from a nearby field.

Quickly angling in that direction, he smiled as he realized that everything had been calculated exactly. He smiled even wider when he heard the chirp in his ear. Pressing the control, he heard his love, Tasha, telling him, "You did it, dear cub! You did it! Now, take the flyer back to Shanandrae, and return Kallain's equipment to him. You'll be far enough away from this disaster that nothing can be pegged on you from a local observer. Then, when you're free, come back to me, my hunter."

He wasn't exactly sure what she meant as his hind paws touched grassy field moments later, but in the nearby treeline there was a flyer rolled back in hiding, it's pilot motioning to him. Pulling one of the shoulder releases, he deflated the parachute and quickly reeled it into his arms as he jogged towards the craft. As he approached, a large side door opened, and he was stunned to see Kallain and his aide both waiting to greet him and help him in. "Welcome aboard, specialist Shadow! It's not every sol that one gets to destroy a monument that has stood for centuries!"

"What?" he asked, now standing aboard the flyer, its door closing.

Melissiana smiled at him and pointed out the window as Kallain removed the chute from his arms. Where the Guide statues had been mere moments before, only a ruin remained, hunks and clusters of metal that weren't even recognizable as the two heroines of the Meeting Den littered the ground and side of the mesa which seemed to be burning like an active volcano. "By the moons," he breathed, shaking his head.

"Yes, it appears as if quite the number of burnable metals were being stored in the facility in addition to the volatile chemical substances," Kallain told him. "Pilot, we are away, please."

The pilot hit his thrusters, moving them out of the tree line and into the open field. In a moment, they were airborne just on top of the trees. "We'll take the first pawful of courses on the treetops at speed, too fast to be seen by those on the ground as they'll only get a brief look. When we're credibly far enough away, we'll take a standard approach into Shanandrae air field. Are you alright, specialist Shadow?"

"I was told to … give you these," he told them, pulling out his ear communicator and giving over his watch control. "They made very good companions; a good field test, at the least."

Melissiana seemed to recognize the distress he was feeling. "Come, please. Sit. I have some drink for you and a light snack. This vehicle also has a facility if you need to go."

"Surprised I didn't running along the top of that thing. Damn, what a sight."

"One I'm grateful for," she told him. "Kallain and I share in the legacy of what you destroyed, something which should never have been built. Did you hear any names while you were inside?"

"Chuffar – a loyal elite."

Kallain nodded and answered, "Went to ground after the Sahnassite dissolution. We didn't know where."

"Well, at least you'll know where to place the marker," the Vulpi told him.

"When we get a little higher in altitude, we'll get a transmission from Attoria – it's already been arranged. They are scouting the damage to the area with drones. In the meantime, please relax and accept our thanks. You've done exceedingly well."

"I'm not sure my superiors will see it that way. I'm not sure they banked on the Guides statue being destroyed."

"My old order signed that statue's destruction order when they tunneled into it. The art exists many times over in smaller forms," Kallain told him, "and I think that if Vanarra or Sahnassa were alive still, they would say that statue had stood long enough."

Shadow sighed and nodded, certain that the beatification that occurred after their deaths wasn't something either of the heroines would have truly wanted, let alone the cults that came to be formed in their names. After a few moments to refresh and re-center, Shadow allowed himself to be escorted by Melissiana to a private terminal in the back of the flyer. After he put on the headphones, she nodded and stepped away after pressing a control on the terminal. Nodding thanks in return, he looked down right into the face of the matriarch, Vanalla.

"Nice work, cub," Vanalla told him, smiling.

"It was a team effort, honestly," he offered. "A team ... I hope I can still join."

"I think you were a member the first sol we saw you," she acknowledged. "I've got Tasha waiting outside for a moment because we do need to talk about a few things. First, damage estimate. Take a look." The image changed to distance shots of the mesa where the Meeting Den had stood. "This is taken from just in front of the lair where the tunnel began. Watch this in three, two, one..."

There was a flash and an explosion of debris at the base of the mesa just before sections of the forest collapsed down into the ground. "Took out a hover trail running between the two mines, but watch this." Just then, a nearby plume of fire and flying debris scattered in front of the camera which wavered given the proximity of the detonation.

"Seems like trams aren't the only things that follow tracks," he noted. "Anyone in there?"

"Two at least; local authorities are sorting through the aftermath right now. Both mine systems seemed to have collapsed. High-speed review of the images shows parts of the forest actually rising up during the explosion event. Here ... here is what's probably going to separate your director's head from his shoulders." The image this time was of The Guides statue, and it showed Shadow crawling out, looking up, and dashing away. Then, zooming out as it kept track of Shadow's progress towards the edge, it focused on The Guides statue. At first, the powerful flash of pressure and flame just pushed the two figures apart, with the joined paws falling away, breaking off. Then, a much more powerful explosion seemed to launch the figures outwards, but even as a frame-by-frame slow motion capture demonstrated, neither statue was built for such rigor and collapsed in upon itself, ripping apart.

"We sorta lost that drone, but here was the view just a few passes ago." The image changed to a giant inferno sinkhole in the surface of the mesa, a chimney fire of dark smoke rising from it. "More than a pawful of New Windston's residents are swearing that the mesa has gone volcanic."

"What about contaminants?" Shadow asked.

"Negative, on all counts, and we've been checking our drones making sure of it – nothing chemical, nothing biological survived the inferno of the reactor going off. Radiation is present in the smoke, but the designers of this reactor took the potential of a high energy explosion into account; the exposures are exceptionally small, only slightly above background. We also have a rain storm which is moving into the area. If a good rain gets that place, it will settle out a lot of worries."

"Not a good place to go exploring, though, once everything cools off."

"No, not at all. We're waiting for the smoke to clear to get an idea of how deep that hole in the mesa goes, but it could be all of one hundred and fifty tracks or more, even with the stuff piled at the bottom. And so," Van asked him, coming back on the screen, "what do you think your director will say?"

"I think he'll be … energetic regarding my choice, very impassioned. He'll probably want my hide, and … with your permission, I'd like to take my leave."

"Fair enough. I took a guess at your pay, and although you know I can't offer you as much right now, there are other incentives to stay." Tasha leaned into the picture, coming up beside her matriarch, now his, as well.

"It's … good to see you, Jayanar," she told him, lower lip quivering. "I … I was worried."

"I think it's my job, dear. Too much stress. I might want to think about a change."

"Oh really?" she asked, her lips drawing into a smile. "I believe there is a very competent intelligence officer here who could use your help, your expertise?"

"Sounds interesting. Quiet neighborhood? Thurians get along there?"

"They do," she assured him. "Good place to raise a family, if you'd like."

"I do," he answered, both of them realizing that she'd asked him to join her, and neither regretting it in the slightest.

Director Geornan de Oterbythe's hard stare fixed him as he stood in the same office where his mission had started. "Thirty dead, the city of New Windston in a panic and temporarily evacuated, the Meeting Den mesa belching out smoke as if it had suddenly become a volcano, and two of the most prized statues on the planet decimated to unrecognizable piles of metal. According to geologists, a carbonized rock deposit is now on fire beneath the surface, *hopefully* localized to the area of the Meeting Den mesa, what's left of it, but making the recovery of anything in that area utterly and completely impossible."

"Given what I recorded, Director, could you see any other alternative? I learned they were about to release a biological weapon in Attoria, and the storehouse of biological weapons they possessed was utterly daunting."

The Perratti sighed and looked back at him. "Politically, it's very hard to see it as that simple. Thankfully, the matriarch of de Gonari who owns that property has told us she will not press any kind of charges and will assist with keeping Thurians away from it, but the select committee is calling for your neck, Shadow."

"Could *they,* from the safety of their offices, see any other alternatives? I recorded the conversation of Loyal Elite Chuffar – have they listened to that?"

"They have, but it hasn't swayed them. They want guiderails on anything like that we do in the future, a minimum of two agents going in together, communication back with the headquarters continually. They believe containment would have worked if we, as they say, were more prepared."

"I was alone with no one else to consult, and the threat is removed. Attorian lives are saved, and in the end, sir, who knows how many others."

"Stop telling me you're right, dammit!" the director shouted, coming to his hind paws. When Shadow's expression didn't change, the director sat back down. "I ... I know you're right. That's not the point of the thing."

"Will my departure from the service calm things down, restore their delicate balance?"

"It would at least place meat on the sacrifice altar," the Perratti sighed, looking away from him.

"Very well. Then, I resign," Jayanar told him, and the director's gaze held him to make sure this wasn't some kind of trick or ruse or asinine comment.

"You're ... serious?" he asked, a little stunned.

"With so much political pressure, you'd have to reassign me away from field work, keep me at a desk until a full hearing was convened taking who knows how long. In the meantime, what I did would be spun and recast and rewritten until I was made to sound like the most incompetent member of the team when, in truth, I just removed one of the major threats on the planet. To get back into any kind of active service, I would have to apologize for what I did, and to be honest, knowing more of the ones living in Attoria who were the targets of the biological weapon, my apology would be a lie. I'm not sorry for it; I never will be. I've seen the way it went with Avalanche in similar circumstances; I have no wish to continue if that is to be my lot."

The director looked genuinely troubled, realizing that Jayanar was truly serious. "We ... won't be the same service without you. Where will you go?"

"Where I can be of use, Director. If the worries are still about Attoria and what it could become, I could be a liaison there keeping an eye out for any problems. However, if they continue to be what I've seen, then living there would be my choice."

"Minus the other matriarchs turning on Vanalla, I can't imagine any circumstance now which will hold them back. True to our word, we're being held to the military airlift for refugees, and word has been circulated through various channels. It looks credible that Attoria might be getting a big bump in population, the last possible from the outside. They'll ... need competent individuals. I do not want you to go, but under the circumstances, you're right. You wouldn't see any field work for two seasons or more."

"In Attoria, I doubt I'll see anything but that," Jayanar chuckled, shaking his head before growing serious. "I ... left my credentials and firearm with the quartermaster. Thank you for the opportunity to serve, Director."

"Thank you for your service, *Shadow*. I'm sorry to see you go," the Perratti admitted, his expression looking bleak. Turning around, the Vulpi left the Director's office.

Two intervals later, Jayanar had time to regret and to worry, and when he pulled out of the trees and in towards the village center, he was doubting if he would actually be accepted. Seeming to sense his concern, the matriarch Vanalla was standing right at the entrance and waved him to a stop. Looking in the back, she shook her head. "Is this all you're bringing with you?"

"It's my hope that there's not that much of my old life I'll require."

"I'm sorry, Jayanar," Vanalla offered, taking his paw in hers. "You deserved better than having to resign in order to save your organization's tail, but we are the beneficiaries, all of us, you and me and Tasha and everyone here. Are you sure this is where you *want* to be, cub?"

"More than anything, Honored One. I never told them that ... you were on that mission with me, but if you'll forgive this, you are a far better guide and leader than those I've served in the past. While I hope that Tasha's love-"

"Oh yeah, cub," Van chuckled. "No worries there – she's bouncing off the walls, almost literally. Hope you're ready for her."

"I'm ... I'm more than ready," he admitted. "I love her. I know how we treated sex in the past, both of us at different times of our lives, but as a mate, I only want for her, but I do also want you to know that I love you, Vanalla. I love you as my leader, as my matriarch."

Van reached over and pulled him into an embrace. "I love you, also, Jayanar. Vosh shared with me the recording you made of Chuffar. Ash and I both listened to it. They intended to kill me first, using me to wipe out everyone I know and love. You kept that from happening, and we both love you, cub, for that. Understand that you are our family now, and if you wish it, before you ever step your hind paw into this community as a resident, you will be family. Will you be kept by and keeper of, Jayanar?"

"I will, Honored One. I will, and I place myself and my soul under your command and order for whatever purpose you would have me serve out."

She parted from him and looked up into his face with earnest affection. "You, cub, are a treasure to us. What can I do for you to prove that?"

He looked away, shyly, and quietly stated, "I ... was without my parents at a very young age. Just call me your ... son, only once. I will call you Honored One, but in my heart, you will be my mother, if it would not be too much."

She put her paw on his chest and looked up into his eyes. "You are my son, Jayanar, and I will not misuse you or your gifts. Please, come, be a part of our family. You have protected us, shielded us, and you are part of us. How much you are part of us is something that you will come to realize only in time, but take my words now as my oath."

"I do," he replied softly, his eyes welling, and he kissed her on each side of her muzzle.

Smiling and threading her paw fingers through his, she led him forward. "I'll send someone back for the vehicle later. I ... have a question for you, my son."

"Mother?" he asked, and she nodded.

"Only when we are beyond the hearing of others, as a special consideration for the rest of the family."

"Of course."

"There is a beautiful Vulpi Faelnar who just might have wandered into the chapel, and even though it is not fully furnished, I think there's a Lupar who is there, as well. She loves you, my son. Do you love her?"

"With every part of my heart that is not owned by you, Honored One," he replied, smiling hugely.

"Well, then. Shall we make official, by law, what you two made official between one another?"

"I am willing, Mother, and I want to, but I want your blessing."

She smiled up at him. "I wouldn't have asked you or arranged it if you didn't already give that. I know you, cub, and not everyone's commitments are made like yours. That doesn't mean I think any less of them."

Just then, Jayanar saw someone approaching and smiled. "Ash!"

"Oh bud, is it good to see you!" the mixed blood offered, coming quickly towards him and embracing him. Letting go, he shook his head, "Damn near scared me to death when they told me what happened after I dropped you off, and I stayed around in one of the drop zones … saw the whole damned thing explode."

"I didn't worry you, did I?"

"Yeah, duh!" Ash said is if it should have been the most easily grasped truth of all time.

"Ash, take his other paw. We need to escort him to see … someone special."

The mixed blood's eyes widened expectantly. "Really?! Oh, wow, is Tasha ever going to be happy. Come on!"

Shadow awoke, not a short time later, but many seasons afterwards, the wonderful recollection of his arrival and acceptance in Attoria a dream which he always cherished. It had been such a powerful moment in his life that even now, almost two hundred and thirty-five seasons old. Vanalla had given him everything she promised, and he hadn't realized how much he had to grow after leaving the intelligence service. As he made his way to the little deck on the small lair he and Tasha shared, he looked out into the morning at a sight that would have seemed implausible to him so many seasons ago. Attoria was a city, and it wasn't a small one. Nearly every open area of the valley had been filled with it, minus the parks and green spaces which were always preserved and tended. Its bustling population had actually grown so large that on the same sol as his own bicentennial, the village of Silarcia had been started, much in the way that Attoria had been, and it, too was now growing and growing well.

There was a sadness that hung heavy over the morning, however, as he remembered that Vanalla de Kyvara, the first matriarch of Attoria had passed away in the night about a moon ago, her cub having done so a moon earlier, still. The many vigils and remembrances were lovely, and atop the memorial hill, the matriarch's own voice had sung her to her final rest, recorded and played every sol in the evening above the graves. Given her instructions, her tomb was not different than that of any other Aelkinda, and the inscription on her memorial said as much. "I am only one of you, nothing more, and nothing less. Never dishonor my life by remembering more of me than there truly was. Love one another; that is honor enough for me."

"I ... I love you, Mother," he told her, softly, looking towards the hill where she lay.

"Jay?" Tasha's soft voice called to him. "You alright?"

Turning around, he looked at the graying mixed blood who had shared his bed and his life ever since he came to Attoria. "Hello, beautiful. Are you feeling alright?"

"Well, I am, but I'm sad to say that this is our last sol here."

"I don't understand," he told her. "Where are we going? I'm not sure I want to go to Silarcia. You've been so sick, lately."

"Well, we both have, on and off. Come inside, lay down beside me, and I'll explain." He did as he was asked, slipping into bed beside her. "Jay, all these seasons, you've known me as you've known Vanalla and everyone else, and you've never known us as anything but normal Thurians. I know you'll think I'm demented or crazy by telling you this, but the Vanalla you loved was truly someone else, someone you would never have suspected. When I tell you, though, if you can believe me, you can tell that I'm not wrong."

"Who ... who was she, love?"

"In outward appearance, she was always Vanalla de Kyvara or Vanalla Ashallo if you knew her before Attoria. Inside, however, she was someone from long, long ago. Someone found her, someone who wasn't a Thurian – ascended, if you like, and gave her a much longer lifespan. She wasn't born in our time."

"She was born before us?"

"Many, many seasons before, my love," she told him, smiling. "You know how you've always told me how impressive she is, how certain and sure and reliable her goals and her heart?" He nodded, smiling at the memory. "She had cause to be. She saved the Vanarrans, in part, my cub, because she..."

"Vanarra? Vanarra de ... Gonari?" He laid back, looking at the ceiling. He had always appreciated her so much – the depth of her insight, her humility, her inner strength which bore up under the most astounding pressures. Those qualities in her, present and truly refined from such a relatively young age made him curious. He had seen so many hints and clues over time that suggested such might be so, his adopted mother never telling him outright, but over time he felt that, at least in her spirit, it had to be true. "She ... she was the real Vanarra de Gonari, the actual one? I have to tell you that I wondered, Tasha; I just didn't think it was possible; I thought that Vanalla was some kind of reincarnation of her – never felt comfortable enough to mention it. She was really Vanarra de Gonari?"

"On the inside, yes. That's who she is, and notice, I said *is* – not was. Those you think we've lost, cub, we haven't. Vosh, Ash, Shenaria, Trax, they're not gone. They live, and what we buried of them is what will be buried for us – resemblances of us that will convince everyone we are truly dead. They will bury us never knowing that we still live, just as you didn't know they still lived."

"Is it ... everyone we knew?"

"Not everyone. Lallie and Dexer are gone as are Racea and Ariasta. Drayash, of course, was many seasons ago. Vidiana, no. Not all are right for this calling, the calling of a second life, as it must be away from the Thuria we know. You, my cub, and I, however..."

"We are to have that as our destiny?"

"We are, if you accept it. I will tell you only that the sky and stars above will open to you, and that we will live – our bodies renewed and capable of exceedingly long lives. We will be those who serve the cause of our kind as we have here, in a place far away where our kind also live and flourish."

"What merit do we have, that I have..."

She put her paw alongside his muzzle and shook her head. "You asked for her to be mother to you. She is bringing you for the same reason she took Ash and she will take their kits. You are brother to Vosh, Jay. You asked for her to take you into her family, and not just de Kyvara – it was more than that. Don't you know that?"

He bowed his head, and tears slipped out of his eyes. "Yes. She's been that to me. She's been that to us?"

"Yeah. She ... she adopted me, too. She also knows that you can let this place go, let our children go and live their lives."

"Will they get the same gift?"

"Cub, how many are there now? How many kits and cubs?" He sniffed and thought. "Forty-seven?"

"No," he contested. "You forgot. Mallie had twins three sols ago."

"Yeah, and so it's forty-nine. That's just from us. All of ours believe in the Creator, and so I believe that all of ours will be caught and blessed by the paradise beyond, but I still wish to serve. I wish to guide others, and you have already." Jayanar smiled. It was only recently that he had to give up his mentoring program, teaching young cubs the life skills they would need, helping them build solid friendships and respect the needs of those friendships as important. "See? Van *knows* you. She knows you'll do well, and she truly loves you."

"So ... what do we do?"

"We go back to sleep, and when we wake up, we will be gone, and two bodies will be in our place. It will be traced back to a sickness we caught together-"

"You knew this was coming!" he accused softly. "That's why we've been staying at home!"

"We've been sick, but we've been keeping it quiet, you see? We didn't want to bother anyone, and since it's after the sols of feasting, everyone just presumes everything is alright. It's the right time and the right way. Medical analysis will show that you died of a heart attack after I died in my sleep – it's a little sad, but not for us. Frankly, I'm looking forward to being able to do physical things again."

"Does this mean ... all things physical?" Jayanar asked.

"Oh yes, cub. You bet," she chuckled, nuzzling into him. "Now, lay down beside me." He did and then looked up at the ceiling. "Have you … ever regretted our lives here?"

"Never," he replied. "I'm saddened that it didn't begin sooner. I'm saddened that I might have only now barely begun to make up for the lives I took when I was being a secret agent. I've never once regretted being here with you or being … Vanarra de Gonari's son."

"Good answer, cub," she said, snuggling into him. "Sleep, now. Lots of work to do … tomorrow."

Chapter 30: The Last Chapter

$\mathbf{J}$ay?" Tasha's voice called softly to him, but it wasn't exactly the voice he was used to, more like that out of a dream. "You awake dear cub?"

"A few more passes might be nice."

"Well," Callanar's voice said, nearly shocking him to full consciousness, "I've only waited the better part of a century – I'm sure I could afford a few more passes for such a sleepy tail."

"What?" Jayanar asked, his voice stronger than he could remember it being in quite a long time as his eyes opened and searched. They found his mate's face first, and he breathed, "Darling! You're beautiful!"

"Well said," Callanar chuckled and caught the Vulpi's glance at that moment.

"Calla ... Callanar? You're..."

"I'm alive, dear cub, yes," he chuckled, offering a paw, "I'm alive, and just a little bit younger than when we first met. Come on, wake up. The truth is that you two were our last couple coming with us, and time is running short."

Slipping up to a sitting position and looking at his arms and paws in surprise, he asked, "Time ... running short for what?"

"For the becoming," Callanar told him, a rueful smile playing across his features. "It's something that will take a bit of explaining, but there are a few in the waiting area ahead of us that will help." Looking around the room, he took in who was there, and all were dressed very nicely: Ash, Shenaria, Trax, Kallain, Melissiana, Callanar, Vosh, and a few others he didn't recognize: three Nephti, a

Faelnar, and what appeared to be a mated pair of Vulpi, to judge from their clasped paws.

Standing up, he looked down at his body. "Is … that why I'm dressed in a suit?"

"Formal occasions call for formal dress, good cub," a female voice he didn't recognize told him, and looking over he saw a Faelnar female – her body young, but in her eyes, he saw exceptional experience and wisdom. "And this is a sol like none other."

"To save you from asking," a female Nephti sighed, shaking her head, "and to again undermine my dear friend's penchant for the dramatic, let me cut to the chase. First, she's Amyra de Gonari, and I'm Rahnahi de Dothnar, both ascended. Second, your body and those of everyone else here have been renewed and improved into a state we call Trans-Thurian; short form – you live a lot longer, are stronger, and have some interesting abilities. Third, your Vanalla is-"

"Vanarra de Gonari," he said with assurance after raising his paw, and they all looked at him. That is, all except Tasha and the two Vulpi standing against the wall.

"Damn you, cub," the female Vulpi said. "I always suspected you might have figured it out, but you never said anything, and you never did anything about it! Oh, my name is Kylie, by the by."

"Nice to meet you," he stated, standing, gently lifting his mate alongside him. "I read many of her works and found similarities in the way both write; I profiled her speech and then checked the lines of her face."

"But why not … confront her or tell someone or…" Callanar was confused.

"It was still so fantastic, Callanar, and without any knowledge that such like this was possible, it was only fantasy or happenstance. Tasha confirmed it for me, as well, just before we arrived here. Look, I knew I was following a leader unlike any since the time of Vanarra, and that was still true. I also have a suspicion about you," he stated, nodding politely to Shenaria who was standing alongside Trax, both looking young. "I'm inclined to believe that you are … her mother, Vanarra's I mean."

"How did you figure that out?" Shenaria sighed.

"You have a real, familial affection for one another, and I might have happened to have read your muzzle by accident when I was using a pair of distance viewers."

"Oops," Kylie breathed, but then walked towards Jayanar, waggling a finger. "Don't think you've pulled off a complete surprise here, cub, because I have some pieces to play in return. Do you know that we had to avert six different attempts to kill you? That secret specialist background of yours cropped up, especially just after you joined us. They were going to kill you, kill Tasha, and/or kill us in various and different combinations."

"Who?" he asked, his brow furrowing. "Why?"

"Everyone from bad guys to your own director. Sad to say that we caused the latter to get retired early – still lived well enough, but it explains why he never called. The bad guys, well…"

"Good riddance, I presume?"

"We didn't kill them, but we guaranteed, successfully I might add, that they would never be a threat to you, ever again. It was a very worthwhile trade; you were an essential fixture in the Attoria community."

"You can say that again, dear Kylie," Callanar offered. "Very true. You brought a toughness and self-reliance and, dare I say, optimism and service-oriented heart that we desperately needed. Attoria is much of what it is now because of everyone in this room, and that certainly includes you, my friend. That is part of the reason why you are here – you can make a difference and, yes, you choose to."

"Part of the reason," a new voice said in the room, a male voice that was strong and certain. Jayanar and Tasha looked over to see a male Nephti with brilliant blue eyes walking towards them; Tasha's grasp on his paw became tight, and awe was clearly in her expression. "My name is Theo de Allarrae, Jayanar. Although, I like the codename Shadow, very much. I am … Vanarra's leader, and her adopted father. You can say that I trained her, even in the old times."

"Thank you," Jayanar offered, nodding a bow. "She was the most exceptional leader I have ever followed."

"And your allegiance to her is absolute, as is true for those here. You are all here because you are the nearest and dearest to

Vanarra's heart and soul, and as Vanarra transitions to a new life, you are the ones she has asked to help her as she finds her way. Also, each of you offered your love, your service, and your loyalty to a cause that will see one of the greatest and most profound changes to Thurian society; for in your time, the cults were utterly dispatched, the houses were restored to an appropriate place in Thurian society, and the innocent among the Sahnassites and the Vanarrans were saved. Thuria found its way past hate and past revenge with your help. What's more, they know they are the better for it. Now, everyone else has had a few moments with Vanarra as she prepares for this, and she can explain it to you. She wants to see you on this side before the change happens; she feels she owes you that. Would you both come with me?"

"Yes, please." However, before they made it to the smoothly opening door, Vosh came up to them. "Vosh?"

"I can now call you by the name I have always wanted to, Jayanar. As you asked Vanarra to be your mother, I am her daughter. I call you *brother*, Jayanar, as I have always wished to."

"My sister?" he asked, and she nodded, smiling. He embraced her, happily.

"Now, there will be time for many happy reunions later," Vosh told him. "Go, now, and see our mother before this change happens so that you may both understand and trust."

Jayanar had always felt strong ties to Vosh, and now he could see why, she felt the same ties to him through their mutually adopted mother. Leaning up, he kissed her on the side of the muzzle and then followed Theo out of the door, Tasha once again holding his paw. A few steps down the hall, Theo spoke, "Jayanar, you are doing very well in accepting this new reality."

"I'm feeling very honored to have a second lease on life, if you will, and to once again be with my friends and those I care about, so thank you. I'm just … uncertain about what I'll be doing, now."

Theo looked over his shoulder as they walked. "I have to admit that I also had a paw in bringing you to this time, and that is because I might have special need of you. It's something we can discuss afterwards, but if you trust Vanarra, and she trusts me, I'm hoping that we can work together, with her blessing."

"With her blessing, Sir, and Tasha's agreement, as well, I believe I would be honored."

"Yeah, that's a good thing to say because he's kind of the leader of a lot," Tasha prompted. "Like ... way more than you suspect."

"Oh, nothing much," Theo chuckled, "a trans-dimensional interstellar, intergalactic, trans-universal alliance made up of billions of different kinds of sentient life forms, all gathered to promote and nurture and protect those emerging species with promise, like those on Thuria. In short, no end of places where help is needed and good souls can make a real and powerful difference. You see, Vanarra is one of my Teldear – it's an old word from my kind meaning student, but it also means the representative of the Allarrae on a world, the Allarrae being my kind, as I'm just being a Nephti temporarily for the purposes of easing the conversation."

"I see," Jayanar replied, reeling a little but having enough presence of mind to make an observation. "And Vanalla, I mean Vanarra is one of these ... Teldear?"

"Indeed she is, a special one – so special I've adopted her as my daughter, so you and I and Tasha here are a family in a way. I don't expect much acceptance of that at this point; you've just met me."

"Still, Sir, I'm ... very grateful for being able to serve your daughter. Beyond my mate, she truly understood and cared for me."

"Still does," Theo told him, stopping and standing in front of a door, "and will continue to, as I. Now, I will leave the details of this transformation to Vanarra to explain, and when she has finished her time with you, join me out here, and together, we will watch while she becomes. She will explain, inside."

"Is this for both of us, Sir?" Tasha asked.

"Of course. Everything I said, as well, please know that. Now, go ahead. You are her last. Everyone else has already seen her and spoken to her."

"Thank you," Jayanar said and then, paw in paw, walked through the door which had slid open for them. They stepped through a short entrance hallway and into a wide, open room that was at least thirty tracks in diameter, and at the far end were four cushions, and on each was seated a different individual. Walking forward, their eyes were immediately drawn to the creature of light – something that looked like Vanarra of old but made of sparkling luminescence, wings protruding from its back wreathing its body in a majesty and warmth that could even be felt. Next to this female form was another, almost as bright, of a gold-on-gold Faelnar.

"Is that ... Tana?" he asked, and instantly he felt the being's glee at having been recognized. Taking a few more steps forward, Tasha and Jayanar could see the last two figures, Vanarra and an unmistakable Nephti sitting right at her side. Vanarra seemed solid, but this Nephti seemed to have a semi-transparent quality.

"Jayanar, Tasha," they all spoke as one. "Thank you for coming."

"Van?" Tasha asked the form on the far left, but all of them nodded.

"You look at the *me* you know, that you are most familiar with, but I am truly all of these ... and more. Please, sit now. We do not have very long, my moment of becoming is nearly here."

Jayanar helped guide his overwhelmed mate to a soft cushion in front of the quartet. "You appear to be one number short," he observed, gently.

Just then, the Faelnar form of Vanalla stood in front of him, in the center of the group. "This was just a disguise I took when I returned to Thuria, for I could not take my true form in public upon the world," Vanalla's voice alone said to him. "Look behind me, dear cub, and see me."

"I'm not sure what I'm seeing, Mother," he told her, and he felt love coming from all of the creatures in front of him.

"Even now, you trust, when all is as strange as it can be. You, cub, exceed my abilities in this. I was not as sanguine about such things when I first discovered them. You see before you all of the aspects of myself that I have gathered over time and carried with me, as a part of me, while I was on Thuria. You see the orphan who became a matriarch. You see my dearest and truest friend before all, before I was accepted by others, I was accepted. You see the one who pledged her soul to my service, and in doing so became mate along with me, and later, became a part of me. Finally, you see the presence that Theo wove into my being to protect me and help me, a gift to heal and to guide. Does that help you?"

"It doesn't hurt having only one to speak with," he offered, smiling, and stood before her. "I ... love you, Mother. I never knew this was the truth of who you were."

"You couldn't know and be who you needed to be. Tasha knew a piece of it, but..." Vanalla looked around Jayanar to Tasha who was still staring at the various forms, overwhelmed. "It's a lot to take in – yeah, I get that."

Hearing the blunt practicality in Vanalla's voice, something he truly loved about her, he asked, "And so you'll become something new? You ... does this mean you will die?"

"No, cub. Not at all. In many ways, my time as Vanalla allowed me the freedom to blend all of the aspects of myself together, so in many ways, this might be closer to the form I attain than those seated behind me. This isn't it, though."

"There are more?" he asked. "How many?"

"Four more. My Vanarra self is the real body present here, and this Sahnassa is one which is present only in spirit. For my dear Sahnassa, waiting somewhere else, she is the real bodily presence while Vanarra is a present only in spirit. She, too, has other companions joining this mix. She has an image of herself which is akin to Tana, and she has a creature of fire that matches my creature of light. There will be eight of us, cub, who join, and together, we will become one collective presence – Vanassa."

"Will Vanalla be a part of that presence?" he asked.

"She is already, and Vanassa ends nothing of who you see before you in her becoming – she is the combination of all. She is not a child; she is another level of being an adult."

"Can ... can I still call her Mother?" he asked softly. "Will she still call me her son?"

"By her first word when she greets you after becoming whole, she will assure you of that just as Vosh and Tasha remain her daughters, Ash her mate, and Shenaria her mother. For a long time, Jayanar, I was afraid of what I would lose in this joining together of souls. Now, I regret that I held it back for as long as I did, but it had to be done."

"It did if it meant that Attoria or Silarcia would lose you one moment earlier," he told her. "Even still, it's … difficult."

"They will not be without help. The lineage of Kallain and Melissiana now stands in my stead as Teldear of Thuria, and they will never be without one. Do you know what a Teldear is?"

"Your … father explained. Does this mean he is my or … our grandfa?"

"It means he loves you, Jayanar, loves you both. In … this way, however, I wanted to thank you. When you asked for me to be your mother, you and I weren't that far removed in terms of age, well that you could see. I was honored, and I remain honored. You two have an amazing future before you."

"Thank you, Mother," he told her, and turning around, he pulled Tasha up to a standing position. She was no longer as overwhelmed as she had been. Instead, she had been transfixed by the conversation passing between them, her eyes running with tears.

"Thank you, Mother," she offered Vanalla, and opening her paws, Vanalla embraced them both.

"My love for you never dies," Van told them, and then, letting go, she nodded once and disappeared.

Looking down into four sets of loving eyes touched both of them so that they put their paw over their heart. "Go now, my children," the quartet said together, a strange kind of light seeming to surround each form. "The time is now that I must become who I was meant to be, and Vanassa is so eager to be with you."

"Soon, Mother," he told them, and then he turned, sensing that along with the love they felt for them both, there was an undercurrent of concern and urgency, of a moment that had been forestalled as long as it possibly could have been.

When they made the door, Theo was right there waiting for them. "Come on. It won't be long now. You two were the last piece," he told them. "Let's go to a place where we can all observe in safety. The others are already there."

"What's dangerous about this?" Tasha asked.

"Well, the true becoming of a creature like Vanassa who is not only ascending but ascending as much as she is – it can create an enormous amount of energy."

"How much is … enormous?" Jayanar asked.

"Well, we're in the middle of deep space between galaxies in an area where no inter-dimensional weaknesses or gravity faults exist," Theo offered.

"And we're right next to where she's going to ascend?" the Vulpi asked as he looked, wide-eyed, into the observation deck overlooking the double walkway which met in a single platform which seemed to almost resemble a beacon.

"Indeed!" Theo replied easily as he nodded to Amyra and Rahnahi as well as the rest of the individuals in the room. "Oh, and did I mention the ship we are in doesn't actually have an active power core; well, not yet."

"I'm not sure what all of that meant," Tasha admitted, "but I'm kind of scared, I have to tell you."

"We're aboard Vanassa's new ship," Theo explained, "and its core will be brought to life by Vanassa's own ascension. It will be permeated with her essence and identity. Both Caloizar and Kylie are coming to live aboard it as more or less permanent residents. Everyone you see around here will have some part with Vanassa, either training her or helping her as she continues to grow and explore. I'm very pleased with the progress my daughter has made, and she will make more, as will so many of you."

"Does this ship have a name?" Jayanar asked.

"Not yet, but I think I have an idea of what it will be. Now, my friends and family. It is time."

As everyone came to the window, they watched Vanarra walking out to the platform followed by the ghostly Sahnassa, the shining Tana, and finally the brilliant creature of light.

"Theo?" Shenaria asked, coming up beside him. "Please, please tell me this is going to be alright."

"It will be, Shenaria. It will," he acknowledged. Jayanar noticed that Ash was also moving closer to Theo, looking worried. Theo smiled at them, nodded, and offered his paws to them. Shenaria took Theo's with Trax on her other side, and Ash with Vosh took his other paw. Jayanar walked up beside Vosh and whispered, "Sister," and took her paw, his own in Tasha's. One by one as the four made their way to the center and stood around what had been an empty central core about the size of a fire pit, the four of them occupying one half of the available space.

Then, four more figures appeared on the other side of the walk and started making their progress to the center. There was Sahnassa followed by a ghostly Vanarra. Following them were creatures which Jayanar and Tasha stared at a fair amount of time before they understood what they were seeing. The next form behind Vanarra was almost like a purple crystalline version of the Nephti, and behind that, a version of the Nephti's form shining with burning fire, its wings a match to those of its Vanarra peer.

"Oh my stars, you can feel it!" Shenaria blurted, and indeed, all of them could feel the pull between the individuals being drawn into becoming one.

"I love them all," Ash offered softly. "I can feel that."

Sahnassa entered the central core, and the moment she did, it started to shine – a glowing white orb suspended between them. Walking towards Vanarra's creature of light, the incarnations of the Nephti took their opposite place across from their peers. They stood, just feeling that moment as the core between them started glowing brighter and brighter. "We are one, the barriers fallen between us, our souls and lives and loves together as one. A moment of meeting, a lifetime of companionship, eons of discovery, and now our moment is here, my moment is here." All of the incarnations in the core looked towards the gallery of their friends and relatives. "We owe you for this honor, for this privilege. You have made our lives shine, and we will always love you for that. I will always love you for that."

At a nod from Theo, everyone at the window bowed, paw in paw. When they rose, those around the core also did so, in unison. Then Vanarra and Sahnassa stepped forward, linking their paws within the orb of shining light, then ghostly Sahnassa and Vanarra did the same, then Tana and her crystalline opposite, and finally the creatures of light and fire reached together touching off a light which blinded every creature there and paralyzed some of them with the immense power, the sense of life and presence which was inconceivably existent in the moment, life-changing in a way that could have never been expected nor could ever be described.

Jayanar's mind was filled with light and love and peace and belonging and hope until he could experience nothing else. It held him as he felt something completing in front of him, a sense that every worry was gone and every hope realized and solidified as inalienable, incontrovertible fact. It was a moment of profound truth and honor and reverence. For what seemed like intervals, he didn't breathe, but he didn't die – there was no pain, only life.

Finally, as if something had realized that it must control the reach of its influence, the tide of power which had overwhelmed was gathered, purposefully gathered, back towards the area in front of them all. Jayanar's head tipped forward, and he nearly bumped the barrier in front of him. Tasha, as deeply influenced by what had happened, actually sagged forward slowly and rested her head on it, panting. "By the Creator," Ash croaked from nearby. "What ... was that?"

"Vanassa," Theo told them, smiling a very pleased and proud smile. Looking forward, he told them, "Hearken to the sol of Vanassa, greet her with kindness and love, and give thanks to the Creator of all that such as we are allowed to behold this."

Jayanar struggled to look into the still shining core which had become a golden, sparkling ellipse of light. Finally, it started to fade just enough so that he could make out fore paws stretched apart as if trying to gather and constrain this mass of energy which had broadcast itself during the joining. Indeed, he thought he could perceive a sparkling wave front which was speeding away from them which had been part of the event.

When his eyes flashed back to the figure in the middle, he smiled. She was beautiful, and she was indefinably "her", the one he loved and followed, the one who had taken the place of every other fallible leader in his life, before. She was dressed in beautiful robes which flowed with energy and light, and her eyes seemed to glow with light of their very own. The two walkways which had led to the center, he noted, were also gone, and only one remained which was directed straight to them.

Theo nodded at the shining individual before him, and with enormous deference and honor, Vanassa bowed to him on one knee. Letting go of the paws around him, he made a motion and caused the barrier in front of them to separate, opening the way for this marvelous creature to join them. When she saw the way was opened and saw Theo nod permission, she almost ran to get to them, those she loved. As she approached, Theo stated, "Ash and Shenaria, you are first. Others follow as you wish!"

Biting her lip a little, Shenaria patted Trax and then took Ash's paw. When she saw her mother and Ash gathered to meet her, all pretense of restraint went away, and the excited and jubilant Vanassa simply crossed the distance in an instant, reappearing as if having sprinted between her mate and her mother. "Oh, I love you both so much!" Vanassa breathed.

"You did it, love! You did it!" Ash cried, holding her.

"Oh, my daughter," Shenaria crooned. "Oh, I love you so much. Now tell me, are you alright? Do you feel … whole? I remember all of those other times-"

"I am perfectly whole, Mother," Vanassa effused. "I can just tell it. This was my time, my time to become! It was just perfect!" Leaning up from her mother and Ash and looking at everyone around her, she breathed out, "You made it that way for me! I felt all of you here! I was, for a few moments, a part of all of you! All of you are part of me! My … my mother, my mate, my friends, my-" and she looked at Jayanar, Tasha, and Vosh. "My son, my daughters." Jayanar couldn't help himself at that moment, he was crying with joy as he stood there, and Tasha was no better. Then, her eyes tracked to Theo. "Me Sha, my father," Vanassa almost wailed. "Oh, thank you, Me Sha! Thank you! I can see so many amazing things, and I see you so much more clearly than I ever have! You are a wonder, my father!"

"You are a wonder, my daughter," he said, coming towards her. Gently, he took Vanassa in his arms and hugged her, but her eyes were wide with happiness and excitement. "You know now the plans I had for you oh so long ago, and how much I care for you."

"I am so grateful, Father! I'm … I'm so grateful!"

"And excited!" Amyra observed, placing herself next in line. "Wow, my former matron, you are something!"

"I'd say!" Rahnahi agreed. "But you've got a lot of training to do!"

"Oh, I know! I know! There's so much I don't know. I mean, I'm barely holding myself in this body!"

"Is that a problem?" Trax asked Theo, softly.

"No, she's stretching her situation a little. She's got a good margin. She's okay."

"There's so much more though!"

"There is, my dear friend," a beautiful and delicate Nephti added.

"Merialla! Yes! Oh, thank you! I know!"

"But you will learn. I know you," the Nephti told her.

"And we will endeavor to teach you, powerful one," a Nephti dressed in elegant yet primitive looking clothes told her.

"Alahari! Oh, yes, I know! I can't wait!"

"My Noble Shade no longer," Kallain noted, coming forward, and Vanassa bit her lip, smiling. "Now, you are our Noble Light, the fire that warms us and the love that lights our way."

"Thank you, Kallain and Melissiana; thank you for sharing this with me!"

The thanks continued for several passes until she had finished and looked towards the rear of the observatory, Caloizar and Kylie walking forward to meet her. "We are ready to serve you, Teldear," Caloizar stated.

"Not only that! Your ship awaits the pleasure of her naming, Teldear," Kylie told her.

"Did it work? Is the ship okay? Everything worked, right?" Vanassa asked.

"It did," Caloizar assured her. "The core is fully powered and self-sustaining. All systems are on-line and ready. It ... only needs a name..."

"The *Vattaria*," she stated, looking at her mother for approval. "A remembrance and an offering of gratitude for those who gave me life."

"Are ... are you sure, love?" Shenaria asked, her blush fur riding high. "Not something to remember Sahnassa's parents or Tana's or..."

"I am of one mind about this," Vanassa told her, "with no reservations and no regrets. All I ask is for your approval."

"You have it, my love, and thank you," Shenaria replied, and at that moment, the ship around them noticeably came to life, thrumming and humming in a clearly ready state. "Oh, my!"

Caloizar nodded. "Activation codes accepted, ship now at one hundred percent readiness on all flight modes, across all systems."

Nodding her thanks to them, Vanassa then looked to Theo. "Orders, Father?"

"Please direct our course to Thuriana, if you will. I believe there are more than a pawful of locations there that would make a good base of operations for you and a shelter for your ship when she's not out doing things. In fact, I think some old friends of yours may have actually made provision for such."

"Training and systems familiarization," Rahnahi observed, "sounds like a good idea to me. After all, some of us just sort of woke up to this new reality." Her gaze was in Jayanar's direction, but she wasn't being unkind. "Some of us might need a little time to walk around and get acquainted with what living in this way actually means."

As, an interval later, Jayanar stood alone in an observation dome at the opposite end of the ship, he knew Rahnahi was correct. The others had congregated together, swapping stories, and Kylie had subtly offered him a way out by suggesting that he explore the ship. "Don't worry. I'll give you space and make sure you don't end up in a weapons chamber or something."

True to her word, he had wandered through the ship and found many different places, including the bridge, and had an introduction to Caloizar, someone he felt an immediate kinship to. Caloizar, after speaking with him for a while, suggested this very observation dome, one that looked out upon the massive expanse the Vattaria was traversing. He could see a galaxy coming closer and closer to him, and it was just utterly compelling to watch. What's more, it made him feel very small against everything that was happening.

He had been gratified when Vanassa had called him her son, and he had felt her love for him. Still, looking into that incredible face was just that, looking into a *different* face. He had seen and felt the joining, and he knew who Vanalla had been, but maybe even more than before, he missed Vanalla. He was a Vulpi, Vanalla a Faelnar, and there was just the hint and echo of what must have initially drawn some of their number into de Caterra service so long ago. When she spoke to him, her whole being was present in that moment, and loyalty and trust were always present. Now, as the galaxy loomed large in front of him, nearly filling his field of view, his doubts and worries grew as well.

"I noticed you were missing," a female voice said, the specific voice he was pining for. He didn't turn around but rather continued looking out at the scenery as the individual bearing that voice approached and stood beside him. They were both silent for a moment as the Vattaria soared above the galactic disk, uncountable stars passing beneath them. "Quite the perspective," she offered. "It … is a good reset for me. I've thought so much of this moment and how big it would be, how grand, imagined all of the individuals who would be here with me."

"Was it not what you had hoped?" he asked, still not looking at her.

"It wasn't what I had seen," she admitted. "Saletta wasn't there – she and Nyssia are getting on so well now they are barely separable and busy very far away. Dynaea is, well, she's breaking in a new Teldear for Thuria. Lyshantor is keeping an eye on Thuriana, so I'll get to see him soon. I saw him ascend, actually. I … thought he'd be there for me, too. Vassia and Laxar are actually waiting for us where we're going, which is okay I suppose. Some other friends, too, from my time away, Almar and Trillias. In the end, my vision of this future wasn't perfect. Still, every one of you here helped shape the moment, and in the end, it was complete, and it was beautiful, and everything went according to plan."

He then turned and looked at her, his eyes widening a bit as he saw Vanalla, the Faelnar, looking out into the stars. "And now?"

"Well, I don't know. This is the part of my history after which I don't know what will happen. This is a real and true future, a one that is on the other side of my predestined moment. I felt so good about what we did in Attoria, and I knew we were doing well. I knew that things for me were moving forward and that my life on Thuriana and my life on Thuria were ending in such a way that I could be whole, I could be complete. So, we are in the space of time where ... I don't know. I'm trying to figure myself out a bit; I've had little previews of what I would feel, what things would be like moment to moment, but this is different. It's different to live that out."

"And so, you are ... uncertain? Did you switch back because you were uncertain?"

"I chose this form because, I think for both of us, it gives us comfort when we talk. I need that, Jayanar. I do. Of anyone, you have known me the least amount of time, and you have known about who I really was not long at all, a few intervals from your perspective."

"Why didn't you tell me?" he asked her, seriously.

"Tell you? What would I have done? Shown you this form?" She changed into the form of Vanarra de Gonari. "Or this one?" She changed into Sahnassa. "Or this one?" Then, she changed into Tana before, after a few ticks, changing back into the Faelnar version. "Our relationship was something special I didn't get from anyone else. You never knew me as anything other than *Vanalla*, the Faelnar, and with you, there was no history and no expectations. You judged me by what you saw me do."

"Which you, though?"

"See, you think Vanalla was a forgery, don't you? You think she was only the mask I used."

"Wasn't she?" he asked, the real source of his worry and concern coming to the surface.

"When you met me, Jayanar, you met Vanassa. Do you know how I know that? You never thought of me as one of the heroes of the Meeting Den or the Most Honored of all Matriarchs or any of that, and you didn't come with any of the *worshipful* filters like the Vanarrans came to me with. We just met because of random chance, but with every interaction, we came closer together, learned one another, trusted one another. I never *had* to show a different self to you. I never *had* to prove anything to you other than being an individual you relied upon and followed and ... loved. Like family, you loved me. From that first sol forward, Jayanar, you met *me*. Callanar is, like you, someone who met me that way and only ever knew *me*. He was my aide, but he was raised Vanarran; you weren't.

Yet, you … chose to be my son! My first ties in and of myself – this self – started in Attoria, and you are my truest one. You mean a lot to me, please know that. When you and I met, I was far less Vanarra or Sahnassa or anyone else than I was Vanassa."

"Can you show me your new self?"

Vanalla nodded, and again, she changed into the mix between Vanarra and Sahnassa. "And so?" she asked.

He looked at her a long while, studying her. Finally, he told her, "You're right. You are very much here, aren't you? I've watched VidStar of Vanarra de Gonari and Sahnassa. It isn't you. You are different, but you are still the one I've known, I think."

"It feels that way. I don't feel any different about you than when I was talking to you during that mission – you remember?"

He nodded. "It felt like we had some little pet whizzing back and forth between us taking messages, at least I imagined it did, but that mission made me realize that if there was ever anything hard that needed doing, tough choices that had to be made, you were the one I wanted to help make those choices, take orders from. I knew you treated all life seriously, with care, and you treated me that way when we first met. I didn't deserve it, no, but you did anyway."

"And so, my son," Vanassa asked him softly, "I need you now, too. I need your help, and I need someone who can't and won't point back to the ones I was and will accept the one I now am. Theo has told me that there is still great work that has to be done, not only on Thuria and Thuriana but many places. Will you stay with me and help me, please?"

"Is Tasha staying?"

"She told me that she would abide by your decision and give you time if you needed it somewhere else."

"I don't need any time other than what I'm spending with you, Ash, Tasha, and everyone else," he assured her, taking her paw. "Whatever help I can be to you, I will. You and I helped foster the hope of Attoria. I'm sure there are other places that need the same thing."

"There are," she said, looking out the window at a planet not unlike Thuria save for its different continents and shorelines.

"Thuriana, our new home base. Where we learn. We'll be settling right there off of the eastern shore of that continent, Altia."

"Like our ocean, but reversed?"

"Yes. Not for every continent, but for many of them; some are named for the oceans or rivers of Thuria."

"What are the cities named for?"

"Many different things. Our base will be in the mountains overlooking a valley, and we'll have the city of Dania below us."

"Dania?"

"Yes, a dame of de Dothnar, back in Rahnahi's time. One of her most trusted and able Honored Dames." She looked at him and held his paws in hers. "Thank you, Jayanar, my son."

"You are welcome, Mother. What does Theo think about me staying with you? He said something about wanting to have me help."

"He does, but he knows we'll need time first. I think that he'll want us to work on a few projects, do some training. Knowing Theo, all of that will fit together somehow. He appreciates you, and he knows I do as well. Vosh, also. My, your sister has some very neat secrets of her own, but I'll let her share those with you."

"I look forward to it. Thank you, Vanassa, my mother, for all you've done for me."

She reached around and hugged him, and he felt the warmth and love coming from her in a way that lit him up inside. Lifting his head, he happened to catch sight of his mate, Ash, and Vosh, standing at the door crying happy tears. "A bright new life, now, for all of us."

The End

Epilogue

Major Tagashar de Kyvara stepped up to the platform to speak before a worldwide broadcast, his seven companions suited up in the same gear as he. Looking out at the expectant crowd, he began his short farewell speech. "Fifteen hundred seasons ago, the village of Attoria was founded as a place for those who some believed deserved no second chance to find a new home. It was a frightening and difficult time, but that time changed Thuria, forever. We learned that the forgiveness we withhold does us more harm than it could ever do those we won't forgive. We learned that … when we do forgive, amazing things can happen."

"We, together, have spent the time since then finding new ways to live and work, and joining paw in paw over the seasons, we have placed outposts for our kind on both of our moons as well as our nearest sister planet. These were our first steps, and they were tentative. We had challenges, set-backs, and disasters, but we recovered. We learned from our mistakes, and we built better. Now, we leave on a new adventure, the adventure of a lifetime – the adventure of all of our lifetimes. We have sent our first faster than light probes to the Vagross Three system in the Fanassaragatti cluster, and after the three-season round-trip journey with their mark one engines, they have returned to us with images of a lush, new world waiting for us to discover and, perhaps, to one sol call our new home. This world we hope to name … Attoria."

"Now, aboard our newest and most advanced vessel, the Hope of Attoria, the eight of us hope to serve by bringing you news of that world in only three … short … moons. Speaking as an Aelkinda, I'm honored in so many ways to be here with those of mixed blood, Lupar,

Perratti, Pantera, Vulpi, Faelnar, and Nephti – a true representation of our world, our hopes, our struggles, and dreams. And so, this sol we set out on a brave new journey of exploration and discovery. We do so with gratitude to all of those who participate with us in this endeavor, and all of the ones who came before. May the Creator's love and protection always be with you, and farewell."

He waved as the crowd around him cheered, and then watched as his fellow space travelers walked down the gangway to the transportation waiting to lead them to the rocket.

The Nephti female responsible for planetary analysis didn't let more than a tick of time go by after the door was closed to turn to Tagashar and sigh, "Oh, you truly brought a tear to my eye, Major! I felt *so very* proud!"

"Geesh, Talla," he groaned. "I did the best I could. They rewrote that damned speech ten times and every time it stunk more than the last. How about this for a speech – you build a ship, we plan to use it, if everything works out, you'll hear from us in three moons. Don't let anyone repossess my lair in the meantime, right?" The entire crew chuckled and nodded.

The Vulpi of their number, Connal, added, "Yeah, I listened real close to that speech, also, and I could hear the doctoring – all the right political muzzle-buzzing and a bit of rubbing the oppositions' collective muzzles in the dung pile for yanking their funding from the deep oceans project for this one."

"Hey, we find a new planet they can live on, they can have two planets' worth of oceans to explore and build huts on the bottom of!" the Faelnar, Grazzar, added.

"Well, I'm voting for this effort; that's why I'm on it," the major offered, shaking his head. "Can't do everything, have to pick. Hey, Talla, any word from the cracked skull of a scientist about the signals he's been detecting?"

"Not much," she told him. "The truth is … I've looked at his data. What he has concerning the Vagross Three isn't completely conclusive as far as what the probes recorded."

"Okay, it's not *conclusive,* but is it … compelling?" Booch, the Perratti of their group asked. He was a young archeologist who had double-majored in archival skills. It was his job to help search the planet for ruins or other signs of artificial structures.

"Hard to say," Talla confessed. "Small blips that repeat every so often on certain frequencies. They seem aligned to the planet's rotation with a few variances, but still, it's pretty weak. I won't rule anything out, though."

"Every image of the trees, the canopy, the deserts shows absolutely nothing at all," Meriasta, their Pantera crew member, told them. "I've been over that survey two thousand times or more, and I know our new Attoria like the inside of my own paw, better even. There's nothing there! It's empty! There is only plant life. There are no signs of animals whatsoever, not even insects."

"It could be anything, from intersecting electromagnetic fields, piezoelectric crystals that are under stress during the planetary cycle, anything," Talla told them. "The short story is that we won't know until we're there. The probes weren't even built to search those frequencies – just picked up what we did find on a side band."

"Then we go," the major told her. "Cussar, is the ship ready?"

The young Lupar down the way answered, "Hope's in good shape. Got the goods on her this morning after the techs finished up. She's all locked in and fueled up. The run back and forth to the edge of the solar system showed no problems whatsoever. Our sexy little kit is ready to run!"

Booch shook his head, looking at the pilot with disgust. "You speak about our ship as if she is your own private hunt, Cussar."

"Hey, I'm not the one who gets all familiar with her. I just tell her where to go; it's Nallax who gets his paws dirty."

"What of it, Nallax? Your report tally with lover-cub's here?" Tagashar asked.

"Every system checks out, and our back-up stores are exactly where they need to be. We could almost build a second ship out of what we're carrying!"

"Yeah, hope we don't have to do that," Meriasta offered. "I just sorta got promised to be joined, so…"

"Well, then you're dead," Cussar told her, deadpan. Her surprise and horror just made him wave his paw in the air. "It's how it always is in all of the space fiction you read. You want to survive, you have to be the likeable rogue, not the tragic love just promised to be joined. There's a term for those characters in the books – dead meat."

"I'm … I'm going to be sick, and then I'm going to kill you, Cussar," the Pantera offered, looking truly unnerved.

"Stow that; we've got a crap load of work to do, and we are not going to do any of it on our own. We stay together. We're only orbital this time – bring samples back to Fireclaw station, take pictures of ourselves with the planet in the background. Come back, write books, get joined, and if everything works out, maybe go again in a season or two or three."

Cussar was undeterred. "Yeah, that sounds alright and all, but I'm planning on meeting aliens."

"I said," Meriasta replied stridently, "there isn't so much as a *bug* on planet Attoria. You can be sure that if we get there, Cussar, *you* will be the most alien thing there … just like you are here, right now."

"Doublecheck your heat shield, flyer-cub!" Connal quipped. "I see scorch marks!" Everyone but the Lupar pilot had a good laugh at his expense.

Intervals later, Major Tagashar sat to the right just behind Cussar, Connal sitting to his left. The orbital shot had gone off without a problem as had the docking with the Hope of Attoria. After the traditional "adjustment" period to weightlessness, they had all regained their equilibrium and were ready for their trip to begin. "Nallax, you ready yet?" Cussar asked, pressing the intercom.

"Everything is set, and I checked it twice."

"Damned, he's fast," Cussar breathed before he shot back, "I show all good on the panels up here, and so I think that means we can leave, right?"

"Ask the boss," Nallax answered. "I can only tell you the motor is running."

"What of it, Major?" the Lupar asked. "We good?"

"We certainly are. Connal, call it in and keep it simple. We've done enough speeches this sol."

"Seconded," the Vulpi agreed, pressing the communications switch. "Base Station Fireclaw, the Hope of Attoria is now underway. Reports back on the interval until we reach the solar system barrier."

"We read you Hope; everyone here wishes you all success, but foremost, we look forward to having you back."

"See you soon. Hope of Attoria, out." They watched as the brilliant orb which had been their home began to recede, growing smaller and smaller as the Hope's engines lifted her smoothly away from Thuria's gravity well.

Tagashar looked at both of his companions in the control bridge. "Good job you two. Let's make sure we do the job right and make sure all of us return home."

"Hey, look at us, we're back with plants and rocks and pictures," Cussar sighed. "Big deal."

"I thought you said this was a big deal, cub," Connal chided. "At least you did to the kits on our last night out."

"It is, but ... the real glory run will be for the first Thurian to set hind paw down on another planet. That ... Thurian is going to be a legend. Damned shame it won't be us."

"Not sure I want to be a legend," the major chuckled. "Tales from my past say that might not end well."

"Fair point," Cussar agreed. "Alright, we've got about one interval until contact. I'll watch the speed and the like. Might want to check with Nallax and make sure we're ready for trans-light once we get out of the shoals and into the open ocean."

"With your permission, Major?" Connal asked, and the major nodded. The Vulpi then unstrapped and pushed off towards the back of the control bridge.

A moon and a half later, the blue flashing light called all of the crew back to their positions to strap in as the Hope would be decelerating to sub-light as it approached the edge of the Vagross Three system. "You've got twenty ticks," Cussar told them over the intercom. "Not like I can stretch this out."

"I'm in," each one of them called back, and by his status board, Major Tagashar could soon confirm that everyone was properly strapped in with ten ticks to spare. "You're good, Cussar. Put on the brakes."

With a few quick switches, the morass of shifting light ahead of them settled into the darkness of the edge of the Vagross solar system, the star burning away, small and bright in the distant center. "Back to sub-light, Major, no problems."

"Nallax, confirm please."

"Same thing, Major, all good here. Hope seems to be in good shape; we seemed to get nudged a bit coming out by something. I'll keep an eye on it. All panels show good right now."

"Damn," a female voice said over the intercom. They all recognized it as Meriasta.

"Something you'd like to share with the rest of us?" the major asked as Cussar started setting the course for Attoria.

"You know those ... piezoelectric broadcasts, weird signals from here that we heard on Thuria and in the telemetry of those three season probes?"

"Yes, Meriasta."

"Listen to this," the Pantera, her voice breaking at the end, told them before switching the TransCom frequency receiver into their intercom. A high frequency and very regular series of pulses, not all of the same length, played through the speaker.

"Regular, steady," Connal noted, and after a moment added, "Repeating?"

"I think so. There are minor ... variations, but there seems to be some pattern to it," Meriasta told them. "And, Major, its source is ahead of us. I think it is coming from Attoria."

"We've got a good three intervals to get there. Talla, Connal, Booch, and Meriasta, see if you can make sense of it. See if there's any chance it's naturally occurring, like a reflected pulsar emission or something."

"Yes, sir," Meriasta said, nervously.

"Gonna be bug aliens, I'm sure of it," Cussar told her. "The brain sucking kind."

"By the Creator, Cussar – you are the living end!" she swore.

"That's my aim," he told her, smugly.

Three intervals later, the crew was again strapped into their seats as the blue green orb of Attoria loomed large in front of them.

"Signal's stronger," Connal observed as the now tense crew waited for the Hope to settle into her orbit around their target planet. They were approaching the lit side of the planet, and although the last three intervals of analyzing the pulsing transmissions and looking through their high-power telescopes hadn't given them any new information, the signal dominated all of their thoughts. Tagashar knew his crew was on edge, anxious – Meriasta to the point where he considered sedating her. She had held it together just well enough and had promised to, no matter what.

"Meri," he asked gently, "can you see any differences on the surface now that we're close in?"

"Nu … nothing, Sir. All … all nominal. Again, no signs of animal life."

"Bitching storm down there," Cussar noted as they approached the terminator into night. Roiling lightning storms were lighting up the clouds in an amazing and exceedingly active display.

"It's beautiful," Talla breathed. "Just like the storms on Thuria. Did you ever see the polar lights, Meri?"

"I'm not looking there, kit," she confessed over the intercom.

Just as the terminator slipped beneath them, Connal asked, "Cus, you see that? The … area where there aren't…"

"Yeah, no stars," the pilot said softly.

"Meri, triangulate that signal again. Give me an exact range and bearing."

There was a brief pause before she answered, "It is in … orbit with us, ahead of us."

"But that's freaking huge!" Cussar told her. "And … what the mange?!" Now in the total dark of Attoria's night side, the shape in front of them began to take on depth and, what's more, started to show lights across its surface. "Is … that…"

"It's not natural. An artificial satellite of some kind," Tagashar noted, his heart quickening.

"Damned big," Connal noted. "About one course across and about a quarter course high."

"Hard to judge closing rates, visually, and I'm not getting a damned thing on the rangefinder."

"Major," Talla told them. "I've computed the pulse width and frequency in relation to its source. It ... they are giving us the distance. We're at about seven point six courses away." A few ticks later, she added, "Make that seven point five." A few ticks later, she said, "Seven point four. We're closing on it."

"It shouldn't be able to stay in our orbit like that," Cussar stated, confused. "It's not going fast enough."

"Yeah, well maybe your space aliens know a trick or two we don't," Connal warned. "Major, we have enough time to break orbit if we want."

"Yeah, not that it couldn't follow us if it ... what's that light in its center?" Tagashar asked.

"There was a brief increase in the distance, but we're closing again. If its rate of approach didn't change, I ... think we're now getting the broadcast from inside the station."

"Station?" Meriasta asked, her voice trembling.

"I don't know what else to call it," Talla told her.

"Still time to break away, sir, if we want to," Cussar said over his shoulder, looking at the Major, anxiously.

Thinking furiously, the Aelkinda commander came to a few conclusions. "Try some basic maneuvering, Cussar – make sure we're still in control."

The ship tilted left and right, rolled gently, and then seemed to slow a moment before picking up speed again. "I have it all, Major. No sign at all that we couldn't get out of here if we wanted to."

"No. They are here. We are here. They've given us the chance to escape but opened the door. Connal, broadcast transmission to them asking for permission to land."

Keying the transmitter, Connal stated, trying to keep his voice from wavering, "This is the Thurian ship Hope of Attoria to the vessel in orbit with us. We request permission to land."

"Any response?" the Major asked, and Connal shook his head.

"Look, sir. I'm thinking the answer is yes." They looked, and the interior of the station ahead, the black hole in its side, had grown lighter, a shade of dark purple and blue, and bright yellow tracer lights moved in ribbons from outside of the hole leading into it.

"Oh, Creator, please ... no," Meriasta breathed into her chest, a tear floating out of her eye and hovering right in front of her.

Talla reached in, pulling it away, and put her paw on the Pantera's shaking paw. "Hold it together, Meri. We're here with you."

"Connal," the Major stated, "notify them that we are following their direction and beginning to land."

After the message had been sent, the station loomed larger and larger in front of them. "Hey, the lights changed – brighter on the top set," Connal noted.

"Crap, I think I drifted," Cussar stated. "Correcting. Talla, I'm having a hard time orienting things up here. Was I low?"

"Yeah, you drifted lower. Aspect changed. It's back again where it was."

"Keep an eye on it, Talla," the Major told her. "Looks like they're helping, but we should check, too."

"Roger that, sir."

As they approached, the lights inside of the landing bay slowly grew in intensity. "Looks like they want us to put down ... over there," Cussar noted. "Whoa!" he said as he felt the ship sinking.

"What happened?"

"Increasing thrusters to maintain elevation. I ... I think we hit some kind of light gravity. If that's so, then I think we should do this with the skids."

"Go ahead. Deploy them. I presume they'll let us... is that one of their crew?" Tagashar asked.

Looking ahead, the three figures in the control bridge saw what appeared to be a creature that walked on four hind legs and had two front appendages. Each of those was holding a signal light. By its movements, it was simply and calmly moving to the location where a landing guide would normally stand. As Cussar started to bring the Hope closer in, the gravity pulling them down seemed to increase.

Their guide started spinning the two lights in a pattern that was vigorous and very clear, especially to the pilot. "Yeah, no shit, Bucky – more thrust! Damn, I feel heavy."

"What's the gravity reading, Talla?"

"Only one quarter; it was building, but it's tapered off."

"Just enough to land," Connal noted, now starting to be more curious than anxious.

"Okay, Bucky's happy now," Cussar observed as the spinning pattern was replaced by movements inviting him forward. "Kind of looks like a purplish bug-"

"Please, Creator no!" Meriasta blurted.

"He seems to be a nice bug," Connal observed. "A little left. Bucky's a bit of a perfectionist, it seems."

"Yeah, well he wasn't wrong. Our aft was starting to drift a bit. Hey, something's wrong back there."

"Nallax!" Tagashar ordered, "give me a status – aft thruster, port quarter!"

"Loss of power, sir. It's failing, overheating!"

"Bucky's seen it," Cussar stated. "Here come a couple of helpers … and the fire crew. Aw mange, that isn't good."

"Is there a fire?"

"Shutting it down. She's burning up! Something very wrong here. I'm checking," Nallax told him.

"I can't stop the spin with what we've got left – it took down the whole freaking set. Hey, what are you saying now?" Cussar asked, his eyes on the landing guide who was now off to his left. The motions took a moment to interpret. "Okay, I got it! I got it, Bucky! Nallax, kill all positional thrusters, shut them off! Just keep our downward thrust."

"Shutting down! Fire suppression systems were successful, but we've lost aft quarter positional and control of all the rest. Like … completely! Crap!"

"Hey, what are those guys up to?" Cussar asked when he noticed two more of the bug like creatures taking position on either side of the craft. Just then, two beams of light hit the hull creating a soft rumble, and their rotating motion slowed. "Well, damn, fella!"

"Hold tight, you," Tagashar encouraged as he saw the bug like creature digging in as he tried to arrest the Hope's spin. The three of them watched as the creature lost his grip on the deck, was pushed back, but then gripped with his hind legs onto a metal bar running along the side of the landing area. They could all tell from the tension in the body of the creature that it was striving hard, and they were gratified as the rotating motion of the ship finally came to a halt.

"Damn, I think we owe him a case," Cussar said, nodding to their benefactor as the ship was slowly rotated back to center up on the lead controller, the downward thrusters still keeping the ship aloft. When they gently drifted back into a correct orientation, the lead controller nodded and gently lowered his signals. "You got it, Bucky. Damn good save, cub."

"How do you know it's a male?" the Vulpi asked.

"Ain't got no boobs," Cussar commented, and the Major couldn't fault his argument. The ship gently settled into position and came to rest, the controller indicating to shut down, which Cussar did at the Major's nod. The creature then held its signals in a what appeared to be a halting or warding gesture, and soon, they understood why as they were all pulled back down into their seats with greater force.

Gritting her teeth, Talla called out, "Three … three quarters gravity, Sir! I … I think they're trying to acclimate us to the station norm."

Nallax called out to them. "More of them, approaching … approaching the aft quarter. Looks … fire crew? Maybe?"

"Get us a view," Tagashar almost grunted, and Connal managed to reach over and flick on the external cameras. There were six of the creatures now, two of them somehow attached to the hull and apparently communicating with the lead controller who had walked around to that side of their vessel. There was what appeared to be a conversation between the creatures before some loud creaking and shrieking seemed to echo through the ship.

Nallax explained it. "They've cooled the damaged systems; looks like … maybe the fuel is gone, too. The … creature is coming forward."

They watched on the camera as one of the creatures started making his way up the hull, passing right over Meriasta's window causing her to scream. The creature stopped, looked down at her, and seemed confused. Talla looked up at him and waved hello, nodding.

The creature did the same in return. "See, Meriasta, it doesn't seem to want to harm us. Wave, okay?"

Terrified, the Pantera waved. The creature looked at her, still confused, and then took a device out of what appeared to be a back-pack. After studying her for a moment, it pulled the rod apart it had removed which seemed to leave some kind of display surface between the halves. Working quickly with one of its grapplers, it made movements back and forth on the palette."

"What do you think it's doing, Talla?" Meriasta asked, still terrified by this never before seen form of life in front of her.

"I ... I don't know, but, well now!"

"Oh, well, yes ... it's lovely!"

"What did it do?" the Major asked, still straining.

"It ... it sketched me, Sir. Kind of nicely done. I sketch a little. Let me ... let me see," she said, and she pulled out a data pad from beside her. The Pantera worked quickly and in less than a pass turned her viewer to face the creature. It leaned closer in surprise, and by its movements, it was clearly excited. It then waved at her, and she returned the gesture, but then it continued along the hull. "Sir, I ... I think these are ... friendly."

"How do you know that?"

Booch spoke up, "They just art-ed at each other, sketched one another."

"I see you, and you see me," Meriasta stated softly. "I'm an individual, and I see you as one, as well. I ... delight in the fact that you see that. That's what it meant!"

"Major," Connal called as the creature appeared outside of the starboard window. Looking in, he waved, and they waved back. Then, the creature took his rod back out and split it, providing them with a viewer. They saw the sketch, but that was soon replaced by an image of the area of the port aft thruster assembly with flashing areas showing the damage. The Major nodded, and the image changed to a diagram showing that the fuel had been removed and special packing had been added around the damaged components as another safety measure. Then, it showed the Hope moving through space and a high energy particle striking them from behind, deflected into their path.

"It's their guess at what happened," Cussar replied, nodding at the creature. The creature repeated the motion once and then displayed another image. This one took a moment to understand, but soon it showed that these individuals knew exactly how many of them were aboard and where they were. It showed a bar slowly lowering, but then flickered to an image of the bar hitting the bottom of the image, and then the individuals on the Hope getting up out of their seats and making their way to the flight controller ahead of them. The creature then pointed at a spot on the wall where the same type of bar was lowering.

"Attention, crew. It looks like they want us to wait here and acclimate to the gravity. They are showing us being able to leave the ship – if I had to guess, in about half an interval."

"Sir, aft cameras show the doors closed behind us," Nallax told them.

"Yeah, and I've got air outside, our pressure and composition," Talla offered before looking up and smiling. "Meri, your friend is back."

They both watched as the creature seemed to sit down on the hull, pull out his "easel" and begin to draw. Feeling a strange kinship to this extremely odd creature, she started drawing in more detail, coloring in the milky blue coloring in its eyes, the purple of the hinges of its four-jawed mouth, and the nearly pink segments of its antennae and mandibles. "It's a very … fierce and primal-looking creature in its own way," she commented, "the bladelike spikes on its face and spikes along the backs of its arms and legs, but those eyes … oh, you can just get lost in them."

"Doesn't look quite *exactly* like an insect," Booch stated.

"The body sort of does," Grazzer noted. "Kind of … suggests the segmentation you see in insect bodies, but it's like their development just took a different turn. This one on the other side of the ship seems to be having a bit of a coaching session with the one who had port duty on our spin. Probably didn't set the device properly, based on what I'm seeing."

"He did seem to strain a bit," Connal commented.

"And look over at Bucky," Cussar observed. "He's just standing on his platform working his damned antennas off, banging away. Mange, probably a crap load of paperwork every time some idiots like us show up … which reminds me." They watched as the pilot took out his flight procedure and started going through the shut down and stabilization procedure point by point. He was about halfway through the checklist when the controller's platform seemed to levitate over, allowing him to crawl up onto the hull.

"Hey, what's up, Bucky?" The creature seemed to indicate the book with the checklist in it, its head canted. "Oh, sure. Here. Take a look." He turned the book around to flip through the pages. After a few of them, the creature waved and then extracted his own display rod, pulling it apart. Turning it around, he showed an image of the Hope of Attoria with gases rushing out of certain release valves. Then flashing stripes crossed the sections, and the image showed the gas discharge stopping. "Oh, okay. Right. Got it! No kick-outs. Okay." The Lupar turned the book around so the controller could see, and then taking a pen, struck through certain steps on various pages. Pointing at the display once again caused the creature to wave and step off the hull back onto his platform. "Taking care of business, Bucky. Dammit; I like you."

The waiting that continued was a lot more pleasant as the crew was able to observe the creatures moving around doing normal duties, although admittedly some of the duties were extraordinary given their complexity or the strength required to do them. Near the end of the time, Meriasta was surprised when the creature gently tapped on the side of the hull and turned its image around for her to see. It was very stylized and showed an immense amount of artistry and insight. The Pantera smiled and nodded and then turned her own image towards the window for him to see. The creature's antenna stood on end, and he seemed to signal to his compatriots working in other parts of the bay, two of which crawled up on the side of the ship and looked in to appreciate the art as well, waving their thanks.

Cussar was just about through with his modified checklist when he saw Bucky take up the signal lights and get his attention. The creature indicated the bar which was at the last and final segment of its traverse. As they were both looking, it ended and disappeared. The creature motioned down towards the floor of the bay and then crawled right down the vertical surface to reach it.

"Okay, everyone. If you're able, I think we have someone new to meet." The crew acknowledged, and Meriasta had to stop her art show to obey the command, the creatures waving and then walking off the hull and springing onto the floor.

Soon, with the Major in the lead, the group of eight started making their way down the gangplank in the lower forward section of the ship, the creatures lined up, standing still, as the crew made their way down. Over the past half interval, they had all gotten used to seeing the strange creatures and were starting to feel and understand the character of each one. Bucky, as Cussar had named him, was standing apart from the others, clearly in command, waiting for them to join him.

"You okay, Meri?" Talla asked.

"Yeah, yeah, I'm … I'm okay, I'm just wondering which one of these was…" Her searching eyes caused the third one down to step forward slightly and raise one of its forward legs, what appeared to be arms to her. When she drew even to it, she raised her paw and very slowly moved it towards the grappler at the end of its arm. With the whole group watching, they gently touched and then slowly clasped one another. "How is it, Meri? You okay?"

"He's extremely strong, but … very gentle," she explained. They let go, and she bowed to him, and not only he, but the rest of his line did the same, mimicking her motion.

They continued walking down the path until they reached "Bucky." The Major slowly offered a salute to the creature who echoed the motion in return. Then, the creature went down the line to Cussar and put his grappler on the Vulpi's shoulder, and Cussar returned the gesture, patting him gently. "Thank you, bud, appreciate the assist."

The creature turned its head and whirred and clicked a response. A new presence in the bay said, "He says thank you, and you get credit for keeping your head in a touchy situation." They all turned to look at what appeared to be a mixed blood from their own planet, something between a Faelnar, a Nephti, and a Vulpi. She was beautiful, nearly radiant, and Major Tagashar was stunned. However, the whirring and clicking was continuing. "He also says you are the absolute calmest group he's ever had a first contact interaction with, and he's wondering if any of you would like a job."

Cussar spoke up and raised his paw. "Tell him I'll sure as mange sign on after my tour on this crate is up. His operation is really tight."

The creature then seemed to break out into nothing short of a full laugh, the other creatures poking one another and joining in the joke. "I ... don't understand," the Major said.

"Simple; they really like your pilot, and they thought his offer to join up was funny. See, they're really good listeners, excellent with spatial awareness and procedures, can work in low gravity and in a vacuum with no problem whatsoever, but Thurians do have a bit of difficulty in understanding them, at least at first."

"But they understand us?" he asked.

"Sure, they've been listening to me for quite a while."

"But ... are you a Thurian?"

"Ascended, but Thurian was how I started," the beautiful creature told them, her smile kind. "My name is Vanassa of the Allarrae. Welcome to Pathion Station, and welcome to one of the biggest discoveries in your history. Now, who we are and what we are about here, as well as what you want to talk about is something we can get to. However, that gear you are wearing looks heavy and uncomfortable, and we have good food and rest, inside. Also, Bucallar says that some kind of high energy particle intercepted your ship and burnt through your aft rear thruster and then created a pulse that weakened the orientation system. He's been working on a way to fix that plus he's got about sixteen structural recommendations based on micro-cracking he scanned. He'd just like someone to work with him on it."

"Major, with your permission, I'll work with Bucky." The Major just looked at Cussar. "Come on, you heard her – Bucallar. It shortens up to Bucky real nice."

"It does at that," Vanassa agreed, smiling. "I have no complaint, but I might see if I can't get you an earpiece so you can understand him. Just please don't let him get started on the war stories, okay? Now, if you'll follow him in, he'll show you where to change and where some refreshments are." The crew started following the six-legged creature down the walkway towards a hatch, but Tagashar stopped. "I ... I feel like we're doing this the wrong way – that we should somehow introduce ourselves and declare-"

"That you mean us no harm?" Vanassa asked him, crossing her arms and looking at him, amused, the Aelkinda ducking his head in a smile. "I already know, Major. Your ship has no offensive weaponry, period, and you're not carrying any weapons. The truth is that we already know who you are. There is not much sentient life in this part of the galaxy, and other than a few colonies we've planted, Thuria is kind of it. We've been keeping an eye on your civilization for a while now, monitoring your broadcasts. We monitored your in-system flights over the seasons and even your trans-light tests. We stationed a satellite about mid-range in your solar system just so we could listen in and relay everything here. We know your whole crew because we saw the news as you were all selected. We even listened to your farewell speech. Suffice it to say that we knew you were coming and were very glad of it."

"But," Cussar asked, "how did you know that we'd come inside and actually ... land?"

"Had not the foggiest," Vanassa admitted, her arms open while she smiled in good humor, "other than a little instinct, let's call it! However, we could have had this whole conversation over what you call TransCom, and then we'd still have invited you to come in. I mean, if necessary, we could have flown a ship out there and docked with you, but you chose the sensible route. You'll enjoy it here, I promise, and then, I think we will have a lot of interesting things to talk about. Now, come on. I promise there's a warm cup of Aster tree tea, roast grazer, and some well-seasoned tuber roots waiting for each of you."

"Hot damn, I'm in!" Cussar almost shouted. "No more eating our own-"

"Shh!" Meriasta cautioned. "Manners, Cussar, please!"

The Major chuckled and agreed, "It would be nicer fare than we've been enjoying. Alright then, Vanassa, we'll join you and ... thank you." Looking over to Bucallar, he asked, "They ... aren't ascended Thurians, right?"

"No, the Kynarra are from another galaxy, pretty far away; very adaptable – they worked out a way to colonize every solid planet or moon in an unclaimed system. I think you're going to find their scientific types real fascinating to talk to. They and many of the other kinds who are here have been looking forward to your arrival for some time. Now, follow him, and he'll make sure you are well taken care of." She clasped paws with each of them as they walked by, but what they couldn't detect was that when the Nephti took her turn, the clasp was just a bit stronger and longer than it was for anyone else.

It wasn't more than a few passes later until the crew was in separate rooms changing. Talla started to undo her suit when a pair of soft paws reached over to help her. "So very well done, kit! They calmed down very nicely. I'd say they are acclimating extremely well, *Teldear*."

Talla smiled upon hearing the voice aloud she had only heard in her mind for the last two moons. She turned and lost herself in the embrace of the one who had sought her out, trained her, and then given her the role of Teldear on Thuria. "Oh, precious kit," Vanassa sighed, holding the diminutive female Nephti close to her. "I've truly missed you, but I was so happy to make it back from Thuriana in time for this!" Vanassa held the Nephti back and looked at her, questioningly. "Hey, but what's with your crew? I don't recognize all of the faces you brought with you. Vassia and Laxar didn't mention any big changes to me."

"Well, there's three of them that I had to nudge onto the disabled list about four moons ago. Cussar, Nallax, and Meriasta are their replacements. Trust me, it was totally for the better; Vassia will back me up on this. If we had been stuck with those others, I would have suggested Pathion station just stay cloaked and not come out of hiding. They were battle hardened from the colonial moon disputes. Shoot first and say hello later..."

"Xenophobia is always a problem, to be sure, especially in an isolated species. There was a little of that with your Pantera, but I think fear is now becoming fascination. I can see our newly met artists will need to get better acquainted, as well. Cussar is itching to learn all about the Kynarra, and I think they share his sense of humor. The others will need to find some friends, too. Spending a few sols on the planet together might also help. I think we'll introduce some of the other species to them and see who makes a connection. They could spend the next half moon or so getting acquainted, taking pictures, getting proof, starting to figure out how they can look at colonizing Attoria. I'm sure your crew will truly appreciate that singular honor." Vanassa helped her put the heavy gear aside and offered her soft, comfortable clothing to wear.

"Oh, thank you! You bet, especially since the landing crew slated to come after us are a real piece of work – wrong sort entirely. This was the right crew, Nassa – right Thurians, right time; it wasn't a hard decision to make," Talla agreed as she quickly dressed. "If you could help us out with a message saying you'd like to see us back, that might help. It's a great crew, and if they are treated kindly and openly, they'll do really well, especially with the hardest piece of first contact."

Vanassa sighed and helped her student put on her top. "Yeah, taking first contact back to everyone else. I'll work out something and put just the right spin on it so it sticks. The Major is the only military you had; think he'll be a problem?"

"No, the Major isn't the suspicious type, and no one is really doing poorly on the trip, so far." Talla then looked up into the eyes of her leader, tears in her eyes. "Nassa, thank you for letting me do all of this. You're fulfilling a dream I had since I was a little kit, and what's more, we can finally do what we've dreamed about for centuries."

"Introduce ourselves to Thuria and help them achieve everything they are capable of," Vanassa agreed as she took the Nephti's paw in hers. "So many good friends put in so much work over the seasons to make this moment happen, and I'm happy and very proud that it is you, Talla, who shepherds them to meet us. You deserve the honor, and you've done a wonderful job."

"Only with your help," Talla told her. Walking over together, they looked out the window of the green and inviting surface of Attoria rolling beneath them. "Such a long trail getting here."

"It's a long history, isn't it? First, it was Me Sha who reached out to Thuria, then I helped with the rights of mixed bloods and later with the Aelkinda-"

"Well, it was ... the different you's actually, right?"

"I never think of it that way, anymore," Vanassa chuckled. "Everyone has a history – I just happen to have several! And now Talla, my dear and wonderful kit, you are guiding them into the age of the stars where they will begin to interact with ones not of their own world – taking the lessons from the past with mixed bloods and the Aelkinda out to the stars. Our kind have come of age, and now ready to begin the next great chapter of the Thurian saga!"

Abbreviated Thurian Reference

Thuria:

Thuria is the fourth planetary body in a sun-centered system of ten planets. Two moons rotate in slightly different orbits in perfect opposition to one another. Fifty-eight percent of the surface is water, with fairly uniform land masses in the temperate zones. While the poles of the planet are covered with ice, there are no land masses there. Each continent, to varying extents, has its mountains, rivers, lakes, and deserts, but much of the land is arable. While rich in minerals, Thuria lacks fossil fuels, so industrialization and technological advancement occurred slowly, over a long period of time.

Thurians:

Thurians are anthropoid mammals standing erect on two legs covered with thick hair or fur, and the color of fur varies. Most major species of Thurian have fur-covered tails of varying lengths. Ears, muzzles, and eyes are generally somewhat larger than those found in most sentient, bipedal species. Teeth and muzzle betray an omnivorous, but predatory ancestry. Front paws are four fingered with one being an opposable thumb. Claws are imbedded within the end of most species paw fingers, and the inside of the paw maintains a relatively thick paw-pad.

Life spans are long, at approximately 250 seasons (or orbits of Thuria around its sun), and birth rates are lower in compensation. However, this elongated life span allows for families to have nine or ten generations alive at one time. Thurians are social and very familial, with allegiance and membership to a family group passing generally through the male, unless the female is titled (member of the family matriarchy). As compensation, the familial leadership is nearly always female. Thurians are fertile by age 15 and generally lose fertility at around 90 seasons. Usually, mating produces one cub (male) or kit (female). Those terms apply regardless of species. Multiple births are not easily supported by Thurian biology. Families frequently will raise one child to full adulthood before beginning again.

Thurian Species:

Anati – (*"a-not-tea"*) any mixed-blood Thurian (derogatory term).

Faelnar – (*"fell-narr"*) Purebred species, generally of sleek to average build, with long, short-furred tails. Fur colors range from brown through golden to shades of yellow. Eye colors include gold, green, hazel, and yellow. Noses are black, brown, or yellow brown.

Lupar – (*"loo-parr"*) Purebred species. A large species (second only to the Pantera in size) with gray to brownish fur, with longer than average muzzles. Eye colors are gray to blue to green. Tails are long, straight or curved, and bushy. Fur color ranges from light gray to black and brown.

Nephti – (*"neff-tea"*) Purebred species, generally of average build. Tail fur is long and thick, forming a wide, long, and bushy tail. Fur colors from light gray to black into dark purple through light purple. Eye colors include silver, gray, and shades from deep blue through indigo and violet. Noses are black, pink, or mottled. Striping is prominent, in shades of white, silver, or grey.

Pantera – (*"pan-terr-uh"*) The largest of the purebred species on Thuria. Fur colors range from light gray to black, with no patterning except on the ear ridges (generally black). Tails are short-haired and only of moderate length. Their muzzle is thicker than most other species. Eye colors are blue through hazel to dark brown and gray. While not as sleek and quick as their Faelnar counterparts, they make up for it in muscle. Noses are usually pale pink to pale grey to black.

Perratti – (*"purr-rah-tea"*) Purebred species. The smallest of all Thurian breeds, on average, but sizes can approach average and sometimes exceed it. Tails are small and covered with short hair. Muzzles are long and almost box-shaped, with fur occasionally draping off the sides down the face and muzzle like an upside down "V". Fur color ranges between black, gray, brown, and tan. Noses are uniformly black. Eyes are silver, blue, hazel, or brown.

Vulpi – (*"vull-pea"*) Purebred species. Fur colors include white, orange-red, orange, red, and gray. Patterning is mostly limited to large variations on forearms, hind legs, muzzle, or tail. Eye colors are blue, green, silver, brown, and hazel. Tail fur is thick, forming a wide, long, and bushy tail.

House Matriarchal Leadership Hierarchy

Grand Matriarch or Matriarch

Honored Dames and Dames

Matrons

All other house members

Thurians Prominent in *Incarnation*
Those of no family house
Fireclaw Destiny – Mixed blood Primal sports star

Trax Lasser – Mixed blood resident of Shanandrae

Shenaria Anasto – Purebred mother of Vanarra de Gonar

Laxar – Former mixed blood acolyte of the Vanarrans

Of House de Orturu (species: Nephti)
Sahnassa (Sahni) – Former Grand Matriarch

Of House de Gonari (species: Faelnar)
Vanarra (Van) – Former Grand Matriarch and Teldear

Saletta –Vanarra's dear friend

Tana –Vanarra's friend and companion, now a Allarraen jewelstone

Kinness – Male mixed blood director of Shanandrae Commons hospital

Mishiph – Elder male, head of volunteer services at Shanandrae Commons

Drayash – Elder male, security guard for the Pinnacle Center Academy

Of House de Dothnar (species: Nephti)

Carinthia de Dothnar – Dame

Pathia de Dothnar – Dame

Coursia de Dothnar – Dame

Shalan de Dothnar – Grand Matriarch

Racea de Dothnar – Student at Dothnaria Academy

Ariasta de Dothnar – Student at Dothnaria Academy

Others:

Kallain de Mistral – Loyal Elite of the Sahnassites

Kylie de Kestrick – former female Vulpi fitness instructor, Sahnassa's friend

Vosh – An Allaraen Terspear space fighter

Temple Master Lashure – Vanarran leader in Shanandrae

Vanarran Select Vassia – Vanarran in charge of the breeding program

Javoth de Bosnar – Minister at the Creator's Path church in Shanandrae

Emmeniama (Emma) de Kestrick – Vulpi psychologist at Shanandrae Commons

Preview of *The Legacy of Aris*

Tarma waited impatiently for Almar's return as she had the difficult task of convincing the refugees from the city not to kill Salmar for threatening to expel them all. "He's the worst sort to act as a leader," she grumbled to herself. When she spotted Almar's swiftile appearing over the horizon, she sighed while thinking in his direction, "You had best be coming with good news on relieving this overcrowding. If you don't, all of these will likely murder one another solving the problem for us. Salmar is the worst possible choice you could have made to act in your stead as leader. We'd have been better off appointing a swiftile or a skitterer."

As she couldn't read him, she knew he couldn't answer her, and she quietly closed her mind to him shortly after offering one additional detail. "The scouts have confirmed Relitha is concentrating her purges in the city right now. She hasn't sent forces in this direction, yet."

When he finally arrived, he was bursting to finish the conversation she had started. "You just don't know how maddening it is to be able to hear your complaints and not be able to give you back as much as I'm getting! I just have to sit on the back of that beast and chew them raw the whole time."

She, satisfied, smirked and said, "Well, then you've had time to listen and ruminate over your choice which nearly cost me my life. That seems a fair punishment. Hopefully, you bring something that looks like relief so you can regain the reigns here and consign Salmar back to the task of frelas harvesting."

"Good news, indeed. We are, by no means, the largest group rebelling against Relitha nor are we the most fortified or well placed, although their leaders believe we would make an excellent forward base. They want to get all of the children and families into their facility as quickly as possible and send skilled warriors here to train the rest."

Tarma startled. "Really? How many are they willing to take?"

"Based on what I described to them, about ninety. We need to start running them to a couple of relay points starting tomorrow. It will take a while to get them out secretly where the guards from the city can't see them. However, their leaders think we'll benefit by acting quickly."

She followed him in as he stabled his animal, patting it lightly on shoulder before letting it eat from the trough. "Their leaders – who are they?"

"You replaced one of them in the castle – Masella."

"It was the Lady Masella, I thought?"

"She forsook that title when freed from her unwanted mate," he explained. "Now, there is a second, and he's a seer who could give Boscar a challenge, maybe even defeat him. His name is Lalerro."

"The princess? Did you see or hear anything of Trillias?" she asked, carefully studying him.

"If they are hiding her, then they are keeping it quiet."

She looked at him with an almost disgusted expression. "Masella was once her caretaker, and Lalerro was her friend when she was a child. The first I knew from Relitha when I was appointed, but the latter Trillias confided to me. I very much doubt either of them would be willing to risk the chance of the queen or her guard getting their claws into that precious hide. If she's anywhere, she's there."

"Well, I didn't see her."

"What were you looking for? Royal robes? A crown?" Tarma chided as she sat down, her arms crossed, and Almar's scales lifted in anger and his color darkened at her remark. "That's as much an answer as I could have wanted." Defeated, he settled and shifted color.

"I'm not that stupid, Tarma. I did keep an eye out for her, but unless they pointed her out or she was all decked out in finery, I wouldn't have actually known."

The older Mayara female looked at him, curious. "You have abilities! You were blind?"

There was humiliated embarrassment in the response. "Uh, yeah. Lalerro is that powerful. I barely could get to within half a day's ride before he shut me down," he confessed.

Tarma considered this for a moment and then posited. "Fine, you have fair points, but you also have eyes and," she stated, her expression turning nearly mocking, "you're young. A young male not even of fertile age but fast approaching it. So, did anyone happen to catch Almar's fancy while he was there?"

Although he tried to still the tremor through his scales, he couldn't. "There were a few good looking young females there, yes," he confessed. "Far more than I've ever seen, but there were more of every kind of individual than I've seen in a long time. I've grew up tending the wind funnels and picking frelas moss out of them. You certainly don't meet many lovely females there."

"True, but you've had an interesting assortment ranged around you here, and there are a few who are quite lovely who have been with you since Relitha's day of terror. Never made you twitch before, not even one of them."

He looked at her, a little worried. "You ... observe me that closely?"

"I observe everyone that closely," she replied flatly. "You saw someone. She impressed you. Describe her."

"It's pointless! We could all be dead tomorrow! Next month!"

She looked at him and wouldn't take her demanding stare away. "It is not pointless to me," she asserted. "I will keep your confidence, but you will confide, nonetheless."

"What does it matter?"

"You want my continued help, you will answer my question."

He stared at her a long moment before his shoulders sank. "She … was fairly slight. Her scales were perfect – softest pink I've ever seen, and her face was just … captivating, not thick or thin but kind and … very delicate. There, that do it?"

"More," Tarma quietly insisted.

His eyes widened in exasperation, but she wouldn't break her stare. "Oh, please! Okay, her voice was very soft, humble, nearly a whisper, and when she spoke with me, I sensed that she wanted to hope in something, wanted to believe in something or … someone. Her eyes were so clear, so dark, and ridges above them and on her cheeks were just so … perfectly sculpted. They made me want to reach out to her, I felt like her cheek would rest so perfectly in my hand. There, have I … embarrassed myself enough?"

"Nearly," came the reply.

He sat down on a bench and closed his eyes, bringing back the memories of her, "Her claws were perfect white, unmarred, her tail spike had the loveliest and most graceful curve to it. Her hind claws were prominent, vital, dangerous. The overlap of her chest scales were … ornate and just intriguing, and she had a little ventral ridges running from underneath her chest coverings downward. I tried not to look or pay attention, but they were beautiful, and I thought – or maybe I hoped – that her chest swelled just a bit as I was talking to her. But, her kindness, the way she spoke…"

She looked at him as he stared off into space, seeing only her. "It is her kindness, Almar, that defines her. It has always been so. That is why I love her," Tarma explained. "That is why Lalerro loves her, and it is why Masella does."

He looked at her, suddenly confused. "No! There was—"

"No one else in that cave who could have captivated you as quickly she. It's not a manipulative skill she uses, Almar – it's who she is," Tarma assured him.

"I saw … the princess?! She is the daughter of Relitha?!"

"And Virmarn," Tarma reminded. "And of Masella and mine, as well. As far as her birth is concerned, although both of her parents were thoroughly horrible individuals, their breeding was sound. Relitha's ancestry was royal, and a good part of that blood remains in her with a rather interesting mix of others. It gives Relitha a commanding and domineering aspect our tamed royal lines do not normally have, but in a pairing with Virmarn, there is an excellent mix between the blandness of the royal exterior and Relitha's overcomplicated mixing of lines. I can read the bloodlines of the royals as well as anyone, which is something you were never trained to do. In the end, though, that makes you dry sand that she inadvertently put an impression into allowing me to see her mark clearly. You have spoken to real royalty, Almar. You have spoken with true nobility."

He stood up, angry, and shouted, "Royalty killed my brother! Royalty sent me to prison and left me to die in a hole! Royalty has culled the innocents like a ripe crop! Damn, Tarma! The only dust here is what you just turned that experience into! She could be the next Relitha!"

"No, she couldn't, and that is what you have missed," she assured him, but then she abruptly stood. "Well, no matter for us right now. We have to save Sal from actually causing himself to get nearly a hundred tail spikes of all manners and graces shoved through his chest in response to his sagacious leadership decisions." Feeling angry and nearly betrayed, Almar reluctantly stood up followed her out of the stable to relay his "good news" wishing that he could have the entire experience erased from his memory.

More to come!

Available soon!

About the Author

James Todd Lewis is a science fiction and fantasy author living in Orlando, Florida with his lovely wife and two children. A native of Warner Robins, Georgia, he is a graduate of the Mercer University College of Liberal Arts and the Great Books program. He's been writing novels and short stories since 1982. At first, he just enjoyed the writing process and the fun of reading his own work. It wasn't until a hard drive crash erased several months of work that his wife, who also enjoyed his stories, insisted on making a printed copy for safekeeping. Seeing his work in print for the first time was quite a moment, and it made him wonder if others would also be interested.

Now, he feels humbled and grateful that others have been entertained by these books – doubly so when someone has been kind enough to post a review!

There is more coming in the Thurian Saga!

LIKE the Thurian Saga on Facebook for updates,

discussions with the author, and more!

Follow the author on Twitter! @hmseagle

Visit the author's website for his essay blog, book descriptions, and more in-depth information: www.jamestoddlewis.com!